Author: Teddy Baire
https://www.teddybaire.com/
Cover Designer: Joan Belda
ISBN:978-1-955410-05-2

READER BEWARE

This novel MAY CONTAIN depictions of sex, assault, murder, blood, gore, the power of hugs and kisses, multiple phobias, and other questionable acts.

CHAPTER 1

Through the darkness of nightfall, a lone ship sailed amongst the waters of the ocean. The reflection of the moon above looked serene over its calm surface. Gentle waves pushed along the wooden ship that Victor and Frenka sat atop as the soft sound of parting water splashed against the hull of the ship. At the ship's railing, he stood alone, looking over the water as the wind blew through his short dark hair. Behind him, footsteps pierced the sound of the wind and the creaking of the ship

"Are you still enjoying the trip?" he asked as he turned to see a beautiful dark-haired woman holding a bottle of wine.

"Yes, I look forward to seeing your homeland," said Frenka.

"How did you convince the king to let you come with me, anyway? Isn't your duty to the prince and all that supposed to take up all your time."

"Prince leave Frenka and take off somewhere. So, I tell king I marry you and will spend time with new husband in his kingdom of Mari."

"And how did he take that?"

"He was very happy and congratulated Frenka. He even smiled, which is rare thing for King. He said that he could not wait to tell Saffron when he returns."

"Of course, he did," said Victor as he lifted his glasses again and started rubbing the top of his nose. "I'm sure this decision will make Saffron hate me."

"Frenka thinks he already hates you. But you no worry, I protect you from stupid prince."

"Of course, you will," said Victor, taking a drink from the flask and handing it back to Frenka. "It's nice to see you're getting more comfortable around me now. You're using 'I' now, instead of always referring to yourself in the third person."

Frenka took a sip from the flask, closing her eyes, savoring the taste. "Prince said that before. He says that Frenka says 'I' when nervous."

"And are you nervous around me?"

"Of course, Frenka nervous, she marry non-mage from foreign kingdom and now off to his home. But just because Frenka nervous does not mean Frenka not happy."

"I make my new wife nervous; that's always a good sign," said Victor sarcastically.

"Husband should make wife nervous. You are man. You need to make Frenka feel lots of things. Nervous, happy, sad, and sexy. Especially the sexy. All of the feelings now. That is your job now, for me and sister wife."

"Really," said Victor with a chuckle. "And what is your job in all of this?"

"The same, sometimes even more." said Frenka as she placed her hand on Victor's. "I learn this from mother. But do not worry, I take you to meet father and mother one day. They show you how to be good mate. They have been together long time. And they will be happy now that I have chosen mate. Father was sad after I kill his chosen mate for me, War Leader Gresham."

"I'm sure he was. What makes you think he'll take kindly to me then?"

"He will. You are war man, and father likes those types."

"War man..." said Victor, allowing a sigh to leave his lips. "I guess I am that, but I wonder if you know just how true your words are."

"You no like being war man?"

"Sadly, no. I have never really been a fan of killing. It's more of a trait that comes with the job than one I actively seek out."

"Shame, you seem good at finding people to kill."

"Gee, thanks." *And just like that, my nice quiet dream life is all but done now.* Victor admired the beautiful dark-haired woman at his side. *What's next, Victor? Now I'm in some type of clan mating ritual. So, I've gone from the dream of marrying the baker's daughter off in the woods somewhere and living off the rest of my life in quiet comfort...* Victor shook his head. *I don't even know what I have anymore. A clan wife, a shapeshifter stalker, and Clarissa. Oh, Queen Clarissa, how am I going to explain that?*

"It will be fine, you will see."

"Frenka, listen, I have something I need to tell you."

"Yes?"

"It's about the Queen and me. She and I; well, we don't have an ordinary relationship."

"Frenka guessed that much."

"You have?"

"Of course. Do you not remember Frenka heard about you and how you become sixth general with no magic? Frenka assumed you fucking Queen to get title. But Frenka sees now that you earn it. You have good mind. Proper for war, I think."

"Yes, well..." Victor scratched at the top of his head.

"You were right in your first guess. But it's not for the reason you think."

Frenka's lips twisted as she looked at Victor, trying to understand what he was saying until her eyes opened wide. "Wait, so you no fucking Queen?"

"No, I mean yes. Well, sometimes. But I can't control it."

Frenka's eyes narrowed as she stared at Victor, "Husband not making any sense. Is Queen to join us and become a sister wife?"

"What? No," said Victor, his voice in more of a panic than he could control. "That's the last thing I could ever want. I have no intention of spending any more time around that woman than I have to. So, whatever you do, don't try to involve her in this."

"Okay..." said Frenka, looking even more confused. "But why fuck queen if you no like her?"

"That is a long story," said Victor, turning back towards the water, placing his hands on the rails, and dropping his head.

"Victor should share the tale, or Frenka will not understand. It is us alone over water. This is good time to trust Frenka with secrets. Unless Victor thinks the fish will spread his words."

"Perhaps," said Victor with another sigh as he turned his head, looking Frenka in her eyes. "The whole story... I don't have the stomach for right now. But the short version is, you know the Sakari bonding ritual, right?"

"The one prince used to link you and Dula-hon."

"Yes. Well, I have a link with the Queen. But it's not the same as the Sakari version. The bonding I am under is a variant that's been modified by the kingdom of Mari. Even more compelling and just as unbreakable."

"So, you must do what Queen tells you?"

"Essentially, yes, but if it just stopped there, then it wouldn't be so bad. As I said, it's a variant of the Sakai's process. The Queen's version affects the mind. So, it's not

4

making you do what you don't want. Instead, it makes you believe that's what you have to do. And you feel compelled to do it as if it were your own thoughts and you will follow through with it, with conviction."

"Frenka confused. So, is it mind control?"

"In a way, yes. But ours is complicated."

"Okay, but Frenka no understand. Why fuck Queen, does she love Victor?"

"She thinks she does, but that's because of the mind control."

"Wait, so Queen under mind control? I thought husband was."

"Yes, I am. I mean... we both are. It was done when we were young. Something happened and the spell ended up being shared between us rather than all of it being on me."

"So, Queen under mind control to love Husband. Husband under mind control to obey Queen. And Husband also under Sakari bond with Dula-hon, who refuses to use it to control her."

"As I said, it's complicated."

"Frenka thinks she may have chosen wrong husband now."

Victor gave a chuckle despite himself. "Well, too late. You're stuck with me. So, get used to it."

Frenka smiled and stepped towards Victor, wrapping her arms around his waist. "Are you giving Frenka commands now?"

"Would you listen if I did?"

"Husbands and wives have their own type of mind control," said Frenka as she lifted herself up and placed her lips against his. And for a moment, under the moon, the two shared a kiss, the smell of salt water on their nose as the taste of each other filled their lips.

"I think that's the only mind control I completely agree with," said Victor after removing his lips but allowing his forehead to stay pressed against hers.

"See, the best mind control."

"Come on," said Victor, not letting go of Frenka's hand. "Let's head downstairs. I want to try to get some sleep tonight."

"Sleep is hard for man who thinks too much. But why not try to kill Queen and free yourself, like Frenka and Gresham?"

"I can't hurt the Queen. If I even try, my body freezes in place as if I've become paralyzed. And even if I did, I'm starting to think that if she ever died, the spell that binds us would kill me as well."

"Too bad, then Frenka will try not to kill Queen."

"I appreciate that," said Victor with a chuckle.

They made their way back down into the lower levels of the ship. The creaking planks of wood sounded in their ears as the ship swayed slightly. Frenka lit an ember of magic in her hand to illuminate the darkness of the ship below as the two made their way forward. Voices could be heard from the cabins around them as they made their way through the ship until finally arriving at their door.

Opening it, they found the ashen-skinned Silk sitting on a cot, a candle on a small table in front of her, and a book in her hand. The flame of the candle flickered over her ruby and emerald eyes as she looked over at them. After their fight, Nahtalli had healed the damage to her face, but on the journey, several scars had reemerged. But no matter how many times Victor looked at her, he never seemed to get used to the soft white grayness of her skin and hair.

"You two left without me again," said Silk, narrowing her eyes at the two.

"You were sleeping," said Victor as they walked in. He shut the door behind them. "And we have a bit of work to do. Don't worry. I'll start including you in the plans as soon as you're able to transform again."

"Yes," said Frenka, extinguishing the mage light from her hand. "I want to see you perform this magic. Dula-hon are not known for transforming."

"Stop calling me that, my name is Silk."

"Oh, sister wife still angry."

"And I haven't agreed to that either. Sharing Victor with you is absurd."

"Okay, no need to start a magic fight aboard the ship. I would like to at least make it to dry land before you two sort out your differences." *At the very least, I'd have the ability to run away.* He sat down on the opposite cot on the other side of the small room. "But have you decided what you want to do now? When we reach Mari, I'll probably start back on another mission. I'm sure Clarissa already has something planned for me. Are you sure this is what you want?"

Silk looked between Frenka and Victor for a moment. Then placing her hand on the book, she nodded her head. "I want to stay with you. But are you sure that I can? Even when I'm able to transform again. Won't you have to tell your Queen about me? And what if Grennok comes looking for me? He won't be happy knowing that I've run away from him."

Victor stretched out, lying over the cot, looking up at the ceiling. "That won't be a problem. My reputation in the kingdom is already a mystery to most. So much so that even if you strolled through the castle with me as you are now, all it would do is add to the rumors that are already circulating about me. You have my word. You will find a home in Mari."

"See, husband is very confident," said Frenka as she laid down on the cot beside Victor, allowing her head to rest on his chest. "Sister wife should have more faith in husband. He is good at keeping promises."

"So, you're saying you have faith in me?"

"I do. You will give Frenka council on how to lead clan."

"I thought the men were supposed to lead?"

"No. In clan, the woman leads. But men offer counsel in war."

"Less burden on me, so I won't complain."

"But it shame bed so small," said Frenka as she allowed her hand to make its way down, resting above Victor's crotch. "Would like to mate properly with husband and sister wife to celebrate union."

"I still haven't agreed to us three... whatever this is. And I most certainly haven't agreed with what you want to do."

Frenka smiled at Silk, her head still resting on Victor's chest. "Dula-hon, not want to join us? Or maybe just not Frenka. She did not mind sharing nakedness with Frenka when she invite her into her home, then bathed her and bandaged her wounds."

"That's... that's not the same."

"Is it not? We share nakedness, and we share man. Frenka remembers you say you want to love Victor and stay beside him."

"I do... but sharing a man with you... As I said, that's not something I can agree with. I don't even know you."

"Oh, does Dula-hon wish to challenge Frenka to be leader of clan then?"

Okay, I recognize this moment. This is the moment where I close my eyes and pretend not to hear this.

"What do you mean challenge?"

"We fight to lead clan. If you wish Frenka gone, then you must prove to be strong enough to lead husband. If you win, then you will lead clan and can cast Frenka out."

Silk closed the book, staring back into the smirking face of Frenka. Her eyes narrowed as her voice took on a serious tone. "And if I lose?"

"If Dula-hon loses, then she accepts Frenka as clan leader, accepts herself as sister wife, and listens to the commands of Frenka."

"And what happens if I don't want to challenge you?"

"Then we fight with words, as we do now. Nothing changes," said Frenka as she lifted her hand back up, patting her hand on Victor's chest. "But Dula-hon, you will understand, that the only way into husband's bed is if Frenka is already in it."

Sweet Goddess, women are terrifying creatures.

CHAPTER 2

In the port city of Malistan, outside of a seaside inn, Dessi, one of the members of the black Jewels mercenaries and Chloe, a friend of Isha's from school sat overlooking the water. The sounds of the ocean rolling over the shore mixed in with the voice of squawking sea birds.

"I won't pry into your business," said Dessi as she took a deep breath of the seaside air. "But I know you're not telling us everything. Those Sakari girls said you attacked Isha. I just need to ensure you won't do it again."

"I won't..."

Isha came out of the door with her cheeks flushed.

"We'll talk about this later," said Dessi, turning her attention to Isha. "Hey, you changed your clothes."

"I had to."

"What did Oscar want with you?"

"He wanted me to use my powers to see how they

worked."

"Oh, okay, I guess... Wait, but doesn't---" Dessi shook her head while biting her lips as she gave Isha another look. "I guess that explains the new clothes. At least tell me no one else saw."

"No," said Isha as she stepped up, sitting down at the table with them. "It was only him in the room. But it was still embarrassing not having any clothes on."

"I imagine so. I'll go have a talk with him about it later."

"I don't want these stupid powers if that happens every time," said Isha as she folded her arms.

"Why do I have to be here?" asked Chloe.

"Mostly to give off the appeal to us being just happy travelers," said Dessi as she looked over the water. "Oscar insisted that you and Isha stay together while you were in our company. We can't have Isha being spotted alongside him or risk someone trying to kidnap her. Us just being three girls makes it easier for us to blend in."

"What about Miss Gregga? I mean Mother," said Isha, looking over at three Sakari women by the ship.

Gregga hugged both the women and gave them kisses before watching them walk aboard the ship. She handed a kingdom man a small bag before turning around and heading back towards them. She waved her hand at the man behind them selling fish.

"Three fish I would like to have."

"Alright, gimme a minute and get you ready."

"I remember those ladies from the camp. Are you sending them away, Mother?" asked Isha.

"Yes. They have given birth and will need to raise children. I send them back to Sakar to do so. Plinth may send warriors back for me to train."

"Plinth? Is that someone you know back in Sakar?"

"Yes, Plinth is leader of Malnoy Clan in Sakar. She old friend. She will help women find place to raise children."

"Alright," said the vendor handing Gregga the fish.

"Here you go."

"I will go back now. Shouldn't be seen with daughter for too long, or people figure out who you are," said Gregga as she wandered off.

As she went by, Isha saw her speaking with a few other young kingdom girls. She had never seen them before, but they all seemed to be acquainted with Gregga.

"And there she goes," said Dessi, turning back towards Isha and Chloe. "So, you two tell me something; what's school like up there in the magic city? Oscar's kept you locked up in that hotel for the past month, so we haven't really had time to talk."

"What do you mean?" asked Chloe. "Fairline and I take classes and go about learning magic."

"You say that as if it's normal," said Dessi with a laugh. "To us mundane people, you all might as well live in a different world. Not everyone gets to play around with magic and fly on airships at the drop of a coin. Most of us here have barely even seen one, let alone ridden one."

"Oh, sorry. I sometimes forget that."

"Really? Aren't you and Isha friends? I figured you'd have talked about all this before."

"How did you learn magic?" asked Isha, "Maggie never said she had any magic friends."

"Maggie?" asked Dessi with a turn of her head. "You mean the girl from Passala."

"Hmm, yes. Chloe's also from Passala."

"Really? Well, that's odd. Two magical street girls, both from the same city. Especially Passala. That place isn't known for having a lot of mages," said Dessi, taking a long look at Chloe. "And with Broderick going around and picking up all the stray girls he can find, I find it odd that he missed a girl like you. Especially with that hand of yours."

Chloe stuffed a piece of fish into her mouth, purposely looking away from Dessi.

"Have any of you gone back to Passala? Are Maggie and

Billy okay?"

"No, not yet," said Dessi, turning back to Isha. "Usually, we stop once or twice a year, but with this whole mess with you and your weird magic... The old man's been having us spread out amongst the local cities until you're ready to head back to school."

"It's not like I asked to be a mage. I wish none of this ever happened, at least I'd be home with Papa now if I could."

"With everything that's happened. We've never really talked about your family before. You mentioned your father, but what about your mother? Was she a mage?"

"I never saw Mama use magic. But she could have been, I guess. She wasn't around much. But Papa wasn't one. He always worked with his hands to make stuff, or he'd be swinging his sword around. You think Mama was a mage?"

"No telling. But from what I know, mages prefer to mate with other mages. Especially if they're trying to have their children inherit a certain type of magic. It would be odd if your mother wasn't at least some type of mage, and here you are with some weird type of magic. Who knows, maybe she tried to hide you away because she knew all the kingdoms would come looking for you. It would explain why you were off across the seas in Green Village."

"That's what father said," said Isha with a frown on her face. "That thing about people trying to make me have babies so they can have them."

Dessi reached over, rubbing Isha's head, "Don't worry about Oscar. I know it doesn't seem like it sometimes—okay well, most of the time—but he's doing his best by you."

"It doesn't feel that way. He locked me in a trunk and made me listen to people talk about all kinds of stuff."

"Yeah, I heard about that from Jacob," said Dessi with a sigh. "Listen, Rana, I mean Isha. I'm not even sure your name matters anymore at this point. Remember what I told you that night after what Molan tried to do to you?"

Isha was quiet.

"I know you don't want to think about it, and now's hardly the time and place. But I want you to think about what I said and what Oscar is doing now," said Dessi, her eyes on Isha. She then sighed, shaking her head. "I guess it falls on me then. Isha, I want you and Chloe to come to my room tonight. I want us girls to talk about something."

"Yes, ma'am," said Isha, lowering her head.

"Alright then," said Dessi, placing her hands on the table and standing. "Come on, you two. It's time to head back." Dessi stood up from the table and made her way throughout the city with Isha and Chloe.

The port city was alive with the movement of people and street vendors. Stone buildings sat along the city's coast, but behind them the architecture changed to brick and wood. Horses tied to stalls and those carrying carriages stomped the soil streets beneath them as they trotted through the city.

"Are we going to Faylon now?" asked Chloe.

"Now? No. Since we've finally gotten Isha out of that stuffy room, I figured this would be a good opportunity to get you girls some fresh air while we have the time. Who knows what the Old Man has in store for us next? So, we may as well take this time to enjoy ourselves and try on a few new outfits. You girls can't run around in your school garbs while you're here, and those rags you have on could certainly use an upgrade."

"What about Mother?" said Isha, "Will she be there too?"

"I'm sure she has her own business to take care of here. And I don't think I'm ready for another shopping experience with Gregga. Don't worry; I doubt anyone noticed us sneaking out. They're still over in Faylon trying to sell first use of your virtues.

The three went down past a few streets before finally turning down a path where many people were out shopping.

"Ah, that one should do," said Dessi after they made their way in front of a store with mannequins for more

14

petite girls and women displayed in their window. "Let's try this one first."

"This reminds me of the Ladies' shop in Passala, the one father took me to."

"Ladies' shop? Oh, you mean Addison. I wish we were there. She'd be able to make you something really special. But we work with what we're given."

"Hello there," said a female shopkeeper behind a desk as they entered. "How are you ladies today? Can I help you with anything in particular?"

"Not yet. We're just taking a look for the moment."

The shop was stacked with wooden mannequins that flowed down the walls. To their left were adult female statues wearing garments of different tastes, and to their right were smaller models, more of the girl's own sizes. Those displayed more frilly children's designs: bows, laces, bonnets, and shoes that matched the outfits.

Immediately, Chloe was drawn over to the dresses, rubbing her fingers over the lacy design along the waist of the skirt.

"Oh, she seems to know her way around," said Dessi with a smile as she stood behind Isha, placing her hand on her back. "Go over and play with your friend. This is a good time for you all to talk. You two have been acting funny since you made it back to camp."

"It's not that. It's just... well... she always gets mad at me, and I don't know why."

"Then now's a good chance to go on and find out why," said Dessi, giving Isha a little pat on the back. "I'm going to have a talk with the shopkeeper over there and see if they have anything nice but maybe a little less fancy. It's not like we're going to a ball or anything."

"Yes, ma'am," said Isha as she took a breath before heading toward Chloe. "Ah... have you worn these types of clothes before?"

"Yes, mother and I used to wear them when going to

town," said Chloe as she looked between the dresses on display. "She always wanted me to look presentable when we went to see Miss Vanessa or when she'd want me to impress the Turner boy, Edrick."

Vanessa? I... I think I remember that name. That was Mr. Goose's wife. "I remember Mr. Goose. He had the house close to that statue in the city."

"What?" said Chloe, turning back to Isha, her head tilted upwards in disbelief. "What do you mean, you remember? You never went there."

"Huh? What do you mean? Of course, I did. I remember how to get there. He's a chubby man. I remember his face."

"What? But how? You never met them."

"Stop saying that! I know what I did. Why do you always pick on me?"

"I'm not pick-" Chloe shook her head, then pointed her finger at Isha. "Fine, then tell me something about Miss Vanessa. What do you remember about her?"

"Well, she's tall... I think. And she once took me shopping in the city; she bought me a dress there. A pink one with a red bow for my hair. I remember that."

Blinking in disbelief, Chloe just stared at Isha as if she had just told her that the sky was purple.

"That's not... how do you even know that?"

"What do you mean? I remember it. That's what happened."

"That's not what happened. I mean, it did, but... Oh, never mind, whatever."

"No," shouted Isha. "Not whatever. You always do that. You don't ever tell me anything. And you always get mad at me," said Isha, stepping toward Chloe with her finger pointed toward her. "I want us to be friends, but you don't tell me anything."

"What? I don't have to..."

"Stop that. I want you to tell me the truth. Why did you try to fight me? Why don't I remember you from Passala?

Why do you act like you know things about me, but when I try to ask you anything, you always get quiet or run away?"

"That's not... I mean... It's not like I want it to be like this."

"Then tell me."

"I can't."

"Why?"

"Because I don't have anywhere else to go!"

"Hey, hey. Calm down, you two," said Dessi as she placed an oversized hat on Isha's head. "Remember, the goal is to not draw attention to ourselves."

Both girls turned around to see the lady behind the counter staring at them before dropping their heads, and turning away, embarrassed.

"I'm sorry," said Isha.

"Sorry," said Chloe.

"It's fine," said Dessi with a sigh. "I figured you both would hash it out one day. Just didn't expect it to be in the middle of shopping." She stepped around them, placing her hands on the girls' shoulders. "Come on, let's go for a walk. It'll help get rid of some of that tension you both seem to have built."

Dessi ushered the brooding girls towards and out of the door with a smile across her lips.

"You two really are a handful. I can't leave—"

Dessi's body went flying to the ground as they exited the building. A man collided with her, planting a blade into her side and tackling her to the ground.

"Dessi!"

Isha barely had time to reach her hand out to Dessi before her body hit the ground. Two men appeared behind her and Chloe, covering their faces with black sheets, the edge of the cloth digging into her throat.

Help... Dessi, please.... someone help Dessi.

Through the cloth came the sounds of her and Chloe's muffled screams as the two men hoisted both girls into their arms. As she struggled, she heard men's grunts and a few curse words. An arm wrapped itself around her waist as she heard a wagon approaching and with the familiar sound of stomping horse. Quickly then she was snatched off her feet.

"Quick, get 'em in," said a man's voice as was tossed inside what she figured had to be a carriage, by the way it shifted back and forth as she was tosses inside. She tried to move, stand, crawl, or anything, but something heavy was pressing down hard against her back.

"They're magic, get 'em in the collars."

Not again. Papa, Father. Someone... please.

Pinned down on the carriage's floor, her hands were pulled behind her back, then Isha felt something cold clamp down around her neck as she struggled to breathe through the cloth over her face. Now she knew the weight above her was a man, his was pinning her beneath him, her ribs pressing against the floor beneath.

Chloe... Is Chloe okay? Arghh... get off me.

Through the floorboard, Isha could feel the carriage's vibrations as it rushed down the road.

"Is anyone following us?" said the voice of a man.

"It doesn't look like it," a woman's muffled voice answered.

"Alright then, get 'em up and hold 'em still. We got this far; we don't need any surprises."

Hoisted up by her wrists, Isha was forced to sit upright, a man's hand pressed against her waist. They then removed the cloth over her face as she shook her head, blinking from the influx of light. She struggled to focus through the tears that watered her eyes.

"Hello there, young ladies. I hope the boys weren't too rough with you," said a dark-haired man in front of them.

Isha squinted her eyes to see around the cabin where there were four men. Two were on either side, and one man held Chloe in his lap in front of her. Her arms were clasped behind her back. There was a collar around her neck and a small amount of blood on her cheek from a gash.

"Who are you? What do you want with us?" asked Chloe angrily as she struggled in the man's grasp.

"Oh, the one with the rotten arm's got some fight in her," said one of the men reaching out and grabbing Chloe's burned arm. "Hah, she's been through a right fun time, hasn't she?"

"Don't touch me," said Chloe, ripping her hand free and slapping the man across the face.

He smiled and reared back his own hand, slapping Chloe so hard that she fell over the lap of the man beside her, hitting the carriage wall. He then grabbed her by her hair, pulling her back to him. She tried to struggle, but with her mouth agape, she could only manage small screams as tears came down her face.

"You wanna go for another try, sweetheart?"

"Stop," screamed Isha. "Please! We're sorry. We'll behave. Please, let her go."

The man looked at Isha, "You stay out of this. This is between..."

"Let her go," said the brown-haired man on the other side of Chloe. "She's had enough."

The dark-haired man stared at the brown-haired man for a moment before he thrust Chloe across the cabin. She landed atop Isha.

"Then you best keep her quiet. 'Cause if she mouths off again, I'll give her more than a slap."

Isha forced herself to be calmed as Chloe latched onto her, her body shaking uncontrollably.

"What... what do you want with us?" asked Isha.

"Us? No, you little money pieces. We want whichever one of you is that special magic kid everyone's talking about. We spent a lot of good coin keeping track of you after you left the city," said the man looking between both of the girls. "Now, which one of you got that special magic?"

Isha was silent as Chloe cried.

The dark-haired man smirked as he reached into his coat and pulled out a blade. Its metal edge glimmered off the sunlight that made its way inside the carriage.

"You, little darlings, might think you're tough, but we'll see how long you stay silent when I start peeling the skin off your bones."

"They told us not to hurt the girls, Salley," said the brown-haired man. "And I don't want them mad at us, especially that big one. He looked scary."

"They only want one girl, and we got two. We might be able to ransom the other one. I ain't giving them both the girls if I can make money off the other. Besides, they're mages, and they just want 'em for screwing. They don't need fingers or toes for that."

"You say that, but if they don't pay us, I'mma let you tell the boss what happened."

Salley stared at the brown-haired man for a moment before putting his blade back into his coat. "Fine. The ones buying 'em are mages, anyway. I'll have them tell me which one of 'em is and isn't their little magic baby. But I'm keeping the other one. If they're from that damn magic school, it means their family's got money."

The girls were forced to ride through the rest of the day, swapping from one carriage to the next as nightfall took them. They finally stopped their travels when the moon was high above them.

"Alright, get 'em out," said Salley from outside the carriage. And soon, the door to the carriage opened. Behind the brown-haired man, the flames from a fire could be seen.

"Come on, you two. Out ya get."

Isha and Chloe just stared at the man, not moving.

"Look, I know this ain't easy. But you two gotta be good 'til we get where we're going or Salley's gonna hurt ya something bad."

"Hey, what's taking so long?" came Salley's voice from near the fire.

"I'm just checking their collars. Don't want 'em casting nothing on me," said the brown-haired man, turning back to the girls. "Now come on. I don't wanna see him hurt no little girls again. He's done worse than that, I promise."

After another moment, Isha slid forward on the seat, standing by the door.

"Now there's a good girl. I promise I'll keep ya safe from Salley as long ya don't cause no trouble."

The brown-haired man stepped aside as Isha poked her head out of the carriage into the night air. Then, turning around, she reached in, and grabbed Chloe's arm by the wrist.

Isha swallowed her own fear. *I have to be strong. I can't be scared.* "Come on. We best do what they say for now. Father... Father will come get us," said Isha, her foot beginning to shake as a stiffness began to creak up her neck.

Chloe wiped the tears from her face and nodded. A bruise was now beginning to show on her cheek from where Salley had slapped her. She followed Isha out of the carriage to the cold grass below. As she stepped down, Isha only noticed then that one of Chloe's shoes was gone.

"Well, the princesses finally decided to join us. Mirow, what ya doing? Link them collars together; in case they make a break for it, we won't have to go looking for both of 'em."

"Oh yeah, right," said the brown-haired man as he grabbed the chain around the collars and linked them together. "You two go grab a place by the fire. We ain't gonna be here long. Might wanna get some rest."

Making their way forward, Isha took notice of the woman asleep above the carriage and the other two men who sat around the fire. One was a bald man, the other: a man with his hair in a ponytail.

Don't look at them. Just look at the fire, thought Isha as they took a seat on the ground a little away from the men. The ground was cold as the dew of the grass trickled between their fingers. She could feel Chloe's hand shaking against hers as she stayed quiet, looking between the men. The stiffness and anxiety had made their way from Isha's shoulders as her teeth started chattering inside her mouth. Taking a deep breath, she squeezed Chloe's hand in hers. "We're going to be fine," said Isha in a low tone, although she wasn't sure if she said it for Chloe's sake or her own.

"How far till the damned hideout?" said Salley.

"Just in the next town over," said the woman nonchalantly as she waved one of her arms in the air. "If we leave when the sun comes up and the horses are rested, we should be there early morning. So, what? You afraid some monsters may come to get you?"

"I'm afraid of not getting my money. Every second we got these little magic babies is another second I ain't got my money. Can't even have no fun with 'em because they paying us for their cunts," said Salley as he tossed a piece of wood on the fire before turning to the girls. "What's it like having magic cunts? You piss magic too?"

Isha narrowed her eyes at the man, her breathing becoming labored as she listened to the chatter. They went on and on, talking about her and Chloe as if they were objects to be used and discarded. *It's like what father said. Everyone's the same. The nobles; them, all of them, only care about what they want.*

"What? You really up for fucking them little rug rats? They barely even started getting their tits. Look like small boys with long hair."

"You touch them girls, Salley, and I'll personally come down there and cut that cock of yours off," said the woman up on the carriage.

"What? You getting all mushy up there? Didn't know you cared, especially after what happened to you back in Sangrel. Heard them boys had fun with you that night."

"And two of them boys dead now. You touch them girls, and you're gonna get to ask 'em yourself what happened to 'em.'

"That's a fact, is it?"

"Stop that bickering, both of ya," said Mirow. "Ain't nobody doing nothing but getting some shut-eye 'til the sun comes up. Now, if y'all wanna fight, y'all can fight after we get our money." He then turned toward the girls. "You two get some rest too. We'll be where we're going by the morning. Grab one of them bags right there if ya need something to put ya head on." He said, pointing to a bag a little farther away from them.

Looking around the fire first, Isha then tried to stand, but her neck collar chain caught, stopping her mid-movement and causing Chloe to fall over. It forced Isha to turn around, bending over to keep them from choking each other.

"Ha, they're like little dogs on a leash," said Salley, slapping his thigh with a laugh.

"Don't listen to him," said Isha, grabbing Chloe by the arm. "Let's go over here." Helping Chloe up, they walked over to the bags. On the way, Isha noticed Mirow's eye following her. The girls sat and laid their heads down.

"Do you think they're really coming for us?" Chloe whispered.

"I know they are. You'll see. Father, he... he is on his way." Isha wasn't sure, but she hoped her words would be true. *Please come get us, Father. You said you wouldn't let anything else bad happen to me.* She took one more glance over at the fire, where the men were sitting. Mirow, she noticed, was still staring at her. Quickly she averted her eyes back up, focusing on Chloe's face, squeezing her hand in hers. *And this is really bad.*

"What if they don't get here in time? I mean, they're after you, aren't they? What's gonna happen to me if they find out they don't need me? They're going to give me to that Salley man, and he's gonna-"

"Shh... don't say that. They might hear you," said Isha, closing her eyes and wrapping her arms around Chloe. "Just close your eyes and try not to think about it. As long as we don't tell them anything, we'll both will be fine. I... I'm not going to leave you."

"Okay, okay... I... I'm sorry."

"For what? It's not your fault we are here."

"No, I mean.... For everything that happened. I... I know that... it wasn't your fault."

"What do you..." Isha's words froze in her mouth as she spotted something in the woods away from them. It was in the brush, covered by darkness. While she could not make out its shape, she could see a pair of golden eyes appearing and disappearing in and out of the leaves. It was only for a moment before they were gone, but they were there; she was sure they were.

Isha felt her breath catch in her throat as the brush suddenly started to shake, and a sizeable puffy bird flew out. It perched above them on a tree limb. In its mouth seemed to be a small rodent. The fowl appeared to be gazing down at them, the image of a large moon behind it glimmering off its golden eyes.

Goddess, I pray, thought Isha as she gazed up at the moon behind the animal. *Please let Dessi be okay. Please let Father find us before... before.... I don't want what happened to me to happen to Chloe. Please come get us, Father.*

Before the girls had realized it, they had fallen asleep.

The following day, the girls awoke to the feel and sound of clanking as Salley jingled that chain around their necks.

"Get up, ya little money cunts," said Salley as he pulled on the chain, lifting the girls by their necks as they struggled out of their sleep, gripping the chains. "Ya know, I think I can get used to this; having my pets chained up."

"Just get your ass to helping to load up. The sun's almost up," said the woman as she climbed atop the carriage, taking a seat in the driver's seat.

He then released the chain, letting the girls crash back down on top of the bags below. "You heard the lady. You two get them bags up and tote 'em to the wagon."

Both Isha and Chloe turned back to Salley with the same look of hatred in their eyes.

"Oh, the brats got some fight still left in 'em," said Salley, squatting back down. "Well, go on. Take a swing. I wouldn't mind giving ya both more of what she got yesterday."

The girls didn't say a word. They just continued to stare daggers at the man.

"That's what I thought," said Salley as he reached forward, playfully patting each girl on the side of their face. "Remember, they only need you for your cunts. I can do what I like with the rest of ya."

"Hurry up, down there." yelled the woman in the carriage.

Salley smirked, "Ya heard her Get to work." Then standing back up, he walked back towards the carriage.

"Come on," said Isha, her voice low as she tried to hold in her anger. "We still gotta do what they say 'til Father comes."

And she and Chloe reached down, picked up the bags they had slept on, and took them over to the back of the wagon, where Mirow was loading the last camp materials. The girls stumbled over, dropping the bag at his feet.

"Alright, go'n hop inside. We'll be there soon enough."

Isha found herself staring at Mirow for a moment. The scar at the side of his face seemed odd. But before long they were taken to the side of the carriage and hoisted inside. After clearing the site, they were on their way down the road once again.

The group sat quietly for the next few hours as the carriage shook around them. She watched as the morning sun passed over the carriage window, and above their heads where she could no longer see. The shaking of the carriage heightened their frustrations as the metal chains between them clinked. The weight of the collars dug into their necks, chafing at their shoulders.

The carriage made a few twists and turns as the sounds of people chattering came from outside. But soon enough it came to a halted and with it the came the heavy feeling of nervousness that found its way into he pit of her stomach.

"Alright, who are ya, and what d'ya want?" asked a man's voice from outside.

"Tell your owner we brought that bounty that he put out," said the woman atop the carriage. "And that we'll be expecting payment immediately."

There was another moment of silence before she heard the sound metal scraping against metal was heard which she assumed to be a gate. Then, with the sound of a pop of the reins, the carriage lurched forward.

"You two; wait here until I can confirm with the master about your cargo," said the man's voice.

"Well, one of you girls is about to meet your new master," said Salley with a smile as he stretched his arms. "And I'm… about to be a rich man."

A few minutes later, the man returned. "Alright, bring 'em out. The master's come to see for herself."

The door to the carriage opened, and Isha was greeted by the scenery of well-manicured hedges. Flowers littered the ground beneath, alongside a pathway that led towards the half-circle stairs of a large manor. Ahead of them stood a woman in fine clothing at the top of the steps between her guards.

"Well, isn't this a pleasant surprise," said the woman, making her way down the steps with two female guards at her side. "I never imagined someone would manage to pull off the theft of the golden child. I'd just put out that bounty as a matter of curiosity. Now, doesn't this just prove you really should just take every opportunity that comes your way. You never know what seeds will bear fruit." The woman looked over the group of kidnappers, bringing her hands together and slowly intertwining her fingers. "And this certainly is quite an accomplishment from a group such as yourselves."

Salley pulled Isha and Chloe forward, tugging on their chain, making them bump against each other as they were forced to stand in front of the women.

"Alright, here they are."

"So, I see." said the well-dressed woman. "But why are there two of them? I was informed only one child of special talent was found."

"Yeah, well. The two of them were together, and we didn't know which one it was. But I figure you have someone who can handle that job."

"Indeed. Just give me a moment," said the woman as she stared down at Isha and Chloe. Then, after a few seconds, she smiled and gestured at Isha. "This is the one with the talent. I must say, I've never seen anything like it. Although the other one is also a mage."

"Well, I guess that solves that issue," said Salley with a smile. "What say you? You got our money or what?"

"Oh yes, I suppose remuneration for services rendered is in order," said the woman, turning back to her guards. "Bring the gentlemen and the lady's reward."

Two men walked out a few moments later, holding a small trunk by its handles. They planted the trunk at the carriage's door before opening it, exposing a large amount of gold.

"Wow, now that's a thing of beauty," said Salley as he pulled out a key, inserting it into the lock that linked the collars around their necks. It clicked, setting the girls free of each other. Salley pushed Isha towards one of the guards who grabbed her. "Take her."

"Such an abrasive man, aren't you?" asked the woman, shaking her head in disapproval. "You simply must learn to treat women better. We are such delicate things, after all."

"Yeah, well ya got the one ya wanted, and she's in one piece. I'll be keeping this one," said Salley as he leaned down, rubbing Chloe's chin while squeezing her wrists behind her back, making her wince. "Truthfully, this is the one I hoped I'd get. I like the proud ones."

The woman with them just shook her head as Chloe's eyes began to water.

"No, stop," shouted Isha as she struggled in the guard's hands. "Let her go. I won't let you!"

"Oh my. Well, this is certainly a predicament," said the well-dressed woman. "I guess these two are friends. That can be useful if one knows how to use it." She turned to Isha. "You there, what is your name?"

"It's Isha; my name's Isha," she said, turning to face the well-dressed woman. "Don't... don't let him take her."

"Well, Miss Isha, if I were to also procure that girl over there along with yourself, would that make you more agreeable to my requests?"

"Yes, don't let him take Chloe. I'll do whatever you want."

"Wonderful," said the well-dressed woman with a genuine smile. "I'll be taking that one as well then. She's sure to be useful come auction time."

"What?" said Salley, looking between the girls with narrowed eyes before his lips turned into a smile. "Fine, but that's gonna be extra."

"Oh, don't worry. I included a bit of extra gold as a sign of good faith. Just take that as extra for the girl."

Salley turned back to the gold before frowning back at the woman. "Spoiled the fun; surely ya wouldn't mind if I asked for something else."

"I think you misunderstand the situation, sir. Instead of having you and your friends killed here on the spot, I am letting you leave with your lives and a substantial amount of gold. Surely you wouldn't be trying to impose on my good nature," said the well-dressed woman, her tone changing to show a bit of annoyance. "Please be aware that I wouldn't mind taking both of the rewards back from you."

The two female guards seemed to twitch as their hands hovered over their blades.

"Salley, you go on and get yourself killed," said the woman with them. "I ain't losing my life because of your stupid ass."

"Yeah, you're on your own, Salley," said Mirow. "I ain't getting killed for you."

Salley looked around before removing his hand from Chloe's face and wrists. And she ran over to Isha, wrapping her arms around her. He then raised his hands above his head with a grin. "Okay, okay. I get it. I'll take the gold and be on my way then. There ain't no need to turn this into a fight. We both got what we wanted. The gold for us and the girls for you."

"Yes, I agree," said the well-dressed woman, her smile resuming on her face. "No need for bloodshed on such a lovely day. In fact, I would like to invite you all to join us for dinner."

"Well, as much as I'd like to stay," said Salley, walking over and closing the trunk of gold. "I think it's best I be on my way."

"Same," said the woman on the carriage, "I'd rather just take my gold and leave. You might wanna leave too. We got you the girl, but I've heard of that Oscar Highland fella from my time in Orios. From what I heard that man is a little too capable."

"Why? Do you believe you were followed?"

"We didn't notice anyone. But if that girl's as valuable as I been hearing, I wouldn't take any chances."

"I agree, and it'd be such a shame to lose my investment. But worry not; my men and I have plans should the need arise."

"Suit yourself then," said the woman as she climbed back up in the driver's seat of the wagon.

"And what of you then?" said the well-dressed woman to

Mirow. "You off on your way to as well?"

"No," said Mirow as he stared at Isha and Chloe. "If you're hiring, I'd like to work for ya."

"Well, that's certainly a surprise. But I don't see any reason why not. I can certainly use more capable men. I suggest you grab your share of the spoils before your companions run away with them. Until the girls are sold, I'm appointing you as their caretaker. Rest assured; there will be a hefty bonus in it for you."

"Fine with me," said Mirow, walking over, re-opening the trunk, scooping handfuls of gold coins into two pouches. One after another.

"Hey, don't take what doesn't belong to you," said Salley, turning back to Mirow.

"Don't you worry, I'm pretty sure I'm not even taking all my share. Just enough to make all this worth it," said Mirow as he held the two pouches of gold in his hand. "Oh, and Salley, I hate you. I would tell you to go kill yourself, but I'm sure that you and that gold of yours will find a way of getting it done on your own real soon. You never could keep your mouth shut."

"Ha, better than being a coward like you."

"You two up there, Fival," said Mirow, looking up to the female driver. "Ya best get away from Salley as fast as you can. Either he'll kill you and take your gold, or he'll get you killed."

"Don't you worry about me," said Fival. "I'll be ditching his ass the next city over. I just want outta here, is all. Be safe, Mirow. Try not to die while playing at being a guard."

"Well then, seeing as things are in order here, I wish you all the best on your journey," said the well-dressed lady.

Salley and the other man walked back to the carriage, again closing the chest of gold and climbing inside. And with a final snap of the reins, the carriage squeaked and rolled out of the manor with the gate closing behind it.

"Now that that piece of business has concluded," said

the well-dressed woman as she turned her attention back towards Isha, "what say you give us a bit of a demonstration of this wonderful power of yours? I'm so excited to see what all this fuss is about."

Isha looked around between Chloe and the guards nervously.

"Now, now, no need to be shy. We had a deal, didn't we? I allow you and your little friend to stay together, and you give me your cooperation."

"It's not... I mean, I can't control it yet. It hurts people. I was supposed to return to school for them to teach me, but I haven't."

"Is that so? Well, isn't that a shame? But, just for demonstration purposes, I'm sure you won't do that much damage. Now, I was told you enhance the power of other mages. Is that true?"

"Yes, ma'am."

"Oh, such lovely manners. So, tell me, how is it done?"

"I, ah... well, I'm not sure, exactly. But I'm supposed to touch a mage when they use magic, and then they're supposed to get stronger, I think."

"Splendid," said the lady with a smile as she turned back to her guards, looking between them. "Which one of you two want to give it a go?"

The guards looked at each other before turning back to the well-dressed woman.

"Not me," said one of the guards. "You heard the girl; she hurts people with whatever she does to them. And I'm not going to be the one she puts down first."

"Same goes for me," said the other guard.

"Oh, come on, surely one of you has a heart for adventure."

One of the female guards shook her head, "I'm your friend and I might work for you sometimes. But that doesn't mean I'm stupid? You're a mage too. Why don't you do it?"

"Oh please, I can't risk myself. I'm the organizer of the

event," said the woman, placing her hand on her chin. "I suppose we can ask around the mercenaries we hire. Perhaps one of them has the gift."

"I think one of the girls in the kitchen has some talent; heard 'em talking about it some days back. Refla, I think her name was," said the first guard. "She might do."

"Oh wonderful, I remember her. She made that delicious pie a day back," said the well-dressed woman, turning to one of her male guards. "Go and fetch this Refla; she's going to become ever so useful." He turned and headed back into the manor. "And for you, little dear, let's get that collar off of you."

The other female guard walked forward and took the key, placing it at the collar on Isha's neck. She twisted it, and it popped off, falling to the ground. She then turned to Chloe, reaching out for her collar.

"Ah, ah. Hold off on that one, for now, just as a precaution. There's no need to risk any unforeseen events occurring. Just her for now."

A slim female in an apron appeared out of the house a moment later and made her way down the steps.

"Yes, m'lady. Have I done anything to displease you?"

"What? No, of course not. You've been the best since I arrived here. Especially that pie you made just the other day. Simply marvelous."

"Thank you, m'lady. Then, if I may ask, why have you summoned me here?"

"Apologies, Refla, but I'd like you to assist us in an experiment."

"Expe... expe... I'm sorry, m'lady. I don't know what that word means."

"No worries, your education is not what's needed. They informed me that you're a mage, and I wish for you to show us some magic."

"Aye, m'lady, I have a little talent, but it's barely enough to lift pebbles off the ground, let alone something to look at."

"No, someone of your limited ability is perfect for what I wish to accomplish," said the well-dressed woman as she gestured ahead of them. "So, please show us your little pebble trick if you would be so kind."

"Ah, yes, m'lady," said Refla sheepishly as she stepped forward, wiping her hand on her apron. She stopped a few feet ahead, raised her hand, and closed her eyes. Seconds later, they heard the sound of rumbling as a few rocks on the ground shook and soon levitated off the ground. The few stones hovered in the air before Refla's outstretched palm. "Is this okay, m'lady?" she said, looking back at the well-dressed woman.

"Yes, but please, hold the stones there for a moment," said the well-dressed woman as he turned to Isha. "Well, if you would be so kind as to give us a demonstration."

Isha swallowed but nodded and walked forward, placing her hand on the woman's back.

"Ah... m'lady, what's happening? What's she doing behind me?" asked Refla.

"Nothing of import. Please keep the stones in the air for us," said the well-dressed woman.

Isha closed her eyes and began looking for her magic. *Okay, just do it like before.* She looked inside of herself and once again found the different colored strands of flowing light. *Just grab some of it and push it into your hand.* Then, reaching her hand out into the strands, they washed over her like running water. She tried holding some but only managed to grab a single strand as it wrapped around her finger. *Find where it connects.* She guided the strand ahead until she found another source of magic and tried combining the two. *And just connect it together like...*

"Why's she got her hand on my..." said Refla, her words cutting off mid-sentence as her eyes went wide and her mouth went agape. Then, suddenly, the surrounding ground trembled for only a moment before a large piece of it burst from the soil, ripping the land apart.

They all stared in amazement at the large piece floating ahead of them, easily towering over the largest man in the area. It rotated in the air, dust swirling around it as if it had its own gravity.

"Amazing," said the well-dressed woman as the smell of burned cloth and flesh filled the air.

Isha came back to real world, opened her eyes, and pulled her hand away from the woman. The large rock that had been pulled from the ground crashed back down to the soil, breaking into pieces as Refla fell to her knees and passed out. Her eyes rolled back into her head.

Chloe was patting her shoulder as the smell of something burning lingered on her nose. She found she had burned through Refla's clothing, revealing that she had left a burn mark in the shape of a small hand the woman's back.

Chloe began was patting the left shoulder of Isha's garment, extinguishing a small flame that had burned away her clothing, exposing her skin beneath.

"Incredible," said the well-dressed woman. "I see why you're the talk of the five kingdoms. That certainly is a gift." She grimaced while looking down at Refla. "Although the side effects seem to have much to be desired."

"I told you I can't control it yet."

"So, I see. But still, you are an exquisite creature. If my own gift wasn't so useless, I might even try to take you for myself. But alas, I've already sent word to our patrons. The auction will start in a day, so that much can't be helped."

"Auction?"

"Yes, dear. There are a large number of patrons interested in your gift. And they are willing to give up a massive amount of gold, influence, and wealth to acquire you. So much so that the poultry amount I just parted with will only seem as if it was a drop in the bucket."

Isha immediately thought back to her days in the trunk inside the room with Oscar and Gregga. Man after man came in trying to buy her. She was even surprised to hear the voice of quite a few women who came to bargain. She started to feel the anger boil up inside her as the metal collar sealing her power once again clamped around her neck.

"Well, come along then," said the well-dressed woman as she turned around and began walking up the steps to the manor. "I suppose we should get something to eat and get *you* a new garment. Have you girls eaten yet? I imagine you haven't. Being smuggled along the road like that, I'd be surprised if they feed you at all."

Upon entering the house, the girls followed the well-dressed woman, spotting odd-shaped items in each room as they passed. For example, a large, curved piece of wood that seemed to have strings connecting the top to the bottom was in one room. Another room just had fabrics of different colors. Then there was a vase, some type of bird in a cage, and many other items that Isha had never seen before.

"I see you're eyeing my collection of trinkets."

"What is all this for?"

"Wonders from around the world, each for sale to the highest bidder. But you, my dear, are the icing on the cake for the event. The star that shines brighter than the rest. Your acquisition may bring about a change in this kingdom's long history. One that I hope to be a part of if only as an usher."

"What do you mean?" asked Isha, blinking, trying to understand what the woman was saying, but her manner of speech confused her.

"Oh, I guess you don't fully understand what your birth means to the world. But perhaps as you grow, you will understand. A pawn princess on the board or perhaps a fifth queen challenging the rest. Oh! I get tingles just thinking about it."

They both entered the main hall of the manor, where a large table sat.

"Ah, soldier, go tell Refla to prepare something... Oh yes, well, I guess that won't happen for a while, will it?" asked the woman, shaking her head. "Well tell the staff in the kitchen to prepare something for our guests here." She walked to the head of the table and gestured to the seat next to her. "Please have a seat. It is so very rare that I get to have guests with such a history as yours. Surely you can regale me with the tales of how you came to be."

CHAPTER 3

Isha and Chloe were lying on a bed together. The soft and fluffy sheets contrasted heavily with the hard metal collars around their necks. The room they were in was just as impressive as the outside of the manor. Expensive-looking furniture and pillows were in abundance all around them.

"Do you really think they are coming?" asked Chloe as she gripped the sheets.

"I know Father is coming. He... he has to. We just need to wait."

A knock came on the door. It swung open and the woman from yesterday walked in. Throughout the entire night, she had never introduced herself.

"Good morning, my two darlings," said the woman as she stepped into the room wearing a nightgown, followed by her two personal guards and Mirow. "I do hope you two had a good night's sleep. Given the circumstances, I want to be as accommodating as possible."

"Why are you doing this to us? We haven't done anything to you," asked Chloe, sitting up from the bed.

"Why? For the money, of course," said the woman, shaking her head. "How so like children to not understand how the world works." She gave a dramatic sigh before turning to one of her guards. "I, too, was that naive about the world, men, and money." She raised her hand towards the ceiling. "Ah, to be young again. First loves, first betrayals, first deals. Ah, such wonderful times."

Father, where are you? Please tell me you are coming.

"Ah, well, let us continue the show. You girls follow me. We must prepare for this evening. Your potential buyers will soon be arriving, and I shall not have you two greeting them looking as if you've just fallen off a haystack. And you, those half-burned clothes will undoubtedly need to go. Let us get you cleaned up, shall we? We have a bath waiting for you," she said, clapping her hands.

Isha and Chloe looked at each other before Isha began easing herself out of bed to the floor. She waited for Chloe to follow suit, and the girls reluctantly followed behind the strange woman as they made their way through the manor.

"Where are we going?" asked Isha

"To whoever's chambers this was before we got here. I didn't take the opportunity to ask. But either way, it serves its purpose," said the woman as they made their way down the hall before entering another large room, where a large tub filled with water sat.

"Okay, wait outside, all except my guards and the caretaker. Us ladies are going to prepare." They all entered the room with both female guards standing beside the door as Mirow went and sat down in a chair near the wall.

Isha looked around the room, noticing the clothing on the bed, then looked over to see Mirow still staring at her like he always was.

"You girls, go on, hop into the bath and get yourselves cleaned. I have some nice clothing on the bed for you both to wear. Go on and pick whatever you like."

"I'm not undressing in front of him," said Chloe, pointing toward Mirow.

"Well, that's a shame. And here I'd thought you'd want to dress up all nice. Those tunics you both have on have certainly seen better days. But it's not you that needs to be clean. It's her," said the woman as she went to a desk and grabbed a brush, pointing it at Isha. "And that one has already promised to listen to whatever I ask in exchange for saving her ungrateful friend." She smiled at Isha. "What say you, dear? Will you do as I ask of you, or will you force me to have your caretaker there come hold you down as they bathe you?"

Isha looked at Mirow for a moment before he stood up and walked towards the window with his back turned to them.

"Oh, well, look. It seems he cares a bit for your modesty. And they say chivalry is dead these days," said the woman with a smirk. "Well, go on then; your modesty is safe."

Isha quickly took off her tunic and climbed into the water. It smelled like flowers. She grabbed a cloth and began scrubbing herself as Chloe walked forward and stood in front of her, blocking any view the man ahead could have if he turned around.

"There we are," said the woman with a smile as she sat down at a table and began applying shades of blush to her face. "But you may want to get accustomed to men gazing upon you, dear. There will be so many important people coming here today for that body of yours. I think that caretaker there will be the least of your troubles in the coming months."

"Is that all you people are about? Money?" asked Chloe, looking around the room.

"Oh, I simply love this part. This is where they try to

teach us about morals," said the woman as she turned herself in her chair and patted her lap. "Go on, child. Give us a speech on morality or doing the best we can for our fellow man."

"Chloe, stop," said Isha, reaching out her hand and grabbing Chloe by the arm. "It's okay, really. They won't listen to you."

"Why…" said Chloe, turning back to Isha as tears began to fill her eyes. "Why aren't you trying to fight them? Is it because I'm here?"

Isha thought back to the days she spent locked in that trunk as multiple men came day in and day out to talk to her father about her. How they would use her, and if they started early and used healing magic, how maybe she could have nine or ten children before she was 'used up.' That term, as disgusting as it was, was now ever clear in Isha's mind.

"No, it's fine, Chloe, I'm… I'm used to it now."

"But it's not…"

"Which clothing do you want me to wear?" said Isha, shaking her head at Chloe.

"Oh well, aren't you just the best commodity I could ask for?" asked the woman, looking back at the dresses on the bed. "Try the white one. I think it'll look good if we put your hair up in a little bow and make you look cute. I bet it'll drive up the price a bit."

"Chloe, can you grab me a towel?"

"But…" said Chloe, looking at Isha with frustration still in her eyes, but Isha just stared at her as if everything was normal.

"It'll be okay, Chloe."

Chloe grabbed some clothing from the bed and handed it to Isha, who stepped out of the water and dried herself. She then walked over to the bed and slipped into a gown; then, picking up the white dress, she brought it back to Chloe.

"Will you help me put it on?"

"I... yes," said Chloe as she helped Isha into the white dress.

Looking at Chloe's face, Isha suddenly felt she had done this before. As if she could remember it, the trying of clothes together. *Why does this seem familiar? Am I remembering changing clothes with Jacinta and Makeba?* "Chloe?"

"Huh?" asked Chloe as she helped Isha get her arm into a sleeve.

"Have we done this before? I feel like this... I feel this is familiar."

"What? No, of course not," said Chloe, her eyes glancing away from Isha's.

"Are you..."

A knock came on the door before Isha could press her question. And through the door came a man's voice.

"The first of the guests have arrived, ma'am."

"Oh, good," said the well-dressed woman. "Time has made its way to us. And we shouldn't keep the moments it grants us waiting." She stood up, walked towards the large closet, and began flipping her fingers through the clothing. "Not particularly a style to my liking, but in times of necessity, one must simply do what is necessary." Finally, she plucked out a sky-bluish dress with golden trimmings. "It's going to be a wonderful morning."

Soon, the girls were ushered back out the room and led upstairs. Mirow held the chains to their collars as they entered a dark room with light shining through a few peepholes in the wall. Releasing their chains, he nodded to the peepholes. Doing as suggested, the girls went forward, peeking through the holes in the wall.

Below, Isha could see a row of seats set up along with a stage made of lumber. She could see some of the guests mentioned in a few chairs and a few others making their way inside.

"Are they all really here for you?" asked Chloe.

"Yes, I know they are here for me," said Isha, her fingers gripping against the wood above the peephole. "I've seen some of them before." Isha's mind returned to her time locked in the trunk, looking through its little peephole. At least two of the men down below had visited Oscar a week ago in that hotel room.

Mirow closed the door behind him, stepping inside, allowing the room to be swallowed by darkness. He stood there, just watching the girls as they looked on.

It didn't take much longer before the room became filled with people as guards set up on each side of the room.

"Welcome, you connoisseurs of marvelous taste," said the well-dressed woman as she took the stage in front of the crowd. "I do hope your travels here were splendid. And, given the short notice of this event, I must admit that I'm surprised to see so many of you have come."

"Yes, yes, we know," said one man in the crowd, waving his hand dismissively. "Can we skip the formalities and get on with it? We all know why we're here. So, bring out the girl, and let's be done with it."

The crowd echoed his sentiment.

"Now, now. She's busy making herself ready for her admirers. Surely, none of you here are the type to rush a lady."

"Let's get on with this farce, so we can get to what we all came here for."

"Always so impatient," said the well-dressed woman with a sigh. But she then waved her hand, and one of the guards brought up a sizeable stringed instrument on the stage and placed it on a podium next to her.

"Unfortunately, because of the accelerated nature of the event, I wasn't able to procure many items of interest, but I have a few that may peek the fancy of someone here." She gestured towards the instrument. "Such as this, a harp of mirroring brought in from across the seas. It is a great device that continuously plays one of five tunes as long as you place a specific type of magic into it." The well-dressed woman ran her fingers on the strings of the harp allowing just a hint of magic to linger around the cords. Responsively, a soft melody began to play by itself throughout the harp, its strings moving of their own will.

Isha and Chloe stared in wonder as the instrument's melody made its way around the room.

"A hundred gold," said a woman in the crowd.

"Two hundred," said a man a few rows ahead.

The bidding had begun, and Isha could see that with every raise, the smile on the well-dressed woman's face grew wider.

For the next hour, the assortment of people below bid on all types of items. Isha and Chloe witnessed everything from a bird with feathers that changed colors according to how a piece of clothing wrapped itself around a woman's arm as she poured magic into it.

A knock came on the door of the room the girls were in. Mirow opened it, revealing one of the female guards.

"It's time," she said.

"Alright," said Mirow, "come on, it's time to go."

Isha turned around, balling her fists and taking a deep breath, then headed towards the door with Chloe following behind her. But as she entered and passed Mirow outside, they stopped Chloe at the door.

"Just her, you stay here," said the man, looking down at her.

"But..."

"You," said Mirow, looking at the female guard. "Keep her here 'til it's done." And with a firm grip on the chain around her neck, he led Isha down the hall. Her last images of Chloe were of the fear in her eyes as the door shut in on her.

The two went downstairs as Isha heard the well-dressed woman's voice.

"And now, what I'm sure you all have been waiting for, the main event of tonight's showing. A girl with a magical power not seen since the goddess herself brought us to these lands. Let me tell you, I have seen these powers for myself, and she was able to make the weakest soil mage able to shake a very mountain to its core. I bring you Isha, the Enhancement Mage."

And with that announcement, they led Isha on to the stage for the viewing pleasure of those who had attended. She just stared out at the faces of the people who had gathered for her. So many were the ones who had come to see her father just days before. It looked like seven or eight, not one or two as she had thought.

"Now, shall we start the bidding at..."

"How can we be sure that she is the one, and this isn't some trick?"

"Guards, please escort that gentleman out. He has now lost his ability to bid."

"What? You can't just..." said the man as a set of guards grabbed him by the wrists and turned him around, pushing him out towards the door.

"Now, while I am a gracious host. One thing I will not tolerate is someone questioning the validity of the items that I have painstakingly worked to procure for these sessions. As some of you here may know, I am a woman who goes to great lengths to uphold her reputation. And as such, you will not be allowed to question that. So, are there any more questions?"

"Not as to the validity of the girl being who you say she is," said a blonde-haired woman holding a fan, "but another question pertaining to the girl herself if you would be so kind."

"And that question is?"

"The girl, how are we to know that she hasn't been damaged already," said a man with a woman beside him. "Her father wouldn't let us see her. How do we know she can bear children, or at the very least remains untouched?"

"Men and their incessant need for virgin goddesses," said the well-dressed woman, shrugging her shoulders. "Fine. Tell me, child, have you ever shared a man's bed?"

"No...," said Isha, gripping her skirts once again. "No, ma'am, I have not." The question instantly brought back thoughts of that night in the tent where Molan assaulted her.

"There, you see, she's taken no man. That is from her own mouth. And perhaps in another two or three more years she might be ready to safely bare a childbirth."

"While her words are clear, I simply must ask for more validation, given the extraordinary amounts of coin we all here are willing to divvy over on this occasion. I think that shouldn't be so much more to ask of you, given the circumstances."

"And what would you have in mind?" asked the well-dressed woman, a level of annoyance clearly growing in her voice. "For her to spread her legs here for you all to have a look? I may be an auctioneer, but as a woman, I would not agree to such a thing."

"No need for theatrics. I have brought a birthing mother with me. She has seen to the birthing of three of my children and those of my housemaids. You may escort her with your guards to a room and have her check whether the child is intact or not."

The well-dressed woman scratched at her head, "The paranoia of men knows no bounds," she said, raising her hand. "Fine, caretaker, please escort the young lady Isha to the back along with that woman there. Take one of the guards with you and see that everything is handled properly."

"Yes, ma'am," said the caretaker as he led Isha off stage.

"But the auction will continue while she is away. I see no need to subdue the bidding while we wait for the men's curiosity to be sated. So, shall we start the bidding at a modest fifty thousand gold?"

Mirow led Isha down the aisle, still holding the chain attached to her neck. Two guards joined them as the midwife followed behind. Along the way, Isha could hear more and more of the people bidding for her, the number steadily rising.

"Alright, this room will do," said Mirow as he stopped by one of the rooms. "Make sure no one comes in," he said to the two guards before escorting Isha and the midwife in and closing the door behind him. "You can use that table. I'll wait over here."

"Now come on, dear. Hop on the table. I promise I'll make this as quick as possible."

Just do what they say. Father is coming. You have to keep Chloe safe. Isha reminded herself as she climbed up on the table, letting her feet dangle in the air. The words repeated in her head as she laid back against the table, her hands on either side gripping against the edges. She turned her head to see that Mirow was staring at her, his dark eyes focused on her as they had always been.

She felt the woman spreading her legs as her hand slid up her thigh. Isha's lips quivered as her eyes began to water. *Father is com… father is.* "I can't," she shouted, "please don't." She said as her legs began to kick, catching the woman off guard for a moment as she grabbed Isha by the ankles, holding them together.

"Calm down, child. It will only take a moment," said the woman, holding onto her, before turning to Mirow. "You, come hold her down."

"No, don't… don't," said Isha in a panic as she saw the man coming toward her. He placed his hand on Isha's chest, pinning her to the table.

"No! No!" screamed Isha as she felt her chest tighten with the weight the man was pressing down on her.

And in a flash, Isha saw the woman reach up to her hair, pull out a small blade, and plunge it at Mirow. The blade sank deep into the man's hand, protruding out the other end as he blocked. Then, removing his hand from Isha's chest, he revealed his own blade and he drove it upward, catching the woman off guard and sinking it deep into her neck. She gasped, her eyes wide. Blood oozed out of her mouth as her eyes focused on Isha one last time before she fell forward, landing on top of Isha, her face across her belly.

"Ahh... ahh..." murmured Isha in shock, her heart pounding in her chest as she freed herself, causing the woman's corpse to fall to the floor. Her mouth widened as she gasped for breath, but before she could scream properly, Mirow grabbed her around the waist with his bloody hand and covered her mouth with the other.

"Shhh... Don't scream, okay?"

Isha's body trembled in the man's hand. She could see the other end of the blade sticking out of his hand as it pressed against her stomach. And ahead of his fingers, sprawled across the floor, was the dead body of the midwife.

"I'm going to let you go now. I'm not going to hurt you, but I need for you not to scream, okay?"

Isha's eyes darted back and forth for a moment, but she nodded.

"Good, I'm letting you go now," said Mirow as he released his grip on Isha and took a step back. Blood trickled down his fingers, dripping to the floor. "Are you okay?"

"What? What's happening? Why... why did she... I don't know what's going on."

"You don't remember me, then? I was afraid you might give away my identity."

"Who... who are you.?"

"I work for your father," said the man as he gritted his

teeth, ripping the blade from his hand, "You... you met me once before, but it was only for a moment. My name's Rebby."

"Rebby?" asked Isha, her mind trying to remember him, but she couldn't think properly. So instead, she turned, staring at the body of the dead midwife. "Why... why did she? Was she trying to kill me?"

"Probably me. Probably you. Who knows? She's dead, and we're alive. We can figure the rest out later."

"We probably have a few minutes before they come for us. So, here, you take this," said Rebby to Isha as he extended the blade the woman had used against him to Isha.

Her hands shaking, she took the small blade, the bloody metal feeling slippery against her fingers.

Rebby walked forward, kicking over the woman's body and freeing his own blade from her throat. "I guess we might be able to escape from the window. I was hoping your father would have found you by now, and I wouldn't need to act, but you can't always get what you want."

"Father... is he coming?"

"I'm sure he is. Or at least out looking for you. You might not know it, but we've gone through a lot of bodies to keep you safe as long as we have. Assassination attempts, multiple kidnappings schemes. Oscar's been quite busy sorting it all out and..." The man began looking around the room and sniffing the air. "You smell that?"

"Smell what?"

"Smoke," said Rebby, stepping towards the window and peering out the side. "Yeah, there's smoke. "Fuck. Someone else is gonna try something. We might have to break the window and make a run for it. Find a few horses."

They then heard the sound of a scuffle outside the door, followed by two thuds as something hit the floor. Rebby stepped back, shielding Isha from the door as the knob began to twist.

"Okay, so I guess that plan's shit."

The door swung open, and there, standing before it, was Dessi, her neck and chin covered in blood.

"Dessi," shouted Isha, but she quickly noticed that Dessi's attention didn't look happy to see her at all.

"Release the girl," said Dessi.

Isha could see Dessi's hands near her and the hint of a blade peeking out of her trousers.

"Dessi, he works for father, he—"

"She's never seen me before... I don't stick around long," said Rebby.

"If he works for Oscar, then he'd be happy to let you go."

"Not until I get confirmation that Oscar is here. Until then, I don't know who you are. Even if the girl says, she does. You could just be wearing someone else's face."

Isha watched as the two stared at each other. "Dessi, he saved me from that woman on the floor. You don't need to fight."

"That true?" asked Dessi, her eyes quickly glancing from the floor and back to the man.

"Not sure who she was trying to kill, the girl or me. But yeah, I killed her."

"And Isha, you trust him?"

"I... I don't know. But I want to."

"Well then, I guess that will just need to be enough then, won't it," said Dessi, sliding the blade back into place. "You say you will only release the girl to Oscar, then follow me. He should be up on stage soon." Dessi then slowly turned and stepped back into the darkness of the hallway.

Rebby clutched a hand on Isha's shoulder, leading her out of the door, where Dessi waited for them.

"You will need to be quiet for a moment. Oscar is waiting for them to finish their bidding,"

In the hall, they passed by two guards dead on the floor. Both appeared to have had their throats slit, their blood leaking out and pooling together over the rug beneath them. Stepping over their bodies, they followed behind

Dessi as she led them forward, Rebby's hand still holding on tightly to Isha's shoulder.

"Seven hundred and fifty thousand gold is the current bid to Mr. Haskelwell," said the well-dressed as they neared the door that led to the main hall.

"Just wait here a little longer," said Dessi as she creaked open the door. To get a better view. "Oscar should be approaching soon."

Through the crack, Isha could see the joy on the well-dressed woman's face as she navigated the auction from the stage; the price continued to grow.

After a long while of bidding, the well-dressed woman clapped her hands.

"And sold to Mrs. Filliana Alogrand of the Greenland Merchant group for the astonishing price of one million three hundred and twenty thousand gold. I'm sure she will make a wonderful girl for young Charlie's upcoming name day. I hear he's almost fifteen now.

"Thank you," said Mrs. Alogrand. "I do so hope you gentlemen are not disappointed," she said as she looked around the crowd. "Simple economics won out, is all. Now, where is the girl? Bring her back out."

"I'm afraid that won't be necessary," came the voice of Oscar Highland as he entered the room, followed by Jacob and two guards.

"You! How did you get in here?" said the well-dressed woman.

"Oh, I figure that's not important right now," said Oscar as he walked up on the stage. "The question you should be asking yourselves is who am I going to allow to leave this room still breathing?"

"Guards," screamed the well-dressed woman. "Seize this man."

The guards that were spaced around the room all drew their weapons and pointed them at the crowd as the door burst open and more soldiers entered, all with blades drawn at the group of people that had gathered."

"What is this…" said the well-dressed woman as one guard grabbed her by the arms, forcing her down on the stage, planting his knee in her back.

"Oh, that won't be happening; you should pay more attention to who surrounds you rather than your little show here," said Oscar as one of his men handed him a chair. He then took a seat on the stage, looking over the crowd, their faces filled with fear and shock. "All your guards are dead, as well as everyone outside this room who isn't a man of mine. Ship pilots, coach drivers, all dead. Perhaps some were able to flee; not all rats can be caught, after all."

"This is preposterous," said a man in the crowd. "You can't hold us hostage. Do you have any idea who we are?"

"No, it seems you don't know who I am. Some of you know do," said Oscar, looking toward one of the men in the crowd. "What say you, Sir. Dollward? I see you've managed to attend this event even after just visiting me a day ago. What of that brother of yours? Where is he this fine morning?"

A gray-haired man stood up from his seat, "After he found out the child was yours; he smartly decided that this event wasn't in his best interest to attend. A sentiment I regretfully find myself now sharing."

"He always was the smarter of you two."

"Unhand me," said the well-dressed woman, writhing under the man's weight. "You can't do this. You filthy, unscrupulous people have no idea the connections—"

"Jacob, my boy. Would you please do the honors?"

"Yes, father," said Jacob as he drew his blade and stepped over the head of the well-dressed woman being pinned down.

"What… unhand me… don't you dar… argh," screamed the well-dressed woman as Jacob drove his blade down into her shoulder with such force that it pierced through the stage, causing the sword's hilt to collide against her back.

"Now, if you don't keep quiet, I'll have my son chop off

your head. Then I'll personally deliver it to that healing bitch of a high mother on a silver platter."

The well-dressed woman's eyes twitched as she moaned, but while biting her tongue, she endured the pain as silently as she could.

"Well, now isn't that pleasant," said Oscar, turning back and looking over the crowd. "Now, where's my daughter? Isha, do you hear me?"

A few seconds later, Dessi and Isha appeared hand in hand, headed toward her father.

"Ah, there you are," said Oscar. "Come up here, child. I want you to take a look at these people."

Isha made her way back on the stage, noticing everyone's eyes on her. She stepped up and took her place beside her father.

He smiled as he looked over Isha's bloody dress. "Well, haven't you had a wonderful adventure," he said as he placed a hand on her chin, inspecting her face. "Eyes are a little red, but not much. Good, you didn't cry this time." He placed his hands on her shoulders, looking her over. "Let's get that collar off you now, shall we? Where's the key?"

A guard took the key from a nearby stand, passing it over. Jacob took the key, unlocking the collar before gently lifting it off Isha's neck, revealing the red chaffed skin underneath.

"There, now doesn't that feel better?" asked Oscar as he saw Isha's lips begin to tremble, and her eyes start to water. "Oh no, not now. You're not allowed to cry yet. You need to be brave for what's to come." He wiped a tear from her cheek with a smile, then brought Isha in front of him as they faced the crowd together. "You all stand accused of kidnapping my daughter. Do you have anything to say for yourselves?"

The crowd murmured amongst themselves before another man stood up, "We didn't kidnap her; we merely came for the-" The man's words caught in his chest as a sword burst from it, his body fidgeting and twitching for a moment before going limp. The guard removed his blade, letting his body crash to the floor. The crowd gasped, and they all stood from their seats in a panic.

Isha tried to turn her face away at the sight of the scene.

"No, daughter, not now," said Oscar. "If you don't want this to ever happen to you again, you will need to look at things like this and face it head-on. Be strong."

Isha shook, her fingers twitching, her nose starting to run. But she did as instructed, lifting her head, watching as the room exploded into a panic.

"That's my girl," said Oscar with a smile as he stood up from his seat, clasping his hands on either side of Isha's shoulders. "Do not worry; I don't plan to kill all of you," said Oscar as the room quieted. Only half of you, and that starts now." He nodded his head, and instantly the slaughter began.

Nobles began casting their magic, only to be cut down before anyone could let off any spells of significance. A sword or spear quickly impaled the ones that did manage to counterattack.

"Nobles never were the best of fighters. All that time being pampered does that to someone. A room filled with mages all dying to the mundane. A shameful sight."

Their bodies were either thrown, hoisted across the room, or collapsed on the floor as blood and steel danced through the air as if in a murderous stage play. A play perfectly set for father and daughter as they stood and watched, one with horror and the other with a gleeful smile.

"Enough," screamed Oscar over the room after enough bodies had fallen lip. And on his command, the soldiers all drew back to their positions, still holding their bloody weapons. In the center of the room, squatted still over a dozen nobles, some cowering with their hands over their hands as their companions lay dead around them in a bloody and sliced mess. "Congratulations," said Oscar. "You will get to live and tell the tale of what happened here so that it will reach the ears of all those who take an interest in my daughter."

The huddled crowd began to look around the room as they rose to their feet.

"So, you won't kill us then?" asked the man from before

"Sir. Dollward, you old bastard, you managed to survive. You always were a hard one to kill," said Oscar with a smile to the man. He had fought while the others cowered. His face and arm were bloody, but there was a fire in his eyes. "I'm sure your brother will be ecstatic to see you after he hears of this." Oscar grabbed Isha's hand and led her off stage. "Well then, as much as I would like to stay and chat with you all," said Oscar, looking over the bloodied crowd. "I think it's time I get my daughter home and put her to bed. I'm sure she's exhausted from these events."

"Wait, Father, they still have my friend, Chloe; they have her upstairs."

"Oh, don't you worry about her. We rescued your friend some time ago. She and those Sakari girls are all out front waiting for you.

"I'll get you for this, you brute," shouted the well-dressed woman, still pinned down to the stage by the blade.

"It really is loud in here," said Oscar, "Do see that everything stays the way it is. I'll return soon. I wish to see my daughter out. Dessi, you will take half the men outside and ensure the girls make it home safely."

"You're not coming?" asked Isha, gripping Oscar's hand.

"Oh, I'm afraid not. They tried to kidnap my daughter. I'm afraid I'm far from done." Oscar stopped near the door, looking at the nobles and dead bodies. "I think what comes next might be a bit much for you. So, I'm sending you home with Dessi. Don't worry. Jacob and I will be along shortly afterward. But you are welcome to stay and watch if that will satisfy you."

Isha looked over the bloodied carnage, noticing the well-dressed woman's eyes still focused on her. She shook her head. "I... I want to go home."

"Of course, you do. Just leave everything to your father," said Oscar as he led Isha out of the room with Dessi. The screams of the well-dressed woman cursing his name in the background.

And as they neared the exit of the manor, the woman's screams began to be drowned out by a crackling sound. Then, as the guards opened the door back to the world outside, Isha's eyes reflected a world on fire. Airships and carriages were set ablaze as heaps of bodies littered the ground, many of which were missing their heads.

Oscar took a deep breath and patted Isha on the back, pointing below. "Go on now; your friends are waiting," he said, pointing to Chloe, who sat on the ground alongside Makeba and Jacinta.

"Oh sister, we come to get you," said Jacinta as the girls stood up with bright smiles.

"Go on, daughter," said Oscar, patting Isha on the back. "They've been waiting for you."

Isha made her way down the steps embracing her sister's arms and Chloe's.

"Oscar," said Dessi. "There was a man there who said he worked for you. But I've never seen him before."

"Yeah, that was Rebby. He's usually on a mission, so you haven't met him yet. But Jacob knows him."

"You don't think you should have told me you had someone watching over her?"

"I needed you motivated," said Oscar, looking Dessi over, seeing the blood still splattered across her neck and chest. "Nothing like a mother desperate to protect her children, is there," he said with a smirk.

"Just be careful, Oscar. If I end up killing one of our own, then it falls on your head."

"I'll remember that. But for now, go and take care of our little problem child. You women folk can comfort her more than I can, right now."

"And what makes you so sure of that."

"Because every mistake I made with you, you and I are going to ensure it never happens with her."

Dessi just stared at Oscar for a moment. "Sometimes, I really can't tell if you love me or if you just hate yourself."

Oscar turned to Dessi, looking her in her eyes. "You finally decided you want the answer to that question you've been dancing around for these last years?"

Dessi bit the inside of her lip for a moment, staring back at Oscar. "I'll wait a little longer; besides, now's not the time." She then patted Oscar on the shoulder and headed down the steps to the girls.

Oscar watched as Dessi escorted the girl through the burning wreckage outside the manor and into an awaiting carriage.

"Bring the box," he said to one of his men. And soon, two men, each holding one side of a trunk, made their way up the stairs. Oscar then turned around and headed back inside the manor with the men following him. They dropped the chest at the room's entrance. It clattered with the heavy sound of metal clashing inside.

"What do you intend to do with us," said one of the women in the crowd of surviving nobles. But Oscar quietly walked around the room, walking back up on the stage. He stepped past the well-dressed woman who was still pinned to the floor and looked over the crowd.

"I said that I would let you all live. But your living comes with conditions. A good many days' journey from here is the city of Orlana. I imagine you all know it very well. I will have you all escorted there in the same chains you dared to place my daughter in. There you will be paraded nude like the livestock you intended for my daughter. If any of you object to this treatment, then step forward, and I'll have you join your companions on the floor beneath you."

The nobles nervously looked around at each other, and the guards still held the blades at the ready.

"I would kindly ask that you all start removing all your clothing, undergarments and all. That includes the ladies as well. You are just as guilty as the men beside you. More so, even."

Slowly, the crowd began to reach for their clothing.

"Surely there must be another way," said a nobleman with small amounts of grey hair on his head. "Each of us here has a substantial amount of gold to offer. Surely we can come to an alternative."

Oscar nodded, and instantly, the man found a blade emerging from his belly. He twitched, looking up at Oscar as blood leaked out of his mouth, and his body crashed to the floor.

"Any of you not fully undressed in the next minute will be killed for wasting my time," said Oscar, not even flinching as he stared at the crowd ahead of him.

They immediately began ripping at the clothing, some going so far as to rip the fabric from their bodies until both women and men stood completely naked, with a pile of bloodied clothing lying at their feet.

"Dollwood," said Oscar as the man finished ripping off his shirt. "How would you like to keep what little pride you have left and not your co-conspirator in their march of shame?"

"I'm not afraid of death, and we've known each other long enough, Oscar. If you want something, spit it out. And if I avoid this travesty of a show without damaging my house, then I shall comply."

"A shame you retired from your post and ended up here. Well-spoken men such as yourself are a boon to their kingdom," said Oscar with a smile. "Stay with my men here. We can discuss the details afterward."

"Now, where was I? Oh yes, public shaming," said Oscar as he nodded to the trunk behind the naked nobles in the door's entrance. "Behind you, you will find a trunk filled with those fancy magic-stopping collars that you all had my daughter in along with a key. Go on and place the collars around your own damned necks and see what it feels like, then hand the key to the guard by the door. You will then be escorted to the grounds, where wagons await you. You wanted to seal my daughter's fate. Well, now you will do the same to yourself."

"What... what are you going to do to me?" said the well-dressed woman, the bloody sword still protruding from her shoulder.

"Oh, I've got something special planned for you. I can't kill a member of that healing bitch's group. But I can think of far worse fates than death. Trust and believe; I have something special planned for the person who made all of this come together."

One by one, the nude nobles walked up the trunk and shackled the collars around their necks. The clicking of a key sealing in any potential magic they might have made them weak as any mundane. After finishing, they were led out of the room, leaving only Oscar, Jacob, and the well-dressed woman remaining in the room.

Oscar sat back down in the chair on the stage. "Remove the sword if you please, Jacob."

Jacob stepped forward, gripping the hilt of his sword and ripping it free from the well-dressed woman on the floor.

"Argh!" screamed the woman as she went rolling around on the stage. "That hurt, you bastard."

"I'm sure it did," said Oscar with a brow raised. "Come on out and bring your mistress a chair."

The well-dressed woman's blonde guards came from behind a corner with a chair. They stepped up on the stage and helped ease her into the seat so that she and Oscar faced each other.

"You know, just because I can heal, that doesn't mean it's not a pain in the ass to do so." said the well-dressed woman as she placed a glowing hand over the wound.

"My son stabbed you where you instructed. Therefore, the blame lies purely on you. I'm sure a leg or hand would have sufficed for my needs."

"And... let there be doubt in my involvement in this? No, it needed to be as real as... possible," said the woman as she winced in pain. But she soon regained her composure. "Now, am I to assume you will hold up your end of the deal?"

"You will be paid well for your trouble, and your secret will be kept from the High Mother. Now, did you acquire the item I requested?"

The well-dressed woman nodded, and one of her guards removed a sachet from over her shoulder, tossing it to Oscar. "It was a pain to acquire on short notice, and considering what you wanted it to do, I couldn't acquire much of it. Apparently, it takes quite some time to make. And she will need to master using it."

"She'll get the time she needs," said Oscar, handing the bag to Jacob. "Then our business here is concluded, Miss Fisdale."

"I'd appreciate it if you'd never call me that name again. It's a relic of a life I no longer live."

"So be it," said Oscar with a smirk. "That's something we have in common, and I understand the need to keep one's identity a secret." Oscar leaned back in the chair. "Rebby, are ya still here?"

"I'm here," came Rebby's voice from somewhere unseen.

"Good, then stick around awhile. I've got another job for ya."

CHAPTER 4

"Why do I always have to hide in the back of the damn carriage?" pouted Silk as Victor and Frenka sat up-front in their wagon, riding into the city Capital of Mari.

"Because you're the only one who stands out," said Victor as he guided the horses by the reins. "Don't worry. Nahtalli said that your ability should return soon enough now that the mental bond has weakened. We can also look to removing it now that we're in the capital. One or two mind mages should be capable of breaking the link here."

"I'm sick of smelling like hay."

"I have a home here; we'll soon..."

"Excuse me, sir," said a man riding up alongside them. "The Queen awaits your arrival in the castle."

"Of course, she does," sighed Victor." I assume you've been waiting for my arrival at the gates."

"Only for the last two days, sir," said the man with a

smile as three other riders on horseback joined alongside them. "She has guards at every entrance of the city. It seems she was quite eager for your return."

"Queen seems to miss you very much, Victor," Frenka laughed.

"Well, I'm happy someone finds this amusing. I had hoped to hide you for a day or two before I had to explain this mess."

"Poor Victor, it best to face problems headfirst. Move it out of sight so that you may focus on real problem. By waiting, you just give yourself more distractions."

"More clan wisdom, I assume."

"More Frenka wisdom. You and Dula-hon are now blessed to have it."

"Says the dumb mountain woman," said Silk. "You will not decide what I am blessed to have,"

"I shall. That is unless you wish to challenge me."

"I will challenge you when I get my powers back. And then we'll see who's laughing."

"Well then, Frenka looks forward to it."

"Ladies, let's leave the talk of mortal combat until after we've had our visit with the Queen."

"Agreed," said Frenka, wrapping an arm around Victor's as they headed off towards the castle at the center of the city.

They traveled through the city with their escorts leading the way. Instead of the main entrance, they were brought around to the stables, where Frenka and Victor dismounted.

"Alright, come out of there," said Victor, walking around to the back of the wagon and removing the drape. Silk appeared in an over-large hooded brown tunic covering everything from her hands to her legs. Victor extended his arms, picking her up and setting her down on the ground. The hem of the over-large outfit dragged along as they headed in.

"Who's this one then?" asked the guard.

"A secret person the queen wants to keep a secret. I'm sure you understand."

"You're the general. It's not my job to question. Just surprised by the appearance is all."

"Not as surprised as I was, I can assure," said Victor as he allowed the men to lead him into the castle, through the barracks where multiple rounds of guards were sitting in their armor around the tables. "Tell me, how has the capitol been since I've been away? Anything interesting happening lately?"

"Nothing much to speak of sir. Just your average mugging or murder for some type of gambling debt. Nothing that ranks so highly as to require your direct action. Unless you still prefer to slum it with the grunts these days."

"You might be surprised. I've been slumming it a lot lately."

The two men continued their casual conversation about the kingdom's ongoings until reaching the castle's throne room. Guards opened the door, allowing them to pass. Then, walking in with the group, Victor quickly noticed Queen Clarissa sitting upon her throne in a mostly empty room except for one or two guards stationed at either side.

"Hello Victor, welcome back home," said Clarissa as she waved her hands. "Guards, please leave us. This is a private conversation between Victor, myself, and his companions there."

Immediately, the two guards left the room, closing the door behind them.

"I am not sure this place has ever been much of a home. But I am here as you requested. And I'm going to assume you have some other errant task for me."

"I do. But that can wait," said Clarissa, standing up from her throne and making her way down the steps. "Surely, you would like to introduce me to your guests. And perhaps also explain why I've been feeling as if something has been tugging on my magical core, as if you've done something curious to affect our link."

"I may have done something."

"And this something, was it perhaps around three months ago?"

"May have been," said Victor as he began to feel an itchy tingle on his neck as the Queen drew closer.

"Oh, poor Victor, always making messes for me to clean up," said the Queen as the gray veins began to appear on her neck, crawling their way up to her chin.

"It's not a mess that needs to be fixed at the moment," said Victor as he struggled to keep from scratching at his neck.

"Oh, is that so?" asked the Queen as she stood before Victor. "Perhaps we'll see to that later, then." She turned toward Frenka, who was staring at her. "Oh, my apologies. Where are my manners? Who are your friends, Victor?" she asked as she took a step back, looking over Frenka and Silk, who was still covered. "My, my, isn't this one mysterious?"

"I am Frenka. I am Victor's wife."

The Queen froze for a moment, her eyes open, her cheeks pursed in, and her brows raised. "Pardon? Did... Did you say wife?"

As ridiculous as this situation is about to become, I dare say that look on your damned face makes it worth it. "Yes, and this one too," said Frenka, gesturing to Silk, who kept her head down and covered. "She Victor's second wife, sister wife." Frenka nodded, giving the Queen a pleasant smile.

Clarissa looked back and forth between Victor and the two women for a moment but regained her composure with a shrug of her shoulders. "I see. Well, haven't you been busy, Victor?"

"It was a complicated journey," he said as his lip twitched.

"So it would seem," said Clarissa as she stepped back in front of Victor, placing her finger under his chin, raising his head, and exposing his neck to Frenka. "Well, little wives,

I assume that Victor has informed you of the ties that bind us."

"He say you control him, but also not to make you his wife. He not like you very much, it would seem."

"Like? Well, I suppose that should normally have something to do with it. But you see these wonderful marks on his neck, and undoubtedly, you've noticed mine. Well, let's just say that they can become quite uncomfortable. Now, as a mage, I can fend off the worse of it, but alas, poor Victor, if he isn't relieved. I'm afraid he could easily just be driven mad." Clarissa smiled and leaned in, giving Victor a kiss.

Victor felt a wave of release take over his body as the veins on his neck slowly receded down into his collar, out of sight. Clarissa's neck followed suit as well.

"Ah!" said Clarissa, taking a deep breath, and savoring the moment. "There really is nothing like it. The freedom you give me."

Clarissa turned and reached her hand toward her throne, and suddenly the metal shook. And next came the sound of metal screeching across the room as the throne twisted and bent in on itself. Clarissa rotated her hand as it stretched toward the ceiling before finally snapping. The top piece was a mangled mess of what it had once been. It hovered in the air before crashing down to the floor, sliding and colliding against one of the room's pillars. The other half was just a spiral of twisted metal that raised toward the ceiling.

The door to the throne room burst open as several guards entered, holding their blades, but stopped in the door frame upon seeing the Queen.

"Hold your position. No need to panic. I was merely taking out the trash." A new throne is going to be made for me this week. I just felt it was time to get rid of the old one."

"Ah, yes, my Queen," said one soldier with a bewildered look on her face. "Ah, would you like us to remove it?"

"Perhaps later, please continue to give my guests and me some time alone. There are still private matters we wish to discuss."

"Yes, ma'am, said the confused guard as she and one of her men bowed, closing the door behind them.

"That's very good, Frenka not even sure if stupid prince could do that."

"Stupid prince?" asked Clarissa, tilting her head.

"Frenka here is one of Prince Saffron's royal guards," said Victor, removing the Queen's hand from his face.

"That child? You took one of his royal toys. I doubt he took that very well."

"Not sure he knows yet. We sort of just packed up and left."

Clarissa chuckled. "Oh, that certainly will provide some entertainment for me later." She stepped toward Silk. "Fine, I accept your ludicrous marriage as long as it does not affect our relationship. But what of this one? Is she another guard? She's been reticent since she arrived. What of it? Can she not speak?"

"Silk," said Victor, "Show her."

Raising her hand to reveal her ashen-skinned arms, Silk removed her hood, revealing her face to the Queen. Her ruby and emerald eyes were as striking as ever. She even caused the Queen to take a step back in shock.

"Oh my, what sort of affliction has befallen this one? A curse of some sort?"

"I am not a curse," Silk said annoyedly. "This is who I am."

"And it finally speaks."

"She is my wife. She is not an 'it'."

"Yes, I see. My apologies. I was thrown off guard by her visage. But if I may ask, why? Surely there must be a story behind this one."

"I'm still figuring that part out."

"I swear, Victor, you never fail to exceed, do you? It

seems oddities and circumstances find their way to you no matter where you go.”

“She says they hired her to protect me from an assassin while I was on the ship.”

“Really? Is this who Wollenhielm hired?”

“Wollenhielm? What’s he got to do with this?”

“They informed me that someone in the capital doesn’t seem to like the way I treat you, so…”

“And you never thought to tell me my life was in danger?”

“Oh, Victor, please. I have saved your life dozens of times now without you realizing it. It would just be a waste of my breath to inform you of every occasion.”

“I see,” said Victor, his tone low and droll.

“You know, the typical ongoings of court life. So, I asked Wollenhielm to see to it and arrange for you to have some protection. But I had no idea this… this wife thing of yours was who he would hire. Tell me, did Wollenhielm contact you directly? I fail to imagine that he knew such a creature as yourself existed and kept it to himself.”

“I don’t know any Wollenhielm,” said Silk, her tone matching Victor’s. “Grennok handled all that stuff. He just told us what to do.”

“Ah, so you have a contractor then? That does make more sense. So tell me, with that skin, you must be an oddity. What are your powers, anything of note?”

“She’s a shapeshifter,” said Victor. “Think; illusion magic without worrying about the temperature or improper sunlight to reflect. A perfect replication of voice and appearance at all times.”

“Oh! Well, that does sound like a useful skill. Show me. This is a trick I’d very much like to see.”

“I can’t.”

“She was injured. The healing process has yet to complete.”

“Oh, well, that simply will not do,” said Clarissa, shaking her head. “But I suppose this would be a perfect time to invite our guest in." She turned around. "If you would be so kind as to introduce yourself."

A woman draped in a white garment walked out from behind one of the pillars.

"You certainly do love a flair for the dramatic, Clarissa."

"Victor, you may not remember her since I don't think you were unconscious the last time you met. But this is the High Mother of the Healing Circle. She's traveled a long way to meet you. It would seem that the girl they sent you off to find has become something of a valuable commodity in the five kingdoms."

"What? How so?"

"I shall inform you of the circumstances, but first, I think we need to have a talk about some red crystals you may have come across."

Victor narrowed his eyes. "And how, if I may ask, did you come across the information that I was looking into them? I can't imagine you just showed up here and started asking the Queen about them."

"That is true. Let's just say that Oscar Highland sends his regards."

"Of course, he does," said Victor with a sigh. "Fine. What do you want to know? Granted, I know little myself."

"Do you know who is making the crystals and why?"

"I believe a radical section of the Church of the Goddess is making them. Not exactly sure for what purpose. But I think they have connections to the Magic School of Latrusa."

"Hmm... And what brings you to that conclusion?"

"We were investigating an underground cavern when we found dozens of bodies with crystals implanted in their skin. Inside the cavern, we found a letter with the school's insignia stamped on it."

"And what did the letter say?"

"I couldn't tell. The words were washed away. And shortly afterward, we were attacked, making further investigation impossible. I can tell you one thing for certain; I am sure those little red crystals can either raise someone from the dead or bring about some type of possession."

"What?" asked Clarissa. "And you've seen such a thing?"

"Indeed, we got our asses kicked by such a thing," said Victor as he unconsciously began pacing. "But back to the girl. What does she have to do with this? She should be safely tucked away in the walls of Latrusa."

"An unknown group attacked the school. Probably that church you mentioned. As such, we've returned her to Father Oscar Highland until things can be sorted and the school can double their security."

"Makes sense. Was there any info on what the girl's powers were? That was the topic of much discussion while I was in their company."

"Of course!" said Clarissa with a smile. "You've been traveling amongst the mundane, so you wouldn't have heard. That girl looks to be the bringer of change. It seems she has the ability to enhance a mage's magical ability. Perhaps even my own. First of her kind, an oddity that may change the shape of our world."

"What?" asked Victor rhetorically as he stopped pacing. "If that's the case, then every mage from here to the western isles will be after her."

"Quite so. I've even heard rumors of that Highland fellow taking bids on who will be the first to cement themselves in her womanhood," said Clarissa with a smirk. "I dare say the poor child is in for a life of being used and mistreated unless we get our hands on her first."

"Clarissa, I encourage you that any schemes you have to acquire the girl be dropped immediately. I don't know what that Oscar fellow has planned for the girl, but I can assure you he's not selling her. And anyone that thinks that is in for a rude awakening. The man is as cunning as I've ever seen."

"Cunning? I've heard he runs a ground of low-rate mercenaries out in the countryside. What is there for me to be afraid of? And a commodity such as the girl cannot be left unchecked, even if I were to heed your counsel."

"I'm afraid I would have to agree with Sir Victor here, Your Highness," said the High Mother nodding her head. "I've had dealings with the man myself. One of which was where he held a blade at my neck. And at the time, I was as protected as any Queen might be. So, I would advise you not to underestimate him. While not a known figure in this kingdom, the man has a reputation for being *effective*."

"I shall take your advice under consideration, then."

Which means fuck us. She's going to do what she wants. Victor turned towards the High Mother. "Since I have given you all the information I have. Perhaps you could do me a favor, High Mother."

"Me? What can I help with?"

"My wife here, the ashen-skinned one. I had a disciple of your Nahtalli look at her. But he could only do so much, and she hasn't been able to use her full power since our investigation. Would you mind having a look?"

"Oh, of course. Nahtalli is a talented healer, but I suppose his understanding of shapeshifters might be limited since they are such a rare breed."

"You know more people like me?" asked Silk in disbelief.

"Now? No, but in the past, I've had dealings with your type before. Every hundred or so years, one or two of you will appear. I've had experience healing them before," said the High Mother glancing at Victor. "But to see you walking about in your natural form and married no less. In the past, your type were called monsters, hunted down and killed. A sign the times are changing."

"Not that much," mumbled Silk.

"Now, let's have a look inside, shall we," said the High Mother, reaching out both hands and clasping Silk on each side of her head with glowing hands. "Yes, I see. Your core is a bit damaged. How did it happen?"

"Fighting something magical down in a tunnel."

"Some... thing?"

"It looked like a person. But people can die, or at least I thought they could. Whatever that thing was has me second-guessing my beliefs on that.

"Well, that certainly raises so questions," said the High Mother before turning back to Silk, "Give it another month or two, dear. It should heal properly, but I could expedite the process if you desire. I can't stay for the entire week needed, but I can create an elixir that will help with her problem. Think of it as payment for the information and what I will ask of you. And while I'm here, I'll take care of those scars across your face as well."

"Of course, you will," said Victor. "Don't you all have someone better to do your grunt work?"

"No one as capable as you, it would seem."

"See, husband. They see you as smart man."

"I'm thrilled."

"Now, don't be that way, Victor. The High Mother has traveled a long way to visit you. The least we can do is hear her out. Go on, High Mother. I, for one, am very interested in what you have to say. This could end up being a potential threat to all our kingdoms."

"Before, I was going to ask that you continue to look into the jewels. I'll also have the school of Latrusa do the same. But since you said it may be a sect of the Church of the Goddess, I would ask instead that you visit the Frothel Cathedral in Usjun. I have a few people inside the church who I can call upon for assistance in this matter. The common people have always viewed healers as symbols of the Goddess, and the church has adopted many of our own. I will start calling on them for information as well."

"And to think," said Victor, looking at Clarissa with weary eyes. "All of this started because you decided to involve me in your mess with King Nevander."

"Oh, stop acting like a petulant child. We have both outgrown the fantasies of any other type of life," said Clarissa with a smirk. "And you cannot say this ordeal has not been fortuitous for you. I mean, really, Victor. Returning with two wives. And here I thought you just disliked women in general, judging by how you treated your poor Queen and lover."

"I wasn't aware we were sharing our situation with others now," said Victor, glancing at the High Mother. "And it's 'reluctant lover.' I did not exactly get a say in the matter, or do you not remember."

"Seeing as you've done the same, I find it highly hypocritical of you to see fault in me in this regard. Besides, as I said before, you were asleep the last time you met the High Mother. She was one of the first people Mother contacted to try and remedy our situation. So, she has known about us for quite some time."

"I think you were barely over fourteen the last time we met. An absolutely adorable child," said the High Mother. "They had you on the table as they tried to undo that bond between you and the Queen. Although it seems after all these years, no progress has been made on that front."

"Oh, I wouldn't say that. Over the years, we've learned to make the most of it. Victor here does what I wish, and I, as Queen, shower him with my love. Regretfully, it's him and him only, which is hardly fair for the rest of the kingdom for this mundane to have a monopoly on my affections. But he's proven useful enough to warrant my attention. However, I am unsure how I feel about sharing him with his new companions. I do not think a Queen should be part of this man's magical harem."

"The Goddess has her plans for us all, it seems," said Victor.

"Unfortunately, but I must admit, having a man do exactly as I say during our coupling does have its advantages." The Queen rubbed her fingers together, allowing a slight bit of magic to form. "Victor dear, raise your hand and tell me you love me."

Victor sighed as he raised his hand above his head, "I

lov—"

"I love you, Queen Clarissa," came the voice of Silk.

Victor's eyes went wide as he slowly turned his head to see Silk with the same astonished expression on her face as she looked upward at her own hand raised above her head.

"Well," said Clarissa, "This certainly is unexpected."

CHAPTER 5

Jacob stood on the deck of an old wooden building, looking toward the sky. At his side a leather pouch hung over his shoulders, resting against his waist. Ahead of him, he watched as an airship made its way towards his direction. They had spent their days in the small village of Pril, a farming village with little to speak of besides the occasional harvest festival. Dirty streets, the echo of nearby sheep, and trees that stood off in the distance. But today, it would serve their purpose.

The airship above him was a small vessel, nowhere near the grandeur of the previous sights of Soulden's or the High Mother's. By comparison, it seemed like a dainty thing; the likes seen by that of lesser nobles. It had a banner like most ships, but not one known to him. As the ship continued its approach, he turned and made his way through the small town, ending up at an inn.

Instead of walking inside, he walked along its walls, making his way towards the back of the building where he found Dessi and Oscar sitting down, watching as Chloe, Jacinta, Isha, and Makeba were practicing their magic on tree logs.

"They've arrived."

"Ahead of schedule, it seems. Dessi, go and greet them. I'll bring the girls along shortly. Jacob will help carry their things."

"Alright, then," said Dessi, dusting off her clothing. "I'll leave the grunt work to you," she said as she passed Jacob, patting him on the shoulder.

"So, ready to say goodbye to one of your children again?" asked Jacob as he walked up beside Oscar, leaning his back against the inn's wall.

"It's more of a need at this point," said Oscar, looking over at the girl as they continued to play with their magics. "This feeling she's been infecting me with since we found her. I've been thinking it over in the time since she's been here. And it can be quite annoying after one realizes it's there."

"Soulden said it was an affinity spell, right? That it only enhances what's already there. So, what's the problem? I kind of like feeling like an overprotective brother. And Dessi's always in high spirits with her around."

"I've been thinking it's that same spell that drove Molan to do what he did. Brute that he was; he'd never disobeyed an order before."

"So what? Are you going to ask them to look for a way to remove it?"

"No, not as of yet. Plus, at the moment, it's probably helping resolve another issue," said Oscar, gesturing back towards the girls. "That little one with the scarred hand. When she arrived, she could barely look at my daughter without a scowl on her face. I had thought to use that kidnapping ruse to bring her under control, but it seems to have worked better than expected. She's refused to leave the girl's side since they've returned from their little adventure."

"You think that's the spell as well?"

"Partly. Rebby said my little girl protected her from some bastard named Salley in their group. That was probably what started off this change."

"Where is Rebby anyway? I haven't seen him since the theatrics."

"I sent him off on another assignment. Unlike Jasper, he doesn't particularly like to be around. So, I keep him busy."

"And yet, Jasper's the one who trained him. How in the Goddess's name did they wind up so differently?" asked Jacob with a sigh. "If Dessi or your little Isha ever find out what you did, they will hate you for it. You do know that, right?"

"Dessi understands that I had a hand in it. Just not to such an extent. And as for Isha, she doesn't need to understand. A father's job isn't to be understood. It's to do what's best. And this little adventure was a growing experience for her. She's not going to be a child for much longer. The fact that we had to go through all of this proves that."

"Still regretting having to do it?"

"We thwarted over a dozen attempts to kidnap the girl, and she doesn't even know it. She just goes along with her day, not a care in the world. Ended up having to stage our own just to stem the tide. It's always a bitter pill to accept one's limitations."

"If being a father is such a thankless job, why take it on?"

"Ask me that question again when you and Dessi have your own," said Oscar, standing up from the back steps of the inn. "Alright, ya little mages in training. It's time to go. Jacob here has come to make sure you pick up your things."

"Have they come to get us?" asked Jacinta as they all ran over.

"Yes, they have. So, come along. Let's get your things ready." said Jacob as he turned around, leading the girls back down the side of the inn.

"Wait. Not you, little Miss Chloe," said Oscar, raising his hand. "I have something to speak with you about."

The girls stared at Chloe nervously.

"Did Chloe do something bad?" asked Jacinta.

"No, of course not. This is just a friendly chat, is all. I've known you three girls sometime now and have had talks with all of you. But I haven't had the pleasure of having a one-on-one talk with this new friend of yours. And I'd like to take advantage of this chance before you all take off into the sky, is all." Oscar opened the door to the inn. "Come along then; I promise this won't take long."

Chloe looked back at the rest of the group before letting Oscar lead her inside.

"Let's head on then," said Jacob as he patted the girls on the back, leading the three into the town.

"What does father want from Chloe?" asked Isha.

"I'm sure it's just to talk," Jacob said as he looked down, seeing Isha with a skeptical face.

"Father never wants to 'just talk.' He always wants something else."

I wonder if you know how right you are, little Isha. "Well, look at you being all skeptical; you're going to wind up being like him one day if you keep thinking like that," said Jacob with a smile. "Momo, Jomo, you girls meet up with Dessi and tell her we're on the way. I still need to talk with Isha before you girls head off. I think your mother's over there waiting for you."

"Okay," said Jacinta, as she and Makeba ran off ahead.

"You want to talk to me?"

"Yeah, it's nothing too important. I'm not even sure it'll work but judging from how your magic works, who knows, it might!"

"Huh? What is it?"

Jacob reached into the pouch at his side and pulled out a magic restricting metal collar.

76

Instantly, Isha stepped back into her mind as images of her time trapped with Chloe flashed into her mind.

"I see you're not too fond of these, are you?"

"No, I'm not. Why... what's that for?"

"I want you to put it on."

"What? Why?"

"I want to show you something. Or do you not trust me?"

"No... I trust you. It's just..." She stared at the collar as it dangled from the chain in Jacob's hand. "Do I have to?"

"I'm not Father. I won't make you. Instead, I'm asking you to put it on. Don't worry. It won't take long. But if you don't trust me, then you don't have to."

Isha looked between Jacob and the collar before reaching out and taking it from his hand, almost dropping it as he released it and the weight fell upon her. She then fiddled with it in her hands before raising it and placing it against her neck.

There you go. Don't be afraid of it. "Okay, now turn around, and I'll lock it on your neck."

Isha did as instructed, and Jacob tightened the lock on the collar before patting Isha on the head. He then reached into his pocket, pulled out a small piece of cloth, and placed it in her hand.

"What's this for?" asked Isha as she fiddled with the collar.

"Try using your magic?"

"What? But the collar..."

"I know. Just trust me. And only a little bit, okay? We don't need you burning up your clothes like last time. I don't need you going nude again, like with Father."

"That's not... he made me."

"I know," said Jacob with a smile, "Just try to focus your magic on your hand."

"But doesn't the collar stop my magic?"

"That's what we're here to find out."

Isha frowned but closed her eyes. Nothing happened

for a moment, but then, with a slight shake, the cloth in her hand began to darken. Then in the center, a small flame appeared, and the fabric caught fire, causing Isha to drop it.

"Ow, it's hot," she said, dropping her hands. "Oh, it worked."

"So it did."

"But why did it burn me? It never burned me before," she said, watching as the flame consumed the rest of the fabric on the ground.

"I'm pretty sure that collar limits only some of your magic but not all of it. Remember that pull magic you showed me," said Jacob, pointing to a stick on the ground. "Try using it on that."

"Okay," she said, quickly extending her hand toward the stick. "Pull," but nothing happened. "Pull," she said again, but still no movement. Isha looked at her fingers. "It doesn't work now."

"I figured as much. I guess our magic works sorta in the same way."

"It does?"

"Yeah, I've had those magic collars on me before. But I found I could still use my powers on anyone I touched. So, when I saw all your clothes get burned off, I wondered if your powers worked the same."

"You didn't have to watch," murmured Isha with a blush, looking away.

Jacob smiled, patting her on the head again. "I'm sorry. I should have turned away. I guess the curiosity about your powers got the better of me. Do you forgive me?"

Isha pouted her lips but spoke softly. "I forgive you."

"Thank you. Turn around so we can get this off of you," said Jacob as he spun Isha around and unlocked the collar, placing it back in the pouch. "Here," he said, handing it to her. "You can keep this one. Try to find out what powers you can or can't use with it on. And if you ever find out why some powers work, and why some don't, tell me when you get the chance."

Inside the tavern, Oscar led Chloe to a table with a pouch on top and took a seat, extending his hand for her to sit down.

"Well then, Miss Chloe, seeing as you're about to take off, I think we should form ourselves a little understanding."

"Wha... what understanding, sir?"

"An understanding as to who you are. I have an idea, but I figure it's best for me to hear it from your lips rather than just speculate."

"I... I don't know what you're talking about. What do you mean?"

"Oh, you're lying to me already, then. Alright, I'll humor you this time. Firstly, according to them little Sakari, the first time you met my daughter, you attacked her screaming; 'it's your fault'. That implies you know each other."

"That was a mistake, I—"

"Secondly, Dessi says that ever since you got here, you've kept your distance from Isha, and whenever you were around her, you'd always avert your eyes. Now, my daughter and them Sakari might not pick up on it yet. I guess that's the pleasures of youth. But I'm far too old not to notice when someone's hiding something obvious."

Chloe sat in silence, looking at the satchel ahead of her.

"You're trying to think of an excuse, I see. But I want you to understand that I won't tolerate another lie out of your mouth. So if you have any plans to return to that little school of yours, you will be truthful with me. Or I'll find a more inventive way to get the information I desire."

Chloe looked back up at Oscar, her fingers beginning to shake. "I... I don't want her to hate me."

"I'm sure you don't. So, I will give you my word that I will not tell her anything about what you reveal to me here. So, do we have an understanding?"

Chloe looked around the room one final time before turning back to Oscar, "Yes, sir."

"Good, then tell me. What is your real name? Because I suspect it's not Chloe."

"Prescilla."

"Prescilla Richards? The daughter of Christol Richards, that supposedly went up in that fire? I guess that explains the hand," said Oscar, rubbing his chin. "How did your father get a hold of Isha? And how did she find her way out of a burning manor to a whore house in lowtown?"

"I don't know, sir, honest. One day father just shows up and tells me to look after her. But she was acting all wonky. She didn't even remember her own name. And there was this guy who was around our home a lot. A gray-headed man, Father called him Eunwalt something. And he kept casting spells on us while she was sleeping."

"Us? So, he was casting spells on you too?"

"Yes, sir, except I was awake. He made me hold Isha's hand and tell him stories while he did it."

"Stories?"

"Yes. Just little things. What was my favorite supper or trips father had taken us on."

"I guess her powers got a hold of that arm of yours, did they?"

"I... I know not it's not her fault now. I know she didn't mean it."

"That's good, you know it. I'd hate to have a misunderstanding," said Oscar as he leaned back in his chair. "Some of the pieces are falling into place now. How long did your father have Isha before the fire started?"

"Only a few days."

"Wait? So, Isha didn't start the fire?"

"No, sir, it had started from outside the room we were in."

"Well, that's something. Then tell me, before the fire,

was anyone acting odd?"

Chloe thought back, "No sir, well maybe. Papa and my sister were fighting. But that happened a lot anyway."

"I'm aware of what happened to your parents, but what about that sister of yours? Where's she in all of this?"

"I don't know," said Chloe, her eyes showing hints of anger and sadness. "The King's men took her."

"Alright, do you know how your father got a hold of Isha? The way she tells it, she was in Greenland and just wound up here."

"No, sir. As I said, Father just brought her home one day."

Oscar stared at Chloe for a moment before standing up from the table and grabbing the satchel, "Alright then, that's all the questions I have. Let's go and get this last bit over with."

"So, you won't tell Isha about me?" asked Chloe as she got out of the chair, following behind him.

"I'm a man of my word," said Oscar as he looked out of the door. "But I'll give you this advice. Secrets will usually lead to the people you love hating you. I know this well. So, if you don't want this coming between you and my daughter then I suggest you tell her sooner rather than later. She's still naive, so she'll forgive any wrongdoings you have committed. It's only the old and bitter who hold on to grudges."

Chloe looked up at Oscar for a moment before turning and looking down the street of the town to see Jacinta, Makeba, and Isha waiting for her while holding bags in their hands.

"Let's go then. They seem worried enough about you," said Oscar with a sigh. "I swear, it's like they down trust me at all." And together, they made their way down the street, meeting up with the girls. "Alright, here's your little friend back."

"What you talk with old man about?" asked Jacinta. "He try to get you to join Black Jewels too?"

"No," said Chloe. "He just wanted to know why I fought with Isha. I... I told him it was a mistake."

"That was funny mistake. You both bad fighting and go falling down."

"Stop that," said Isha, butting in. "And besides, we're supposed to get better at school."

"All come along; let's head over to that ship then," said Oscar as they ventured through the town. On the outskirts, their ship hovered over the grass before the trees, where the girls saw Gregga and Dessi waiting on them.

"I can see I'm the least loved in this so-called family pairing," said Oscar.

"A father provides, but it's a mother's love that brings them back home," said Soulden as she walked up behind Oscar.

"Says the woman with no children to speak of."

"A woman needn't have a child to know how to be a mother. It is something every woman shares. If not the experience, then most certainly the nature." Soulden stood beside Oscar and watched as the girls gathered around Gregga and Dessi, chatting away with smiles on their faces.

"You sure? I've seen some terrible mothers in my time. Not all children of war come from nonexistent homes."

"I can imagine," said Soulden. "But a Sakari mother is an odd thing, I will admit. In any case, it's good to see all my students are in one piece. You can never be too careful with Oscar and his methods."

"I imagine there are many rare sights for someone stepping down from your high horse and visiting us common folk walking amongst the dirt. I see you've followed my instruction and not come in your giant eye sore in the sky."

"Yes, I'm not so foolish to not know that it would draw attention. As such, it is now hovering over a nearby city and will pick up a girl of similar stature to your Isha and take her on a romping trip through the skies before dropping her off somewhere out of the way. That should serve as a proper distraction for all interested parties. But I trust you haven't had too much trouble keeping your alleged daughter safe."

"More than enough trouble," said Oscar, looking over at the girls. "They're your problem again now, and I trust you to keep them safe until they're returned."

"I've doubled security at the school, and there will be no uninvited guests during the rest of the semester. Anything, and I do mean anything, that approaches unannounced will be blown out of the sky long before they reach us. We've even attached our training group to the school to limit travel."

"Glad to hear it," said Oscar as he tossed the satchel to her.

"What's this?" asked Soulden as she opened the bag, pulling out a red fabric. "You want me to make a dress?"

"Not enough in there for that, I'm afraid. You see, I've had my daughter show me that magic of hers a few times. And it seems that she has a bit of a bare skin problem, what with it burning all her clothes off. That fabric ya got there responds to magic, I've heard, and doesn't burn easily. I'm sure you've got someone up there who can make something for the girl that doesn't leave her bearing herself to the world after every time she uses her magic."

"How?" said Soulden with a curious look on her face. "This is Valen cloth. How did you get your hands on it? Only royalty of the Viskan Islands has it."

"I know a lady who collects rare trinkets, and they were indebted to me for a favor. I trust you'll make good use of it."

"I refuse to believe someone owes you a favor that isn't the result of blackmail. But I'll accept it all the same. Since I have been trying to find a way to fix that particular issue."

"Then a solution to both our needs."

"Alright," said Dessi, walking over with a smile on her face while holding Isha's hand. "The girls are ready to go."

And they all walked over to the ship, where a large square piece of wood sat below the vessel's side.

"Take care, daughters," said Gregga as she kissed Jacinta, Makeba, and Isha on their foreheads. "Until the next time we meet." Finally, they all said their goodbyes.

"Come along, children," said Soulden as they all stepped onto the wooden platform.

"What? No fancy device to hoist yourself onto the ship this time?" asked Oscar.

"Sadly no, this ship does have such amenities, but...." Soulden raised her hand, and their wooden platform shook, levitating off the ground. "I am quite resourceful when it comes to staying on my high horse, Oscar."

"So it would seem," said Oscar with a smirk. "A high and mighty bitch through and through."

"Say farewell, children," said Soulden as the girls waved, reiterating their goodbyes as the platform rose above the ship, setting down where Oscar couldn't see and shortly afterward, taking back off into the sky.

"Well, there they go again. I would say that now is a time for us to gain a bit of a break," said Jacob with a stretch. "But you were never one for that. So, you care to inform us on what's our next course of action?"

"First, we head back over to Orlana. There is a bit of punishment that will need to be put on display," said Oscar, turning and walking back into town. "Second, I've received an invitation from an old friend, and I want to see what he has to say before I make my next move."

"You know, when someone mentions a friend, they often refer to someone who thinks fondly of them. But with you, I can never really tell if it's someone who actually thinks fondly of you, which I admit is rare these days, or if it's someone you're going to ask me to kill in the coming months."

Around an hour later, the girls were wading through the

air aboard the ship, once again looking over the land below.

"We been in sky a while, how long until school?" asked Jacinta.

"Shouldn't be too much longer," said Soulden. "I assure you our pilot is capable enough. It's the vessel itself. It's not exactly meant for speed or comfort. If we were in my vessel, we'd be there by now, but this is the price of secrecy."

"Is Leo, okay?" asked Isha.

"Physically, yes, but... well, let us just say that I think it will do him good to have you girls back. This hasn't been an easy experience for anyone involved in that mess."

"What about Tree Sakari?" asked Makeba. "Has she been, okay? I want to see her again."

"That I cannot answer to. While we are now certain that the tree was what they were after, we still do not know why. You spoke with her when you last left, so I can only assume she is still okay. We have repaired the tree to the best of our ability, including Mr. Caudbell and Tannor, who have been heading the recovery. But without being able to speak to it as you all can, there is only so much information we have to go on.

"Only Sister Isha can talk to her," said Makeba, looking over at Isha. "She makes it so that we can. But I also wish to learn magic to talk to the Tree Sakari."

"Don't look at me like that. I don't know how I do it either. I just push magic into the roots, and she talks to me."

"I would have to assume it's because of that enhanced magic you have. But now that you're back and the school is not in chaos, we will focus a lot of our efforts on unraveling the mystery of your gift."

"Oh, there's school," said Jacinta as the girls all turned to see the spire of the marble school sticking out above the clouds. But as they rose into the sky, they saw something behind the school. Another large land mass in the sky hovered along with the school. It was covered in dense forest and scattered between the trees were different colored houses. The sight was as odd as the floating school itself and connecting them were two massive chains that swayed gently.

"What is that?" asked Chloe.

"That, dear children, is the training island. Remember the large chains that were around the docking area? Well, that is what they were for, to link the training grounds to the school. We typically leave it high above the clouds since there is no way to properly navigate the island. But with things the way they are, I decided it was best to go and retrieve it. That is where you will receive a decent amount of your combat training."

"It must take lots of magic to make ground float like that."

"Not as much as you might think. The hard part is bringing it up when we need it. The rising takes considerable magical energy, but once it is airborne, it takes far less to sustain it."

Isha could see that around the sides and underbelly of the island were these large vats of red liquid that were attached.

"It even has trees," said Makeba with a smile as she pointed toward the island. "Maybe Tree Sakari can live there."

The ship turned through the air as it approached the city, but unlike before, it flew over the city and hovered within a foot of a moss-covered building. Here, closer to the city, Isha noticed that the leaves of the trees looked duller than before. Their once-lush vibrant greenery now seemed more withered and malnourished.

"This ship does have its advantages when compared to my own. It means we can do things like this." She walked over to an opening in the wooden railing of the ship and stepped down onto the house's roof. She then turned around, inviting the girls to join her. "Come now, don't be afraid."

One by one, they dismounted the ship with their belongings. Then they made their way over to a stairwell and finally down into the streets of Sceana.

"It's good to be home," said Soulden as the ship took back off into the sky and behind the castle. "Now, how about a nice walk to the school, shall we?"

"Why trees look bad now?" asked Makeba, looking over the city. "They look as if they are dying."

"Yes. That is something we were hoping you could inform us on as well. Ever since the attack on the school and the damage done to the Trailage Tree, it seems to have had a negative effect on the city's forestry."

"Where people at?" asked Jacinta as she looked around the empty streets of the floating city. "They will be returning starting tomorrow. I did not want to bring you girls through a sky that would be filled with airships. I'd prefer to avoid having you involved in that security mess. Also, there's someone here to meet you."

"Oh, is it more talking statues? I liked those."

"What talking statues?" asked Chloe, looking confused.

"Fortunately, no. I've had enough of explaining things in that room to last a lifetime. Instead, this should be just a pleasant visit. Merely the greeting of an interested party."

"Oh, it secret person then?"

"One could say that."

Isha listened as Jacinta and Soulden carried on with their conversation. Her sister truly seemed to be glad to be back. Then, after a bit of walking, Isha found herself staring at a tree as they passed it, and without thinking, she veered off toward it. She stepped off the street into the grass, placed her hand on the tree's bark, and began channeling her magic into it. She then closed her eyes and waited, but no response came.

"Is she there, sister?" asked Makeba, "Did you speak with Tree Sakari?"

"No, not yet," said Isha, turning to see the group waiting

on her. "I guess we are still too far away?"

"Well, the tree is still there. If you like, I will take you up to visit. Last time you were able to speak to her directly, so we'll have a go about it again. Although I wish I could take this journey with you."

"We have been practicing with sister a lot. Now we no longer hurt her when we push magic into her."

"Does Isha not burn you when she uses her powers?"

"She burn once. But then it only gets hot. We want to try more, but Mother makes us stop after she burns Makeba's finger. But it's fine if we share small magic."

"Both of you should be careful," said Chloe, lifting her burned arm. "Your mother was right. You don't want to end up like me."

"Is that so? I've never heard of any mages other than healers pushing magic into someone else. Perhaps that's why we assumed you were one," said Soulden, looking down at Isha as she returned.

"So, I won't be able to heal then?"

"Honestly," said Soulden as she continued to lead the group through the city streets. "I have no idea what you can and can't do anymore. Your magic could turn you into the next shadow king or the Goddess herself. But I suppose that's another mystery I will have to look into while you're here. Between the attack and the revelations you girls provided, this year has certainly been one of my most taxing."

They continued making their way through the streets until they reached the main road leading up to the school. There, Isha saw guards in royal blue waiting at the steps, standing as the girls approached, their metal armor shining in the midmorning sun.

"Ah, so you've returned," said one of the guards. A tall man with a hint of gray in his beard.

"We have," said Soulden. "Sorry about the wait. The ship we used was quite slow."

"We understand, but she awaits your presence inside

Sir. Caudbell's office?"

"Caudbell, really? Oh, I do hope he's not trying to have her participate in one of his experiments," said Soulden as she walked up the steps and into the school. The hallways were empty, but Isha could see that the problems for the forestry continued inside the school. The roots that made their way through the walls were now smaller, with pieces of the bark that protected it now peeling away and falling to the floor.

"It really has gotten worse," said Isha as she rubbed her hand over one of the roots, watching as even the slightly touched shed some of its protection.

"Yes. Our best efforts to resolve the issue have turned out to be less than successful. That is another reason why we opted to have you return to us early."

As the group headed upstairs to the second floor and stopped at Caudbell's door, Isha couldn't help the feeling of dread that flowed through her.

"Girls, try not to cause any immediate trouble. You are about to meet the Queen."

"Queen?" asked Jacinta, "Should we be wearing puffy dresses?"

"I'd hardly think so," said Soulden with a smile as she opened the door and allowed the girls to go in. Inside, they found Caudbell sitting at a table, and on the opposite side of him sat a beautiful woman in a royal blue and white dress. Atop her head sat a silver crown. At its three peaks sat three beautiful blue gemstones.

"Oh," said the woman, "They've finally arrived."

"Sorry for the delay. It was..."

"Yes, your ship, I heard," said the woman as she turned around in her seat, never once moving her folded hands from her lap. "I told you I would allow you to use my vessel if you desired. I would have much preferred to meet these three..." She stared at the group of girls. "I was informed there were three, but I see four."

"Yes, the other one is their friend."

"I see," said the Queen with a smile. "My name is Yasmine, and one of you must be the magical child with all the kingdoms in an uproar."

"That Sister Isha," said Jacinta. "She is the enhancer girl that burns people."

"Hey! Don't say it like that."

"Yes, Isha. A mage with the power to make other mages stronger. That sure is a rare thin; so rare in fact, that I've never heard of it. So, I've come to see this for myself. Would you mind a demonstration, please?"

"I… I can't control my power yet." Isha looked down at the floor. "I… I do burn people."

"Oh, I've heard. Mr. Caudbell has been informing me quite a bit about the outcome of your gift. How it leaves you nude and the subject unconscious on the ground. But I have a fair amount of experience dealing with large amounts of magical power. I think I shall be just fine. But as a precaution…" The Queen outstretched her arm with a closed fist before extending her index finger. "Instead of trying to push power into me, let's just have us try touching fingers."

"Are you sure, your highness?" said Soulden as she placed her hands on Isha's shoulders. "This is quite serious. I was out for days after my ordeal, and I still have the scars on my back to prove it."

"Oh yes," said the Queen as she held up a black crystal. "This has been provided to me by your gracious Mr. Caudbell. He assures me that it will handle all the excess magical flow, if for some reason I can't control it. Now dear, if you would be so kind."

Isha looked up to Soulden, who nodded her head and let go of Isha, allowing her to step forward. She then extended her arm, placing her index finger against the Queen's.

"Wait," said Soulden. "If we're going to perform tests, then I won't waste an opportunity to see if this works." She said as she reached into the satchel that Oscar had given her and pulled out a small piece of cloth. "Here," she said as she placed the fabric between the queen and Isha's finger.

"And what's this?" asked the Queen.

"A gift from her father."

Isha looked up at Soulden with eyes wide. "What is it?"

"Just try to use your magic a little, and we will see," said Soulden as she stepped back.

Isha looked back to the Queen as she nodded, then closed her eyes and began her search again. Finding the stream of magic and its interwoven strands was quicker this time. Then, grabbing a hold, she began to look for any other signals, and there it was, a short distance away from here but stronger than anything she'd felt before. It was a power that pulsed like a heartbeat. Every pulse felt like a vibration through her. It felt like she could touch it, the thought almost making her lose hold of her sense of the magic she had gathered.

Moving forward in her mind, she reached inside the pulsing orb and planted the magical string she had gathered. Isha watched as it took the strand and began to feed off it, growing wider, the pulsing coming quicker.

Isha opened her eyes to see the irises in both the Queen's eyes had turned completely white, her jaw trembling as if she was freezing cold. Isha began to pull back.

"No... child," said the Queen as she grasped Isha's finger. "I... I... am in... control." She said as the black orb in her other hand began to crack. "I see... I see so much." The Queen gazed around the room as if she'd never seen it before. "It's beautiful."

"My lady, your hand," said Soulden.

Isha looked down to see the reddening of the Queen's hand. She quickly snatched her finger from her grasp. The Queen gasped and threw herself back, falling to the floor.

"My lady, are you alright?" said Soulden, stepping forward to help the Queen.

"No... it's... it's alright. I was simply lost in the moment of it all," said the Queen as she stumbled to her knees and stood back up, keeping her fist closed. "I was not expecting so much. If I hadn't limited my own, I suspect that I would still be on the floor now."

"You are the first to stay conscious when connected to her," said Mr. Caudbell, "Please tell us. What was your experience?"

"It was... What's the proper way to say it? It was as if I could *see* magic, like strands of thread from a sewing needle. It pierced all of you; or flowed through you might be the correct way to explain it," she looked at Isha, "Except you," The magic flowed around your body as if it was afraid to touch you."

"Fascinating," said Caudbell, "I'd love to hear more, perhaps after we get that hand of yours treated."

The Queen opened her hand, revealing the burn marks that scarred and blistered her palm. "Though I was able to withstand the power, it's seems clear that I am not immune to it's price."

"But it appears that the cloth was," said Soulden as she stepped forward, kneeling to pick it up. It wasn't burned; the heat that Isha put off had shown no trace of affecting it. "Well, this should come in handy for you," said Soulden as she looked at the now somewhat burnt collars and shoulders of Isha's tunic, shaking her head. She then turned and gave the satchel to Caudbell. "Think you can make something that will give our girl here some security?"

"Well, I'm not a seamstress," said Caudbell after opening the pouch. "But I'm sure we can find a way to make something for her."

"I can see this power of yours being a problem for anyone trying to keep any sense of modesty," said the Queen with a smirk. "If I could, I would like to ask you to be a guest at my castle, but I can't guarantee your safety, even there. Especially when the rumors of this Queen's Bane person running amuck. No, I fear that as word continues to spread about your gifts. You won't be truly safe anywhere other than this sky fortress and perhaps not even here."

CHAPTER 6

In an old two-story house in the city of Mari, Victor stood with his military coat in his hands, rubbing the fabric between his fingers. With his back against a wall, he listened to the coughs of the weak, ashen-skinned woman in the room next to him. To his left on a table was a vial of some white liquid and a half-used bottle of June dust.

The room was lit only by a single candle. Frenka sat by a bedridden Silk's side, wiping her forehead. The ashen skinned assassin unable to move and shaking uncontrollably

"Why... why are you... still here?" asked Silk, her finger clenched on the bedsheets and eyes barely open.

"Sister wife sick," said Frenka as she removed the sweat-soaked rag, rung it out, and dipped it into a cool pail of water before placing it back on Silk's head. "It is head of clan's job to make sure you do what you are told and get better."

"I will fight you. I won't accept this."

"Maybe... but you not fight now. Now you rest and get better, then maybe we fight."

"And how is our patient?" asked Victor, walking into the room with a smile.

"Damn you," said Silk. "I should never have let you... convince me to drink that stuff."

"The High Mother said this would be the side effect. You probably still have another day or so before the medicine's run its course. Then we can head out," said Victor, sliding his arms into his coat sleeves. "You both enjoy yourselves. I'll be back this evening. I still must fill out some reports at the castle."

"I see husband out," said Frenka as she stood, following Victor to the door.

"See that she continues to take her medicine," said Victor, his voice lowered. "She can be stubborn."

"Frenka knows. She will take care of sister-wife. But Frenka worried for husband. You say someone in castle try to kill you. So, why go there now?"

"Well, Silk said that, and the reason I must go is that I would still like to find out who tried to have me killed. Usually, I wouldn't care so much, but with you both here, it complicates things."

"Really?" asked Frenka with a smirk. "Does husband worry about his wives now? Afraid we weak women?"

"Not you, especially. I have a good sense of what you're made of," said Victor, turning his head to the opening of the room where Silk lay bedridden. "But that one, she's a lot weaker than you. And I'm not talking about her magic."

Frenka reached forward, placing her hand on Victor's face and forcing his eyes to meet hers. "Frenka knows this. I lead clan. I will train her. You trust Frenka on this. She will be strong. You will see."

"And there you go, always so certain on everything."

Frenka leaned forward, giving her husband a kiss. "You go now, husband. Be man and go protect what is yours. It is man's job."

"I'm not sure I'm being encouraged or belittled," said Victor before giving Frenka another kiss. "Either way, I will do what feels right." He then left Frenka and Silk at the small house in the city and made his way through the city of Mari.

He didn't go more than a few houses down before he was greeted by a familiar face in uniform, sitting down at a fountain in the center of the town square.

"I was wondering when you'd get here," said Sergeant Coral.

"Why are you always the first to greet me when I come back to the city?"

"Probably because I'm the only one who cares about you," said Coral as he stood, shaking Victor's hand and patting him on the back. "How you been, friend? Still off enjoying your adventures? Whatever happened to the man who was supposed to retire, get married, and go live in the woods somewhere?"

"Our wonderful Queen happened," said Victor as he continued his way through the streets with his friend. "And the next thing I know, I'm gallivanting through the country-side of Burlus."

"At least tell me you enjoyed the women over there. Or did you keep yourself stuck in your war talk the whole time?"

"Well, on that front, progress was made. I apparently got married. Twice."

"What? What do you mean twice? You got two wives or something?"

"Yes, they're back at the house now."

Coral abruptly swung around on his heels and tried to make his way back before Victor grabbed hold of his shoulder.

"Are you seriously going to hide your wives from me after I spent the better part of a decade trying to get you to pay attention to any woman?"

"You will get to see them, eventually. One is at home sick at the moment and the other is taking care of her."

"The least you can do is tell me their names. How can I brag about my friend and his polygamy and not know their names?"

"Their names are Frenka and Silk, and I'd appreciate it if you didn't brag about me just yet. I would prefer to keep this a secret for a little while longer. I don't think I can afford any mistakes just yet."

"Huh, why's that? Something going on that I should know about?" asked Coral, his voice taking a serious tone.

"Apparently, someone in the capitol arranged to have me assassinated. One of my wives is the one who prevented that from happening."

"As much as I want to be jealous of you marrying some badass assassin of assassins—and we will talk about that later—but for now, tell me everything you know, and I'll start looking into it."

Really couldn't ask for a better friend than you, thought Victor as they made their way through the streets of Mari. On the way to the castle, Victor informed his friend of everything that had happened since he left.

"There's more to be said," said Victor as they reached the castle steps. "But that's the short version of what happened."

"Alright, I get the gist of it. I'll start looking around and asking questions. But when all this is over, expect me to harass you about everything I've missed."

"I wouldn't expect anything less. Just let me know what you find, even if it's small."

"Don't worry. I know how you think. I'll keep a journal or something," said Coral as he turned to walk away. "Welcome back to the war, Sixth General."

"It's a shame on my life that I must return, Sergeant,"

said Victor as both men shared a laugh. He then turned back towards the castle, opening the door. Inside he saw a few maids and guards standing around, but no one of note. *Well, if this is a war, then I will need to get a hold of the logistics of the battle,* thought Victor as he headed back to the barracks. *I doubt someone of low rank is trying to kill me. What would be the point? So perhaps an up-and-comer, or maybe one of the other generals. They never did take a liking to me.*

As Victor made his way towards the barracks, he could hear the men and women cheering as the sound of metal clashing against metal grew louder.

"Are the boys and girls out having a good time?" asked Victor as he stepped inside.

"Oh, ah," said one of the men, about to stand.

"Be at ease. This isn't an inspection; just looking for Sir. Dunwitty. I would like to ask him some questions."

"Dunwitty? He's out with the boys getting their morning training done."

"Thank you," said Victor as he stepped forward and out of the door. After taking a look around and seeing a man and a woman engaged in swordplay ahead of them in a training circle, he spotted Dunwitty standing with his arms folded as he watched them spar. Victor crossed the place, "Dunwitty, do you have a moment?"

"Yes, Sixth, what brings you back to our humble area? Looking to refresh yourself?"

"No, sadly, I was never the best at sword combat. I never had the frame to engage in brute force for long amounts of time."

"Alright, then, what can I help you with?"

"I'm curious as to what the other generals are up to. Figured I'd come ask you."

"I mean, I know something about their engagements. But would it not be best to go to the capitol building and ask? They should be receiving regular updates there."

"I shall, but I often find that while reports have their

place, it's often the soldiers themselves who have the sense of a man. Words can only convey so much without hearing the emotion behind them."

"So... you wish to have my perspective on them personally. Is that it?"

"Yes, despite my position, I spend most of my time in the field. In fact, I've only just recently returned from a mission. So, the people I met a year or two ago might not be the same as I remember. I'd like a refresher on them before I step back into politics and offend someone accidentally."

"Ah, I see. I guess the world of politics even exists for the high military."

"Unfortunately, that is the case. So, what can you tell me?"

"Well, the First went along and is probably still in Bolgrad, to my knowledge. He never really leaves there unless the Queen calls for him."

"Yes," said Victor, thinking about his last meeting with the First and how he and the Queen lured him into that room.

"The Fifth is around the castle here somewhere. She and the Queen have been holding meetings of some sort."

"Well, at least that much is the same. She's the only one who stayed as reclusive as I did. And the others?"

"The Third and the Forth are stationed at the border to Ursjun."

Of course, they are. Someone needs to be there if shit goes south with the Starlight Queen. "They have them together down there? That must be a pain to deal with."

"Yes, I heard that they force their garrisons to compete in mock battles. A few of their men have even died from it."

"What about the Second?"

"The Second was stationed at the border to Burlus around three months ago."

"Thank you, Captain. That's just the information I needed."

"My pleasure, sir. But if I may ask, what brings you back? It's well known around the castle that you've always avoided the capital as much as possible. Choosing battles over court politics..."

"Well, that's certainly true," said Victor with a smile as he walked around the training area. "I mostly find it all so tiring, at least on the battlefield. I'm sure they just want to kill me." He looked up at the castle. "Here, I don't know what they want to do."

The Captain nodded. "Yeah, that is true. But I imagine it's the same in most kingdoms. So, I doubt there's much you can do about it."

"I agree. That's why I stayed away as long as I did."

"So, what will you do now?"

"Oh, I'm sure our wonderful Queen will send me off to brown-nose with some annoying family sooner or later."

"Yeah, I heard something about you becoming an ambassador."

"The royal ass kisser and dog to go and fetch things. What a glorious occupation to have."

"Ha," laughed the Captain as they reached the door back to the barracks. "You certainly aren't like the other generals if you refer to it like that."

"Thank you for the information, Captain. I hope to see more of you around the capital during my short stay here."

"Same to you, Sixth."

Victor then left, going back through the barracks into the castle. *I can already tell this is going to be a long day. But if I can just move, find out who-*

"Well, if it isn't the little General," said a familiar voice. "I was wondering when I'd get the pleasure of seeing you again."

Victor closed his eyes for a short moment and took a breath. "Hello, Fifth, nice to see you still in good spirits," said Victor, turning around to see a woman in court dress with a fan in her hand.

"Not as good as you, I'd assume," said the Fifth as she walked up to Victor, the back end of her dress sliding across the marble floor. "Off galivanting through the countryside, fighting off bandits and whatnot. And you even managed to find two homely-looking girls to take you in, apparently."

"I see you've been talking to the Queen," said Victor, trying to hide his annoyance.

"Of course, I'm who she confides in when she's feeling annoyed," said the Fifth as she stood in front of him. "And my, oh my, did you annoy her. The poor girl was almost in tears. To think her little toy would go off and get married, and to barbarians no less. Shame on you, Sixth, to play with the heart of a Queen. I dare say you should be hanged."

At least she didn't mention Silk's shapeshifting. "And you would be the one tying the noose around my neck. Have I mentioned how glad I am to see you having fun with all this?"

"Oh, I am. I'm curious to see how this will play itself out. And as far as hanging you, I think you shall do a well enough job of that yourself. But I will admit, it will be fun to watch you struggle."

"And you mean to tell me you are not going to try to interfere."

"No more than I usually would, I assure you. After all, the Queen is my friend. And I do so want to see her happy."

"And what of my happiness?"

"Your happiness? Please. A mundane strategist who finds luck on the battlefield. You should be thanking the goddess herself the Queen uses you for her pleasures and still allows you to roam free. On several occasions, I suggested that she lock you up until you can be of use to her. A much simpler way to handle a man who only really has one real use."

"It's nice to see your narcissist nature is still intact," said Victor as he walked ahead, staring at the still mangled throne on the floor. "Tell me, what have the other Generals been up to? Your honest opinion. Preferably without the self-righteous charm."

"Oh, the grand strategist wants my opinion. What's changed? Surely you haven't started to value anyone's opinion other than your own."

"I am in the belief that one of the other Generals tried to kill me."

The Fifth grew silent as she stared at Victor for a moment. "And your proof of this is?"

"An assassin who saved me."

"And you did not mention this to Clarissa; why?"

"The link that binds us. It may cause her to act... questionably. So, I would prefer to find out the truth before she does."

"Yes," said the Fifth, "I can see that being an issue. But if that's the case, what makes you think it's a General? And if it is, are you not suspecting myself? Clearly, you know I hold no special fondness for you in our ranks."

"No, but you love Clarissa. So, while it's possible that you may have ordered the attempt on my life, I find the probability low. And as you said, you would just lock me up if you could."

The Fifth then turned, walking up to Victor, reaching for his face, and patting his cheek. "Ever the little thinker, aren't you?" She stared into his eyes, a child's curiosity on her face. "What must it be like to be so small and weak amongst giants?"

"I would have preferred to live a small and weak life, but the giants brought me into it."

"So, we did. We must all have our forms of entertainment after all," said the Fifth with one final soft tap on Victor's face before stepping past him. "But your assumption about me is correct. I have no need to see you slain. It would simply be a waste of good entertainment. So, what do you desire of me? Because I can tell you, none of the other Generals are that fond of you. They find your mundanity an offense to their sensibility, even more so since you are in an equal position of power with us."

"I merely ask that you inform me of any plots against me you may happen to come across. You're in their company often enough. Perhaps one will confide in you."

"And what will you do? Surely you wouldn't suggest the clipping of one of the most powerful mages in the kingdom. A wonderful plaything you might be for the Queen, but I would never sacrifice our power for you."

"You say that, but an opening in the ranks of power. You're the lowest of the Generals, besides myself. A mundane and, by all means, a charlatan. The allure of taking a higher seat couldn't have escaped your attention in these years." Now Victor stepped closer, whispering in her ear. "And to gain a higher seat, you would need the support of another General. And you would, of course, have mine."

"Sweet, tempting words. But I'm loyal to the kingdom."

"Of course, you are. We all are. I'm merely speaking of possibilities that may or may not happen."

"And in return for these... possibilities?"

Victor stepped back, "I only ask for you to lend me your ears. So that I may protect my own life. A noble goal, I imagine, for you to protect the life of another General."

The Fifth stood silent momentarily but smiled, "I shall think about what you said. Perhaps you will prove more useful than a toy after all." She then stepped forward, "Until next time, Sixth, may you stay in good health." The Fifth performed a slight bow, but Victor could see the mischievous grin across as she turned, leaving the room.

I think I'm going to be sick.

CHAPTER 7

The girls followed Soulden, allowing her to escort them again into the school's heights.

"Will Queen person be okay?" asked Jacinta. "She no look well."

"I'm sure she will," said Soulden as they passed through the orange rings of light on their way upward. "She has her guards with her. And after her experience with our young Isha here, I can't very much fault her for electing to take a rest after that showing."

Soulden led them through the shadowy upper levels as they went down a dark corridor until they reached the light at the end. And there, Isha once again saw the damage that had been done. Over half the trees were uprooted, their trunks now over in a corner against the wall. In their spaces now were much smaller trees, younger ones which, unlike the other larger orange ones, still had their green leaves.

"We've been trying to repair the damage that was caused," said Soulden, shaking her head, "but progress has been slow without a connection to the tree itself."

Isha couldn't help but look up at the large tree that once stood proudly in the center of the domed room. Now, it seemed to be barely holding on. Half of its large limbs had been cut. A few seemed to be growing back slowly. But the luster of its orange leaves had diminished to a pale brown.

"You can't fix Tree Sakari?" asked Jacinta.

"We are trying," said Soulden, "but none of us were around when these three were grown here. While we know how to maintain it, none of us know how to fix whatever is happening here. So we were hoping you girls could provide some information on that now that you've returned."

"Sister will ask Tree Sakari what is wrong?" asked Makeba, looking at her sister. "And then we fix?"

"I... I can try. But I don't know what I can do."

"No one expects a miracle, child. We all just hope for an answer," said Soulden as she led them through the small green trees towards the large maimed one in the center.

"Oh, good, you've brought them," said Caudbell, appearing from the other side of the tree, followed by Tannor. "I was hoping they would pay a visit here today."

"Hello there, girls," said Tannor with a smile as he walked to Makeba. "There's been some development on that crystal you worked on. Would you like to see it?"

"Crystal? Wha... oh, the shiny rock. I didn't break that one. What did it do?"

"Come, I will show you. It started spreading through the crystal."

"Perhaps another time Tannor," said Soulden, "Firstly, I'd wish for the girls to try out their skills on our little problem here. Their insight might speed along the healing process. This school has felt oddly different without its influence."

"Oh, yes, of course. My apologies. It seems I was overly excited. Perhaps some of Caudbell is rubbing off on me
105

after all."

"Will you give it a go once again?" asked Soulden, patting Isha on her shoulder. "See if there's anything you can find?"

"I'll try," said Isha as she stepped forward, placing her hand on the tree's bark. She could feel the coldness on her skin as she ran her fingers through the ridges between the bark. It felt rough and hard, but as she closed her eyes and began to focus her magic, she could still see the light inside; not as bright as it once had been, but it was there.

Hello, Lonta'Mar, are you there? I... I've come back to visit again. Can you hear me?

You... you... came... back. The words slowly flooded back into her mind.

Yes. I, ah, I brought Makeba and Jacinta. Can we come to visit? I think it'll be okay this time.

Yes... you visit. I... open... way.

Isha turned around to her sisters. "She says it's okay. We can go there now."

"Okay, we go now," said Makeba, walking forward with Jacinta and taking a seat amongst the tree roots.

"Ah, how I wish I could join them," said Caudbell, rubbing his hands over his knuckles. "The experience alone must be amazing."

"We tried that, remember?" said Soulden, shaking her head. "I think I remember the result of which was you being laid out on your back for four days in recovery."

"Yes, perhaps it's something to do with the girls' connection with each other; how they refer to themselves as sisters. Or perhaps it's because they're all female, and the tree is just incompatible with males."

"All wonderful questions," said Soulden, patting Isha on the back towards her sisters, "but ones that will wait for another time."

Isha sat amongst the tree's base with Jacinta and Makeba, placing her hands over the roots. The girls smiled at her as they put their hands over her forearms. Isha felt their warmth as their magic began to flow over her skin. It was a feeling she had grown accustomed to over the numerous times they'd practiced together.

"Let us go, sister," said Jacinta as she rubbed Isha's arms with her finger.

Isha then closed her eyes, focusing her magic on the tree. And inside the darkness of her mind, there it was once again. The orange light still flickered. Then, allowing her magic to flow outward through her, she reached out and touched the light.

Instantly, she found herself back inside the world of the tree. Lying on the ground, she looked around at the white fog covering the area. Then, blinking, she sat up and began looking around the void, and there before her, sat Lonta'Mar. She was on the ground, staring back at Isha with her arms wrapped around her legs.

"Hello, Lonta'Mar," said Isha as she nervously looked around for her sisters. "Where are Makeba and Jacinta?"

"They're here. They speak to me the same as you. But cannot bring together, too tired."

Two fuzzy images appeared in the cloudiness around them. Each showed her sisters talking to a version of Lonta'Mar in their own space. Jacinta had sat down in front of the other Lonta'Mar, and they were speaking, while in Makeba's image, she was walking around the squatting girl, patting her on the shoulders and playing in her hair.

"What is Makeba doing?"

"She says she is trying to fix me, but I am not sure if anyone can. I am so tired since the people came and cut me. Since they pulled at me."

"But we want to fix you. The people... the people outside have planted more trees. But they aren't turning orange."

"I cannot reach those trees; they are not part of me. They do not respond to my call."

"They need to be Sakari trees. Is that it? Would you be fixed if they got more Sakari trees?"

"I don't know. Nothing feels... em," Lonta'Mar moaned, "This feels.... This feels better." She closed her eyes as her head began to sway. "More, please.... more."

"What? I don't... I don't..." said Isha as she watched the small Sakari girl's head bobble up and down as if she were in a trance. "What's wrong?" Then, suddenly, the mental world they were in dimmed, and the images of her sisters swayed. She could see Jacinta looking around nervously, but Makeba now had her arms wrapped around Lonta'Mar in her area.

As the world around them dimmed, Isha found herself back in the darkness. A feeling as if she was falling had taken over. To her surprise, after opening her eyes, she found herself back in her body with Soulden staring down at her.

"Children, children, are you okay?"

"Huh," said Isha as all the other girls began to stir from their slumber. "Is it over?"

"I'm happy to have you both back. I was wondering when you three would return to us."

"What you mean?" asked Jacinta as she lifted herself from the roots before turning around and helping Isha up.

"You girls have been out for over twelve hours. It's night out now."

"What?" asked Isha, "But that was only a few minutes."

"Perhaps it's different now," said Caudbell, rubbing his chin. "Time may flow differently for you when inside, wherever you are. But tell me, what did you do in there? The tree leaves glowed for a moment but then went away."

"Nothing, we just talked. But... ahh.." Isha turned to Jacinta. "Did it take that long last time? I don't remember us being in there for hours."

"Maybe," said Jacinta with a shrug of her shoulders. "I not remember."

"What about you, Makeba?" said Isha, turning around to see her sister sitting amongst the roots. "Makeba, are you okay?"

"Huh, oh yes. I fine, sister," said Makeba as she struggled to rise, but halfway up, she collapsed back down against the roots.

"Makeba," shouted Isha. "Are you okay?" She reached down with Jacinta and hoisted her sister to her feet.

"I fine, just tired now. Tree Sakari took too much. Head hurts now," said Makeba, her head slumped forward as her sisters held her up.

"What?" said Isha in confusion. "What did you do?" But it was too late. Makeba had passed out.

"Makeba!" screamed Isha.

"Sister!" screamed Jacinta.

"It's alright, child; it's just magic poisoning. Her body's just taking a nap, trying to recover," said Soulden looking around. "Someone grab the girl; we shall escort them home. We're done here for today."

"I'll take her," said Caudbell as he reached down, picked Makeba up, and hoisted her into his arms. "Let's go, shall we? We shall continue this another time."

"Well, aren't you considerate," said Soulden, leading them out. "I'd have guessed you'd want to have them perform more of your experiments."

"Oh, I do, but they are students first. And their safety and health are more paramount than my curiosity."

"Words I most certainly respect, although unexpected from you."

"Your words resemble that of Tannor's'. Do I really come off as someone who's only concerned with his research?"

"Oh, very much so. But I assure you. We all appreciate this side of your character."

They all left the room, Caudbell with Makeba in hand, and took the lift back down to the main floor, escorting the girls home.

"I must wonder why Makeba here is the only one of the three girls that has experienced the side effects of too much magic," said Caudbell as the Sakari girl bounced along in his arms. "Was there something different between you three?"

"I'm not sure, but inside, Lonta'Mar said something about how Makeba was trying to fix her somehow. But I don't know what she did."

"Well, whatever it was, it drained her if she's out like this. Soulden, I would guess that whatever this girl was trying was also the reason why the leaves of the tree began to glow. I'll look more into it when we ensure the girls are returned."

"There's the Caudbell, I remember. It didn't take long for you to reemerge."

"The pursuit of knowledge never rests, Soulden. In a school, this is especially true."

The moon hung in the night sky, casting its gaze down upon them as they passed through the floating city's streets. The chill in the night air nipped at Isha's shoulders as they made their way home.

Outside, they saw the familiar face of Rima. She was there, planted on the windowsill as she often had been.

"Oh, so the miracle girls have returned. Welcome ba... What happened?"

"She's just sleeping," said Soulden. "It seems we've worked her a bit too hard today, and she overused her magic."

"Let me come down and get the door," said Rima, disappearing into her room. The sound of footsteps hitting the wooden beams echoed through the house walls before she opened the door for them. "Please come in."

"Thank you," said Caudbell as he stepped inside, walking over and laying Makeba on the couch. "I think she'll be fine. Just allow her to rest for the night." He rubbed his hand over her head.

"Oh? Did something happen?" asked Rima.

"We're not sure, but all this can wait 'til tomorrow," said Soulden as she and Caudbell turned to leave. "You both take care and come visit me tomorrow if you find the time."

"Yes, ma'am," said Isha as she and Jacinta knelt by their sister on the couch.

"Thank you for bringing them home," said Rima as she escorted Soulden and Caudbell to the door.

"No worries, dear. Tell me, how has he been?" asked Soulden in a low voice that the girls couldn't hear.

"He's getting better, I think. But… losing Elena hurt him real bad. He doesn't really speak that much now. Mostly keeps to himself. But he's been coming home with bruises from training with Higgins."

"Higgins? Yes, I assumed that would be the direction he would take." Soulden sighed. "Well, let us hope having the girls returned to him will lift his spirits. Because I'm afraid there are some wounds that even he can't heal on his own."

Rima closed the door behind the two, turning back to the girls as they sat with worried looks over Makeba. Closing her eyes, she took a deep breath and stepped forward. "What say I make you girls something to eat, huh? I'm sure you all must be hungry."

"Is Leo back? Is he here?" asked Isha, looking around the room.

"He's here somewhere, I think. He hadn't told me he was leaving," said Rima, looking up to the roof. "He's been spending much of his time on the roof at night lately. So, he might be there if he's not in the back."

"I'll go check," said Isha as she walked down the corridor to Leo's room. She slowly creaked open the door, but inside there was only an empty room with clothing on the floor. Then, turning around, she made her way back. "He wasn't there."

"Then I guess he's up on the roof."

Isha took another look at her sister, asleep on the couch. "I'm gonna go see." She then turned and headed outside, closing the door behind her and making her way around the house. There, she saw an old wooden ladder that passed her window and led to the roof. Walking forward, Isha grabbed the side of the ladder, shook it a bit, testing its safety, and looked up, seeing only the stars above.

Her heart sinking into her stomach, she placed a foot on the beam and started the climb. Each step made a deeper pit in her stomach until she finally reached the top. Her head peaked over the edge, and there he was, asleep with his arms stretched out,   his brown hair, that was once long and curly, was now short. She swallowed her fears, stepped onto the roof, and crawled over to him. He was covered in bruises, a gnash on his bottom lip, dark spots under his eyes, and he seemed thinner than before. Along his right eye were three large scars that hadn't properly healed: one across the top, two across the bottom. The scars spread across his face. She could see them between the strands of his hair.

Isha wanted to speak, to say something. Anything, but no words would come out. Only the sound of the night's wind came through the nearby trees as it roamed over them both. The breeze tickled at her skin as she reached out and ran her hand over his head, lifting the short hair from over his closed eyes.

She sat there a while and watched him as he slept, thinking about the short time she had had with Elena. She remembered how they used to joke together and the time she walked in on them kissing after class. Instead of speaking, she chose to lay beside him, resting her head across his outstretched arm. Isha then gazed up at the stars, noticing how brightly they shone.

Others were dim and could barely be seen. But they were there, even if only in the night sky for a moment. And maybe that's all that matters.

With thoughts of the past in her mind, the world slowly went dark as the stars vanished from sight. Instead, it was replaced with a soft dream of her being held by her papa as she sat in his lap by the fire, his voice in her ear as he read to her.

"And the warrior maidens Isha and Rana rode into the kingdom of Taluna on the backs of their starlight horses," said a large man with a book in his hand as he sat with a small girl in front of the fire. "Isha, with her red hair the color of fire. Rana, with her green hair, the color of nature. They both challenged King Kalmojin and his armies."

"Do you think they will win, papa," asked a small, button-nosed version of Isha as her father bounced her on his lap, rubbing his thick beard against her face, tickling her.

"Of course," said her papa, but as he laughed, his playful voice began to change, replaced with something thick and billowy. His brown wool clothing was transforming into a black garment and cloak. And as she looked at his face again, it was no longer her papa, Eulan Hasher. But now, it was Father, Oscar Highland. He held her in his arms as she leaned back against the chair—that same knowing grin across his face.

She looked around, and no longer was she in front of a cozy fire. Instead, she was back in a tent. Oscar reached over, grabbed a book and placed it in her lap. Opening it, she could see the pages were smeared with blood. She couldn't read the story anymore. The blood was covering the words and was now over her hands.

Isha's breathing quickened as she tried to wipe the blood away.

"No... no, it's okay, it's okay. This is who ya are now. This is who ya are," came her father's voice as he rubbed his own bloodied fingers over hers. "You're my daughter, and this is who we are."

Isha looked over their hands, so red with blood, as Oscar brought his other hand around in front of her and placed in them the jeweled dagger. Its ornate metal shone as the jewels sparkled in front of her.

"My daughter."

Isha's eyes opened wide, broken from her sleep. Above her, she no longer saw the star-filled sky but instead were the wooden beams of her room that she had grown accustomed to. It was now morning as the sun shined through the window, and by her side was Jacinta, her arms wrapped around her.

A bad dream, a really bad dream.

Lifting her head, she looked ahead to see the jeweled dagger on a small table next to the wall, along with the toy horse Oscar had carved for her. Ahead of her, she saw Makeba sitting on the floor. Her legs were crossed in front of her, with her eyes glowing slightly gold.

"Makeba," said Isha, a bit of worry in her voice. "Are... are you okay now? Do you feel better?"

Makeba was quiet for a moment but slowly nodded at her sister. "Hello, sister. Yes, I fine now. Still tired is all. Is sister, okay?"

"Me? Yes, I... I'm fine. I just had a bad dream."

"Sister sure? She looked different while dreaming."

"Different? I don't understand." Isha moved her arms around. "I feel fine."

Makeba nodded again and then smiled. "Okay, then. Good morning, sister. Last night you were tired like me. So, Leo brought you back and put you in bed."

"Leo?" asked Isha, her mind speeding back to the night before, of her falling asleep next to him with the stars above. "Is he home? Did you see him? Speak to him?"

"We saw him, but he spoke little. He seemed sad. We think losing Elena hurt him a lot. He healer, but face has scars now. Can he not heal them?"

"I don't know. I didn't get to talk to him."

"Maybe he need creamy person like you."

"I don't know, maybe. I just wish he would have woken me. I will try to talk to him today," said Isha as she removed Jacinta's arms from around her and crawled out of bed. "Wait," she said, remembering Makeba and the tree. "When we were inside, what were you doing with Lonta'Mar? I saw you. You went around patting your hands on her. She said you were trying to fix her."

"Yes, I try to fix Tree Sakari, but I was not strong enough. Instead, I go to sleep."

"Wait, what do you mean? Do you know how to fix her?"

"Hmm," moaned Makeba as she looked up to the roof. "Not sure if I know how to fix. But thought she could not fix herself because no more orange Sakari trees. So maybe if I give her Sakari magic, like I do with sister, she will get fixed. But she takes too much, and I go to sleep."

"Wait, so Sakari magic is different?"

"Yes, that is why we have markings. They let us use magic. Sister Isha remember, she ask about them during wash."

"Oh... yes, I forgot about the markings; they allow you to use magic. How?"

Makeba shrugged, "Not understand everything, but Aukube would know. She has marking too. She is older and helps us learn our magic."

"Aukube? She taught you?" asked Isha as she thought about the Sakari healer. "What about ahh... Mother. Why doesn't she know magic?"

"Mother says she never had gift. That why she brought Aukube along to teach us."

"Oh... then not just anyone can learn Sakari magic then?"

"No, few Sakari mages back in Sakar. Why? Does sister want to learn Sakari magic now?"

"Ahhh. I just thought maybe, if I could help you with the tree, maybe that would help if we could do it."

"Sister would need Sakari markings. Only one who can

teach is Aukube, but she back with mother."

Isha looked down at her sister as she sat on the floor. But then she remembered the root that had come out near her bed. Then, walking over to it, she placed her hand on it and closed her eyes.

Lonta'Mar, can you hear me? Are you there? But no response came back to her. Isha sighed and turned back to her sister. "Come on. I think we should go and tell Soulden. She might figure something out."

CHAPTER 8

"I really don't think this is a good idea," said Mova, sitting down at a tavern with Dekol, Saffron, and Laura. The merry laughter and good cheers surrounded them from the tavern's patrons.

"What?" asked Saffron with a smile as he slid a mug of still-foaming ale over to Laura. "Have a drink, my wife. It will warm your belly and make you cheerful."

"What do you mean, 'what'? You tell us another shape-shifter attacked you, and now you have us out here in the sticks again."

"Yes, it certainly was a surprise," said Saffron, still wearing the same joyous smile.

Mova threw her face in her hands while shaking her head. "This is why I never enjoy making these trips with you. Why didn't you just invite Frenka and leave me out of it?"

"She's too far away back in the kingdom to summon for, and you were on hand. Come now, stop being such a baby. The fresh countryside air will do you some good."

"Laura, will you please say something to your husband? Try to bring some reason to him."

"Ah well, I do not believe it will be such a terrible trip," said Laura as she poked at the foaming ale before lifting it up and taking a sip. She quickly removed it from her mouth, making a sour face. "Oh, that is disgusting. Do men really enjoy this?"

"Enjoy?" asked Saffron as he looked at Dekol. "I'm not sure that's the word we'd use. But even though it tastes like piss, it's not really piss… probably." He then turned to Mova. "And why are *you* complaining? I brought a lot of the proper supplies this time."

"One of the few times you've listened to me. Isn't it about time you gave all this up? You're married now. A prince should not be gallivanting through the countryside while on his honeymoon."

"We're just going to investigate the rumors of the red jewels," said Saffron. "It's not as if we are starting a war. Do not worry. You will be back in a cozy castle with your maids in no time."

"Ah! Goddess, you're so infuriating."

"Now, let's get started before the sun goes down." He stood from his table and headed out the tavern. The midday sun glowed over the city of Favrov; a brick city of respectable trade. The dirt streets were as familiar as anywhere else he'd seen. The key resources went into building the people's homes as they should have been.

"What's the first step then?" asked Dekol.

"Mova, take Laura with you and ask the city's patrons about the Clergy of the Goddess here and hint about any red jewels. Dekol and I will visit the chapel here and perhaps make a sizable donation to the Goddess if she can provide us with wisdom."

"The real wisdom would be to take our asses home," said Mova as she stepped toward Laura, wrapping her arms around the princess. "But fine, come, Lady Montavia. Let us do our part and let the boys here play their little hero games."

"Be well, my wife," said Saffron with a wave. "Try to learn from Mova. She's a bitch, but she's dependable."

"Oh, shut it."

"Now that they're gone, you want to tell me what you really have planned?" asked Dekol, his face clearly suspecting something more.

"My lady wife admitted wanting to go on an adventure."

"And you decided hunting down the jewels would be the best opportunity for this?"

"It's better than when I got involved with those black widows. I doubt we'll end up naked, hanging from a rooftop this time."

"And the reason we're doing this, rather than hunting down that second shapeshifter?"

"Three reasons, actually. One, I've had quite my fill of shapeshifters at the moment. That is especially true if we count that shadow mage. Two. It can change into anyone, which would make it almost impossible to track down. It could be right next to me, and I wouldn't notice. Goddess, it took your image, and even I couldn't tell. And I know you better than anyone." said Saffron, throwing his arms up.

"Fair enough. And the third?"

"The third? Well, I fed it some information it found interesting, and if it's going where I think it's going, then it may all work out in my favor."

"Alright, so we're headed to the chapel then. How are we going to do it? Will you go as yourself or..."

"No. Royalty has its place, but people tend to become more standoffish when they realize who I am. I shall change my appearance on the way."

"And you didn't think to change it beforehand?"

"No one out here would recognize me except people who have been to the capital. And even then, they would second guess themselves."

"What about Laura?"

"A new princess? She has an even less chance of being spotted. Only the Duke will know her. And I doubt they are dumb enough to try anything. So, all should be in order."

"Okay, then, let's be on our way."

And together, the two men made their way through the city. Saffron ducked into a nearby alley, casting magic to change the appearance of his face to that of a dark-haired man with brown eyes.

"How do I look?"

"About as ugly as you were before, just with darker hair."

"You really do have just the worst sense of taste. This is still quite a hard skill to pull off. "

"I'm not a magic user. So, the nuance and sense of awe are lost on me."

"Fine, fine, smart ass. Let's just go."

The smell of burning lumber and molten iron filled the slums of the city, no matter which turns they made. In the markets, they could see numerous trinkets that metal masons had made on display for sale at the various stalls.

"A city renowned for their craftsmanship in armor, and yet during times of peace, this is what they make," said Saffron, stopping to inspect a small round saucer and a cup.

"I'm sure Harrowhil would enjoy it if another war were to commence considering the number of high-grade armorers under his employ. Will you also be stopping in to see him?"

"Depends, but I can't imagine he would know anything about these jewels," said Saffron, leaving the piece and continuing his way through the city. "Unless they're mounting them to metal bracelets or something. Otherwise, I don't see a possible connection."

"Victor said that they were mounted into the flesh of the victims. So, are you planning to strip down every clergyman you see?"

"Well, that depends on how attractive the clergywomen are, I'd imagine. Or at least that's what I would say if I weren't married."

"Really? You actually plan to live up to your vows? That's quite the unexpected turn. Why the change in morals?"

"It pains me to think that my best friend thinks so little of me."

"I have reason to think so little of you."

Saffron chuckled, "Yes, well. I've recently come under the impression that Laura might be more than she appears. So, this honeymoon romp of ours will also serve as a test of sorts."

"Perhaps marriage will be good for you after all," said Dekol as they turned another corner, spotting the chapel ahead of them.

"Glad to hear you approve, but now we will need to get *you* married, my friend. Then we can watch as our children grow up together and become mortal enemies."

"I think I shall continue to enjoy the unattached life a while longer."

"Stubborn as always," said Saffron as he walked through the arched gate of a picketed fence up to the stone chapel steps. To their left, they saw a robed man in a flower bed holding a wooden pail of water as he scooped it out with a dipping spoon, spreading it out amongst the petals.

"Oh, hello," said the man. "May I help you?"

"Ah, hello. We've come to see the leader of this church. Is he here?"

"Oh, that would be I," said the man, placing the pail on the ground, then stepping toward Dekol and Saffron while wiping his hands on his robe, smearing dirt across the fabric. "Kemlor Austine of the Goddess's Valor, how may I help you two gentlemen?" He shook both Saffron and

Dekol's hand in greeting.

"Hello Kemlor, my name is Zeon Hilde," said Saffron. "I'm here investigating the disappearance of some people from the local towns."

"Oh my, they disappeared, you say? I hadn't heard of such a thing."

"Really? I thought it would have been common knowledge by now. Has no one come to pray with you about such things?"

"No, perhaps one of our other members may have received news, but it hasn't yet reached my ears. How many have disappeared so far?"

"To my knowledge, a little less than a dozen or so. Not enough for the city guards to take notice of, but enough for a concerned party to ask me to look into as a personal favor."

"Ah, I see. Well, if I can be of any assistance, I will be," Kemlor Austine gestured toward the chapel door. "Please, come inside, and we will discuss this further."

"Thank you, Sir. Austine," said Saffron as he followed the man. The inside of the chapel was filled with rows of benches across a wooden floor. Light shone through mosaic glass windows, the colors providing a soft rainbow effect through the streams. And up ahead, the focal point of all attention, was a statue of the Goddess holding a bowl in her hand.

"Now, what is it exactly that I can help you, gentlemen, with? Was one of our own taken?"

"Yes, it is true that some of the clergy have also gone missing along with some town's folk."

"I do so hope they are found. Do you have any leads?"

"Not sure currently. But Kemlor, how many variants of the Church of the Goddess exist now?"

"What? Why hundreds, I would assume. It doesn't take much to form your own branch. The Ostmanchal believe that all should be allowed to worship the Goddess as they see fit and are likely to be approved as long as they follow its three main tenants." He lifted a finger as he proceeded to name them. "One, it is accepted that the Goddess wants the best for mankind. Two is to accept that all the world's gifts should be shared equally among mankind. And three, to accept the love of the Goddess in all its forms."

"All for the betterment of mankind."

"Yes, that's how... wait, you don't think one of our branches was involved, do you?"

"That's merely one of our guesses, but it is possible. What if one of the branches had decided that the best way to serve humanity would be to start kidnapping or murdering people?"

"What? That's absurd. The Ostmanchal would immediately renounce such a group and order them hanged. As much as it shames me to admit it, the records show that such things have happened in the past. And it was always the council heading the Ostmanchal that would enlist the aid of anyone who would put down such atrocities."

"I've never heard of such things happening to the faithful."

"That is because the Ostmanchal is very thorough and expedient in wiping out such things. We are to serve as a light to the people and will not permit vile acts done in the Goddess's name. I imagine the High Chancellor herself would lead the charge personally if such a thing were to be found out today."

"I see. I guess we have no choice but to visit the Ostmanchal. Although I will admit, I'm not especially looking forward to the trip."

"Oh, if you just wish to see the council members, they will be in the Holy City of Diohil in the coming months to inspect a new main chapel."

"Is that so? Then that will save us a long, arduous trip for the most part. Although heading north will surely be a pain. Thank you, Kemlor Austine. I will relay your assistance to the council when I meet them."

"Thank you, Sir. And I hope that you find those responsible for the disappearances. Whether they be clergymen or not. Anything vile that is done in the Goddess' name must be dealt with hastily. Losing the faith of the common folk will surely lead us on a path from which there will be no coming back."

"Kemlor, has anyone else been through here? Another worshiper on a pilgrimage or the like?"

"Yes, Favrov, is a stop for many on the way. Three Kemlors have passed by here in the last few months; all of notable repute. Why, even prince Saffron and his lady wife just recently visited the city and apprehended some bandits."

"What?" asked Saffron in genuine confusion. "Did you say Prince Saffron?"

"Yes. He and his wife were here a week or so ago. I even managed to speak with the man myself."

Saffron looked at Dekol, but Dekol looked just as confused as he did. "Did the prince say what he was doing here?"

"Apparently, he was out with his lady wife, showing her the entire kingdom. They were surrounded by guards, of course."

"And you said they apprehended some bandits?"

"Yes. They had been plaguing the nearby towns, and the prince brought them into the city, bound in ropes. He took the reward, which I must say was no small amount, saying that he would distribute it to the poor villages affected by the banditry."

"Of course. Prince Saffron has always been known for his generosity." It felt weird talking about himself like this. While not adverse to praise, it felt odd praising a version of himself that he had never met. "But on our earlier topic, can you tell me a bit about the Kemlors?"

"Of course," said Kemlor Austine, walking over to a table and pouring some wine. "Would you like some? It has been blessed."

"No, but thank you. What was that about the other three Kemlors?"

"Oh yes, the first was Sister Grebble. She stopped by on her way to the capital. I believe she was to have an appointment with the King of Burlus."

"The King? Did she mention what they would talk about?"

"No, I'm afraid not, and I never pursued it."

"I see. What about the other two?"

"The other two were Sister Pilan and Brother Kolgin. Pilan was on her way to Latrusa, while Kolgin headed towards the holy city, wanting to get the council's attention. I believe he wants funding to open up his own temple."

"I see. And these other two; are they fairly popular Kemlors?"

"Huh? Oh, yes. Sister Pilan has been with us quite a while and gathered quite the following on her pilgrimages throughout the years. She is well known for her travels through different kingdoms. And Brother Kolgin has an even larger following, which is surprising, as he is a recent addition to the clergy. But I suppose that is why he wishes to seek funding for a chapel. Then, of course, he would need to establish his own sect if the people began following him. We all worship the Goddess in our own way when we hear her calling."

"New? I thought being a Kemlor took years to earn that title. How long did it take him?"

"Typically, yes, but Brother Kolgin was hand-chosen by one of the council. He apparently was a researcher at Sceana, that fancy magic school, beforehand. So, I would assume he'd done some work there."

"That's odd. Does the Church of the Goddess receive many mages?"

"Some, yes, but I wouldn't call it a common occurrence. Mostly, our masses are filled with the mundane. But I think you are mistaken. Brother Kolgin isn't a mage. He was a researcher."

"I see." *I suppose one does not need to be a mage in order to study magic. That mundane general knew a lot about magic himself.* "What about this Sister Grebbe? Anything you can inform me about her?"

"Grebbe? She's been with us for over twenty years and has been a mentor to many future Kemlors that have come this way. She's even one of the few candidates to be considered for the council when one of them steps down."

"Thank you," said Saffron. "Your information has been quite helpful. I must admit I'm surprised. I thought you would shun us for accusing your fellow brother and sisters of the kidnappings."

"The goddesses' will is all that matters, gentlemen, and the people trust we will lead them according to her will. If someone out there leads the people astray in her name, they must answer for that crime. Be they a beggar, a brother, or a sister. In our order, there is no higher crime than a false prophet."

Saffron and Dekol left the chapel and headed back out into the streets.

"Well, that was certainly informative," said Saffron, looking towards the building tops ahead of him as the sun shimmered off behind the trees of distant fields.

"He didn't seem to be hiding anything from us. You think he was lying?"

"No. Probably not," said Saffron as he led Dekol down the street. "He was all too willing to give up information to protect his relationship with the Goddess. But while he may know nothing, that doesn't mean that someone else here doesn't. This is one of the cities where it was reported that people first started to disappear, so perhaps the girls have had better luck."

The two men traveled through the city, continuing to ask questions to the people and any robed figures they came across. But their answers were much the same as Kemlor Aistine had given them. Then, after wandering, they found Laura and Mova sitting in the nobles' quarters having lunch.

"Well, don't you ladies look comfortable," said Saffron as he walked up.

"We are," said Mova, sliding out of a chair. "Have a seat."

"Thank you. While not our original goal, a piece of interesting information has passed our ears. Apparently, we have imposters of myself and my lady wife gallivanting across the kingdom."

"What?" said Laura, confused. "You mean like people pretending to be us?"

"Exactly, and apparently, they walk around with their own guards."

"Really?" said Mova, looking unimpressed. "You mean even the imposters realized that even a fake royal prince would need to have guards? I dare say that represents poor planning on a certain true royal heir."

"Nonsense. I doubt that group has such fine warriors as Dekol and yourself protecting them."

"Are you not worried about them, Lord Husband?"

"Not especially. They seem to be no more than thieves. Time catches up to all thieves, and we have our own concerns to worry about. Speaking of which, I don't suppose you two have made any progress on the current situation."

"Oh, but we have," said Laura excitedly. "Turns out that there were Kemlors in the city here from the last few months. And each of them had those little red stones you were talking about."

"What?" asked Saffron, looking genuinely surprised. "How did you find that out?"

"Apparently, bringing your wife along was quite handy," said Mova with a smirk. "One of the nobles here is a heavy donor to the Goddess and gives funding to Kemlors on their pilgrimages.

"I just told him I wished to know more about the Goddess, and he grew excited to help us. He even had some of the red stones." Laura pulled a red jewel from her pocket, showing it to Saffron and Dekol, before plopping it down into her husband's hand. "See, he was even willing to give me one."

"Apparently, this stone came from a Kemlor named Disdale, but the other two also had stones," said Mova, finishing up a piece of fruit. "I'm thinking if we ask around, we can find out where they went."

"I don't suppose he said what they were used for."

"He said that if you channel your magic into one, it creates a pretty white color inside of it. Mova and I tried it, and it worked, but other than that, it didn't do anything else."

"I wish you would have waited before you tried," said Saffron, raising a brow at his wife. "I'd hate to lose you to some freak accident. But still, this is good work. I'm honestly surprised."

Laura smiled back at her husband. "I wish we could have found out where the Kemlors went. But the Duke did not know anything. Apparently, all pilgrimages are different."

"On that, I believe we can help. We have the location of where the Kemlors went."

"Good," said Mova. "But here's a question I've been wondering since we left the Duke's manor. If all pilgrimages are different, then why are three Kemlors showing up here around the same time, each of whom was involved with these stones?"

"True," said Saffron as he rubbed his thumb over the jewel. "The obvious conclusion would be that they are working together. So, for now, let's just work under that assumption."

"Okay then, what's next on this journey of yours? We have three Kemlors, so I'm going to assume we're going after one of them."

"Yes, one is apparently off to meet with my father. Which in itself brings to mind all sorts of questions. But that will be looked into at a later time, although I doubt I'll get a straight answer in any sense. So instead, we shall head to Diohil. One of them is supposedly going to meet with the Goddesses council there."

CHAPTER 9

Days later, after returning from the capitol, Victor stepped inside his home, bag slung over his shoulder, to see Frenka sitting at the table reading a book.

"Hello, husband," said Frenka, looking up from the book, standing up, and coming to greet Victor. "Did you find the man you were looking for?"

"No such luck. My days have been filled with the mundanities of catching up with troop movements, supply shipments, and deciphering cryptic messages. What about Silk? Has she awoken yet?" said Victor looking at the closed door.

"Scars are healed and not coming back. That is good, and her fever left her this morning. So maybe she wake soon," said Frenka as she stepped forward, giving Victor a kiss.

Victor found himself quite enjoying her kisses. The

softness of her lips. The way her hand would graze his side. To him, Frenka didn't seem the type who'd offer intimacy easily, but to those whom she did offer it to, there was a lot of it to give. Although this time, she smelled a little different. Not so much the forest and nature smell, this time the smell was more subtle.

"So," said Victor, after a moment of savoring her kiss. "What are you reading?" He stepped inside, walking over to the table.

"It is the history of Mari Kingdom; I wish to know more about husband."

"Is that so?" asked Victor as he sat down in the chair, dumping the bag on the table. He then reached up, pulling Frenka into his lap and wrapping his arms around her waist. "Well, it's true we haven't had time to enjoy our marriage. I've been sleeping at the capitol these last few days trying to catch up. But tonight, I think I'll sleep in my own bed."

"And tonight, you accept me? I wish to be with my husband."

"And you shall, but first, you're going to do something special for me," said Victor, tightening his hand around her waist and kissing her on the neck.

"Really?" asked Frenka. "Then I will be a good wife. What does husband want me to do?"

"Well," said Victor as he ran his hand over the clothing around her breasts. "You can start with transforming back into yourself."

Frenka's eyes opened wide as she leaned away from Victor's kisses and stared at him.

"You really thought I wouldn't notice?" asked Victor with a smirk.

Frenka tried to stand up and push herself away, but Victor held his grip firm, keeping her planted in his lap.

"I'm sorry. I just thought..."

"Oh no, you don't. I'm not letting you run away from this. You started this game. So, you're going to finish it. I am not letting you go until you change back."

Frenka sighed and slumped her shoulders before her skin began to change from a pink to a pale white and then back into the ashen skin of Silk. Victor felt the change in weight across his lap and the shrinking of her waist in his arms. He couldn't help but notice the size difference between the two women. Whereas when she was Frenka, her feet were solidly on the floor, even in his lap, in her own body, they dangled in the air.

"I… wasn't trying to be…" Silk looked away from Victor. "I just thought you'd prefer her more."

"Frenka has her appeal," said Victor with a smirk before reaching up and sliding his hand across Silk's chin and giving her a long kiss. "But then, so does a little ashen-skinned murder princess. And I'd much prefer it if you wore yourself when we are alone. Not anyone else."

"If you say so," said Silk, still with disbelief in her eyes.

Victor then looked over Silk, who was still in Frenka's clothing, which now flopped loosely on her. "How did you get Frenka's clothing anyway? I don't remember her carrying extras."

"She took a bath and put on your shirts before she went to sleep. So, I just… well, I wanted to try it on." Silk patted the now loose chest area of the garment. "She's a lot more womanly than me."

Victor chuckled, "I don't think breasts are the standard for how you judge being a woman."

"Then you don't know much about women. Looks, eyes, breasts, we talk about these things. Beauty and femininity are as much of a weapon as magic is."

"The world of womanhood seems like a treacherous place," said Victor, shaking his head. "I imagine that's why the Black Maidens are so feared."

"Are you going to let me go now?"

"No."

"What? Why not?"

"I've grown somewhat comfortable with you in my lap. You're quite warm." Victor thought he could see a bit of a blush on her ashen skin. "Why? Are you not comfortable?"

"No... I mean, yes, I am. It's just, I'm not... I'm not used to people like you. Well, you know. You weren't this clingy when we were hunting those clergy people."

"And you weren't my wife back then. And now you are. You also didn't have a home. And now your home is with me. So, excuse me while I exercise my husbandly right and cuddle with my wife." Victor rubbed his head over her shoulder, his hand running across her neck.

"Okay, okay," said Silk with a laugh despite herself, "I understand."

"Now, tell me. Did you ever learn to cook anything in all that assassin work of yours?" asked Victor, looking at the bag he dropped on the table.

"Not especially," said Silk as she eyed the bag suspiciously. "Why, what did you bring?"

"A bit of beef, fish, and flat wrap bread from the market along with some Solan herbs and Morlakine spices. Figured I'd have a Fontaine Wrap for dinner."

"Fontaine Wrap? Sorry, I've never cooked that before."

"Well then, I suppose it's time you learned how to make one of your husband's favorite meals," said Victor, sliding Silk off his lap. "Come on then, while our so-called clan leader is asleep, I can show you."

"Wait," said Silk as she let go of Victor's hand, headed off into the room, and came back wearing a tunic but with a smile.

"Ready now?"

"Yes."

They both then made their way into the kitchen as Victor plopped down the bag again and took out the ingredients as Silk ignited the wood inside the stove with a spark of magic.

"Magic certainly is useful for cooking," said Victor as he placed the fryer on the stove.

"Where did you learn to cook?"

"My mother taught me," said Victor, "Okay, so take some of the herbs and grind them up in that mixing bowl there."

"Your mother? I thought boys didn't learn to cook," said Silk as she took the bowl and grinder and began mushing the herbs.

"I was always the curious type. After helping the rest of the men, I'd go home and watch mother cook. She'd let me help if I nagged her enough," said Victor as he squished the meat with a rolling pill over and over. "It's a skill that came in handy when I was on campaign. Most of the boys never knew how to cook. And the women were from noble families, so they had their maids do it in the past. I became popular really fast."

"Have you been in a lot of wars?"

"I've seen my fair share. We've both killed people for one reason or another. Just the circumstances of how we got to that career are different. What about you? Have you ever had to impersonate a cook or a baker?"

"No, it's usually noble people. Grennok would want me to kill or seduce people in order to affect some trade, or merger, or something. A lot of it we didn't understand. So, sister and I would just do as we were told," said Silk as she finished the grinding, showing Victor the bowl. "Is this, okay?"

"Yes, that's fine. Now mix in the Morlakine spines and grind them again," said Victor as he flipped the meat over and began rolling it again. "Your sister, what is she like? Do you have similar personalities?"

"Hmm, no, not really. I mean, she looks like me. But she's more attached to Grennok, I think. She was always happy to go on missions and kill people."

"You said her name was also Silk? Why not have separate names?"

"Grennok just never gave us names. It was always you 'go here and do this' and 'you, go there and do that.' And it's not like we ever needed other names. We always knew who we were even if no one else did."

"Well, I think it's too late for me to start calling you anything else. But, maybe if we can get your sister away from Grennok... Any idea how we can find her? And preferably in a way that she won't feel the need to kill me."

"No, not unless I go back to Grennok. I told you before that we can sense each other when we're close. That's usually how we meet. And she's not a bad person; she's always been protective of me."

Yeah, that's what I'm afraid of.

"Always taking the more dangerous missions and leaving me with the easier ones."

"Such a loving sister," said Victor, sliding the piece of meat over in front of Silk. "Okay, that looks alright. Take a decent amount and spread it over the meat as if you were sprinkling sand from your hand."

"Okay," said Silk, doing as instructed.

"I am happy to see that you're okay. After you took that medicine. I must admit that I started to worry for a while," said Victor as he handed Silk the roller.

"I should have never taken that stuff," said Silk, taking the roller and rolling the spices into the meat. "It tasted horrible, and I swear I've never felt so weak before in my life."

"Well, you had Frenka to look after you. So, at least you weren't alone."

"Wish that I was. She sat over me with that smug look on her face the whole time. And when she thought I was asleep, she would sing some weird clan song about The Fires of Palgamon."

"She sings?" asked Victor with genuine surprise in his voice. "That's a surprise."

"You've never heard her?"

"No, I guess the occasion never came up. How was the sound of it? Was it pleasant, or would you describe it as the wailing of a dying cat?"

This time it was Silk's turn to laugh, "Goddess, you're an ass sometimes."

"So I've been told."

"It wasn't bad. It's just," she stopped rolling the spices over the meat and turned to Victor, looking him in his eyes. "Listen, what do you think of all this?"

"What do you mean?" said Victor, taking the meat and placing it on the stove, watching as it began to sizzle.

"I mean her and me and all this sister-wife stuff. I'm not used to people caring about me other than my sister, and here you two come along. You took me from the prince, and with her washing me when I'm half-dead, then sitting over me when I was sick like that. It's not.... well, it's not normal."

"You keep saying that, but who's normal are you referring to? The people whose face you wear or yourself. I mean, look at me. I'm essentially a magical slave of the Queen. And you say you've spent your life locked in the darkness with your sister. Perhaps you have worn other people's faces for too long. So, when you ask about normality, I'm not sure we've been that for a long time. If we ever were."

"So, you think I should just accept what she's saying."

"No, I think you should stop trying to be who you think you should be and just be who you are."

"Fine," said Silk. "I won't complain about not being normal anymore. But you still didn't answer my question."

"And that was?" asked Victor as he watched the fat from the meat leaking out onto the fryer.

"About this whole sister-wife thing."

Victor took a breath, smelling the savory smell of the meat mixing in with the spices as he stared up at the ceiling, "In truth, I've been thinking about that since we left the ship. And I've more or less come to terms with it. That I care about you, and I care about Frenka. But honestly, polygamy seems more trouble than it's worth, especially if you and she continue to argue as you do. But I won't cast either of you from my side either. If you're willing to put up with me, I'm willing to live my life trying to see you both taken care of. Well, as long as you'd have me."

"So just like that, you get two wives? You won't doubt it anymore?"

"My grandfather once told me it's a woman's right to choose. And if she chooses you, just try to make sure you're worth the choice. So, for the most part, I think I'll just follow along with his teachings. So far in my life, they haven't led me astray."

"I still don't know, "said Silk, staring down at the meat. "I meant it when I said I want to be with you, it's just-"

The door to the guest room swung open as Frenka walked out wearing the shirt of one of Victor's military uniforms. Her bare legs were exposed, and her long black hair was wild and loose as she rubbed at her eyes coming over to them.

"Husband cooking for Frenka. It smells good, and sister-wife help," said Frenka as she walked behind them, coming over and kissing Victor. She then stepped to the side, wrapping her arms around Silk and kissing her on the cheek, squeezing the ashen-skinned woman in her embrace. "What you make?"

"It's dinner," said Victor as he watched Silk's body freeze in Frenka's embrace. Her face looked confused as if she didn't know what to do. Victor placed his hands on Frenka's shoulders and turned her around, making her release her cuddle grip on Silk. "There's some wine in that cabinet over there, Miss Clan leader. Set three cups on the table for us. The food will be ready in a moment."

"Yes, husband," said Frenka as she sleepily walked her way forward.

"And Silk, can you set the table? There should be some trays in the cabinet behind me."

"Huh, oh yes," said Silk as she walked to the other side of Victor and opened the cabinet.

"It's your choice, Silk. If you wish not to be involved with us anymore," said Victor in a low tone. "I will keep my word and find a place for you to live happily even if it's not here." He then picked the meat up with a metal instrument, slid it along a saucer, and took it over to the table where Frenka was putting out the wine. And as Victor began to cut the meat, there came a knock at the door.

They all looked at each other

"Husband expecting company?" asked Frenka.

"No, this late in the evening, I shouldn't be," said Victor as another knock came from the door. "Silk, hide for a moment, and I'll check." He walked towards the door. "Who is it?"

"A concerned citizen coming for a night's visit," came Queen Clarissa's voice. "I'd appreciate it if you would open the door."

Victor narrowed his eyes but made his way over and unlocked the door, opening it. And there stood Clarissa with a hood over her head with two women in street clothes that Victor recognized as guards from the castle.

"Finally, you two go for a walk," said Clarissa to her guards as she stepped into the home without permission. "Close the door, Victor; I'd prefer no one to know I've come here tonight."

"Shayla, Milborne," said Victor with a nod to the two female guards as he felt his body move on its own as he closed the door, and an itch began to stir on his neck. He saw Silk poke her head out for a moment before ducking back. "Why are you here?" he said as he began to unconsciously scratch his neck, following behind her.

"A bit of business is all," she said towards the table, looking at the food. "Oh, you've cooked again. I do miss your meals. A man who can cook properly is a rare thing these days."

"You come to join, maybe enough for four," said Frenka, a smirk on her face as she plopped her elbow on the table,

138

mounting her head on her fists as she looked the Queen up and down.

"No," said the Queen with a sour look. "Sadly, I must return to the castle soon. I've only come to give Victor this medicine and his orders for his next assignment."

"What assignment?" asked Silk as she stepped from behind the kitchen counter and came to stand beside Victor.

"And there's the other one," said the Queen. "The assignment I wish for him to handle. I need him to travel down into Frontsdale inside of Dresha. We had arranged for a pickup and safe transport of goods, but we lost contact some time ago. I want Victor to find out what happened and retrieve the cargo."

"Dresha?! Are you insane? That entire country hates me. If I'm spotted anywhere near there. I'd be..." Victor narrowed his eyes. "You know that. You don't intend for me to go. You're trying to use my wives."

"Oh, and what makes you think that? I've already sent the Fourth and the Fifth out on their own missions, and this is the type of mission I can't send my army at risk of inciting another war. So, I'd prefer not to repeat that tragedy or our past. And considering your involvement in that debacle, I'd imagine you'd feel the same."

"What's going on, Clarissa? What's so important that you'd..." Victor's eyes opened wide for only a moment as he bit furled and bit his lips while shaking his head with disgust written all over his face. "I knew it. It was you."

"Whatever do you mean, Victor?" asked Clarissa, her face looking at him with an innocent smugness.

"The Starlight Queen's child. I knew you had something to do with that mess."

"Oh, please, Victor. I'm merely asking you to travel there and pick up a package. And if the package just happens to be a small infant baby with significant magical potential, then so be it."

"Why? Why drum up the risk of a storm that we barely

survived the first time? Do you know how many times I came close to dying in the last war?"

"So, see to it that we don't fall into another one. An anonymous third party was used, so they would have no link to us even if caught. We were to meet them in their own country and with men that didn't directly work with Mari."

"And you think sending a general, whom the entire country hates for killing their beloved Grand General is a good idea."

"As I said; if you can't do it, perhaps someone else can," said Clarissa, glancing over at Silk. "Perhaps someone with the ability to appear as anyone. Someone skilled at infiltrating a foreign kingdom and the high levels of nobility."

"No," said Victor, the anger thick in his voice.

"Tell me, oddity," said Clarissa, brushing off Victor's anger nonchalantly, "has that shape-shifting power of yours returned yet?"

"Yes, it has," said Silk, annoyed. "But it's not you who will decide what I will do with it. I don't work for you."

The Queen laughed, "Dear, everyone in this kingdom works for me, whether they know it or not."

"That's not part of our agreement, Clarissa," said Victor, finding a way to calm himself. "So, I'm going to respectfully decline letting you make use of my wife."

"Oh, that's cute. You're the one who gave me control over her the moment you did... whatever it was that was you did," said Clarissa pointing her finger at Silk. "You, oddity, transform for me."

"What? No? Why should I?"

"Hmm, so it seems she can refuse my orders," said Clarissa, "Victor, kneel before me."

Victor felt his body jerk downward, his knees beginning to stretch as he leaned forward. Even the thought of trying to fight it brought a sense of pain to mind. The longer he tried to fight it. The more it felt as if his arms and legs were attached to stones, and he was sinking into water.

He dropped to one knee, giving in before looking over and seeing that Silk had assumed the same position. The sight of her performing the act instantly ate at him as his chest grew tighter.

"Oh, so that's how it is?" said the Queen with a raised brow.

"Clarissa, stop this," said Victor through clenched teeth.

"It only works if I order Victor to do something. Interesting," said Clarissa as she stepped forward and looked around the room.

"I'm warning you, Clarissa."

"Let's see if this works, then. Victor, transform into that mountain woman you seem so fond of."

There was a moment of silence in the room. But nothing happened as both Victor and Silk stayed knelt on the floor.

"So, it doesn't work that way either," said the Queen with a smile across her face.

"Silk, I'm sorry about this," said Victor, the muscles in his shoulder tensing up even more as he began to stand. His body felt like it weighed three times as much as it did before. "I did... warn you... Clarissa." Victor clenched his fists as he stood up, folding his hands in front of him as he looked down at Clarissa. His body felt cumbersome as his throat began to warm, and his bones began to ache.

"What are you doing? Stop that! Get back down before you pass out."

"I... refuse," he muttered through clenched teeth. The ache in his body worsened as a sharp stinging sensation struck his right eye. He could feel the gray veins creeping up his neck and over his jaw. He tried his best to stand firm but couldn't block the pain from his mind. His only solace was the look of panic that began to creep onto the face of Clarissa as her own gray veins started showing on her neck, mimicking his own.

"What... you really want to challenge me on this?" said Clarissa, the panic Victor saw earlier now creeping into her voice. "You… you know this hurts you far more than it hurts me."

"Maybe… but I… can live with this. And we both know how this ends. There's only so… much… that you can block."

"Fine… you wish…. to… to choose them over me. Fine. Then suffer. Victor, dance for me. This instant!"

"I refuse." The pain now struck in both his eyes.

"Victor, sing for me!"

"I… re…fuse."

"Vic…tor," said Clarissa, her eyes beginning to twitch and water. "Jump… for me!"

"I…." he breathed out through clenched teeth, "re… fuse."

"You… sure about… this Victor?" said Clarissa as she looked downward. "It's… not just us… any… more."

Victor followed her gaze to see Silk huddled over on the floor, shaking. The gray veins up to her cheeks. But she didn't speak. She didn't say a word. She just silently endured while curled up on the floor. *I can't give in now. I'm sorry, but if I give in, she'll rule our lives forever. And I won't allow that to happen. We're setting the ground rules for our future right now.* He turned back to Clarissa and smiled. "This is… marriage."

"You… stubborn oaf," said Clarissa, who was now visibly shaking as a tear fell from her eye. "Just… just do as I tell you, damnit!"

"I… refuse… you," said Victor, noticing Frenka, who was still in her seat, just watching as the ordeal unfolded. She seemed unbothered by the whole show and was just watching as if it was another day.

"You… dare," said Clarissa, gripping Victor by the collar with both hands. "You… annoying man. You refuse to… see me. You… come back… with your whores. And you… think… you can just… be rid of me." She squeezed the fabric in her hands, tightening it around his chest. "I won't… allow it."

"Not.... your decision."

"You don't... get a choice," said the Queen, her eyes glazing over. Then, as her lips began to quiver, she found herself lying against Victor's chest, looking up at him. "Kiss... me. Submit... to... me."

"We will... die... first," At this point, Victor's whole body felt as if it were on fire. His eyes watered, his hands felt numb, and it was taking everything he could to just stand up. *I won't pass out. I refuse. Stay conscious, damnit. Stay awake.*

"End this... Kiss me... Now!" demanded Clarissa, her breathing labored in front of him as she lifted herself onto her toes, trying to place her lips on his. "I... command you."

"I..." He said while the strain made his head wobble as he tried to speak. "Re... fu..." but before he could finish, out of the corner of his eye, he saw Silk rise to her feet. "Wha..."

Victor and the Queen turned to her only to see the gray veins spiraling over her face. She jumped forward at Clarissa, forcing her to the floor and landing on top of her.

"What... get..." were the only words Clarissa could mutter before Silk sunk her mouth onto hers. Their lips smushed together as Silk grabbed the Queen by the hair, holding her down as she forced herself onto her.

Instantly Victor felt the release of his body giving way to freedom as his mind went blank, and he fell to his knees and watched as the world went white. His last image was of a wide-eyed Queen Clarrisa struggling under an ashen-skinned assassin, their faces planted together.

Frenka sat at the table, watching the ordeal play itself out. The blade meant to cut the meat for their dinner was now beneath her hand as it lay on the table. Victor's body crashed to the floor as Silk jumped on the Queen, pinning her down; their lips pressed against one another.

"Argh," muttered the Queen as she forced Silk off of her as she lay on the floor coughing. "How... dare you?"

Silk rolled over gasping on the floor, looking up at the ceiling, her chest heaving as she struggled to breathe.

Frenka stood up from the table, the knife hidden behind her back as she walked over to them.

"Sister-wife and Queen's lines go away." She looked down at Victor and squatted over his passed-out body. "Husband too, his lines are gone." She began rubbing her hand over his face, inspecting it, and sliding his hair back behind his ear.

"Yes, well... a dreadful way to alleviate our condition."

Frenka looked over to the Queen. "Today will be Queen's last day ordering Victor. You will now ask for Frenka's permission."

"Ha! You dare to think that you can give me orders. Do you forget whose kingdom it is that you are in, whore. Weakened or not, I could snap my fingers and wipe you from existence."

"Frenka knows you strong. King strong too. So is stupid prince. But Frenka feels that she will break promise to her husband today," she said as she gripped Victor's hair, lifting his head up and placing the blade at his neck.

"Frenka, what are you doing?" yelled Silk at the sight as she struggled to rise from the floor.

"Stop! No! What are you doing?" said the Queen as her eyes went wide with terror at the sight of Victor with the blade at his neck.

"I promise husband not to kill you. And not to make you sister-wife. But as wife, we are only ones who give husband orders. Not Queen."

"You dare," spoke the Queen with venom on her tongue as her eyes narrowed, her magic growing so heavy that she could see it seeping from her body like a mist. "You." She looked back at Silk. "Both of you. Who are you? Nothing! That's what you are. You just appear out of nowhere and think you can just do as you please." Her fingers clenched as the floor of the house began to shake. "You wouldn't dare. You know nothing of him; nothing of us."

Frenka's eyes stayed focused on the Queen as the house began to shake.

"I know husband hates you. And now you will leave husband be, or I will take husband away from you. It is a wife's duty to free her husband."

"I will do no such thing. But you, you will not leave this house alive unless you release him, right—"

Frenka slid the blade across Victor's neck, dropping his head to the floor as a slew of blood spewed forth.

"No!" yelled the Queen as she quickly crawled across the floor on her way over to him, placing her hands over his neck and began channeling her power, trying to hold in the blood flow. "No! No... Please..." Once again, the veins on her neck began appearing as the white in one of her eyes went completely black. "You... you... bitch. Damn you." Suddenly, a wave of force erupted from around the Queen that shook the house. It sent Silk flying back against the wall as the windows of the house burst out, and a large hole burst forth from the roof.

But Frenka shouldered the sudden blast of power before placing the blade over Victor's heart.

"You strong, but you not healer. If I stab here. Then you not fix that. Even really strong Queen cannot bring husband back from this. And it take time to get real magic to stop me. Time Queen not have.

"No! Please..." pleaded the Queen, the magic emitting from her blood-soaked hands, keeping the blood inside Victor as she focused on keeping him alive. "He can't die. I can't let him die."

"Then you let him go," said Frenka sternly as she watched the veins on the Queen's neck making their way down her arms onto her fingers.

The Queen bit her lip as tears came down her face. "I

can't. Why don't you understand? I just can't…"

Frenka twisted the blade into the fabric of Victor's shirt; the cloth, giving way to the sharpness of the blade.

"Stop. I'll give you anything. Anything you want. Just not him. I can't give you him," The whiteness of the Queen's other eye was slowly turning black as the roots of her hair began turning gray.

"Then Queen and Frenka work out deal. Because if not, I stab, and no healer coming in time to save."

CHAPTER 10

Days later, Isha, Makeba, and Jacinta left the heart house with Rima, the other healer of the house, waving at them from the door. They joined in the morning rush of other students, all headed to their morning classes.

"They still look at sister funny," said Jacinta.

"It's fine. I'm used to it now," said Isha as she looked around. But she could feel the eyes of the other students now upon her. She would catch them eyeing her up and down every morning.

"Hey, over there," said Freedo as he ran up to the girls, holding a book in his hand. "Hey Makeba, you girls doing okay? I was worried you wouldn't come back."

"We needed to take sister away after bad things happen at school."

"Yeah, everything's been so crazy since those people showed up, and your sister got them freaky powers," said

Freedo, scratching his head, embarrassed. "Oh, I'm sorry, Isha. I didn't mean to say it like that."

"It's fine. I don't mind."

"Hey, Makeba, can I come over tonight? My father showed me this cool magic. I'm able to freeze water now."

"I am not good at water magic."

"It's fine. It's mostly just how you concentrate wind magic on a small area. I really do think you can do it."

"Fine, you can teach. But I still not be your woman."

"What? Nooooooo," said Freedo in a nervous chuckle as he looked around. "I just want us to be friends, is all. You know and spend time together. I have even been studying books on the Sakari people, see." Freedo held up the book for the girls to view. On the cover was a Sakari woman and a kingdom man with a blade clenched between his teeth as they swung on tree vines. "Is it true that you get around by swinging from trees in Sakar? Because that sounds so cool."

"What?" asked Jacinta. "That crazy. You crazy boy. Where you find this book?"

"What? My father gave it to me after I told him about you two," said Freedo as he looked at his book, disappointment evident on his face. "You sure you don't swing from trees?"

Isha just watched as her sisters went on to spew answers, trying to correct Freedo's perspective of their Sakari culture, although some of his misunderstandings forced her to try to hold in a few bouts of laughter.

"Hey there," said one boy, walking up to them. "You're Isha, right? My name's Hillow. I heard about you. You're the one who can make other mages stronger, right?"

"Another person come to see sister," said Jacinta, shaking her head. "But sister already has man. So you go away now."

"What?" said Hillow with a smile, undeterred. "I'm just being friendly. And besides, we're both students here, so we might as well get along."

"No, thank you," said Isha, not looking at the boy as she

kept her head down, moving forward. "I don't want to make any new friends right now."

"Ah, come on. Don't be like that."

"No," said Jacinta, turning to the boy, and halting him by placing her hand on his chest. "If you want sister, then you must get her from Leo. He sister's man now."

"What?" asked the boy as they left him behind, "That lecherous teacher. You can't be serious."

"Stop telling people that," said Isha as Jacinta caught up.

"If sister no want men to come to her, then she must get man, so they leave her alone. Even if it is lie. Many people scared of Leo now. So this is good."

"What was that about?" asked Freedo, looking back at the boy.

"Sister gets lots of looks from people now. She has become the talk of school," said Makeba. "It is very funny."

"Well, it certainly doesn't feel fun," said Isha.

"Well, I'm a man," said Freedo, placing a thumb to his chest. "I can be your fake man if that helps."

Jacinta instantly started laughing, "You not really man. You maybe-man. Not strong type. Can't protect sister. So no good."

"What? That's not true. Just because you're both stronger than me doesn't mean I'm weak. You're both just freaky strong, is all." Freedo folded his arms in front of him. "And you live with Isha. Who is to say she's not making you stronger just by being around her?"

"Oh, he blame sister for being weak man," said Jacinta to Makeba while giving Freedo a smug look. "That not manly thing to do. This is why you no good for Makeba."

"Why you... that's not fair. I'll show you I can be a man," said Freedo as he puffed, he continued to puff up his chest and reached down, grabbing Isha by the hand. "Come on, Isha. I bet no boys will talk to you if I'm here." Freedo then led Isha off to the school while Makeba and Jacinta laughed and giggled alongside them.

Inside the halls, students shuffled back and forth in their school garbs as they made their way to their classes. More eyes followed Isha, but to her surprise, no one tried to talk to her as Freedo led her to the classroom door.

Tannor was at the door waiting for them.

"Hello, girls," said Tannor as he noticed Freedo holding Isha's hand. "Oh my, I wish I was so bold at such an early age."

"Hello, Mr. Tannor," said Isha, "Are you going to be teaching the class now?"

"Me? Oh goddess, no. I'm not sure I could handle it," he said as he reached inside his garb, pulling out a piece of golden rope. In the center of it was a circular silver cradle, and within the cradle, there sat a tiny gem with a seed inside. He then showed it to Makeba. "Do you remember this?"

"Oh, that the rock I did not break."

"One and the same. Would it be alright if I asked you to wear this around with you for a while?"

"I do not mind. It is pretty."

"Good," he said as he knelt down and placed it around her neck, tying the ends together. "When you have free time, can you just start channeling your magic into it? It doesn't need to be a lot. I don't want it to affect your classes. But just when you have some free time."

"Okay. I will do this."

"Thank you. Well, I should be on my way. Every second I leave Mr. Caudbell unsupervised is another chance he has to destroy something." He then left the girls with a wave and headed back down the school hall.

Makeba couldn't help but try to channel a bit of her magic into the jewel around her neck. It glowed purple in response to her magic as it began to hover between her hands.

"Come on," said Freedo, leading Isha into class. "We don't want to be late." She could feel his hands shaking nervously as he led her up the steps and to their seats.

"People really are looking at you funny," said Freedo, letting go of her hand and dropping his head. "It feels weird."

"I'm happy someone agrees with me. My sisters think that it's funny."

"Really? It doesn't seem that way to me."

"What do you mean?"

"Like just then with that guy; Jacinta made sure to keep him away from you. I mean, yeah, she was laughing, but if it was really enjoyable to her, do you think she would have done that."

Isha looked over at her sisters, who were talking about something she couldn't hear.

"You are probably right. I still don't understand them," said Isha as she turned around to see Freedo staring at her. "What... what's wrong?"

"I just thought that... well, aren't supposed to be afraid of men and all. That's what Makeba said. But I just realized you didn't mind me grabbing your hand."

"I..." Isha stared at her hand while rubbing her fingers. "I guess... I guess I don't mind then. I wonder if that's because you like Makeba and not me."

"Hey," whispered Freedo as he looked around the class. "It's fine if they say that. But if you start saying it out loud. Then people will start thinking it's true."

"It is true, isn't it?"

"Well... yes, but I don't want her to know that. She's always smug whenever she thinks she's figured something out."

"Okay, class," said Miss Webblebottom. "Today we are going to talk about practical uses for magic and... Yes, Dayvon, what is it?"

"Can we talk about Isha's magic? Is it true she can make other mages stronger?" asked Dayvon as the rest of the class echoed his sentiments.

"Well, I guess it was too much to ask that we might avoid that topic. But yes, after extensive testing and the hospitalization of several faculty members, we can confirm that it is true that Miss Highland does indeed possess the ability to increase our power by a substantial amount. But Miss Highland is forbidden from using her powers unless directed to by Headmaster Soulden."

"What? Why?" asked Dayvon.

"Because everyone she's used her power on has passed out on the floor or ended up in a coma for a week. So, I'm afraid you all will have to wait until she is properly trained and can control her powers."

Isha felt the eyes of the class turn to her, each looking curiously hungry as if they had found a new toy. But her uneasiness of the situation was quieted as she felt Freedo's hand again squeeze hers.

"Well... too bad for you all," said Freedo as he stood up, looking over the class. "Because Isha's already promised that I get to go first. So, you all stay away. I'm going to be taking care of her from now on."

Isha looked up at him with wide eyes as Freedo smiled. But as she looked around the room, she saw the same shock in the eyes of the other students. That is, except for Makeba and Jacinta, who looked at her with mischievous smiles.

"Stop that," whispered Isha, her face beginning to redden as she reached up, grabbing Freedo by the arm and pulling him back down to the seat beside her. "It's embarrassing."

"Oh, sorry. I thought I was helping," whispered Freedo. "You think it worked?"

"What worked? Why did you..."

"Well," said Miss Webblebottom. "That was quite the declaration of love."

Freedo's eyes went wide "Of love?" he mumbled under his breath. "Wait, that's not—"

"You be sure to take good care of Miss Isha," said Miss Webblebottom with a smile. "Perhaps your affection for her will help her keep her power under control. Goddess knows no one in the faculty could."

"But... but... I... I mean," Freedo turned back to Isha, who was looking down at the floor with her face reddening. "What, why are you blushing?"

"Good job, Freedo," said one of the boys in class with a laugh. "When she learns her powers, you've got to show us, okay?" The rest of the class echoed the boy's sentiments in between their giggles and laughter. Freedo just looked over the class with a dumbfounded expression on his face.

"Okay, class. Now that the issue with Miss Highland's power has been settled, let us all focus on our own powers. Who here can tell me how we find our limits regarding our magic ability?"

"Isn't that when we get headaches from using magic too much?" asked Serpene.

"That's correct, but that's the effect of what happens when we use too much magic. I'm asking specifically about the limits of your magic. Anyone can use magic until their brains shut down. I mean, what is the difference between a strong mage and someone who makes themselves stronger?

"You mean like power then?" asked Marlene.

"Yes," said Miss Webblebottom as she grabbed a wooden ball from her desk. "Let's say we want to make this magic ball float. Like so," The wooden ball began to float above her fingers. "Now, if we do this for hours and hours, eventually, we will tire. That's the same for every mage. But what's different for every mage is the effort required to make the ball float. Some of you might find the action easier than others. That will be based on your innate strength."

"But we all are here to become stronger, right? So won't we all be the same when we graduate?"

"I think you misunderstand what stronger really means here. We can't make you stronger. Your body will have a natural limit for just how much magic it can handle," said Miss Webblebottom as she raised a finger. "Now, this certainly increases as you get older, and your bodies grow into adulthood. But after the age of twenty or so, you will be about as strong as you're ever going to be."

"Then why train at all if we can't get stronger?"

"You can become stronger, but the strength you gain will pale compared to what actually makes you stronger."

"I... I don't understand."

"Because what I teach here isn't to make you stronger. But instead, I will refine the magic you do have, making it more effective and precise. And through that efficiency, you will become more powerful mages."

"Wait?" said another boy in class. "Then what about Isha? She makes people stronger right? Can't we just use her to make us stronger?"

The class turned, looking at Isha again.

"And that is why our little Isha has become the topic of all the kingdoms. The first mage with the power to strengthen other mages. Life is going to become quite interesting for you, young lady." Miss Webblebottom gave a smile. "And you too, young Master Freedo. Be sure to take care of her if you plan to be her suitor."

"What?" said Freedo, looking around the class as they giggled again.

The rest of the class went by with the occasional tease of Freedo's and Isha's coupling. When classes were over and before Freedo and Isha could become flooded with the questions the course seemed dying to ask, Soulden appeared at the door.

"Miss Highland, I would like you and your sisters to join me."

Isha stood along with Makeba and Jacinta before she glanced back down at Freedo beside her, "Thank you, Freedo. I'm okay now."

"Huh... oh, okay, no problem." Freedo tilted his head to look over at Makeba. "Is it okay if I come to visit today?"

Isha smiled, "Yes, I think it's fine. Makeba might not say

it, but I think she likes you."

"Really?"

"I think so. I mean, she never talks to any boys besides Jacob. And she doesn't seem to mind talking to you."

"Yes," said Freedo with a smile. "You're right. I... I'll be over tonight then."

"Okay," said Isha, before making her way to the bottom of the class where Soulden was waiting for them.

"It seems your friend arrived around an hour or so ago," said Soulden as she led the girls out into the hallway.

"Aukube, here?" asked Makeba excitedly.

"Indeed. I asked Mr. Caudbell to escort her to the tree. I imagine they are waiting there for us now," said Soulden as they stepped onto the platform again, lifting them up, and taking them into the school's upper levels.

Once again, Isha found herself going through the orange rings. Again, the marble walls passed around her till she finally returned to the dark corridor.

She didn't take the time to look through the doors as they passed, but she could hear the echoes of something knocking against the walls. It thudded, the bass so deep she could feel it in her bones as the vibrations bounced off the walls of the dark hallway. From a few of the dorms, she could hear the sounds of both men and women screaming.

Isha chose not to ask questions as she was more concerned with meeting with Aukube again.

"What happening here? So many screams," asked Jacinta, curiosity taking control of her mind. "Why big tree not below? Instead, we must travel up high to see Tree Sakari."

"Oh, tests mostly. Our more secret tests. You three wouldn't know of it, I'm sure. But all the magic schools compete against each other regarding academic finds and prestige. We classify ourselves as the best magical academy in the land. Still, we can only do so based on the quality of the students that graduate from here, along with our magical discoveries. Otherwise, we'd be no better than any other magical school."

"So, this school special?"

"It is when compared to the others, yes. We consistently produce innovations. You three yourselves, add to this."

"We do? How?"

"How?" asked Soulden rhetorically, "Do you three not realize how special you are? Surely you must. Two budding Sakari girls whose magic can be trained in our own ways and Isha, whom all the kingdoms are looking at as some golden broodmare." Soulden turned back to the girls. "Oscar informed me of that little adventure of yours. And I ensure to have it so that no situation like that ever befalls you again. And if by some chance it does, you will be competent enough to deal with it. And as such, I have asked Mr. Higgin's to give you special attention in your training."

"Oh, the big loud man is good at fighting?"

"Of course. As loud as he may be, he is very talented in the art of combat. Both magical and mundane." She then looked at Makeba and Jacinta. "And you two are fierce in your own right. I remember that day on the ship. I shall also look to you to ensure she is trained correctly."

"We also want sister to get be better fighter. Bad people try to take her a lot."

"Hey! They had Chloe too. What was I supposed to do?"

"Speaking of which, where is Miss Richards? I know you two had your rocky start. But I was under the impression that you two had become fast friends."

"She's back at home now," said Makeba. "She wanted to stay with us, so she moved her stuff today. Her and sister have become friends now."

"That's good to hear," said Soulden as they entered the domed room again. "Perhaps you all will cause me less trouble now. Your antics were quite the experience to explain to the council."

Ahead of them, the orange tree still stood in terrible

shape. Its limbs were still cut, and the subsequent trees that were planted to try and help it had still not yet been accepted. Ahead of them were Aukube, Caudbell, and Tannor. They were sitting on a blanket on the floor, a tray with leaves from the tree between them.

"Hey, Aukube," said Jacinta as she and Makeba ran over to greet their teacher.

"Hello, I did not believe I would be seeing you girls so soon. I must admit, I was surprised when Oscar and Gregga came to me asking that I visit this sky kingdom."

"We have been having the most wonderful conversation about theories as to why the tree hasn't healed itself," said Caudbell, picking up one of the orange leaves from the table.

"Sakari forestry has different demands than those in your kingdom's lands. The air is thinner back home, and the trees have adapted to the climate. But since your land does not have that restriction, it affects the tree differently. I imagine if you tried to grow a Sakari tree of this nature down below. The abundance of air would only serve to poison it over time rather than feed it."

"We theorized that," said Tannor. "That is perhaps one of the reasons our forebears had this school placed in the sky is exactly because of this situation. Up here, the air is thinner and would be similar to the mountainous regions of the Sakari lands."

"You believe this entire school is up in the sky because of this tree?"

"If you consider all the surrounding context, it does make sense," said Caudbell. "I mean, look at this school as a whole. The abundance of plant life in such a modern city is unheard of. The harmonious nature between forestry and construction is quite interesting. For example, have you noticed that on the rare occasion when one of the houses might fall into a bit of disrepair, say when a block around the foundation breaks or crumbles away, it will often be a thick vine or root that will fill in that crevice? Even before our service people have had a chance to inspect it."

"If the entity inside the tree can control the forestry throughout the school," said Soulden, looking up at the tree, "why are these smaller green trees even necessary? Should it not be—"

"She," said Jacinta, looking up at Soulden displeased.

"Pardon."

"Tree Sakari is girl, not an 'it.'"

"Yes, my apologies then," said Soulden, turning back to Caudbell. "Should she not be able to draw in what she needs from the surrounding forestry? After all, it is not as if there isn't a fair amount."

"That is unknown because while this appears like a typical Ren'lock tree in my land, orange leaves as massive as this size are not common at all. It has been changed since it came to your land."

"And do we have any idea the exact changes our forebears made?" asked Soulden.

"Sadly, no. Records from that far back are surely lost, even within our own halls," said Caudbell, shaking his head. "If only Retallia were here. He would surely know more."

"Who is Retallia?" asked Isha.

"Another one of our researchers," said Soulden. "He handled the upkeep of the forestry here before he left. A job that we all believed to be mostly self-correcting to our knowledge. So we never really required much of his research."

"Yes. That was a mistake," said Caudbell. "I assumed he left because his research never yielded any results. But he did love plants. You would often see him planting new types of forestry around the school and houses."

"You two never looked deeper into his notes," said Tannor. "He was trying to find a way to have the trees themselves cast harmonious spells and correlate them to the different times of the day. It was his own research that led to the color-changing trees we installed in Orlana."

"Has his office been cleared out yet?" asked Soulden. "Perhaps, there is something there to help."

"Yes. Unfortunately, when he left, he took the majority of his notes with him."

"Shame," said Soulden, looking down at Makeba. "I guess our only current option would be that trick you pulled to make her leaves glow. But after seeing how weak that made you, I must admit that I am hesitant to ask you to revisit that situation."

"I am curious about that," said Aukube. "What did you do, Makeba?"

"I give Tree Sakari magic. It is the same that I do for Sister Isha. But Tree Sakari took too much. It hurt, and I went to sleep."

"Now, I am even more hesitant to allow you to repeat that action. Magical poisoning is something we take seriously," said Soulden. "But why did it not take magic from you two? I mean, all three of you were in there."

"She try with me. But I not let her," said Jacinta. "I was not sure if I get magic back."

"She didn't try with me," said Isha.

"That's probably because Sakari magic and Kingdom magic are different," said Aukube, "or should I say we access magic differently? The markings on our bodies allow magic to flow into us and our bodies change it into a magic that suits us." She looked up at the tree. "But I do not think a dozen Sakari mages would be able to fix this tree. She has been damaged very badly."

"What if sister got markings? Would she be able to do Sakari magic then?"

Aukube took her gaze from the tree down to Isha. "Most likely, no. She has a kingdom body. Only those that lived in Sakari would be able. We are one with the land. We have eaten from the land the tree grows on; fed off the animals there. No matter where we go, that link ensures that we belong to Sakar. But your sister Isha has no such connection to our home."

"That shame. I want to fix Tree Sakari to talk more with her. She knows a lot about old Sakari ways."

"Wait," said Caudbell. "There may still be a way." He rubbed his chin while looking back and forth between the girls. "The Sakari's problem is the mental exhaustion from using too much magic, correct? And Isha's problem is that her magic isn't compatible with Sakari magic. Well, what if we used Isha as the filter for the magic that the Sakari draw in? They seem not to suffer the burned flesh whenever she uses her powers on them. So, I think it's worth a shot."

"That is a misunderstanding, it seems," said Aukube. "Isha has, in fact, burned the girls. It is just less frequent than with your kingdom people. Out of the ten times we had them connect their powers; the girls felt an abundance of heat twice. Fortunately, we were there to stop any real damage."

"Yes, it is hard to change Sister Isha magic into ours. It feel too different."

"Perhaps Isha's affection for the Sakari acts as a mental block to protect the girls," said Caudbell, picking up a leaf and twirling it between his fingers. "Fear has often been the cause of many magical creations and disasters."

"The key word being 'disaster,'" said Soulden. "And I would prefer not to risk the occurrence of another one."

"I may be able to do something about the magic transfer issue," said Aukube, looking at Makeba. "You and your sister have the same link to magic. So, I would just need to add Isha to that link. That is, if you girls are okay with strengthening your bond. Because once done, it cannot be undone. Isha will have a permanent link to you and you to her. Blood in and blood out."

"I think it right thing to do. Sister Isha is Sister Isha," said Jacinta

"I would not mind Sister Isha joining us."

"Wait... what's happening? What is... I mean, what is this link?"

"Oh, sorry," said Aukube. "We have gotten ahead of ourselves. "Links are the markings on the back of Jacinta and Makeba. What we used to make these markings was ash from the land of Sakar. We then bleed both girls, mixing their life force into a bowl until it turns black. And with that, we engrave the markings that they have now. And because of this, they share magic between the two of them. We simply wish to add you to that link."

"What? You... you have to bleed me?"

"You? No, that is only to form the link. The link already exists. We only wish to add you to their link. So we will need to bleed them again. And then mark you."

"Will... will the markings hurt?"

Aukube gave a cheerful smile. "Oh yes, very much so. All three of you will be in much pain until the link is finished."

"What?" asked Isha, the look on her face not hiding her fear as she stared at the adults before turning to her sisters. "And you want to do this?"

"Me and Makeba talk about it already," said Jacinta. "We want sister to have markings like us since that night with Mama in the bath. That makes us true blood sisters. But never good time to tell Sister Isha. Now we have reason to. Also, it will be good to save Tree Sakari. So, it is good thing to do now. She will teach us more old Sakari ways."

Isha took another look at the tree and then at the look on her sister's faces before she slumped her shoulders. "Do we have to do it now?"

"Oh, no. I must gather everything, perhaps in a day or two. You need not worry. It will take some time."

"I still feel worried."

CHAPTER 11

Victor awoke to the sound of humming around him. A soft melody comforted him in the darkness of his mind as he stirred from his sleep.

"Oh, he finally awake now," came Frenka's voice. "Sister-wife, come. Husband has awoken from sleep."

Victor's eyes shot open as the memories came to him. The pain of disobeying Clarissa still lingered in his spirit as he reached over and clenched his hands on his chest. The hatred of her trying to control him was so fresh on his lips that he could taste it. But with the opening of his eyes only came the pain of trying to adjust to the room's light. Everything was blurry and he couldn't focus. He tried to bring one of his arms up to shield his eyes but found the action more laborious than he anticipated.

"Welcome back, husband. Frenka wondered when you would wake."

A wave of relief came from Victor that he didn't expect as he heard Frenka's voice. "How long wa..." he tried to speak but felt an intense burning sensation on his throat that immediately stopped him as he grabbed for his neck. There he found some type of patch wrapped around his throat.

"Careful husband, you not heal yet."

Heal? How bad was the bonding's price this time? "Are you... okay? Where's Silk? Is she... okay?" Victor's voice spoke horse as he struggled to sit up in bed, turning his head and listening to any sounds as his eyes still showed blurry and gray.

"Yes, Frenka is fine."

"I'm here," came Silk's voice from nearby. "I'm okay now."

Another wave of relief hit his heart after hearing the woman's voice. He exhaled and released the strain on his body, relaxing back into bed.

"Here, husband," Frenka handed Victor a cup of water. "Drink this. It will help with your throat."

Taking the cup to his lips, Victor began to drink, the liquid providing a cooling sensation to his burning throat.

"Why husband's eyes gray?" asked Frenka, a worried tone in her voice.

"One of the... results of dis... disobeying her orders. It will pass soon. It has before."

"So husband has refused Queen before?"

"On occasion... I have refused orders. The results of which... were much the same as this. But it goes both ways. She suffers from my refusal... as well. Silk, are still here? Did you recover well?"

"Yes... It hurt, but I used magic to numb it as much as possible. But the way... the way you feel compelled to listen to her. It is hard to think clearly."

"I... am aware," said Victor, the grayness finally beginning to leave his eyes as the world slowly began to come

163

back into focus. But as his vision finally cleared, he found himself disbelieving the sight before him. Silk sat in a chair near the head of his bed. She wore on of his military uniforms. It looked ridiculous on her, trousers that dragged down to the floor across her feet. And the arms were too long for her, falling over her wrists and covering her arms.

Victor raised a brow as he looked at her with squinted eyes. "My vision has come back, but-"

"Don't look at me like that," said Silk, frowning down at him. "You were out and needed to be seen around the castle."

"A lot has happened, husband. But now Queen will no longer give you orders. That matter now settled."

"What do you mean? And... what happened to my throat?" asked Victor before coughing and taking another sip of water from his cup.

"Frenka slit husband's throat," said Frenka with a tone of cheerful humor in her voice.

Victor coughed out his water at the declaration and began gasping for breath, his eyes starting to water. "You... you what!" was all he could manage as he continued his fit of coughing while slouched over the side of the bed.

"After sister-wife kiss Queen, she was upset and did lots of shouting. So, I told her that she was not allowed to give you orders. Your life now belongs to Frenka. Instead, she must come to me with requests. Then, I will decide if you do."

Victor turned back to Frenka, his eyes still watery. "What?"

"Oh, she laugh at Frenka. So to show her, I simply walk over to half-dead husband and slit his throat. When the blood came, I make her hold blood in with her magic and refuse to allow healer until she agree. She started crying, but she agree. And now she is Victor's third sister-wife."

"What..." Victor began coughing again as he reached for his throat, the inside quaking as if on fire. "You... didn't."

164

"Frenka did."

"I told you specifically that... I didn't... want that."

"You did... and you also told Frenka not to kill Queen. But one of two must happen for husband to be free."

"And what... and what did you do in all of this?" asked Victor to Silk in the harshest tone his voice would allow.

"Sister-wife did nothing. She listened to what Frenka had to say. It was Frenka's decision." She stared Victor in the eyes as his face twisted with the emotions his mind was going through. "You are angry at Frenka."

"I am," said Victor as he watched Frenka, her face as calm as it had ever been. But noticed her rubbing the back of her knuckles.

"You belong to Frenka now, not Queen. I need her to understand."

"So... to do that... you tried to kill me."

"Yes, husband. Frenka will do what she must to free husband. That is what a wife is. Husband will not live as slave, nor will he allow us to."

Victor closed his eyes and took in a deep breath. Again, he could feel the burning sensation passing down his throat, except now it had a partner near the temple of his head. It was a sharp pain that made his shoulders tremble as if intensified the more deeply he breathed in. It was bothersome—more than bothersome; downright painful.

Just the thought of it. To make a decision like that... I've traded one slave master for another. Do what feels good. What a fucking load of... He then opened his eyes and stared directly at his wife.

"Leave."

Frenka took a short breath and nodded before standing up from her chair and turning to go until Victor grabbed her wrist. She turned back to him, a hint of a tear in her eye.

"I'm not telling... you to go back to your kingdom. Just... just give me time to think about this. What you have done... I must think. And I need more time. And I can't do that and look at you right now."

"Frenka... Frenka will go out today." She nodded before wiping her eyes. "Give husband time to make decision." Frenka then turned to Silk. "Please take... take care of husband today." And with one final look at Victor, Frenka left out of the room, and shortly afterward, Victor heard the door to the house open and close.

Victor closed his eyes and took another breath, trying to embrace the pain in his throat, and become accustomed to it, only to open his eyes again and see Silk staring back at him.

"Okay... what do you want to say?"

She sighed. "I don't know," said Silk, staring back at him. "I don't know what to say. I mean, I think I understand why she did what she did. But after everything. I wanted to kill her. I mean, I was angry. But you're still alive. And the Queen agreed to not give you, I mean, give *us* orders anymore. So many things happened that I don't understand. Like when the Queen transformed and..."

"What?" shouted Victor to his instant regret as he leaned over the side of the bed, coughing.

"Are you okay?" asked Silk, rising from her seat, but was stopped by Victor raising his hand.

"I'm... fine. I'm fine." He raised himself back, regaining control of his breathing. "What... do you mean... transformed?"

"Well, not fully. But her eyes went black, and her hair started to turn white." Silk stared at Victor curiously, "Is... is that not normal for her?"

"No... She can't transform. That's never happened before."

"Maybe it had something to do with you almost dying." Silk placed her hands over her chest. "I mean when it happened, I felt this weird feeling inside of me; like something was tearing at me. But when I saw her, she was going through something bad. Those gray veins were all over her body, not just her neck."

"I... I don't know. I've never seen anything like that before." *I don't want to think about any of this anymore. My new wife slit my throat, and Clarissa is... I don't know anymore.*

"Do all Sakari bonding rituals end like that? I mean with her... well... whatever that was?"

Victor sighed, "No. The bonding ritual with the Queen and I... well, it's different. A complication altered the spell when it was placed on us. So, we are still bonded. But the pain is shared between us when I refuse her order." He gestured towards Silk. "It seems you've inherited that bit. But we don't know what else might happen in our bonding. And I spent most of my life away from her, trying to not find out."

"Well, that might be hard now."

"A little harder since I'm back here. But I'll leave again soon enough."

"No, I mean. Frenka made her your third wife when you had your throat cut."

Victor closed his eyes again, performing a soft growling moan in his throat. The vibration felt weird. It was as if there was a foreign object right against the skin inside his neck, and no amount of coughing would clear it. "I just think... there had to be another way."

"Victor, how long have you been with the Queen like this?'

"I don't know, sixteen, seventeen years. Why?"

"And in all that time, someone as smart as you never figured out another way."

Victor just stared at Silk for a moment. But he couldn't think of a response. "So, I am to just accept this as my new way of life now?"

"You did with us. And we did with you. Do you think Frenka did that to hurt you?"

"No, but I'm not sure she did it thinking of me either. She just... just does things. It feels like I'm just around for the fallout."

"Victor, a lot has happened. But that was the deal they made. The Queen wouldn't let you go. So, Frenka and her made a deal that she and the Queen would work together if the Queen would submit to not giving you orders."

Victor placed his hand over his face and began rubbing in frustration. "This will never end." He then threw his head back, looking to the ceiling. "Fine, and where do you stand in all of this? Any wisdom from the assassin? At this point, your advice is as welcome as any."

"No. After what I saw last night, I just don't know what to think anymore. I saw a Queen submit to a mountain woman on a marriage proposal over the dying body of her husband. And honestly, Victor, I don't want to think about this anymore." Silk stood and crawled into bed beside Victor laying on top of him and placing her head against his chest. "I have just decided that I want to be with you, and if this is your life, then I will be with you through it."

"It sounds ridiculous to think about, but hearing you say it out loud is even more ludicrous. But don't worry. I can't let you off the hook this easily. You're a part of this now. So, tell me, what do you think I should do about our mountain wife?"

"Why ask me? She's *your* wife," a smile spread across her lips as she patted his chest.

"No... she's *our* wife. And apparently so... so is that bitch Clarissa. And as an equal wife, you get an equal say. I'm not letting you not have an opinion here. If I'm in this shit hole, then so are you."

Silk sighed again. "Frenka is a good person, I think. And she accepted me. Even if she thinks I'm something called a Dula-hon. And she cried after the Queen and her healer left. She didn't let me see her, but I could hear her through the walls, her trying to hold her breath, the sobbing. But I don't know what or how she thinks. She might try to kill you again because of some stupid clan rule. But if she does, I told her that I would kill her myself."

"Does that mean she stays?"

Silk closed her eyes, taking in a deep breath, "Yes, there are many things I dislike about her. But I can see that she loves you. In her own way. So does the Queen." Silk just shook her head. "I remember you telling me you wanted to marry a simple woman. Do you think you've done that now?" She looked up at him sticking her tongue out, playfully biting the tip.

Victor couldn't help but start laughing at Silk's face. "Oh, goddess. That dream surely is long gone. If anything, you're the most normal out of the bunch." He shook his head. "My father and mother would surely spin on their heads at the sight of my wives."

"Your parents? Are they still alive?"

"Oh... yes. They both live down in Greywill. Thankfully, very far away from all this madness. When I acquired my wealth as a General, the first thing I did was set them up as far away from the capital as I could. They spend their days by the coast now."

"You've never talked about your parents before. What's it like to have parents?"

"What's it like?" Victor looked at her curiously before remembering her situation. "Yes, well. Not all parents are great. You might have done better by not having them. But mine were normal for the most part. My father was a lumber master, and my mother helped him design things, like patterns for handles and tables and such. When we get the chance, I shall introduce you to them."

"Really? I mean..." Silk looked herself over. "Will... Do you think they will accept me?"

"It'll be a shock at first. But they already know about Clarissa, sort of. I didn't hide that from them. I'm sure an assassin with shape-shifting skills will take some time." Victor patted Silk on the back. The rugged fabric of his military outfit spoiled the moment a bit, but it was enough.

"They'll adjust, but let's not open with that when you meet them."

"You really intend to keep your word about trying to give me a home?"

"That's... the plan," said Victor, lifting the sheet and rolling out of bed, trying to stand. He placed his feet on the floor and stumbled over to the wall, catching himself.

"Stop! What are you doing?" asked Silk as she hurried out of bed over to him, taking his arm and trying to support his weight.

"I need... to stretch my legs. Can't stay in bed all day," said Victor, making his way to the door.

"Fine, but you might need to brace yourself. Frenka and the Queen, they sort of made a mess when you were down. They yelled at each other. I protected us, but they... well..."

"Mess?" Victor opened the door. "What type of..." His eyes went wide as he stared at what had once been the living area of his home. Now, it seemed as if his home was the remnants of what was left after a war and proper pillaging. The corner walls near the door were completely gone, and he could see out into the street as people walked by. Furniture had been uplifted around and was now embedded in walls and above his head. Victor, in disbelief, looked upward and could see the sky through a giant hole in the roof.

"I warned you."

"Wha... I mean... But..." said Victor as his brain failed to comprehend the leftover carnage in front of him.

"They yelled at each other a lot."

CHAPTER 12

Early in the morning, in the dorm of Heart House, Jacinta, Makeba, and Isha lay on the floor looking over their textbook. Around them were empty plates and a few discarded nightclothes they had yet to pick up. Rima placed her finger on the book page that showed a woman's body.

"Okay... To heal a mundane is different for us because they do not have magic in their system. Instead of channeling our magic inside of them and trying to mix it with how their magical core works like with a normal mage, we isolate our magic on the affected area and form a magic core on the point we're healing. Do you understand?"

"I... think... so," said Isha with a confused look. "It kind of makes sense."

"Why Leo not here to teach?" asked Jacinta, looking around. "We not see him so much since we get back."

"Yes, I wonder that myself sometimes," said Rima as

she rubbed her hands over her cheek and sighed. "But I'm sure he will be back eventually. At least, I hope so. I'm not exactly the best teacher. And I'm not sure how to get Isha to use healing power. I mean, don't you have some type of enhancing magic power? Are you even sure that you can heal anymore?"

"I don't know." Isha looked at her head. "I mean, Leo once said that only healers can take in another person's magic, and I can do that. So, maybe I can."

Rima groaned. "How did Elena make all this look so easy? All this cooking and cleaning and teaching. It's exhausting."

"Rima not strong. Rima is rich girl. Why Rima no have servants come do things for her?" asked Makeba.

"Because I still have my pride. Even when I was at home, I used to help our servants out in the kitchen. Okay, well, maybe not that much, and it was only with the cakes. But still, I helped. And I want to be more like Elena and be more capable. Besides, even if I wanted to, this school wouldn't allow it, especially after the attack where whoever that was came disguised as Miss Evangale's servants. The school has locked out guests unless specifically granted by Soulden, and I don't think having my servants here qualifies."

There was a knock at the door.

"Who is it?" asked Rima as she stood up from her seat and walked over to the door.

"It is Aukube, I have come for the girls."

Rima opened the door, and Aukube stepped inside, spotting the girls on the floor with their books.

"Hello, Aukube," said Makeba, standing and walking over to her. "Did you make markings for Sister Isha?"

"Not yet. I do not know if you want to do it here or under the tree. Since the ritual requires ash, I assumed it would make sense to use the ashes from a burned piece of the tree itself. But I wanted Isha to ask the tree for its permission first."

"I... I can ask. But I cannot talk to her here. She will only hear me if I go there."

"Then I was right to come ask. I have been shown around the school and have been treated very nicely. I will be with Soulden when you girls are ready to begin. I shall also ask for a table for Isha to lay upon." Aukube turned to Rima. "You may come too."

"Wait," said Rima as Aukube turned to leave, "you... they said you were a healer. Is that true?"

"Yes. That is true. My art is healing."

"Can you help me? I mean with their training. I am still learning myself; all I can do is teach Isha what I know so far, and it's not really that much."

"Hmmm. The Sakari healing method is different from the kingdom healing, I think. But if Isha will be doing the link. Then perhaps my training will be of use. But I have a duty to the tribe." Aukube turned around, looking down at the girls once again. "But teaching our leader's daughter may be best for the tribe." She then nodded. "We shall see. I will make the decision after we see how linking works. This is the first time a Sakari has tried linking with the kingdom people. Maybe it will not work."

"Yes. I understand. Thank you."

Aukube then left the building, making her way out into the streets.

"Okay, so you girls should go and get ready for classes then. Hopefully, they will have everything prepared by the end of the day.

"All right," said the girls as they headed back upstairs into their room to change clothes.

"Does sister think Leo will be okay? He is always sad-faced when we see him," said Makeba, handing Isha her blue skirt.

"I hope so. I mean... He doesn't even come home anymore. I only see him when he comes to heal some from class."

"We go visit Leo today then," said Jacinta as she pulled her shift over her head, tossing it aside before sliding on the top of her school uniform.

"What? But... he acts like he doesn't want to see us. I mean, he doesn't even speak."

"Too bad. I want to see him. And so do sisters. We will not let him run away."

"Can we just do that?"

"Yes, we can. I war sister, so that means we will."

"But this isn't a war."

"Yes, it is. Sister just does not know what war is." Jacinta slid on her skirt before sliding her feet into her shoes. "But sister Jacinta will show you. War comes from many places."

"What does that mean?" Isha slid on her stockings. "Is this more Sakari things?"

"This woman thing. Mother teach us." Jacinta walked over to the door. "Come, we not be late for class."

"Alright. Don't rush." Isha finished putting on her shoes and made her way over to Jacinta as the girls headed downstairs. As they exited the door, they merged into the crowd of similar students that stirred for the day with the morning sun rising.

Once again, they found Freedo waiting under a tree. He came over and held Isha's hand as he had done every morning since the start of school.

"Hey, you three," said Freedo as he came over and held Isha's hand as he had done every morning since the start of school.

"Hey, Freedo," said Isha. "You know you don't have to do this anymore. No one really bothers us now."

"Maybe not. But they could be just waiting for me to go away," said Freedo, looking around a bit before turning to Makeba. "Hey Makeba, guess what I learned. I can do illusion magic now."

Makeba frowned at Freedo, "You lie, Freedo still bad at magic."

174

"Are you sure?" asked Freedo with a smug grin that looked to actually annoy Makeba.

"Fine. Then show. If you can do, then I will do better."

They all stopped at the castle steps, standing to the side so the other students could pass. "Freedo removed his hand from Isha's and held it up for the girls to see.

"They all stared at his hand as a small bubbly light began to form across his palm. It fluttered a bit before it began to spread out and finally formed the shape of a green leaf.

"Oh! Weak mage boy can do it," said Jacinta with eyes wide as she turned to Makeba. "He beat you sister. Now sister Isha will have to marry him," Jacinta giggled.

"Hey. Don't call me 'weak mage boy.' I tried really hard to... Wait, what do you mean Isha has to marry me?"

"Jacinta, you stop that." Isha turned to Freedo. "Forgot about her. But that's really good. Don't you think so, Makeba?"

Makeba bit on her lower lip while staring at the green leaf floating above Freedo's hand. "It looks okay." She then slowly reached her hand and poked at it.

"Hey, don't do that. I'm not—" the image popped as Makeba's hand slid into it, bursting it into a thousand small images of glitter flying up into the air before quickly disappearing.

"Oh, pretty," said Jacinta as she watched the explosion.

"Ahh," yelped Freedo as he shook his head and started fluttering his eyes as if he had been staring at something for too long. "Now, I won't be able to make another one for at least an hour. It's so hard keeping that image in my head." Then, when he opened his eyes, he found the girls staring at him.

"What?" asked Freedo defensively.

"You will teach Makeba how you do this magic."

"Really? I mean..." Freedo coughed. "Sure, I will. But only if you promise not to call me weak mage boy. Oh! And you have to teach me more Sakari stuff."

Makeba and Jacinta looked at each other for a moment and then nodded.

"Fine. You not weak mage boy no more," said Jacinta, pointing her finger at Freedo. "You will be *okay* mage boy."

"What? Come on, at least call me by my name."

"No, you not ask for that," replied Makeba, "Now come, okay mage boy. We late for class." Makeba and Jacinta then turned and walked up the steps into the building.

"Hey, that's not fair," said Freedo, following behind.

Isha couldn't help but giggle as she followed behind them as they headed through the halls into Miss Gallows' class.

"Okay, class," said Miss Gallows as they all entered the room, taking their seats. "Okay, class, today's topic of discussion is magical animals. We hear about them in the stories of old; like how the Shadow King kept two magic cats as the guards of his throne room. But I'm sure none of you have seen any magical animals."

"That's not true," said Marlene. "My aunty can make her dogs do things with magic."

"Oh! And what sort of things?" asked Miss Gallows.

"He can make it bark and go get things."

"No. That, child, is magical control, or at the very least a well-trained animal. Tell me, was she able to manipulate animals in other ways? Perhaps, your auntie is a mind mage then?"

"Yes, ma'am."

"She's using her magic to control the animals. That's very different. No, I speak of an animal with its own magical core. An animal that can use magic at its own will. That is what a truly magical creature is."

"What? You mean like a dragon out of the fairy tales?" asked another boy in class.

"We've actually looked into dragons before. But we haven't found any proof that they ever existed. But even if

176

they did, I'd be hesitant to refer to them as magical creatures. All the old tales say they only breathe fire from some type of gland in their throat; much like a snake that spits out venom or a skunk that hits you with its scent. There's nothing much magical about that, now is there?"

"Okay," said Serpene, raising her hand. "Do you mean that there are animals that can cast magic like we do?"

"Exactly. Although it is rare in the five kingdoms. They are a bit more common overseas. Now, can anyone tell me what stops an animal from being able to use magic? Because, as we have discussed before, magic is all around us. And if so, why haven't the birds and the bears we find out in nature been able to harness the power as humans have."

The class was silent for a long moment before one of the girls raised her hand.

"Is it because our brains are different?"

Miss Gallows clapped her hands. "Good job. It looks like someone has been paying attention." She began to pace in front of the class. "That's exactly the conclusion we have come to. The human mind can access magic and filter it in a way that most animals can not. We have even performed experiments in the past where we tried to channel our own magic into animals, and the result, more often than not, ends in the fatality of the animals. Not only can their minds not filter magic, but it also seems that they do the exact opposite. To protect themselves, animal minds actively block magic."

"Then why does my aunt's mind magic work on her dog and pets?" asked Marlene.

"That we do not know. Mind mages are few and far between, so we haven't had the chance to properly examine that particular skill. But I have heard that mind mages slaughter their way through a dozen or so animals before they can properly control them. But that is all hear-say."

"That's terrible. I was hoping I'd get to talk to the animals one day," said another girl in class.

"Well, perhaps you will be the first mage to learn how to do such a thing." Miss Gallows turned her attention to Jacinta and Makeba. "What about in Sakar? Do they have magical animals where you girls are from?"

Jacinta and Makeba looked at each other for a moment making sure she was talking to them.

"Not sure. Mama says we have them. But we not remember them," replied Jacinta. "But, we have big animals that eat men. And the bad people we feed to them."

"Well, that certainly is not a pleasant thought." Miss Gallows grimaced. "But perhaps somewhere in the world, there exists a creature outside of man and woman that is able to cast spells at will."

The class continued as Miss Gallows gave her lesson on magical creatures and under what specific circumstances they might be created. All the while, Isha struggled to focus. Her mind was on Leo. Why was he coming home late? Why was he avoiding them? Did he blame her in any way for what happened to Elena?

Finally, the image of a bell appeared above the class, as it usually did, and the sound of a ringing came, signaling the end of the course.

The girls left class and headed upstairs on the way to Soulden's office.

"Wait," said Jacinta, stopping in the middle of the corridor. "We go see Leo first. We tell him about linking."

"He... he might be busy," said Isha, hesitating about seeing Leo again.

"Yes. I think it a good idea too," said Makeba as she grabbed Isha's hand and led her off towards Leo's office.

"But what if he doesn't want to come? He's... he's—"

"He will come," said Jacinta. "Leo will come if we ask."

The girls reached Leo's office door and knocked, but no answer came. Jacinta tried to open the door, but it was locked.

"You see," said Isha, dropping her head. "He's not even here."

Jacinta frowned. "Let us see," said Jacinta as her magic began to twirl around her fingers and into the lock on the door.

"What are you doing? We shouldn't do that."

"Sister, hush. We do this." There was a clicking sound as the door lost its rigid hold and swayed inwardly. "There." Jacinta placed her hand on the door, opening it.

"How did you even do that?"

"Door has dust inside. I move dust. It unlocks. We learn when playing with old man's chests."

All three girls peeped inside to see Leo in front of his desk in his chair, asleep. The girls stepped inside, with Makeba holding only Isha's hand tightly as she led her inside. Jacinta closed the door behind them as they moved more into Leo's office.

"We shouldn't be here now," whispered Isha.

"No, he should know. He will want... Oh, the pretty girly boy asleep too." whispered Jacinta as she spotted Pavel on one of the beds in the room. "That's why we not see him in class. He sleeps here with Leo."

But why are they sleeping? Does Pavel just normally sleep here? Isha turned from Pavel and back over to Leo, who was leaning back in his chair, his eyes closed, with the sunshine coming through the window shining down on him. There were bags under his eyes. The scars across his face and neck were still just as present as she had seen that night on the rooftop. *What are those for?* Thought Isha as she noticed two opened vials on the desk beside him.

"We wake him," said Jacinta as she made her way over to Leo and began shaking his leg.

"Wait, don't..."

Leo's head bobbled back and forth

"Leo, wake up. You come with us."

Leo moaned as he was awakened from his slumber,

turning his head away from the light as he began squinting his eyes, trying to focus. "Huh? What? What's... going on?" He shook his head as he focused on Jacinta ahead of him.

"Leo, wake up now."

"Jacinta? Wha... what's going on?"

"We come to get you. You come to watch over Isha during linking."

"The wha... what linking? Isha? Something wrong with Isha?" He looked ahead at Isha, still squinting his eyes. "What's wrong now? Did you get into another fight?"

"No... that's not... I mean... we wanted to know if you were busy since you haven't come home."

Leo planted his head into his hands as he rubbed his face. "How many days has it been?"

"A lot of days. So, you come now and watch over Isha. Make sure she safe."

"You said something about linking. What are they talking about?"

"Ahh, well, I'm not sure. But they want to give me their markings so we might be able to heal the tree. I think."

"You think?" asked Leo as Jacinta turned around, showing Leo the markings on her back.

"She get these like us."

"Wait, but won't that hurt? And who's doing the marking? We don't have anyone at this school that specializes in Sakari markings."

"No, we invite our teacher, Aukube, to do it. She healer like Leo."

"Wait, stop. There's a Sakari healer here now? Then why do you need me?"

"Because Sister Isha feels better if you there," said Jacinta with a bit of a harsh tone. "Why Leo not been coming home. He running away from us now?"

"No... I..." He began rubbing his forehead in frustration. "I've just been busy, is all."

"Then you come watch over Isha while she do linking."

Leo looked over at Pavel, who was still asleep. "I'm not sure I can right now. I need to stay here."

"Is pretty girly boy sick?"

"Yes... I mean, no... It's complicated. I gave him something to sleep, but it's probably best if I stay here to look after him for the rest of the day."

"Oh, okay. It's fine," said Isha, unable to hide her disappointment. "You don't need to. We know you're busy."

"Don't worry," said Leo, standing from his chair and making his way over to Isha and Makeba, who were still holding hands.

"Everything is going to be fine, I'm sure. This linking thing is something the Sakari do, right? Then I probably wouldn't even be able to help much since I don't know much about their magic. But do not worry, I'm sure the Sakari healer will take care of you. Afterward, maybe she can even teach me a few things." He rubbed at Isha's head with a smile on his face.

As Isha looked at Leo, she felt that he looked a lot worse than she thought. His eyes were heavy with lack of sleep, and his words were slurred as he spoke to them. He hadn't even healed the bruise on his cheek that wasn't there the last time she saw him. It had turned a bit reddish-purple.

He looks so sad and tired. "Okay," said Isha. "Come on, they're probably waiting for us by the tree. Bye, Leo." Isha turned around as Jacinta came up beside them.

"I... I'll see you, girls, later," said Leo as they left the room.

"Leo not really Leo anymore since Elena die," said Jacinta as they made their way down the hallway back towards the stairs. "Now he all quiet and speaks softly."

"He loved Elena," said Isha. "We all did, and I miss Elena too. But I don't... I mean, I don't know how to make him feel better. He doesn't come home anymore."

"Oh, I forgot to tell Leo about Rima," said Makeba. "I will go tell him now. Meet sisters downstairs."

"Rima? What did…" and before Isha could finish her words, Makeba had already taken off back towards Leo's. Isha turned towards Jacinta. "Do you know what she meant?"

"No, but Makeba been spending time with Rima in her room, sometimes. I not know what they do there."

"Really? I didn't know that."

"Sister been busy. Guess Makeba been busy too."

"And what about you? Have you been busy too?"

"I always busy. It hard looking after reckless sister."

"You're talking about me, aren't you?"

"Of course. Makeba quiet type. Easy. But Sister Isha crazy type. Burn things down and get into fights and get lost in big house. It makes me worry a lot."

"That's not…" Isha thought to herself about everything that had happened. "Well, it's not like I'm trying to do it."

"It fine. We look after Sister Isha; we have decided."

"Why did you two decide to make me your sister? Was it because of that blood right in the tent back then?"

"That is because we did not want to kill sister. So we accept her."

"What? What do you mean?"

"Sister Isha shared with us her first kill, remember?"

"Yes," Isha frowned. "I remember that. I don't think I can ever forget."

"We share in the blood of Sister Isha's first. To make her our sister. Otherwise, we would have to fight Sister Isha for taking kill that belongs to us. But since you are sister, it is okay for you to take kill."

"What? But… I mean… what about Father? He was there too."

"Old Man? Yes, but he leader. He always has right to kill, just like Mama. But you were not leader or Mama. You were just Rana, then. We had talk with Mama about should we kill sister. But Mama say Old Man pay price. And Uncle Funny Man bring you to us. So we not want to kill you. So we accept
182

you as sister, and then Mama accepts you as daughter."

Isha's mind whirled with this information as they made their way to Soulden's door. She knocked, but no answer came. Opening the door, they looked around, but the office was empty.

"She not here," said Jacinta as she peeked in, gazing around the room.

"Maybe she's already downstairs." Isha then closed the door, with both her and Jacinta heading downstairs to the first floor. The hallway was mostly clear except for one or two students as the girls made their way toward the platform. Ahead they saw Soulden waiting by the pillar at the center of the lift.

"Ah! I was wondering when you girls would arrive. I had thought of meeting you here after class. How foolish of me to assume you would head here after your day was finished."

"We visit Leo first to see if he would come. Make sure Sister Isha stay safe."

"I see, and judging from the absence of the man, I'm assuming you could not convince him."

"No. He said he had to stay and watch pretty girly boy."

"Pretty girly boy? Who might that be?"

Isha sighed. "She means Pavel; she and Makeba refuse to call him by his name."

"Ah! Mr. Hemmington. Yes, I guess he does have a fair face."

"Why he always sick? He miss class a lot too."

"Yes, Mr. Hemmington was unfortunately born with an excessive amount of talent for magic and a body that isn't well suited to use it," said Soulden as she glanced at Isha. "Not unlike your situation, my dear. That power of yours also needs to be tamed. But Mr. Hemmington, his illness is because of its abundance, whereas your issue is because of a lack of understanding. We've never seen yours before, so that ensures that your training will consist of much trial and error."

"Old Man afraid sister burns down camp. That why he sent us here."

"Yes, well, after that episode we had together and the little hand-shaped burn marks on my back, I realize Oscar had a legitimate reason for thinking that way."

"Why you not get Leo to heal you?"

"I merely asked for an inspection. After it was found that I was fine, removing the burning marks seemed trivial when compared to setting the school's affairs in order. Perhaps one day I will take the time to have them removed." Soulden looked around. "Where is the other sister? I was under the impression the tree of you would... ahh, there she is."

Makeba appeared by the steps, then made her way over to them, and stood on the platform next to Jacinta.

"Okay, now that we're all here, shall we be on our way?"

The girls nodded, and Soulden placed her hand on the orb at the center of the platform. The girls once again took off into the sky.

Okay, okay, this is going to be okay. Everyone's going to be there. I... I don't have any reason to be afraid, thought Isha as they made their way upward through the levels of the school until once again stopping at the entrance way covered by roots. As the platform stopped, Isha felt a heavy feeling in her stomach. *I can do this.* She took a deep breath, facing ahead as the vines parted for them to enter. *I can do this.*

"Well, come on then. I'm sure they're waiting for us. I for one, have never seen a Sakari linking process, or for that matter, I haven't seen any of the Sakari rituals. I think this will be an enlightening experience and getting the Trialage Tree back in working order would do us all some good. The forestry around the school has been greatly affected by its damage."

Making their way through the dark corridor, Isha couldn't help but notice that it was darker than usual. Along the path through the doorways, there was no light shining through. All the rooms adjacent to the hall were empty. And the lack of sound except for their footsteps echoing off the walls made their walk feel all the eerier to her.

Ahead of them was a dim light that felt as if it beckoned them. After their walk through the corridor, Isha returned to the domed room where half the trees looked worse than they did before. Only half were orange, and the ones once green were turning brown. Some even looked to be dead as their leaves lay beneath them, leaving the trees appearing barren.

"It looks bad now," spoke Jacinta as she stepped forward through the wilted-looking trees.

"Yes, sadly, our attempts to integrate more forestry for Trialage Tree to assimilate still bear no fruit. That is why your assistance would be most helpful in this matter, as I'm afraid we are out of options."

"I hope it works," said Isha.

As they made their way forward, they spotted Aukube sitting with her legs crossed on the floor next to a fire-lit lantern on a stool. In front of her was a thin but long table adjacent to another smaller table holding a saucer, and to her side was a brown leather bag next to a long-curved blade.

"Hey, we ready now, Aukube," said Jacinta, running up to their teacher. "Hello, you too, other lady."

"Other lady," said Miss Huffles with a giggle. "Though your time in my class may have been short, I would at least ask for you to remember my name."

"I'm surprised you decided to join us today," said Soulden.

"After you informed me of such an event, how could I not come? Honestly, rarely have I seen you pace throughout the night instead of coming to bed. The last time I remember such a thing was when you were first named headmistress of Sceana, and even then, you weren't as jittery."

"Well," Soulden coughed as she straightened her

shoulders, "of course, I might be a little nervous. This is one of our students, after all. If this method does not work, I fail to think of the next step we could take to try and heal the Trialage Tree." Soulden looked around the area. "Where are Mr. Cauldbell and Tannor? I assumed they would not want to miss a magical procedure such as this."

"Ah, you mean the two men who were here," said Aukube. "I sent them away. I do not think Isha would like being naked around them while I search for her links."

"I have to take my clothes off!" yelped Isha.

"Yes, I will search your body for where I can find your link. For Jacinta and Makeba, it was on their backs, but for you, it could be anywhere. Perhaps a breast or a leg. Once found, that is where I set the markings."

"Oh..." Isha suddenly started looking around, uncomfortable about the situation. "Are... are you sure they're gone?"

"Yes, I made sure they leave. One was very passionate about staying, even saying he would blind himself."

"That was probably Caudbell," sighed Soulden. "For as knowledgeable as he is, he can be quite inconsiderate when it comes to his experiments."

"Since all are here, we should start," said Aukube, reaching to her side, picking up a curved blade at her side, and standing up. She then walked over, reached upward, and grabbed hold of one of the branches of the Trialage Tree. Then, she clipped some of the lower hanging branches with a quick set of swings.

"How does this work?"

"Isha will link with her sisters and share their power. From then, we will take their blood. But we will also need the bone of the tree if we wish for them all to share. And if this tree is alive as the children say, then perhaps it shall also work to service it."

"Perhaps?" asked Soulden, looking up towards the Trialage Tree. "That's not a very definitive answer."
186

"Few things in this life are certain," said Aukube as she placed the branches on the saucer. Then with a wave of her hand, the saucer ignited and began to burn away the stems.

"I not remember burning things," said Jacinta as the fire illuminated the surrounding darkness.

"Well, I had already prepared the ash and oil during yours and Makeba's linking. But here I will make it fresh," said Aukube as she watched the flames devour the branches. "Okay, Isha, come and sit at the table and remove your clothing, and we shall begin.

Isha took a deep breath and stepped forward. Then taking a final look around, she began to disrobe until nude and sat down on the bench with her back facing away from Aukube. Then, attempting modesty, she covered her chest with her arms.

"Okay... now what do I do?"

"You do nothing now, child. Now it is up to me to find what needs to be found. I have never inspected kingdom people for links before, but if they are there, then I will find them." Aukube extended her right hand, pressing her index finger against Isha's shoulder blade as magic began to whirl around the finger, finding its way over her skin.

She closed her eyes and stiffened as she felt Aukube's cold touch against her. But shortly after the touch came a strange feeling. It was as if she was taking in a breath without actually breathing. Instead, she felt like the air was entering her lungs, forcing her chest to expand. And then the feeling began to move inside of her, following along with the movement of Aukube's finger: First, down her arm and to her fingers as Aukube lifted her elbow, then back up to her shoulder, then down her back to her waist, and repeating the action on her other side.

Why does it feel so different than when Jacinta and Makeba push their magic into me? I wonder if... And just like Miss Huffles had taught her, Isha focused her mind and went inside of herself, looking for the magic. The practice had

187

now become much easier for her to navigate over time. Inside, she could clearly see her own magic and the weird stream of magic she could tap into. While her own magic seemed like a swirling blue ball of magical strands, the odd stream of magic she saw was like a river stretched as far as her mind's eye could see. But farther away, beyond them, and moving closer was a type of smokey gray magic that had entered her mind. It made its way forward, the threads of magic reaching out as if searching for something. It came closer to her in a swirling motion, passing through her body as it poked at the random spaces around her.

I wonder how Sakari magic is different from normal magic. Is my magic different? She focused in on Aukube's magic as it poured into her. It felt the same as it had before. She remembered the times she would come and perform healing on her leg after she had taken the arrow. It was cool and soft. The way it flowed over her skin felt inviting and careful, as if she wasn't trying hard at all. *How does she do it so easily? I have to really try to use my magic.*

"Isha... Isha... Do you hear me, child?"

"Huh?" said Isha, startled back to the real world as she opened her eyes to see Aukube and her sisters staring at her. "I'm sorry. Did I do something wrong?"

"No, child, I ask that you lay down on the table and allow me to check you."

"Oh... ah, yes, sorry," said Isha as she shifted her weight, turning on the small wooden table. She stretched out her legs and laid down with her hands still covering her chest.

"Okay, now don't worry. We will be done with this part soon. I must inspect to ensure where your links are. Just be calm, child."

"I... I'm calm," said Isha as she closed her eyes again and went back into her mind, trying not to think of her embarrassment. It didn't take long before she was back inside herself. The light blue sphere was ahead of her again. But now, the gray magic was sliding over the top of it, poking at it carefully. It seemed as if it was testing it. A poke to the left side, then one to the right. It slowly and methodically poked at the spinning blue orb, making it react to its touch. Then, in a few spots, she saw her magic light up inside the sphere, turning from a light blue to a bright white for a moment before turning back blue. Every time the white light would come, she would feel a sensation. She wasn't sure where, but she definitely could feel it.

What does this mean? She thought as she embraced the feeling. *Are these the linking things they were...* She felt another cold sensation on her shoulder, and then it was hot again. *I guess I'm going to find out. I mean, it doesn't feel different. But what does it mean to link with Jacinta and Makeba? Will I be able to use their golden eyes or that soil magic they use? I probably should have asked before all of this—*

"Leo," his name came into her mind from somewhere outside.

I wonder if Leo is really okay. I cried when Elena died. But Leo, I never saw him cry. Do boys cry? I've never seen Papa cry, not even when Mama would go. I wonder what Leo is doing now. Still checking on Pavel, probably. Is he really that good at magic? I mean, he's learning with all of us. And I've never seen him do anything special. Maybe he can-

"Leo, wait," spoke the voice again.

I wonder if there's anything we can do to make Leo feel better. I'll ask Rima when I get back. She's known him longer than-

"Sister up," came another voice into Isha's mind.

Sister? With those words, Isha pulled herself out of her own mind, back into the real world. Then, opening her eyes, she began squinting as the fire's light stung her eyes, but soon the world came back into focus as she saw her sisters looking at her.

"What's wrong? Are we done?" asked Isha as she turned to face Aukube.

"Oh, sorry," spoke Leo's voice. "They asked me... ah...

to come."

Isha turned her head around to see Leo squatting down with his hands in front of the fire. His weary eyes were showing the solemn face from before. His lack of sleep seemed even more present in the darkness, with the flames illuminating his face as he stared intently into the fire. She sat up with a smile at seeing him. "You came." But quickly realized the air around them seemed cold, even with the flame nearby. She looked down and was instantly reminded of her own nakedness. She tried covering herself but wasn't sure where to put her hands, so she just walled herself up on the small table.

"Sorry, dear," said Soulden. "We didn't hear him walk up to us; the next thing we knew, he was behind us."

"I'll leave now," said Leo as he took a deep breath and stood back up. "Sorry to bother you, ladies."

"No," said Isha, and before she realized it, her arms were reaching out to him as he stepped away. "Please... please don't leave."

Leo looked around, unsure.

He's going to go away again. He hasn't even come home since we got back. What do I do? What would Elena do? She... She always knew what to do.

"But-"

"No buts. Stay, please." Isha once again found the words leaving her mouth. "I... I want you here. Just... even if you don't want to see me—"

"What? That's not... I just wanted to make sure you were okay."

"Then just sit by the tree. Aukube will start soon, and I want you to be here for it."

Leo looked around at all the women.

"It seems you've gotten your answer, Leo," said Soulden with the hint of a smirk across her face. "You are in this with us now."

Leo just glanced between the women looking confused.

Then with a sigh, he turned and walked over, taking a seat at the side of the Trialage Tree, facing off into the darkness. "I will wait here until this has finished, just to ensure everything goes well."

Ahh... what am I doing? Isha turned towards a surprised Aukube. "You can start again. I'm ready now."

"There... there is no need. I have found the links I need. Your body has a fair amount more than I am accustomed to finding."

"It does?"

"Yes. Now all that is left is for you to decide on the designs of the markings. Your sisters only needed one marking to link with each other. But you will need three because you will be linking to them and the tree."

"Three? Will they be like Makeba's and Jacinta's?"

"That depends on you. The design must be a certain size. The shape, you can decide, yourself."

"Oh, I not know that," said Jacinta with a smile. "Sister, get three. She can get picture of three crying people."

Isha frowned at her sister, "Oh, stuff it. Don't make jokes. Turn around and show me your markings if you want to help."

Jacinta gave a large smile before she and Makeba walked over to Aukube, removing their tops and showing Isha and her their markings.

"Do the markings mean anything?"

"Yes, sister," said Makeba. "We were told I have the night flower and Jacinta has the day flower."

Flowers? Thought Isha as she stared at the design of the marking on her sister's back shoulders, realizing that she had never paid much attention to her sisters' markings before. *They kinda look the same. But the inside is different.*

"Would you also like markings similar to your sisters?"

"I don't know," said Isha as she turned around and looked back up at the tree. "Is there another flower or tree?"

"Yes, there is a third flower. Had their mother had the

gift of magic, I suppose she would have it. But seeing as she does not and you do, I think it would be perfect since you are their care-sister."

"Which one is that?"

"In kingdom tongue, hmm," Aukube rubbed at the side of her mouth as she began to pounder. "I suppose the right name would be 'the twilight flower.' The space between light and dark."

"Where will the marking be? On my back too?"

"They can be, you have several places that can be used, but the true link will be here," said Aukube as she placed her finger at the center of Isha's collar bones. "Because your links are scattered, I shall move the markings to match. This way should make the connection stronger."

Isha took her hand, placing it on the spot below the neck where Aukube had shown her, and took a deep breath, closing her eyes. "Will... will it hurt?"

"Yes, it will take time, and it will hurt. But that is why you have us here," said Aukube, nodding over towards Leo, who was sitting with his back against the tree. "And he seems worried enough about you."

Isha took another look at all those around her before nodding her head. "Okay, what do I have to do?"

"You? Nothing. You have done all you can. The rest will be on your sisters and me." Aukube stood and stepped towards the flames on the burning branches. She then waved her hands over the fire as they all watched the flames die down. "Jacinta and Makeba, are you girls ready?"

"We ready," said the girls as she walked over and extended their hands to Aukube.

"Yes. We will be able to heal tree Sakari," said Makeba.

"Good," said Aukube as she grabbed her curved blade and stood, stepping to the girls. She held Jacinta's hand first and placed the blade over her palm, quickly slicing through the skin. Jacinta bit her lip as blood began pouring from the wound. She then repeated the same action with Makeba as both girls raised their bloody hands over the bundle of ashes, allowing their blood to flow down on top of the grayish-black ashes as a few embers crackled beneath.

Isha shivered at the sight, clenching her fist to stop her hand from shaking as she watched. Aukube then walked over to Isha. And after one final glance at her sisters standing over the ashes, blood dripping from their cut hands. Isha took a breath and extended her hand to Aukube.

"No child, that was their part to play. Yours will come soon. Now, lay down on your stomach and leave your back open to me. We will start soon."

Isha did as she was told, lying face down on the wooden table, her arms placed under her chin.

"Good," said Aukube as she reached to her left, picking up a vial and a small saucer. The vial had some type of black liquid that, even when picked up, there wasn't much movement inside the glass container. The fluid looked thick and ominous as Aukube popped the cork and poured a small amount onto the saucer on the smaller table next to Isha. The liquid came out in a thick creamy drop, pooling on the saucer, and when finished, Aukube took it over to the fire's remains, reached in, and grabbed some blood-soaked ashes in her hands. The orange heat from the fire was still alive as embers flew up around her fingers.

"Sister Isha will be okay; it not hurt so bad," said Makeba.

As Aukube spread the bloodied ashes over the liquid, Isha watched the mysterious liquid as it seemed to devour the ashes. So much so that it seemed to melt inside as Aukube grabbed three more handfuls of ash. Each handful sunk into the black liquid but seemed to not increase the volume on the saucer. She then stepped back to Isha, setting the saucer beside the table. Isha couldn't help but stare at the unmoving black liquid, its calmness not showing a trace of the ashes that had been dropped into it.

"Look away, child," said Aukube, as she reached inside her own robe and pulled out a needle of a fairly large size that made Isha's eyes widen. "The process will not get any easier by watching. Instead, close your eyes and focus on the world around you." She then dipped the needle into the liquid, and Isha watched as the black liquid pooled around the needle, seemingly climbing up the metal on its own accord. Then, Isha decided that closing her eyes was a good idea, and she tried to stop her body from shivering.

It wasn't long before Isha felt the cool touch of Aukube's fingers as her hand crossed her shoulders and the back of her neck. And then she felt it: beside her soft finger came the hardness and sharpness of the needle. And it wasn't long before a sharp ping of pain made her twitch and clench her fists as the needle pierced her skin. Once, twice, the number began to add up faster than she could count. The sound of tapping coincided with each new ping of pain as Aukube drove the needle over her body.

As she tapped over her skin, Isha could feel the blood sliding down her skin. Despite the liquid being cold, everything about this started feeling hot. As she breathed in, it began to feel impossible not to focus on the pain. The vibrations against her rippled through her neck, making her teeth chatter.

"Do not focus on the pain, child," said Aukube in a calming voice. "Let your mind go."

Isha struggled to force her mind past the constant pecking on her back. That was until she felt another hand grab ahold of hers, followed by a hand on her leg, and then something larger and warm against her thigh. Makeba had come to rest her face and arms across Isha's leg as Jacinta took hold of her hand. Soon a calmness came over Isha as she felt her sister's magic flowing over her leg and arms. Then, focusing on them, she could forget the pain and drift back into her mind.

Time in the darkened room passed as Aukube went about her work, engraving the markings on Isha's body. Even the oil from the lantern dried out, causing Soulden and Miss Huffles to each cast mage lights that hovered in the branches above Aukube as she worked.

Satisfied with her efforts, Aukube lifted Isha up and, with her sisters' help, placed Isha onto her back and began work on the skin above her collarbone, the bloody needle sinking over and over into Isha's skin.

"She seemed so afraid before," said Soulden, peeking over. "But she doesn't even seem to be awake now."

"Yes, she is away and has left her body in our hands. This is a good thing. The process will go smoother if she trusts us."

"I'm afraid to ask how it can be bad."

"There have been a few times it has gone incorrectly," said Aukube as she turned and smiled at Makeba and Jacinta, who had already closed their eyes and were still holding onto their sister. "But I think that shall not be the case here."

"Let's hope not."

The tapping continued for hours as Aukube went about her work with methodical patience. Every few minutes, she would dip the needle back into the black liquid to soak it again but would always return to her work. Several times through the course of the next hour, Isha would need to be rotated as the markings took hold.

In her mind, Isha had forgotten about the sensations that had just previously rattled her body. Once again, she was swallowed back into the darkness of her mind. She was confused about what was happening to the ball of light there. One of the threads had now wrapped its way around the light, but it didn't consume it. Instead, it looked as if it was feeding off of it. Or maybe the orb was feeding off the gray thread; Isha couldn't tell the difference.

Why is it doing that? I don't understand any of... stopping her thoughts; Isha felt something else enter the space inside her mind. Focusing into the darkness, she saw another gray thread as it wormed through the area approaching the sphere of light. It began to poke the sphere much like the previous one, and just like before, it lit up wherever the thread touched. And with every touch, Isha could feel something inside her responding to it.

Letting curiosity get to her, she moved through the space, getting closer to the orb of light as she watched its light glow between the grayness. As she neared it, she could feel the warmth coming from inside. She reached her hand out towards it and watched as the glowing light streamed away from it and began circling her fingers. What was even more surprising was that small pieces of the gray threads had also broken away and intertwined with the orb's magic as it flowed over her fingertips.

Feeling safer now, she pulled herself towards the orb, allowing the magic to flow over her body as she tried to peer inside the slowly swirling mass. Although its glow was a little bit bright, she could still see. Her hands sunk into the magic, and the farther they went in, the denser it became. Soon, it felt like she was trying to slip her fingers inside a ball of yarn. The outer layers were easy, but inside it was packed too tightly. Struggling, she managed to inch away at an opening into another layer. Inside, she could see something. Moving her face closer, she tried to peer inside. And to her surprise, there was a person inside. But the surprise was that the person inside looked exactly like her. It was like staring into a mirror. The other version of herself floated inside the sphere as if weightless, her eyes closed, and arms cradled around her legs. Isha watched herself floating as if lifeless.

I don't... I don't understand. Is this normal for a mage when they look inside like this? Do they all see themselves? Thought Isha as she watched her other self rotate around inside the sphere. But one thing that she noticed was that even though the gray threads had made their way over and around the orb, they hadn't made their way inside. Instead, the strands mixed in with the other layers of magic, just skirting the orb's surface. Isha watched as the strands intertwined with each other. *I'll need to ask Aukube what this means. I don't know what...*

Isha turned her attention back toward the other version of her, only to see that her eyes were now open and staring back at her. She froze as she caught a glimpse of her own face staring back at her. But there was a startling difference. The version of herself inside had grey eyes, and with a few blinks, she started to speak.

A word was spoken, but Isha couldn't hear her other self. Instead, a gust of force came through the darkness like a strong wind blowing through her mind. It was so strong that it detached Isha from the orb of light and carried her off back into the darkness. She struggled to control herself as she was spun into her mind's darkness. At the mercy of the unknown force, she went floating back as all the light faded away.

Isha's eyes opened, gasping for air in a panic. Then, trying to catch her breath, her blurry eyes began to focus, and the world around her came back into view. Above her were the orange leaves of the Trialage Tree that was alive with two glowing orbs of magical light illuminating the area around her.

"Welcome back, little one," said Aukube as she appeared from out of the darkness around the tree.

Isha blinked as she took a gathering of her surroundings. Her sisters were over on a sheet of cloth. Both girls had fallen asleep on the floor. Turning her head, she saw that Leo was still sitting on the marble floor, arms crossed with his back against the tree.

"Are you okay?" asked Leo, still worried. "Do you... do you feel as if anything is wrong?"

"Wha..." spoke Isha, her mouth feeling a bit hoarse. "No, I... I don't think so. I feel..." The moment Isha tried to move; the pain struck her instantly. Her chest, shoulders, and back felt like they had been set ablaze. A sharp pain coursed through her upper body. Quickly, she sat up, breathing heavily as she felt the magic inside of her being pulled and tugged at. The sensation was as if someone was stretching her arms out, pulling at her from both ends.

"Isha, are you okay?" repeated Leo with worry apparent in his eyes as he made his way over to her and Aukube. "Is this supposed to happen?"

"Careful now," said Aukube, handing Isha a cup of water. "It will pass. Your body is trying to find harmony with your sisters. I gave them both sleeping water to make it easy on you. But you need to be awake to allow your body to find its balance."

"It... it hurts," said Isha as she clenched her teeth, her hands tightening into fists over her chest as her body began to sweat.

"Try to calm your magic, little Isha. This should pass. It will take time for your body to adjust to the sharing of magic."

"I... I'm trying," said Isha as her body trembled. "It's just not... working."

"You are receiving magic from your sisters, and they are receiving it from you. Over time this connection will feel normal and... Argh," yelped Aukube as she tried placing her hand on Isha's shoulder but quickly pulled it back. Turning her hand over, she saw the redness of her palm as if the skin had been warmed over a fire.

"I'm sorry. I... I didn't mean..." Isha caught Leo staring ahead. She turned to see a small white light floating in the air. It hovered there in the distance, a bit away from them. But then it was joined by another as white ball of magic seemed to emerge out of the marble floor and join beside it.

"What is..."

"No, no, I can't... I can't control it when it gets like this," said Isha as she turned back to look up to Leo and Aukube. The scent of burning wood was now in the air as the table she was on began to smoke and darken around her thighs.

198

"When it gets like what?" asked Leo looking around as more white orbs of magic floated up from around the floor. "What is all this?"

"This is Isha's power," said Aukube, "but I did not know it could be so unnurtured. She should summon it inside of her, not outside."

"How do we stop it?"

"I... don't know. It only happened once when Isha forced her magic into a man named Molan."

"And what happened to him?"

"He burned alive from the magic."

Leo looked down at Isha as her eyes continued to flutter from green to white. "And what you did to Soulden, those burns on her back are when you forced this into her?"

"I... I don't remember."

Leo grimaced, noticing that as more and more white orbs appeared, some began floating towards Isha. He watched as a nearby orb made contact with her skin and went inside her arm.

"Oh no, the girls," said Aukube as she stood and pointed to where Makeba and Jacinta were still asleep. "They're sharing magic now." She pointed as a few of the magic orbs began breaking off and heading towards the sleeping girls. "I don't know if bonding is complete. They... they, I don't know what's going to happen." She turned back down, looking at Isha. "Isha, you must stop them. You sisters are sleeping and cannot contain so much magic when asleep. The mind... the mind is not prepared. You will burn them."

"I'm trying. It... just won't listen to me. It's too much to control," said Isha; her eyes squinted in focus as she tried to contain herself as more and more magic began to fill the area.

"This will all stop if she has an outlet to push her magic into, right?" asked Leo. "Were both healers? Can't she just push it into us?"

"Use your eyes," said Aukube. "Where would I send it
199

all? The magic must go somewhere. I do not know enough combat spells, and I can only heal so fast. If I tried to take in so much, it would burn me alive, like it did Molan."

Leo took another look around the room before reaching to his waist, grabbing at his shirt, and lifting it over his head. Then, exposing the bare skin of his upper body, he tossed the clothing to the floor before extending his hand toward Isha. "Remember those hugs we used to do every morning? You wanna try doing that again?"

"This amount of magic," said Aukube, looking around. "Even your headmaster, by her own words, felt that it was too much."

"Well, I'm not as versed in war magic as Soulden. But in terms of healing, outside of the High Mother and my brother, you would have difficulty finding someone stronger than me." He then turned back to Isha and knelt down on one knee beside her as she huddled on the small wooden table. "You ready?"

"But," said Isha, looking at his hand warily. "I'll... I'll burn you."

Leo's face took on a melancholic smile as he glanced at Jacinta and Makeba, the orbs of magic getting closer. "Better me than them. I promise you. Even if it burns, I'd barely even feel it." He then reached out his other hand and slid them under Isha's shoulders. Instantly his arms began to redden. "Now, come on. Let's get this done so we all can go home."

Looking at Isha Leo's smiling face, her emotions finally broke as she let go of her knees and allowed Leo to lift her up into the air as he stood back up with her cradled against his chest.

"I'm sorry... I'm sorry," repeated Isha as she wrapped her arms around his neck, and he held her in his arms.

"There's nothing to be sorry about," said Leo as his skin began to sear.

"I'm trying to stop it. But it... it won't listen to me."

"It's okay," said Leo as the skin around his face and neck turned red. He stepped forward and began circling the tree with Isha in his arms. "Don't try to hold it back. I want you to just let go. Take as much of the magic as you can and give it to me, and I'll do the rest. Can you do that for me?"

Isha took a deep breath and nodded her head.

"That's a good girl."

Releasing her control, Isha allowed the magic to consume her as if guided by a flowing wind. The small white orbs of magical light hovering above the floor began making their way toward her and Leo. Inside the darkness, the two paced, surrounded by the encroaching light. Slowly swirling around them, small amounts of the magic veered off, entering Isha's body. She felt like each piece of magic soaked inside her, her body tremble as it tried to contain the power. But as she trembled in his arms, she could feel Leo taking away the magic from her into him.

Surprised, she began to lift her head from his shoulder, but before she could, she could feel his hand on the back of her head, holding her in place.

"This isn't something for you to look at, Isha. Just close your eyes, focus on controlling the magic, and let me know when it's done, okay."

Isha nodded, but as her heartbeat slowed, she began to realize the scent around her was a strong odor of burning flesh. It was the same smell that she remembered from the night in the tent when Molan had come to attack her.

And there, underneath the Trialage Tree, surrounded by the lights of Isha's power, the two stood for what seemed like hours as both their bodies glowed white, infused in magical light.

"I... I think I'm okay now," said Isha, as she opened her eyes to see her own arms and Leo's shoulder covered in blood. Surprised and not knowing how long it'd been, she tried to turn towards Leo but instantly felt his hand on the back of her head again. He clutched the back of her head, pinning her chin to his shoulder.

"That's... good," said Leo, his voice sounding garbled and weak. "Time... for... sleep."

"Wha... but," said Isha confused, but quickly found her world turning blurry. Her eyes instantly felt heavy, her body limp in Leo's arms. And within seconds, Isha was fast asleep as Leo carried her back to the small table where she had laid before. It was dark now that the white lights were no longer around them; the only light source was once again the flame of the pan that had been relit.

Aukube was beside Jacinta and Makeba, but she began making her way back to Isha and Leo when she noticed him bring her back and lay Isha down on the table.

"Are... those two... okay?" asked Leo in his tortured voice.

"Yes, they absorbed some of the magic. But they do not seem to be badly affected by it. A few burns, but I shall heal them. What about Isha, have you— Oh! Sakari Mother, you... your..." Aukube froze as she saw Leo.

His left side was completely burned as his skin blistered and leaked pus. The burns went from his stomach up his chest and around his neck, covering half of the left side of his face. The most horrible point was that there was a hole in the flesh of his cheek where she could see the side of his teeth and tongue. His left eye was completely seared to the point where it was barely there, and the left side of his head had the hair and skin burned away to the point where she thought she could see a piece of his skull.

"She shouldn't... see me... like this. It... only make... it worse for her," said Leo as he looked down at his left hand, clenched Isha to his chest. The skin on his arm and hand had been burned away, allowing him to see the tendons beneath as his own magic flowed over and into the burned areas.

"How... how are you still standing with those wounds?"

Leo took his gaze from his bloody, scarred hand and turned his attention to Aukube, his magic dancing at the edges of his face where the burns met his flesh as it tried to repair the damage. "I... don't... know."

CHAPTER 13

Saffron stood beside Mova with his back against a wooden fence in a small country village on the outskirts of the city of Burlus. They were waiting to the left of a small wooden house amongst a dozen similar homes scattered down a wooden road surrounded by forestry. The smell of dirt and leaves was thick in the air as the few town folks that could be seen went about their day through the streets.

"Why did we make a stop at this... place?" asked Mova, frowning as a man holding the reins of a cow walked past them, giving her a grin. "Couldn't you have chosen a more distinguished city? Something like Hilik or Malengal. Not this," she gestured out over the small town. "Whatever this is."

"Still haven't embraced the country bumpkin lifestyle, I see," said Saffron with a smirk as he took a deep breath and exhaled. "I would think you would be more acquainted with the environment, given how many of my trips you've joined me on. Remember that time in Doval when he had you dress up as a beggar? There, you seem to accommodate yourself quite well."

"That was to stop bandits who had raped and pillaged for months. And if possible, I prefer not to do that again. It took forever to get that mud out of my hair."

"Oh, is that why you cut it? I do seem to recall it was around that time when you cut off those golden locks your father was so proud of."

"In fights, if someone gets close, they often try to grab and pull my hair. So it was the practical thing to do."

"Well, women always told me beauty is its own battle. But really, Frenka has long hair. I'm not sure she's ever complained about it."

"She also has control of fire magic, so anyone who tried to grab her would end up burned alive. That's not the same for my magic. And I prefer close combat anyway."

"That's a shame; I kinda liked your long blonde hair. The contrast with Frenka was always an eye-turner. I always thought of you both as my warrior maidens."

"I'd prefer if you didn't include me in your thoughts with Frenka. Fantasy or otherwise."

"You two never got along. Why is that?" Saffron turned to look at Mova. "You're both two powerful mages; I'd expect you two to get along well. You know, that feminine companionship and all that?"

Mova laughed, "What? You mean like you and Dekol. No thanks. We don't need to be friends to do our job. Which, by the way, you are constantly finding new ways to make it more difficult than it needs to be." Mova pointed out to the trees. "Really, you dragged Laura along on this, then dump her off in the woods with Dekol."

"I did not dump her with Dekol. Goddess, if anything, she's safer with him than she is with either of us."

"And what if your devoted bodyguard decides to run

off with the prince's new wife?" said Mova with a sly smile. "Dekol is quite the man. I've seen a few ladies around the castle eyeing him."

Saffron chuckled, "Dekol? I fairly say that there's a fairly higher chance of you running off with my wife than him."

"You seem pretty confident about that. Are you sure? I mean, not every—"

"Hello, Sir," said a young man who appeared from around a corner with an older male companion beside him as they began approaching the two. "Hello, Sir."

"The boy has no tact whatsoever," said Saffron, shaking his head.

"Sorry for our late arrival, Prince Saffron. There was an incident over in Kervick that required our attention."

"You haven't been on many missions, have you, lad?"

The young man turned to his partner, looking confused. "Well, no, sir. Is it that obvious?"

"Well, when on missions like this, I would prefer it if you didn't call out my name. We're probably safe here, but it's best not to take any chances."

"Oh, I'm sorry," said the boy, realization coming into his eyes. "My mistake."

"It's fine. I imagine it's the mistake of those that are green. I'm sure my companions would have many a tale to tell of my mistakes, said Saffron, shaking his head. "Now, tell me, what news do you have for me of the ongoings of the capital?" Anything exciting?"

"No, your highness. Although your father seems quite displeased with your sudden decision to relocate your honeymoon so quickly after your wedding."

"Yes, I'm sure he's all torn up with worry," said Saffron shaking his head. "Tell me, has Father taken court with any Church of the Goddess members recently?"

"Why yes; a sect did come to the castle some time ago looking to speak to the king. I'm not aware of what they spoke of, but I remember them being in the castle for a few days."

"So they've gone then?"

"Yes, sir. They were only there for a short time. They were led by a woman, I believe."

"That's something to think about," said Saffron as he noticed the older man that had appeared to be looking around oddly. "Is there something I can help your friend find there? He seems to be on the lookout for something."

"I'm looking for Lady Laura," said the older man as he turned back to Saffron. "I am to report to Lord Dunblane on her well-being. We've received reports that you had taken Lady Dunblane across the countryside and were battling bandits."

"Yes, that rumor. There seems to be an apparent group of impersonators going around the countryside doing good deeds in our names. While I am flattered, I do find the act a bit eccentric."

"I see," said the older man with a brow raised at Saffron. "So you say, but are you not galivanting across the country-side with my Lady?"

"Well, yes. But I assure you we haven't run into any bandits."

"Yes, and where is my Lady now if she is not in your company?"

"She is off with my man Dekol. You needn't worry. She's been well looked after."

"Young Master Hargriff? Yes, I was acquainted with his father. But I must insist on seeing the princess before I go."

Saffron sighed. "Well, I suppose it would be hypocritical to try and dismiss a guard dog of the princess when my own is out with me. Fine, walk with us for a while. We shall meet up with them soon," said Saffron as he eased himself away from the fence onto the dirt road and began walking down into the town. "So, tell me, lad; what have my other two guards, Frenka and Thaddius, been up to? Have you seen either of them recently?"

"No, sir, Frenka left the castle some time ago. And Sir Thaddius was only in the kingdom for a day or two before leaving shortly after the clergywoman came."

"It seems father is making use of my toys again," said Saffron with a frown as he turned toward Mova. "How did you keep from being sent out on father assignments?"

"I merely explained to him how I was the only one of your guards who had any sense of reason. Thaddius is a musclehead, Dekol is only loyal to you, and Frenka is a mountain woman with questionable morals. How could he afford to send me away?"

"Ever the clever strategist."

"And yet, here I am following your dumbass through the countryside like some low-life peasant. Clearly, I'm not as clever as you think I am. And I'm surprised you looked so afraid of our guest there. Is it wise for a prince to show fear to his subjects?"

"In my short life, I have only met two types of people who care nothing about titles. The first are Barbarians and the other are fathers who acts, thinking they're protecting their daughters,

Mova laughed before waving her hand in front of her face to try and alleviate the stick to the city.

"Your view of the common people really is one of disdain, isn't it?"

"Oh, do not misunderstand me. I understand the need for the common people. The crops, the taxes, the labor, the military, and the fresh crop of babies born into the kingdom to fight the next war. But that doesn't mean that I need to be around them." Mova sniffed the air. "Or smell them, for that matter."

"I must say that your sympathies for the common people are unmatched. I'm surprised people don't confuse you for the goddess herself."

"I don't need to sympathize with them in order to protect them. But perhaps they sympathize with pigs; it would explain much here."

"And here I thought I was supposed to be the pompous royal. Oh, there's my lady wife now, it seems," said Saffron as he spotted Laura and Dekol approaching from behind a house and turning towards them. They both held bags in their hands, Dekol carrying the heavier of the two.

"Hello, husband. Are these—" said Laura before she placed her bag on the ground and ran up, jumping into the arms of the old man that had accompanied them. "Oh, Sir, Helrick. How have you been? I have missed you."

The old man smiled as he held Laura around her waist, hoisting her in the air. "I'm faring well. Your mother and father have asked that I check in on you to ensure you're still enjoying your marriage."

"Oh, that's right," said Laura as she was placed back on the ground. She then quickly stepped over to Saffron and wrapped her arms around him. "Yes, I'm enjoying it so much. My husband has even decided to take me around the kingdom for our honeymoon. Have you two ever met before?"

"This would be the first time we've met in person. But I have heard stories of the prince and I've seen him at the rare palace ball once or twice. His activities are well known in the kingdom."

"Yes, well," said Saffron, feeling a sense of impending judgment from the older man that eerily reminded him of his father. "I can assure you that I am upholding the ideals of a model husband. Miss Laura and I are having quite the journey, and it's only just beginning as we are now on our way to Diohill."

"Diohill? Yes, I suppose you could head that way from here."

"Laura, who is this man to you? I assume one of your guards."

"Who, Helrick? Well, I suppose you could say he was my teacher. He taught me how to read and how to control my magic and, well, everything really. Father and mother were always busy, so Helrick took care of me when they were off at war. If it wasn't for him, I probably would never have been able to go camping with Father."

"I was the young lady's training instructor for most of her life," said Helrick, "I taught her combat magic, courtly living, amongst a slew of other things in preparation for the day that she would ascend to womanhood. Although I must admit, I was surprised when I received word that she was supposed to marry you, Prince Saffron."

"Oh, you aren't alone there. It was a surprise to me as well. But now it seems like a pleasant surprise. You have trained her well. She has been much more than I had any right to expect when given the mundanity of the other ladies I am forced to hold court with for father's machinations."

"Oh, I assure you, it's not just your father. All nobles have their schemes," said Helrick, looking around the area. "Tell me, are there no other guards or perhaps a coach to ensure Laura's safety on your travels?"

"No," said Saffron, "I think it is best to travel lightly and without the excesses provided to someone of my station. A few horses and casual dress allow us to move throughout the kingdom without taking too much notice. The blade is only drawn for those we recognize as a threat or opportunity. Given as we are now, we'd only need to worry about the occasional bandits and not some well-organized attack."

"A sound reasoning; hiding in plain sight," said Helrick with a nod before stopping. "I have gained what I needed. I shall not keep your company any longer."

"What? But you've only just arrived," said Laura in protest. "Why leave so soon?"

"Apologies, Miss Laura, I merely wanted to ensure your well-being upon my return. I have a business to attend to in Vontal and saw a slight deviation to come and see you as a nice respite from my orders. Do not worry, child. I shall return soon, and you should focus on your new husband, not this old man." Helrick gave her a smirk as they headed to a nearby stable that housed a group of horses.

"I am focusing on my husband," said Laura with a frown. "I mean, at least I'm trying to."

"Then that's wonderful. I'm sure all this responsibility being thrust upon you so fast hasn't been easy," said Helrick as his partner brought back their horses and climbed atop his mount. "But I've no doubt you will handle yourself well. You are Fravline's daughter, after all. You both carry that fire in your eyes."

"Be safe, Helrick. Tell father I miss him if you see him before I do."

"Will do, little Laura. I'm pleased to see you are enjoying this union. But, I must admit, your father was quite worried after your mother arranged it with the king. But you seem to be pleased with how everything has turned out. And to you, young prince, take care of your wife. She means an awful lot to me."

"I intend to ensure her safety. My main concern now is for my wife to enjoy her honeymoon."

Helrick looked down into the prince's face before looking over into Laura's, and a smile came across his face. "A honeymoon stroll through the outskirts of the kingdom dressed as commoners. Perhaps you two are a perfect union, after all." Helrick turned his horse. "Come lad, let us report back." And with those words, Helrick and his partner headed back through the town.

"Well, I suppose we should also head back on the trail. Diohill is still a fair bit away."

"That's only because you refuse to get us an airship."

"What's the point of a journey when there is no journey?"

CHAPTER 14

"Are you really going to do as she asks?" asked Silk as she, Frenka, and Victor sat around a large wooden table in a stone room inside the castle. There were dressers on each side of the room along with suits of armor that had the three roses of Mari etched into them. From the ceiling hung giant blue banners with golden roses embroidered on the fabric. As far as meeting rooms when, this one was one of the nicer ones of the castle.

"Yes, unfortunately, things have grown too big for me to ignore now. Preventing war is my main goal. And if word gets out of Mari's involvement with the child's abduction, that would surely lead to another war with Ursjun, and I would rather not relive those days."

"Husband, I help you in this, and you will forgive Frenka?"

"I've already forgiven you. You don't owe me anything.

I'm alive and apparently in a better position," said Victor as he reached up, rubbing at the scar across his throat. "Although, I would appreciate it if my wives would stop trying to kill me."

Before Frenka could respond, the door to the room opened, and in walked Queen Clarissa, her royal blue dress adorned in golden trinkets shining in the morning light. The gold across her wrists and neck matched the ensemble.

"Thank you all for coming," said Clarissa as the doors closed behind her, and she made her way to the head of the table.

"Well, we couldn't do this at my house, not with the giant hole in the side of it," said Victor, giving a narrowed glance over a Frenka who remained silent.

"Oh my, haven't our builders gotten that mess sorted by now?" she asked as she waved her hand dismissively. "They must be busy with other projects in the city. I'm sure they will have it fixed once you return."

"I'm sure," said Victor with an understanding sigh. "Fine, let's get on with it. Tell us what you know."

"So demanding. But I suppose a man must be as he sits amongst his harem." The Queen smirked at Victor. "Tell me, are you enjoying your newfound freedom? It seems to me you've just traded one master for three. But men have always been a greedy lot, even if it was to their detriment."

"Need I remind you that all this results from your constant meddling and politicking? And once again, you're using me to clean up your messes."

"Now, Victor, don't blame a woman for your mistakes. It's quite unmanly." The Queen gave a glance between Frenka and Silk. "How do you two deal with him at night? At least our couplings were more the occasional passion. But to live with the man. Surely you both grow weary even now."

"We and husband are fine. We have understanding," said Frenka, the annoyance in her voice clear as her fingers tapped the table. "Queen-wife will tell us what she wants now."

"Queen-wife?" asked Clarissa with a raised brow. "Yes, I suppose I am that. You barbarous mountain people certainly have a way of simplifying complicated situations. A trait I admire, believe it or not." She turned to Silk. "And what of you, changeling? Are you willing to do the bidding of your new Queen-wife, also?"

"I am helping Victor, not you."

"Ahh, but they are one and the same, aren't they? Because what is good for me is inherently good for Victor."

"Just stop with the antagonization and tell us the information you've received," said Victor in an attempt to stop any more bickering.

"Fine," said Clarissa, with a smirk across her face as she revealed a piece of parchment and slid it across the table towards Victor. "We have scouts in Diohil awaiting the arrival of the leaders of the Church of the Goddess. Two have arrived, and the rest are on their way to the summit meeting. Amongst them have been seen a large supply of those crystals in wagons. Needless to say, we can't exactly force the leaders of the Goddess' Will into anything. The last thing we need is a war with an entire religion shared across the five kingdoms."

"And what do you expect me to do? Kindly ask them to reveal their secrets?"

"I expect you to continue your role as our ambassador. I've sent word that we wish to have a Temple of the Goddess erected in the capital city. You are to meet with Brother Misseus and discuss when and would lead such a prestigious chapel here. The temptation of having the main chapel in a capital city is too much for them to pass up."

"Your schemes will never end, will they?" asked Victor as he took a deep breath.

"Now, should you really be asking me that question considering you are the one who taught me to think strategically? I'm merely putting your lessons to good use. Really,

Victor, I'd think you would be proud of me."

"Victor was your teacher?" asked Silk, the curiosity controlling her.

"Oh yes. I never took to Mother's brand of leading a kingdom. But during our late nights together, Victor would pound the information into me; amongst other things," she blew Victor a kiss, "During the war with Dresha, it was Victor whom I allowed to handle the course of the war, to the great shame of the other Generals. But they simply weren't getting the job done. Victor had the wonderful idea that instead of attacking their food supply head-on, our men should infiltrate supply lines, and instead of destroying them, we would inject a slow-acting poison into their food supply. As a result, thousands of soldiers, women, and children died without lifting a finger. And that's not to mention that wonderful feat of defeating that horribly barbaric war bride of theirs."

Frenka and Silk turned to Victor with looks on their faces that Victor couldn't tell if it was disgust, reverence, or just shock.

"Oh, so I take it you two didn't know. Such a shame, Victor, keeping such a juicy secret from your wives," said the Queen with a mischievous smile. "The other Generals have never taken kindly to Victor, but what could they say after such feats in war? Even if it was done in a way that they considered to be underhanded. The Queen shook her head in mock sympathy. "I'm afraid that's who we've fallen for, ladies. A man who is known as a walking war crime. Victor Krill, The Demon of Flowers."

"Are you finished?" asked Victor, weary of the Queen's games. "Just get on with it. I do believe you have something to say about the child."

"Yes, I suppose we should move the conversation along. Well, as before, I would ask my apparent... sister wives to perform a boon and retrieve the child, bringing her back here. She should now be just about a year old."

"And this child, is she not the Starlight Queen's child?" asked Frenka. "Why you not return her? Will only lead to more war if found out."

"War with whom?" asked the Queen as the smirk across her lips grew into a smile. "You're a mountain woman, and as long as you don't specifically name your connection with Burlus, who would guess such a thing." She turned to Silk. "And this one can be whoever she desires. If you're caught, there isn't a single thing to tie this back to Mari."

"And what will Queen-wife give in return?"

"Oh! And here I thought allowing you to share in this sister-marriage thing would be enough of a gift. But fine, I am a Queen before I am a wife. So tell me, what is it you two want? Gold? Land?"

"Silk wishes to live as herself here, not wearing others' shape. You will make this happen for her and another."

"What? Do you want her to be able to walk around like that? Why the questions alone would cause scandal enough for those to wonder if we are performing experiments to recreate the monsters of old. And did you say another? Another one like you? I do believe some things are best kept in the shadows."

"Then maybe if we find baby, Starlight Queen will help us. Maybe even give husband home there." The room was silent for a moment as Frenka's words hung between them.

"I can see that we are going to have just a marvelous time getting to know one another," said the Queen, placing her elbows on the table and interlocking her fingers. "I must admit, I'm not accustomed to bartering like this. It most certainly isn't a pleasant feeling. But fine, I will see that our little whatever-that-is sister-wife will have accommodations with her friend. Tell me, this other one for whom I'm to make arrangements for, is she also another of your secret wives, Victor?"

"No, merely the sister."

"Are you sure? It seems you've gotten into the habit of

collecting women. Far be it from me to hinder you in your goal of capturing spouses."

"I think I've had quite enough, thank you," said Victor as he reached up, lifted his glasses, and began rubbing between his eyes in frustration. "When am I to leave for Diohil, and how will I be traveling?"

"I have arranged to have an airship take you there under the guise of a transport ship, sending supplies in celebration of the Day of the Goddess. It will be an important event, so I figure some fanfare will be needed."

"I appreciate the effort. Have you received any reports on what the red crystals are used for?"

"No, they were brought into the main chapel, and while I have received reports on their movements, we have no word on what happened to them once they were moved into the innards of the building. But I trust you will be able to enlighten us on that. You've always been so useful when it comes to finding out other's secrets."

Victor sighed, "Fine. Is there anything else?"

"Well, certainly. That is all the kingdom business," said Clarissa as Victor placed his hands on the table, ready to leave. "Now, now, Victor. Just because we are done with kingdom business. That, by no means, indicates that we are done with our meeting." The Queen folded her arms. "And I dare say that we most certainly have a lot to discuss."

"And I take it you're not content?"

"You would be correct. You may be content with having a blade at your neck, but I most certainly am not."

"That won't be happening again. It has already been discussed. It's not something for you to concern-"

"Not my concern? You can't be serious. If not for me, you would be dead. Sacrificed to gods at the hand of some barbarous mountain woman."

"It was not sacrifice," said Frenka in protest. "It was to protect husband; you try to control. No longer will this be allowed."

"And you think that you have any right to tell me what is and isn't allowed, you savage Burlus bitch. If not for-"

"Stop!" yelled Victor, his voice rumbling around the room. "This is exactly why I ended up almost dead on the floor with half my home destroyed." Victor pointed his finger between the two women. "I get it. You two won't ever choose peace. But we're here now, so try to deal with it without violence."

"As if such a thing were so simple."

"Then make it simple. I'm stuck in this the same as you are. And it's not as if you aren't benefiting from this. You and this baby theft thing are highly likely to bring us all down."

"Fine. But even you must know that this can't continue forever."

"Maybe not, but we have more pressing matters to attend to than you two not liking each other. But now, I have a question of my own. I was told that while I lay bleeding on the floor, you began to change. What was that about?"

"I don't know."

"Clarissa, this isn't the time for-"

"I said, I don't know. I've tried to look into the matter. But it's not as if you or I were ever pushed that far before. Sometimes, I feel things when you're away, like a tinge of the power creeping into me. But that was something completely different. And I doubt either of us wishes to recreate the event just to analyze it. I'd like to think we both experienced enough of that when the bond was formed."

Victor slouched back in his chair, "On that, we both agree, I prefer never to be poked and prodded like that again."

"No offense, but I would like to know more about my mission," spoke Silk in a soft tone that stole the moment.

"Oh, did I not inform you of the happenings then? You and... that woman will make your way into and past the Kingle's border and head into Dresha. There, you will head into Chrisjak, and you, my dear, will assume the visage of

218

an old man with a specific cane and wait by the fountain. You will be approached by our man who will give you all the information you require."

"Are you sure he's still there? When was he last contacted?"

"I'm told that he was contacted two days ago. Which is when I originally made my attempt to speak with you three. But that attempt was ruined, and now I'm afraid you must operate on a few days' old information. But I am glad to see someone taking a proper interest in their assignment. So, perhaps the boon I shall do for you will not be unappreciated after all."

"The border is half a moon ride from here. Will you also be lending them a ship?" asked Victor.

"Of course, although they will be smuggled on a basic transport ship for supplies to a nearby city. I can't risk loaning an imperial vessel and having them catch the attention of nearby spies and perhaps being followed on their mission."

"Fine, let's just get all this over with. It's not as if I'm not interested in the mystery behind these jewels," said Victor as he stood up from the table. "If there is nothing else, I'd like to be on."

"No, Queen-wife will do something for Frenka now."

"Did I not just agree to-"

"That was for Sister-Wife, now you must do for me."

"Alright," said the Queen, her eyes narrowing. "Tell me, what is it you want?"

"Tell us why you wish to have baby."

"What? Is that all? Why would I not want the child of another Queen? Aside from the power the child holds, the political leverage alone, should the need arise, would be the largest piece I could hold. Surely even you can see that."

"Yes. I see that. But I also see that you not telling all truth. So, Frenka wishes to hear you say it. Frenka is Prince royal guard. She hears the King talk. But you probably not tell husband. But you will now. You will say it."

Victor turned back to the Queen; his face lost in confusion. "What is she talking about?"

The Queen was silent in her chair for a moment as she looked at Frenka. "I can see now that we shall never make amends."

"Clarissa," said Victor. "Tell me what she is talking about."

The Queen closed her eyes and sighed. "Men are truly idiots. Women are not fertile forever, Victor. Even ones with as much magical energy as I have. And while I have been able to put off the concerns of my childlessness for some time, that time is fast diminishing. But unlike all the other Queens, I have a unique problem: You and your accused mundanity."

"Queen needs magic baby or risk losing kingdom," said Frenka, tapping her finger on the table.

"Quite so. At one point in time, I had thought I could just suffer through the coupling with a high lord and conceive a child of significant magical talent. But, you see, Victor, this spell that we share causes me to become excessively violent towards any whom I choose to give myself to who isn't you. As a result, I've had to cover up some naughty things in attempting to conceive. Unfortunately, poor Lord Delvon didn't live long enough for his cock to turn fully hard. Thankfully that Queen's Bane rumor served us well on that."

"Queen plans to have baby with you. If baby is magic, then good. But if baby is not, she will pass Starlight Baby as her own."

"But that baby is almost a year old. No one would... nooooooo," said Victor in a low drawl as his words slid out of his mouth.

"That mountain woman is smart, isn't she," The Queen smiled as she stood from the table, a hand across her belly. "While that incident between us a few nights ago gave me a scare. We are indeed safe." She took a breath. "I had planned to tell you later, but congratulations, Victor. You are going to be a father."

"That... that is why you had me visit you before sending me out on this mission. You planned it; you planned all of it."

"As I said, you should be proud. You are the one who taught me to always think ahead."

"But..." said Victor. But he couldn't think of anything else to say.

"Come along now, husband," said Frenka as she grabbed Victor's arm and began leading him out of the room. "Queen has told you the truth. You will think on this now."

"Yes, I suppose there is me that we all need to think about. But do try your best on this, Victor. These jewels, they may be nothing more than some new religious mandate, but I'd prefer it if you were careful. After all, I would like the father of my child to be alive."

How long? How many months? But she kidnapped the child before then. So she knew even beforehand. But how long has she been-

"Oh," said the Queen as Victor opened the door. "Do try not to take on any more wives on this trip. There should be a limit to a man's selfishness these days."

Victor left the room with a solemn expression on his face to the sounds of the Queen's laughter behind him. Along the way, Frenka and Silk, who had taken on the appearance of a blonde woman, had to guide him out of the building as he continued to lose focus.

"Are you two okay with doing this?" asked Victor as he left the castle. "I mean, there's a baby. I mean, she wants to steal a baby."

"Are we okay?" asked Silk, looking at Victor, confused. "You look like you can barely walk, and your face has gone whiter than mine."

"I am. Okay, I'm not. But I can put that aside for now. I

think. I just need to focus on something else. She wants you to kidnap a baby."

"Not kidnap. Bring baby to her. Baby already kidnapped," said Frenka. "And I would like to know baby safe, not being hidden in maybe unsafe place. We bring, then Queens will bicker."

"I've done worse," said Silk as she turned to Victor. "And apparently, we both have. Why were you so against me killing in Molask when you have killed so many? I'm not afraid of killing."

"Of that, I am aware. I understand the need to kill, but I've only killed when the need arose, or I had no choice. The slaughter of a random Goddess member or guard would not have served any purpose."

"It would have sped things along. Sometimes, being slow will get you caught."

"Then I can only leave that to your judgment, but I'd ask you not murder unless the need arises for it. I imagine the death toll between us three is already high enough."

"Where we going now?" asked Frenka.

"Home or what's left of it. My supplies are there, and I would like to lie down."

As they passed through the streets, it wasn't long before they were back in front of Victor's house. The wreckage his home did nothing to improve Victor's mood. He just stared at the damage for a moment before walking up to the hole in the wall and stepping inside.

"With magic, it shouldn't take long to fix," said Silk trying to comfort Victor.

"Perhaps not," said Victor as he headed towards his workshop at the rear end of the building. "You two gather what you need. We'll stay at a tavern and discuss everything that needs to be done."

"You think Queen can be trusted? Maybe this mission to be rid of wives."

"There's always a chance, but no. She will try to use you

like she does everyone else," said Victor as he opened the door to his storage and stepped inside. Then, reaching up, he turned the nob of an oil lantern, and with the sound of a click, it ignited, revealing the room. He then grabbed a belt satchel from a hook on the wall and laid it down on the wooden workbench in front of him. Surrounding him were the familiar sights of the tools he had used over the years to help him in whatever assignment the Queen had asked of him.

Okay. So what am I going to bring? She says this mission will be that of an ambassador, but so was the last, and we *ended up against bandits, mages, and whatever that thing in the cave was.* Victor smirked as he heard the sounds of Silk and Frenka outside as they rummaged through the house. *But I guess it wasn't all bad. You never really know how life will turn out. They are my salvation through the lunacy of my life.*

Shaking his head, he tried to remove them from his mind, back to the job. *First, I'd be foolish to think that I won't run into any trouble.* He grabbed four small vials of crushed Alagon powder and placed them into one of the pockets of the satchel belt. *There might be a combative sect within the Goddesses' will, or at worst, the entire leadership could be involved. What a horrid mess that would be.* He then stuffed a few black balls and some sharp caltrops into separate pockets as he heard more shuffling sounds from his wives. *I wonder if they might need anything. Silk probably wouldn't take the Alagon powder since she fears being near it. Maybe Frenka then, she seems...* Victor froze in his movements as a smile came over his face. *Really, Victor, you're trying to protect a magical shapeshifting assassin and an even more magically talented king's guard. He finished packing a few more items in his pouches and headed back into the kitchen to see Frenka and Silk sitting in the chairs.* Apparently, the rustling sound from before was them lifting his overturned dinner table.

"What's this?" asked Victor as he looked over the house once more. "Have you decided to clean the house? I'm afraid at this point that it would amount to just wasted effort until the repairs are done."

"Come sit, husband," said Frenka as she pushed her leg out, extending a chair to him. "We wish to discuss matter with you."

Victor frowned as he noticed the serious expressions on their faces but walked over and took a seat at the table. "Okay, conversations like this never end well. This isn't about the baby, is it? If so, can we wait until—"

"You have been husband for almost three moons now. And you have now accepted this role, yes?"

"Yes, I don't see a point in denying it now. I accept that I am a husband to both of you." *What is with this tone? It feels like I'm on trial.* He glanced over at Silk to see her rubbing her fingers together. *What are they so nervous about? I'm the one about to have a damned baby. Is there another clan ritual I don't know about before a mission?*

"Then does Husband not find his wives attractive; maybe only Queen?"

"What! No, why would—"

"Then why haven't you tried to sleep with either one of us."

"What? I mean... It's not like I haven't thought about it. We've just been busy. You ask about this now? After that whole thing with Clarissa?" *Is this what this is about? Has it really been three moons since we left Burlus?* "Besides, weren't you two arguing about this on the boat ride over."

"Yes, and we decided to share husband. When husband gave us rooms, we thought he would visit us at night, but our beds remained cold."

"That was only one night, and I had my throat slit the next day, or don't you remember?"

"First night home is plenty time for husband to bed his wives."

So you're just going to skip over that whole slit throat part. Victor placed his satchel bag on the table and lifted his glasses, rubbing his eyes again. *Stop, don't argue. It won't help.* "Look, I agree. I probably have not been as attentive to your needs as I should have been. But it's not as if I didn't have a good reason. You two constantly fought on the boat ride over, and from there, it was a long and dusty horse ride to the capital, where you two also argued half the way. It was exhausting trying to keep you two apart."

"Women argue; we set rules on who owns husband."

Owns? What? Am I a slave now? "Either way, there was no time. What was I supposed to do; ask one of you to look away while I plowed the other behind a bush?"

"Maybe," said Silk sheepishly.

"A real man would," said Frenka confidently.

Okay, this conversation is truly happening, thought Victor, as he looked between the faces of both women. "Fine, What? You both want to fuck me now? How about here, on the floor, so the people walking by can watch us through the giant hole in my wall?"

"Do not be foolish. House still has many rooms with beds and doors."

Victor just stared at Frenka for a moment. Her eyes never wavered as she looked at him with eyes expecting his answer. *She's really serious. Is this normal? Am I just supposed to fuck at her leisure to show some type of clan male dominance or something? Ah! This is ridiculous. Now what? Do I just take her when I'm expected or risk whatever backlash comes from denying this?* Victor stood up from the table and took a deep breath. "Fine. Then if you've both decided on this. Then who will it be? Far be it for me to deny my husbandly duties any longer."

"Both. Husband has made wives wait too long. Now you will please both to make amends."

Both? Victor turned to Silk, "And you agree to this."

Silk stood up from the table, looking at Victor. "Frenka and I have come to an understanding on this."

When? You were fighting all the... no, don't think about

it. That would only bring us problems if I were to guess when you two decided on this. "Okay, we're really doing this," said Victor as he started walking toward the intact part of the house. "The room in the far back will do." Victor's heartbeat quickened in his chest as he listened to the echoes of Silk and Frenka's footsteps behind him. *Let's hope this doesn't end like the last time two women tried to seduce me. A knife at my...* Victor's face took on a pained expression as he clenched his teeth and squinted his eyes as the realization came to him, and he reached up, rubbing at the scar on his throat. *Life really is just one big circular joke.*

They all entered the room at the end of the hall as Silk closed the door behind them.

"Silk will help me undress, husband," said Frenka as she reached up and began unbuttoning the top of Victor's shirt, working her way down. Silk then joined her as she came over and placed her hand on Victor's face, letting her thumb linger on his lips as she stared into his. Her blue eyes flickered for a moment from blue to green.

You don't have to push yourself to do this, he thought as he tried to allow himself to be carried away in the moment. *Damnit don't think about this. Just embrace it.* Victor noticed Frenka fiddling with the third button on his shirt for an extended amount of time. *She's being gentler than I expected...* He glanced down at Frenka and caught her taking the button loose and rebuttoning it in his shirt. *What the hell is she doing? Is this some type of teasing?* He turned to Silk as she began to fiddle with her own shirt. Her hands shook as she undid the buttons of her own attire with her blonde hair dangling over her shoulders."

What's going on? Why are... Argh, I'm an idiot.

Victor grabbed hold of Frenka's hand.

"Wait."

"What wrong?" asked Frenka, taken aback by his movements.

Victor turned toward Silk, "Why are you still wearing

that? Change back."

"What? I am," Silk looked down at the floor. "I thought you'd like me this way."

Victor reached out and grabbed Silk by the face, his hand clenched around her cheeks to the point where it made her lips pucker. "When did I ever say I preferred you like this? When we are alone, I want you to wear yourself. And I will not have our first night together spoiled by having you wearing someone else's body. Change back, now."

Silk's eyes began to water as she glanced between Victor and Frenka.

"You heard husband. Best you do as he says."

Victor felt the bone structure soften as Silk's form shortened in his grip. The soft sound of popping came as he released his hand, and Silk's golden hair turned white, and her pale ashen skin returned beneath her clothing.

Frenka stepped forward and reached out, grabbing Silk's arm, pulling her forward, and embracing her before swooping behind her. "There you see, husband accepts you fully now. No need to hide," she said as she reached inside Silk's loosened shirt and began to rub her hand across one of her breasts. All the while looking back at Victor, but the look on Frenka's face wasn't that of lust. Instead, it was something akin to determination, something that needed to be done and done the right way.

You clever woman. I really have no idea what goes on in that mind of yours. Is this why you were pressuring me so hard?

Frenka placed her lip against Silk's ear, gently biting it before giving Silk a kiss on the cheek. "Go forward, Sister-Wife. Finish undressing your husband."

CHAPTER 15

In Heart House, Isha stood alone in her room, a heaviness on her breath as she tried to focus. Sweat dripped down her face. A sharp blade in her hand matched the assortment across the edge of their bed. In front of her, against the wall with three blades around the outer circles, hung the training board that Jacob and Dessi had made for her. She slid her right foot forward with her arm extended back before whipping it downward, releasing the blade from her hand. It flew quickly across the room, striking into the second outer circle of the board, embedding itself into the wood.

Why am I not better yet? I should be better, thought Isha as she walked over to the board.

"You're still at it, I see," said Rima as she entered the door with a plate of warm food. "I would say it's not normal for a healer to practice like this, but I guess you're not really a healer anymore, are you? Not that you ever were."

Isha frowned back at Rima before walking back to the bed, "He hasn't come home yet, has he?"

"No," said Rima, following behind Isha. "Not yet, but he said he will be home in a day or so, just as soon as his wounds heal. So, just be a little more patient. He hasn't tried to hide it from you, so I don't think he hates you or anything."

"I... I just wanted to apologize."

"And you will... when he returns. Now come on and eat. I took the time to make this for you, and I promise that learning to cook hasn't been easy."

Isha looked at the food on the tray and, beneath it, the few remaining cuts on Rima's fingers that were still healing.

She bit her lips and nodded as she walked over, took the plate, sat in a chair beside the bed, and began eating. The moment the food touched her tongue, she started to inhale it, her mouth taking in another bite the moment she finished the previous one.

It... it tastes like Elena's cooking.

"Well, I guess that means I got the recipe right," said Rima with a smile as she poured a cup of water for Isha. "Now, take a drink before you choke."

"Mhmm," moaned Isha before taking a gulp from the cup, followed by a deep breath. "Why? I mean..."

"You mean, why does my cooking suddenly not taste like burned trash?"

"No... I mean... I wouldn't say it was that bad."

"Well, Leo was here a few nights ago to check on you."

"He was?"

"Yes, and while he was here, he gave me some of Elena's cooking notes. I've been practicing. But who would have known cooking was so hard? Apparently, you have to mix things together at the right time to get the taste right." Rima waved her hand dismissively, "It's all such a pain, really."

If he came, he should have woken me, thought Isha with a sour face. *Why does he keep treating me like...* Isha closed her eyes and shook for a moment with a moan before she began rotating her right shoulder, trying to stretch it. It felt tight, but this tightness wasn't from the blades. Since she had received the markings, she could feel when either Makeba or Jacinta used their magic. A hit of magical vapor would appear on her back when they did so.

"Is it happening again?" asked Rima with a look of concern on her face.

"Mhmm, Jacinta is using her magic again; I can feel it."

"I can see the magic gathering behind you," said Rima as she nodded to the flow of magic behind her. "But I don't understand how it works. Are you sending magic to them?"

"No, I mean. I don't think so. I... I just feel it when they use magic."

"Have you tried using that special magic yet, the one everyone's so interested in?"

"No, they told me to wait until the markings have healed properly. I'm not allowed to use magic until then."

"Ah, that's why you've been up here throwing things against the wall and not going to class."

"That, and I promised Dessi I would."

"Dessi, huh? I've heard you talk about her before," said Rima, turning back to the board and looking at the chunks of wood missing from the target. "I'm guessing she would be proud of you. You're definitely hitting it."

"But I can't hit the center like I'm supposed to; like she does."

"Give it time, you will get there. I guess the same could be said for me and my cooking," said Rima as she reached over and grabbed one of the blades, gently tapping the top of her finger against the sharpened end. "It's not as good as Elena's, but I'd like to think I'll get there one day."

A loud thud from outside followed by the sounds of someone talking took the girls out of their moment with each other. They both headed over to the other side of the house into Rima's room, poking their heads out of the window. There they saw Soulden, Freedo, Jacinta, Makeba, and another boy Isha didn't know. But what really stood out was the large marble statue that now sat in the front of the Heart House underneath the limbs of its only tree.

"Oh, there sister with Rima," said Makeba as she noticed them from below.

"Sister, come see. They make new Elena from stone," said Jacinta with a smile and patted the statue playfully.

New Elena, thought Isha as Rima and she looked at each other for a moment before heading back inside. Down the stairs, both girls went out of the front door where the group was waiting for them. Barefooted, Isha stepped onto the grass and over to her sisters to gaze up at the stone creation they had brought. And sure enough, it was a statue of uncanny likeness to Elena. She was kneeling in her hooded school garment with her hands cupped together. In them, she held the basic design of a human heart.

"Where did this come from?"

"That would be me," said the boy they had brought with them. "I was there that day, as was one of the students sent to retrieve some herbs from Salamander House. After her heroics, I felt it wouldn't be right to not honor her somehow."

"Well, you certainly did a wonderful job," said Rima as she reached up, feeling the curves and structure of the statue. "I'm surprised you were able to capture her likeness so well."

"Ah, well, you can thank that fellow Leo for his contribution to it. He was instrumental in getting down the finer details of her face."

"Leo was helping?" asked Isha.

"Yes, he's been helping me for the last few weeks, late into the night. Although recently, he's been showing up covered in bandages. I offered to postpone but he insisted on pressing on. He was passionate about this; I'd often come into class early and find him still there staring at the paintings I used for references."

After hearing his words, Isha immediately began looking around. "Is he here?"

"No, sadly, after finishing the piece, he withdrew himself from the art area, and I haven't seen him since. He said that he had to focus on healing."

"Oh," responded Isha, a disappointed expression across her face.

"Now, dear, give Leo some time to heal. I imagine it's far more than the burns he's suffering from now. Elena was a loss for us all, but I imagine for him, the loss was far more devastating. He will come around soon, I assure you. He even came to me to ask to be there when we attempted to heal the tree."

"He did?"

"Indeed, and speaking of which; how are you feeling? Do you feel any different now that the ritual has been completed?"

"I... I don't know. I feel fine, I think. But my back feels funny whenever Makeba or Jacinta use their magic."

"Yes. That Aukube woman of yours said such a thing would happen for a while. I have granted her special permission to live underneath the Trailage Tree for the duration of her stay here. Since it is apparently of Sakari origin and responds to their magic specifically, she has opted to stay and feed the tree the occasional supply of magic until we can find a more stable solution."

"We want to feel Sister Isha's magic," said Jacinta. "So, we wait until healing is done then we might get white bubble magic too."

"White bubble? "Yes, I guess it does look like that to you," said Soulden with a smirk as she turned back to face Isha. "Well, speaking of your magic, I have something for you." Soulden lifted the pouch strap over her shoulder, handing it to Isha.

"What is it?" asked Isha, accepting the bag curiously.

"A gift from your father. Open it and see what it is."

Father? Thought Isha with a sense of worry before removing the flap on the bag and taking a peek inside. *Clothing?* She reached in, grabbed the cloth, and pulled out three pieces of fabric. It resembled the outfit she wore while fighting with her sisters in the circle. A top that exposed her midriff, a small skirt that would probably come down to her knees, and a small undergarment underneath that she caught Freedo staring at for a moment before turning away. "Father sent me clothing?" asked Isha while holding the clothes out and looking at them curiously.

"That he did," said Soulden. "But this particular clothing is unique. It's a fabric made out of special cloth that only the royalty of a family in a faraway kingdom can use. How your father managed to get a hold of it is beyond me. But Oscar has always been deceivingly resourceful."

"What special clothing do?" asked Jacinta as she poked at it. The cloth swayed, shimmering in the sunlight.

"Well, this particular clothing has the ability to absorb and respond to a person's magic after it has had the proper time to adjust to it. While worn, it supposedly feeds off the wearer's magic, becoming almost an extension of the body. Or so I've heard; I haven't tried it myself." Soulden reluctantly admitted. "But the hope from your father and I is that your magic will absorb into it and not burn it to ash. Oscar was quite annoyed with the thought of you being stark naked every time you used your powers."

"Oh, sister, get magic clothes. She always gets mad when clothing come off after fight."

"Of course I do. How would you feel? You're not the ones naked every time you use your magic."

"Why? You naked when we take bath together."

"That's not the same thing, and you know it," said Isha, annoyed by her sister's teasing as she turned back to Soulden. "Do you think it will work?"

"Only one way to know for sure. Aukube said you should be perfectly healed up in another day or so. We'll test it out then, shall we? I'm sure it hasn't been easy being cooped up here and not being allowed to use your magic."

"It's fine. So, will I get to go to class soon?"

"Yes, and I'm sure everyone misses you."

"It will be good for sister to be back in class. It is boring now," said Jacinta with a pout. "No one fights, just talks too much. Sister makes class exciting. Talk to trees and get into fights."

"That's not... okay, maybe it is true. But you're making it sound like I'm trying to do these things."

"Oh," said Freedo, chiming in. "They still have us playing with the pink goo, but most of us have gotten it by now. And Pavel was looking for you. Mr. Higgins did not assign him a new partner since he was told you'd be coming back to class soon."

"Yes, we do lessons with pretty girly boy until sister comes to class. He and Makeba have race to get pink goo off. And I fight him in class a lot. He good, but I better."

"Stop that. I hope you're not calling him that in class."

"She does," acknowledged Freedo. "But Pavel has people who follow him around now, so it's hard to talk to him outside of class."

"What do you mean?"

"I suppose I should explain that," said Soulden. "They are his guardians of sorts. I do believe you all know that Pavel has a perceived destiny amongst a certain sect amongst the Will of the Goddess. After the previous attack, allowing them access to guard over here was a concession I needed to make to continue his studies. They are perfectly trustworthy, I assure you."

Isha remembered her time in the castle, where she found Pavel talking to someone about an attack. Which was then followed up by an attack on the school. *How can she say that? I told her about the attack, and it still happened. But it wasn't Pavel who attacked the school. Was it? I mean, they came with the blonde girl's mother. Unless, maybe, they were all*

234

working together. And Pavel is always with Leo, but Leo isn't... Isha began shaking her head as the frustration. *No stop... just... just think about the tree. I don't want to think of this now.*

"Is everything okay, child?" asked Soulden.

"It's fine. Can... can I come to see you tomorrow?"

"What? Of course. You can join Miss Huffles and me tomorrow for brunch if you wish. You already know where to find us?"

"Yes, ma'am."

"Well then," said Soulden, clasping her hands together. "I suppose that's it for our little expedition to drop off this tribute to Miss Elena's bravery. The day is growing old, and I wish to get back. Come along, you two. Let's leave the girls alone for the evening."

"Bye," said Freedo.

Isha was surprised when he gave them all hugs before walking off with Soulden and the boy pushing the cart that brought the statue.

"Well, you three have certainly become close with that Freedo boy, which one of you is his little girlfriend?" asked Rima.

"We all Freedo girlfriends," said Jacinta. "But he really likes Makeba and maybe Sister Isha, but I think he worries about Sister Isha as we do."

"Freedo is good boy. Not a man yet," said Makeba. "He is weak still, but maybe he will become a man one day. Then maybe it would not be so bad to think of him as mate."

Isha blinked her eyes in surprise. *She's not getting mad? Does she like Freedo now? Wait! Do I like Freedo? I mean, I don't hate him.* As she and Rima talked about boys, Isha stared at her sister for a moment. *How is she not embarrassed? I would be.*

"What is wrong, sister?" asked Makeba, finally noticing her sister's gaze on her. "Do you wish for me to do something?"

"Huh? Ahh, no. I was just thinking, is all," said Isha

as she turned to go but caught another glimpse of Elena's statue for a moment, staring up into its face. Looking up, she felt as if Elena was there, telling her not to run away from her thoughts. *I know. I promise I'm trying. I'm going to do better. And I'll try to see Leo tomorrow if he doesn't come home. Even if he doesn't want to see me.*

"Come on, you two. Let's head back inside," said Rima as she patted the girls on the back, leading them back into the house. "I even cooked again."

"Yuk," said Jacinta, sticking out her tongue. "We ate at school. We okay."

"Hey, stop that. I'll have you know that I have been practicing. Even Isha thought it was good."

That night Isha stayed up late waiting for Leo to come home, but he never did. Finally, as the frustration took over, she got up from her bed, put on her clothes while her sisters were asleep, and headed off towards the school. The moon was high in the sky, hiding behind the soft bluish clouds in the night skyline. The pale bluish glow cast down the streets leading towards the castle where classes were held. Its marbled surface glimmered in the night as the moisture in the air gave off an otherworldly appearance. The castle looked eerie, as if the shadows around it were alive, spiraling over its spire and down into its lofts.

Through the midnight air, she made her way through the streets towards the castle until she reached the steps to the doors. Feeling unsure, she looked around. No one else was in sight, only the shadows and a slight breeze. To her, the darkness seemed even more unsettling than she would have liked to admit. But determined, she placed her hands on the door, and with a push, it creaked open. The moonlight shining through the door and the windows into the hallway gave her path a slight illumination.

She heard a creak behind her and turned to look, but nothing was there. Just an empty street. She stepped inside, allowed the large door to close, and made her way through the castle. She had been in the school the night before, but tonight seemed ever more unsettling. Gone were the twinges of light from the roots protruding in the walls. Instead, it was replaced by the cold loneliness of an indescribable void. Since the tree was damaged, and she could no longer talk to her, everything seemed so lifeless, which only compounded during the night.

I really hope we can heal the tree when I am able to use the magic again.

She felt a need to kneel and place her hand on one of the roots. To at least try and communicate with the tree. But she was forbidden from using magic until her markings had been healed. So instead, she stepped forward and made her way through the corridor, allowing her finger to graze across the hard bark. She hoped that the gesture itself would provide a sort of comfort to Lonta'Mar and maybe herself.

She reached the stairs and made her way up, footsteps providing soft echoes off the nearby walls. Then, up the first flight, she turned and made her way up to the second floor where she knew Leo's office was. Making her way down the hall, she stopped at his door and touched the handle. With a press, the door swung open, but as it gave way, she saw that the room was empty, his chair sitting in the dim light, along with the beds.

Not here. Where... he said Leo spent time in the art room. I think that was on the second floor, here... somewhere. Feeling uneasy but now more determined, she made her way down the hall, peeping into door after door, trying to find the art room. *I wonder what classes these rooms are for. Probably for the second-year students.* Making her way to the next room, she looked through the door's window and saw him there. As the boy earlier said, Leo was sitting on a stool. His image between the shadows and moonlight came through a ceiling hole. In front of him sat a painting of what Isha could only assume to be Elena. Slowly opening the door, she felt a coldness run over her ankles. Looking down, she realized she couldn't see her own feet. It was as if the shadows consumed them, forming a black mist that blended in with the shadows.

"I guess I shouldn't be surprised to see you here," came Leo's voice as she looked back at him.

"I... ah," said Isha in a moment of confusion. "I just thought... I mean." Now seeing him there, Isha didn't know what to say.

"Come here. You should see this," said Leo, as she stared at the portrait. "I was thinking of bringing it home when I came back."

Isha stepped inside, the black mist around her legs disappearing as if it was seeping outside into the hallway.

"What was that? More magic?"

"What was what?"

"That ahh..." Isha struggled for a moment to describe what it was. "There was something cold around my legs... I think."

"Well, it is nighttime, and it does get cold up here. I would have assumed you'd gotten used to it by now. But come over and tell me what you think."

Letting the matter of the black mist go, Isha stepped over to Leo. As she made her way closer, she couldn't help but stare at his bandaged head and neck. She could see half his head was covered as the wraps crossed his left eye, covering half his face. Even underneath his clothing and down his arm, the right side of his body was wrapped in bandages.

"What... I mean... Did I-"

"No need to worry about it now. I'm mostly healed up. Just another day or so, and the numbness will be gone. Then, after some cream work, everything will be back to

238

normal when I have the time. After that, I might be able to do it myself, but well, I'm not in the best condition to perform that work on myself yet."

Cream work? Thought Isha as her mind returned to when Dessi took her to a creamer. She remembered the pain that her small mark had caused her and the writhing and suffering Dessi went through on the man's table as he removed her scars. Looking over Leo's bandaged body, she shuddered at the thought of how much pain it would take to heal him properly.

"I... I'm sorry. I mean..."

"There you go dropping your head again. I did what I did for my own reasons. And it all worked out," said Leo as he turned back to face the portrait. "We're both still alive. That's all that matters."

As he spoke, Isha could see the sadness in his eyes and turned to view the portrait. To her surprise, it didn't look like the statue they had brought earlier, with its stoic and graceful face. Instead, the portrait was of the side of Elena that she remembered the most. A sweet smiling young woman, set to a backdrop of vibrant red and orange colors behind her. In the center of the colors was the image of Elena holding out a tray of food in her apron.

"She really did like you girls," said Leo. "She said it was like having little sisters. Since she only had brothers back at home, she enjoyed every day with you girls."

As Isha listened to Leo and stared at the portrait, a world of feelings began to flow from inside of her. And even though she tried to fight it at first, it was as if every heartbroken word from Leo's mouth seemed to break her spirit even more. And what was once the hint of a tear in her eye was now becoming a stream of emotions that poured down her face. Isha soon found herself once again wrapped inside Leo's arms as he held her, allowing her to cry on his shoulder as she grit her teeth and clenched the fabric of his shirt.

"It's okay. I've got you," said Leo as he held Isha against his chest, looking for a sort of comfort himself from the feeling of loss. "Cry as much as you like. I promise you, I've done my fair share here."

CHAPTER 16

Out in the forests of Burlus, the moon rippled across the lake as Mova and Laura bathed in the water. Up on the bank, there sat Dekol and Saffron beside the women's discarded clothing as Dekol tossed a small piece of wood on the fire between them.

"Have you figured out what you will say once we get there?" asked Dekol as he poked at the fire with a twig. "The inner circle of the Goddess has talented mages and healers. If you wear a disguise, it won't take long before you're found out."

"I've been pondering that," said Saffron as she turned to gaze at women wading in the water. "I believe it is best that I simply introduce myself, title and all. Their main capital is in Burlus after all, so I can't imagine my name not holding some sway over a certain level of their guard. At least enough to get us past the main hall's doors."

"Are you going to contact your father when we arrive or ask for assistance from the local guard? That may be required."

"I shall alert them to my presence and some of my intent. But having them accompany me to the cathedral, perhaps not. That might be construed as me storming the gates of a holy temple. If I was to lose faith with the people, I'd ask for it to be done at a slow pace rather than me attacking the main figurehead of a whole religion. No, there has to be another way."

"You're not going to try to get us all killed again, I hope."

"Oh, please. I'd imagine we've been through worse than..."

"All right," said Mova as she stepped out of the lake, the water sliding off her naked body as she came close to them. "You two jump in. I will appreciate not having to smell your stink for a while."

"And here I assumed you enjoyed the smell of real men," said Saffron as he turned to her. "Where is my lady wife? Have you left her to wade the waters alone?"

Mova gestured back toward the water. "Your darling bride is a bit shy about showing off her body."

"And of which it seems you are not," said Saffron as he gave Mova a glance over. "You've always had a lovely figure. Why haven't you found a man for yourself yet? Are you afraid of marriage? I can assure you it is not as bad as it seems. I, for one, am quite enjoying my newfound responsibilities."

"Yes, plowing your wife in the bush while Dekol and I keep guard, what a wonderful life I live. And I'll pick my own mate when I'm ready," said Mova as she channeled a small amount of magic, using it to conjure a bit of air the flow across her body, causing the water on her skin to rise up into the air pooling into a water bubble. She flicked her wrists, sending the bubble splashing in Saffron's face.

Saffron just sat there momentarily as the water dripped over him, falling to the ground below.

"You know, I'm not sure all this wetness came from the lake."

"You're right. I pissed in there a bit."

Saffron began spitting and frantically wiping the water from his face as Dekol turned away from him, trying his best to contain his laughter.

"You are just the worst."

"That was a joke, you idiot. Now go and coax your wife out so I may have my time around the fire without your eyes ogling me."

"Your personality is a mixture of an ill-mannered shrew and constantly annoyed house cat," said Saffron as he stood and began taking off his clothing. "But I will comfort my wife. I doubt you would understand what comforting a loved one actually means." Then, taking off his shirt and trousers, he stood there as naked as Mova before turning to Dekol. "Would you mind joining me, old friend? I imagine you're more of a reason for my wife's reluctance than our dear house cat. And I think a shared sense of embarrassment will liven up the night."

"I don't think comparing yourself to me has ever worked out well for you before," said Dekol as he stood and began undressing.

"Who's comparing? I have a wife, and you do not. So, I stand to think I'm already leaps ahead of you," said Saffron as Dekol undid his shirt, unbuckled his sword belt, and placing it on the ground before dropping his pants and walking over beside him, both men standing naked by the water.

"It seems that you have gained weight, Saffron," said Mova as she gestured to the naked men and then downwards. "Tell me, why doesn't a man's cock grow with the rest of him?"

"I guess you would think that way," said Saffron. "Your breasts would grow if you picked up weight. But a man must be sturdy and built like a rock. Ever unchanging, so that we stand the test of time."

"And you showing off yours and Dekol's cock to your new wife is part of that unchangingness? What if she starts having ideas about that close friend of yours? I'm sure you've heard stories of princesses and their loyal servants."

Saffron turned to Dekol, who gave him a shrug, then turned back to Mova.

"Perhaps, if it was you, Mova, who would try seduced my wife, but then again, I hardly think of you as a loyal servant. More of a forced conspirator. But I think I might enjoy the sight of catching you and my lady wife in bed together."

"Just go and wash that decrepit cock along with that decrepit mind you have," said Mova, shaking her head as she walked over to their drying clothing.

Saffron smirked before turning back to the water and spotting his wife threading water, just staring at them. "Come, my lovely wife," said Saffron as he extended his arms toward Laura. "Do not hide yourself from me. Allow me to observe your beauty as the water removes itself from your figure. Unlike Mova, I'm sure it will actually be a pleasing sight." Saffron's words were immediately followed by a thunk on the back of his head as Mova struck him with a small rock.

There was a moment before they saw Laura slowly making their way toward them.

"You really enjoy embarrassing people, don't you?" whispered Dekol.

"Modesty is only for the people you don't trust, and you and I might as well be the same. But, since she's my wife, then I'd wish for her to shed a small amount of her modesty for extra security," said Saffron in the same low whisper. "I ask that you protect her as you always have me."

"And you know you don't need to ask."

"Perhaps. But a bit of formality amongst friends is still appreciated, no?"

"It is."

Although coming closer, Saffron still saw his wife's hesitation to lift herself from the water.

"Is something wrong, my dear wife? Why do you hesitate to embrace your husband?"

"Can... can Sir Dekol not look away?"

"I'm afraid he cannot. For Sir Dekol is a proud and bold man, and so is your husband. Now, come, my dear wife. Here we stand before you. Our cocks in the wind for you to see. I once asked you to treat Dekol as if he were me." *Although at that time, it wasn't Dekol but a damned assassin. But now's not the time for semantics.*

"Come to me with no shame, proud of the bodies the Goddess has given us, and embrace your husband."

"You really are enjoying yourself too much," said Dekol, continuing his whispering.

Laura took a breath before finally stepping out of the water, exposing her naked self to the men. Stepping forward and using her arms to cover what little she could, she stepped into Saffron's waiting arms as he embraced her, giving her a kiss.

"I suspect that was quite embarrassing for you."

"I... I admit I'm not accustomed to how open you all are around each other. Should... should I also be this open around Thaddius?"

"Thaddius?" said Saffron with a twist of the lips in thought. "I suppose not. Although a loyal man, he's not the same as Dekol here or our house cat Mova."

"Oh, that's good," said Laura with a sigh of relief. "Wait, ah, why a house cat?"

Saffron released his wife from his grasp with another kiss. "I'm sure you will understand soon enough." He stepped to the side, gesturing to the fire.

"I'll go get dressed now," said Laura, passing them on her way toward Mova.

"Well, now that that bit of business is well and done," said Saffron as he placed his hands on his hip and stretched his back. "How about we attend to ours then? What do you say to twenty gold for who makes it to the other side first?"

"Just say when."

"I see you've survived another one of your Lord Husband's whims," said Mova as she handed Laura her clothing.

"Yes," said Laura, taking the dried clothing, "Is it... I mean, is he always like this?"

"As long as I've known him," said Mova with a sigh as she watched both men diving into the water and begin swimming across the lake. "Yes, that's pretty much the way of him. Dekol is a lot more stern but allows himself to be carried along with Saffron's stupidity."

"Do they not worry about the noise?" She looked around the wooded area. "What if someone were to come for us?"

"There's nothing around us at the moment. I can feel the vibrations in the air with a decent sized area around us, even past the road. If there was a person nearby, I would know it."

"You specialize in air magic?"

"Yes," said Mova as she flicked her wrist at Laura, performing the same trick from earlier. The air swirled over her body, pulling the few droplets of water away from her skin until a small bubble appeared that she sent splashing to the ground.

"Oh my," said Laura, shivering a bit after the wind hit her. "That is a useful spell."

"It has its uses. But you're a mage. Did you learn any combat magic under your father? He is a General; I can't imagine him not teaching you basic self-defense."

"No," responded Laura quickly. "He did try... And I have learned some. I was just never that talented in it. Oh, but don't misunderstand, I can defend myself. It's just that I'm not my sister."

"Either way. We are as safe as can be here," said Mova, pointing towards the men in the water. "Despite their foolishness, you know how powerful your husband is. And Dekol... well Dekol is Dekol."

Laura slid on her pants. "I had the impression that Master Dekol was not born with magic."

"No, he wasn't. But I'd guess if I were to fight Dekol seriously, I'm pretty sure I would lose," said Mova as she stood once Laura was dressed. "Come on, let's clean the men's clothes in the water and wipe away their smell. It won't take long for me to dry them by the fire."

Both women grabbed the men's garbs and walked toward the lake.

"Can I ask you something personal?" asked Laura as they reached the water and began dunking the men's clothing.

"Sure, what is it?"

"You are from one of the eight noble houses. Your Mother is General Pathos. Can I ask why you became a guard? You didn't need to, with your mother in her position."

"In truth, I had no intention of accepting the role of one of Saffron's guards. Would you believe my only plans were to someday become a noble lady and have some lord's babies? I would spend hours imitating how my mother's friends would speak."

"Then what changed?"

"One day, my father was visiting one of the lower stations in the countryside: a lesser lord. And Father used me to entertain that lord's daughter as he went about his way in discussion with the woman, leaving us to attend to ourselves. Well, I'd guess that we were being watched by some petty thieves who had designs to use for ransom. So they'd snuck into the manor, killed two of the lord's guards and some staff, and took the lord's daughter and me. Not that they had much trouble since I could barely summon the wind at that age."

"What happened? How did you escape?" asked Laura, her eyes wide with intrigue.

"Apparently, a wandering knight just so happened to be on her journey and heard of the situation. While my father was planning to pay the ransom, she swooped into the bandit's base, and in only a few seconds, she managed to kill them all." Mova smiled as she thought back to her younger days. "My father was shocked to have us returned to him before he could do anything, and needless to say, my dreams had changed. Especially when I found that the knight and I shared the same affinity for magic. And here I am."

"And what happened to the knight who saved you? Do you know?"

Mova smiled, "She became my father's mistress and taught me how to use the sword and my magic. Then sometime afterward, she gave birth to my sister."

Laura just looked at Mova with unbelieving eyes.

Move smiled as she lifted the clothing from the water, stood, and walked back to the fire. There they draped the men's clothing over a stick by the fire. "One can never truly guess how one's life flows. Turns out that same knight dreamed of the life of an easy-going noble."

"Does... did your mother not object?"

"Would you object if Saffron were to invite Frenka to his bed? Not that she ever would," said Mova as she whirled a bit of magic over her fingers, sending a small gust of wind downward, draining the men's clothing of the heavy water before the breeze fluttered in their campfire.

Laura was quiet for a moment as she bit her lip, then sighed, "Maybe I am just like my mother then."

"You don't need to worry about Frenka. She has never had the—" Mova quickly turned her head, looking towards the trees. "Someone's coming into the woods."

"What? Are you sure?" said Laura, looking around nervously.

"They're there, and it's a bunch of them, and they're moving fast," she tried to focus more as she closed her eyes. "Not exactly towards us, but not away from us either." Opening her eyes, she hurried back down towards the water. She placed her hand on the surface and began channeling magic, releasing a wave of magical force inside. Then turning around, she walked over to Laura, handing her a sword. "Come on, let go and see what's going on," she whispered.

"What? Me? You want me to come with you?"

"Yeah, it'll take a while for the men to get back and get dressed, and I'd rather surprise them than have them surprise us."

Laura swallowed nervously but nodded her head. And with a final look back at the lake where she thought she saw the heads of both men being still in the water, she followed Mova into the brush of the trees.

Mova dashed off into the trees with Laura following behind her. She was surprised by the young princess' speed as she kept pace, dashing between the twigs and branches while staying surprisingly silent. Although dark, the moonlight above them did an alright job of illuminating the night. They focused their eyes as they pressed forward.

"Okay, the first group will be here soon," said Mova as she crouched near an open in the wooded area with Laura soon beside her.

"What... what's happening?" asked Laura as she looked around nervously.

"There," said Mova with her finger pointed ahead. "I can feel three people ahead. They'll be appearing soon."

And within a minute, Mova's words came true as a robed woman holding the hands of two young girls came out of the forest, the brush parting around them in a flurry of broken sticks and leaves as they hurriedly made their way forward.

"Why are they running?" asked Laura

The woman ran over to the other side of the opening,

forcing the girls into the bush before coming back out to stand in the clearing. Soon out of the clearing came half a dozen men, all panting and breathing heavily as they stepped towards the woman. Their clothing was worn and shabby, much like the locals from that area.

They began to speak, but Mova and Laura were too far away to hear. With a snap of her fingers, Mova sent forth a small breeze, and a few seconds later, she began to catch their words.

"Just give up. Tell us where you've hidden them, and we'll let you go."

The woman didn't speak but instead turned and ran back into the woods.

"Oh, for the Goddess... catch her. Don't allow her to escape," shouted the man who had stepped forward. And without hesitation, the men chased after the woman with their pitchforks and shovels.

"Wait here," said Mova, turning to Laura. "I'm going to follow them. When it's clear, go and check on the girls over there."

"What," said Laura looking around nervously. "But..."

"It's fine. The men will be along shortly," said Mova, placing her hand on Laura's shoulder. "They will find their way here." And without another word, Mova turned and took off, following the crowd through the wooded area. With the help of the wind behind her, it didn't take her long to catch up to them as she darted between the trees while still keeping her distance from the group.

The robed woman shuffled between the trees trying to dodge the men before they finally caught up to her again. Digging her feet into the soft ground beneath her, she began frantically looking around at the men.

Mova quickly reached into one of her pockets and pulled out a small, tied pouch. Releasing the string that held it, she poured a small amount of gray ash into her hand. As her fingers began to glow, the ash lifted and was carried off into the air.

"No more running, Sister. You're coming back with us. And you're going to tell us where you've stashed those girls."

"I won't hand them over. They aren't yours anymore."

"They're not..." said the man in a tone of frustration as he rubbed the side of his face. "Just grab her. We're taking her back with us. We're leaving." The men all move forward, closing in on the circle they had formed around her.

"Excuse me, gentlemen," said Mova as she stood and stepped out of the shadows, making herself known to the men. "I don't think I can allow that."

"What?" said the man as they all turned toward Mova. "Who are you?" He then turned back to the robbed woman before making up his mind. "So, you had someone helping you this whole time?"

But the robbed woman just stared at Mova silently.

"Sorry, but you're wrong. I have nothing to do with this woman. I was camping nearby and heard you all chasing her, which led me here."

"You expect us to believe that? A woman," the man looked around, "out here, camping by herself," He shook his head as Mova watched the robbed woman place her hands over her nose. "Okay, enough, we won't be fooled again. Grab that one too, and let's... let's." The man's words trailed off for a moment before he started to wobble on his feet.

"Hey... hey, what's wr..." said another man before collapsing to the ground."

The leader of the men saw this and frowned. "Wha... what have you...," were his final words before passing out on the ground, followed by the rest of the men.

"There we go," said Mova as she cautiously stepped over one of the men's unconscious bodies toward the robbed woman. "Well, now, I think you and I should have a little talk."

A few minutes later, a bare-chested Saffron stood beside a similarly disheveled Dekol, alongside Laura and two small girls she had plucked out of the forest. He stood for a moment and raised his hand in the air. Then, feeling the breeze flow over his skin, he pointed to the left of them. "She's this way."

After traveling a short distance, Saffron saw Mova standing with her back against a tree with a robbed woman sitting down on a log in front of her. When the two girls beside Laura saw her, they broke away and ran to the woman, wrapping their arms around her.

"Thank you for bringing them back to me," she said.

"No worries. It was our pleasure to help."

"Are... are they dead?" asked one of the girls as she stared out at the bodies of the men on the ground.

"No," said the woman in a comforting tone, "they are just sleeping. This woman is a mage, and she put them to sleep."

Saffron surveyed the area, "You always were the more peaceful type. As a mage with the same affinity as me, I always wonder why you try to avoid fighting so much."

"You mean charging recklessly and foolishly into things we are rarely ever prepared for?" said Mova shaking her head. "No, I prefer not to be slathered in blood and soil and exhausted from fighting for my life. Especially after I've just had my bath."

"Suit yourself," said Saffron as he placed his boot on one of the unconscious men, rocking him back and forth. "It hardly seems sporting to dispatch them while they are like this. But it's not as if we are equipped to escort these men to the nearest town's barracks." Then, finally, he turned to the robbed woman. "Care to inform us why these men were chasing you three in the forest in the middle of the night."

Mova stepped forward, "She's escorting the girls to be members of the faithful. One of the girls is the daughter of a nearby lower-town noble. He had hired the men to retrieve them as they ran off."

Saffron looked at Mova with a raised brow but shrugged his shoulders, "Trying to escape from the grips of one's father then?" He stepped forward, patting one of the girls on the head. "Well, I suppose you couldn't have found a more stalwart ally than myself."

"So... so you won't make us go back then?" asked one of the girls, her disheveled hair dangling over her face.

"Of course not. In fact, as luck seems to have it, we are on our way to the city of the faithful. So, I see no reason we shouldn't escort you along the way." Saffron gave a glance to Laura. "That is, if my darling wife wouldn't object to us taking a small detour on our trip. It is her adventure, after all."

"What..." said Laura as Saffron gave her his attention. "No, I mean, of course not. I think... I think that would be the right thing to do."

"And thus, our adventure continues." Saffron rolled the unconscious man over with his foot. "How long will this lot be out? After learning that they are some lesser lord's somewhat loyal troops, I'd hate to be forced to explain who I am to them. Even if they would be unlikely to believe me, given our current attire."

"The dust should only last for another half hour or so before they begin to wake."

"Well, that seems like enough time to grab our things, adorn proper attire, and be on our way."

CHAPTER 17

Isha, Makeba, and Jacinta stood before the tree with Aukube, Leo, Caudbell, and Soulden standing behind them.

"Are... are you sure it's okay to use my magic now?" asked Isha as she looked nervously back at the group while holding up a white orb of light in her hands.

"Yes, enough time has passed. You should be ready now," said Aukube. "But Leo and I are here just in case. Now is the time for you to try."

"Yes, please do," said Caudebll. "I am eager to experience what this marking technique has done to augment the connection between you and your sisters. Your control seems to have improved. This is a recent development."

"Calm down, Caudbell," said Soulden with a frown on her face. "You seem more excited than the girls are."

"Of course, I am. And unlike last time, I simply cannot be forced to miss out on another development. The research is far too valuable."

"Come, sister," said Jacinta as she reached out, touching Isha's white orb of magic and absorbing it into herself. She laughed. "Oh, that feels funny."

"Jacinta!" yelled Isha. "How... That could have burned you. You didn't know-"

"Fascinating," said Caudbell. "She can take the magic wholly without the subject's permission."

"I know sister would never try to burn us. I trust her magic is the same now."

"But-"

"I wish to see Tree Sakari again. We have waited long enough. Let us go and fix her now."

"That's easy for you to say," said Isha as she glanced back at Leo. He seemed better, although his body was still wrapped in bandages. He gave her a smile, acknowledging that she should try.

Isha sighed. "Okay."

"Good," said Aukube. "You should not need to touch each other for you girls to feel each other's magic. So, Jacinta and Makeba, each of you girls, walk forward and place your hand on the tree. When you feel your sister's power, you should try to draw it in and push it into the tree."

"Will this really work?" asked Soulden. "Filtering her magic through those Sakari?"

"The tree seems to accept Sakari magic, but it is only a guess. Sadly, if it does not, I cannot think of anything else that will."

"So, we pretty much have no other choice," said Soulden, shaking her head. "Well, let's just hope, I guess."

"Go on, Isha," said Aukube. "Your sisters are ready."

Isha then stood still with her hands at her sides and balled her fingers into a fist. She closed her eyes and went into her mind again, trying to find a deeper strand of the magic. After such a time of purposely avoiding using her own powers, it took her a moment before she was back inside the dark place where streams of magic flowed freely around her. But eventually, she made her way there and found herself again in front of the spiraling orb of magic she had seen before. Hesitantly, she moved back away from it, remembering the sight of the other version of herself that was inside, how it had stared at her. Instead, she found her way towards the loose strands of magic floating nearby. Reaching out, she allowed the magic to entangle itself around her hands until she could feel it coursing through her.

"I have it," she said as she returned to reality, seeing her sisters with their hands on the tree, ready with anticipation. "Okay, here goes," she said, and with one final swallow of nervousness, she channeled the power into herself. Unlike before, where the power would well up inside her, she could now feel it pulling itself out of her.

Looking ahead, through her sister's clothing, she could see the tattoos on her sister's body. A surprise to her was that Jacinta and Makeba's markings had now turned white and were putting off the slightest glow from their bodies.

"Oh, it... it does feel weird having sister power," said Makeba as she stretched her shoulders.

"Yes, Sister," said Jacinta. "Come, let us try to heal Tree Sakari now."

There was a small moment of pause in the room as hope and anticipation swelled. Each of them looked up at the tree. One moment of nothing, then another, and another. Then came a breeze that began to rustle the dulled leaves of the neighboring smaller trees. The wind rattled them, lifting the leaves from their branches and sending them spiraling around the large tree. Some got caught in the girls' hair as they began to dance around the room.

The orange glow of the leaves began to fill the room, and the Trailage Tree started to shine an abundant light that highlighted the room.

"Well, it looks like something is happening," said

Soulden as she turned to Leo and Aukube. "Do you two see anything?"

"The tree is taking in the magic," said Aukube as she stared up into its branches, her eyes focused on the magic inside. "It is good, but it takes in a lot of magic, it seems. I worry about girls."

"Isha," said Leo, looking worried, as he stepped in beside her. "Are you okay? I can see the magic flowing around you; if you're tired, then..."

"No," said Isha, assuredly. "It feels weird. I can feel Jacinta and Makeba. I mean, I feel them taking the magic. But it... it doesn't hurt or anything."

"Okay, if you say so," said Leo, the worry on his face still ever-present as he turned toward Makeba and Jacinta, who were still forcing their magic into the tree. "What about you two? Are you still feeling well?"

"Yes," said Jacinta. "It not hard to use sister magic, but it feels funny like magic is there, but also it is not."

"No," said Makeba, "magic is there, just in different place. You need to hold it."

"What do you mean hold? You are not holding magic. You put magic into tree."

"No, you hold magic for tree."

As the two Sakari sisters bickered, a smile came across Leo's face. "Well, if they can argue like that, I guess they really are fine." He turned back to Isha. "What do they mean by holding magic? Do you store it up inside them?"

"I... I don't know. I mean... I don't think that's what I am doing. I'm just finding the magic and touching it."

"Touching?" said Leo with a raised brow. "We really need to progress your training in magic so you can understand exactly how your powers work."

"Yes," said Caudbell, chiming in. "Oh, on this, we agree. We simply cannot find the proper explanation with her limited vocabulary. Unfortunately, because so much has happened, your training's been lacking. But I will get with

Soulden and prepare something special for you three."

Isha grimaced.

"Hey, I see that look, young lady. This will be good for you. Every mage should learn how and why their powers work. Even the oddities like you."

"I guess," said Isha with a frown. "It's not that I don't..."

You hear me? I am feeling much better now. I am not feeling tired. I... feel awake.

Isha quickly began glancing around the room before looking up at the tree.

"Is something wrong?" asked Leo, noticing the confusion on her face.

"It's the tree... ah... she says she is starting to feel better now."

"Oh," said Leo, taking a look at the glowing tree. "Well, that's a good sign. You did say that you could talk to it. I remember you saying that you needed to touch it."

"I do... I mean, I used to. But I guess I don't anymore. Or maybe it works as long as one of us touches her."

"Well, let's ask," said Leo as he turned to Makeba and Jacinta. "What about you girls? Can you talk to the tree?"

"Yes, Makeba and I have been talking to Sakari Tree for a while now."

Leo turned to Isha, "Can you hear what they are talking about?"

"No. I never knew they were talking to her."

"I guess even your power has limits as to what it does. But, it's good that your new clothing has taken to your powers. I'd imagine it's quite a pain in the butt to be naked every time you want to cast that magic of yours."

"It is." Isha admitted as she thought back to her time in the hotel where Oscar had demanded that she give him a demonstration of her powers. "But using my powers on the tree never caused that to happen to my clothes."

"That may have been because of how fast the tree absorbed your magic," said Caudbell, rubbing his chin as he placed his other hand on the tree. "I was there for your display with the Queen. Even she could only absorb so much. But the Trailage Tree is probably the perfect receptacle for your ability. Especially now in its current state. As vast as it may be, your power may only be a drop in the bucket of what is needed to fully heal it."

"I never thought to check beforehand," said Leo. "But given how much you are giving it now; it does make sense."

"Is everything going to be—"

'Sister,' said Jacinta. "Tree Sakari wishes for you to visit."

Isha turned, looking up unsurely at Leo.

"Go on," said Leo with a smile. "We will have plenty of time to talk later. You should be with them now." He nodded to the Sakari girls ahead of them.

Isha turned back and began walking toward her sisters, joining them as she placed her hands on the tree's bark. She could feel the tree's warmth against her fingers as it took in the magic at the tip of her fingers. And with closed eyes, she found herself taken away. When she opened them, she again found herself inside the space the tree had made for them. But now, instead of mostly white foggy surroundings, the area had more of an orange accent that reminded her of the colors of the glowing leaves.

"Oh, sister, here now," came Jacinta's voice as an image of her began to appear alongside Makeba.

"Welcome, Isha," said Lonta`Mar, appearing beside her sisters, "I am happy that we get to meet again. I could see you but could not speak to you."

"Sorry,' said Isha, as she stepped forward to meet the girls, "I was told not to use my magic."

"Yes. Your sisters said you were sick," said Lonta'Mar, stepping forward and placing her hand on Isha's shoulder, looking worried. "Are you better now?"

"Yes, I… I think everything is okay now," said Isha as she began to look around. "Why does everything seem different now? Are you okay now? Will you be able to heal if we keep doing this?"

"Yes," said Lonta'Mar with a smile as she spun around. "I feel much better now. Before, I felt bad and did not feel the other trees. But now I feel much better. Cannot feel all the trees. But soon, I think I will."

"Good, I was worried that—" Isha's mind jumped back to what happened to her the last time she went inside the tree. She began to look at her hands. "Will... will I be okay being in now? I mean... last time I was here, it hurt me to be here."

"I... I do not know. But you may see," said Lonta'Mar as she waved her hand, and slowly in the air appeared the image of the girls outside the tree with Leo and Soulden looking worriedly over them. "Who man who looks over you? Is he the mate?"

"No," said Jacinta with a frown. "Isha not pick mate yet. Leo not bad man, but he weak and not warrior."

"He's not weak," said Isha, defending Leo reflexively before she realized it.

"She always protective of Leo," said Makeba with a smirk on her face.

"I'm not. And stop that. We're not here for that. We just need to make sure Lonta'Mar is okay."

"I think I shall be okay. I am feeling better. But, I think it will take much time before I feel like I was."

"That's good," said Isha, letting out a genuine sigh of relief. Looking around the area, she realized that even though she could see her body, she didn't feel anything. She made a fist, and even though she knew what it would feel like, she didn't feel her fist clenching. There was no breeze of air here. She didn't even feel the breath leave her body as she spoke. The feeling was similar to when she went inside herself and searched for her magic.

"What is wrong, Sister?" asked Makeba, taking notice of Isha's curiosity as she rubbed her fingers against themselves.

"Huh? Oh, it's nothing," said Isha, returning to her senses. "I was just thinking about this place. We haven't really been able to spend much time here. It reminds me of when I had to search for my magic. But it's really bright here."

"What sister mean?" asked Jacinta, confused. "It always bright when we go into magic land."

"Magic land? Is that what you call it? So, when you go inside ah… magic land, it's always bright like this?" Isha watched as her sisters and even Lonta'Mar all nodded. *Is Sakari magic different from mine? I never asked the others what their magic looked like.*

"Leo looking at us now,' said Jacinta, pointing her finger at the floating image above them. "It not good to make him wait long. He needs to heal like Tree Sakari."

The girls turned their heads to see Leo huddling back and forth between them with a nervous look on his face.

"I think we should head back now," said Isha to a sad-faced Lonta'Mar. "Oh, but it's okay now. We will be able to visit you a lot more now that everyone knows about you. Maybe even tomorrow."

"Really?" asked Lonta'Mar, the hope, and excitement in her voice matching the expression on her face. "Okay, I'll send you back now."

And with a gasp of breath, Isha found herself back into the world of the school, looking over to Leo, who was inspecting Jacinta, who, after she came back to reality, jumped at him wrapping her hands around his neck.

"We back. Leo get nervous for us."

"Ow," grunted Leo for a moment as he held Jacinta in his one good arm as she pressed herself against his mangled flesh. "Welcome… back. Are you girls okay? How do you feel?"

"Yes," said Soulden. "I remember hearing that you vomited blood the previous time you performed such an act."

Isha inspected herself, looking over her arms and taking deep breaths. "I think… I think I'm okay. I mean, I feel fine."

"That's good. But you were in there for around three hours," said Soulden.

Three hours. But it only felt like a few minutes.

"For the rest of the day, let's have you limit your magic. We still don't know the exact limits to what you can do, and we don't know exactly how much magic the tree took from you."

"Oh," said Isha upon hearing Soulden's words. "Can I ask a question about magic?"

"Of course. What is it?"

"It's about when we go inside to search for our magic. Is it bright in there?"

"Bright?"

"Yes, as if there is a lot of light around you."

"Well," said Soulden, placing her hand on her chin. "Yes, I imagine it is. I mean, I don't have any issue finding my magical core. But after years of using magic, you hardly need to look inside yourself to pull your magic out anymore." She turned her attention to Leo and Mr. Caudbell. "I imagine both you gentlemen are the same."

"Yes, my magical area is illuminated well."

"The same for me."

"What about seeing another you inside the magic orb? Is that normal?"

"Another you? No," said Soulden, looking down at Isha curiously. "Is that what you see when you venture inside of yourself?"

"Yes," said Isha with a nod of her head. "It's dark, and when I looked inside the magic, I saw another me inside."

"Amazing," said Caudbell. "I never considered asking you what it felt like when you ventured into your own magic." He placed his hand on his chin and began to pace back and forth. "I mean, who would? Even among other oddities, no one has reported any substantial differences while discovering their talents. But to see an image of oneself. That certainly is..." Caudbell stopped pacing, stepped back toward Isha, and leaned down to give her a close look. "Tell me, are you able to speak to this other version of yourself? Does she act the same as you, or is there a difference?"

"What? I... I don't know. I only looked once," said Isha, dropping her head. "I was... I was afraid to try again."

"Well, I imagine you would be," said Soulden in a soothing tone as she placed her hands on Isha's shoulder. "That must have been quite the shock. But that also is something we can look into later. For now, I'd like for you girls to rest. There's no need to solve all the world's mysteries today. So, Leo, if you would be so kind, please escort the girls back home and see that they are rested. We shall renew their efforts after you've inspected them and concluded that they are in fact, healthy enough to continue."

"We feel good, and sister not in trouble like last time," said Jacinta with a smile as she walked forward.

"Feeling fine and being fine are two very different things. Trust me, that's something you will become keenly aware of as you three get older," said Soulden as she began to lead the group out of the room. "You girls embrace the joys of your youth while it's afforded to you. None of us here are blessed with the immortality that the High Mother is graced with, so we must take care of ourselves."

CHAPTER 18

"Is that really all that has come to the table?" asked Oscar as he sat back in his chair, looking annoyed.

"Ah, yes, sir," said Amos, looking nervous."

"You had to assume this might happen," said Jacob with a laugh. "You did parade a group of stark-naked nobles through the streets of Orlana. It's easy to imagine that a fair amount of people would be hesitant to hire a group that would do that. But on the bright side, I think it also means your message to the other nobles was received perfectly. We haven't received any word of anyone going after my freshly crowned sister."

"Just because we haven't heard any word of it, does not mean there aren't plans. Fear only drives others to mask their intentions with caution. She's too valuable a tool to be used for those with power to not want to use her."

"You mean like you plan to?" asked Jacob with a knowing

look. "Tell me, what plans do you have for her when she gains proper control of those powers? As wonderful as it is to watch you play the doubting father, you always have something else in that head of yours."

"That's a question that can only be answered after she's gained control of her powers and we see exactly what she can do. Soulden said she could make any mage stronger. But is it one mage or one hundred mages at the same time? When that question is answered, I'll know what to do with her."

"Well, I can't imagine she'd get the same treatment as I did," said Jacob. "Whoring your son out to the noble women for coin wasn't exactly a very fatherly thing to do."

"We need to coin. And you knew the price when you became my son."

"That's true, but having her laid up with child most of her life doesn't seem fitting for your tastes."

"No. She'd be useless to me in that way. And there is no guarantee that her children would have that power of hers. I could end up wasting years of effort on that."

"Her effort or yours?"

There was a moment of silence as Oscar gave Jacob a look.

"Everything I do to or for that young one will be for her best interest, but I will not be kind about my way of doing it. This world isn't made for those of any type to be coddled. Or have you forgotten how she was found? Sold to be used by a magistrate for the exact thing you would accuse me of."

"Ahhh! Excuse me," said Amos, somehow managing to look even more nervous than before. "Should I leave or...."

"Yes," said Oscar in a harsh tone. "But go and report back to Pilgrim that we refuse his offer. Tell him we lack the manpower to deal with his discord with rival Dukes. Tell him to ask us for assistance in a real war. And take that new one with you: you can teach him how it is done."

"Ah. Yes, sir," said Amos before hurriedly leaving the

room.

"You seem more aggravated than usual," said Jacob. "I can't imagine my usual prodding has you this wound up. Are you feeling the burden of becoming a doting father, worrying about his daughter as she's run off to school?"

Oscar drummed his fingers across his lap, "Tell me, have you noticed something strange in the five kingdoms recently?"

"What do you mean? There hasn't been any uprising or..."

"No... I mean, like a feeling. The type of feeling you get when the world's about to change. Like when the Shadow King came into power. Originally there were eight Kingdoms. Then after the war with the Shadow King, there were only five. The land suddenly went from eight queens down to four and a king."

"That was before my time; and yours, for that matter. The only time I know of is now, and nothing seems different that I can think of."

"Really?" said Oscar. "Red crystals implanted in bodies by a religious cult. The child of a Queen lost out in the world. This Queen's Bane fellow killing nobles. And whatever Rana is. None of this seems strange to you?"

"I hardly think the death of a few nobles signifies such a great change. Dessi herself just recently killed a clan chief and the son of a Duke. The brother of whom now works for you under the pretense that it was done by someone else."

"A suggestion you brought forth and I granted after you pleaded with the sister. You may remember that the contract was for two dead brothers."

"I saw no reason to kill him when he could be of use to us. You, yourself just assigned him to a mission with Amos."

"I make use of the tools I have, even the ones I had no intention of ever having."

"Ever the practitioner my father is," said Jacob as he leaned back in his chair, rubbing at his forehead. Then came a knock at the door, and before the men could reply, it opened, and in came Dessi wearing the ornate outfit of a lady.

"I see you both are enjoying your father-son time."

"Dessi, since you've come, can you inform Father that he is paranoid?"

"About what?" said Dessi after grabbing a piece of meat from Jacob's plate and popping it in her mouth.

"He seems to think the world around us is changing, as if the five kingdoms will be torn down tomorrow."

"Tomorrow might be a bit of a stretch, but something certainly is happening. Most of the noble ladies in town have been whispering about it. How no one noble wants to make any waves with the other, in fear of not knowing what side they should be on when it all happens."

"Well, it's nice to know my son can at least pick an intelligent woman. Despite not being able to be a man of observation himself."

"Hey," said Jacob. Looking offended at Dessi, "I thought your job was to support m.,"

"I will," said Dess, "when I think you're right. It just so happens that at this moment, I don't." She patted Jacob on the shoulder. "Now come along. You're needed to give Amos some words of encouragement."

"I am?"

"Of course. It seems your father here has tasked him to spend days and nights alone on the road with a fellow who he feels might just be after his chastity. I think the poor boy feels his virtue is in jeopardy."

Jacob frowned, "Why must I be the one to comfort him?"

"Because it was your idea to wreck my well-thought-out plans for your own selfish reasons. Now, it's your responsibility to ensure that all of that wasn't simply wasted effort."

"Well spoken," said Oscar with a grin. "The boy must clean up his own messes."

"I see why father never felt the need to adopt you," said

Jacob with a sigh as he stood. "What's the need when you both are already so similar." He shrugged his shoulders. "Alright, where's the lad?"

"He was down by the well outside last I saw him. I'm sure he hasn't gone far."

"I'll be on my way then," said Jacob with a reluctant smile as he gave Dessi a kiss and headed out of the door."

"Perhaps I'll take a peek," said Dessi with a smirk. "This may indeed be worth watching."

"Leave the boy to take care of his mess," I have a job for you."

"Again? Do you not think that perhaps you might send someone else? You do realize that I don't have that magical endurance that Jacob or Isha have."

"I've already sent Friva ahead of you. You're going to mean up with her. So I, in fact, did send someone else."

"Oh," said Dessi, biting her lip. "But before that, I have a question about Isha."

"And what might that be?"

"When she's done with all that magical training, tell me what you intend for her. You avoided the question last time. But now I think I want an answer, given that we just sent her back to that school."

Oscar eyed Dessi for a moment before nodding his head. "The magical training is just a start. She'll have control, but she won't really know the taste of battle. After a year or so, I plan to give her to Addison or maybe Rahila. They trained you and a few others, so I see no reason not to continue that trend."

"So, after pawning her off on Soulden, you wish to pawn her off on those two."

"I take it you have a better suggestion unless you wish to train the girl yourself, and we both saw how that ended."

"No. I'm saying that a lot happens there that you aren't aware of. Many nights crying alone in my room, my fingers bloody and my skin raw. Yes, I learned a lot, but that doesn't mean I didn't suffer. And that girl has already been through so much, and you don't know much is left before it breaks her."

"She's tough. The girl can handle it, the same as you did."

"I didn't handle it," said Dessi, her voice raising louder than she intended. "Don't you see that? You don't know how many nights Jacob spent trying to fix me from what they did to me down there."

Oscar was quiet for a movement. "Then, do you have a better solution?"

"No! I just," she shook her head, "you once said that the reason you never accepted me as a daughter is because you had already failed me. Well, if that is the case, then learn from it. Don't fail her as well. Care for her better than you did for me."

He tapped his fingers over the desk. "If I said I'd consider it, would we be able to move on from this conversation?"

"Fine," said Dessi, shaking her head and taking a seat in the chair that Jacob was previously in. "What am I needed for?"

"Information. I've got people in different areas, but it's not enough. When whatever happens does happen, I'd prefer not to be caught in it."

"Given the state of things, I would say that's impossible. The people are on edge with the murders happening in the kingdoms. I heard that Queen's Bane fellow uses shadow magic. Do you think that's something? "He goes around calling himself the one true king. I remember hearing stories about another shadow user from the past that claimed something like that."

"Yeah, the Shadow King. But unless you start seeing walking corpses covered in shadows, then it's just another random shadow mage. They're still a few of those running around."

"I don't remember you ever trying your hand at getting

one. We've run across a few, but you've always kept them at a distance. Seems like a type that would be useful, given what you're involved in. And maybe I wouldn't be so overworked."

"We're all overworked. You're just not around enough to see it."

"And whose fault do you think that is?" said Dessi as she slid down into the seat, her body beginning to feel exhausted. "Oh well. No use fighting it any longer. But I still expect a hefty payment. Your son chose an expensive woman."

Jacob made his way down the steps of the building and through the front doors to the city's streets. Then, taking a few quick steps, he made his way to the side of the building, where he saw a few men by the well, but not Amos. But after a quick glance around, he found the boy sitting alone by the bench with something in his hand. Stepping closer, he could see that Amos had his father's carving knife and was doing a terrible job creating whatever he was making.

"That's a focused face you are making there. Are you perhaps going to be leaving us and picking up the woodworking trade?" asked Jacob, nodding to the disfigured piece of wood.

"No, sir. Your father, I mean the captain, has been teaching me," said Amos shaking the piece of wood in his hand. "I'm no good at it, though. Things never turn out well."

"Give it time. Nothing's ever easy in the beginning. And you'll get plenty of time to practice on your way back to Duke Pilgrim. And Henry should be good company. You are both around the same age, so you'll have much to discuss."

"I doubt that," said Amos with a shake of his head.

"What? You two not getting along?"

"No... it's not... I mean... He likes... well, you know... he likes men."

"Yes... you're afraid you're going to fall in love with him?

I wonder if you're his type."

"What? No! I most certainly am not?"

"Are not to which one? That he likes you or you liking him?"

"Wha... ba-ba... both."

"Then I see no reason why you two can't work well together."

"But the other men. Ever since the captain has assigned me to look after him, they... they've been spreading rumors about me. About how I... I...." Amos grimaced, "About how I liked being buggered."

"Yeah, I got that for a while myself."

"You did?"

"You haven't been with us long enough to have known him, but I once had a friend who preferred male companionship. So, I got the same treatment you're getting now."

"And what did you do?"

"Oh, we'd argue and fight, either each other or whomever father pitted us against on the battlefield. But he'd always say that I'd stop caring about who he went to bed with after he'd saved my life a couple of times."

"And did you? Stop caring, I mean?"

"Yeah, I did. He was right about that," said Jacob with a smile. "When you're bloody and beaten on your back looking up at the sky as war rages around you, you really don't care much about who saves your life."

Amos gave Jacob a frown. "That's your way of telling me to just do it, isn't it?"

"Not mine. I'm just telling you a story. How you live, your life is up to you."

Amos sighed before standing up from the bench, looking around, and spotting Henry, who was now over by the well. He then took a deep breath. "Well, I'll be on my way then," and he made his way through.

A moment later, Jacob felt a hand pat him on the back as Dessi stepped in beside him to give him a kiss.

"Are you done giving your words of encouragement to poor Amos? The daring tales of love between two impressionable military boys," said Dessi with a chuckle.

"Ha-ha," said Jacob as he walked back over to the door of the building. "He reminds me of myself not too long ago. And if I remember, you weren't too keen on Mallory, yourself."

"Well, that was because he had a crush on you. He always used to pick fights."

"Yeah, you two never did get along. He said he would argue with you 'til his dying day. Seems he was right about that," said Jacob, as he picked up his sheathed blade beside the door. "He was right about something else too."

"Oh, and what's that?"

"That I would one day be happy to grab ahold of his sword," he then held the blade out for Dessi to see. "Although, I doubt this was the one he had in mind."

Dessi giggled, "Well, since we are talking about swords, come with me for a moment. Your father has pissed me off and given me a new mission. So, I'd like your opinion on something."

"Oh?" asked Jacob with a smirk. "And what's that? What special assignment has the old man wrapped us in this time?"

"Not us, just me," said Dessi as she led Jacob into the building and up the first flight of stairs. "But it's nothing too dangerous this time; just gathering intel from Mari."

"The last time, it was nothing dangerous I found you half-dead in a forest with a small child in your arms."

"That's part of the job. What's wrong? We've patched each other up before. The Goddess has seen me sit at your bedside plenty of times. Remember after Duvall? I was afraid you'd lose your leg."

"I remember," said Jacob with a frown as he entered the room and began looking around. "What do you need me for? You want to talk about the..." He turned around to have Dessi press a finger over his lips.

"No, I said I needed you. If I'm going to be gone on this dangerous mission for a while, I think it'll be nice to have as many memories of you as possible before I go."

"I thought you said it wasn't dangerous."

"You never know what could happen. Better safe than sorry."

"Dessi," said Jacob with a sigh as he stepped back. "You know I want to, but..."

"I know," said Dessi, interrupting him as she stepped forward, not allowing him to gain distance from her. "I know what's going to happen, and I'm saying it's okay. And to be quite honest, after dealing with Oscar, I need this."

"Was it that bad?"

"Bad enough."

"You know what will happen. Every time we try, it always ends the same."

"Better to try and regret than not have you at all. And who knows, maybe you can control it now. Have you been practicing?"

"And how am I supposed to practice that without you?"

"Oh," said Dessi with a smirk as she placed her hands on Jacob's chest, pushing him backward and causing him to fall on the bed, looking back up at her. "So, you do need a bit of practice then." She climbed on the bed as he lay there, straddling him. "All you needed to do was just ask." She smiled as she placed her hand on his midsection, finding the space between trousers and vest, and began roaming her fingers across his stomach.

"Now you know that's not... emm," moaned Jacob as Dessi's fingers found their way from the softness of his belly to the ever-growing hardness of the mound of heat between his legs.

"Oh, it does look like you're ready for some practice after all," she said as she methodically rubbed her thumb against his cock. Playfully but tightly, she allowed her finger to stroke it as she leaned down on top of him, looking him in his eyes as she could see and feel his frustration building. The way his body tensed, the slight bite of his lip, she knew exactly the right buttons to push. "I guess we could stop here, and I could find... ohhhh!"

In an instant, Dessi found Jacobs's arms wrapped around her as she spun around in a flurry of hair and soft bed linens. Then, before she realized it, she found herself in the opposite position, flat on her back with Jacob above. His breathing was deep. She could see his chest heaving through his shirt, his eyes narrowing as he began to look her over. The longing in his eyes seemed ever more apparent as the seconds grew between them.

His hands found their way to the corners of her waist. As they followed the curvatures, the caress of his fingers caused her to give out a small moan as she arched her back in need of him. Only to then feel herself pressed firmly against the bed as he lay on top of her, his lips against the side of her neck as his other hand made its way through the strands of her hair, then finally gripping the back of her head, she gasped at the sensation of his lips pressing hard against hers. The familiar smell of a mix of sweat and dried leather soaked into his skin. She'd quickly come to prefer this smell over the smell of all the lords' manors. The only aroma that pleasured her now, was his.

He pulled his hands off and lifted himself from her body while gazing down at her. It was there she could see it, at the corner of his eyes, a hint of blue magic. And behind it was worry, hesitation, and just a small amount of fear... for her. But as his hands trembled at her side, she knew he was barely controlling his longing... his longing for her. She smiled while reaching her arm up, placing a gentle hand against the side of his face.

"You aren't going to stop now, are you?" she asked with a smirk. "I thought you…" she took in a deep gasp of surprise as Jacob grabbed the sides of her shirt, ripping the cloth free of its bindings, sending the flimsy buttons that once held the garment flying across the room and exposing her breasts to him. "Ah, that was new. Your father's going to have to buy me another."

CHAPTER 19

Inside a well-furnished house in the kingdom of Mari, Victor stood in his kitchen overlooking a piece of meat as it sizzled on top of a pan. The savory aroma filled the atmosphere of the home as Victor made his way through the kitchen. As if called by the temptation of food, Silk appeared on the steps wearing the nightgown of what was probably the lady of the house. She was again wearing the appearance of the blonde woman instead of herself.

"Isn't it our job to cook for you?" she asked as she came over with a smile, standing beside him and looking down at the food.

"I think you've been spending too much time around the noblewoman," said Victor as he leaned down, giving her a kiss. "And why are you wearing that look again? Is it that hard to be yourself even when we're alone?"

"It's not that... I mean... I know you don't mind my

appearance. It's just... I think it will take some time before I'm used to it; being around you and not feeling odd. But in time, I will. For now, this just feels better."

"As long as you don't think I prefer this you over the real you, then it's fine. And when we're in bed," he patted Silk on the bum, "I much prefer the other you."

"I always thought that if I ever found someone, they would enjoy the fact that I could wear other bodies. I mean, aren't men like that?"

"Many are..." his face twisted in thought. "Okay, maybe most are. But if you want to try that later, perhaps. But I won't have our life together start with you wearing other faces."

"I understand," said Silk with a laugh. "You two are so different."

"Who?"

"You and Frenka. You can't just say what you want, and that's all Frenka ever says."

"And you are there to bring us balance," Victor skewered a small piece of meat, lifting it near Silk's lips. "Here, taste this and tell me what you think. I added a few different spices."

Silk blew on the meat once before taking it in her mouth. "It's swooot," said Silk with a smile and her mouth full.

"Good, I was hoping you would like the taste. But unfortunately, I still don't know much about you. And we still have a few..." before Victor could finish his words, there was a knock at the door. "And it seems I never will." Victor dropped his head before giving a sigh and heading for the door as he heard Silk give a giggle. To his surprise, he felt a sense of happiness as he placed his hands on the door handle.

"Well, it's about time," said Coral as Victor opened the door to him. "How long do you expect a man to wait outside his home? Have you no decency?"

Victor chuckled at seeing his friend in the chilly morning

air before stepping to the side and letting him in. "You were supposed to be on your way to the country with the wife and kids. Why are you even still here? And you could have just entered. Don't you have a key to your own home?"

"I do," said Coral. "But what type of friend would I be to burst in on your honeymoon without the proper invitation?"

"The kind of friend who's doing just that right now,"

"Yes, well. At least I have the courtesy to knock," said Coral before his nose cleared and he took in the fresh scent of Victor's cooking. "Oh, someone made breakfast. I don't suppose you'd spare a meal for a friend in need, who you so haphazardly put out on the street."

Victor chuckled as he walked over and patted his friend on the shoulder. "Why not? You used to eat all my damned food before anyway. Silk, would you mind if my friend here joined us for breakfast?"

"No, of course not. I'll fix him a plate."

"Hello there," said Coral. "Silk is an interesting name.

"Yes. I get told that sometimes."

"So... what happened to your grand entrance back home? Decided that the capital was too hard for you to leave?" asked Victor as he and his friend took a seat at the table.

"Ha! Not in this lifetime. It just so happens that her royal highness sent a shipment of sucking-up wine to the Dukes of the lower region. And room for one of her loyal subjects, be they in the military or not, wasn't something they could not accommodate. So instead, I leave on the morrow when the next ship leaves for Ravenholm, and from there, I'll acquire a horse and make the day's trip home."

"Well, I'm sure that wine was very important."

"Fuckin' hell it was. And now I'll be days late on my way home."

"Sorry to hear about your trip," said Silk as she placed a place of warm food in front of Coral. "Hopefully, you will be on your way soon," said Silk with a smirk and a suggestive look.

"Oh, don't worry, Miss I know where I'm not wanted," he said as he took a moment to gaze up at Silk. "But since I am here. Victor, aren't you going to introduce me to your lovely wife? You shouldn't go hiding such a lovely lady from the world. Tell me, have you and Victor decided on how many children you plan to have?"

"Children?" asked Silk with a hint of surprise before she glanced back at Victor. "We haven't talked about that, actually. But I wouldn't mind, I don't think."

"A topic for another time," said Victor, happily willing to change the topic of discussion before looking at his friend and then back at Silk. *Not the time, old friend. Although, if I could tell anyone, It would be this idiot.* "Actually, you do have a point. I think it is time I introduced you to my wife. But first, I have to tell you something else."

"Oh, yeah?" said Coral before picking up a piece of meat with his finger and popping it into his mouth. "What's it about? Another super-secret mission from the Queen?"

"Somewhat. The Queen is pregnant. If my memory serves me, her baby should be along in the coming month."

"Well, congratulations to her royal pain in the ass. What poor Duke did she end up with? Probably someone from the Bervillian family. Everyone knows they've been trying to get closer to the Queen." He scooped up another piece of meat, taking it to his lips.

"It's mine. The Queen will be having my baby, unfortunately."

The piece of meat in Coral's hand dropped to the floor as he turned to look at his friend. His face twisted before slowly reaching out and grabbing Victor by the collar. "Why, have you gone mad?"

"What do you mean, why? You know my situation. I couldn't control myself."

"No, with your wife, you're not supposed to be able to control yourself. But the Queen, really? Do you just like punishment?"

"Sometimes it seems that way. But just stop. I just told you because I knew you wouldn't tell anyone."

"Well, of course not. And who would I tell even if I could? I'd either be locked away or laughed out of the kingdom." Then his eyes opened wide. "What... what about your wife? Is she in danger being here like this? You can't just have her here and have the Queen accept it."

"Victor and I have come to an understanding with the Queen, there is no need for worry."

"Understanding? Does the Queen even know what that means? Seriously, Victor. I don't like the idea of you putting your new wife in a situation like this."

"Rest assured, old friend, she is safe here. If anything, I'm the one in danger."

Coral then turned to look at Silk. "And you are okay with this?"

"I am. It is the choice I have made. And I am happy here with Victor."

Coral shook his head, closing his eyes for a moment before finally sighing. "Okay, fine. So apparently, you are going to have a princess for a daughter. A plan, I think, puts you both in danger. Is there anything else you wish to surprise me with? I might as well die of a heart attack while you are out here giving me unneeded stress."

"Well, since you are so willing, Silk, could you show my friend who you are?" said Victor with a smile. "Who you really are."

"What?" asked Silk, blinking in confusion before looking back at Coral. "Are you... are you sure?"

"With him, yes. This man would die for me. In fact, he has tried, twice if I recall."

"Yeah, well, don't go making a habit of having me sacrifice myself for your hide. Remember, anything happens to me, and you're the one who will look after my children along with that little upcoming princess." Coral just shook his head before popping another piece of meat into his mouth. "I swear if I had never met you. My life would be as peaceful as a spring-filled morning."

Victor gave a playful grin towards Silk. "If you don't mind, my wife. But I think it would be nice for you to have more people whom you can trust, and despite his dimwitted appearance, I trust no man more."

"Backhanded compliments are still hurtful, you know," said Coral as he pointed his finger at Victor.

"No, I don't mind. I trust you," said Silk.

"Just what are you two talking ab..." Coral's eyes went wide as Silk's form changed before him. The sounds of soft popping as she stretched her shoulders. The nightgown that she seemed to fill out before was now over a more petite woman. Her ruby and emerald eyes stared out of a skin that appeared to be made of the whitest powder. "Wha... wha... wha."

"Oh, honey, I think you've taken his breath away. I told you your natural appearance was your most beautiful."

Coral slid his chair from beneath him, knocking it over as he stood up from the table, taking a step back. "Is this... is this some kind of illusion ma... Wait, no. You said natural appearance. Victor, what's going on?"

"Sergeant Coral Dolphif, my dearest friend, I would like to introduce you to my actual wife, an ex-assassin, blessed with the ability to change her body into the form of anyone she pleases."

"Assassin? You mean... But you.... But how?"

"Oh, she tried to kill me, and we fell in love."

"I did not try to kill you. I protected you, remember?" said Silk with a solemn face.

"My apologies. She protected me from another killer. Remember the assassin I asked you to look into? Well, this is the one who stopped it. And now we're married. Although I must admit, I'm a bit surprised by your response. Given what we've been through, you must have known that something like this would happen."

"Something like this? Who can predict something like this?" said Coral as he made his way back to the table, staring intently at Silk while rubbing his chin in contemplation. "And… you naturally have this appearance?"

"Ah, yes. This is who I am," said Silk, looking a bit bashful as the man's eyes began to look her over.

"Amazing," said Coral, "I knew you would find yourself a special woman, but goodness me. Who could have predicted this special? Tell me, what attracted you to my idiotic friend?"

"What?" asked Silk, looking confused. "You… you're not afraid of me."

"Afraid? Of Victor's wife? Madam, if I were to be afraid at this point, I would have no right to call this man my friend. Has he ever told you the story of when he had us fighting trees that could uproot themselves?"

"What? Is that true?"

"In a way. It was a form of illusion magic placed on our platoon during my time in the field."

"Illusion or not, it felt real enough," said Coral, crossing his arms over his chest. "Tell me then, how does it work? What does it feel like to transform your whole body? You seemed to get smaller. So, can you become as tall as a house or as small as a baby?"

"No, it's a strain to go taller or shorter than I am now. The more I go, the harder it gets. As for what it feels like… Oh, let me see your wrist," said Silk as she reached out for Coral's arm.

"No, no, no, no," said Coral as he quickly jumped back. "I was just curious, is all."

Silk looked in surprise as he jumped back from here. "Oh… I'm sorry I… I should have asked first," said Silk with a shamed look down at the floor. Which caused Victor to give his friend a suggestive look of his own.

"What? Oh no, it's not like that, ma'am," said Coral in a

quick attempt to apologize. "I was just a little surprised, is all. And I've always been jumpy like that. You can ask my wife when you meet her. It took six months before I would allow her to touch me."

"Yes, I do remember you having quite a bit of trouble while courting her," said Victor in agreement.

"See. So, I think you and Victor are having a much better start than I was. Tell me, what do you like so much about him?"

"Huh?" blurted out Silk, snapping out of her depression and beginning to think as she turned back to look at him. "Well, he is nice, and he treats me well. And he's smart." Silk patted her wrist as she struggled to think of the proper words.

"Those are as good a reason as any I've ever heard," said Coral with a smile. "You don't need some grand message from the Goddess to love someone. You just need to know when being around someone feels a whole lot better than being away from them."

"Is that your years of experience talking?" asked Victor.

"Nah, just good old-fashioned common sense."

Then came the sound of a yawn and the creaking of wooden beams as Frenka came down the stairs in a similar nightgown to the one Silk was wearing.

"Oh, and who's this now?" said Coral, watching closer as Frenka made her way downstairs. "Did you hire a maid to care for you both on your honeymoon, or is this just another assassin you've managed to pick up?"

"Frenka is no maid," said Frenka as she walked over beside Silk and Victor. She gave Silk a kiss on the cheek before giving Victor a kiss on the lips. "Who is this man, husband?"

"Husband?" asked Coral with a squinted eye as he looked at the three.

"Coral," said Victor. "Allow me to introduce you to my other wife. Her name is Frenka. I do believe I did inform you that I had two wives."

"You did? I mean… I thought you were joking. I… I think I need a seat," said Coral as he picked up his overturned chair and walked back over to the table, sitting down again. "And you're all okay with this, Miss Silk?"

"Me? Why ask me?"

"Who else would I ask?" said Coral, throwing his hands up. He then glanced around the table before placing his head in his hands. "Perhaps you're right. My friend here seems to have switched allegiances to the Kingdom of Lunacy. I imagine he will have more wives the next time I see him."

"Maybe another wife would be good for husband," said Frenka, rubbing Victor on his chin and looking into his face lovingly. "But one who waits at home. Maybe not killer. One to look after the children we will have."

"I have enough, thank you," said Victor, shaking his head. "I'm not even entirely sure I'm ready for this with you two. Let alone the thought of having children. Which I will apparently have soon." He then turned to Coral. "You know, having someone I can talk to about this feels refreshing. And I can have you babysit my daughter."

"To the Goddess, I will. How much of this do you plan to drag me into?"

"The same as our days on the battlefield. So, I'd say all of it. You are in it now, old friend. There shall be no rest for either you or me."

"Did you forget I have my own kids and, hence, my own problems? How selfish can you be?"

"Husband will do fine," said Frenka, taking a seat in Victor's lap. "I would not choose the weak man who could not."

"Seems like you're going to have your hands full, Victor," said Coral with a chuckle as he stood up from the table. "Now more surprises. I want out of this madhouse. So, what's the next mission? If I know the Queen, she already has some other place to send you."

"Us and Queen have come to understand each other," said Frenka. "But sadly, myself and Sister-wife, we will go soon. Off to Ursjun and husband, off to another city."

"Yes, I was made aware of some sort of understanding. And to be honest, that sounds like her. But why Ursjun? We're not starting another war, are we?"

"Nothing that serious, just the acquisition of a resource."

"And that is his way of saying that he doesn't want to tell me. Which, at this point, I must admit I'm a bit grateful for. Keep the rest of your secrets. I don't want to hear anymore."

"Really?" said Frenka, "You not want to stay longer?"

"I get it. I know where I'm not wanted. Even if it is in my own house. I'll stay at an inn tonight and head out tomorrow."

"You could just stay here. It's not like you don't have extra rooms."

"And hear whatever you three are getting up to at night? No. Your friend, I may be, but that does not lift me above the emotion of jealousy. An inn will do me fine. I still have a few things I can take care of before I go." Coral gave the ladies a bow. "Come on, see your old friend out, won't you?"

Frenka lifted herself from Victor's lap as he left for the door with Coral, closing it behind them when they were outside.

"Everything all right?" asked Victor. "You were jumpier in there than I expected you to be."

"Yeah, well. How could I not be? That was a lot to throw at a person all at once," said Coral as he just stared out over the city. "Victor, that ashen-skinned assassin, the one you called Silk, I think I've heard of her before."

"Really? I've never come across such tales."

"That's because you never looked. I'm not sure how many she's killed. But it's a lot. And what about her handler? I'm not sure the people who own her will just be willing to let you take her away."

"Yeah… I get your point," said Victor as he began rubbing the bridge of his nose between his eyes in frustration. "You know, you're not supposed to be the voice of reason. That's usually my job."

"Given your situation now, I'd say you've been failing at your job for quite some time."

Victor glanced back at the house. "I suppose that's a fair point. Perhaps I'll be able to negotiate the release of her. I have a fair bit of money saved up."

"From the type of people who kill people for money? Is this really the great Victor Krill, the one known as the great tactician, saying these words?"

"Okay, okay. I get it," said Victor, dropping his head and raising a hand to stop his friend from berating him more. "You're right. But what do you want me to do? I'm not sending her back to that. Not after everything she's been through. The girls clutched onto me with every bit of hope she has left."

"And, of course, it's your job to shelter her."

"It is. I'm making it my job," said Victor, his tone harsher than he expected it to be.

Coral sighed, "All right, I'll see what I can do then."

"What? You're going to help? After complaining about how dangerous it is?"

"Of course. I also have a vested interest in seeing the great Victor Krill struggling through married life," said Coral as he turned to go. "Just remember you've chosen this life and everything and everyone that comes with it. I hope you're prepared."

"I hope so too," whispered Victor under his breath as he waved goodbye to his friend.

CHAPTER 20

Isha sat on the floor of Heart House in her school uniform with her legs crossed. In front of her sat five small plants in potted vases, each with different color leaves. To the left of her sat Leo. His body and half of his face were still bandaged as he watched over her. And at the table behind her sat her sisters as they read a textbook.

"Why do I have to do this?" asked Isha as she outstretched out her hand toward the plants, trying to send her magic into them. "I thought they said I wasn't a healer."

"No, they said they don't know what you are, other than you can make other mages stronger. You may also have the ability to heal."

"Sister Isha will heal the trees like she does the Tree Sakari?" asked Jacinta, looking up from her book.

"That's the idea," said Leo with a nod. "And since you've fallen behind on your studies, I'm going to make sure we find out what you can and can't do. And not just me; I've informed the other teachers as well. You girls will be put in a hard crash course on magic."

"I still don't understand what I'm supposed to do," said Isha as a stream of white magic left her finger and began wrapping around one of the small plants.

"I've clipped some of the branches of those trees. We are just going to see how it reacts to your magic. Nature is magic in itself. It will take what it needs from the environment around it to heal itself. That includes strands of stray magic that..."

Suddenly the plant in front of Isha burst into flames as she yelped, sliding herself backward away from it. Leo quickly grabbed a nearby bucket and placed it over the tree, smothering the fire.

"Wha... wha... Did I do something wrong?"

"No. It just seems the tree... wasn't able to make proper use of the magic," said Leo with a cough as he fanned away the small amounts of smoke on his face. "It's why I've set up different types of trees for you to practice on. So don't worry yourself too much over..."

A knock at the door interrupted their training.

"Come in," he said with another cough. "And leave the door open."

The door swung open and inside stepped Chloe, also wearing her school uniform and carrying a bag. She fanned at the smoke as she covered her nose.

"What happened?"

"Nothing. Just a small house fire," said Leo as he clapped his hands together. "Okay, girls, off to class with you. I'll be in my office later today. Come see me there after class if you want."

"Wait," said Chloe as she stepped over and handed Leo the bag she had with her.

"What's this?"

"My clothing, I was told I could start staying here now."

"You were?" asked Leo's as he looked over at the girls. "I guess we do have the room. So there shouldn't be a problem."

"Thank you. I had intended to move in before, but so much has happened. I still have a few things I need to get."

"Sure. I guess the more, the merrier, and it will be good to have smiling faces around. And that will give me more opportunities to properly inspect your arm. I'll get you a room ready, so go on and head off to class."

"Okay," said Chloe as she walked to the door, stepping outside.

The other three girls gathered their things and headed out the door, joining Chloe in the street with the rest of the students.

"Why Chloe still wrapped?" asked Jacinta looking down at Chloe's arm. "Leo say he fix you."

"I am... I mean he did... It's just that the skin is still sensitive, especially to the air up here. It just feels better to leave it wrapped for now."

"Can you do magic now?" asked Makeba. "Won't wrappings make it hard?"

"I can... sort of, but it's becoming easier the more I practice."

The girls made their way into the castle, following the crowd of students as they made their way through the woodland halls. The forestry of the building seemed lusher now. The leaves seemed brighter, and the roots that flowed through the walls had a green mossy look rather than the dull brown from before. So, they walked until they finally reached Mr. Higgins' class. The class was typical, with all the students talking amongst themselves. But standing over in a corner was an assortment of weapons that adorned the back wall.

"Hey guys," said Freedo as he walked up, holding a wooden sword in his hand. "We're going to start playing with weapons today." He began waving the small wooden sword around before pointing it at Makeba. "I'm going to show you how strong I am."

"You not strong, but I think I will teach you how to fight," said Makeba as she walked forward, grabbing Freedo by the hand and leading him off towards a corner of the room.

"I go to. Other friends are there," said Jacinta before she made her way through the room.

"Alright, you little babies, today's the day we start official combat training and where I'll teach you how to defend and attack using more than just your fists and rubber balls," said Mr. Higgins as he glanced back at Isha and Chloe. "So all of you, go over to that wall and pick out a weapon you like. They're all made of wood, so you won't end up killing each other."

Along with the rest of the class, Isha and Chloe made their way over and began looking over the weapons rack. There were swords, shields, long sticks, wands, and many things Isha had never seen before. One was just a large round wooden ball that she couldn't understand how it was used as a weapon. She reached for one of the sticks, weighing it in her hand.

"Are you going to be using a staff as your magical weapon," came a familiar from behind her.

Isha turned around, still holding the stick, to see Pavel smiling back at her. He was followed by the same boy and girl that seemed to follow him everywhere.

"No. Jacinta is good at using sticks. She and Makeba train with them back at ah... home. But I'm not really good at using them."

"That's no problem. Have you decided what you are going to use?"

"What? No... I'm still trying to decide. I just picked this one up first, is all."

"I'm thinking of using the sword," said Pavel as he picked up one of the wooden sticks. "Everyone back home uses one, so I think I've just gotten used to holding one."

"Do you know what this one is for?" asked Chloe as she lifted the wooden orb from the floor, holding it against her chest.

"I think that's a Soil Orb. It's something only mages who control Soil Magic can use. I think they fill that with magically enhanced dirt and can control it and send it flying through the air."

"Oh," said Chloe, looking a little disappointed. "I guess this would be something Makeba or Jacinta would use then."

"I don't know," said Pavel. "Those two seem pretty good at those little blades they carry around."

Isha turned toward Makeba, who was over in a corner with Freedo playing with sticks and her mind drifted back to when they met, and they insisted on teaching her the game Krump. But that ended up being more of a torture method than a game.

"Both Makeba and Jacinta will do what they like," said Isha as her eyes drifted back down to the floor, scanning over the other random trinkets that were supposed to be weapons until she saw two circular-shaped pieces of wood with a strap linking the two.

"Alright, you little babies, pick out your weapons and bring your butts over here and line up," said Mr. Higgins, standing in the middle of the floor.

The students followed his order, grabbing their items and making their way over with Isha holding the circular wooden disks by the strap linking them.

Why did I pick this one? I don't know what it does. Isha began to look around at all the other students. Chloe stood next to her, holding two short sticks. And down from here were her sisters. Jacinta held two short wooden blades, much like the ones she'd seen her use before. Makeba, to her surprise, was holding one of the large wooden orbs between her arms. *I guess she did find the one that wasn't meant for Krump.* Next to Makeba, she could see Freedo holding a bigger sword than before that seemed too long for him.

"Okay, to start off, we will have people with similar weapons face each other. All of you find yourselves a weapons partner to square off with. Swords with swords, polearms with polearms, and whatnot." Mr. Higgin's clapped his hands together once again. "Come on, move it." The children shuffled around the floor, pairing up as instructed until only Isha and a few other students had chosen weapons that no one else had. Even Makeba, who had selected the orb, had found herself a partner in Marlene, who had done the same.

"Alright. The weapons you're holding will be your weapon for the next week. After which time, if you feel that it does not suit you, you will be allowed to change. Until then, become acquainted with your weapons and the partners before you. So start practicing now; the formal training will start tomorrow after I assign you your instructors."

As the sounds of sticks being beaten against each other rang throughout the room, Mr. Higgins turned to the few that had chosen weapons that no one else had. He rubbed his chin as he looked over the students. There were four altogether, all of whom were girls. Isha noticed that one of the girls was Serpene. She was holding a small stick that housed two orbs on either side. The other two girls both had old weapons. One was a rope with pieces of wood sticking out of it, and the other looked to be just a box.

I didn't notice that one before. I wonder what's inside.

"Every year, there's always a few that pick the odd weapon or two. So, there's four of you this time, aye?" asked Mr. Higgins as he began pacing in front of the girls. "Halcion Orbs, Spiral whip, Seduction box, and…" He stared at the weapons in Isha's hand for a moment. "I was told about you. Do you still get nervous when men approach you?"

"What?" asked Isha, taken aback by the question. "No… I mean… sometimes. But I'm okay if I know them." She dropped her head, looking at the floor. "I think."

"Then tell me, do you even know what that is in your hands?"

"Ah, no, sir. I just grabbed them. I wasn't really thinking when I did."

"They're replicas of Nova shields. You're only supposed to use one, while on your other hand, you're supposed to wield a blade. Why'd you bring two?"

"They were together... I thought... I thought they were weapons."

"Look to the wall, child. Does it seem like the others are together?"

"No, sir. I... I'll go put it back."

"No," said Mr. Higgins, stopping Isha in her tracks. "I said you're to use whatever weapons you brought back from the wall. That includes you too. It's not unheard of for someone in the field to use two shields. I'll be damned if I've ever seen it. But at the very least, you'll learn how to block, I guess." Higgins rubbed at his chin as he continued to gaze down at Isha. "And given that trick you pulled off with Soulden, this might end up being something."

"I can help her practice shielding. My mother uses Halcion orbs. I promise I won't hurt her," said Serpene.

"Yeah," said Mr. Higgin as he took a deep breath. Your weapon's probably the best suited for starting it off." He turned to Isha. "You, try wrapping one of those straps around your hand until the shields are tight across your fist."

"Like this," asked Isha as she attempted to do as Mr. Higgins said.

"No, hold on," said Mr. Higgins as he stepped forward, adjusting the shield. "Now make a fist on the strap. That's it. Now hold it out." He stepped back. "Now channel your magic into your hand, letting it seep into the shield."

Isha paused for a moment as the large burly man stood over her, his hands over the shield. Again, she felt the tightness in her chest. *He's not Molan. I'm not scared. He just wants to help me.* Her chest began to tighten as he loomed over her. *I can do this. I'm not afraid anymore.* Controlling her breathing, Isha focused as hard as possible, trying her best to push down the anxiety. *Focus. I just need to push my magic into this. Don't think about anything else.*

Isha, once again, did as she was told, closing her eyes and calling forth her magic. The wooden shield began to light up, and at its center came a white light spreading out in a circular pattern. Like waves over the beach before crashing upon the shore, so too did the magic escape the sides of her shield before vanishing out about a foot away from its edges. She opened her eyes, amazed at the rippling waves of energy.

"I'm doing it," said Isha as she stared at the waves of energy in front of her face.

"Good," said Mr. Higgins, taking another step back. "Now, point it in Serpene's direction, holding it out in front of you. Good, just like that." She then turned to Serpene. "Okay, toss a few blasts over this way."

"Okay."

Isha watched as other orbs at the end of the small shaft lit up. Serpene then shook the top orb in Isha's direction and launched a perfect sphere of magic the same size as the sphere housed in the grip of the small stick. The orb of magic floated gently and smoothly through the air in an arch before crashing harmlessly into Isha's shield and exploding into a thousand small fragments and vanishing."

"Very good," said Mr. Higgins as he picked up one of the practice swords from a nearby wall. "I see your parents have taught you to control your magic very well. But as for this one." He turned to face Isha. "Keep that shield up, honey." He charged his magic into the wooden sword, making it glow a dark green. "I can already tell she's going to need some work." He placed the sword on Isha's outer shield and began to press against it. Instantly she could feel the drain on her as the magic was pulled out of her as she tried to hold the shield.

It's hard, thought Isha as she clenched her teeth, trying to hold her shield in place.

"Plant your feet, girly. Things are going to get way harder than this, especially for you and that weird power of yours."

Isha struggled to keep her stance as she pressed forward, trying to keep herself from being pushed back. The drain on her magic was more than she'd felt before. It was causing her body to shake.

"There, that's it. Yes, put some force behind it. But you need to always remember..."

And in an instant, Mr. Higgins stopped pushing his magic into his sword, and Isha watched as the force she was exuding before now sent her flying forward as the blade pierced her shield and went past her face. As she lost control and fell, Mr. Higgins extended his sword arm, catching her against his forearm, and holding her up.

"That wasn't bad. You might be a half-decent mage after all," he pushed his arm forward, allowing Isha to balance herself once again and release the magic from her shield. "Remember, magic blocks magic, but not the mundane. And because some magical attacks can become physical, always use the main part of your shield to block, not just the outer magical wall. Got it?"

"Yes, sir," Isha said with a nod as a bit of determination crept into her voice. She wasn't sure, but she thought she saw a smile on Mr. Higgins' face. But if it was there, it was only there for a second before he had her raise her shield again, and the training resumed.

The class practiced with their weapons. The sounds of wooden sticks rattled against each other as bodies hit the floor, followed by the sounds of grunts and moans from the children as they struggled through their first lesson.

Hours later, they all were in a tired, sweaty heap on the floor. Even Jacinta and Makeba were huddled around their sister, breathing heavily, as Jacinta rested her head on Isha's lap.

"Alright, today was a good warm-up. All of you go wash yourselves or head home."

"Big man too strong," said Jacinta. "Why he not be tired?"

Pavel, who was nearby with Freedo, chuckled. "Mr. Higgins is a master at fighting magic. He could probably fight all day and not be tired."

"Well, I want to kick him down."

"I think that's most of us. But you're welcome to try. I'd certainly watch."

"Pretty girly boy, not so pretty now," said Jacinta with a frown as she pointed at Pavel, only to have Isha wack her on the side with her hand.

"Stop that. No teasing," said Isha as she turned her head to look at Pavel. And it was true. His face was red, his cheeks were flushed, and his hair was sticky with sweat that clung to his forehead. "Sorry about that."

"No, it's, argh," Pavel moaned as he stood up. "It's fine. I should probably go and wash up. I have to go see Leo after classes, anyway."

"Okay, see you next time," said Isha as she watched as the rest of the class was getting up to leave. "I guess we should go too." Isha tried to move, shifting her weight a bit, but the soreness and exhaustion won out, and she once again rested her back against the wall. "Maybe... maybe just a little longer." She allowed her body to slump back into rest before feeling something graze against her wrist. Looking down, she saw a small root begging, curling around her finger. Then, with a sigh, she took hold of it and began channeling her magic.

Hello. Can you hear me now? The Tree Sakari's voice came into her mind.

I... I can hear you. Thought Isha with a verbal sigh. *I know we promised to come to see you today. But we can't really move now.*

Are you okay? Are you in trouble?

No, just tired. We can't really move right now.

Oh, no need to come the long way. I can bring you here.

Isha smiled at the thought of not having to move as she closed her eyes. *I wish you could. That would be... wait, what?* And before Isha could respond, she opened her eyes, and there was nothing but blackness. The castle had once again consumed her as she felt herself being moved around by a force she didn't understand. The whole thing was disorientating, as she couldn't even perceive which way was up or down, just that she was moving in some direction. Suddenly, Isha found herself on the floor as a small breeze rolled off her face. She opened her eyes to see that she was again in the domed room with the trees all around her.

"Sister was brought here too," said Jacinta's voice.

Isha turned her head to see Jacinta a few feet away from her, lying at the base of one of the other trees.

"Where's Makeba?" asked Isha, catching her breath as she began to peer across the room.

"I am here, sister," said Makeba, her head popping out from behind the Trailage Tree.

"That was fun, sister. Can the tree Sakari send us anywhere in castle?"

"I don't know. You will need to ask her yourself," said Isha with a moan as she lifted herself from the floor and stumbled over to the tree where Makeba was. "Come on. We promised to visit her." Isha sat back down at the base of the tree with her sisters and held her hands. Jacinta and Makeba sat beside their sister, each interlocking their fingers with her as small roots from the tree crept over their legs and waist.

Isha had become familiar with the feeling after she and her sisters had visited the Tree Sakari several times. She knew the feeling now and just where to look, and with the right push on her magic she could access, she found herself once again inside the world of the tree where Lonta'Mar was waiting for them.

"Hello again," said Lonta'Mar. "Can we play again?"

"Sure. What game would you like to play this time?" asked Isha as she began to stretch. *At least I'm not tired here. I just wish I wouldn't feel so sleepy when we leave.*

"I do not know. I was hoping you could teach me more kingdom games, one like the stick game."

"That wasn't a game. That was just Jacinta and Makeba doing their practices," said Isha as she once again looked around the open space. "Lonta'Mar, why does it always look like this here? Are you not able to change it?"

"I... I can, but it never stays. It always changes back when I do something else."

"What do you mean?"

Lonta'Mar closed her eyes and began to think, "It is hard to explain. I do not know many places, but..."

Suddenly the world around Isha shifted beneath her feet, and in an instant, she was standing in the space behind the school castle beside the pool area in the garden or the moving hedge maze.

"Wow," said Jacinta. "You can change world here. Tree Sakari is like the spirit mother."

Isha was stunned to see the new world around her. It didn't seem precisely like the place she knew behind the school; some things felt weird. Looking down, she could see her bare feet on the stone, but she could not feel its coldness. She could feel the touch of her own skin as she rubbed her fingers together, but not the wind between them as she moved her hand around. Curious, she knelt beside the pool and dipped her hands into the water. Sure enough, she could feel its coldness, and her hand was certainly wet after pulling it out of the water.

"I can change things. But since I do not understand how many things are, it is hard to keep the places solid here."

"So... if you understood, then that means we can play in all kinds of fancy places?" asked Makeba as she went around, touching the plants along the edge of the marble area.

"I... I guess so."

"Oh. Do you remember Sakar? Can you make Sakar?"

"Yes, but only a small part. It has been so long that I have forgotten many things."

"Then we help you remember," said Makeba with a smile as she walked over, grabbing Lonta'Mar's hand. "Try. Let us go back to Sakar. I wish to show Sister Isha what our home looks like."

"Then I shall try my best," said Lonta'Mar as she closed her eyes.

And just as suddenly as before, the world's colors began to change as the ground beneath her feet morphed, changing from gray to brown and finally to green. Isha could only stare in amazement as she found herself in a lush forest. The smell of nature filled her lungs, and she could feel so much more than before. From the light on her skin that shone through the branches above her to the wet morning dew on the grass beneath her feet, she was just so aware of everything. She even felt the blades of grass prickling between her toes.

"We're home, we're home," said Jacinta and Makeba as they ran around rubbing their hands on the trees.

Isha genuinely couldn't think of a time when she had ever seen her sisters so gleeful. The way they rubbed their hands on the bark of trees to the leaves on the small plants was a rare sight. But to her, it felt like an entirely new word. So many plants and trees that she had never seen before. Their leaves all had different shades and colors, from pinks to reds and purples, that all seemed to mix in with each other.

"Is this what your home looks like?" asked Isha as she fiddled with a plant leaf.

"Yes, sister will need to see more," said Jacinta as she stepped around a tree exploring. "The rivers and homes and…. Oof." Suddenly Jacinta went falling, landing on her bottom.

"Sister?" asked Makeba as she hurried over. "What's wrong?"

"Something there," said Jacinta as her sister knelt beside her. She pointed to the space in front of her. "Something there. It stops me."

Makeba frowned, not understanding, how she could look ahead and see the rest of the forest but, when extending her hand, she was stopped by some sort of invisible wall.

"Is this what you mean by you can't remember much about your home?" asked Isha as she walked over, placing her hand on the invisible wall that stopped them from going forward.

"I'm sorry," said Lonta'Mar with her head down, looking ashamed. "I… I try to remember more. But I can't. I know there is more of home, but this is all I can do."

"Then we help you remember," said Makeba as she walked back over to Lonta'Mar, wrapping her arms around her. "Sister and I will help. We remember home."

And just as promised, Isha watched as the three Sakari girls discussed their home. They began walking around the small wooded space as Makeba and Jacinta described the area ahead and how they thought it would be. Hours had passed before the girls finally decided to take a break.

"That's probably enough for today," said Isha. "We probably need to go home soon."

"Yes," said Lonta'Mar in agreement. "I… I must think about everything now. Remembering home has been much harder than I imagined. But you will come back again, right?"

"Of course."

"Okay, then I'll send you back now."

And in an instant, Isha's world went dark, and when she opened her eyes again, she was again in the domed room with the colorful trees. She looked down at her legs and watched the branches that had once covered her recede into the tree's bark, freeing them to stand. She stood and found her body aching. She bent over, taking a breath. From this position, she watched a bead of sweat drop from her face down to the floor.

"I am tired. I wish to sleep now," said Jacinta as she began to stretch and rotate her arms.

We were in there for hours, right? Why are we still sweating? How long has it been out here? "Yes, I think we should all go home now." Isha then leaned over, placing her hand on the tree. *Lonta'Mar, is time different in there than out here?*

I... I do not know. I have never been out there.

"Do not forget. We must visit Leo also," said Makeba.

"Okay, first Leo, then bath."

Leo is the man who came with you before? The one with the scars?

Yes, that is him. We promised to go see him. Isha looked over her arms and felt the sweat at the back of her neck. *Although, I wish I could take a bath first.*

Okay, then I can send you to bath.

You can? What do you... and before Isha could finish her thought, she found herself knee-deep inside of the floor and sinking fast.

"Oh, it happening again. Where we go this time?" asked Jacinta.

Isha's last sight was the smile on her sister's face as she looked around in wonder before the world went black.

Once again, she found herself being moved through this unknown space inside the castle to wherever she was headed.

I don't think I will ever get used to this. Lonta'Mar... are you there? She waited for a response but no answer game. *I guess not. I wonder where she is sending...* She then felt the fresh air against her face and opened her eyes. To her surprise, she looked down into a pool of water, and at the center was a person with blonde hair bathing their body. *Oh, no!* Thought

Isha as the panic settled in with the realization that she was exiting from the ceiling. "No, no, Lonta'Mar. Lonta'Mar, this is the wrong... Ahhh!" She screamed as the ceiling released her and she plummeted into the bath water, causing a huge splash.

"What in the, ahhh," came the sound of a voice as Isha emerged from the water, splashing about, trying to catch her breath. Her eyes filled with water as the world appeared blurry.

"Isha? Is that you? What are you doing here?" came a familiar voice.

"I'm..." She coughed as she wiped the water from her eyes. "I'm sorry. I didn't... I mean... She didn't..."

"Well, we're probably in trouble now," said Pavel's voice.

"I'm sorry, I'll..." said Isha, her eyes clear, and she saw Pavel standing before her completely naked, his long hair draped over one side of his shoulders. But on his chest, there was something not suitable for a boy. He had breasts, perhaps around her size. Isha blinked in shock as her mind tried to comprehend this Pavel in front of her. And even without willing herself to do so, her eyes unconsciously drifted downward towards the other region of his body where she unmistakably saw what knew was undoubtedly a part of a man.

"But... but..." Isha blinked, only standing in shock. "I mean... you have..."

Pavel just placed his hands on his hips and smiled at her. "We really are going to be in so much trouble."

CHAPTER 21

Saffron, Laura, Dekol, and Mova sat atop their horses. They made their way over the hilltop countryside, escorting a horse-drawn wagon. Atop that carriage sat the woman Mova had rescued, and in the back were the two girls she had with her.

"So, Miss Latrisha, are you sure you'd not wish for us to accompany you to the Holy City?"

"No, it is fine, really. I will stop at the commune in Derkstone and take service with my sisters and brothers there before moving on to the Holy City. I will ask that Shepard Latrisha looks after the girls for their training until after I return."

"Are you going to leave us?" asked one of the girls, her head poking out from behind the wagon covers.

"Only for a bit. I did promise to oversee your training, but I have a mission in the Goddess's city that I must attend to." She patted the girl on her head. "Do not worry. I shall return in one or two weeks. Then I shall be with you until your training is complete."

"Is it normal for you to follow a trainee through their courses?" asked Saffron to stave off the boredom of the open road.

"Usually, no. Typically we would just take the faithful to the temples to be trained, and any missionary would be on their way after they've settled. But I wish to have these girls accompany me in my efforts. I think it would be more influential to have these two with me. Many other children in different cities might have an issue trusting adults who wander into their towns, whether they be faithful or not."

"I applaud your dedication to the faith. But surely you see the danger in what you are doing; three females traveling the countryside alone. Are you not provided protectors when you're on a mission? Surely the circumstances we found you in are a testament to the need."

"The council ensures that all members are taught basic self-defense in case trouble arises. But you are correct. There is the occasional word of our brethren that have fallen victim to banditry, and as you say, the females that were caught were not given the same quick mercy as our male counterparts."

"Then why travel alone?"

"The will of the Goddess calls us all in different ways. Who are we to decide? We simply go where we feel we are needed.

"But the faithful cannot help all the impoverished children in every city," said Laura with a sad look. "How do you decide who to help?"

"Each missionary is only allowed to bring in five recruits each year, or else the chapels would overflow. It may be harsh, but we must choose who we think would be the most loyal to the faithful. These two girls will be my last of the year. The rest of my time will be spent teaching them and having them follow me on my journey until the day when they are ready to branch out on their own."

"A truly selfless life you must lead, Miss Latrisha," said Saffron as they rounded a hill and spotted the city ahead. "And there is the city Derkstone. Just as dirty as I remember it from years ago."

"Then it is a place where we can do the most good," said Latrisha.

"What say you, Mova? You've certainly been quiet on our trip lately. Barely a complaint about the tough roads, the foul smells, or just normal disdain for anything unclean. I must ask if you are feeling alright. I expect the silent treatment from Dekol, sure. But from you, it makes the journey a little more unnerving."

"Nothing to concern yourself with. I just grow weary of the road and wish to soak myself in a warm bath, even if it is in a pig sty like this place."

"Well, let's not keep you from your cleansing hopes," said Saffron as he signaled the horse to go forward. It wasn't long before they were in the city. An older dwelling with what seemed to have over a hundred years of history that showed through its chipped brick foundations and dirty streets. The people were a mix of the impoverished and the semi-dressed merchants that had found their way to scrounge out a living in the aged city. High brick walls that were probably meant to keep out raids from a time when the town was prosperous—surrounded the city.

"The chapel is up ahead towards the left and past the corners," said Latrisha as they approached a fork in the road. "I shall go and inform the clergy of our arrival and get the girls settled in with something to eat. Please do stop by for a visit before you leave. I'm sure the Shepherd would like to thank you personally for saving us."

"I shall accompany them," said Mova. "If any place has clean water to bathe in such a city as this, one would think it to be the clergy."

"Yes, I do not think that will be a problem."

"I would like to join you," said Laura hurriedly.

Saffron shrugged while shaking his head. "Well, I can't say I'm surprised. Please, take care of my wife. We shall meet up with you two later then. But, for now, I shall try to find suitable arrangements for the night. I think it will do us all some good to sleep in actual beds for a night. Be well, ladies."

Saffron and Dekol made their way down one side of the fork while Mova and Laura escorted Latrisha and the children through the streets towards the chapel.

"Oh, how I so look forward to the chance to wash my hair again," said Laura excitedly.

"I thought you were excited about this trip. I was told that it was your adventure, after all."

"Well, yes, I am," said Laura admittedly. "And although I would never complain about it to my husband, it is not as if I enjoy the feeling of bugs crawling on my skin. I just do not wish to trouble my husband after he has gone to such trouble to take me on this journey."

"The dutiful wife. I sometimes wonder what that feels like," said Mova as they approached the chapel. It was a large brick structure inside of a gated brick wall. They could see many robbed members walking in and out as two members stood guard by the entrance.

"Hello, brother Ivan," said Latrisha as she approached.

"Hello and welcome back, Sister Latrisha. How were your travels?"

"Well, brother, I have brought two who wish to join us."

"These two?" asked the man looking between Mova and Laura while rubbing his chin. "I did not know the Master required such seasoned examples for her work."

"No, these two are my escorts. I have two young ones in the carriage here. I wish to have them clothed and fed here while I complete another missionary request in the Holy City. I was hoping the Mother would not mind."

"Oh yes, of course, come in. Mother is in the main building and should have just finished prayers."

"Thank you, Ivan," said Latrisha, and with a snap of the reins, the ladies made their way onto the temple grounds and up a dirt road path with budding trees on either side. As they approached the chapel, they could see that service was indeed just ending as many robed figures were leaving the building. And there, on the steps, giving out her well wishes, was a robed brown-haired woman.

"Hello there... Latrisha is that you?" asked the robbed woman.

"Yes, Mother, I've returned," she said, stopping the wagon in front of the chapel before hopping down. "I hope everything has been well."

"As well as one could expect in a town such as this," she said as she spotted Mova. "Oh my, it seems we have guests. And quite a distinguished one at that. Mova Grailwood, a face I haven't seen in some time."

Mova gave a half-hearted smile. "I see you have found a new calling in the Church of the Goddess, although I must admit, that is an unexpected turn."

"The Goddess calls upon us all in the strangest ways," said the woman before spotting the girls Latrisha brought with her being escorted out of the back on the wagon. "Oh, well, who do we have here? Such sweet-looking little girls. Come along then. No need to stand out in the sun. Let's get you girls sorted then, shall we?"

Following the Mother's lead, they were escorted into the chapel. The scent of smoking incense floated through the air as they walked through the aisle. To their sides, were rows of worn wooden benches. The chapel was old and probably used repeatedly throughout the decades as needed. Ahead, behind the podium, was a stone statue of the Goddess. She stood with her hands outstretched towards where a crowd would usually sit. The concrete around her hair and arms had been chipped, and over her bodice hung a golden cloth.

It draped over one shoulder, making its way down to the floor, where an assortment of candles were lit at her feet.

"Do you really hold service here?" asked Mova with a raised brow.

"Why, of course," said the Mother with a smile. "I doubt the Goddess cares where her words are spoken." She then turned and waved at another woman. "Grettal, please see to it that these children are fed, bathed, and properly clothed."

"Yes, ma'am," said Grettal as she escorted the two girls away.

"May I ask to join them?" asked Laura. "The road has been quite long."

"No," said Mova hurriedly. "Perhaps we should..."

"Oh, do not worry," said the Mother, interrupting, "I assure you that this place is quite secure. She will be safe within our walls. That is, of course, unless you think we are not capable of offering our protection."

Mova looked around the room again, seeing a few other robed female clergy members, and sighed. "Go on, Laura. I will join you soon enough. But, first, I wish to talk with the Mother."

"Ahh, okay," said Laura, now slightly hesitant. But she was soon dragged by her arms by the two girls as they led her off, following Grettal.

"Well then, now I suppose we may speak a bit more freely," said the Mother as she and Latrisha turned and walked away, expecting Mova to follow. "Tell me, Brenthelin, what brings you to our humble home?"

"My name is Mova now," she said, following behind the Mother.

"Of course, it is, dear. I hope things have been going well with you in that capital," said the Mother as she made her way into a hallway stopping at a thick wooden door with a torch next to it. "You always were a fan of the shinier things, I suppose."

"And I see you're still taking children from their homes

and forcing them to do your work for you."

"Oh, you make it sound so diabolical," said the Mother as she slid a key into the door. The lock clicked, and she opened the door to reveal a stairwell. She grabbed the torch from the wall and began to make her way down. "We do what we must. Granted, very few are magically talented, and none since have had your particular skill." The Mother sighed, "It really was a shame you decided to leave us."

"I think you are misremembering how things ended for me," said Mova as she began to hear the sounds of thudding impacts and the moans of children.

"Am I?" asked the Mother innocently. "Perhaps the years are catching up to me after all."

They reached the bottom of the steps where another door awaited them. Opening it, Mova found that it led into a large open area underground. It was alight with torches placed along the four walls of all the support pillars that held the building above. In between them, hanging from the wooden support beams, were sandbags held by chains, and in front of each were young girls with sticks. A woman ahead gave the order to strike the bags. Each blow caused the chains to jingle, providing an eerie sound that echoed in sync throughout the enclosed area.

"How many?" asked Mova.

"Oh, enough. But I'm curious. How did you meet Latrisha? As nice as it is to see a promising student of the past, I hardly think we sent an invitation. And yet you show up at my door with a fresh princess in tow."

"The prince is also with her, along with another man," said Latrisha. And there are rumors of your group sharing your goodwill from village to village. I must say, from the stories, I expected you all to have more guards with you."

"I guess it would have been too much of an expectation to hope you would not know who they were?" asked Mova with a frown as she looked at Latrisha disapprovingly.

"Oh, she looks a bit different. A little make-up and magic

to smooth out her features. But she is who she is. But do not worry. As I said, your charge is safe with us. Now back to my question, how is it that you've come across our doorstep?"

"The original story was true. Just the play was backward. Your servant Latrisha was about to kill a few men who were pursuing her. I simply intervened so that no one would be killed.

"How did you know who I might be back then?" asked Latrisha.

"The fighting stance you took. It was Kru-lin, wasn't it? That style is most preferred by Mother here. And certainly not something your average clergy member would know. I assume you keep small blades tucked in the sleeves of your robes."

Latrisha lifted a shoulder, then jolted her arm downward quickly as a blade slid into her palm. She then raised it for Mova to see as the shine from a torch glimmered off of it as they passed in the shadows.

"But back to our previous discussion," said the Mother as they turned down a corridor leading to off-sitting bedrooms. "Why are the young prince Saffron and his Princess making their way through the countryside? There has been no word of a royal visit to play kiss ass with the local lords. So, I would have to assume that this is more of a spur-of-the-moment decision."

Mova was quiet for a moment, trying to decide what to say.

"Oh, don't worry," said the Mother waving a hand in dismissal. "As I said, we have no desire to harm your precious charges. In fact, you might be interested to know that your king has entrusted us to look into those disappearing villagers. Something about crimson crystals, I do believe."

"And have you found out anything interesting?" asked Mova as they entered a small room of parchment and quills, wherein the center sat a desk and a few chairs.

"Oh, are we sharing information now?" asked the Mother as she sat at the head of the desk and gestured for Mova and Latrisha to sit. "I think that's a wonderful idea. But you first; I do love listening to stories."

Mova sighed, "And I suppose pleading to your love of king and country will not persuade you to release this information to me?"

"Afraid not. You should understand that here we have our own allegiances. But you're welcome to not share if you prefer. We can have one of the girls bring us down some sweet cakes. I do remember those being your favorite."

Mova tilted her head upward as she stared at the ceiling while tapping her foot on the floor. Finding no answer, she took a breath and refocused her attention back on the Mother. "Fine, but only one story."

"Oh, good. Latrisha, close the door, would you, dear? Secrets should be kept between friends after all," said the Mother as Latrisha stood up and walked toward the door. "Then the story this time is what group of circumstances led to you betraying us."

CHAPTER 22

Victor lay on the floor of his friend's house, strands of hair covering his face as he focused on the chandelier above him. The way the daylight shimmered off the crystals was somewhat mesmerizing. The reflection of the house's colors shifted just so slightly that he couldn't focus on anything for more than a moment before it shifted again.

What am I doing? What do I have to do? Red crystals that are doing goddess knows what. Link to a splinter group of the church. Little girl with unknown powers sent off towards the magic school of Latrusa. Magical school is apparently attacked by an unknown group. Then there's the matter of the stolen child of the Starlight Queen. Which I am having my newfound wives assist in the kidnapping of. And of course, I will need to...

"What are you doing?" asked Silk as she descended the stairs.

"Just thinking," said Victor as he turned his head to look

at her. She was back wearing the face of the blonde girl and was wearing a blue dress.

"Do you always think on your back like that?" she asked with a smile as she knelt beside him. "And what is it you're thinking about?"

"You, me, Frenka, the world, a kidnapped child, my own child, and a small girl in a magic castle,"

"Seems like a lot to think about," said Silk as she looked over at him. "Here, let me try." She lifted the edge of her skirt just a little as she straddled him on the floor, then pressing herself against him, she laid her ear over his chest."

"And this is supposed to help me think? I think it has the opposite effect."

"Not you. Me," said Silk as she closed her eyes and took a deep breath. "I'm listening to the way your heart beats. Thump thump... thump thump."

"Is it really so pleasing to hear; the sound of a confused man's heart?"

"You're never confused. Ever since I've met you, you've always had some type of plan."

"I think you're confusing improvisation with planning. In truth, most of my plans fail. I just keep trying new ones."

Silk rubbed her face against Victor's chest before turning her face upwards and giving him a kiss. "Then be sure that you keep trying so that you come back to me. I do not wish to lose this feeling I have inside of me."

"Oh," said Frenka as she stepped in front of the two. "Is husband inside of you now? Should Frenka join in? Would not mind another before trip."

"What?" said Silk, startled as she tried to stand but clipped her foot on Victor's slide, causing her to trip and fall into Frenka's arms.

"Frenka was just making joke, but if sister-wife wants, maybe we have time before husband's ship leaves."

"And once again, it's sounding as if I have no say so on the matter," said Victor as he lifted himself from the floor.

Frenka waved her hand dismissively at Victor as she looked at Silk." Well, perhaps this time we do not need husband."

"No," said Silk, stepping back. "I'm... I'm fine now."

Victor smiled as he knelt, grabbing his satchel from the floor and draping it over his shoulder. "Then let's be on our way, shall we? My ship is probably being loaded as we speak."

Together, the three left the house and began making their way through the city, with Victor taking special care to take a path that led past his own home, which was currently having its destroyed side and roof rebuilt.

"It will be fixed by the time husband returns. So husband should not worry."

"It's nice to see you still have your optimism."

After walking, they arrived at the royal airship's courtyard. Where several airships were docked in their V-shaped docking stations or hovering just above the ground next to loading towers. It didn't take Victor long before he saw his ship.

"I guess this is goodbye for now," said Victor as he stepped forward, turning around to face his wives. "I feel as if I should say something romantic and uplifting, but in truth, I just want you both to be safe. And I'm sorry I dragged you into this mess."

"The look on husband's face tells us how he feels. It better than words now," said Frenka as she stepped forward, giving Victor a kiss. "Now, good man husband go be hero and let wives be villains."

"Remember... remember the promise you made," said Silk. "I'm supposed to be able to walk around the capitol as myself. I won't... I won't let you forget that."

Victor smiled as he looked down at his wife, who fidgeted with her fingers. "I won't," he said as he leaned down, giving Silk a kiss and pressing his forehead against hers. "I'll be waiting for both of you when you return." He then raised back to his full height. "Be well, my adventurous wives. Take care of each other. Because at this moment, you're all I hold dear in this world."

And with those final words, Victor made his way towards the loading tower, following a group of passengers as he climbed up the steps. At the top, he stepped over the loading plank and found himself unable to control himself as he made his way over to the ship's railing to look out at his wives from above. Seeing that, they gave their final waves as the ship gave a lurch and headed off into the sky.

CHAPTER 23

"So, explain this to me once again," said Leo as he paced back and forth in front of Isha and Pavel, who sat on one of the cots of his office. His tone reflected one of exhaustion and frustration.

Isha couldn't help but notice that his bandages appeared looser than they were that morning. Perhaps he had been treating himself when they intruded on his time. He had always kept them covered, not allowing anyone else in the house to see what damage had been done.

"She fell from the ceiling, down into the bath where I was," said Pavel with a smile. "It was rather impressive. I hadn't known this school was studying teleportation. I had heard it was only theoretical magic."

"That's because it is. No one has mastered teleportation magic, and the few who have tried, never lived long enough to perfect it. And even given Isha's ability, I doubt the Goddess also gave her the ability to teleport. This world can only be so unfair in the handing out of its gifts. So..." Leo looked down at Isha, "that leaves the question of how exactly you got there."

Isha glanced over at Pavel for a moment before dropping her head and remaining silent.

Leo caught the glance over at Pavel and sighed. "Fine, we'll talk more about this when we get home. But I need you to understand, you cannot tell anyone about what you saw in the bath. Pavel's condition isn't to be known by anyone. Do you understand?"

"Yes, sir," said Isha, still keeping her head down. "I'm sorry, Pavel."

"I think you're scaring her," said Pavel as he placed his hand on Isha's back. "Don't worry; you're not in trouble. Someone was bound to find out sooner or later. I'm actually happy that it was you. It gives me someone else I can talk to."

"No, I didn't mean..." Leo sighed while rubbing his face. "You're not in trouble. Although I still wonder why it's always you that finds your way into my office over and over again."

"Can I ask a question?" asked Isha.

"Sure. At this point, what could it hurt?"

"Pavel... are you... I mean..."

"Am I a girl or a boy?"

"No! I mean... well, yes, if you don't mind me asking."

"Hmm," moaned Pavel, placing his hand on his chin. "I wondered that for a long time myself. But honestly, I think I'm both: having a body like mine isn't so bad." Pavel raised one of his hands with their palms upward. Their eyes narrowed as a red orb of magic appeared above their finger, then slowly, half of the red sphere began to change from red to green.

"You can use two types of magic at once?"

"Not quite," said Pavel as they raised their other hand

and forced another green orb of light above their palm. "I can... I can use three."

Isha could see Pavel struggling to hold all three forms of magic as their arms began to shake and they grit their teeth. It was only another moment before the magic Pavel held lost its orb-like shape and fell apart, washing over his hands as it vanished into the air. Dropping his arms to his sides, Pavel began taking deep breaths.

"Are you alright?" asked Isha, placing her hand on Pavel's arm.

"I'm fine... It happens... when I use too much magic at once."

"Pavel's body has the reproductive organs of both male and female," said Leo, sitting at his desk. "A phenomenon which apparently allows him to access different magics equally. Usually, we would train in all magics, and even then, he would need to cast one magic instead of another. But Pavel here doesn't seem to possess that limitation."

"But I don't know if I can do oddity magic like mind or shadow stuff."

"Is that why you were sick a lot? You were sleeping when we came to visit Leo."

"Oh... that," said Leo, looking away toward the window. "It's true that I need to monitor Pavel's body to ensure he is growing correctly and there aren't any problems. But that was... hmm... that is to say."

"It means I get bad stomach aches during certain times of the month," said Pavel with no hesitation.

"Oh," said Isha. "I get those too. It really is... it... it..." Then the realization of what that meant suddenly struck Isha. "But... but. That means..."

"That I can probably have babies. Yes, I was surprised as well when Leo told me that."

Isha blinked in shock as she stared into Pavel's face. The way he just smiled at her as if he was just telling her about the weather. But unconsciously, Isha's eyes moved from his
318

face to his slim shoulders; over his chest or was it her chest. Then her eyes drifted lower until she glanced at his crotch.

But he has man parts. Does that mean that behind it, there is...

"Would you like to see it again?" asked Pavel with a laugh.

Isha's eyes widened as Pavel's words snapped her out of her daze. "Huh, what? No! I mean, no, thank you. I just," She fumbled her words for a few more moments before she dropped her head again, feeling shame and only managing to squeak out. "I'm sorry."

"You do apologize a lot," said Pavel as he reached over, taking Isha's hand. "Don't worry. It was a surprise to me some years ago. But I've come to accept this is just who I am."

"Yes," said Leo, interrupting, "in terms of oddities. You're both exceptional in your own way."

"That's why I don't mind Isha knowing my secret. We have different powers, I think, but maybe her body is like mine. And I can help her when she starts growing a penis herself."

"What?" blurted out Isha, her eyes wide once again. She quickly turned to Leo in fear.

"No, that's not going to happen," said Leo, shaking his head in disapproval at Pavel's obvious joke. "Don't listen to him. Pavel was born the way he is now. People don't grow extra pieces after they are born."

Isha turned her attention back to the gleeful Pavel. Her face was now flush red as she began hitting him on his shoulder. "That's not funny. I believed you."

"I'm sorry," said Pavel, playfully shielding himself, trying and failing to contain his laughter. "I couldn't help myself."

Isha stopped her soft blows and turned away from him, her cheeks puffed out in stubborn refusal to accept his apology.

"Well, one thing's for sure. Your sisters may have been right about me being a girly boy," said Pavel as he raised his hand, looking over himself. "But I'm not exactly sure which part is more than the other."

"And speaking of your sisters," said Leo, placing his hands on the desk. "You can't tell them about Pavel. This stays between us. You've told me you've already had people try and kidnap you. We certainly do not need any more unwanted attention diverted towards this school."

"I won't," said Isha remembering how that woman had kidnapped her and Chloe and had her up on the stage as all the people stared at her. *If Father hadn't come for me, what would have happened?* She glanced back at Pavel. *Would Father save him if I asked him to?* But then, a more chilling thought crept into Isha's mind as she began to think about the type of man he was. *What would Father do if I told him?*

"Okay, that's enough for today," said Leo. "Let's all head on home. And Isha, when we get there, we still have to discuss how you ended up there in the first place."

"Yes, sir," said Isha, hopping down from the bunk with Pavel, then exiting the room. The hall was empty as they had stayed beyond the regular school hours.

"I guess we're done here. My house is on the way, so we can walk together."

"Okay."

As they left the castle, Isha could see a full moon high in the sky, peaking above the clouds. Once again, she turned around to view the marble castle in the moonlight. It shone as usual, but now it didn't seem so bright. Instead, it felt more shadowy to her. It was as if the shadows from the clouds didn't match with the shades on the castle. They seemed as if they were moving according to their own will.

"Did you forget something?" asked Pavel.

"Huh? Oh, no, sorry," said Isha, turning back to Pavel. "We can go now."

"The world becomes a strange place at night," said

Leo as they then began walking through the darkened city streets of the floating school grounds. The streetlamps lighting their way home.

"Have you decided what you will do when you graduate?" asked Pavel.

"Not really. Father just sent me here after I gained my magic. But I guess he will find something for me to do."

"Oh, I forgot, their something I need to check on at him," said Leo. "You two can make it fine on your own, right?"

"Ah? Okay, yes, we'll be fine," said Isha, curious as to what Leo had to rush home and see.

"Good," said Leo, he then gave a nod to Pavel before rushing off down the street. "Have fun."

"So, you have nothing you want to do?" asked Pavel.

"Huh? Oh, I mean, I would like to go home. But I don't think there's anything left for me anymore."

"Where's home?"

"Greenland."

"Oh, I don't think I know that place."

"That's what a lot of people say. But I'm told it's really far away and will take a long time to get there."

"At least you have your father here with you. I never got to meet my folks."

"He's not... I mean..." Isha didn't know how to or if she should explain her situation. "Then who took care of you?"

"My caretaker, Miss Kolim. She was more of a mother to me. But the group always looked after me and taught me magic and how to use a sword. A few of them even knew about my body. But the rest saw me as the Child of Destiny, whatever that means."

"Child of Destiny?"

"I think I told you about it before; how many people believe I'm supposed to stab the shadow king in the heart when he returns."

"Oh. But what about you? Do you believe that?"

Pavel stopped next to a bench. "I think you're the first

person to ask me that. Usually, everyone just tells me, 'It's your destiny,' or 'you will be a great hero.' What about you? Do you think your magic makes you special?"

"I don't know. I never thought about magic until I discovered I had it."

"Then we really are kind of the same," said Pavel as he decided to sit on the bench under the streetlamp's light, patting the space next to him with his hand. "You mind if we sit? It's not often that I get to talk with someone like this."

"Do you not get to talk with your friends?" asked Isha as she stepped over, taking a seat. "I mean those two that are always with you?"

"What? Frokal and Delaine?" asked Pavel with a laugh. "They are more my guards than they are my friends. They are like everyone else back home. They see me as some special type of savior. I mean, they don't even know about my body's condition."

"Oh? I... I just thought since they were with you so much. Do... do you not have anyone whom you can talk to?"

"Not especially, no. I mean, Lady Soulden knowns, Leo, and the weird fellow Mr. Caudbell. But I don't like the way he looks at me. I feel he'd cut me open if they let him."

Isha giggled, despite herself at the description of Mr. Caudbell. "He... he looks at me the same way too."

"Yes, I figured that might be the case. But now I don't think it'll be so bad." Pavel placed his hand over Isha's. "I mean, I'd like to talk with you more, since you know my secret and all."

The sudden touch of Pavel's hand surprised Isha for a moment. But she didn't shy away from him, and the two just looked at each other for a moment.

"Pavel, um... can I ask you something?"

"Of course. What is it?"

"Did you... I mean... well... Did you know that the school was going to be attacked?"

Pavel pulled back, removing his hand from Isha's, the

surprise on his face obvious to her.

"Wha... what makes you ask that?" asked Pavel as he turned his face away from Isha instead of looking down at the stone road before them.

I hope I'm doing the right thing. "One night at school, I heard you talking with someone. They were telling you about an attack. Were they talking about the school? Did you know about it?"

"So, someone was there that night. I remember no one was there when I went into the hall."

"That was me, I was there."

Pavel leaned back on the bench, looking up into the stars. "Of course, you were. You're just everywhere." He then took another look at Isha before dropping his head. "Okay, you're right. I knew or at least, I was warned about it."

"But how? Why didn't you tell someone?"

"I did. I told Soulden. But somehow, she already knew or at least, had suspicions. She came and asked me about the attack, and I told her everything I knew. Not that it did any good. We still ended up fighting them inside the castle. That's when they blew that hole in the wall and hopped on their ship, taking pieces of the tree."

"Oh. I didn't know you were inside fighting when they attacked. I thought that..." said Isha as she caught Pavel staring at her again. "What? Is something wrong?"

"You know about the tree as well, then, it makes sense since you heard me talking about the attack."

"What? What do you mean?"

"When I mentioned the tree, you didn't seem surprised. If I said that to someone else, they'd ask, 'What tree?' But you didn't do that."

"I... I've seen the tree," Isha admitted reluctantly. But didn't dare to reveal that there was a Sakari girl inside of the tree.

"Of course, you have," said Pavel, shaking his head. "Are

you just a lightning rod for secrets at this school? Because you certainly find yourself in a lot of places."

"I don't do it on purpose. Things just happened."

"Well, either way, I'm happy you're here. Because of you and your sisters, not many people think that I'm weird anymore."

"Why did people think that?"

"My group… some people think they are a cult. It made making friends hard when I got here. But then you came and broke that girl's arm, and suddenly everyone forgot about me. That was one of the reasons I wanted to become friends with you. I figured you might need one. But maybe we both did," say Pavel with a smile as he stood up from the bench, turning back to Isha and offering her his hand. "Shall I walk you home, my lady?"

Isha looked at Pavel's hand for a moment before nodding her head with a smile. She then gave him her hand as he pulled her up from the bench. "I think I'd like for us to be friends." And the two-headed back down the streets. They talked a bit more about their studies and what they hoped to learn in class, but it was just small talk. Soon they arrived at the door to Heart House, where Pavel stared at the statue of Elena erected in front over the lawn and under the tree.

"I really am sorry for what happened to her. I didn't know Miss Elena well, but she seemed like a nice person."

"She was. She was really kind. I'm really—"

The door opened, and Jacinta peeped her head outside. "Oh! Hello sister, welcome home," her eyes glanced down and noticed that the two were still holding hands. A sly and smug smile crept over her face before she darted back inside.

"Sister home and she pick pretty boy as mate. They kiss face in door."

"Jacinta, stop that," said Isha, stepping a foot inside the house to see Leo, Freedo, Makeba, and Rima all staring at her. "It's… it's not like that."

"Does…," said Pavel, failing to control his laughter again. "Does that…. mean I won't be getting a kiss then?"

Isha turned back to him, her face and cheeks red with blush. "Stop encouraging her."

"I'm sorry. But I really do find it hard not to," said Pavel, regaining control of himself. "Will you forgive me?"

"Fine," said Isha with a sigh. "I'll see you in-" Isha's words paused in her mouth as Pavel, to her surprise, quickly stepped in and planted a kiss on her cheek. Instinctively she reached up, placing a hand where he had kissed her, her eyes wide with shock.

"I'll see you in class tomorrow," said Pavel with glee as he took off into the darkness, a bright smile across his face.

Isha turned back to see a surprised look on everyone else's faces.

"I must admit. I didn't expect that turn of events, especially after the meeting we had earlier," said Leo.

"It's not… I mean… He just did that."

"I know. I saw," said Leo. "I must admit. I'm a little jealous. But maybe it's for the best if you find someone your age. And you two do have a lot in common."

"That's not what I meant."

"I guess you won't need me to walk you to class anymore," said Freedo.

"Fine. I give up," said Isha, pouting. Her cheeks puffed out as she walked over and sat on the sofa with her arms folded. "Go on. I don't care if you make jokes anymore."

"Ahh! There, there, princess," said Leo as he came over, wrapping his arms around Isha. "Come on. Let's start your lessons."

After a few moments, Isha was sitting on the floor with the five different colored plants in front of her.

"Okay, you want to tell me how you ended up falling through the ceiling in that pool area?"

Isha looked around a moment to make sure she and Leo were alone.

"The Tree Sakari. Remember we told you that she can move us throughout the castle?"

Leo folded his arms, "I remember Makeba saying something about that after Jacinta came to me crying that night. You were pretty banged up. But I just thought she meant they took the platform down."

"No. Lonta'Mar can really make the floor and walls open and take us inside. But I think she isn't fully healed yet. So, maybe it's probably not working properly right now."

Leo shook his head, "At this point, it would be just foolish of me not to believe you." He leaned back against the sofa. "Okay, try not to go anywhere the school doesn't want you to be."

"Huh, what do you mean?"

"This school is a place of learning, sure, but there are dangerous places here. Typically, we keep those places locked up. But since you can now walk between walls, the typical safety procedures don't apply to you. And given your knack of ending up where you don't belong... just be safe, okay?"

CHAPTER 24

Victor stood atop the airship as it sailed through the night sky. Looking back, he watched as the pilot switched herself out with another woman. Together he'd noticed four women taking the pilot role since he'd boarded the ship. The way the red orb glowed as they sank their magical power into it was something close to mesmerizing. A glow that was mirrored by the side of the ship glowing red. Its fluids pulsed with the changing of the pilots.

I wonder how many pilots they actually have aboard this ship. Is there a fifth? I remember one pilot telling me that it took something akin to ten years to learn to properly pilot these things. But once you learn, you become invaluable to any kingdom with a heavy reliance on trade. So, in fact, all of them.

As he looked through the night sky into a sea of darkness only illuminated by the moon and stars above, he couldn't help but think of another place that floated in the sky. A place where the world's supposedly best mages would go to train, and his involvement in hunting down a small girl and escorting her towards the ship that took her there.

How many war orphans have I seen now? Children were cast out into the world after their parents were killed because some noble ordered it. I guess me and that old bastard aren't that different. How many children have I made weep at the loss of their mother or father? And that poor girl clutched to my fingers as she shook at the sight of any burly man with the hint of a beard.

For a moment, Victor thought about the implications of what that meant about his own manhood before shaking the thought from his mind.

Perhaps, children just take to men with glasses.

"Enjoying the night air?" asked a husky voice behind him.

Victor turned around to see an older bearded man with glasses and a gentle smile across his face.

"It's a pleasant enough night. How about yourself? May I help you?"

"Just an old man looking for company and conversation if you would indulge me," the older gentleman stepped beside Victor. "You seem to be a military man. Perhaps we could share stories to pass some time on our dreary trip."

"How did you assume I was a military man?"

"Thirty years of service. One tends to recognize the subtle hints in a person's posture. The way you place your hands behind your back, the straightness of your legs, the spacing of your feet, always a certain distance apart. Clothing can only hide so much of who we are, young man."

"So, it would seem," said Victor with a genuine smile. "Alright, then tell me, weary traveler, what brings you on this trip to the Holy City?"

The older gentleman nodded to a young boy who had fallen asleep on the deck with his back against the cabin wall.

"That little man over there's called Xelon. He's, my grandchild. I have him traveling with me to show him that there's more to the world than there is back home."

"I suppose he's not one for nighttime viewing."

"Not yet. The young never have an appreciation for life. Only after about two dozen years and a few deaths that hit too close to home does one begin to realize their own mortality. I doubt I'll live to see him come to such a realization. But like I remember my grandpa's lessons, I'm sure he'll remember mine."

"You have a pleasant way of thinking."

"Do you not have any children? Not a wife waiting for your return?" asked the old man as he took a pipe, lighting the embers inside by snapping two pieces of metal together attached to rings on his finger.

"No children. No one back at home at the moment. But there are these two ladies that I've grown quite fond of in the past few months."

"I see, you're on your way then. A bit of advice from an old man: When you decide which one you wish to marry, be swift and honest with the other. It's better to rip out the blade and let it heal than leave it in and risk the plague. A woman's wrath can be a terrible thing."

"You sound as if you speak from experience," said Victor with a smile. The sweet smell of the leaves of his pipe tingled his nose. It was light but soothing.

"I like to think I was quite the bachelor in the spring of my youth."

Victor nodded to the boy. "You said that you were experiencing the world with your grandchild there. Where are his parents?"

"My daughter and her husband have two other girls to distract them, both of whom have the gift of magic. My grandchild there, being a boy, wasn't as fortunate as his sisters."

Victor nodded his head in understanding. A boy who

dreamed of being a grand mage only to find himself without any magic to speak off. And a grandfather determined to show him another way he might be able to live. "The world is big, and we all must find our place in it."

"Agreed," said the old man. "That we must." He stretched his shoulders. "Thank you, sir. I've enjoyed this little night conversation. But it seems as if my grandson over there is in dire need of his cot, and I should probably turn in as well."

Victor nodded to the old man as he patted his pipe before walking over to the boy, waking him as they made their way downstairs.

Children huh? A shape-shifting assassin and a woman who not so distantly cut my throat. He placed his hand on his neck, rubbing at the scarred skin. *I guess I should have a creamer look at this. Or perhaps this suits the look of a man who's supposed to be a military commander.*

"That is a very bad scar you have," said a heavily accented feminine voice from nearby.

Victor turned to where he thought he heard the voice, but nothing was there.

"I would think that it was too deep to survive. Yet here you are?" said the voice, her accent as heavy as the darkness surrounding him. "I was told you no mage, so how you survive?"

"I got lucky," said Victor, who reached for the dagger at his side, underneath his coat, only to realize that it was gone.

"You won't be needing that now. Blades are dangerous things. It's best to keep them away."

Victor dropped his hands to his side as he narrowed his eyes. "You have my weapon, which means you were close enough to kill me, and you didn't. So, what is it you want?"

"Ho ho, you smart man, this is good. But I already knew this. You lace blade in Alagaon stone. Would catch some others but not me. I better than most."

"So it would seem. But are you going to tell me what you

want?"

"I'm curious. First, I was told to find you. Then I was told to kill you. Then I was told to protect you. You very confusing man." The voice paused as if taking the time to consider something. "Why so confusing?" said the voice, seeming to whisper in his ear from a distance so close Victor felt as if he could feel her breath on his skin.

"Having assassins protect me seems to be a common occurrence in my life."

"Really? Then do tell where last assassin be. Did they die?"

"I married her."

Slowly from around him, Victor felt the wind blow. Here, inside the protective space of the ship, where he knew no wind should have blown, came the sound of laughter.

"This is true. Your face, it does not tell a lie. And fresh scar across throat may be proof of this." More laughter came from the anonymous wind. "I think you will be good target, funny man. But you no marry me... Maybe last assassin go crazy. This is what I think."

"You've asked me a question. But what if I have a question?"

"Yes. You would have many questions, I am sure. So I grant you one since you make me laugh."

"Why does the person who hired you want me dead?"

"Oh, so you ask a 'why' but not a 'who.' I know not the answer to either. Boss, order you dead, then I receive word for you to stay alive. Very confusing, but also very interesting. Much more of a challenge to keep one alive than make them dead."

"Really? I think I've been doing a good enough job keeping myself alive."

"Have you? When old man try to poison you with pipe, you not do good job. I make immune by tingle on back of neck. Then I poison him. Believe the boy to be his apprentice, but he bad assassin. They both die soon."

What? Thought Victor. "Did you kill them?"

"No. Only gave them the sea belly. But old man is old. He may not survive the shits."

"I didn't realize assassins had qualms about killing their own."

"My own? No, I am as far from him as the sun is from the moon. If kill, they might send another. Instead, wound them their pride. Let them know they are inferior. Then they tell others if attack you, I may not spare them."

"So, wound the hound to scare the pack?"

"You have the way of it, yes."

From one assassin to another. "Fine, I accept that you mean me no harm at the moment. So, what am I to call you? I figure since we are now together. We should at least know each other's names."

"I have no name. It changes like the days. Call me what you wish. There may be time when name is needed."

Always up to me to think of something, Victor thought of Silk and smirked. "Fine, how about Muslin."

"Hmmm," came a soft moan. "Yes, Muslin, you may call me this."

"Well then, Muslin. Do you know where I am headed? Or what my mission is?"

"You go to city of your Goddess. I do not care why. But you will do well to keep yourself out of trouble. I save you, but I not told to die for you."

"Noted."

"And if order's change, then I kill you, even if I find you to be funny man."

"I'd never expect you not to."

"Good, then we have understanding. I sleep now."

And with a gust of the wind from where there should have been no wind. The voice and the assassin's presence vanished, leaving Victor on the deck along with the pilot as they veered off further into the night sky.

I really think I've had my fill with assassins.

Days later, the ship finally arrived at the Holy City. Stepping out of his quarters and onto the ship's deck, Victor could see the golden arched roofs of many prestigious buildings along the deck were most of the crew and passengers. They docked near one of the loading towers, extending the bridge towards the ship. Victor hadn't spoken to the assassin again since that night on the ship, but he also noticed he hadn't seen the old man or his supposed grandson. But above deck, he did see them now. They were at the head of the line, looking significantly worse for wear. The older man's eyes were sunken with dark circles around the edges as he leaned on the side of the ship's railing.

It seems he survived.

The older man glanced around before stepping onto the tower bridge and catching sight of Victor. Victor gave him a nod and a smile, but the old man turned his head away. A look of disgust on his face as his supposed grandson led him across the bridge and down the tower.

"Are you still there, Muslin?" asked Victor in a low voice, but no response came. *I guess I couldn't really expect a response,* thought Victor as he scanned over the crowd of people. *The voice was female, but it's not as if that provides much assistance. That's all of the crew and most of the passengers.*

Shaking his head and discontinuing the thought, he joined the group of exiting passengers and made his way down the ramp. The city's streets were just as beautiful as the building they flowed through. Water drains on each side of the road. In the middle of the street were several designs etched into a large circular marble disk surrounded by cobblestone. It was a pattern Victor found that was mimicked on every road he made his way through. However, each symbol inside the circular marble disk was different than before.

I wonder what they mean; perhaps they represent the noble houses spread throughout the city.

The city was huge, easily bigger than the capital cities of Burlus and Mari, and at the center, for all to see and worship under, was easily the largest statue of the Goddess herself. She held a blade that pierced the ground and was as wide as a house and perhaps a dozen or so stories high, in one hand. Her other stone arm rested over her belly as if sheltering a child that had yet to begin showing. She wore a long dress draped over her shoulder and fell to the streets below, spreading out towards the streets. The stone fabric made its way into fountains or turned into stools for the people to rest. To circle the structure on foot seemed as if it would take an hour at the least.

"Some things never will never cease to be amazing," said Victor, looking up at the statue. The streets grew more and more lively as Victor traveled through the city, getting closer to its heart; a grand temple bigger than any castle he'd ever had the privilege to see. It stood in the shadow of the giant statue, shielded from the evening sun by her stone dress. Occupants from the building shuffled in and out, up and down the numerous flights of stairs that lead up to its doors.

Okay, I've arrived. What is my course of action? *Confront the council about the crystals in the bodies of citizens hidden beneath their temples? Sounds like a quick way to be tossed into another dungeon and labeled a heretic. First, I need information.*

Victor glanced around at the city, at its people in well-dressed garbs and clean roads once again before setting off on his way. It took most of the day circling through the streets before he finally stopped at an incense shop. The name Genlin was expertly etched into a wooden sign that hung from a metal rod protruding from the wall. He twisted his lips, looking up at the sign with squinted eyes.

Shaking his head, he entered through the shop's door. Inside, floating through the air, was a stream of light pink smoke that hovered just below the ceiling. It smelled of some sweet plant or perfume that he couldn't quite place but that somehow seemed familiar.

Ahead of him was the front desk, but no one was behind it.

"Welcome to Grenlin's," said a familiar voice in a tone that suggested that he couldn't be bothered to care about who had entered. "What d'ya want?"

Victor turned to the corner of the room to see a man sitting down with his boots on a table. The man's head was down. His eyes were closed, and his arms were folded across his chest.

"I came looking for information, but it seems I've found only a lazy lout with no sense of courtesy."

The man slowly opened an eye to get a look at Victor before chuckling.

"Well, if it isn't the old commander. What brings you to my humble little shop? I hope you're not recruiting for another one of your suicide missions. I'm out of the game now. You'll find only smoke pots and quiet evenings in my future."

"The shop may be humble, Grenlin, but you never were," said Victor as he walked over to the table and pulled out a chair, taking a seat. "I'm in need of a bit of information. Can you tell me about any strange dealings in the city?"

"Strange? What isn't strange about this city?" asked Genlin as he reached into the inside pocket of his vest and pulled out a brown glass vial. He placed it on the table, sliding it over to Victor. "Not that I don't trust ya being the jackass that I think ya are. But better to be sure, and with ya being who ya are, it shouldn't mind ya none."

Victor nodded his head in understanding before grabbing the bottle and uncorking it. He turned it upside down and put a decent amount of white pounder onto his hand. Then, corking the bottle back and sliding it back across the table, he dabbed both of his shoulders with the white powder.

"That's nice. Need to be sure of no trickery," said Grenlin as he placed the bottle back inside his vest's pocket. "Now, what ya be needing to know? The city's got its fair share of boy and lady whores. Schemes and plots and whatnots. Noble families vanishing from their homes. Or do ya believe in the hidden treasure inside of that eyesore of a goddess statue?"

"Let's start with a broader question. Have you noticed anything odd about the city in the past year?"

"Was what I just said not odd enough of ya. Ya really do have high standards for fuckery, don't ya?" said Grenlin as he placed his hand on his chin and began thinking. "A few more killings than usual, but with them robbed fuckers and their grand holy meeting coming up, you'd expect more foolishness. Hmmm. A few moons back, some fuckers tried following me. Not sure what they intended, but I scared them off well enough. Some second-rate mages looking to test themselves, I'd bet. Wounded one good, and the rest ran off."

"You ever been attacked in the city before?"

"A few of times when setting up shop here. Couple of rival shops thought they'd try their luck at running me out of town. They soon found themselves with more trouble than they'd wished for, and it's been quiet since 'cept for that night with the fellas."

"And the nobles, were they mages also?"

"Ya know any nobles that aren't?"

"A fair point."

"What, ya think people are going about picking off mages now?"

"Not sure. A while back, I found that a sect of the church of the Goddess was going around kidnapping the common people from the town they had temples in."

"So what? Ya think they've moved up from cooks and housewives to mages now?"

"Seems that way."

"Well fuck. Why's my life always gotta turn ta shit when ya come around? I don't work for ya no more. Go find some other poor bastard to fuck over."

"Isn't it customary for old war friends to meet to share stories over drinks?"

"That's only true if crazy old commander hasn't tried to kill us over and over," Grenlin pointed his finger at Victor. "Ya know we all hated ya at first. Non-mage captain ordering mages to their death. It never felt right. Felt more like punishment for something we did, but we never figured out what."

"Just bad luck. It wasn't my decision to become a captain, or commander, or even a general for that matter."

"Yead, so ya have said. Word comes that Queen made you these things. At first, we thought ya were fucking Queen, but then we thought better. The Queen wouldn't stoop so low. I think she keeps you as a pet to show off to nobles. Like a fancy dog after it has learned its tricks."

"And you think you're any better?"

"No, we're all dogs. But the Queen would not show me off. Probably doesn't even know I exist. But she knows you exist. So, what is it you will be asking of me? Not much I can do now since I became spy. And if you try to sneak into the Holy Castle, then you're stupider than I thought and may as well kill yourself to save them guards the trouble."

"Is it that bad inside?"

"Yes, many people, many spells. One wonders: why kidnap mages when the church has powerful mages all their own?"

"None of this makes any sense. All we know is what they are doing. We still have no idea why."

"There is no we. I left to get away from you. They could be working to revive the Shadow King, and I still not help you. I give ya the information as agreed, but this time your craziness will not involve me."

"Fair enough, then can you inform me where I might stay the night and to whom I might inquire more about the church's activities without being noticed?"

"Oh, you will be noticed," said Genlin with a laugh. "Everyone who comes to the city is known by someone or another. Some come to use the church for money or power. Others come to the city for business or power. All is known eventually, but it is who you are known by that matters. And there are few that being known by isn't so bad as long as you do not mind the company you keep."

"You left the regiment early. I'm no longer who I was. I know the world isn't black and white. I've done many things in the years and associated myself with people you would find it hard to deal with."

"That so? We will see. If true, then I will not see your body hung from one of the town outposts in the coming days. There are a few places you could go. The first is Madam Silvie. She provides the flesh for those who will pay. Look for the Umbridge House and tell her what you wish to know. She does not usually deal in names, but if she asks, tell her truthfully. To lie to the Madam Silvie is not done. She knows a lie. And bring gold. She likes the sound of it."

"And the others?"

"Lady Brunline, she finds herself as an instrument of the Goddess, sent to punish the wicked. This will be hard. She will require a guilty man or woman; someone who she thinks requires the Goddess's punishment. But if you bring her this, she will offer you anything."

"Anyone else?"

"Brutil, a man who works at the weapons yard. Big man, he will want to fuck you, and for you to call him daddy while he does so."

Victor just stared at Grenlin for a moment.

"The man knows things. And I did not know if you were in hurry; Brutil will be the fast way, I think."

"I'll keep that in mind," said Victor with a grimace as he

stood from the table. "Goodbye, Grenlin. Your company was just as pleasant as I remember. Try to be safe. The kingdom would so hate to see such a fine man as yourself caught up in this mess."

And with a swirl of a magical finger, Grenlin opened the door, and Victor saw himself out, hearing the door close quickly behind him. He was barely two steps away from the door before he felt a breeze tingle his ear.

"Oh please, say we go visit this Brutil first. I very much would like to see," said Muslin's voice, drifting over his ear softly.

"Then I'm afraid I must disappoint you. First, I will look for a place to rest and perhaps a strong drink. I suddenly feel a headache approaching."

CHAPTER 25

"Hold it, girl," shouted Mr. Higgins. "That's it. Keep your feet planted. Buckle your knees. Yes, like that. Now, lean into it with your elbows."

Isha gritted her teeth as she clutched the buckler in her hand. The magic protruded from it as large mounds of dirt and rock crashed into it. Ahead of her stood Jacinta and Makeba, both dirty and breathing heavily with sweat dripping down their faces. Each Sakari girl stood beside a large trough filled with a mixture of dirt and clay. And in the center of them stood an equally exhausted Chloe.

"Again," shouted Mr. Higgins.

The Sakari girls planted their hands into the troughs, letting their magic seep inside, coursing through the dirt and clay. It began to move and shift around their hands. Then, as if on cue, both girls brought up two large mounds of spherical dirt. But despite the newly created rocks floating
340

above their hands, the girls seemed to struggle to lift them above their heads.

"Now, launch another volley,"

Chloe's hands and arms began to glow a light blue as she stretched her hands out warm, letting her magic flow over the balls of dirt above the Sakari girl's heads. And bending their knees, Jacinta and Makeba launched the balls into the air.

"Arghh!" grunted Chloe as she added her force to theirs, assisting in the balls through the air towards Isha.

Isha watched as the small boulders headed to her. As instructed by Mr. Higgins before, she grit her teeth. With one shield over her hand, the strap dangling by her knees, she channeled all the magic she could into it. The first boulder hit with a thud that dropped her to one knee as it exploded against her shield, sending dirt and dust flying all around her.

I can do this, I... can do this.

Her arms felt heavy. Her knuckles felt raw from bracing up against the back of the shield after each impact. But with no time to rest, she grunted and tried to stand with the shield forward, pushing as much magic as she could into it. Then the second boulder came. It was launched higher than the first. and it struck harder than the first. Isha's power gave out as her shields broke apart, and the boulder exploded against the buckler with such force that it knocked her back. Pieces of the boulder slid off the shield and flew past her, breaking apart on the mat behind her. But she couldn't regain her footing after the impact and fell, sliding over the floor. The buckler escaped from her grip, rolling across the ground beside her.

"Sister okay?" asked Makeba as the girls ran over to Isha, helping her sit up.

"I'm..." she winced as she tried to move her arm. It had taken the front of the blow and was now shaking. She began rubbing it, trying to get the feeling under control. "It's...

okay. I'm okay. I just need... a minute."

"No," said Mr. Higgins, stepping over and looking down at the girls. "You're not. That's enough for today. You four have done well enough. and I've been instructed to keep teaching you after classes, but you can only go so far before you begin to break down. So, take tomorrow off and give your body time to recover. For now, go wash up and have that healer take a look at that arm."

All the girls eagerly agreed as they helped Isha to her feet and left the room, leaving Mr. Higgins behind to clean the mess. The halls of the school were once again empty as the settling sun could be seen through the classroom windows. The girls made their way down the hall and headed down a flight of stairs that led to a bathing room; the room she had fallen into where Pavel's secret was revealed.

"So tired," said Jacinta as she began stripping off clothes on her way to the bath when they entered the bathing area. Dropping her clothing on the floor, she slouched towards the water before falling in.

Makeba followed suit as Chloe locked the door behind them.

As Isha began removing her clothes, she caught Chloe staring at her.

"What? Is something wrong?"

"What? When do you get those?" asked Chloe, pointing to the markings across Isha's back. "Those are like the markings that Jacinta and Makeba have."

"Oh," said Isha, turning her head, trying to see over her own shoulder. "I guess you haven't seen these since I got them. And you're right; these are the markings the Sakari use. It allows me to share the magic I have with Makeba and Jacinta without it hurting us. And they can share theirs with me."

"You three must be really close," Chloe said hesitantly as she reached forward. "Can I touch them?"

"Ah, sure. I don't mind."

Chloe slowly placed her hand on Isha's back and shoulders, running her fingers over her skin where the markings were. "It's pretty. But didn't it hurt to do this?"

"It did," agreed Isha as she let the garb around her waist drop to the floor. "But I think I would hurt them a lot more if I didn't do it. And I don't want to hurt them any more than I already have."

"You really see them as your sisters, don't you?"

Isha smiled over at Jacinta and Makeba as they began splashing about in the water. "I really don't think I'll ever understand how they see me. But since we've met, they've protected and looked after me. And rarely ever complained, even when I was being a bit selfish. I don't... I just don't want to mess that up. Not again."

Before long, they had all stripped and were sitting on the bath steps, their bodies submerged in the water up to their necks.

"It good... that sister find bath here," said Jacinta as she frowned while she stretched her shoulders. "Much bigger than house bath, and we not have to walk back sticky."

"I also did not realize there was a bath down here," said Chloe as she looked around at the statues against the wall. "How did you find it?"

"Sister always finds new places," said Jacinta as she swam over to one of the two fountains in the shape of a giant fish that fed the bath. "I wonder where water goes. We in sky, so no lake to give us water, but school has lots of water."

"It probably more magic," said Makeba, lifting her hand from the water and examining it. "Water is clear like new water. So it not from lake. Maybe they catch the rainwater and keep it for bathing."

"Makeba," said Chloe, "What's that thing around your neck?"

Makeba lifted the golden rope, holding it up in front of her. "This magic crystal. I push my magic into it. But so far, it does nothing but glow for a while. It is very pretty, though."

"Tannor man, give it to her," said Jacinta. "But he not come back yet. So I guess we keep. Come, sister. You have dirt in hair."

"Maybe... owe," winced Isha as she tried to stretch her arms in the water.

"Are you okay, Fairline?" asked Chloe as she slid her way over to Isha.

"Huh? I think so. I mean, my arms hurt a bit, is all."

"No... well, yes, that too, I guess. I mean... you've been looking tired a lot these days. You even fall asleep in class."

"Oh. I guess I have. But I'm okay, really. I think... I think I'll be good after I get some sleep."

Chloe looked around the bath as Jacinta and Makeba began washing each other's hair underneath the fish fountain. She then closed her eyes and took in a deep breath before sighing it out over the water. "Fairline, can I talk to you about something?"

"Okay, is something wrong?"

"No, it's not... I... I just never thanked you. You know, for what you did when they took us."

"It's okay. You would have done the same thing for me, right?"

"I don't... I don't know what I would have done. I was... I was just so mad at you."

"Yeah. I'm sorry too. I don't know what I did, but I must have made you pretty mad," said Isha, only for her to turn and see that Chloe was looking at her as if she had seen a ghost. "What? Did I say something weird?"

"Do you... do you really think you did something?"

"I mean... well, didn't I?"

"No!"

"But... then why were you mad at me?"

"You... how are you like this?" Chloe brought her hands out of the water, placing her palms over her eyes and splashing water over her face. "Why are you like this?"

"Chloe, are you-"

"Arghh, Fairline, listen," said Chloe as she reached over, grabbing Isha by her shoulders. "It's my family's fault you're here."

"Wha... what do you mean?"

"My father, he brought you here. I mean, well... I think he did."

"Chloe, are you alright? It was my father who brought us back to the school."

"Not the school. I mean all of it. You said you were from some other place, right? I think it was my father who took you away from that place. I don't know what happened, but there was a fire and... and... my mother she... and father." The words caught in her mouth as she began fumbling words, her eyes tearing up at the edges. "I'm sorry. I'm... so sorry."

Isha just stared at Chloe. *That can't be... I mean... The night of the fire. It wasn't... But I remember being with Papa, and then the men attacked. Then I was in the castle... and the fire.* Images of the night of the fire began flashing through Isha's mind. But she couldn't get a clear picture of anything. Images of her father's face kept changing between a rough brown-haired bearded man and a clean-shaven dark-haired man.

"Fairline... Fairline."

Why... why can't I remember his face? No, this isn't right. I remember... I remember being chased from our home. Papa wasn't... Suddenly the image of an old man appeared in Isha's head. He had a thick gray beard. Out of the fog of her mind, Isha heard the sounds of her name being called, and she took one look at Chloe's worried face and muttered the word, "Sister," before the world started to blur.

"Fairline are... are you alright?"

"Stop, no... I can't remember his face. I just... I just need a moment," said Isha as she placed a hand over her face. As her head started to throb, she felt as if her stomach was in knots, almost to the point where she wanted to vomit. *No... something's not right. I... I shouldn't feel like this.* She forced herself to stand up from the water, clutching the bath's side so she wouldn't fall over. "Jacinta... Makeba, can you please help me home? I feel... I don't feel right."

The Sakari girls swam back to their sister as Chloe helped her out of the water. Haphazardly, they put back on their clothing, helping Isha into hers, and made their way out of the school and back home, where they found Leo sitting on the roof looking up at the stars.

"You girls are home late, Enjoying the..." Leo's words paused in his mouth as he looked down at the girls holding up Isha. "Okay, what is it this time?" said Leo with a sigh as he walked to the side of the house, making his way down a ladder.

"Not sure. Sister Isha say she feel bad, so we bring her home," said Jacinta, a worried look across her face. "We practice with Mr. Higgy man. He say to look at her arm."

"Well, at least you brought her home this time," said Leo as he walked up, placing his hand on Isha's forehead. "I was getting tired of having to come rescue you. Humm. You do not seem to have a bit of a fever." He turned to lead them inside. "Okay, come in and lay her on the floor."

They followed Leo, doing as he said as he placed his hand over her head and heart, closing his eyes, letting his magic seep over her. Then, after a few moments, Leo removed his hands and looked at Isha with a smile.

"It seems you do have your limits after all."

"What... what do you mean?" asked Isha, her chest still heavy and her head throbbing.

"Magical exhaustion, this is what it looks like. Even with that weird power you have, the effects still apply to you."

"Sister was not using white magic power," said Makeba, wiping a line of wet hair from Isha's face. "Higgy man said not to use it and instead she should use normal magic first, so she gets stronger."

"Higgy man? Is that what you call Mr. Higgins? I can't imagine he took kindly to that. But maybe it is a good idea to have you focus on your standard magic first. Relying too much on a magic none of us really understand might cause you problems later."

"Higgy man say the same."

"Higgy man," said Leo with a laugh. "I'll never get used to that." He then looked at the water droplets over his hands and then looked at the girls. "Why are you all wet?"

"We took bath at school, that when sister get sick."

"Well, you're home now. You girls escort Isha upstairs and help her change. She should be okay after a night's rest. Thankfully, she didn't exert herself too much. I've seen extreme cases that have put someone under for a month."

"I guess... I guess I should go then," said Chloe as the Sakari girls helped Isha back to her feet.

"Go where? You live here now, or have you forgotten that?"

"No..." said Chloe quickly as she glanced toward Isha. "I should... I mean, I left a few things back at my old dorm. I should probably go and get them." She then turned and headed out the door at a quick pace.

"Well, that was strange," said Leo, turning to the girls as they made it to the steps. "I don't suppose you want to tell me what that was about."

"I will," said Isha, tiredly. "But can I sleep first?" *I don't want to think about anything anymore.*

"Go on. Tomorrow then."

Isha hobbled her way upstairs, allowing her sisters to wipe her hair down and roll her into bed. They then joined her after changing clothes, wrapping their arms around her.

"Jacinta, Makeba?"

"Yes, sister."

"I don't... I don't think... It's just... thank you. I really don't know what I would do if you both weren't here with me."

"Sister would cry," said Jacinta as she snuggled up against Isha. "But we cry together now. Better than alone, I think."

And with that thought and the warmth of her sisters around her, Isha fell asleep in their arms.

The next morning Isha awoke to find that she did indeed feel better and that her headache had passed. Downstairs she heard something heavy being dragged across the wooden floor. The screeching from it ended with a loud thud as whatever it was had been dropped. Curiosity getting the best of her, she went out into the hall and heard the cheerful sounds of her sister's voices.

"Well, I'm happy someone is enjoying this mess," came Leo's voice. "Who is going to clean up the leaves? I mean, look at what it did to the floor."

Isha poked her head downstairs to see Leo shaking his head at what appeared to be a small tree that was sitting in the middle of the house where the sofa had been. But this tree was familiar. Although it was small and barely even reached four feet in height, the trunk was thick and sprouted up through the floor. Its leaves, which Jacinta and Makeba were touching and inspecting, were a fluorescent orange, the same as the Lonta'Mar's tree inside the magic school.

"Oh, sister, awake," said Jacinta after spotting Isha up the steps. "You always sleep long when we not wake you."

"What's going on?" said Isha as she stared at the tree.

"Makeba got Tree Sakari to make us a little tree here, so now we not have to go all the way in castle to visit her."

"She can do that?" asked Isha. *I guess she can. I mean, she can move the roots around.* Then another thought hit Isha.

348

"Wait? Makeba? Can you talk with Lonta'Mar without me using the magic?"

"No, not real talk, But I find out that she can hear me when I talk. I just cannot hear her. So, I asked her if she could make us a tree, so that we see her more often. And now we have baby tree."

"You could have asked first," said Leo, shaking his head. "Or, at the very least, not put it in the middle of the house."

Stepping down to the first floor, Isha watched as the tree seemed to sway slightly as if some type of wind was in the house.

"Can we really use this tree to visit Lonta'Mar?"

"Oh, okay. So I'm just going to be ignored," said Leo, before tossing his hands up and turning around to grab a bag from the table. "Well, there's no school today, so you girls can stay here and play with your little tree. I have to go to my office." Leo then walked over, giving each girl a kiss on the forehead. "Bye-bye, babies. Don't destroy the rest of the house while I'm away."

Jacinta and Makeba all smiled at the gesture, but Isha found herself blushing a bit as he left the house. Thankfully for her, her sisters were too enthralled with their new tree to notice.

"Does sister feel better now? Can we visit Tree Sakari again?"

After eating, the girls sat beneath the small tree and held hands. Isha then began channeling the magic inside of her. The wooden boards beneath them began to creak and bend as from the openings came the roots of the tree as if seeking out for them and began sliding over their bodies before their minds were taken away once again.

Upon opening her eyes, Isha found herself back in the forest area Lonta'Mar had imagined for them before. However, the area seemed vaster than before, and the colors looked slightly livelier. She spotted Lonta'Mar ahead as she appeared from behind a tree with a smile.

"We come back," said Jacinta as she and Makeba walked over to the other Sakari. "Small tree was good idea. Now we can visit much more."

"Yes," said Lonta'Mar. "I did not know if I could make another of myself in such a small place. But I tried really hard."

"This is good. Now we can show you more of Sakari and Henlik."

"Henlik? What's that?" asked Isha.

"Henlik is big city in Sakar. We will get to show sister also, so this will be good."

"I would like to see that," agreed Isha, genuinely curious as to what a Sakari city might look like. Looking up into the extremely large trees, she couldn't help but imagine that perhaps they live high up in the trees in woodland cities.

Soon the Sakari girls were off into the forest with Isha following behind. Jacinta and Makeba spent time explaining things to Lonta'Mar about the forestry and colors that she had forgotten. They would occasionally switch back to speaking Sakari when Lonta'Mar didn't understand what they were trying to say, a process in which Isha was not completely lost as her sisters were teaching her the language.

They spent hours expanding the invisible walls within this world they had created until they all were tired, deciding to take a break underneath one of the trees.

"We did lots today, you remember much more than before."

"Yes, I am starting to remember many of the plants and…" Lonta'Mar's words froze in her mouth as she stared off behind the girls."

"What's wrong?' asked Makeba, looking confused at Lonta'Mar.

They all followed the Sakari's gaze only to see a strange

bug flying in the air behind Jacinta. It had four green wings constantly flapping as it made its way between the girls, leaving a small green mist behind it that reminded Isha of the glow of magic when they used it during training.

"Oh, a Vasque. I remember Uncle Funny Man used to catch them for us," said Jacinta reaching out her hand, trying to get the insect's attention as it hovered between the girls. "But he always had trouble since he no had magic. You did well to start remembering them."

"I... I did not know I remembered them," said Lonta'Mar. "I just... maybe I do remember. But it's hard. Did they respond to magic?"

"Yes," said Makeba with a smile. "Vasque wings are magic. If you have magic, then they come to you at night." She then extended her arm towards the creature, just like her sister. The creature did not come to her. Makeba frowned, looking at her arm. "Can we not use magic here?"

"I... I don't know," said Lonta'Mar. "I never needed to try before."

Jacinta leaned over, then placed her hand on the soil beneath her and closed her eyes. But after a few moments of nothing, she frowned. "My magic no work here either. That no fun."

Makeba folded her hand in front of her while closing her eyes. "I wonder why magic no works here.

Isha attempted to do the same. Remembering the feel of her magic, she tried channeling it into her fingers, but as the others had said, nothing happened. Just an empty feeling where her magic should have been. *But aren't I using magic to come here?*

"This no fun," said Jacinta, tossing the dirt from her hand. "You should try," she said, pointing at Lonta'Mar.

"I don't have magic," said Lonta'Mar, looking nervously at the three girls.

"What you mean?" Jacinta pointed all around them. "Is not all this magic? This is magic world."

"No. This is just what I made. This isn't magic… is it?"

All the girls just stared at Lonta'Mar, confused, not knowing exactly what to say. They had never actually spoken to Lonta'Mar about what exactly magic was.

"Ah, Lonta'Mar," said Isha. "You see the other people doing magic in school. Don't you watch them sometimes?"

"Yes, that is how I learn to speak. Do you mean that I can do magic also? So it's not just for soft-skinned people?"

"What about when you move the roots around the school or take us into the wall?"

"That not magic. I just move things. Like this," Lonta'Mar began to wave her arm around and wiggle her fingers. "It is the same. I move things. But it is true that making new tree was hard. I never do that before."

Isha stood up and stepped over to Lonta'Mar, reaching out and taking her hands in hers. "Lonta'Mar, I think you have magic. You just don't know how to use it."

"Oh," said Jacinta, looking excited. "That means we get to teach her."

"But will we teach her Sakari way or Kingdom way?" asked Makeba, standing up and walking over to Lonta`Mar. "She is Sakari, and the tree is from Sakar, so I think we should teach her Sakari magic.

"Agree," said Jacinta.

"Can I do anything to help?" asked Isha.

"No, Sister, wait for now," said Jacinta. "Finding Sakari magic different from Kingdom magic. "We no have Aukube here, but we sure we can teach."

"Okay," said Isha feeling a bit left out. "If your sure."

"Yes, we sure."

Following her sister's suggestion, Isha stepped back, sat back down on the ground, then watched as her sisters laid Lonta'Mar on the ground, letting her head touch the ground. They then dug up the soil around her body and began pushing it against Lonta`Mar arms and legs, allowing it to cover her hands and feet. Makeba then stood up and glanced around before running around the forest area, breaking off the twigs from a few trees and laying them over her body.

"It is a shame we have no water here," said Makeba, "But maybe we will not need."

For the first time, Isha could see that Lonta`Mar was nervous. Her hands were shaking some of the dirt free as she looked around. Makeba also saw this and placed her hands over Lonta`Mar's face, closing her eyes.

"Kula… Kula san tru ish sla Hulig," said Lonta'Mar, her voice shaking

How… How I know magic come, thought Isha, trying to remember her Sakari words.

"Bole fo Makeba ala zul. Wole ma huol tam tu untet un Makeba," said Jacinta.

Like Makeba and I. Thought Isha, only managing to translate a bit that time.

Makeba and Jacinta leaned over Lonta'Mar, placing the temple of their heads against hers, and began to whisper in unison. Isha couldn't hear the words as they were spoken too low. The closeness of the three seemed to calm Lonta'Mar down, but the effect was the opposite for Isha. This was the first time she felt truly separated from her sisters as they huddled close to each other over Lonta'Mar, whispering in a language she barely knew.

Feeling a bit self-conscious, she brought her knees to her chest, wrapped her arms around them, and watched as the girls recited their words. Isha wasn't aware of how much time had passed, but she didn't see much of a change.

I wonder if it can work here, thought Isha as she looked over the forest again. *Maybe she needs real things. All of this isn't real, I don't think. It's like a painting that hasn't been finished. But if they did it out…*

Suddenly the sound of a loud crackle tore through the wooded area.

What? asked Isha to herself, quickly standing on her

353

feet and beginning to look around. There was nothing around her that she noticed to be any different. She then turned back to her sisters, only to see them still in the same kneeling position over Lonta'Mar. Then suddenly, another crackle, and now paying attention, Isha recognized this sound to be that of thunder.

And upon realization, Isha felt a slight breeze blow through the trees above her, which had once been a clear blue sky; she saw the encroaching glimpse of dark clouds moving in.

"Ahh, Makeba, Jacinta, is this supposed to happen?"

The Sakari girls stayed in their position. Suddenly a white light zipped through the sky, followed by another loud thunderclap, and the small breeze that just came through the trees was now picking up into a fierce wind that shook the trees around them. Isha watched as the huge lumbering trees above her began to sway back and forth, rocked by the incoming storm. And then, as she knew they would, the first droplets of rain came cascading down around her.

The howl of the wind blew through the trees, followed by the leaves that had been pulled from their branches. Then, a blinding light flew past her, striking a nearby tree, the thunder ringing through her ears as she covered her head. The fear was beginning to well up inside her as her knees began shaking. But before any more panic could grow, she felt a hand on her shoulder.

Turning around, her hands still over her ears. Isha saw Makeba and Jacinta staring at her.

"What? What's happening?"

"She learn magic," yelled Jacinta. "But she takes time to learn to control. We go now." She then turned back to Lonta'Mar and waved.

"What? What do you-"

And just like that, Isha's world went white, and in an instant, she found herself back on the floor of Heart House. In front of her sat the tree, but it was now different than before. Instead of its glowing orange leaves, there were now leaves that were glowing a deepish blue color.

"What happened? Is she okay?"

"Tree Sakari learn her magic," said Makeba, "but she not know how to control it, so she sends us back. We can go back when she learns."

"I tired now," said Jacinta as she leaned back, laying on the floor and stretching her legs. "I want to sleep."

"But... I mean, is she okay?" Isha pointed at the tree. "Why did the leaves change color?"

"I do not know why tree change," said Makeba, as she followed her sister's actions, relaxing on the floor. "But we think she will be fine. She has magic now. It is always hard when one learns magic. Hard to learn to control. But she will learn. She is smart Sakari."

Isha suddenly felt tired.

"Oh, you girls are out already?" said Rima, sitting in a chair with a book in her lap. "I expected you to be in there all day? I see empty plates. Have you eaten breakfast? If not, I can try to make you something."

"Breakfast?" responded Isha. "It's not breakfast time, is it?"

"It is unless you think dinner should be served in the mornings. And what did you girls do to the tree? When I came in, it was orange. It's certainly prettier now, although I doubt Leo's going to be happy. I think it's going to glow in the dark unless you girls can turn it off."

"But... it can't be morning. We were in there all day."

"What's that? You've only been in for a few minutes. Maybe a little under half an hour. I've barely started my book."

Isha stood and began to walk towards the door, unable to believe what she was being told. She placed her hand on the knob and opened the house to the outside world, only to see that the morning sun was still early in the sky.

CHAPTER 26

The next day Isha and the girls were preparing for school. Jacinta and Makeba had just finished getting dressed, and once again, Isha sat on the floor trying to slowly channel her magic into the different colored plants, hoping that this time, they would not catch fire. Behind her, still penetrating the house's floorboards, stood the tiny tree. Its orange and deep blue leaves shimmered like a fire flickering in the night.

"Okay, you girls, come and get breakfast," said Rima as she set the table.

The girls all sat down at the table and began eating.

"You getting better at cooking," said Jacinta. "And you no longer bleed over food."

"Oh, ha-ha. I'll have you know I haven't cut myself in over a month. I'm just happy Elena wrote down her notes on how to cook. It was hard enough to learn where I had to go to order all the ingredients I needed. Apparently, I need to order the food a month ahead of time for the school to bring it up here."

Isha popped a piece of breaded cabbage into her mouth, smiling at the memory of Elena. She was indeed getting better at cooking. It was starting to taste like the cooking she had before. "Can you teach me how to cook now?"

"I suppose so. It's only a matter of mixing the spices at the right time. Oh, and getting the heat right, or you'd burn the meat. But you can help me with dinner after school. I'll even pick a little apron for you to—"

Their conversation was interrupted by a knock at the door.

"Oh, were you girls expecting your friends this morning?" asked Rima, as the girls responded by shaking their heads. "Who is it?" she shouted.

"Headmaster Soulden," came a muffled voice through the door. "I've brought a bit of company. Are the children home?"

"Well, I figured they would stop by eventually," she said before yelling, "One second," and made her way over, opening the door.

"Sorry for the interruption," said Soulden as she stepped inside the house, followed by Caudbell and Tannor. "But there has been a development with the... Oh my..." Her words paused in her mouth as she spotted the tiny tree in the center of the house. "What's this?"

"I guessed someone would be making their way here about this tree eventually," said Rima as she turned back around and headed towards the table where the girls sat. "Would you care to join us for breakfast?"

"What? I mean, how did you get this tree here?" asked Soulden.

"Amazing," said Caudbell. "Is this the same phenomenon that happened to the Trialage Tree, but in miniature form?" He turned to the girls. "Tell me, what led to such an occurrence? I must know."

"The tree being in our home is apparently Makeba's doing. I think," said Rima, shaking her head. "The explanation wasn't very clear. Did Leo not tell you about this yesterday? I assumed he would."

"No," said Soulden. "I was occupied yesterday. So, I may have missed him. Mr. Caudbell cornered me this morning and informed me of the changes to the Trialage Tree. I just assumed I would come here and ask since these three seem to always be at the forefront of things." Soulden stepped forward, rubbing her finger across one of the tree's leaves. "And it would appear I was not mistaken."

"It takes too long to go to castle to visit Tree Sakari," said Makeba. "So I ask her to make it, so we visit her here. And she make this tiny tree for us."

"I see," said Caudbell, "It was an issue of convenience." He began rubbing his face. "I wonder if it has the same properties as the Triage Tree in the school. If so, this might be a potential risk. While it would be amazing to have another tree. It isn't exactly secure to have it growing out in the common areas."

"Well, seeing as this happened because it wanted to be closer to the girls, I think we would have quite the issue convincing a sentient tree to move."

Caudbell coughed. "Yes, well, I see your point on that." He turned to the girls. "Tell me, this color change in the tree's foliage," he pointed to the leaves, "is this the work of another tree being made?"

"I think colors change because we teach Tree Sakari magic," said Jacinta as she stuffed another piece of food into her mouth.

"Excuse me, what?" asked Caudbell, his glasses hanging from his nose. "Did you just say you taught the tree... magic."

"Yes, we teach her magic."

"What type of magic exactly did you teach it?"

"Not sure now. Tree not talk to sister Isha since she

learn. But that fine. Sometimes it take days for body to calm down after learning Sakari Magic."

"So..." Caudbell squinted his eyes and took a deep breath. "If I understand this correctly, you three created a new Trialage Tree and then taught it Sakari magic, but you're not sure what type of Sakari Magic it learned?"

"Hmmm," moaned Jacinta, trying to understand his words. "I think so."

Caudbell then turned to Isha, hoping for more of an understanding. "Can you add anything to this?"

"I think that's everything, sir," said Isha, not knowing what else she could say.

Caudbell then stood up, adjusted his coat, and took a deep breath, gathering himself. "Right, well. I guess that's just the way of things, then. If you ladies would excuse me, it seems I have a mountain of things to consider about what I know about magic." He then turned and promptly headed through the house and out of the door.

"Is he... is he mad at us?" asked Isha.

"Who Caudbell?" asked Soulden, a rare smile across her face. "No, he's simply a bit frustrated, is all. Since you three have arrived, you have given him quite the workload." Soulden shook her head. "I must admit it's been a while since I've seen him this flustered."

"They have a way of doing that," said Rima, "They've had poor Leo so busy that he hasn't had time to be as depressed as he used to be."

"I'll take that as a blessing then. He was distraught after the attack. If he's been in an occupied state of my mind, then I'd like to assume he's come to terms with it." Soulden then turned back to the tree, flicking one of its leaves with her finger. "But that still leaves us with this and what to do about it. I'll sit here and try to think of a solution, but until then, I do believe it's time for you girls to get to class."

"Oh, that's right," said Isha as she, Jacinta, and Makeba finished their food and headed toward the door, only to see

Freedo pop his head inside.

"Hey, I came to get... where'd that tree come from?" said Freedo, before Makeba grabbed his arm as they led him out of the doorway into the streets to join the rest of the morning's students.

"Let us go. We will not want to be late," said Makeba. "Today, I will beat you again."

"Hey, you just got lucky last time, and don't try to change the subject. Where'd that tree come from?"

"It magic tree. It come from the ground," said Jacinta.

"Well, obviously, it comes from the ground. All trees do. Wait! What do you mean, magic tree? Are all trees magic to Sakari?"

Isha just shook her head. She didn't know how to begin to explain everything to Freedo everything properly, so she just let him have his own understanding of everything as Jacinta and Makeba continued to tease him. The four of them made their way to Miss Webblebottom's class, all sitting together alongside Chloe, who was already there.

"Okay, class," said Miss Webblebottom, after everyone was seated. "Today, we're going to go over condensed magic. Does anyone know what that is?"

"I do," said Marlene. "That is when you make spells smaller so that they become stronger."

"Very good. That is correct to a certain degree. But there's so much more you can do with it if one were really to use their imagination. So, how about a demonstration, shall we?" said Miss Webblebottom as she pointed towards a large wooden orb in the corner of the room. "Now, how many of you know how to use elemental fire magic?

"I do," said a few students as they raised their hands.

"Okay, now, how many of you can use fire magic without reciting any words during r beforehand?"

"I can," said Pavel, being the only one to raise his hand."

"Ahh. Good. But do not worry about class. You all will be able to perform wordless incantations in time with proper training. Until then, I shall give a demonstration." She then extended her hand out in front of her as a small fire ignited in her hand. The flame danced on each one of her fingers. "Now, this is fire magic. Simple in nature, but if one were to concentrate like so," the flame over her fingers changed color, from orange to a bluish purple, "you will just need to pour your magic," she brought her other hand over the flame, locking it between her fingers, "then you would just need to direct it... and..." she pointed her hands towards the wooden ball and opened the cage she made between her fingers, and a loud crackle erupted through the classroom as a bolt of lightning jolted out from her hand, striking the large wooden ball.

The whole class jumped in their seats at the display, with praises of 'wow' and 'amazing' circulating throughout the room.

"There... you see?" said Miss Webblebottom, catching her breath. "Now, a mage who is naturally attuned to fire magic will be able to do that far more easily than I am able to. But that is one of the many things that can be done with condensed magic and a little effort. Would you like to see another?"

The class unanimously agreed to see more magic.

Miss Webblebottom couldn't help but smile at their eagerness. She then turned back to the now flaming wooden orb. "Now, my natural affinity is air magic, and as such..." She raised her hand, bringing up her entire arm as it began to glow a shade of light green. Then she stepped forward, bringing that same arm low, before snatching it back up again. An explosion of wind shook the room as a torrent of air slid from the teacher's hand in a crescent shape, exploding against the wooden orb, putting out the flame and cutting it in half.

"There, you see. Not a bad way to use it, if I do say so myself. Although I guess I am a bit out of practice. So, who here wants to learn more about condensed magic?"

The entire class raised their hands, even Isha, and they would spend the next few hours understanding the basics of magical manipulation; how the body exerts magic while simultaneously concentrating it on a singular point. A feat that the girls all found out was far harder than their professor made it out to be.

At the end of class, they all began to leave the room.

"Ahh... Isha," said Chloe, reaching over and grabbing Isha by the arm before she could leave. "Can I talk with you for a minute?"

"Okay, is something..." Then Isha's mind flashed back to her time in the bath, where Chloe had tried to tell her something about her father.

"Sister not coming?" asked Makeba.

"Oh, ah... no. You three go on without me, I have to help Chloe with something."

"Sister gonna be getting into more trouble?" said Jacinta with a smile. "She does this a lot."

"No, I'm not. Stop your teasing."

Jacinta's smile widened. "We go and leave sister with her trouble." She then grabbed Freddo's and Makeba's hands. "Come, kingdom boy. We can still do fighting practice in the blue room."

"What? That's not fair," Freedo protested as he was dragged out of the room.

They both waited until the rest of the students left the room before Isha spoke.

"I don't remember everything you said before. But do you know what happened to me and why I'm here?"

"No..." said Chloe as she turned around and began walking further into the classroom towards the teacher's desk. "I mean, I don't think I do. But I know you were in my father's manor the night of the fire. I was there too, but I escaped to The Goose's house."

The Goose? thought Isha, her mind flashing with the image of a portly man's face and the flashback to that night after the fire when she had tried to go to his house. But even though she knew his face, she couldn't remember ever having met the man. "Do you know why your father had me there? All I remember is falling."

"No, he... he never told me anything. He just had this old man with him. He was a mind mage. I was told that he was to give you some of my memories."

"What?" said Isha, completely confused. "How? Why would he do that?"

"I don't know the old man, Father called him Eunwalt, I think, he was supposed to do it. All I had to do was place my hand on your head, and he would do the rest. But when he tried, something went wrong, and that's when... that's when your magic..." she began rubbing her fingers over the burned skin of her arm. "It burned us, and then everything caught fire."

Isha's mind flashed back to that night. How she had woken up and found herself standing outside of the burning manor. And how, out of panic, instinct, and fearfulness, she found herself hiding in the brush after hearing guards screaming, "Find the girl." Her mind thought back to her escape. *How did I know about the hole in the water? Or where that Goose person's house was? Are these her memories?*

"Isha?" said Chloe. "Are you... are you alright?"

"There... there are things I think I remember. But I shouldn't remember them."

"Like what?"

"Like I remember the burning manor, there was an older ahh... manservant, I think. His name was Hemlin. He was there that night."

"Hemlin?" said Chloe anxiously as she ran up, grabbing Isha's shoulders. "Was he alright? Did they hurt him? Please tell me he's alive."

"I don't know. I just remember him being outside of the fire."

"Oh," said Chloe, releasing Isha's shoulder and dropping

her head. "I remember that. I was in the bushes behind the carriage. Hemlin saw me but told me not to come out, so I ran to the Goose's house. The soldiers tried to chase me, but they couldn't fit through the hole in the wall."

"That's... That's what I did. There was a hole in the wall by the water that led up to the fountain."

"Yes. Father used to let me swim there. That's when I found it. But how did you know that?"

"I don't know. Maybe the mind mage, he gave me some of your memories. I knew some of the city streets too. I knew where the Goose was. But I didn't know the other parts of the city." Isha frowned while looking down at the floor. *Why did I not think about this before? Everything seemed familiar then.*

"Father never really let me go out in the city, except when Hemlin would take me to other nobles' houses or to the Goose's. They are the ones who hid me from the guards after the fire."

"I went there that night. I remember seeing someone in the window."

"What? Did you not try to enter?"

"No, I... I thought they would give me to the guards."

"They wouldn't do that," said Chloe defensively. "They hid men the whole time. Even when that inspector man came to the wine house. Mr. Goose did his best to protect me."

"Inspector man?"

"It was a man with glasses from the kingdom. He came looking for..." Chloe's mouth went agape as she pointed her finger at Isha. "You... you were who he was looking for."

"Glasses?" And Isha's mind instantly went to Victor Krill, although he had said that he had broken his glasses in pursuit of her. She couldn't think of anyone else. "Was his name Victor Krill?"

"I don't know. I don't think he ever said."

"It must have been him. He's the one who rescued Dessi

and me from the city."

"Dessi, she's the lady from the camp when I went with you, right?"

"That's her," said Isha as she began to recant the story of what happened to her after she escaped from Duke Richards's manor on that fiery night. How she was taken in by Broody, sold to the magistrate, rescued by Victor, and somehow found herself calling Oscar her father." The last one brought another realization to her. "Oh, Chloe, I'm sorry, I didn't... I mean."

"About what?"

"Your parent's... I mean... what happened to them."

"Oh," said Chloe with a sigh as her shoulders slumped, a sadness filling her eyes. "It's okay now. I know... I know it wasn't your fault." She brought her arms together in front of her and began rubbing her wrists again. "I don't know what my father was doing. But whatever it was, it made the king mad at us, and that's why they came. That's why... that's why..." Chloe's words continued to fumble in her mouth as tears began to well up in her eyes.

But as she tried to find herself, Isha stepped forward, wrapping her arms around her.

"It's okay. You can cry."

"I'm not... I'm," said Chloe, giving a futile attempt to free herself.

"It's okay," said Isha, placing her head on Chloe's shoulders. "My parents are gone too. You can cry. I promise I won't tell anyone. I cried a lot too when I lost my Papa." Holding on to Chloe, Isha thought about how Makeba and Jacinta had been there for her when she needed them and how Chloe didn't seem to have anyone like that for her. *What would have happened to me if they had been there?*

For a moment, the room was silent, and Isha felt Chloe grow still.

"Chlo-" and she felt it before Isha could finish saying the girl's name. The feeling of a cold liquid hitting the side of her neck only to be followed by the sounds of a whaling of pain that had seemed to have been bottled up for longer than she could know. Chloe's weight gave way, forcing Isha to carry her as she lowered herself to the floor. The room seemed to grow darker as she felt Chloe's hands grip the back of her uniform; she continued sobbing softly, echoing off the walls and back onto them, making it seem as if the walls were sharing her pain.

They held each other until their will to stay upright faded alongside Chloe's sobs. Holding each other's hands, they rested on the floor, their hair a tangled mess between them.

"I'm sorry," said Chloe, her eyes still watery as she sniffed. "I didn't mean to cry so—"

Isha laughed while squeezing Chloe's hand, "I remember you telling me I apologize too much. Now you're the one doing it."

Chloe laughed despite herself, "You're right. I've made a fool of myself. I've become you."

"Hey," said Isha, playfully hitting Chloe, "That's not nice."

"No, I suppose it's not," said Chloe, sitting up from the floor and whipping her eyes. "But I think I'm okay now. I think we should probably get going before-" she began looking around the room and towards the wall. "The door's gone! And the windows are closed."

"What?" asked Isha as she also lifted herself, turning toward where the door was supposed to be. But instead of the wooden door, she only saw a marble wall. She then turned to the opposite side of the room, where the windows were now high in the air, where no one could see inside. She hadn't noticed before, but the room was now a lot darker than it had been during class.

"What? What happened?" said Chloe nervously.

Isha looked around, confused for a moment until she saw the familiar orange glowing in one of the roots near the ceiling. Now, it had a hint of blue inside of it. *I guess that means she's okay now.* Isha then stood up from the floor, began dusting off her uniform, and smiled. "It's okay now, Lonta`Mar. Can you let us out, please?"

"Who's Lonta'—" said Chloe as a soft, gravelly sound was heard, and both girls watched as the marble walls shifted, revealing the glass windows behind them, allowing the sunlight to once again shine clearly into the room. Then this was followed by the opposite wall shifting at the base level, revealing the door to the room.

"We can go now?" said Isha as she stepped forward, placing her hand against the door.

"What? What was that? What happened to the wall?"

"It's a long story. I'll explain on the way home," said Isha, as she opened the door to the sounds of students walking through the hallway. The two girls made their way to Heart House, with Isha explaining to a bewildered Chloe how she met with Lonta'Mar.

Eventually, they made their way home, where Chloe stood at the door in silence for a moment as she looked across the room to the small glowing tree in the center of the home. To the left of it was Leo, who was sitting in a chair with a book across his lap.

"Welcome home," said Leo, "Please come in and witness the annoying miracle of this intruder plant that has decided to take root in our home." A few of the blue leaves switched to orange as if in response to Leo's words. "It does that when I talk badly about it." He then turned to face the tree. "Which I will continue to do no matter how many colors it turns. I know you hear me in there, you freeloader." The tree flickers from that blue to orange several times over. "That's right; you better feel bad about it."

"You can understand her?" asked Isha entering the house and walking over to him.

"What? No, of course not. But I know she hears me in there, and that's good enough," he reached over, brushing aside a few of its leaves. "And starting tomorrow, you're helping Rima make breakfast. Magical tree or not, if you live here, you're doing chores like everyone else."

Isha watched as the roots that were scattered through the lower level of the house shifted.

"It really is true," said Chloe, stepping inside and staring at the tree. "This tree, it really is alive."

"That it is," said Leo, still seeming annoyed. "Our little Isha here just has this undeniable affliction for involving herself in things like this."

"Hey," said Isha in protest, "it's not my fault this time. Makeba said she was the one who did it."

"Yeah, well. It's not like you-" Suddenly, the door opened with Jacinta and Makeba entering the home. "And there're your accomplices."

"Oh, sister home already," said Jacinta as she and Makeba walked over. "Do you know if Tree Sakari is okay? Can we see her again?"

"Oh, that's right. You said it was a 'she,' didn't you? Why am I not allowed to have another man in the house?" The three shifted a few branches as if laughing at Leo.

"I think she's okay now," said Isha looking into her sister's eyes, seeing the hope in them. Even Makeba, who was usually the more reserved of the two, seemed just as excited. *They've been so happy lately. But I guess every time they go inside, they get to go home.* And then Isha felt a pang of sadness at the thought of going *home* and how she would feel if she could go back to Green Village and see her father again. But just as quickly as the idea came, Isha shook the thought from her mind and smiled. "Okay, let's try to go and see Lonta'Mar."

"And leave me out here to attend to our guests," said Leo, as he closed his book. "Fine, you three go and play." He then turned to Chloe. "I haven't checked on that arm of yours in a while. Go grab a chair from the table and sit down. I'll give you a look over."

"Okay," said Chloe, watching as Isha, Jacinta, and Makeba sat by the tree and held hands. "But what are they doing? Are they going somewhere?"

"Just watch. It'll be easier than trying to explain it."

And with that, the roots once again sprang up from the floorboards and began wrapping around the girl's bodies. Except this time, it was to the horror of Chloe who jumped back in fright. And once again, the girl's minds were taken away to the Sakari world inside the tree.

Inside, Isha found herself alone, standing in the lush Sakari forest. She could now hear the sounds of running water.

"Jacinta? Makeba? Are you here?"

"Over here, sister," came Makeba's voice from nearby. "We are here. Come see."

Following her sister's voice, Isha made her way through the brush until she came upon a stream. Where, down from her, she could see the three Sakari girls looking down into the clear water.

"Look, sister, pilcar fish," said Jacinta as Isha walked over to them.

"Pilcar? I've never heard of..." Isha glanced down in the water to see the fish glowing a light shade of blue. "Wow. Sakar has fish like these?"

"Yes," said Lonta'Mar. "I had forgotten. But Jacinta and Makeba remind me of them. There are many others I wish to remember."

"Yes," said Jacinta. "You must remember the Juju fish. They are the tasty ones."

Isha knelt by the stream's edge and ran her hand through the water. She could feel the coolness against her skin and hear the sound of the moving water as she waved her hand through it. But for the first time, she noticed that the forest, although lush, was quiet. She had never noticed before, but now with the sound of the water, she realized that the forest was dead. There were no animals or insect sounds like one would constantly hear if moving through a forest.

"Now, you show us your magic," said Jacinta, her words snapping Isha out of her daze.

"Yes, I can move water now," said Lonta'Mar as she raised her hand, and it began to glow. From the stream came a bubble of water holding the glowing blue fish inside. It slowly dripped tiny droplets on the ground as it went floating around the girls before finally stopping at the side of Lonta'Mar. "I think I can do more, but it makes me tired to try. So, I had to sleep."

"Let me try. Let me try," said Jacinta with a smile as she knelt, placing her hands on the soil. It was only a moment later that her hand began to glow, and Jacinta raised it up, pulling with it a large piece of soil that began the spiral around her arm before she released it, letting it fall back to the ground. "Yeah, we have magic again."

Makeba followed suit and found that she could also use her magic.

Then, realizing that all their magic worked, the three Sakari girls turned to Isha expectedly.

"What? Why are you looking at me like that?"

"It's sister time. She use magic now."

"But I'm already using magic. That's why we are here," said Isha. *And I don't know what will happen if I try using it more here. Probably something bad. And I'm tired of getting in trouble.*

"Sister does not wish to try?"

"No, it's not that, it's just—"

"Sister scared. But we are in Tree Sakari world. It safe here."

"I'm not scared," said Isha, frowning at Jacinta. "Weird stuff always happens to me."

"Then you use magic. Show you not scared."

"Fine," said Isha, glaring back at her sister. "But if anything happens, I'm going to tell Leo it's your fault." *I just know something terrible is going to happen,* thought Isha before closing her eyes and going inside herself. Doing it inside of the Sakari world felt different. Usually, she would focus on her thoughts until she drifted away. But she felt she was already inside herself, so she was forced to go deeper till she reached another place inside.

It took some trying, but eventually, she found her way. There was her magical core, the sphere-shaped magic where her enhancement magic seemed to come from. She remembered the last time she came this close to it. That was when the other version of her stared back out at her. Hesitantly, she stepped forward, reached out, grabbed a strand of the spiraling magic, and released her mind.

Opening her eyes, she found her sisters staring back at her.

"Okay, there, did anything happen?"

"Is sister using her magic?" asked Jacinta.

"I am using it," said Isha. "I mean, I think I did it right. It did feel a bit weird, but I'm sure I'm using it now. Makeba, show me your back."

Makeba did as asked as Isha looked at the back of the uniform and saw her marking. They were still black and not glowing. "Are you trying to use magic?"

"I am trying, but I feel nothing. Maybe sister's magic does not work inside since she uses it to bring us here."

"Ahhh! That's not fun," said Jacinta.

"Too bad," said Isha with a shrug of her shoulders and a smile. "It looks like-"

And suddenly, a large throom sound shocked the world around them as a small piece of the Sakari world above the water near them turned white, seeming to morph and absorb the color of the world around them.

All the girls jumped back in shock as the white light began to ripple like a stone tossed in the water.

Its color began changing from white to gray and then to a deep black. And then, from that blackness, came a hand and then another. Both gripped at the ripple's end until finally, a face emerged from it; a face they all knew too well. It was the face of Isha. This new Isha groaned as she pulled herself free from the ripple, which seemed to be trying to suck her back in. She moaned and struggled until most of her body was free. They could see that Isha was also wearing the same school uniform as them. And with one final lurch and grunt, the other Isha freed herself from the ripple of black light, falling face and belly first into the stream of water. The ripple of light disappeared above her after she had freed herself, restoring the world to its normal state.

"Ahh, sister. How you make other you?" asked Jacinta as she pointed toward the other Isha face down in the water.

"What? I don't know. I told you this was a bad idea."

"Is this new sister dead?" said Jacinta as she cautiously stepped into the water and began poking the other Isha on her head."

"Hey, stop that! We don't know—"

"Ahhhhh!" gasped the other Isha, quickly bringing her head up from the water for air; a gesture that startled Jacinta and sent her falling on her butt in the water. The other Isha looked around, panic clearly on her face until her eyes settled on the Sakari girl in front of her, and the two just stared at each other for a moment. "Why are you here? Are you okay?

"What?" said the other Isha. "Who are you? No, wait, I know that face. You're Isha, aren't you? Was it you? Are you the one who brought me here?"

Isha just stared at the other version of herself. She might have had the same face, voice, and body, but the way she spoke seemed more like a noblewoman with an accent. She then squinted at Jacinta, blinking to get a new crop of water from her eyes.

"No… you're Jomo, and that one over there is Momo," she then glanced over at Lonta'Mar. "I don't know that one." Sitting up in the stream, she began wiping the wet hair from her face before turning to Isha. "Where are you finding these Sakari? Are we still in Ellendor?"

"I'm sorry," said Isha. "But who are you exactly?"

"What?" said the other Isha before looking around at her surroundings and seeing everyone staring at her. Raising her hands to inspect them, she frowned and then looked at her reflection in the running water. "Oh, I see. I guess you would ask that, wouldn't you?" She then stood up from the stream, wringing the water from her hair. "May we step out in the sunlight, please? I'd hate to explain everything while soaking wet."

"Yes, there is a spot nearby. No need for me to change my world," said Lonta'Mar as she turned and walked into the woods with the other Isha and the girls following her.

"Splendid."

It only took a minute before they were out in a clearing, where the sun shone down upon them. The other Isha immediately removed her school outfit, revealing her small clothes.

"Now, I'm sure you all have a few questions, the first of which I'd guess would be who I am. Well, my name is Grettaline Vasmir, and you, little Isha, have been stealing my magic."

"I have? I mean… so this magic that lets me make other mages stronger is yours?"

"It most certainly is. And you've been sharing it willy-nilly with everyone, it seems. My magic is meant for only the strongest mages," she said, placing a hand on her chest in pride. "Why, the lower variants would simply either pass out or burst into flames."

"So you are a person inside of sister?" asked Jacinta tilting her head.

"It would seem so."

"But why you inside? And why you not come out till now?"

"Bugger if I know, deary. I don't remember much. But I do remember that when little Isha gets really nervous or scared, I pop out. But when she calms back down, I disappear again. It's an all-around pain being locked away like that. This is the first time I've been able to speak, honestly." Grettaline placed a hand on her hips and pointed a finger at Isha. "And speaking of which, I expect a thank you for saving you from that brutish man who tried to have his way with you. Served him right that he should be burned to a cinder for what he tried. And on a child no less."

Isha's mind quickly returned to the night in the tent when Molan tried to take her. She remembered the feel of the knife plunging into the side of his neck and then everything going white.

But I don't understand. If you are inside me, why?"

"A question we both would like to know the answer to," said Grettaline looking over her clothing.

"Oh, ah... thank you, I guess. You know for what happened with Molan."

"Think nothing of it. The brute got what he deserved," said Grettaline as she began to survey her surroundings. "Now, where are we, and why have I been given a copy of your body? Is this some mirror magic to hide from people? If so, it would be smart. There were many people after my magic, but only one was truly worthy of it. My husband was quite the man, you see."

"We inside tree," said Jacinta, as if that explanation would answer all questions.

"Excuse me?"

"This place is inside of Tree Sakari," said Makeba. "You come out here."

Grettaline squinted. "Now, when you say 'inside'... does that mean we are not in the real world?"

"This is a place I make for them when they come to

play," said Lonta`Mar.

"We come here to visit her," said Isha. "But I need to use your power; that's the only way to do it."

"My power? You mean you're using it now?" asked Grettaline as Isha nodded. "But how does my power allow you to... no, that's not important now. What is important is what happens to me when you leave this place and go back? Do I just go back to sleep inside of you again?"

"I... I don't know."

"Of course, you don't," said Grettaline, the frustration clearly showing in her voice. "Then tell me, is Queen Silvanna still the Queen of Mari, or has her daughter Phillipa taken over? One of them might be able to assist me if I were to get a message to them."

"I don't know. I don't know all the Queen's names," said Isha honestly. "But I did meet the Queen of Latrusa. Her name is Yasmine. Other than that, I just know that Burlus has a king, but I don't know his name."

"Burlus has a king? Preposterous, what man would be allowed to rule any kingdom, let alone Burlus?" said Grettaline with laughter till she looked around, seeing the confused faces of everyone else. "Oh, sweet Goddess, you're serious. Just how long have I been gone that the seven kingdoms have come to this?"

Isha watched as Grettaline sat down on the ground, burying her face into her knees. Seeing an image of herself so distraught was so confusing to her. And with that, she didn't have the heart to tell her other self that there were only five kingdoms now. Not seven.

"I thought kingdom land only had-"

"Ah, Grettaline," said Isha, cutting off Jacinta before she made things worse. "Do you remember where you came from? I mean, before being here?"

Grettaline took a deep breath before looking at the fake world above her. "Not much, really."

"What about before, you said you had a husband?"

"I did. But now, everything seems so blurry when I try to remember him. But it's starting to come back to me, I think. I remember we used to be friends with some of the Queens."

"You say you helped sister when Molan man attacked her," said Makeba. "You kill people before?"

This question shocked Isha as she didn't even consider that. But indeed, Grettaline had said that.

"What? No, I mean, maybe I have. I don't remember."

"Then maybe you good fighter," said Jacinta. "Sister bad at fighting. I was thinking we should teach her," she waved her hand around. "And here would be good place to teach."

"But... I don't. Why? Are you all in danger? I mean, I remember a few times you've used my power. But are you girls in some type of trouble? Are you not safe?"

"Sister is daughter of Old Man. He training her for war."

"What? No!" yelped Grettaline as she stood. "You can't. What if something were to happen to you? What would happen to me?"

Isha looked away, "It's not like I have many choices right now."

"What do you mean?" Grettaline quickly made her way back over to Isha. "What's going on with your girls? I... I remember those Sakari girls. They had their faces covered in blood and... and... there was a body inside of a tent."

"Ahhh," said Lonta'Mar with a yawn. "This has been fun time. But I still not fully recovered from learning magic. I need to rest again. So, I will send you back. But it was fun meeting the other person who looks like Isha."

"What? No? You can't just—"

And just like that, the world again turned white, and Isha found herself back at Heart house, looking up at their colorful tree.

"Oh! That was fast," came Leo's voice.

Isha turned to see Leo holding Chloe's arms in his. "What? What happened?"

"Nothing. I'm just inspecting Chloe's arm to make sure the healing is progressing as it should. You three have only been in there a few minutes," said Leo with his usual smile. "What happened? Was she not home?"

CHAPTER 27

Saffron, Laura, and Dekol rode along the streets of Jensky, with Dekol holding the reins of an extra horse.

"I must admit, besides the occasional harassing beggar, this has been quite the lovely honeymoon galivanting through the countryside. I dare say even if I wasn't masking my image, I might still be able to walk around unnoticed. I doubt anyone out here has been to the capitol to spot me," said Saffron.

"I did not think our kingdom would be such a dangerous place," said Laura, looking around the city.

"Everything is dangerous if placed into the proper context. The capital even has the occasional murder. Lord Masterdane's recent demise should be proof of that."

"Yes, but in the city, there are guards. Here it is more lawless. I understand that not all can just uproot from their lives and come and live in the capital, but to live like this…"

"And to some of those here, living like this is its own kind of freedom. The shackles of nobility is a bondage that many would trade in exchange for the personal freedoms that living such a life out here grants them."

"You seem pretty free to me," said Dekol. "The way you act around the castle, one would hardly think of you as a prince."

Saffron chuckled, "True, but that is merely a facade; an attempt to bring about such annoyance that the act itself would grant me a semblance of freedom. But I still remain a servant of the kingdom."

"My Lord Husband seems very different from your father."

"Ahh. Now there is a statement that warms my heart to hear. You do know how to spoil your husband, don't you?"

They finished passing through the city and made their way to the chapel, where they found Mova out on the grounds using her magic to help dry sheets of the clergy as they hung from strings connected to poles.

"Well, this is certainly a sight I am not accustomed to seeing," said Saffron. "Our dear friend seems to have taken a liking to the Will of the Goddess."

"Shut up, you idiot. You're late."

"Getting supplies seemed to take a while longer than anticipated. Are you ready to leave, or have you decided to give up your duties as a guard and live the life of the faithful?"

"The Mother here wishes to speak with you. She has information of what she thinks is happening to the clergy involving those jewels."

"Is that so?" said Saffron, dismounting. "Well then, I guess we shouldn't keep her waiting. Dekol, stay here and look after my wife and our supplies, won't you? It seems I am scheduled for a mid-morning confession."

"This way," said Mova, with a sigh as she led Saffron through the grounds.

"So, you want to tell me what all this is about?" asked Saffron as he watched the robed figures going about their day.

"What do you mean?"

"Mova, you stayed the night in a dirty cathedral instead of coming back. If you were here, you probably slept in a cot instead of coming back to a—while not the cleanest—tavern, mind you, it still had a soft bed. And we both know you are a stickler regarding your amenities. So, you not coming back means something else is wrong."

"As I said, the mother here has some information you might find useful."

"Fine. I trust you. Even though I can see you're not telling me the whole truth. I just doubt that now would be the time you would choose to turn your back on me."

"Is that why you asked Dekol to stay back?"

"I said I trust you. But unfortunately, that doesn't mean I trust the rest of the clergy here."

Mova was silent as they entered the chapel where at the head of it, beneath a statue of the goddess, sat the older woman from the night before. She sat at a table with a book in her hand and a dozen half-lit candles standing across the table.

"Oh, good," said the woman, "you've come. Please have a seat." She gestured to a few seats in front of her. "Don't mind this old lady not standing to greet you, your highness. It's not so easy to get up these days."

"Don't worry about the formalities," said Saffron as he grabbed a chair and took a seat. "And how did you know I was the prince?" He glanced over at Mova.

"I've made many trips to the capitol in my day. I remember the fresh bundle of mischief you were when you were fresh out of your wet clothes. On more than one occasion, I saw your poor maids trying to get a handle on you as you led them on a chase around the castle. Those poor girls sure had their hands full with you," she said as she wagged her finger at him.

"Yes, well, I'm afraid some things never change. I cannot say that my search for mischief has calmed down in all these years."

"Really? I would have assumed that new wife of yours would have tempered you at least a little," said the woman as she grabbed one of the candles from her side and reached over, using the flame to light the wick of another. "I do so hope you treat her better than her father did. Those beatings he used to give her, such terrible things. I like to think that being married to you would help her forget such things."

"What?" asked Saffron with a snarl across his lips that he couldn't control.

"Oh, you didn't know?" said the woman, a look of mock surprise across her face. "Well, I suppose it will take some time for her to speak to you about that. My father was also quite the disciplinarian. Never once did he spare the rod," she sighed, "no matter how much we begged him to."

"You seemed to be well informed for a member of the clergy. Is it wise for you to go around spoiling the secrets of others?"

"Well, I assure you these are just things I've heard, rumors in the wind. As clergy, we do hear so many things. And besides, you're to be king one day. I think it prudent for you to understand the type of man your father-in-law just might be."

"Noted. I shall try to remember this kindness you offer."

"I'm pleased to hear that."

"Then tell me, what have you heard about any red jewels that might be implanted in the bodies of clergy members? Perhaps a rogue sect of the will of the goddess."

"Oh, yes. There have been whispers about such things. But I believe you may be thinking a bit too small."

"And how is that?"

"Words are spoken that this small group is no longer a

small group and has spread through much of the faithful.”

“Impossible. The capital would have heard of people being abducted and experimented on if it was so widespread.”

“Yes, perhaps they would have. But I said nothing of experimentation. Only that a certain sect of the faith is no longer so small. And I doubt any capital in any kingdom keeps such track of changes in the faithful.”

Saffron thought for a moment as he began to look around the room. “Why are you telling me this? Aren’t you, yourself, a member of the Will of the Goddess?”

“Let’s just say that we are but another small sect of the Will of the Goddess. We all do her Will in our own way.”

“Right,” Saffron looked up at Mova, who just shrugged. “Fine, well, we are on our way to the holy city to perhaps inform ourselves as to why and, for that matter, *how* that mysterious sect is implanting these crystals in the bodies of their devotees. Any information you have on the topic would be appreciated and, of course, rewarded.”

The old woman gave a smile that unsettled Saffron. “The church is always appreciative of any assistance we can receive. But I’m afraid if you are going to the capital to look for answers, you may be searching in the wrong place. Such Places such as that are no place to truly hold one’s secrets. Instead, you must look further away.”

“And this further away place, I assume you will tell me where it is?”

“Towards the edge of your kingdom is a city called Ghemlon. We recently had a sister return from a visit there. Of which, she informed me of a few peculiar things. Many of our brothers and sisters were there. Many more than one small town on the outskirts of a kingdom should have. And not just that, but apparently an abundance of mages as well.”

“Ghemlon? That city is governed by Duke Pinkle, one of the lesser nobles.”

"If I were you, I would go there looking for my answers rather than chasing ghosts in the holy city. But that's just an old woman's opinion. You are free to do as you like. After all, the rumors of your impersonators certainly imply that they are."

"Wait! You know who they are?"

"Just a group of poppers and one or two talented mages; no one whom you should be concerned about now."

Saffron stared at the woman for a moment. Before standing from the table. "I appreciate your time. When I return to the castle, I'll see to it that the clergy or at least the part of it that isn't tainted is rewarded properly, Mother..."

"Oh, I'm Mother Ralhila and no need, child. Just hand it off to your guard Mova there. She knows how to reach me personally. So often, our valuables and trinkets are lost in their supposed delivery."

"Of course," said Saffron, nodding before leaving the chapel into the sunlight. "And I suppose you'll not wish to tell me who that old woman really is? Because if she's truly a Mother, then I'm the goddess herself."

Mova was silent.

"So, I assumed."

"Are we ready to leave?" asked Dekol as they approached the horses.

"Yes, but it seems I must apologize to my dear wife. Would you mind a side trip to the city of Ghemlon?"

"Of course not, dear husband, although I do not know much about Ghemlon."

"Nothing to know., really. A dukedom in the outer layers of the kingdom. It was awarded to a lesser noble for trade negotiations. A few villages surround it, but it's mostly farmland. It is on the way to the holy city, so it shouldn't be more than a day outside our travels."

CHAPTER 28

In the late hours of the holy city, the moonlight glistened off the wet streets, reflecting its roundness in the puddles as Victor made his way forward. But, as with all other cities, the unsavory activities would occur in darkness. Choosing not to take the main roads, he made his way through the city's backstreets and picked up a tail as a few men had decided to follow him.

Their wet footsteps splashed on the watery roads as Victor moved between houses from one street to another.

So, it's two of them. No, three, there's a smaller one, thought Victor as he stopped and stood before a large manor in the city, where a sign read 'Umbridge' across the gate.

"Alright, what are ya having?" asked one man at the gate. "Boy? Girl? And what age?"

"I wish to have a meeting with the lady of the house, Madam Silvie."

"Oh? And what makes you so special? The Madam don't just speak with just anyone."

"Tell her that a high-profile client has arrived and that he's come with gold."

"High profile, eh," said the man as he peered out of the gate, looking at Victor. "Alright, ya seem dressed for the part." He veered into the shadows behind Victor with a raised brow before opening the gate and allowing him access.

"Thank you."

"Don't thank me yet. You better hope you're as high profile as ya say, or I'm going to have to throw ya back out there with them fellas that seem to be waiting on ya."

"I assure you. I am worth your Madam's time."

The man led Victor to what appeared to be a modest house on the manor grounds. It was fully wooden, contrasting with the stone and brick buildings throughout the city. But here, in the greenery of this gated area, it seemed at home. It was two stories tall with a porch with an awning over it where there were a few empty seats.

"Take a seat," said the man as he gestured to one of the chairs. "I'll go and tell the Madam someone has arrived." He then opened the door and let himself in.

"Thank you," said Victor, sliding himself down into a seat by the door. As he turned to watch the man enter, he caught a glimpse of two naked men sitting on a couch together before the door closed.

Well, this part was simple enough. If I'm lucky, this will be my only stop for the night as I'll have no need for the other options. Victor sat for only a few moments before the door opened, and out stepped a middle-aged woman in a stunning black and gold dress. The black faded into the shadows as the gold lace shone in the moonlight.

"And who do have we here?" asked the woman as she looked down at Victor. "A new face has arrived."

"Hello," said Victor, standing from his seat, only to

realize that the woman was taller than him and by no small amount. "I hope you don't mind. I've come to—"

"You wish to gain information that you think I may have."

"Ah, yes… That is correct."

"Humph, I guessed as much. The look in your eyes, there is no lust in them. A bit of surprise, but who isn't surprised when they first meet me? I am quite eye-catching. And men find it off-putting when they are not able to look down on a woman."

"But nonetheless, you are still quite beautiful. I would imagine it is a mixture of both."

The Madam laughed. "You do not deny and instead choose to flatter. Well, now, aren't you a smart boy." She walked past him and gestured to his seat. "Please sit. I would enjoy a bit of conversation that isn't just talk of cunts and cocks. And I think you will provide me with such. Tell me, what brings Victor Krill to my humble place of business then, hmm?"

"You know who I am?"

"Oh, of course. The holy city sits on the border of both kingdoms. So, I've made it my business to know both kingdoms' important and influential people. In fact, I've even offered the services of my establishment to a few of the Generals of Mari. Would it surprise you to know that more than one or two of them truly dislikes you? Some would even call it hate. A young magically deprived man being allowed in their hallowed halls. Oh, they were absolutely scathing."

"And I wouldn't suppose you'd be willing to inform me of who this or these persons might be?"

"Oh, sweet boy, look where you are. This is a place of secrets. And I doubt you have the coin needed to pry that name…" she raised her finger with a smile. "Or names from my lips."

"I figured."

"But you're not here for that. You're here for something

else."

"I'm looking for information on some clergymen."

She laughed again, "You hardly need my help with that. No, you're looking for something more specific."

"Yes. Red crystals in the city. Have you heard anything about them? Or, more specifically, a clergyman named Retallia Kolgin."

"Oh, that name," said the Madam, leaning back in her chair and looking ahead. "Yes, that one did enter the city recently. Apparently, he's a bright star to those who worship the Goddess."

"You sound as if you don't."

"My dear, I worship coin and currency. I lost my love for the Goddess long ago, after finding that she has no love for a woman such as myself. I hear he is to have a meeting with the leaders of the faithful soon. That is why he is in the city; him and his little followers. I do not know where or when the meeting will take place, but most certainly before the day the Goddess arrives."

"I see," said Victor as he leaned forward in the chair and reached into a pocket inside his coat.

"Oh, keep your coin, young man. I do believe it won't be needed unless you wish to enjoy the pleasures of my establishment."

"I think I may be a bit busy tonight," said Victor as he stood.

"Of course," said the Madam as she gave Victor another look-over. "You have honest eyes. Not usually the type for pleasure houses. I was once like that and being out here with you for a while provided me with a nice respite from the debauchery that is my business."

"You told me you worshiped coin, yet you refuse mine?"

"No, I said I worship coin and currency. The two are not always the same. And I have learned a few times that having a general of Mari owing me a favor or two has come in handy when exporting certain goods."

"And will doing you a favor cause me to lose sleep at night?"

"You? No, I suppose not. But it may leave a sour taste in your mouth. Paying back a debt usually does."

"On that, we agree," said Victor as he stepped off the porch. "Thank you for your time. I have a few more places to go tonight."

"Really? Well, be careful. The night often brings out the worst in people. Unfortunately, the holy city is not immune to this truth."

"Yes, that is what I'm hoping for," said Victor, then he made his way down the walkway and out of the gate back into the city streets. Taking a look around, he noticed that the group who were following him before was gone. He then turned and once again began walking through the streets. It wasn't long before he picked up some company.

With a few quick turns, he went into the alleyways between the houses.

Alright, let's see how this works out. Victor took another turn into a darker alley, reaching into his cloak and pulling out some items that rattled in his hands before dropping them on the ground. They clinked against the stone road as a few glimmered in the moonlight. He then found the darkest place he could and pressed his back against the wall, trying to stay silent.

Three men followed behind him shortly after, pausing at the entrance, and began looking into the shadows.

"Where'd he go?" asked one of the men.

"How should I know? I've been following you."

The previous man sighed, "Just look ahead. He looked like he might have been carrying something. You saw how he went into the Madam's house. For sure, he must be holding some coin on 'em?"

"But he was only in there a few minutes. He might not have had nothing."

"Or he just might not've been able to keep his cock

hard for long. You know how them nobles be. Could have a thousand whores on 'em and wouldn't have been a good shagging between the lot of 'em."

A laugh between the men came as they made their way forward into the alley. They poked in the darker areas of the path with their sticks as they made their way closer to where Victor was hiding.

"Hello," said Victor, stepping out from the shadows into the moonlight, "am I to assume that you gentlemen are the entrepreneurial sort?"

"The what? You making fun of us?"

"He's asking if we're businessmen," said the man furthest to the left. "And yeah, we do dabble in a bit of business. We're like a charity. Don't suppose you'd be willing to part with some of that gold you're carrying?"

"To be honest, I would if I thought it would go to someone who was actually in need," said Victor as he took a step back. "But you three gentlemen already seem quite well-fed."

"Oh, come on now," the middle man said as he stepped forward. "How 'bout the four of us have ourselves... what is it, can't you see I'm..."

"Hey, hold on," said the smaller man on the right. "Ain't they supposed to be scared of us? 'Cause he don't seem scared?"

Well, that one's uncommonly smart for his type, although this does seem familiar.

"What? Are you seriously scared? It's only one of him and the three of us."

"Oh yeah, what about Plummy and his crew? Heard it was four of them, and one woman did 'em in."

"That one was a mage. And I don't see no tits on this one."

"Men can be mages too, you dumb fuck."

"Who you calling a dumb—"

"Gentlemen," said Victor, raising his hands, gaining the

men's attention. "There are people trying to sleep at this late hour. I would expect robbery to be much quieter."

The smaller man of the group snarled while gritting his teeth as he looked at Victor for a few seconds. "Fuck this. It don't seem right. And what don't seem right probably ain't right." He threw up his hand, turned around, and began walking off. "

"I'm with him," said the man on the right. "Friskal's usually right about things like this." He then turned around, following the smaller man.

The last man in the center of the group watched as his colleagues began to leave, then turned to face Victor. "You got lucky tonight, fucker. You best thank the Goddess for your luck." Then he finally turned and left, following behind the other two."

"Well, that's a surprise," said Victor under his breath.

"Truly smart thieves they are," said the whisper of the assassin's voice as it soothed over his ear.

"They don't usually have that much sense. Maybe it's a sign of the times."

"Perhaps. But this means no captive for that Madam person. So, only option left now is Brutil fella and his love for men's butts. I think I shall enjoy watching."

Victor closed his eyes with a sigh. Then with renewed interest, he walked forward, taking a small leap over the traps he had placed before turning the corner in an attempt to catch up to the men. It didn't take long as he found them walking up ahead, still arguing.

"I still think we could have had 'em. Would have been a good score for us," said the tallest man.

"Yeah, well, I trust my gut," said the one they called Friskal. "And my gut was telling me that he was nothing but trouble. Better to give up on a score than to be—"

"I'm sorry, gentlemen," said Victor. "But it seems I shall be in need of one of your services tonight."

The three men turned around, their eyes narrowing as

they stared at Victor for a moment.

Friskal frowned as he bit his lip. "I fuckin' knew it." And with no hesitation, the smaller man turned and took off running down the street, an action that, after a moment of realization, caused his two compatriots to join in as they all took off.

Oh, *you must be fuckin' kidding,* thought Victor as he gave chase after the three men. The pursuit led through the streets towards a fork in the road that caused the three men to split up. The smaller and the taller veered to the right and the other to the left. Victor followed behind the two.

Even with his best efforts, Victor barely closed the distance between the two men.

Dammit, I'm really not cut out *for running like this. Even the smaller one is faster than I'd expect,* thought Victor as the other two ahead made their way into another fork in the road, splitting up once again. Friskal, the smaller one, turned left as the taller one kept straight. *Fuck.* Victor followed the taller man.

Down an alley, the two went between the buildings as the man ahead threw trash, wooden beams, and clothing back at Victor, anything in an attempt to slow him down. From one alley to another street, back to another alley. Despite taking a chance to walk the streets to gain knowledge of the city, Victor had no idea which part of the city they were in, only that he needed to catch the man ahead of him.

The two turned down a dead-end street with several houses.

"Groggy... open the door, you bastard," screamed the man with all his might as he continued his mad stride forward.

Up ahead, Victor saw the light emerge from one of the houses as a door opened. He pressed harder in a final attempt to catch the man, but with a leap up the steps, the man flew past the door into the house. Immediately after him, the door slammed shut as Victor twisted, slamming his back against it with a loud thud.

Victor heard the sliding of a wooden bar to barricade the door.

"Go, go, go," came the man's voice from inside as soon came to the scampering of feet echoing away from him.

Of course… they have a back door. Victor placed his hands on his knees leaning over to catch his breathing, sweating beading down his face as his hair hung loose. *Great… now what am I…* Victor spotted the smaller man from earlier down the alley from the corner of his eye. *Both bastards had the same idea, uh?*

Friskal's eyes met Victor's for only a moment before he quickly turned back down the alley.

Oh, no you don't, thought Victor, and with a deep breath, took off running after the man, chasing him through the alley and back into the street. There, he saw the smaller man up ahead. *Why is everyone damned fast?* Victor followed behind the man, but as he passed by a smith's shop, luck seemed to be on his side as Friskal slipped, fell, and went crashing into an unlit furnace, knocking over a few chairs.

Victor finally caught up to the man writhing on the floor by a slew of buckets gripping the back of his head and uttering obscenities.

"Okay," said Victor with a huff after catching up. "Friskal, was it? I… think we should give up on this game of chase." He reached down, grabbed the man by the collar, and lurched him up, only to catch a face full of water from the buckets the man had grabbed. The man then elbowed Victor in the stomach, forcing him to let go, and he dropped back on his hands and knees before taking off again.

"Fucking Goddesses… wraith," said Victor as he gripped his side and gave chase after the man once again. He followed him toward a street that stopped ahead as it was boarded off and split into a street toward the left and right. The man continued running forward. Victor was now quickly catching up to him and soon found himself an arm's length away. As he reached out, the man dropped to the ground and slid into a hole beneath the boards, with Victor hitting the boards, but was too slow to brace himself properly. "Ahh," he grunted as the wooden fence rattled, stopping him in his tracks.

He looked down at the small hole in the wood the man had slid through and turned around, jumping up, grabbing the wood, and beginning to lift himself over. But as his head emerged over the boards, he could only see the man's shadow turn the corner, hobbling away. Finally, with exhaustion filling his body, he let go, allowing himself to drop back down.

Screw it; there must be an easier way than this, thought Victor gasping for breath as he began making his way back down the street. *What side of the city am I even on right now?* He looked around the shadowy city, not recognizing any of the buildings. He sighed. *How long is it going to take me to find my way back to the hotel?* "Hey... hey, you there, Muslin?"

No answer came.

Of course not. Gone when it's... thought Victor, before turning a corner and seeing a wooden wheelbarrow in the middle of the street. But the weird thing was that someone was sleeping in it. Victor frowned but made his way forward. The man's body was limp in the barrow. After getting close, Victor noticed that the man inside was one of the men he had been chasing. The one who had gone the other way after he had pursued the other two. He now lay unconscious with a bruise on the right side of his head.

"You do not look so well," said the assassin's voice in the wind.

"You could have told me you were going after the other one."

"Oh my. Is this how the Mari people say thank you? Such bad manners."

Victor sighed. "Thank you."

"That is better."

He then stepped behind the wheelbarrow and grabbed the handles, immediately feeling his exhaustion again as he lifted it. "Don't… suppose you'd want to give me a hand with this."

"Really? You would ask a frail, helpless woman to lift such a thing."

Victor looked down at the unconscious man again. "If you're frail and helpless, then what am I?" He then lurched the barrow forward and began pushing it down the street. "Can you at least give me directions to that Madam's house? I seem to have lost my way."

Victor made his way down the street with the words of the assassin whispering into his ear.

It took some time, with the wheelbarrow, for Victor to arrive at a house at the center of a forked road. It was a bricked manor with pillars holding up an awning above the door. And on each pillar was a torch that burned brightly in the night. Victor looked around some of the other houses that were in the area. None of them had lit torches.

I hope it's not too late for them to accept visitors. Victor made his way up the steps, then turned to the unconscious man in the barrow. He moaned but was still soundly out of it. *It's not as if I can just come back later.* He faced the door again and gave two hard knocks. There was no response. He knocked again, this time with three hard knocks.

"Who's there?" came a husky voice from the door. "And what do you want?"

"Would you believe me if I said I was a servant of justice, and I've come bearing gifts?"

"Well, that certainly is a bold statement," came a woman's voice. "Open the door. Let us see what the night has brought us."

The door slowly opened, creaking on its hinges, and out of the shadows only stepped a mountain of a man with half of his face laced with markings. Dark lines that started at the top on his head, coming all the way down to his chin.

"Oh, step back. You're scaring the poor man," said a small woman who stepped out from behind the man. She was wearing a nightgown and had a book in her hand. "Oh my! Haven't you had quite the night? Did you get caught out in the rain? And here I thought that had passed hours ago."

"I thought bathing with my clothes on would be an exciting change from the normal routine."

"A sharp tongue." said the woman with a smile. "But I do remember hearing you saying that you brought gifts."

Victor stepped to the side, gesturing towards the man in the wheelbarrow. "A would-be robber of yours truly. I just apprehended him and thought you might have more use for him than the town's guards."

She bit her lip, "Well then, how kind of you. Would one of you grab hold of our friend there?"

And then, from behind her, another mountainous man appeared, his face also marked similar to the others, and made his way past Victor. With just a single hand, he picked the man up by his shirt and dragged him back inside the house.

Where does she even find men that size? Does she grow them here?

"I thank you for your gift. But, please, do come in. I assume you want something in trade," said the woman as she looked up and over past Victor. "And will your friend there be joining us? She's been staring at me quite intimately since I came out to greet- oh, and there she goes. A shame, I think she would have also been something interesting to speak to."

"You could see her?" said Victor, a look of genuine surprise on his face.

"Of course. I was taught to see through such low-class illusions when I was still a child. Could you not?"

"I'm not a mage, unfortunately."

"And yet you show up at my door bearing gifts? Oh, this will be an exciting tale. Follow me." She turned, leading

Victor inside the house, where she snapped her fingers, and a dozen candles spread out around the lower level ignited. "You can leave us here. I wish to be alone with my guest."

Without saying a word, the large man turned and walked over to an open door and down the stairs where Victor assumed the unconscious man had been taken.

"What will you do with the man?"

"Oh, him? You said he tried to rob you? Well, do not worry. From this day forward, thievery will be the farthest thing from his mind. My men and I will see to his training. But tell me, what brings you to my doorstep this evening? You aren't from here just to try and share my bed, I assume."

"Yes, ahh. I was told that you or Brutil could provide me with some information."

"Humm, yes. I can see why you came to me. Brutil is certainly a well-informed gentleman, but for a man who doesn't enjoy the company of other men, I imagine you were in quite the predicament."

"So, you can see why your assistance would be," Victor reached over, grabbing her hand and squeezing it gently in his, "greatly appreciated."

"Well now," said the Madam with a slight smile and giggle, "I certainly will do my best. What is it that I can help you with?"

"The Holy Circle is having a meeting soon. I would like as much information as you can give me on it and perhaps a way that I may attend such an event."

"Oh, is that so? I would have never assumed you to be such a devotee of the faith."

"I'm not. I imagine I believe as much as the next man. But this is a more personal endeavor. There is someone who will be there that day in the discussion, and I wish to listen in on what is being said."

"I see. Well, that's certainly possible. I've assisted the Servants of the Goddess on many an assignment. I'm sure if I were to ask, they would grant anyone I deemed appropriate access. It's still a few days away, so you can give me some time to organize it, and I ask that you... that you... You know, it just occurred to me that I never really got your name."

"I am Victor Krill, Final and Sixth General of Mari."

"Really?" asked the Madam with some shock. "I would have never guessed. To think, two of Mari's generals visited me in one day. What are the odds?"

"Two?"

CHAPTER 29

Isha lay face down on the ground, the side of her face squished against the dirt. In front of her were Makeba and Lonta'Mar just staring at her.

"Sister is getting better, I think," said Makeba tilting her head.

"I don't know," said Lonta'Mar, shaking her head. "She still gets knocked down a lot. And she has been fighting for many days now."

Isha gritted her teeth, clenching her fist full of dirt as she pushed her up off the ground. Then, twisting herself, she rolled over to see Jacinta bouncing up and down in front of her. They had asked Lonta'Mar to create the white clothes she had worn the last time they had fought each other that night in the circle.

"Sister getting better," said Jacinta. "She harder to throw now. But still not good enough to beat me."

"I know that," said Isha, taking a deep breath and rising to her feet. "Now, let's go again."

Jacinta looked at her sister for a moment before shrugging her shoulders, planting her feet into the dirt, and extending her arms. "Sister, come."

Isha then stepped over to her sister and assumed the same pose before reaching in, trying to grab Jacinta's arm. But her sister knocked her arm away, sliding herself forward, and placed her palm to Isha's face, trying to force her off balance. Isha quickly slid to the side, grabbing Jacinta by the wrist, then spun around, trying to swing an elbow at Jacinta's cheek. But her sister ducked, flipping over and grabbing Isha by the foot, taking it out from under her. By instinct, Isha released her sister's wrist to soften the fall's impact with her hands.

No! My back is open. She thought as she quickly turned around to prevent any attacks from her sister. But she was unprepared to see Jacinta's entire body in the air above her and even more unprepared for the impact of her sister's butt as it collided with her rib cage, knocking the wind out of her. Isha heaved and tried to gasp for air as she felt Jacinta's hand clutch hers, pulling it around her neck and beginning to tighten around her throat.

"Mula-ru," she squeaked as she tapped against her sister's arm, signaling their fighting to cease.

Jacinta rolled off her sister and stood up as the latter gasped for breath, doubled over in pain, clutching at her ribs.

"Why does sister want to fight so much now?" asked Makeba as she walked over with Lonta`Mar.

"Sister been acting weird since she summon other sister inside of her."

"She's not... she's not our sister. I... I don't know who she is."

Jacinta frowned. "Does sister not trust other person inside of her then? Is that why you not use magic here anymore?"

"But does not sister use special magic to come here and visit Lonta'Mar?' asked Makeba.

"It's not that I don't trust her," said Isha, sitting up on the ground, trying to steady her breathing. "Okay, maybe I don't." She rubbed her hair in frustration. "I don't know. It's just weird. And she doesn't come out unless I go and get her. So... so, I just needed some time to think about everything, is all." She waved her hand around. "And time is slower here now for some reason, which I don't understand. First, it was faster, then Lonta'Mar learned magic, and now it is slow. Nothing makes sense anymore. So, I just thought I could come here to think."

"Okay," said Jacinta sitting down in front of Isha. "So, what we do now?"

"Now: I catch my breath. And then we continue teaching you more kingdom words. And you can teach me more Sakari. I still get lost when you both start speaking to Lonta`Mar."

"Ahhhh! Noooo..." moaned Jacinta as she laid back on the ground, outstretching out her arms and legs. "But that so boring."

"Is, but that *is* so boring," scolded Isha. "Why do you refuse to use your in-between words? Makeba has already gotten most of them down."

"That 'cause Makeba always been good at boring stuff. In between words take too long to say. Kingdom tongue has too many long words."

Makeba walked over, placing her hands on her hips as she stared down at Jacinta, "You promised Uncle Funny man. So, you will do this."

"I know... I know."

Isha smirked. It wasn't very often that she got to see Makeba scolding Jacinta, but now that it was two-on-one, she would listen.

"Who is this Uncle Funny Man?" asked Lonta'Mar.

"He was who Momma chose for us," said Makeba. "He was silly, but good man who made Momma laugh. He also gave us Isha as new sister. So, he did well."

"Yes, but he died," said Jacinta. "Now sister is the caretaker and will pick man for us. But she slow to pick."

"Oh!" said Lonta'Mar, turning to Isha. "There are some boys at the school. Do you not like any of them?"

"Why," asked Isha with a sigh, "do you always bring that up? No. I don't like anyone. Well, at least, not like that. When I do, I will tell you."

"I think sister not honest," said Jacinta. "You kiss pretty, girly boy."

"That not.... I mean... I did not," said Isha, getting flustered. "Pavel kissed me." She waved them over. "Enough of this. Come on, let's practice our words, and then you three can teach me more Sakari."

The four girls then sat down in a circle and began their lessons. Makeba and Lonta'Mar's grasp of the kingdom tongue was improving daily. Even Jacinta, with her stubbornness, was making progress, although she'd purposely try to use as few words as possible when communicating. But for Isha, Sakari wasn't the easiest to master. The pronunciation felt odd, and how she had to move her tongue when speaking took longer than she would have wanted.

After another three hours of speaking lessons, the girls called it a day, saying goodbye to Lonta`Mar. And in a flash of white light, Isha once again found herself sitting in her school clothes under the small tree in their home.

"Welcome back," said Rima, sitting at a nearby table with a book in her hand.

"We're not late for class, are we?" said Isha as she tried to stand up and found herself stumbling over, using the back of the couch to catch herself."

"Careful," said Rima, standing up from the chair and walking over to Isha. "No, it's still early morning." She helped straighten Isha up and placed a hand on her forehead to feel her temperature. "You look exhausted. You were only in there for a few minutes. Are you sure going inside that tree is safe?"

"I'm fine. It's fine. Is Leo here? I... I need to tell him something."

"No, he left early this morning. I'm sure if you leave now, you could catch him in his office before classes start."

"I'll go then," said Isha before turning to her sisters. "I'll meet you both in class."

"Does sister not want us to come with?" asked Makeba.

"No. It's okay," said Isha as she headed for the door. "I'll meet you both in class." She then opened the door and headed off towards the school. On the way, she saw one or two students lounging about in the early morning sun, but for the most part, the streets were empty. Even the school was empty.

I wonder if he will be upset with me again. thought Isha as she made her way up the steps and towards Leo's office. She had come to his office many times in the past year for treatment or just to talk. Even though he had scolded her many times, he had never turned her away. She placed her hands on the door and took a deep breath. I just need to tell him the truth. She opened the door and stepped inside.

"Leo, I have something I need to..." Her words caught in her throat as she stared at the sight before her.

There at his desk sat a shirtless Leo. The skin on the left side of his chest and stomach was a red mess of burned flesh that stopped at his neck. In front of him, across his desk, were several bloody instruments she had never seen before. In his mouth, he clenched a leather belt. He held his arm firmly planted against the desk, and in his other hand, he held a bloody metal item that held a loose flap of the burned skin still attached to his arm.

The image of the burned fresh pierced Isha's mind. The thoughts of her in that tent that night, Molan on top of her.

"I... I... um, I mean... I just want to," muttered Isha as

she turned to run away. "I'm sorry."

Leo quickly spat out the leather strap from his mouth. "Stop!" he shouted. "Lonta'Mar, stop her."

Isha's body fell forward as she crashed to the floor in the middle of the doorway. She turned her head to see that her feet and half of her ankles were now deep within the floor of the castle.

"Alright, keep her there," said Leo as he walked forward. He took one look outside into the hall and closed the door as Lonta'Mar dragged Isha back inside the room before letting her go and raising her back above the floor. "You're always trying to run away."

"I'm sorry. I didn't know," said Isha, keeping her eyes firmly focused on the floor. "I mean. I didn't think you would be.... would be..."

"That I would be peeling my own flesh from my body?"

"Did I... is that what I did to you?"

"Isha, look at me!"

At his words, she closed her eyes and clenched her fists.

"I really hate to do it this way," said Leo as he knelt, grabbing Isha by her side and turning her over. She tried to worm her way free, but he pressed down hard against her chest, holding her in place with his good, unburned arm. "Stop moving. I have enhanced strength, remember, and it doesn't seem as if you've learned that trick yet."

Isha placed her hands over her eyes as she could feel them begin to water. "I'm sorry, I'm sorry," she mumbled repeatedly. "Please don't make me. Don't make me look."

"Oh, momma bear, I could really use you right now," muttered Leo in a low tone. "Isha. Stop. Stop. Look at me. It's okay. I'm not mad at you. I'm not going to hurt you. It's me, Leo. Remember?"

Isha tried controlling her breathing, and with clenched teeth and watery eyes, she gazed up at Leo.

"That's it. Just stay calm and—"

Isha glanced back down at his burned chest until Leo

removed his hand from her chest and cupped her chin in his hand.

"No. Focus on my face 'til you calm down," said Leo in a soft tone.

The two stared at each other until Isha finally began to relax.

"I... I should go."

"No. You're here now," said Leo in a serious tone. "So, I think we should work on getting you used to the sight of me. Now, stand up."

Isha did as he said but forced herself to look away from him.

"Am I that hard to look at?"

"No... it's not... There was... I mean... There was this man... he... he tried to," said Isha, her mouth quivering as she tried to finish her words.

"Molan, right," stated Leo, calmly.

Isha's eyes went wide, but she didn't say anything.

"There was a night that Elena found you crying on the floor. You and she talked about what happened to you before you came here."

"She... she said she wouldn't," said Isha biting her lip.

"No, she said she wouldn't tell your sisters and she kept that promise. But remember, it was both our jobs to look after of you girls. So, she figured it'd be best to tell me so I wouldn't mistakenly dig up those scars." Leo took another look at the scarred flesh on his chest and arm. "I guess I failed at that too, huh?"

"It's not... I mean, I should have knocked first. It's my fault."

"It's no one's fault. Now, turn your eyes here. I want you to look at me."

"But..."

"I know. You burned him as you burned me. Except that I'm here because I care about you. Not because I want to hurt you. Now come on, look at me."

Isha slowly turned her head to look at Leo. At first, focusing on his healed face. Then her eyes made their way to his neck, where the burned flesh was still a red hue. The layers had melted on top of each other, giving a gruesome view of the nerves and veins beneath as folds of flesh had melded on each other.

She struggled to continue looking at him as she bit down shakily on her bottom lip, squinting her eyes to not focus so much on the disfigured flesh above her. But focus she did as Leo grabbed her hand, placing his thumb into her palm and moving her fingers against his chest. The skin was soft and loose as the flaps of it moved beneath her fingers.

I did this. It's my fault.

"Stop blaming yourself," said Leo, as if knowing what she was thinking. "I spent a long time blaming myself for what happened to Elena."

"But that wasn't your—"

"Just like this isn't yours."

"That's not the... I did that to you."

"Did you try to?"

"No, but—"

"Then that's all I care about. I promised Elena that I'd look after you girls. And I intend to keep that promise. Will you help me?

"Me? What can I do?"

"Well, I need to remove this burned flesh to begin the regrowth process. But it's time-consuming."

Isha couldn't help but look over at his other arm at the peeled, loose flap of burned skin hanging from his wrist. A sight that quickly made her look away again.

"It would be nice if you would help me," said Leo as he lifted himself from over her, standing to his feet and turning back to his desk. "I can't make you learn this. It's never pretty when you cut into someone and-"

"No," said Isha, as she struggled to her feet, taking a deep breath, still facing away from him. "I... I want to learn. I...

I just need a moment." She swallowed a bit of bile that had entered her mouth from the previous sight. Then, leaning forward, she placed her left hand against the wall to steady herself, moaning as she gripped at a new sharp pain in her stomach.

"I'm sorry," said Leo, noting her with her hand over her belly. "Did I press down too hard? I didn't mean-"

"No... no, it's," Isha sighed. "It's the other thing."

"Other? What? Oh!" said Leo, realizing what she meant. "When you get older, there are some herbs you can mix into a drink that prevents... well... either way, you will have to wait before you can take it."

"I'll be fine. It's not bad."

"Okay then," said Leo, taking a seat once again in his chair and placing his arm outstretched over the top of the desk. "Let's get started. You may want to grab that bucket over there; almost everyone pukes the first time they see someone being cut into."

"I'm fine," she said before gathering herself and making her way over to stand beside Leo.

"Alright, grab that blade there. The smaller one with the blunt back. This part isn't going to be pretty. But I can focus on stopping the bleeding and the healing if you do the cutting."

Isha reached over, grabbing the blade in her hand along with a towel. It was next to a bowl of water on the desk. Among all the sharpened knives, Isha saw a golden necklace. An ornament that looked like a leaf with a jewel inside was attached to it, but the gold had been melted somewhat. Putting the trinket out of her mind, she focused on what was in front of her as Leo reached his other hand over, placing it on top of hers. He then guided her hand to his arm, showing her where she needed to cut.

"Small, just do a small light cut beneath the skin."

"O... Okay," *How do I know what's just beneath the skin?* Isha pressed the blade where he instructed. *Not hard, not hard, not...*

And following Leo's instruction, she learned to cut away some of the burned flesh on his arm. She had never watched Leo heal himself this way before. The way the blood moved over his wounds was unsettling. But she found it somewhat beautiful how new strands of flesh began to comb over themselves into the bloodied areas from where she had cut the burned flesh away. They were like strands of hair that were weaving onto themselves. It reminded her much of the strands of magic she would see inside herself. How they layer over and through themselves, forming the orb of magic that housed her other self. Although gruesome, she found it mesmerizing.

Outside of a few instructions, Leo was as quiet as he could be, concentrating most of his efforts on healing. When he was done with one small section, he would either ask for a drink of water or instruct Isha on how to cut him again. Despite her words earlier, an effort required her to use the bucket. A young woman on her monthlies and cutting human flesh did, in fact, seem to make for a very unsettled stomach.

Sometime later, Isha found herself with her head down on the desk in front of Miss Webblebottom's class.

"Are you okay, Isha?" asked Chloe, looking over at her, worried.

"Sister, not feeling well today."

"I'm just tired," said Isha as she sighed into her folded arms.

"Okay, class, today we are going to talk about the negative effects of magic on our bodies. I'm sure you all have felt the exhaustion after a long playing session with Mr. Higgins. Do you remember why?"

"Because the magic we take in also poisons us," said one

of the girls in class.

"Very good. That is correct. If you push yourself too far, what happens?"

"We pass out," she answered again.

"Yes, normally. But it can go further than that. I believe I spoke before about how the brain shuts down itself as a safety function to stop one from using too much power. Well, sometimes, that is not true. Sometimes the mind pushes past its limit and can drive us into madness."

"You mean like going crazy?"

"Yes. Or, in a more technical term, Magical Lunacy. It's rare, but in a moment of extreme desperation, a mage can be pushed past their limits, resulting in a mage's death. I bring this up because of the previous events when our headmaster Soulden Fegmont was willing to give her life for her unconscious students, and she pushed past her limits to achieve higher levels of magic at great cost to herself."

"That's when Isha used her magic, right? That's when Isha used her magic and took her clothes off?"

The class giggled, and Isha frowned at the boy.

"Yes, Miss Isha did save Soulden with her unique brand of magic. But that was the outcome. Soulden willingly pushed herself, accepting death in order to save her students. Isha merely prevented her death. Now tell me, have any of you witnessed Magical Lunacy before?"

"I have," said one of the girls below Isha. "My uncle was in the war. Momma said they fought together in some war and during one of the fights, he went too far, and now he can't speak anymore."

"That can happen. The poisoning can reach a point where the brain can't clean itself. In fact, many during the past battles have found themselves crippled by pushing themselves beyond their limits, some losing the ability to walk or move their hands. This is why it is important, even here in school, to ensure you know your limits."

"We can just get Isha to use her power on us. That's why

she's here."

"No, I am not. I don't belong to you," said Isha, the frustration of the day taking control of her.

"You aren't from a noble family," said the boy. "You only got in because of your power. If not for that, you wouldn't be here."

"Now, now, class," said Miss Webblebottom, "I guess we couldn't skirt around this forever. Okay, class, how many of your parents have mentioned Isha's power to you?"

The entire class raised their hands, except Pavel and his group. Isha was surprised to see Freedo raise his hands as well.

"And what did your parents say? Don't worry. I won't tell them. You can share it with the rest of the class."

"Father told me I should become friends with her," said Serpene, "and when I told him we are already friends, he said I should bring her to our home."

"That's better than my mother," said the same boy from earlier. "My parents said I should try to marry her. As if I would ever, I don't care what type of power she has. I will marry a princess and help rule a kingdom."

"You shut up," said Freedo. "Or I will make you so ugly; no princess will even look at you."

"You can't speak to me like that. All you are is her tag-a-long. I've seen you follow those Sakaris along like a puppy. You should be ashamed. But maybe you know that no girl in the kingdom would touch..."

The boy didn't even get to finish his sentence before Freedo was on top of his desk, leaping off it at him.

The class erupted into cheers as Freedo, and the boy tangled with each other.

It took some time, but the class finally calmed down after Mr. Higgins's appearance. The teacher came in and split the boys apart. Although Isha did notice a bit of a smirk across his lips as he led Freedo away to the other side of the room, separating the boys. After everything was settled, the class continued with Mr. Higgins there to keep the peace.

Eventually, they all left to go home, and Isha couldn't help but spend the entire time thinking about her encounter in Leo's office. She wasn't mad at him. She just didn't know how to feel.

I know it's my fault he's burned like that. It's just… it's just hard to think that I did that to him. Papa used to say, 'it doesn't matter what you intended to do. It matters what you did.' So maybe I should tell him I'm when I get back.

"Something wrong with Sister Isha?" asked Makeba. "You have been looking down all day. Do you not feel good? Is it your moon blood time?"

"What?" said Isha, brought back to reality. "No. I mean, yes, but that's not it. I'm… I'm tired, is all. I just want to go to sleep."

"Maybe asking Freedo to carry sister home was good idea," said Jacinta. "He acted like man today. I was surprised."

"I don't need him to carry me," said Isha as she thought about Freedo. "Although I didn't expect him to jump over the desk."

"Yes. Even weak Freedo still a man."

"He's not that weak," said Isha. "He's been coming by to help us with our magic a lot. Doesn't that mean we are weak too?"

"Sister weak. I am not. He teaches you. I would have learned without him."

"Uhhh-huh," said Isha, looking unconvinced as they made their way to their house door. "Either way, I just want to sleep and not think about anything." Isha then opened the door to Heart house and saw there were no candles lit. *I guess no one's here. I'll just apologize to Leo tomorrow. I mean, if he wants me to help… with that. Then I should. I need to take responsibility for what I've done.*

After taking their baths, the girls headed up the stairs to the bed, snuggling up against one another as they closed their eyes and went to sleep.

Isha found herself in a dark room, Leo's desk in front of her. The bloody tools she used to cut away at his flesh were laid out on top of it. Even in the dark, them seemed to sharp, the metal half covered in crimson. She reached down and picked up one of the blades, holding it up in front of her face. The blood on the blade leaked down the base before pooling at her thumb.

"It's your fault," came a voice out of the darkness.

Isha quickly turned around, turning her head from left to right, trying to peer out into the void.

"Who are you?" She said, but no response came. Instead, she felt the blade in her hand become heavy. Then, looking down, she noticed that the blade in her hand was no longer the smaller cutting blade but was now the jewel-encrusted dagger that was given to her by her adopted father.

"No, this isn't real. It's not—" Isha's words froze in her mouth as she looked up to find the man that she killed in the tent with Oscar now standing in front of her. The dead man's eyes were black as blood poured from the sides of his mouth.

"You killed me."

"No... You're not real. I'm not afraid of you. You were a bad person. Father said so."

His body limped forward in the darkness, until he stood over her. "You murderer. Everyone you touch will suffer the same fate as me."

"That's not true. It's not. I won't."

"Did you protect Elena? No, they came for you and now Elena is dead. They will come again and more will die."

"That's not... they came for the tree. They didn't come for..."

"You know why they came. You know..."

Teddy Baire

"You're not real. You're not real. You're not..."

CHAPTER 30

Her eyes opened. The world was blurry for a moment as the sleep slowly faded from her eyes. She blinked, then began moving her fingers in the sheets. Her body was warm. She glanced at her own body to see it wrapped in an entanglement of the arms and legs of the Sakari as they lay together. Her eyes surveyed back and forth as she gathered it all in. Then slowly, she reached her hands over her body, interlocking her fingers, and began rubbing them together, taking the time to embrace the feeling.

"Well, this certainly is unexpected," she said as a smile crept across her face.

Being careful not to wake them, she untangled herself from the Sakari girls. She grabbed a small nightgown left hanging over one of the chairs and found the fabric was a bit moist to the touch. Throwing it over her body, she exhaled in satisfaction as the cloth slid down over her body.

Taking one last look at the sleeping Sakari girls, she stepped out of the door in the hallway, closing the door behind her. Looking around at the wooden walls in interest, she stepped forward only to stop suddenly and let out a slight moan as she clutched at her stomach.

"Oh my. Aren't you just a growing girl?"

Making her way down the dark hall, she could see a light-bluish glow from downstairs. She took a few steps down and, peeking between the wooden railings, she saw a small tree with glowing blue leaves. The magic seemed to flow off of it like a tiny blue mist. She stared at it for a moment in wonder before noticing that, beside the tree, sat a sleeping young man with a book in his hand.

She scanned around the room for a moment more before spotting the door. Then, as quietly as she could, she went down towards it. The creaking of the wooden beams of the stairs seemed to echo in the night atmosphere in the house. But trying her best not to wake the man, she made her way to the door, opened it, and stepped outside into the cool night air.

Her eyes went wide as the life-like statue of the Goddess towered over her, and behind it sat the glimpse of the moon and clouds that seemed so close that she could touch them. She stepped forward, placing her hand on the statue, quickly realizing it wasn't the Goddess. Or at least not the Goddess that she had remembered.

Have they changed what the Goddess looks like now? They've made her younger and with shorter hair. She ran her fingers across the etched named plate at the statue's base. *Elena? So, they've given this Goddess a name and placed her in the sky? Well, that's certainly a fair amount more than they did for the old one.*

She gazed around at the trees and other houses off in the distance.

I wonder what other things they've done since I've been away. And with that thought, she began making her way down the streets of the floating city.

Despite the many places she could have gone, all roads eventually led to the school. The giant castle that stood above all the other buildings was an image that could not be ignored, and in the shadows of moonlight, it gleamed as if it were crystal. It certainly took her attention.

In her amazement of it all, she stopped to close her eyes and appreciated the feel of nighttime—the feeling of the wind on her skin, the tingling sensation of it flowing through her hair.

So perfect.

She raised her hand as a small stream of white magic began to swirl around her fingertips before vanishing into the air. Then, as if being called from all around her, small white orbs of magic emerged from the ground that hovered just above her feet.

Good. I was about to worry that perhaps this body was volatile. But it seems to match well. I just need... Her breath froze in her mouth. Her eyes widened and another smile crept between her lips. *It's here.* And she stepped forward, allowing the white orbs above her feet to dissipate, the magic flowing back into the ground beneath her as she made her way towards the school.

Up the stairs, pulling on the door's handle until it squeaked on its hinges, she opened the way before her. *No one here? No guards? Are things really so peaceful that they would...* She stopped in the hallway before tilting her head down, looking at her bare feet. Then, kneeling, she placed her hands on the marble flooring, moving her fingers back and forth.

"It's under me. I feel it." She looked around, but in the darkness of the ill-lighted hall, she didn't see any stairs. "How am I..."

Before she could finish her sentence, she realized she couldn't move her hands or her legs and that the floor was getting closer. No, not closer; the floor was swallowing her.

"What... what is..."

She was then swallowed whole. Her world turned to a darker shade of black as the stone compressed around her body. A sense of fear quickly took hold of her. *Where am I? What is going on? Is this some sort of trap?* She tried summoning her magic but felt as if the moment she did, it was just being sucked away before she could use it. *No, I won't be taken back. Not now. There must be a way free.* Her mind raced with thoughts of escape, but she wasn't sure how long she was in there. She just heard the sound of humming. It vibrated in her, a soft, comforting sound that began to thrum through her body.

She moaned as she opened her eyes, blinking as they began to fill with a reddish light. Then her moan turned into a gasp as her eyes fully opened, taking in her surroundings. She found herself on hands and knees in the center of an oval room. And there before her, protruding from below, was a massive red crystal. It was easily over a hundred times her size. Crawling over and leaning on top of it, she placed her face against its surface, feeling the warmth of the power that seemed to flow through it.

"It's here," she said with joy. "It's really here. It didn't go to waste. The sacrifice... it wasn't... it wasn't for nothing." She rolled over, the warmth of the crystal on her back as the light from it shined, peeking through her hair. It shone on the ceiling above her as she stared at the slowly shimmering lights. It felt like she was under a red ocean looking up through it into the sky. "But why is it here? No one should have been—"

She felt herself slipping down the crystal. Confused, she quickly looked down at her feet and saw that the floor was once again pulling her back in. "What? No. Not again." She tried her best to grip the crystal and hoist herself free. But to no avail. The floor continued sucking her deeper inside. "No, curse this wretched place and its walls. I mustn't be—"

Her words cut off again as she was engulfed in darkness.

The tightness around her body shifted her more and more. But this time felt more hurried than before. The shifting was stronger, more consecutive. She knew she was free from the grasp of the castle when she could feel the cold night air on her skin again and the chilled marble floor beneath her fingers.

She opened her eyes, finding herself on her back, looking up at the ceiling of the hall she was just in a moment ago. She then rolled over on her hands and knees as she clenched her fists. *What a cruel joke to show me that and then snatch me away just as...* Her thoughts paused in her mind as she saw a set of golden eyes peering back at her in the shadows. From the corner of the eyes, magic vapor flowed around it as the eyes swayed up and down as they came closer.

Now, what monsters must I deal with? Is this some cruel prison made to torture me? Well, if so, then I will not be so easily... She turned around to see another set of golden eyes coming towards her from the other end of the hall. *Since when is a school for children haunted by beasts? Is this what those girls were supposedly being trained to fight? Well, if so, I shall have it known that I am no slouch myself. And I will give you ruin before I allow you to take me.* She stood to her feet, gathering her determination. *I'll show you. I have not been granted this body just to hand it over to death.* White magic began to leak out from both her hands. "I'll show you just who... wait, you?"

She blinked as, out of the darkness, came one of the Sakari girls. The gold of her eyes faded away as she stood before her.

"Enough, you come home now," said Jacinta with a serious tone.

"Yes, we take sister home," said Makeba from behind.

Sister? Yes, I am wearing this body. I guess there's no need to harm them when I can just play along. She raised her hand and smiled. "Do not worry about me, sisters. I was just out

417

for a walk. You both head on back. I shall come home soon enough."

"No, not Sister, speaking now. The one inside sister. You come home now and give us back Sister Isha."

I must not have said it how she would have. *Perceptive little babies, aren't you? What were their names again?* "No, Makeba. I am Isha," she said as she clutched her nightgown's neckline with a beggar's face. "Do you not trust me?"

"I am Jacinta. Not Makeba, and you will come home now," she said as she came closer, lowering her stance and assuming a fighting position. "If not, then we will make you."

Grettaline sighed, "Well, it was a fifty-fifty chance. Figured a girl had to give it a go." Then she dashed to the side, opening one of the nearby classroom doors. Dropping to her knees in the darkness, she crawled forward, hiding behind the desks and peeking out in the moonlight as it came through the window. She looked around for another door, finding one up ahead. But before she could make her way towards it. She blinked, not believing what was happening. The door was getting smaller. No, not smaller, the wall itself was now consuming the door and closing any chance of an exit she had.

Is this place cursed? Does it have a will of its own? She patted the floor below her, ensuring that it was still solid. *Will I be spirited away again? Are there only certain places I can move to?*

In fear of being trapped by the building again, she waited for what she knew would come. She didn't have to wait long. Both Sakari girls entered the room. That odd golden glow returned to their eyes for only a moment as they stood at the head of the room.

"You not hide from us. We have been on hunt before, and we see you."

"Of course, you have," said Grettaline, stepping out from under one of the desks, her white nightgown glowing in the moonlight. "I do not wish you girls harm. But I will not just be ordered back as if I am some child, no matter the circumstances of my appearance." *Perhaps this cursed place will be less likely to take me if these girls are my hostages. Subduing one of them may be my best option.*

"Then we take you back," said Jacinta.

"You leave me no choice then," said Grettaline as she raised a hand and pointed at the Sakari girls. "You did ask for this but try not to burn yourselves too badly." A white stream of magic left her hand before vanishing. Then suddenly, the same white orbs of magic from earlier came out of the walls and the floor. Dozens of them appeared around the classroom, illuminating the darkness in their glow.

Jacinta and Makeba just stared as the orbs raised around and in front of them.

"I did try to warn you girls. But if you would be so kind as to—" said Grettaline, watching as Jacinta reached out an arm towards one of the white orbs of magic. "Stop that. My magic can't be..."

Jacinta took the orbs of magic into her hand as the magic on her began to glow. "Sister teach and give us white magic." Then, squeezing her hand, her fingers sunk into the orb of white magic. The marking on Jacinta's back began to glow white as she absorbed it into herself.

Grettaline clenched her fists. "That shouldn't be possible. My magic isn't something that other mages can just take as they please."

"Our magic now," said Jacinta with a smile as she and Makeba reached out, absorbing the magic from a few nearby orbs of magic.

"Fine," said Grettaline through gritted teeth. "No more of this farce." She then brought her hands up to her chest as all the orbs in the room gathered toward her. Many of them absorbed into her body as the chairs and desks of the classroom began to shake and rattle. "I warned you." Then with the sound of breaking wood and rattling bolts, all the chairs and tables freed themselves from the floor and lifted into the air.

The Sakari girls watched with eyes wide as the classroom's furniture floated above their heads and around their sister.

"I hate being this forceful, but you girls need to be taught a lesson," said Grettaline as she pointed her finger at the Sakari girls, and a set of tables flew at them. The tables hurled through the air as the Sakari girls planted their feet and waved their arms, sending out a wave of magic that collided with the tables, deflecting them to each side of the room.

Grettaline smirked, "Fine. The hard way is always better."

The Sakari girls split up, running to different sides of the room, narrowly ducking and dodging a new set of thrown furniture. Makeba caught one of the thrown tables by its legs and spun it around while channeling her magic into it before launching it back at Isha's body. It crashed against the chairs and desks spinning around her. Grettaline gritted her teeth as the force of the impact made her bones rattle, the splintering pieces of wood flowing past her.

"Why you little, argh!" screamed Grettaline as her hair was pulled. Jacinta had landed on one of the spinning tables above her and had reached in, grabbing her by the hair.

"You bad fighter, like sister."

"Bad gather... huh," said Grettaline as she tilted her head, reaching up and grabbing Jacinta by the wrist that held her hair. "I have you now." A chair came flying in, striking Jacinta on the head. Then, feeling the grip on her hair loosen, Grettaline launched the table Jacinta was on into the air, sending the staggered Sakari flying back, landing with a thud as she slid across the floor into the wall. Jacinta screamed as her leg bent, pinned between herself and the wall, only to then have dozens of desks and chairs pile down on top of her.

"I warned you, little—" said Grettaline before the sound of crashing wood shook her as a table crashed against the shield of spinning chairs around her. The force of the impact caused her to stumble to the side as each desk crashed against her makeshift shielding.

"You give sister Isha back, now!" screamed Makeba as she spun, placing her hands on desk after desk, launching them at Isha's body.

"Just give up," shouted Grettaline before lashing back out, sending a wave of furniture at Makeba as the Sakari tried her best to dodge a chair flying by that crashed into the wall beneath a window. The two clashed more, but Makeba dropped to her knees by a wall after barely avoiding a thrown chair.

"I have you now," said Grettaline as a furniture mountain descended on the Sakari. Then, trying to catch her breath, Grettaline relaxed as she dropped the few remaining pieces of furniture circling her. "You... you girls should have listened." The room grew silent as the classroom now sat in a mess. Each side of the room had stacked furniture on top of each Sakari girl. "Serves you right," said Grettaline with a smirk of satisfaction before turning around, only to see Makeba in front of her with her fist drawn back. She appeared like a ghost from somewhere unseen.

And before Grettaline could think, she felt Makeba's fist as it struck her on the chin, staggering her, which caused a few of the nearby chairs to spin wildly out of control, tumbling across the room. Regaining her balance, she swung her arms at Makeba, who easily dodged the attack. Then Makeba stomped on her foot and struck her on the shoulder before punching her in the face again. The sprawled-out furniture seemed to shake with each blow Makeba landed on her sister. Finding herself outmatched in hand-to-hand combat, Grettaline lurched forward. Her hand reached out, trying to grab the Sakari by the hair. But her arm was knocked away by the wrist and catching a knee to the stomach for her efforts, Makeba knocked the wind out of her. Her mouth gaped open as she crouched on the floor, gasping for breath, her saliva drooling to the floor.

"You and sister are both bad fighters. Give her back, now," said Makeba standing over Isha's body and looking down at her.

"Why?" said Grettaline with a cough as she tasted blood in her mouth. She spat. "So you can lock me back up. I'd rather not." She lunged upward, surprising Makeba and wrapping her arms around the Sakari. "I bet you can't dodge this."

Makeba tried to break free, but it was too late as a table came flying in, colliding with both girls, sending them flying downward, rolling and tumbling over each other. They both struggled with each other as they went rolling but were broken up by Grettaline crashing shoulder-first into the teacher's podium while Makeba crashed into the front desk next to it.

They both lay there for a moment. But with a gasp, Grettaline rose to her knees, now clutching her arm. She looked down beside her feet at Makeba, who was now lying face down on the floor, and then across the room at all the scattered desks that still housed the other Sakari.

Enough of this. Stay there on the floor. I refuse to have any more to do with either of you, thought Grettaline as she grunted, realizing she could no longer move her arm, and turned to make her way towards the door. But she felt something grab hold of her ankle. Turning back around, she saw Makeba still on the floor with an arm stretched out.

"Why?" screamed Grettaline. "Just... let... me... go."

"Sister, no, go... away," moaned Makeba, her face still pressed against the floor with one eye open.

With her one good arm, Grettaline grabbed hold of the side of the podium, pulling it forward with all her might, sending it crashing down on top of Makeba while also

422

falling back down on her butt beside her.

Grettaline sat there for a moment, trying to catch her breath before closing her eyes, leaning back her head, and letting out a scream of frustration. With her chest heaving, she felt exhaustion taking over. *No, no, not yet. I refuse to...* She opened her eyes to see the other Sakari falling from the ceiling and, with no energy left to move, Jacinta crashed down on top of her, landing on her stomach. The impact sent Jacinta rolling over the floor as she bounced off his sister's body. Grettaline found herself doubled over in pain after the impact. Her feet digging into the floor, her head pressed to the same; she screamed with tears running down her face. *Why? Whyyyyyy... just let me go.* She looked towards the wooden door to see that it was now broken open, and she could see out into the shadowy hallway.

With what willpower she had left, Grettaline tried crawling forward with her one good arm, her body and knees scrubbing against the floor. But it wasn't long before she felt Jacinta clawing at her and crawling onto her back. Grettaline rolled over as the Sakari girl straddled her, and she swung at her with her good arm. Jacinta caught her arm easily, holding it by the wrist. With one eye barely open, there with the moonlight behind her, Grettaline looked up to see the darkness covering the Sakari girl's face.

"I hate you... I hate... both of you," said Grettaline through the tears full in her eyes as she wiggled under the Sakari's weight.

"Give... sister," said Jacinta as she reared her head upward, "back," and with thunderous force, brought her head down as hard as she could. The two girls' skulls collided with a thud that echoed throughout the dark room. And then there was silence as the moonlight shone down on the girls, all passed out. Isha beneath Jacinta, their foreheads still glued together with Makeba next to them, the podium on top of her, but still holding her sister's leg.

CHAPTER 31

Prince Saffron's group arrived on the road leading to the city of Ghemlon. From the road, it seemed to be a city under many repairs. All the houses except for the Goddess's temple and what appeared to be the dukes' homes were all the same. As the group drew closer, they noticed a large group of shirtless men beginning the making of a stone wall that looked as if it would encircle the entire city. Behind them was a group of female mages assisting with moving the heavier blocks. A few of the more skilled mages were shaping the stone blocks with their magic.

"I wasn't aware Ghemlon had the coin to recruit so many talented mages," said Saffron, looking on as they passed the workers. "I doubt they are all homegrown. It seems your friend may have been right, Mova."

"Perhaps your Lord Father is providing assistance in

restoring the city?" said Laura innocently.

"No. I would have been informed of a restoration of this sort. Father would have taken the time to painfully inform me as to why such a thing is or isn't needed. Or, at the very least, there would have been murmurs around the castle. I may have been on the road a while, but something like this would have taken months of planning."

As they approached the makeshift gate to the city, they saw that the two houses on either side of the street before entering were made of stone. Behind them were unkempt dirt streets and the wooden houses they had seen from the side road.

The citizens mostly dressed in typical commoner hand-me-down garbs. Sprinkled between them were the occasional robbed members of the church of the goddess. Some were preaching the will of the Goddess on the streets to anyone who would listen, while others were just helping with a random assortment of things that needed to be done around the city; washing clothing with the wives of the city, or hauling lumber for one of the many houses that were in disrepair

But to Saffron, there was something different in this city compared to any other impoverished dukedoms. The people here didn't seem to have the sadness that a life of this nature tended to bring.

What is it? Something in their eyes. Something willful, maybe? No, that's not right. It's as if... It's as if they are moving with purpose. Yes, that's it. Their eyes have a purpose, thought Saffron before turning to Mova. "I don't suppose you hear any whispers of anything interesting nearby."

"With this many people around? It would be a waste of magic to even try."

"Then I guess we are here to play the role of information gatherers once again."

"We are fairly sure the church is up to something. Why not just grab one of them and make them tell us?" said

Mova.

Saffron chuckled as they turned the corner. His laughter halted along with all of their horses, and they all froze at the sight before them. The street ahead was filled with robed members of the church; a number that looked to be easily over a hundred and many more could be assumed to be behind the buildings, out of sight.

"They're so many," said Laura. 'What... what do you think they're all doing here?"

"It would appear they are praying," said Dekol, stone-faced.

"Mova," said Saffron, blinking his eyes in disbelief, "do me a favor. If you do decide to grab ahold of one of their members for an interrogation, please do me the courtesy of not mentioning our names."

"So, what do you want to do now?" asked Dekol, still looking over the crowd.

"I suppose we should continue as planned. We shall pay the Duke here a visit. Surely, he can't claim ignorance about their purpose with this many of the clergy in his vicinity."

"Even so, do you really expect him to offer up the truth?"

"Perhaps not, but if we know that it is a lie, then that gives us a hint of what the truth might be."

"Well said," said Dekol as they turned their horses around. "The Duke's manor is up ahead, but it seems we'll have to take the long way around."

The trio turned back, making their way down the previous street, following the roads circling the city's outskirts. On each street passed they would see a dozen or more of the robed figures scattered about. It felt like the cycle repeated until they finally reached the gates to the Duke's manor.

The grounds were not that large, even though usually a Duke lived in what some would consider a small castle. This Duke's dwelling was just a large two-storied wooden building with its own stables.

"What'daya want?" asked the man at the gate. He had a

tone of authority in his speech, although he was more or less dressed in rags. Although he did have a hat that seemed a bit too large for his head as it fell to one side.

"Is the Duke or the Duchess in? I wish to speak with one of them." said Saffron.

"No, the Lord's out. But the Lady is here. And who are you that you think you can just speak to her without an invitation?"

Saffron looked at the man for a moment, considering his question. *I suppose honesty would be the prudent choice at the moment.* "I am Prince Saffron of Burlus. These three are my escorts."

The guard laughed. "You must be kidding. And what would the prince of Burlus be doing out here? Coming to see how his peasants are doing?"

Saffron waved his hands, and slowly the magical illusion he had used to alter his appearance washed away as if water had been splashed over his face. He'd waited for a moment in anticipation but saw the man narrowing his eyes at him. *What am I doing? It's not likely this man has ever even been to the capital, let alone seen my face.*

"Yeah, well. I ain't never seen the prince. You could just be some crazy mage. We got a lot of them running around here now."

"A fair point, but allow me to counter," said Saffron with a grin. "Perhaps I am not who I say I am, and you are right to suspect as much." He raised a finger, pointing it at the man. "But let's say that on the small chance that I am, indeed, Prince Saffron; what do you think your Duchess will do when I inform her that one of her subordinates turned me away at the gate."

The man's mouth twitched as he bit his lip, looking back at Saffron. "Alright, you speak all fancy-like. You might be him. Follow me then, but don't try anything. We got men inside."

"I appreciate your hospitality," said Saffron, urging his

horse to follow after the man as he led them inside the grounds. *When reason doesn't work, appeal to their self-preservation. You taught me well, Leonardo.* On the way, Saffron did indeed see some of the supposed men lofting around the grounds, which were just as unkempt as the rest of the city; broken wheel barrels with month-old hay inside and shrubbery that hadn't been trimmed in ages. It was all pretty worse for wear.

"Who ya got there?" asked a man from the second-floor steps as they approached the manor.

"Fella here saying he's the crowned prince. Even got some fancy magic on his face."

"Prince of what? Ain't no way some high noble like that's making his way all the way out here without her lordship hearing about it," said the man, as he looked over at the group. "No offense to whichever one of ya is supposed to be our majesty.

"Non-taken," said Saffron with a raise of his hand. "You and your friend here as wise to be skeptical and are honorable for trying to keep your master free from mischief. I admit my trip here was a bit unexpected."

"Do we have guests?" came a voice as the door to the manor opened, and a tall regal woman in fine clothing stepped out. Although her face still seemed to hold the air of youth, her age was given away by the white hair sprinkled into the brown mane atop her head.

"Ah, madam," said the man up the stairs, the tone of his voice changing as the woman appeared out of the door behind him. "This fellow bellow claims to be... ah well, he says he's—"

"The crowned prince of Burlus," said the Duchess with a smile. "Accompanied by his guards Mova, Dekol, and Thadnot Thaddius." She took another look and smiled. "Oh my, Princess Laura. Had I known I would be receiving such guests, I would have made my home more hospitable."

"No, Duchess Alonna. The shame is mine for appearing

before you without an invitation. I apologize for the burden, but we have been on the road for quite some time. May I trouble you for your hospitality?"

"Oh, yes. Where are my manners?" said the Duchess before turning to the man that led Saffron in. "Lemmy, do take their horses and see that they are fed." She then turned to the man next to her on the steps. "Henrick, I'd wager Sally is almost done with supper. Please, do go and help her with setting the table."

"Yes, Madam," said both men as Saffron and his party dismounted their horses and made their way up the steps to greet the Duchess.

"Now, please, do come in. I would like to say that it's rare that I receive such company, but in truth, in all my years, this is the first I've ever received a visit from the royal family," said the Duchess as she led them inside his manor. "Tell me, what brings you so far from the capital? I hardly think I require much of the kingdom's attention."

"Mostly just inspecting the city," said Saffron as he looked over the home. It appeared quite as he imagined from the outside. Wooden floorboards squeaked when he stepped on them and stale air from some unseen mold mixed in with the scent of lumbar and old furniture. "When we arrived, we saw quite a large group of mages along with an alarming amount of the clergy."

"Take a seat, please," said the Duchess as she led them into a room with a large table. "And yes, the clergy have been here for a little over a month now. They seemed interested in building another chapel here. The mages they brought with them are here to speed the process along and have been quite helpful to the townsfolk."

"We've noticed. They seem to be renovating the entire city, including the building of a town wall."

"Yes, they wanted to start with my home," said the Duchess as she gestured around the room. "This is a far cry from the palace or many other Dukedoms. But I insisted they start with helping the people—first, the entrance to the city and then the wall. We have no shortage of rock and stone out here. Might as well take this rare opportunity and make use of it."

"Very practical," agreed Saffron as three women entered the room holding food trays. The youngest of whom walked over, serving the Duchess her plate.

"Ah yes, this is my daughter, Marian," said the Duchess as she patted the girl on the arm. "Come take a seat with us, dear. You've done enough for now. Come meet the prince."

"Yes, mother," said Marian, pulling out a chair and taking a seat at the table.

The girl was young, Saffron noticed, perhaps around the age of fourteen or fifteen with the same brown hair as her mother's and the same jawline.

"Much like me, my daughter here has the gift of magic. My other daughter was not as fortunate. She takes after her father, you see."

"Where is your husband? I didn't notice him around the grounds."

"Off in the countryside, seeing to our affairs," said the Duchess, flipping her hand dismissively. "I'm sure he shall return in a week or so. His trips can be quite time-consuming." She then turned to Laura and smiled. "Congratulations, by the way, Princess Laura. I heard the wedding was beautiful. How are you enjoying your new title? I do hope your new station hasn't been too hard on you."

"Ah, no, Duchess. I'm afraid it all hasn't really sunk in yet. We are still on our honeymoon."

"Really? And you've chosen to come here? I hardly think out here in the sticks is what I would consider a suitable romantic environment," said the Duchess looking accusingly at Saffron. "But even out here, I have received word of your husband's unorthodox actions. You were known as quite the ladies' man Prince Saffron."

"Tales of exaggeration, I assure you."

"Oh, no need to be coy," said the Duchess with a smile. "Your father was much the same when he was a prince. But I swear, how he ever found favor with your mother was the greatest secret of Siena."

"You went to school with my father and mother?" asked Saffron, his interest peaked.

"Oh yes. I even knew your father, Dekol, a gallant man. A shame about the rebellion." The Duchess shook her head disappointedly. "But such is the way of men; always looking for a woman to bed or a head to lob off its shoulders."

"I am grateful to the king for allowing me a position in the capital," said Dekol, as if he were just stating the color of the sky.

"Yes. I'm sure you are," said the Duchess as she reached over, wiping a strand of hair from her daughter's face. "You know, prince, I had once planned to introduce my daughter to you on her sixteenth birthday. But one cannot fault you for choosing your lovely bride." She placed a finger under her daughter's chin, lifting her face. "But she really does take after me. The spitting image of myself at that age."

"Your daughter is very lovely," said Saffron, appeasing the Duchess. "I'm sure she would have stolen my heart had it not already been taken."

"Yes, sadly, my daughter will never be a princess. So other roads must be traveled."

"Excuse me, Duchess, a question if I may?" asked Laura, interrupting the conversation.

"Yes?"

"Does this city handle any trade? You said your husband was off handling the financial affairs."

"What's that? Oh. Yes, well, we do handle a bit of trade, but not much outside of the stone from the mountains and lumbar. The grounds here aren't fertile enough for wine. But the people here are hard-working, so we find a way."

"So, you don't trade... anything? With the kingdom directly, I mean," said Laura, her eyes shifting over to

431

Marian. "So... nothing... of value... grows here. Well, not anything that can't be found somewhere else. Rock and stone are as commonplace as water and air."

The Duchess placed her hands together, "So, am I to assume that if we were to supply something of value, the kingdom would be open to a more... intimate trade agreement?"

"If something of value were to be acquired, why, I'd imagine the king would be hard-pressed to not at least listen to any desires you might have."

"Hearing that puts my heart at ease," said the Duchess, placing a hand over her chest. "We do try so hard to ensure the best for those around us. Why, it's one of the reasons, I was so grateful to those clergymen. They, too, see my vision for the people here."

"Yes, my Lord Husband said earlier that he wishes to go out and visit your fine city. Sadly, I think I've had enough of a journey for one day. If I might trouble you for a hot bath, I am in dire need of one."

"Oh yes, I'll have a room made ready for you immediately and have some hot water brought in," said the Duchess, turning to her daughter. "Please show her highness to the guest room and see to it that she is looked after. Who knows, you and she might even have some things in common."

"Yes, Mother," said Marian meekly before standing from the table. "Right this way, your highness."

Laura and Mova excused themselves from the table, leaving Saffron and Dekol with the Duchess.

"I'm sorry things aren't as nice as they are in the capital," said Marian, turning the corner and stopping at one of the doors down the hall.

"Do not worry yourself, dear. For the last few nights, I've been sleeping in tents and bathing in lakes. Your home is lovely, and I'm grateful for your consideration."

"Thank you, your highness. I... I will go and see to getting your water ready," said Marian before heading off

432

down the hall and around the corner.

Laura and Mova entered the room. It was significant for the size of the home. Scents had been lit in an attempt to mask the smell of wood but instead only mixed with it to provide a sweet foresty scent. There was a single large bed against the room's back wall, a rug in the middle of the floor, and several oil paintings on the wall.

"I guess at this point, I should consider myself to be your personal guard," said Mova as she closed the door behind her.

"I suppose it does seem that way. I'm sorry to have you shepard over me during this time," said Laura as she walked toward the window. Outside she could see one of the clergy members handing a basket filled with what looked to be black jewels to a house staff member. "If you prefer, I can ask for another when we return to the capitol."

"No, I find myself quite enjoying the company of another woman besides Frenka."

"Have you two never seen eye to eye?"

"We do our jobs. Your husband's still living, after all, despite his countless attempts to do the contrary. But Frenka is more of an uncontrollable force. Our nature just clashes, is all," said Mova as she stepped over, inspecting one of the paintings. "Speaking of which, you handled yourself well there with the Duchess. I think even Saffron was taken aback."

"You think so?" asked Laura with a sigh. "I merely imitated what I thought my mother would do. "She said the courts would be filled with politics and schemes and that I should prepare myself." She shook her head. "Father and mother would often counsel me in mock situations and tell me how I should act."

"So you weren't serious about taking that Marian girl as Saffron's concubine?"

"You remember when you came to me and told me about the prince's feelings for Frenka? I had never noticed it before, but it became obvious after you brought it to my attention. Even during our wedding, I think I caught him staring at her. I believe it was then and there, I accepted it."

"Well, Frenka has always been Saffron's weakness. I doubt there is another one of her."

"Perhaps not, but as I said, my mother taught me that people seek out those with power. Do you know I'm only married to Saffron because the King feared my father would start another rebellion?"

"No, I was aware that it all felt quite sudden, so I figured there was some reason behind it."

"Oh, Father would never do such a thing. But mother was able to convince the King that it might be possible. So they agreed to marry me to the prince in order to maintain relations," Laura gave a laugh as her shoulder sagged. "Mother was so proud of herself that day. She told every detail about how she and the King spent hours bartering the terms of the trade. And now here I am, a princess because of it."

"Perhaps I should cast a silence spell on the room if—"

"I've already done it. The moment we stepped into the room."

"What? But I didn't see you cast anything?"

"Yes, I've become very good at casting spells in secret," said Laura as she walked over, sitting down on the bed. "And when I spent those two months locked in that dungeon after watching that thing take my face and my voice. I realized that this world holds some truly horrible secrets."

"I think my lovely wife just agreed to me being the lover of the Duchess's daughter if she had anything worth trading for it?" said Saffron as he left the Duchess's manor on foot, heading out into the city.

"Perhaps. But you've seen court politics; do you

disapprove?" said Dekol.

"I mean... Well, I had hoped to shelter her from it. If only for a little while."

"She seemed to handle herself well enough."

"That she did. Tell me, is this one of the mysteries of marriage?"

"You expect me to answer that with any sort of tangible evidence?"

"Well, you grew up with your father and a mother. I lost mine most early. Surely, you have more information than I."

"And so does the Duchess. And look how that's working for her."

"A fair point."

"What? Having regrets so soon?"

"Hardly, it's just... I'm beginning to wonder who I have tied myself to. Did I marry a timid woman, or did I marry a conniving countess?"

"Maybe she, herself, is still figuring that out. It's not as if she spoke behind your back. Which probably means she wanted you to see her. I've known many men who were not even afforded that luxury."

"If that is your idea of comforting me, I'm afraid the act is moot."

"Then take solace in the fact that all things come to light. Who she is or isn't shouldn't matter much. It's not as if you can change a person's nature. She'll reveal herself to you eventually. Everyone does."

"Perhaps you're right," said Saffron as he patted Dekol on the back before waving magic across his face with his other hand to change his appearance. "Now, hold still. It's always harder changing the faces of others than it is my own. Unless you prefer to look disfigured."

"What? In a city where hardly anyone has been to the capital, you expect them to know who I am?"

"Honestly, I'm not sure about anything anymore. But it never hurts to be a bit cautious. There, done. Come along, then. We've got a city to explore."

Dirt roads were plenty in the city of Ghemlon. Its people were working hand-in-hand with the clergy at rebuilding an entire city. Smiles and conversations spread around the corners like water flowing from a stream. One side had people discussing contradictory beliefs about the origins of the goddess; another had a clergyman giving another man advice on preparing for the birth of his wife's first child.

"So where should we start first?" said Saffron, shaking his head. "I'll be honest. Now that we've arrived, I'm not sure where to go or even what questions to ask. I had expected the Duchess to be more hesitant. But she openly admitted to working closely with the clergy. I could have prodded more into the situation, but I think it would be best for my wife to rest comfortably for a night or two."

"How considerate of you. Well, when lost, look for a guide," said Dekol as he walked over to one of the clergy-women. "Excuse me, ma'am, we just arrived in the city and are looking to help. We don't know anyone here or where to start."

"Oh! You'll be looking for Miss Lorman. She should be out by the gate. She's organizing the city's reconstruction. I can take you to her if you'd like?"

"Would you? We don't wish to be a burden on you."

"No! Of course, not. We are here to be of service under the eyes of the goddess. Come, follow me," said the clergy-woman as she led the men through the streets towards the city's gate.

"And now we have a name and a purpose," whispered Dekol.

"That we do, old friend."

CHAPTER 32

Lonta'Mar, Makeba, Jacinta, and Isha looked down the hill over a field of tall Sakari trees. Four giant pillars floated above the ground, towering over the trees in the distance.

"We cannot go there yet," said Lonta'Mar. "I do not remember it all. But soon, maybe I will. I think."

Between the pillars they could see the semblance of a city, its walls, and buildings made of white stone. In the center was a huge building, its cone-shaped head sticking out above the rest of the city. The sight was beautiful, but the moment was soured by the reason they had returned to the world inside the tree.

"Sister Isha, bring her out now," said Jacinta, a solemn tone to her voice.

"I don't know how to, or even if I can," said Isha, the nervousness apparent in her voice. "I mean, the last time was just-"

"Sister Isha, bring her out now," repeated Jacinta, her tone harsher than before. "Sister, my responsibility. Other one not allowed to be in control again."

"I know, but maybe we could just talk to her again? You don't have to fight."

"We will talk. But if she no listen, then we fight."

"But... but what she... I mean... I don't want you getting hurt again."

Jacinta just smiled back at Isha. "Sister, trust me. I make this better now."

Isha stared at Jacinta for a moment before taking a deep breath, closing her eyes, and exhaling. "Okay, I'll try." *Oh, please don't let anything bad happen this time. I'm me. I'm me. I'm not her.* Isha chanted in her mind repeatedly as she went inside her mind and searched for the magic that wasn't hers. It took a moment to find it this time. It was deeper inside than usual as if it were trying to hide. But it was there. Isha once again grabbed ahold of it and began pulling it inside her.

Opening her eyes, she took in the magic, and like before, a tear in the world began to appear. It was small at first, but as she drew in more power, it grew larger and larger until it was double their size and floating above their heads.

"Where is she?" said Jacinta, noticing that no one was coming out of the portal.

"I... I don't know. Maybe she..." Isha then felt a tug on her magic. "Wait!" Then, she reached out her hand, closing it into a fist, before snatching it back down to her side. And suddenly, Grettaline fell through the portal, landing on the ground in front of them with a thud. A little to her surprise, Isha saw that she was wearing the same training garb as they were. *Does that mean in here, she will just wear whatever I think I am?*

She landed with a cough and a face filled with dirt. "Can you not," she yelled as she rose on her hands and knees, "find a less dramatic way to summon me?"

438

"No," said Jacinta, her tone unchanged, "We talk now."

"Well, you probably think we should," said Isha's double, standing to her feet before Jacinta. "But I see no reason to explain myself to you. I may be trapped here in your supposed sister's body, but that does not make me beholden to you in the slightest."

"Protecting sister Isha is my job. You not allowed to take her and run away."

"Well, haven't you done just a stupendous job at that so far," said Grettaline, pointing towards Isha. "Forced to murder a man in whatever blood ceremony thing that was. Almost raped by a brute savage. Narrowly escaping being crushed by an airship. And those are just the events that I was awake for. Who knows what other tragedies she's had to endure while under your so-called protection?"

"You in sister's body. You part of sister. Do you accept me as leader?"

"What?" said Grettaline with a hardy laugh. "You? Lead me? Preposterous! I'd sooner follow the lead of a pig."

"Then we fight and see who will lead."

"What?"

"I fight Sister Isha and Makeba for right to lead as war-sister. But I not fight you. So, you accept me as war-sister and follow, or you fight for right to lead."

"I think we can firmly say that I do not recognize myself as your *sister*," said Grettaline as she looked around at the rest of the girls and then down at her own clothing. "And why am I dressed in this revealing outfit?"

"This gear. We fight and train. Easy to move," said Jacinta, crouching low and digging her toes into the dirt.

"What are you doing? Do you want more of what happened last time? Or is your memory too short to remember that it took both of you before?"

"Before, I not want to hurt Sister Isha. But now, I really want to hurt you."

"She's serious," said Isha, feeling a bit of worry for her

counterpart. "And your magic will not work here."

"Don't be preposterous. You can't lock me out of my..." she said as she raised her hands and then looked at her fingers in shock. "What? What have you done?" And before she knew what was happening, Isha saw her counterpart flying through the air, her face plummeting back down, colliding with the dirt. Grettaline yelped as Jacinta planted a knee into her back before twisting her arm.

"It true," said Jacinta, looking at Isha before smiling, "I can hurt you here and not hurt sister Isha. No magic works here unless Tree Sakari allows it. She not understand many magics, but she understands pain. So, you will understand pain."

"Get off. Of. Me. You unruly child. I will not be—argh!" she screamed again as Jacinta twisted her arm even more before finally letting her go and stepping back, assuming the same fighting stance as before.

Grettaline struggled to get up, clutching at her arm. Her dirt-ladened face now held eyes that were unmistakably filled with hatred as she stared ahead at the Sakari in front of her.

"You think you can just bully me into submission? Is that it?"

"Say I am war-sister, and you listen to Jacinta."

"Never. I will not take orders from a child."

"If Jacinta child, then you also child."

"I am most certainly not. And I will not be treated as such," she said before jumping at Isha, swinging her fists in the girl's face. Jacinta easily deflected the motion, bringing her hand up and catching Grettaline's arm. Then, with a twist, she sent Grettaline falling forward and tumbling over on the ground with Jacinta landing on her back, grabbing her by the hair, and wrenching her neck back.

"Say I am war-sister."

"Never... you, savage."

Makeba shook her head before turning to Isha. "She

very stubborn and bad fighter like you."

"Hey! I wasn't that bad," said Isha as she watched the ordeal unfold, "was I?" Watching a version of herself get tossed around by her sister felt odd. It was as if she was watching the past events of her life play out in her mind. And it looked just as painful as she remembered it being. So much so that she couldn't help but flinch after every slam, twist, and punch.

They stood there for half an hour watching as Jacinta continued to beat on her doppelganger to the point where she couldn't help but feel some sympathy for her.

Lonta'Mar closed her eyes for a moment as the fight waged on. "Leo. The Leo-man is calling for you to come back. He says classes are starting."

And with one final thud, the doppelganger fell to the ground on her side, coughing and clutching her stomach with Jacinta staring down at her.

"We do this every day until you accept and listen to Jacinta," she said, her voice cold and unfeeling.

Grettaline could only moan as she lay there on the ground.

"Send us back now," said Jacinta as she turned to Lonta'Mar.

And the world went white.

Isha opened her eyes to see the small colorful tree glowing in front of her. But with that sight came a massive headache that caused her to squint her eyes. She placed her hands on her face.

"Welcome back," said Leo, sitting in a chair at the table, finishing his breakfast. "Honestly, why do you girls insist on attending class in your condition?" He stood up and walked over to Jacinta, who raised her arms for him. He placed his hands under her elbows and helped her to stand up. With one of her legs stinted and bandaged, she had to stabilize herself on the other as Leo handed her a walking stick. "Your leg is still broken, and healing magic can only do so much. You will still need to stay off it for a week or two as I heal the bone."

"I know. I will, I promise," said Jacinta. Moreso than her body, her tone and face were completely opposite of what it has been inside the world of the tree. Here, she looked tired and defeated. She had looked like this for the last few days since her fight in the classroom with Grettaline.

Isha had woken up a day after the fight and she had, in fact, been herself. Even with her injured leg, Jacinta dropped to her knees and repeatedly apologized to Isha, claiming she had failed as a war-sister. Looking at her now, Isha had never seen her sister in such a defeated state.

Turning toward Makeba, one couldn't say she was doing much better. Her arm was in a sling, and Leo had told her that her shoulder had a fracture. Isha, having the lesser of the injuries, woke up to find that she had a large knot on her head. Apparently, Jacinta's headbutt while Grettaline had control of her body was delivered quite hard.

Halfway through telling Leo all the odds and ends of the story, he just told them to go back to bed.

One by one, he tied the golden sashes around the girls' waists as they stood before him.

"Okay then, if you're so determined, then off to class you go," said Leo as the girls all headed out. "Ah, Isha," he said when they reached the door, "stay a moment. I have some to discuss with you."

"Me?" said Isha, giving a nervous glance at Jacinta and Makeba before walking back to Leo.

"You girls go on," said Leo. "She will be along shortly."

Makeba looked confused for a moment but did as instructed, leaving Isha with Leo.

"Okay," said Leo as they left. "I'm not going to pretend to understand everything that's happening with you. At this point, I'm not even sure what to tell Soulden anymore." Leo scratched his head as if looking for the right things to say. "Look, just... just try to look out for those Sakari girls, okay?

Especially Jacinta. I know she acts tough, but I don't think she's as strong as she puts on."

"What do you mean?"

"I mean..." Leo rubbed his face in frustration. "I mean, it's... it's like, none of us know what it means to be Sakari. Those girls call you their care-sister. I don't know exactly what all that means. But they sure take it seriously. Maybe they have responsibilities that we don't understand."

"I... I will try."

"That's all I can ask," said Leo as he placed his hand on Isha's head, tussling her hair. He then nodded toward the door with a smile. "Off you go then. I'm sure they're waiting on you."

Isha made her way outside in the morning light, and the three of them hobbled their way to Mr. Higgins's combat class.

"What in the Goddess' name do we have here?" said Mr. Higgins as the girls lined up with the rest of the class. "I'm supposed to teach you little babies about war, but judging from the looks of it, these three should be teaching the class."

The class giggled at the comment as Freedo ran over toward them.

"Are you okay?" asked Freedo, looking over the girls and reaching out for Makeba's arm but pulling his hand back before touching her. "What... happened?"

"We... we got in a fight."

"You mean a war?" corrected Mr. Higgins, gesturing to the girl's injuries. "Fights don't usually end up looking like whatever this is. And don't you three belong to Heart house? One usually wouldn't expect our healers to walk into class with the most injuries."

"We still can fight. You teach?" said Jacinta, undeterred by the class's giggles.

"Really? Are you sure about that?" asked Mr. Higgins as he walked over, standing before Jacinta. "Cause to me, it looks like you can barely stand. I know the look of someone who's barely holding on."

Isha looked over at her sisters, one's leg wrapped, the other's arm in a sling, then over to the rest of the class, who was obviously staring at them. *I guess we really do look bad.*

"Now, where are those friends of yours," said Mr. Higgins, turning to the class. "Pavel, Chloe, Serpene, and Marlene, come over here. When fighting, you'll be expected to look after the one beside you. These girls are your friends, and they've fallen behind in class again. So I'm entrusting you all to bring them up to speed."

"I can do that," said Freedo happily as he turned to the girls before pointing to a nearby corner of the room. "Let's go over there. Help me get the training rocks, Pavel." He dashed off to a part of the room that had a trough filled with rocks.

The group followed Freedo's instructions, making their way to the corner as he and Pavel made their way back, carrying the spherical rocks cradled in their arms. They all sat down on the floor in a circle. Jacinta had a bit of a hard time with the maneuver, but Freedo was happy to assist.

Isha was surprised to see Jacinta not protesting as Freedo took hold of her arm and lowered her to the ground.

"Okay," said Freedo as he sat between the Sakari girls, handing them both a rock as he took one into his own hands. "Now, both of you use soil magic. But you're not supposed to do that here. Instead, we are supposed to strengthen our bodies with magic like this."

The girls watched as Freedo held up the rock in his hand, beginning to squeeze it. Slowly, lines appeared on it where his fingers gripped the side. And then they heard it: the crackle as it began to break. His fingers penetrated until the rock burst in half as its top fell to the floor, and all that was left in Freedo's hand was dust, dirt, and small chunks of rock.

"Strong," said Jacinta, her eyes wide as the dust dropped

away from Freedo's hand. "And you teach us how to do this?"

"Yes."

"Freedo is actually the best in the class," said Pavel. "He's the one that taught me what I was doing wrong."

Freedo's face brightened in light of the praise, only to be made dull again as he turned to see Makeba squinting her eyes at him. "What? Why are you looking at me like that?"

"Why you suddenly good at magic?"

"What do you mean, suddenly?" said Freedo in protest. "I've always been good at magic. You just don't want to admit I'm better than you."

"Nooooooo," said Makeba, in a long, suspicious groan. "You weak. This must be trick or something."

"I swear, why must you think so little of me?" said Freedo as he reached down in frustration, grabbing Makeba by the wrist of her good arm and placing a small rock in her hand. "Now, close your eyes."

"Fine," said Makeba, doing as instructed, even if hesitantly.

"Okay, now I'm going to place my hand on different part of your body and—"

"What you mean, you touch Makeba?" she said, whipping her head around.

"Just... just trust me for once, okay?" said Freedo with a sigh. "I need... you to send as much magic as you can over to wherever I touch, okay? Can you do that for me?"

"Fine, but you watch where you touch."

"Yes, yes. I will."

The exchange was quite humorous to those around them, but Isha saw the reddening on Freedo's face and wondered how much he was enjoying himself, if at all. But She decided to keep her thoughts to herself as her sister followed his instructions.

"Okay." said Freedo, placing a hand on Makeba's knee, then on her waist, then to her neck on both sides before moving to the elbow of the arm that held the rock, then the wrist and finally he grasped her fingers in his. "Now, squeeze," he shouted in a commanding tone.

And they all watched as the rock in Makeba's hand cracked.

"See. It works," said Freedo with a proud smile as he sat back down.

"It not break," said Makeba, looking disappointedly at Freedo.

"Of course not. It was your first time doing it. It even took Pavel a few days before he got the hang of it. Mr. Higgins says that we will be able to strengthen our whole bodies one day and do things like run faster and longer."

"I want to try," said Jacinta. "Can you show?"

"Huh? Oh… ah yeah, sure," said Freedo as he reached forward, grabbing another rock and handing it to Jacinta. Then he stepped behind her. "It only makes the strength you already have stronger. So, if someone is bigger than us and does it, they will be stronger than us, even with magic. But it's still really cool."

The girls tried several times, but neither Jacinta nor Isha could crack the stone as Makeba had. Soon the image of a bell appeared above class, and they left into the crowded halls of the school with Freedo standing to the injured side of Jacinta so that she would have plenty of room as they made their way.

It wasn't long before they reached Miss Webblebottom's class, where Soulden was waiting at the door.

"Hello, you three," said Soulden as she gave the girls a look over. "Leo informed me of your injuries. But hearing about it and seeing you three are two very different things." Soulden shook her head. "And, of course, they would request to see you all during this moment."

"Someone wants to see us?"

"Yes, you girls remember the chamber I took you three to when you first arrived?"

"The one with weird statues?" asked Jacinta.

"Yes, well, they wish to see you again."

"How they see us, and we not see them?"

"That... that is a very complicated question. If I were to go into detail on how reflections work when mixed illusion magic and image transfers, we would be here for some time. But rest assured, they can see you." Soulden then led the girls down the hall after the students made their way to their classes and onto the lifting pad. Placing her hand on the orb, the platform lifted, taking them up above to the highest levels of the school.

There they walked into the walled garden room as before, the roots and veins now having grown higher up the statues. Ahead of them were the huge stone doors that began opening as they approached. This time, the difference was that the lamp in the center of the room had already been lit, illuminating the darkness inside. Above her, sha could see the statue along the running water.

"Are you all here?" asked Soulden as they stepped into the room.

"Some are," said a voice from the shadows which Isha that was from the heart statue. "The rest will arrive soon enough."

The girls stepped down to the center of the room, with Isha shouldering the weight of Jacinta's leg on herself, their feet splashing in the small amount of water beneath them as they stepped forward under the light.

"Oh my," said the familiar voice of the high mother. "What has happened to you girls?"

"I second that question," said the bull statue. "If I recall correctly, the first time you brought them before us, the other one was on crutches, and now one of the Sakari seems to have taken that role."

Soulden sighed, "I am aware. And I admit these girls," she glanced back down at the girl with a brow raised, "have proven quite dedicated to finding themselves in curious circumstances. I still believe Sceana is the best place for them to learn."

"The school's ability to teach is not a question. I'm curious about the girl's ability to survive its teachings. Judging by the look of them, it is not high."

"Alright enough, scolding the headmaster," said the heart statue. "We only wished to see the girls, questionable health aside, and hear how the training of her gift was going."

"Yes, well, as stated, she can significantly increase the capacity of a mage to wield magic, and it seems to completely negate the effects of the overuse of magic. The problem lies within her controlling or limiting her power as almost any mage she enhances passes out shortly after or even during the process."

"But it was reported that those Sakari girls there are unaffected by this?" said the bull statue.

"Yes, but they were affected beforehand to a certain amount. To negate those effects, we had a senior Sakari related to the girls come to the school to perform a ritual that seems to allow the girls to use the power without negative effects."

"Yes, but your report didn't specify how the ritual was performed."

"I… actually was not in the room. The ritual was private between the girls and their elder."

Isha thought back to the night under the tree when she had the markings placed on her body. She remembered Soulden being there in the beginning. *Did she leave? I think I remember her being there.*

"I see," said the bull statue. "That can't be helped now, I suppose. There is another reason we asked for you to be here. We are still looking into the attack on the school. The real question is, how did they know about the Trailage tree? While it's not a secret amongst certain staff members, it's certainly not well known enough to have made it to such organizations as that attacked without someone purposely leaking it."

"I thought the same," said the heart statue. "But I can't imagine who would give out that information. And keep in mind, we are a moving school in the sky. So, someone would have given out our location. And recently, within the time frame of the attack, for us to be caught unaware. And then there's the poison they used; it was found to have been made in one of our own labs. Whether it was from the soldiers that accompanied Mrs. Evangale or someone already here, I can't say."

"Even so," said the snake statue. "I think it would be wise to operate under the assumption that the school is currently housing a traitor. Even if that is not the case, we can't rule it out."

"Agreed," said Soulden. "As much as I dislike the idea of thinking of one of our own as a traitor, I do feel it is necessary now."

"We still don't know what exactly they were after. I mean, we know they took parts of the tree. But why? We don't even know exactly how it was created. I doubt that they would."

"And recent discoveries regarding the trees lead me to believe that any attempt to recreate it would end in failure," said the bull statue.

"Yes, you said that the tree was sentient. How was this found out?" asked the Snake statue again.

"One of our healers. Leo found a way to communicate with it and has been doing so each day since."

"Has he discovered anything of value?"

"Not as of yet. Currently, he just asks it to do things like handing him utensils or books. But it is still early. I'm sure over time, we shall discover more."

"I'm sure. Do keep us updated. The last few months' events have given us room for pause. Below you, there are still claims of people disappearing from the outer lands of the kingdoms."

"Yes, those reports have reached me as well. I'll admit that I find them quite disturbing," said the voice of another statue.

"These are trying times indeed. I shall keep you updated on any future discoveries. But I must return the girls to class now. Their recent activities have gotten them behind in their studies."

And with nod and farewell from the stones. Soulden and the girls left the room as it went dark.

"Why did you lie in there?" asked Isha.

"A few reasons," said Soulden as they passed the statues and stood on the platform. She then placed her hand on the platform, causing it to relight and send them downward. But along the way, she causes the platform to stop and suspend itself in the air. "I have reason to believe that one or more of the council members may have been the cause or a co-conspirator of the attack on the school."

"So, the statues are bad people?" asked Jacinta.

"No, not all of them. But perhaps one or two."

"Why? How do you know?"

"The light in the room. When we entered, it was on. I am the only one in the school who speaks to the council, and as such, I prepared the room before I came to retrieve you girls. But I distinctly remember not igniting the lamp."

Isha remembered the light was on when they entered.

"And do you remember when we entered, a few of the council members were already there? They could have been talking to someone beforehand."

Isha tried to recollect which statues spoke to them when they entered but was unable to. "Should we do anything?"

"No, I'm afraid this will be on me to investigate. Has anyone approached you, girls recently, or have any of your friends started acting weird?"

"No. I don't think so. The only ones who visit are Mr. Cauldbell and Mr. Tannor. And Rima went back home."

"Yes, I received word on what happened to her father

and mother. A terrible tragedy," said Soulden as she glanced down at the girls, pity in her eyes. "Do... do you know... I mean, why it happened?"

"No. Do you know why?"

"No. I don't think I do. But I suppose all will be revealed in time," Soulden sighed as she patted the girls on their shoulders. "Come on then. Let's get you back to class. And Makeba, afterward, you can join me in my office. I think we should start your training as a ship's pilot."

After class, Isha went home alone as Jacinta opted to stay with her sister. She had been practicing the magical strengthening with a rock she took from class, but no matter how much she tried, she couldn't break it. The attempts persisted all the way until she made it home. There, she found Leo outside, sitting under the statue of Elena.

"Welcome. It's rare to see you coming home by yourself."

"Makeba is training with Soulden. What are you doing out here?"

"Just enjoying the sunlight. It's a peaceful day."

A small breeze came through, lifting a few leaves off the ground and into the air. She hadn't paid attention before, but he'd let his beard grow out to a short stubble that accentuated his sharp jawline and contrasted against his deep green eyes. Isha thought he was quite handsome.

"What's wrong?" asked Leo. "Do I have something on my face?

"Huh? Oh, no, it's nothing. Ahh, I should probably go. I still need to practice my magic."

"Okay then, I'll be in after a little while. You want to help me make dinner?"

"Yes. That's fine," said Isha, a little flustered as she made her way inside the house and up the stairs to her room.

Why was I thinking about him like that? I mean, I like Leo.

And he's nice to us. But... he and Elena. She began pacing around her room for a moment. *No... stop. I need to think about something else.* She looked around and spotted the throwing board that Dessi and Jacob had given her. It still had a few blades stuck in the wood from earlier practice sessions.

She quickly walked over to the board, snatched the blades from the target board and walked to the other side of the room.

Don't think about it. She took a blade in her hand and lifted it above her head. *Focus on the target. Control your breathing just like in class.* She launched the blade, and it didn't even make it to the board. Instead, it hit the floor and sliding up against the wall below it. *Damn it, stupid Leo, why does he have to be... why does... he always have to be nice?*

She shook her head, grabbing another blade. *No. I like Leo. But that doesn't mean I love Leo. I don't know even what love is. I mean, I love papa, but I don't love Leo like I love papa.* She took another blade, raising it above her head. *Argh, stupid Leo.*

She swung her arm as hard as she could, releasing the blade. It left her hand with such force that it whistled through the air, impacting and completely shattering the target board and wall behind it, opening a hole in the wall so that she could see the sunlight outside.

"Oh no," said Isha before running over to the wall, and grabbing the shattered pieces of the target board. "Dessi, Jacob, I'm so sorry."

"What was that noise?" screamed Leo from downstairs.

Isha then heard his footsteps on the stairs, coming closer. Each step seemed to match the beating of her heart as she looked at the broken piece of wood in her hands and then up at the hole in the wall of the house. The door to her room opened, and Leo stepped inside, looking around with wide eyes until he focused on the carnage on the floor. Then he also looked at the hole in the wall.

CHAPTER 33

Prince Saffron and Dekol were out in front of the city with their shirts removed as they labored over large stone slabs.

"I must admit," said Saffron, sweat dripping down his magical mask, "keeping up this facade along with the physical labor has been... quite taxing." He then dropped another large rock near the wall, where a woman came over and smeared its side with a sticky substance before a nearby mage gracefully lifted it into the air and placed it amongst the higher wall stones.

"You could have disguised yourself as a mage," said Dekol as he watched the blocks float in the air and be placed amongst the higher-level wall, "then you wouldn't have to labor as much."

"What, and leave you to enjoy this grueling exercise all

by yourself? I'd never." The two headed back over to where others were shaping the blocks and took a seat amongst the larger stones. "Besides, I'd prefer not to draw unwanted attention to myself and a random mage appearing now would, by sheer curiosity, draw attention."

"What do you wish to do about Thaddius?" Dekol nodded over as their compatriot came into view from out of a nearby house. "I'd assume he's involved with the clergy here for some reason or another."

"I haven't decided yet," said Saffron as he bit his lip. "No matter how hard I try, I can't see him as a traitor. If it was Mova, maybe. Goddess, I could even see Frenka being rebellious, but Thaddius? That man's been loyal to father and me longer than any of you."

"Perhaps the king has him infiltrating the group."

"That is a nice thought. I haven't had much for him to do lately, and father has always been known to make use of people he thinks are floundering. But still, it's not as if I can just stroll over to him, remove my magic and declare, 'I am your prince, now tell me all your secrets.'" Saffron shook his head. "At the least, I would find out if this is one twisted scheme by father, or at worst, I'd find myself at the mercy of one horribly furious male attendant and an entire religion—a large number of whom seem quite experienced at hurling large stones."

"What are you two talking about over here?" said a friendly woman as she approached them.

"Oh, mostly about how the sun exists only to increase our suffering," said Saffron as he noticed the rest of the workers now heading into the city. "Where is everyone going?"

"The Kemlor wishes for us all to gather before the chapel. I think she wishes to make an announcement. You two should come as well. We will be serving water and bread to those that are hungry."

"How can I say no to that?" said Saffron as he and Dekol

headed into town with the lady.

The city was just as lively as before. The crowd filled the streets before the little wooden chapel. Saffron and Dekol found themselves on the roof of a nearby home to watch the proceedings down below.

Before the disheveled chapel on a wooden crate stood a woman in the typical white robes of the clergy with three similarly dressed people on either side of her, which Saffron assumed were her guards.

"Thank you all for coming again," said the woman, her voice flowing over the crowd, carried by a magical wind that seemed to be boosted by those around her. "We know it hasn't been easy for you here and we thank you for your continued hospitality in welcoming us to your city."

Dekol tapped Saffron on the shoulder before pointing downward. Following his finger, Saffron saw Thaddius making his way through the crowd toward the Kemlor.

"Okay, big man. Are you going to give us something?"

"I know times are hard, but we have accomplished much together. And soon, it will be revealed why. The holy city will soon announce a wave of changes to how this kingdom will change. And this small town will be one of the chosen cities at the center of this change. But as more proof of this, I have invited someone from the capitol to speak."

Thaddius's imposing size seemed to part the smaller people in front of him until he was standing next to the Kemlor.

"The King has sent me down here personally to ensure that you all are well taken care of. He feels the pain you all have suffered through over the years. So much so that, not just myself, but the crowned prince, Saffron, and his wife, Lady Montavia have just arrived. Now, I had planned to speak to you all, but I feel that you all would feel more belief if the princess herself were to speak to you."

Thaddius turned around, the door to the wooden chapel opened, and out came a few more robed figures followed by

Mova, escorting and holding the hand of a very well-dressed Laura.

What in the Goddess's name? Saffron's fists clenched around one of the wooden beams of the house.

"Hello, people of Ghemlon," said Laura as she walked forward, her hands placed in front of her. "My husband and I, upon our arrival, took a tour around the city and have seen the progress you have made. However, we have seen something more important than that. And that is the fortitude of its people—the tents laced throughout the outliers of the city; the feeding ground meant to house such a labor force. You are all the pride of the kingdom."

"Your wife is well-spoken," said Dekol.

"So I see. But the question is, why *is* she speaking?" said Saffron.

"You think she's being forced?"

"Could be. Or it could be that it's not her, but if it isn't, then there doing a dam good job." Saffron licked his lips in contemplation. "If Thaddius were betraying me, why not take them hostage? And if they are, why expose them like this? Surely, locking them inside the Duke's manor would have been a better trap."

"By now," Laura continued, "I'm sure it has reached the ears of everyone here of how my husband and I have traveled through Burlus righting the wrongs of those who have terrorized the people of our kingdom for so long. Even at this very moment, my husband is off visiting the surrounding towns, expressing his passion for what you all are doing here, and attempting to gather more people for our cause. But, until he returns, I shall be glad to lend an ear to anyone who wishes to speak. While I am not as all-knowing as our Goddess, I do hope that my ear will provide you some comfort in the coming days. May the Goddess bless Burlus."

The crowd cheered as the princess waved her hand before being escorted back inside the chapel. The clergy then began to allow the citizens of the city to form a line, wherein, one-by-one, each would be allowed in to speak with the princess."

"What do you want to do?" said Dekol as the rest of the crowd began to disperse.

"What can we do, but wait and see where she goes after all this? It's too risky for me to pretend to be a peasant and visit her."

"Was that really the princess?" asked a woman nearby. "I guess they were truthful; they are really going to change this city. Why... we might even be as well known as Orlana."

"Excuse me," said Saffron, stepping into the conversation. "We just arrived to help on the wall. "What does she mean? Is something special happening in the city?"

"Oh," said the woman, giving her attention to Saffron, "well, none of us know for sure. But the city's been abuzz with rumors about how it might become one of those magical cities. You know, like the ones them fancy nobles live in. Who knows, we might all become rich, and I can end up being one of them nobles myself."

"Really? Oh, I'd love to see that," said Saffron. "You think they're really going to do it?"

"Don't know, but with them building that wall and now, with the princess being here, surely this old city ain't gonna be the same no more."

"That's true," agreed Saffron. "Maybe we'll all get to be nobles." With a goodbye, Saffron climbed down from the roof to the street below.

"You always were bad at imitating the local dialect of the common folk," said Dekol with a smile across his face.

"Really? And here I thought I did fairly well back there. Either way, it seems we are at a standstill until my Lady wife is alone."

CHAPTER 34

Victor stood atop a bridge looking over one of the waterways that flowed through the city's edges. Around him, filling the streets of the city, were people celebrating the Day of the Goddess as magical winds carried floating lanterns through the air. Each of these lanterns was trailed by a colored piece of cloth. Each color represented a request for the Goddess—for luck, for peace of mind, and for love, among other things.

"You go there, I do not wish to follow," said Muslin, her voice whispering into Victor's ear. "Tried to enter the night before—too hard, too closely guarded. Places like that tend to hold many secrets. Secrets that people would kill to keep secret."

"And here I was thinking we were a team."

"No team. I was given order to protect. You make it back out alive, then I'll protect. But in there, you are alone,

General."

"Does that mean if I survive, you will finally reveal your face to me?" asked Victor before hearing a small laugh.

"Perhaps, but perhaps not. Good luck, General. I shall wait to see you or see your corpse," said Muslin, and with that, the small breeze across his ear vanished.

"Back on my own again," said Victor as he stepped to the side of the bridge and began following the waterway into the city. The water was as clear as a sky above, forming a constant flow that circulated around the city before heading off to a river that fed into an ocean miles away.

The holy city was living up to its name today. Hundreds of small symbolic tokens and statues were spread across the city for people to see. In the streets, artists painted portraits of couples standing at the Goddess's feet or at the hem of her gown. Above Victor's head was a clear blue sky that seemed perfect for the day. He wasn't sure if they had a group here strong enough to manipulate the weather to their liking, but given this city's resources, it would not be surprising.

"Are you ready?" asked one of the large men from the house as he approached one of the houses with a green door.

"I am. Are you sure you can get me in?"

"Yes. The madam knows several ways inside. But you wish to go in unnoticed. This will be the best course. Come inside." The man opened the door, allowing Victor inside before closing it. Then walking over to a wall, he pressed on one of the wooden planks, and Victor heard a clicking sound. Then, after pressing his hand against the adjacent wall, it moved aside, revealing a passage that led underground.

"That's a neat trick."

"The city has many tricks, some more dangerous than others."

"And is this one dangerous?"

"For others, perhaps, but not you. Madam has said to

keep you safe 'til you reach the temple. I will be your guide."

"How fortunate for me," said Victor as he stepped inside the cavern leading underground. "I don't think being noticed will be a problem if it does happen. But, if possible, I would prefer to avoid it."

"I understand. The madam, too, prefers her discretion."

They moved silently through the twisting underground passage. Victor trailed behind his escort, but whereas he found the cavern a bit enclosed, he wondered how the big man maneuvered through it so unbothered. His broad shoulders seemed to almost be touching each side of the cave.

If it gets any tighter here, I'm afraid my guide will become lodged between the walls. "What did you do with the man I brought to you? If you don't mind me asking."

"The madam does what she pleases, and afterward, she calls for us to retrieve them. She has not called for us yet, so that is still unknown." *She had expressed an interest in you, claiming you to be some Demon of Flowers. But seeing as you came to her with a gift and provided entertainment, she has decided to acquire your trust for perhaps another time.*

"I am grateful."

The cavern grew colder the deeper into it they went. The chill tingled at the back of Victor's neck, a feeling that reminded him of the Muslin who apparently saved his life back on the ship.

"I know that many cities have underground passages, but this one seems a bit more complicated than the usual affair," said Victor, thinking about his previous encounter with the weird magical attacker in a cave. But these catacombs seemed to stretch on forever with openings leading to unknown dark places.

" The city is vast, and many tunnels lead to nowhere or somewhere," said the large man as he turned into another dark cavern. In the flickers of their torch, Victor tried to

460

search for any identifying markers on either side of the walls as they passed. But all the walls seemed the same.

I wonder what system he is using to know where to go. Is it magic? No, he's using a torch, and if he were a mage, there wouldn't be any need to hide it from me. I don't think.

"We have arrived," said the large man as they entered a vast open space in the cavern. The tunnels jutted out in every direction. Victor couldn't even imagine where they all led to."

"Okay," Victor looked around, "is there a certain tunnel I'm expected to go through or...?"

"No," said the large man handing Victor the torch and a satchel. "You wait here. When there is an opening, you will be escorted up." He then turned to leave, walking away in the darkness.

"Escorted by whom?"

"I do not know, but they will come when it's time."

Before Victor could ask another question, the man had gone off into the shadows.

Okay, maybe he can see in the dark. Victor waved the torch around in the darkness. He then shook the satchel given to him and heard a liquid woosh inside it. *I may starve, but at least I won't die of thirst.* He sighed. *What a wonderful life you lead, Victor. From dungeons of kingdoms to catacombs beneath holy cities. You certainly are a far cry from being a woodworker.*

Sitting there in the dark; the torchlight had gone out after the first hour or so. The second hour is when a bit of paranoia began to set in.

He took a few sips of the liquid inside the bag, which was just water, to quench his thirst. The moist air inside the cavern did its fair part in keeping his throat moist.

After some time, the sound of the cave changed from an ominous tone to more of a relaxing hum as if it's just telling me to accept my cruel fate. The water dripping from the ceiling, the sound of a four-legged creature that found its way down here, all cumulates together in a melody of the depressed.

As Victor contemplated his life's choice or lack thereof, he heard a sound. A grating noise echoed off the surrounding walls, assaulting his ears from all sides as, slowly, a hint of light shone down upon him. As the grating grew louder and louder, the hole above opened, and a full stream of light pierced the darkness.

"Hello. Are you down there? Speak up. We haven't much time."

"I'm here," said Victor.

"Stand aside, and I'll toss a ladder down."

Victor stood to the side as a rope ladder came tumbling down, its wooden planks clinking together before hitting the cavern floor. Then, with a deep breath, Victor grabbed ahold of the rope and began his ascent.

Above, Victor was greeted by a young blonde-haired boy in a white robe.

"My name is Kenkel. Are you Mr. Krill?"

"Yes, why? Were you expecting someone else from that pit you pulled me out of?"

"Well, no."

"It's fine. I just have a funny way of accepting one's hospitality, is all," said Victor as he gazed around the room. It was some sort of storage room—brick walls and barrels of some type of liquid were stacked on top of each other. "Where am I?"

"In the kitchens, sir. They often leave me back here to clean up." The boy reached into a satchel at his side and pulled out a white robe. "You'll be needing this. They have guards at the doors, but hardly anyone checks for identification once you're inside. Still, you'll need to dress the part. If anyone asks, you are my older brother, Fenkel Hottingberg."

"Much appreciated," said Victor as he took the robe, dawning it over his own clothing. It fit surprisingly well. Standing still, Victor couldn't even see his boots underneath.

Following the boy, Victor headed up the steps and

out of the kitchen into the main structure of this gigantic building. As one would expect of a building known as the headquarters of the Goddess, it put to shame even the finest castles. Floors of pearly marble, so clean on one could eat off of it and not expect a crumb of dirt between their teeth.

The central chamber had four pillars that held up the domed roof. Each pillar was embroidered with a line of gold that spiraled from the floor to the ceiling above.

"Okay, the meeting will not be starting for some time. But I can get you into—"

"Kenkel, there you are. You're needed in the chamber of scrolls. There's still work to be done. Come along."

"Oh, ah, one moment," said Kenkel, looking nervously around, grabbing Victor by the arm and escorting him up the steps of the main hall. "Stay here for a bit. The meeting of the headmasters isn't for another hour or so, but it will take some time to direct you there. I shall return shortly."

Not seeing a way out, Victor allowed the young man to escort him into another room. Upon entering, it was fairly obvious that this was the holy chapel's main library. The smell of old paper and dried ink drifted into his nose the moment he entered the room. Ahead of him was a mountain of books and parchments. The shelves were filled, but the overabundance spread to the floors and nearby wooden tables.

"Okay, now hold the rocks in your hands," said a woman's voice as Victor made his way through the library. "Yes, like that, Matthew."

Victor passed a bookshelf and saw a woman standing in front of a table where a few men and women sat. Her hand was outstretched, and a small rock floated above her palm and glowed.

It does make sense that they would have their own magic users and teachers.

"Now, it will take some time, but focus as much as possible. There's no need to... Oh, hello," said the woman, spotting Victor. "Are you here for training as well? I hadn't realized I'd miscounted."

"No. I'm sorry, Miss Gippal," said Kenkel, coming from behind Victor and waving at the woman. "He's new, and I needed to step away for a moment. Sorry to interrupt your class."

"Don't worry, Kenkel. Will you be joining the next group?"

"Yes, ma'am. I am to receive my magic sometime soon, I hope," said Kenkel before escorting Victor out of the room. "Sorry about that. It took a moment to get away."

"I see. Will you not get in trouble for skipping out on your duties?"

"I have someone covering for me. I'll return after I've escorted you safely to the observation room."

While walking through the stone halls, Victor felt somewhat curious about the teaching of magic in the home of the Goddess. "Are you also a mage, Kenkel?"

"Me? No, not yet. But soon, I will be. The Goddess has granted many of us here the gift of magic."

"I see, and how old are you?"

"Sixteen, sir."

"I see." Victor thought back to the second general of Mari and the story of how his magic also came in his mid-teens. *I suppose he still has time for his magic to appear. It is not written in stone that magic must appear in the early years.*

They went up two flights of stairs, entering a room with small hex-shaped holes in the wall through which Victor could look and see a round table with chairs below. Ahead, Victor could see two more identical rooms.

"What is this place?"

"This? This is where some of us come to watch the proceedings. Kemlors from all over the five Kingdoms come here once a year to discuss what they wish to accomplish or what hasn't yet been accomplished. Sometimes they get into arguments, especially if some of the group steps too far outside of the Will of the Goddess."

"I see. Will there be others here?"

"No, sir. Today is a closed meeting. You are only allowed because the madam requested it. She has been very loyal to the Goddess, and many Kemlors go to her for support."

"I'm very grateful to her for allowing me this viewing." *If she's such a friend. Why was I brought in through a cave?*

"You are to wait here 'til then. Please do not leave. I do not wish to have any misunderstandings on my behalf if you are found. I will retrieve you after all the affairs are in order." Kenkel handed Victor the satchel around his shoulder. "Inside is water for you and a few apples if you need."

"Thank you."

"Of course, sir. I shall be off now," Kenkel said before closing the door behind him.

"Okay," said Victor as he took another look out of the holes in the wall. "I guess I'll just wait."

CHAPTER 35

Nighttime had finally fallen over the city of Ghemlon. Laura and Mova rode through the city back to the Duchess's home.

"How are you feeling?" asked Mova.

"Exhausted," said Laura, her head slumped down as the carriage bounced along the dirt road. "I still don't understand why so many people wanted to talk to me—to tell me those things."

"By 'things,' are you referring to the woman who claimed her husband was possessed by evil spirits or the man who believed his son to be the reincarnation of the Goddess herself? Although, there was that one woman who grew angry at her husband for sleeping with her sister. But I guess family affairs out here are a lot closer than in the capital."

Laura began rubbing her face in frustration. "Why

would they reveal such things to me? The scandal alone would have me mortified."

"I'm afraid 'scandal' out here means less than it does in the capital.

"You're from a noble house, and yet you know so much about the people out here... Has Saffron really had such extensive trips to the common lands before?"

"Saffron's always been one for *adventures*. I've met many a nobles' son who proclaim their grand deeds, but in truth, very few have ever accomplished anything, really. False bravado to ensnare would-be suitors or lonely wives."

"And you're not ensnared by this? You *are* a woman."

"Bravado fails to impress after you've killed a few people or had your face pounded into the dirt a few times."

"So, there is no one around the capital who has your interest? As Saffron's guard, surely you've attracted the attention of men."

"Do not misunderstand me, Laura. I've taken a man to my bed when I've felt the need for it. But I have not been inclined to have him stay around."

"Him?"

"What?'

"You said 'him.' As in singular. So, there is only one man?"

Laura just stared at Laura for a moment. "Tell me, is it just normal for court gossipers to be so attuned to specific wording?"

"Mother says that what people don't say often speaks louder than what they do say. And that, we as nobles, need to be able to listen for both.

"Another reason why I was never meant for that life. I find that I never had the ear to become a countess."

"The man you sleep with, is it Sir Dekol?"

"You think I should sleep with Dekol then?"

"No, but... your voice. It softens when he and you are talking. It's not as commanding as you are with other men that I've seen you speak to. You even speak to my Lord Husband in an abrasive tone. Dekol is the only one whom you seem to be soft around."

Mova tilted her head and continued staring at Laura as if deciding what to say. "Are you sure your magic is mind magic?"

"Mova," said Laura with a smile, "you were the one who tried to warn me about my lord husband's affections for Frenka. A woman, by your own admission, whom you can't seem to see eye to eye with. But I've never seen you have a genuine conversation with any other woman."

"So, you would like me to share my male interests with you?"

"What I would like is a lady friend in the capital, one who isn't a maid paid to agree with me. If I'm being honest, I'd imagine no one better than you. Could you not open up to me also?"

Mova turned away from Laura, facing the carriage wall and folding her arms in front of her before closing her eyes. She began tapping her fingers on her elbow for a moment before speaking. "Dekol. We... we've shared each other's beds a few times."

Laura's eyes went wide. "Really? So, I was right. Does my Saffron know?"

"No. Dekol keeps it to himself," said Mova, still with her eyes closed but a bit of a blush showing on her cheeks. "And I expect you to do the same, Princess. This friendship or ours will need to go both ways."

"Of course. I promise," said Laura, the excitement clear in her voice. "Is there anyone else in the capital? Has it only been Dekol?"

"No one else—only Dekol. I've never been with anyone else."

"Ah! So, you do love him?"

"What? No," said Mova, opening her eyes and turning to Laura. "I never said that. He's just the only man worth sleeping with."

"Are you sure? I mean, surely, I'm not one to judge. Saffron is the only man I've lain with. But that's politics. I was never afforded the luxury of picking my own mate. But you... you have, and you've chosen Dekol. Do you not think that is a form of love, if not the real thing?"

"Well, no. That's... that's... I don't want to speak of this right now."

"Okay," said Laura with raised hands in surrender, a smile across her face as she clapped her hands together. "You've shared enough. We're almost there now."

Leaving the carriage at the base of the old manor, they made their way up the steps. The whining of the wooden steps was even louder in the quiet of the nighttime air.

"Welcome back," said the Duchess as she stood before them with her daughter. "I was wondering when you'd return. My men gave word upon your arrival. You will find a fresh bath warm and awaiting you in your quarters. Has your husband returned with you?"

"No, but he should return tomorrow or the day after, I hope. Thank you for the bath. After today's events, I really am in the mood for one. And thank you for the use of your dress."

"Oh, don't worry about it, dear. It was an honor to have you wear it. Goddess knows I cannot fit in it the way I used to. So, seeing it work in all its glory does the heart good. I was just surprised when that Thaddius fellow arrived and asked you to accompany him."

"Yes. He is one of my Lord Husband's guards along with Mova here. We've been discussing matters pertaining to the kingdom and I've had the privilege of speaking to your subjects today."

"Yes, one of my men told me of your speech today. I am so glad to hear you are on our side."

"And so am I, but if you will excuse me, I really would like to get some rest myself."

"Oh, of course, dear. Go right along." She turned to her daughter. "See to the Princess's needs, won't you?"

"Yes, Mother."

Together they made their way through the house and into her room where a large tub of steaming water waited for them.

"I am grateful for this," said Laura with a sigh as she cast a Silence spell over the room. It was done so effortlessly that she needn't even raise her hand. "Can you please help me out of this? I feel a bit too tired to undo it all myself. Ah, your name was Marian, wasn't it?"

"Yes, my lady," said Marian as she walked over and began undoing the back of Laura's dress until it hung free, slumping over her arms.

"You enjoy your bath. I'll take a look around," said Mova.

"Alright," said Laura as she stripped free of her clothing and handed the ensemble to Marian, who took the dress and lay it across the bed as Mova left the room, closing the door behind her.

Laura stepped into the tub, moaning with relief as the warm water washed over her skin. Closing her eyes, she embraced the heat and stretched her shoulders. But her moment of relaxation was quickly taken away as she felt something wrap around her neck. In a panic, her shut eyes opened and her body froze.

"Is something wrong, my Lady?" said Marian as she began rubbing a warm cloth over the base of Laura's neck and then over her shoulders.

"Oh my… you just startled me, is all. I seemed to have forgotten you were here in my rush for a bath," said Laura as she reached her hand up, placing hers over Marian's. "You need not bathe me. I can manage that much myself."

"No, my lady. If it is okay with you, I wish to. This is what my mother wishes as well. She wishes for us to become closer."

"Yes," said Laura, removing her hand and letting out a

sigh of a different kind. "I'm sure she does."

"I'm sorry. I just assumed. Would you prefer it were I to leave?"

"No. This is fine," said Laura, allowing Marian to bathe her. "Tell me, are you okay with what your mother wants for you? You do know her plans for you and my husband, don't you?"

"I do. Oh, but I would never dream of becoming Queen or anything. Mother just wishes for me to improve her station. She thinks that if I lived in the capital, it would happen."

"And what do you think? Are you okay with giving yourself to your mother's cause?"

"Well, I... I'm sorry, my Lady. I don't know what to say."

"No. I suppose not. Do not worry yourself," said Laura as she leaned forward, letting Marian wash her back. "I'm merely reflecting on my own situation when I look at you."

"Did you not wish to be a princess—to marry the prince?"

"I honestly do not know. I mean, I think I am in love with Saffron now. But like yourself, this arrangement was made by my mother. She is the reason I was able to marry my husband."

"Mother... she... she was to be a princess as well. She and King Montavia were lovers. But something happened, and she ended up here. When Father's gone, she... she drinks, and she talks about it sometimes."

Laura leaned back, shaking her head. "Yes. Let us both pray that we do not turn into our mothers." She closed her eyes and stretched her neck as Marian brought the warm cloth to her side and began going over her chest. Laura was enjoying the feeling of being bathed, feeling the water move over her body. "Tell me, do you imagine men do this?"

"Do what, my Lady?"

"Having other men bathe them?"

"I... I do not know. I've never heard of it before. Does the prince allow other men to bathe him?"

The water shook as Laura couldn't help herself but laugh at just the thought of someone bathing Saffron. "No. But he does have a peculiar relationship with his guard Dekol. But I doubt the two would go so far as to bathe each other," said Laura as Marian pulled her away. "Thank you, dear. I suppose-"

Laura's eyes went wide as the palm of a hand found its way over her mouth and an arm across her lower neckline. Her body jolted in the tub, sending a wave of water sliding over the edge and splashing against the floor.

"Calm yourself, Lady Laura," came the soft whisper of Dekol's voice, his lips so close she could feel his breath against her ear.

Her heart pounded in her chest as her eyes darted back and forth across the room, whispers of what was once escaping between the fingers across her lips.

"I am going to release you. But I need you not to scream. Nod your head if you understand."

She nodded her head.

"Good. Now, I am not a mage. But I think your Silence spell is broken. So, I want you to cast the spell again to ensure no one is listening."

Laura raised her hands from the water and began to focus on the spell. Admittedly, it was a fair amount harder to concentrate on the spell now than before, but soon a faint shimmer flowed over the room's walls and without another word, she felt as the fingers left her lips and the arm retracted from her neckline.

With freedom once again allotted to her, her mind instantly shifted to her husband. Quickly she twisted in the water, turned around, and sat up on her knees.

"My Lord Husband? Is everything alright?"

"He's fine. He sent me here to speak with you."

Feeling a sense of relief, she took in a breath and sighed, placing her hand over her chest, which coincidentally made her realize her own nakedness. She looked up to see that

Dekol wasn't looking at her, instead he was stepped near the wall and was peeking out the window. She looked to the floor and saw Marian was passed out, still with the warm towel in her hand.

"Ah, Dekol, about that... well, you bathing Saffron. You do understand that was just lady's gossip, don't you?"

"He's over there," he said, pointing his finger, "on the outside of the gate. Saffron isn't the stealthy type. So, he asked me to come speak with you."

"I... I'll take your word for it. I'm not really in much of a situation to move about freely," said Laura as she slid back into the water.

"No, I suppose not," said Dekol as he came back, taking a chair and sitting in front of Laura, his green eyes ever staring into hers. "I wish to speak with you, Princess Laura, about today's events. We saw your speech with Thaddius and the other woman."

"Ahh, yes. I can explain that."

"Yes?"

"The madam, that is the Duchess here, met with Thaddius and informed him of our arrival, I think. I told him that Saffron was off visiting the countryside with you and that I wished to rest."

"And the speech?'

"At first, he only wanted me to meet with that Kemlor woman. Her name is Niskcalla. But they asked me to give a speech of encouragement to the townsfolk here. I did not see a reason to refuse. Mova thought the same."

"Did they say what they are doing here or reveal anything to you?"

"No. Nothing besides that they wish to bestow the blessings of the Goddess on everyone. I told them that Saffron would return in a day or so. Oh! I asked Thaddius why he wasn't joining us, but he said he was doing official work for the king."

"I see," said Dekol as he rubbed his chin.

"Is it always like this with you all?" asked Laura as she leaned her neck back, looking upward at the ceiling. "All this sneaking about and kidnapping and things of that nature?"

"Yes, when the need calls for it."

"I am beginning to understand why my lord husband advised that I grow accustomed to you seeing me naked. At first, I thought it was a jest, but it has grown truer by the day. Is there a reason for it, besides the interrogation, I mean?"

"Currently, Mova watches over you. Sometimes it will be myself. In some moments, I will be by your side, even in moments like this where you wish to wash yourself. Saffron said that your life is above his own. He'd not allow himself to live in a world where you perished before he did."

"Is... is that because of what happened to his mother? I've only heard rumors but-"

"Someone is coming," said Dekol, looking towards the door. "I should go."

"Wait, what? How can you tell?" said Laura as she turned, her eyes following Dekol as he walked over to the edge of the room, lifting a mat and a few planks of wood, showing an opening in the floor before jumping down inside. She never even heard him land below or the wooden beams fall back into place. He was just gone, with no sound of his departure.

The door opened, and Mova walked in, holding a key in her hand.

"Are you still in your bath? I assumed you would be done and in bed by—" she drew her blade, spotting Marian asleep on the floor, and looked around. "Is everything okay? Are you safe?"

"No, no, it's fine. No, I... I was just about to finish," said Laura, recasting her silence spell for a third time over the room after Mova had closed the door behind her. "You should have stayed. You just missed him."

"Missed who?"

"Dekol, he was here, startling the life out of me."

"Dekol was here? How did he... no. Did he do that?" said Mova as she collected her thoughts and nodded to Marian on the floor. "What did he want? Why haven't he and Saffron returned yet?"

"They saw me giving my speech to the townsfolk here and wanted answers."

"Ahh, that would have raised a few questions," said Mova as she grabbed a towel from the back of the chair and held it out for Laura. "Wait," she smirked. "So, Dekol was here while you were in the bath?"

"Yes, and at this rate, he's going to have seen me unclothed more than my own husband," said Laura with a frown. "But you were right."

"I was? About what?"

"He is very, 'matter of fact.'"

CHAPTER 36

"You girls ready?" asked Leo as he sat in front of the small tree with a book on his lap. Over on the couch was Chloe looking over some notes.

"Yes, we're ready," replied Isha as all three girls, both Isha and Makeba, helped Jacinta down the stairs where her crutches lay against the wall. She turned to Leo. "What were you doing?"

"Just reading to our little tree friend there," he said, closing the book. "Apparently, she likes mystery novels. She's terrible at picking out the killer, though. Ouch!" He yelped as a prickly root poked at his ankle. "What? You think I'm wrong? Then who do you think killed the maid? Hold up one branch for Dr. Harold, two for the cook, or three for mage's assistant."

Two branches raised upward from the tree.

"You *would* pick the cook. I swear, you have no

imagination. It was obviously Dr. Harold. He was the one who inspected the body. Perhaps he lied. Did you ever think of that?"

The whole tree twisted a bit from left to right.

"I think it's the cook to," said Chloe.

"Well, I guess we'll just have to read on and find out who's right," said Leo before turning his chair towards the girls. "Alright, get over here."

They did as Leo asked, with Isha standing before him first. Reaching towards her, he began removing the wrapping from her head, causing her to wince at the pain.

"Is it better yet?" she asked.

"Let's have a look and see," said Leo, calling forth his magic and placing his hand over her forehead. "Yes, you have a small scar that can be taken care of later, but the skull beneath has healed well enough. You shouldn't need the bandage anymore."

Isha stepped to the side as Jacinta came forward. Leo took hold of her leg and his magic flowed inside her as, he slowly began to press on her knee. She gritted her teeth in a frown, trying not to show that the pain was getting to her.

"Now you, on the other hand, you will be on crutches for another week or so."

"Why week? I feel good. Don't need… Arghhh!" Yelped Jacinta as Leo pressed a little harder on her knee.

"You were saying?" said Leo as he released her knee and placed a hand on her shoulder. "Look, I let you girls do as you please for the most part. So, I feel partly responsible for you three are always getting into messes. But I'm going to have you listen to me when it comes to your health."

"Not fair. I do not like this."

"And I don't like playing the adult anymore than you like me trying to be one. But it's just us here now. So, bear with it."

Makeba stepped forward, wiggling her arm in the sling. "Feels better now. Not hurt as much."

"Good, Let's have a look then," said Leo, reaching for her arm and repeating the process a third time. "Hmm, that's surprising. It's actually mostly healed. Take your arm out of the sling and move it around for me."

Makeba did as instructed, rotating her arm, curling it, then making a fist. "Is it good?"

"Yes, surprisingly so. I guess you just heal fast. It's uncommon, but I've met a few that responded well to healing."

"So, I no longer need arm wrap?"

"No," said Leo, taking a glance at Jacinta. "But keep it on for another day or so, just to make sure that it heals properly." He then placed his hands on his knees before standing up. "Well, you four still have a little time before school. Would you like me to make you some breakfast?"

"Can I help?" asked Chloe.

"Sure. It's good for your fingers to practice with the little things."

"We go back into tree now. I not done teaching other Isha," said Jacinta, her voice stern.

"Yes, you said something about that. Are you sure it's safe in there?" said Leo, turning to Isha. "What are the odds that you go in and the other one comes out?"

"I... I don't know. The last time I was sleeping, or maybe it was the dream I had. But I don't think she can come out while I'm awake."

"Okay," Leo sighed. "Just be careful, okay?"

Leo and Chloe watched as the three girls sat down on the floor and the markings along their bodies began to glow white.

The girls were again met inside the tree by Lonta'Mar, who had changed the surroundings a bit. Instead of solid ground, there was now a large circle pit. Jacinta, now with the full movement of her body, climbed down. Isha channeled the magic, and her double again came out of the portal, landing on the ground in the pit.

Grettaline took one look around and narrowed her eyes before turning to see Isha staring down at her.

"Are you really going to allow this? Are you all sadists? Have you not grown tired of my suffering?"

"I don't want to do this," said Isha honestly. "But I don't want to wake up and find myself somewhere I don't know. But maybe, if you are too tired from fighting Jacinta every day, you won't come out."

"Is that what you think? You think I can just summon myself forth in your body whenever I desire it?"

"Then how... why did you do it? And where were you taking me?"

There was a moment of silence between the group of girls.

"Fine, "said Jacinta, taking a step forward in the pit. "You no tell, today I break leg, like you did me. Then you heal, and I do it again."

"Fine, stop... just... stop," said Grettaline, her hands outstretched in front of her to stave off Jacinta's advance. "I'll tell you. I... I really wasn't going anywhere. What would you do if you suddenly woke up in someone else's body? Are you truly just going to stay put?"

"Lonta'Mar said there was a big red jewel that you saw. How did you know that was there when none of us did?"

Another moment of silence.

"Speak," shouted Jacinta.

"Fine! Fine, I... I can sense magic. I am not as strong as I was, but if some power is nearby, I can sense and draw from it."

"What do you mean 'draw' from it?" asked Isha.

"Have you truly never wondered how my power works? I mean, really? I can feel it when you use it, you know."

"Yes, I thought about it, but no one knew anything. It just worked."

"Goodness, the naivety of children. The short of it is that our bodies are constantly drawing in magic—from the air, from the ground. It's not a lot, but it's constant. That power can then be channeled to enhance other magical things."

"What magical things?" asked Makeba.

"Yes, I'm sure you've seen the result of pushing too much magic into something that can't handle magic. They end up burning alive because they have no output for it. Another thing is that if you can control it, you can, for a while, make things that are not magical, magical. But that is another matter altogether."

"Why you tell sister so much now and not before?" asked Makeba, looking into the pit.

"Well," said Grettaline, glancing back at Jacinta. "Outside of not wishing to be assaulted again by this beastly sister of yours, and after thinking it over, I realized it was simply in my best interest to be forthcoming."

"Then you behave now? You will accept Jacinta as leader and listen?"

"I will not accept you as my anything," replied Grettaline. "But I will promise to not try to leave if I ever find myself in your body again. Or at least I will not go far. You cannot simply expect me to be a slave to circumstances neither of us can control."

"I not sure. You try to run away before. You may be lying now and—"

"No, it's okay, Jacinta. I... I want to trust her. I can't blame her for what she did. I was the same, remember? Waking up in the duke's burning building, I also ran away. It would be unfair of me not to expect that from her," said Isha, turning back to her double. "We don't want to hurt you."

"I want to hurt her," said Jacinta.

"Okay, but please don't. I want us to start getting along. And maybe we can find a way to get you out of here. I don't know how, but I think working together is better than always fighting."

"Then do we have a deal?" asked the Grettaline. "Will you stop with this absurd abuse?"

"That wasn't my idea. The fight you had with my sisters—you hurt them. So, before we can become friends, you will need to apologize to them," said Isha.

"What? That one up there perhaps," said the Grettaline before gesturing back to Jacinta behind her. "But you expect me to apologize to this absurd beast and expect things to just be all wonderful?"

"It's the only way we can start over. Otherwise, Jacinta will just keep hating you."

Grettaline stared up into Isha's face for a moment before sighing. "Goodness, you really are children, aren't you?" She shook her head. "Fine. Look, I'm very sorry to both of you. I misbehaved and caused you pain and suffering. I very much wish that you can forgive me and hope that we can be friends. There!" she said. "Did that satisfy you?"

Jacinta then walked past Grettaline, intentionally bumping shoulders with her as she took hold of her sister's hand and was lifted out of the pit.

"Guess not," said Grettaline before Jacinta turned around and reached out her hand for her.

"Come."

CHAPTER 37

Saffron sat on a hill overlooking the city of Ghemlon.

"Have any idea what you're going to say?" asked Dekol as he patted the side of a horse.

"For once, Dekol, I haven't a clue," said Saffron as he plucked a piece of grass, twisting the blade in his fingers. "Either I accuse my own guard of treason, or my father is doing... well, I honestly don't know what he's doing."

"As I see it, we have little choice. We searched the town and couldn't find anything."

"That doesn't mean that the bile in my mouth tastes any better," said Saffron as he stood up, tossing the blade of grass into the wind. "Fine. Let us go and have this mystery revealed to us."

"And what of your lady wife?"

"Best to leave her with Mova. If, by chance, something unfortunate occurs, I will not go to my grave with the knowledge that I led my wife to hers," said Saffron as he mounted his horse alongside Dekol, and they rode off into town, no longer wearing their magical masks. Instead, they were back to being the royal prince and his trustworthy guard.

It wasn't long before they reached the entrance to the city, where the workers were still building the wall.

"Excuse me," said Saffron as he made his way over to the one in charge. "I'm here looking for someone—a large military man named Thaddius."

"Oh, you mean the big guy. He's in town at the chapel visiting the Kemlor today. Are you two here to join as well?"

"Perhaps, but at the moment, we're old friends of Thaddius and wish to pay him a visit."

"I see. Well, just ask anyone where the old chapel is, and you'll get there."

"Thank you," said Saffron as both he and Dekol went into the town, obviously knowing where the chapel was. It did not take them long before they were off their horses and walking up to the chapel.

"Hold," said one of the many women standing outside the building. "The chapel is off limits for the rest of the day."

"I'm sure," said Saffron. "But, I'm here to see Thaddius. Can you please inform him that the prince has arrived?"

The lady gave Saffron an odd look before turning to her companion, who nodded back at her. "Yes, ah, your highness. Please wait here while I go and retrieve him."

"Yes. Please, go on. I shall wait."

Saffron came to the eerie realization that he and Dekol were surrounding as the eyes of every clergy member around them now focused on him. *Into the belly of the beast, as they say.* He saw Dekol's hand hovering over his blade, and his fingers lightly began tapping the hilt. *I hope this doesn't turn to bloodshed. I wonder how many of them are mages. And if they'd join in an attack with Thaddius, I might be in some trouble even with Dekol here. Mova would have... no, it's best she stays guarding Laura.*

"Well, I was wondering when you would finally arrive," said Thaddius as he came out of the door—his loud, deep voice commanding everyone's attention. "I wondered if you had gotten lost in the countryside."

"No such luck, I'm afraid, old friend. But I must admit, I'm curious as to what brought you out so far into the kingdom. You can imagine my face when my wife told me you were here."

"Oh, that I can, prince. But one can ask of you the same question. A honeymoon out here in Ghemlon? Even I fail to see the romanticism in it. But then again, you never were the predictable sort."

"Well, I like surprises," said Saffron while noticing a few of the clergy stepping closer. "So, are you going to invite us in, or must we converse in the sun?"

Thaddius was quiet for a moment before he nodded. "Yes, come in. Tell me, when was the last time you spoke with your lord father?"

"Father?" asked Saffron as he entered the old chapel, its rickety wooden holden a far sight from anything one would call hospitable. "Not since the wedding, I'm afraid. You know how he is—always wrapped up in some matter."

"Yes. I see," said Thaddius as he stopped and turned around. "Then, unfortunately, I'm afraid you will need to stay here for a while," said Thaddius as several clergy members followed, closing the door, locking them inside.

And the walls start closing in. "Thaddius, what are you doing?"

"Apologies, your highness. I shall ask for you to stay with us here for a while—until certain matters are sported."

"And if I were to refuse your request of forced hospitality."

"Then you will be subdued. I'd prefer not to oppose you here," said Thaddius, taking a glance at Dekol. "As strong as you might be, I am no small mage myself, and it will take time for you to gather your power. Time, I assure you that you do not have."

"I'd have never taken you for a traitor," said Saffron, a tingle of anxiety going down his spine as he slowly began to call forth his magic.

Thaddius raised a hand to show an unwillingness to want this fight. "I ask that you rethink your situation, your highness."

"Honestly, I'm not feeling as if I can trust you at the moment, Thaddius. So please forgive me if I decline the offer."

"Men are always so quick to distrust each other," came a woman's voice as she walked in from a side room. Like all the others, she wore a white robe with a hood over her head. "Your Highness, it is very nice to meet you. I heard so much about you from your lovely wife. In fact, I recently sent a few of our men to go retrieve her for us. Now, what would she think if she were to arrive here and find her husband and his own guard fighting amongst themselves?"

At the mention of his wife, Saffron let slip the hold he had on his magic.

"You're the one in charge here?"

"I am. Although saying so doesn't exactly mean that I am in charge. But, nevertheless, I would claim myself to be a partner," she said as she walked up calmly and stood beside Thaddius. "One of many that are invested in the future of the five kingdoms. Why, you yourself are one such partner, even if you do not yet realize it."

"Oh, am I now?" said Saffron, folding his arms. "I never heard of a partner having the well-being of his wife threatened. Does that sound like an equal partnership?"

"It was not a threat—merely a way of asking for a bit of patience and understanding," said the Kemlor before gesturing to the door she came from. "May I ask you to join me? All shall be revealed soon."

Saffron frowned and turned to Dekol.

"Alone, please. Your friend there can stay with Thaddius."

"Of course," said Saffron as he gave Dekol a pat on the shoulder. "Shall we be on our way then?" He stepped forward, making his way toward the suggested room with the Kemlor following behind. Opening the door, he found an old man in robes sitting down at a round table with two extra chairs. His hands lay flat on the table in the direction of each chair.

"Please, have a seat," said the Kemlor before turning around. "Thaddius, please ensure that we are not disturbed."

"Yes, ma'am," said Thaddius, not taking his eyes off Dekol.

"Now what? I assume you expected me to make an appearance here, given the extra chair."

"Of course not. I'm merely taking advantage of an opportunity. Before you, Thaddius sat in that chair. But given the circumstances, I feel a more direct line is in order." The Kemlor gestured to the old man. "This here is Feldhiem; he is a mind mage. A rarity even among the highest nobles, but he saw fit to join our cause and allow us the use of his services."

"How very generous of him."

"Yes, it is. Now Feldhiem, do you still have the connection?"

"Yes, my lady."

"Good," said the Kemlor as she sat down, placing one of the man's hands in hers. "Now come, join us, your highness. There is someone you must meet."

Saffron sat down, also taking hold of the man's hand. "Fine, let's be on our way then."

"Feldheim, if you would be so kind."

And as Saffron relaxed, he felt his mind being taken away into a white void. When he opened his eyes again, he found himself up high on the side of a mountain. In front of him was the sky, the sun rising in the distance over the Kingdom of Burlus. It was so detailed. He could see the small villages below. The small farmers having their oxen pull the soil plower, the women washing their clothing in the river that ran through the south valley. It was a perfect image of the countryside of Burlus, and straight ahead in all its glory was the capital city, basking in the morning sun.

"I was surprised when they told me you'd be coming to," came a familiar voice. "But, I have to admit you always did have a knack for finding your way into things."

The voice took Saffron out of his moment of calmness, and a feeling of annoyance overtook him. He then turned around, narrowing his eyes at the man in front of him.

"Father."

CHAPTER 38

Even through the thick stone walls of the Goddess's temple, Victor could hear celebration from the streets around him. He lay on the floor, looking up through the center glass dome atop the roof. Above it were mirrors that guided light inside. Seeing how they were turned; he could see that it was near sunset.

How much longer? Surely, they don't intend to conduct their meeting after nightfall. Although if they do, then perhaps there will be fewer people around, and I can find an easier route to leave. I highly doubt I will find my way back out of those catacombs.

When Victor heard movement from down below, he was taken out of his thoughts. Moving to his feet, he placed his back against the wall as he peered to his side out the hex holes to the room below. One by one, the room filled with men and women, young and old, who were escorted by their guards. And one by one, they took a seat at the large circular table.

"I must say, I am quite excited to hear this year's announcement," said one of the older men as he took a seat.

"Yes, I agree," said a young woman sitting across from him. "I heard that they were trying to establish a chapel in the Sakari Wilds. I've heard of the trouble they've had getting a foothold there. I look forward to an update on that endeavor."

As they all poured in, one man, in particular, caught Victor's eye when he took his seat. It was the Kemlor that he had met in the village where he and Silk had barely escaped.

When they all were seated, one man made his way through the middle aisle and between the circular tables. His footsteps echoed off the walls as he made his walk up the steps to stand in the center of them all.

"Ladies and gentlemen, I do so appreciate you coming." said the man as he gazed over the room. "Although there seem to be a few more empty seats than one would expect. But I guess that is a sign of the times, is it not? Serving the Goddess rarely ever allows one time for relaxation or meetings. I'm sure that is something we all can agree on."

The room murmured in agreement.

"Now, there is much business to discuss. So, I would suppose that we should get along with it?'

"Where is the High Councilor? Shouldn't she be here for this?"

"Oh yes, right. The High Councilor was up late preparing her speech for the people below. She may be here shortly. But I enlisted to allow her some rest for the time being."

More murmurs of the crowd's approval echoed through the hall.

"Now, the first topic of—"

"Excuse me," came the voice of Kemlor Kolgin. "But I have a pressing matter to discuss before we begin the proceedings."

"I see, can it not wait until the main affairs have concluded?"

"Perhaps, but I believe what I have to say will impact all other proceedings. And as such, in an effort not to waste the council's time, I would kindly ask to speak first."

"Yes, I see. If you feel it is that paramount, then please step up, Kemlor, and say your peace."

"Thank you," said Kemlor Kolgin as he raised from his seat and made his way up middle aisle. Then he stood before them. "I apologize for the abrupt change in the order of things, but some things are best done with haste."

The crowd nodded, although there were a few murmurs of discontent.

"Many of you know me, but still, many of you do not. My name is Retallia Kolgin, and like many of you, my path to the Goddess has not been an easy one. I was born outside of a poor fisherman's village in Mari named Bloated Betty. Not the most flattering name, I'm sure."

The crowd laughed again.

"But even being the poor child that I was, the Goddess decided to bless me. One day, a traveling war mage for hire found me playing with puzzles on the docks and took a liking to me. Afterward, he gave my mother a few coins, and the next thing I knew, I was on my way throughout the five kingdoms."

"One day, I would be in a poor farmer's village. The next, I would be tending to the wounded in the tents near a battlefield. There, I found the Goddess as the dying would ask me to pray for them as they went on their journey. Although I wasn't born with the gift of magic, I learned much about it. Some of you here yourselves, the Goddess has blessed you with the gift of magic."

"I was fascinated by it. My benefactor would try to explain it to me, often staying up late into the night. And on the battlefield, I was privileged to see a multitude of talents. From earth magic that made the ground quake beneath our feet to wind magic that could control the weather. Even magic that healed a broken bone in a fraction of the time it would take otherwise."

"My curiosity grew as I grew older. My benefactor, at night, would teach me to read and, in different towns, would purchase books on magic."

"Well, as we all know, the life of one who lives in war is seldom long, and my benefactor found his way into a grave. Although, to his credit, it wasn't a blade or magic that killed him. Unbeknownst to us, it was a poison that had made its way into one of our food supplies."

"To this day, I do not know if I've ever prayed as hard or for as long. But in that same tent, treating others, was a man who would also change my life—a researcher for the school of Scena. And it would be there that I would discover a miracle of the Goddess that would change my life forever."

He reached for the nape of his neck and undid the binding over his cloak, letting it hang over his arm as he revealed his body to all those in the room. The entire room gasped in shock as he stood before them. Across the top of his chest were five red jewels, all of which were embedded into his flesh.

"What... what have you done to yourself?" asked one of the men in the room.

"Do not be afraid," said Retallia. "I wish this to be a demonstration of the research that I have dedicated my life to."

"Research?" said another woman. "You've desecrated your own body, and to what end? To parade this atrocity on the day of the Goddess?"

"No, but to reveal another miracle the Goddess has revealed to me. Bare witness," said Retallia as he then held out the cloak that was just draped over his shoulder. The Kemlor closed his eyes, smoke began to appear, then the robed burst into flames. The Kemlor tossed the burning robe into the air as it was quickly consumed, allowing the ashes to fall over him. "This is the gift I wished to bring to the council."

"Oh my," said one of the older men as he stood up from his seat. "My boy, what have you done?"

"I've developed a way for every mundane in the kingdom to use and control the gift of magic that had previously been awarded only to so few."

"Have you lost your mind? Do you realize the implications of this? No kingdom would stand for it."

"They will if they have no choice. Think of it, sister. No longer will families starve just because they do not have the manpower to farm. Rivers can be diverted to new croplands without the need of the kingdom's assistance."

"Brother Kolgin, even if that is so, you must understand the delicate power balance that this will upset. No kingdom will allow their power to be threatened by such a thing."

"Wait," said another woman in the room, "let us not jump to conclusions. I, for one, wish to hear more about this. Many things can be kept secret for as long as needed. This might well work to the Goddess's favor."

"This? This sacrilege?" said a member of the clergy.

"Tell me, Brother Retallia," said the speaker. "Just how did you come to this discovery?"

"Thank you, Sister Hematin." He gestured to the room. "And I understand. You all have a right to be fearful. The price of this power does come at a heavy price, but not a fatal one. It merely requires that those with the abundance to do so, to share their gift with those who can not."

"With an abund... You mean mages? Are you saying a mage must willingly give you their power?"

"Not their power but their blood, for it is the house where their power to control magic lies."

The room was quiet for a moment as the mirror above redirected down onto the Kemlor, highlighting the crimson jewels embedded in his chest. And in that same breath, the room came to the realization of what had to be done to achieve such power.

"You... you've gone mad! You expect mages to give you their blood so that you... so that you—"

"No, the process will not work with the blood of any mage whose magic has already settled. It will only work with the blood of those whose magic has not yet been shaped."

"Wait! So... if that's the case then..." said a woman, her voice trembling. "That's... that's children? You're talking about taking blood from children?"

"Yes, but it is only enough to replenish the supply," said Retallia. "And I know how it sounds. It sounds monstrous. But we are not murdering them, simply gathering what is needed to access the power."

"Even if that's the case," said another man, "what parent would willingly offer up their own child for such a barbarous process? Even if we claim it is the Goddess's will, surely the majority will fight back. No! This must not be allowed to be carried out. You must destroy any findings you have. If any of this were to get out, the sheer implications of it could destroy everything we have built."

"That is your concern, brother, and I respect it. But what say all of you? I have placed myself on display for you all; shown you what is possible; given you a glimpse of what will be possible. Are all of you willing to waste this opportunity to help those who need it?"

"I admit this is unorthodox," said a woman raising her hand. "But you must admit if we were able to bless the masses with magic, even if it is only a small amount, think of what could be done with this."

"No! Think of the repercussions. What noble house is going to stand by and let this happen? They might even brand this entire council as traitors."

"I agree this is too great a risk," chimed in another clergyman.

"But considering the potential here, it may be a risk to *not* pursue this. Even if it must be done in secret, I think this line of research is too valuable to be destroyed.”

Victor listened as arguments for and against this research were thrown across the room. But eventually the room settled down and began discussing the Kemlor's proposal in a more orderly fashion. Many stated the potential of such research while others voiced their concerns until finally, after what seemed like an hour, it ended.

“Okay,” said the speaker, “all those in favor of keeping this line of research by the Kemlor open?”

A dozen or so hands we raised.

“And all those against?”

Another set of hands were raised. Victor didn't need to count to see that it was enough to outnumber those in favor.

“I am sorry, Kemlor,” said the speaker, “but the council has voted.”

“I ask to bring forth a vote to remove Brother Retallia from his position as Kemlor and asked that he be excommunicated from the order of the goddess,” said a clergyman, standing to his feet.

“Now, brother Askel, that seems to be—”

“Don't you see? We've all decided this is a bad idea. But if this were to leak out, if the kingdoms were to find out what was discussed here today, having this man still in our company would be a hindrance. I'm sorry, Brother Retallia, but this is for the safety of us all.”

And once again, a vote was called for. And not surprising to Victor, they voted against Retallia Kolgin.

“I'm sorry, brother. I truly am.”

These fools, thought Victor. *There's no way this ends with him just marching off into the sunset. Anyone willing to implant those things in their body and experiment on the living… do you really believe that words alone will quell his desire? I've seen zealots before, and this…*

“I understand, speaker. You are doing what you think is right for the Will of the Goddess, and no one here can't deny that as such. As I also did what I thought was in the best interest of the Will of the Goddess and the people I serve. And as such, right now, I have organized the kidnapping of as many children from every magical school in the five kingdoms as possible. It will take place simultaneously, and they will be sheltered at—"

"You what!" shouted the Speaker, as the crowd gasped and shouted.

"You fool."

"You wouldn't."

"You couldn't."

"But I have. While the council itself may be against this plan, the people whom I serve are in need and willing to accompany me on this journey. And when we're finished, no kingdom will take up arms against us for fear of losing their children."

"Guards! Guards! Take this man into, argh!" gasped the Speaker as a sword pierced through his stomach.

For those that claim to represent the will of the people. They certainly aren't well versed in the habits and traits of their own, thought Victor as he watched the man's body fall limp on the table.

"What have you done?" asked another Kemlor as a guard grabbed her by the shoulders, forcing her back into her seat.

"I'm doing what needs to be done," said the Kemlor as he turned to the rest of the room. "And to the rest of you, I thank you for your service to the goddess, but unfortunately, your pilgrimage in this new future ends here."

And with a nod of his head, the room burst into chaos. Guards turned against their Kemlors, and blood flew freely across the room. Some tried to fight back, but this was not a room filled with warriors. Even those with magic talent were descended upon by more than they could manage.

Bodies were sent flying as white robes were stained with red until only the dozen that had sided with The Kemlor were left sitting in their seats, guards pointing their weapons towards them. Alongside them were the two who had decided not to vote on the proceedings, a young woman, and an older man with gray in his beard.

"A horrible deed, but one that needed to be done. Sadly, I think the bloodshed must continue," said the Kemlor, turning to the two that did not cast a vote. "I am sorry to force you two, but I will need an answer as to whom you serve. I would hate to kill a father in front of his daughter or visa-versa. But we are at a turning point today."

"I... I wish to follow the Kemlor Retallia on this journey," said the woman.

"And what of you, brother Jakil? Will you join as well or share the fate of those who have not?"

The older man sighed. "Do you know why I did not vote, Kemlor? It is because I cannot say whether what you want to do is right or wrong. From the moment you revealed to us your findings, I assumed this would be one of the outcomes." He looked around the room. "The others, the ones who did not appear today. I assume you have already killed them?"

"No, on the contrary, they have all seen my vision for this new day and are the ones who are helping to secure relations with the magic schools. I could not have done this on my own after all."

"Then I will not assist or be a hindrance to you."

"Father!" screamed the man's daughter.

"No, Thessia. This is my decision to make," said the older Kemlor. "I wish to play the role of the observer. But if that answer is unsatisfactory to you, then you may come and place a blade to my neck yourself. I have not lived a life of regrets. If it ends here, then I shall accept it. But I ask that you do not punish my child for her father's selfish actions here."

"The observer? Humph. I suppose even the Goddess must have a witness." Retallia stepped forward, placing his hand on the desk in front of the two. "I shall permit it, but if the role of the observer is one you wish to play, then I will ask that you take a vow to never speak against or for anything involving the Goddess."

"I accept."

"What do you intend to do now?" said Thessia, looking over the dead bodies laid across the tables and floor. "These people all had followers. How will you explain the disappearance of so many of us? And what about the High Chancellor? Are you going to kill her two? The people-"

"The people will accept this as the Will of the Goddess," said a young woman in fine robes and a crown on her head as she entered the room. She took one look around the room before shaking her head. "So many were against it. That truly is a shame."

"Your majesty, High Chancellor," said one of the men in the room. "Why... why?"

"Ah! Brother Jillian, I am glad that you survived. And to answer your question, it was merely a matter of resolve. When Kemlor Retallia proposed this idea, I had him locked in the dungeon for a month and planned to behead him. During which time, I visited him many times and asked the simple question, 'why?'. And without anger, he pleaded for the health of the people we serve. He spoke with such devotion that, over time, a question appeared in my own mind, and that was 'what if?'."

She looked around the room.

"What if the people were given the gift of magic? What if we could substantially improve their living conditions? Do we not owe it to ourselves to try? Even if the means are not ideal, the outcome is worth the risk."

"Even so," said one of the male clergymen. "If you had appeared and endorsed this, if it came from your lips, then surely so many would not have had to die."

"No. I believe this was also a test of the Goddess, and a test for brother Retallia. If he wished for my co-operation in this, then he would need the strongest conviction to see it through—to stand upon this stage and proclaim his intentions without relying on my name to protect him. And if halted, have the conviction to see it through." She placed her hands on Kemlor Retallia's shoulder. "This is a conviction we will all need to have because the path ahead will not be an easy one. I say this, not to you but to myself as well, I am willing to sacrifice my very self, if need be, in order to further this goal."

"But you need not be alone in this," came the familiar voice of King Montavia as he entered the room. "Burlus will provide assistance and sanctuary to all who wish to make their way to my Kingdom."

The room grew louder with talk as those gasped at the sight of the King.

Even Victor stood staring at the sight. *Why? Why is he involved in this? What is the benefit of spreading magic for him?*

"When you leave here today," said King Montavia. "I want you to spread the word that Burlus supports the spread of magic through the common folk, that their King will do everything in his power to ease the suffering of the people."

"Rest assured, my council," said Retallia. "Your faith in me has not been misplaced. I have done all I can to ensure that we have every chance to succeed at this. But the hard part, the most grueling part, will be done by you—those that are left in this room, the true believers in the goddess's will. So, I ask that you go forth and spread this message throughout all the kingdoms."

There was a moment of silence as all the remaining Kemlors glanced at each other. But it didn't take long before a decision was made.

"We accept this challenge, High Chancellor, and we are grateful for the opportunity," said one of the Kemlors.

"Thank you all. You may all take your leave now," she said gesturing towards the door. "There are still a few matters I wish to discuss with Kemlor Retallia and King Montavia."

Victor watched as the remaining Kemlors began leaving

the room.

"Ahh! Not you, Brother Jalik. You asked to be an observer. I'm afraid that you must stay."

The old man nodded and looked toward his daughter.

"Go, Thessia. I shall be along shortly."

"Yes, father," said Thessia before giving Kemlor Retallia a weary look and heading out of the room with the rest of the Kemlors.

"Now then," said King Montavia. "I guess there is still one final thing that needs to be discussed before we begin."

Now what? You've essentially performed a coup of an entire religion. Just how deep does this—

"Yes," came a familiar female's voice.

Victor grit his teeth as he looked ahead and watched as a section of the concrete footing began to transform, revealing the figure of Lady Brunline, sitting with her hands crossed."

Shit, thought Victor as he looked towards the door.

"Sixth General, Victor Krill," said the King, his voice booming over the room, "if you would be so kind as to come and join us."

"It does not seem as if I have any choice in the matter," said Victor as he heard the footsteps outside of the door. *Think Victor, how are you going to get out of this?* The door opened and several guards stepped in.

"If you come along, you will not be hurt."

"I'm sure you mean I will not be hurt for the moment," said Victor as he looked them over, noticing blood still on their garbs after their massacre of the people below. He then threw his hands up in submission. "I surrender. I shall accompany you."

The guards escorted Victor down the stairs, surrounding him on either side as they made their way into the gathering room.

"Welcome, Mr. Krill," said King Montavia. "It seems our paths are destined to cross yet again."

"So, it seems. But I must admit, you seem to always be the one in a position of power."

"Those who foster power must do what must be done to ensure its prosperity."

"Who is the man, King Montavia, an ally?" asked the High Chancellor.

"No, but a potential piece on the board in negotiations with Mari. Allow me to introduce you to Victor Krill, the Sixth General of Mari and preferred pet of their Queen," said the King.

"Oh, I've heard of him. This is the Demon of Flowers. He looks a bit worn out," said the High Chancellor.

"My apologies, High Chancellor. I was not under the impression that we would be meeting today." Victor looked over to Lady Brunline, who smiled back at him. "If I had been informed, I would have dawned a more formal attire."

The High Chancellor laughed, "I'm sure. But do not worry." She waved her hand around the room, highlighting the dead bodies. "Today has been a day full of surprises." She then turned and bowed to the King. "If you will excuse me, I must go and finish preparing the speech for the coming days."

"Yes, of course," said King Montavia. "We will see to matters here."

Victor sighed as the High Chancellor left the room and turned back to Lady Brunline, who made her way down the steps to stand beside the King.

"Do not appear so disheartened, General," said Lady Brunline. "I promised you a viewing of today's proceedings, and I have delivered on that promise."

"Yes. I suppose it was foolhardy of me to assume you would not inform them of my trespassing. I suppose my mind was distracted at the time by other worries."

"Yes, few options can often close off the mind. But Bruhil might have also turned you in. He is also a very devout man. He just shows it differently. But in the end, we are all but a tool, one of many that distribute the Goddesses justice."

"And you think this is justice?" asked Victor, looking at the carnage of the room.

"A sacrifice for the future. One you should be well served in. Tell me, that title you carry, Demon of Flowers, how is that any better than what was accomplished here today?"

"That was war."

"And this is not? We are in a war for the prosperity of the people. It sounds as if you are deciding which option suits you best rather than accepting the truth. Wars are decided by those with the power to do so."

"And justice is often judged by the ones with the power to deem themselves worthy," said Victor.

"Well said, and we are so very worthy," said Lady Brunline. "A king who looks after the well-being of so many. And the High Chancellor herself, who is as close to the Goddess as one may come. If not them, then who truly is worthy of being a judge? And as such, they have decided. I am just saddened that I will not be the one to give you the goddesses justice."

"Yes, I'm sure you are," said Victor.

"Truly," said Lady Brunline, turning back towards the King. "I have done my part. I entrust that you will do yours."

"Our deal remains," said King Montavia.

"Then I shall retire. Good luck, General. I hope we meet again,' said Lady Brunline as she left the room.

"And then there were two," said Victor as he looked at King Montavia and Kemlor Retallia. "I understand the Kemlor, but why would you involve yourself in this, Montavia? What could you have to gain by aligning yourself and siphoning the blood of children for this madness?"

"Survival," said the King, his voice as calm as if he were looking over a peaceful sunset. "You may not remember the lesson you gave my son in our dungeon, but your insight into politics was not lost on me."

Victor looked confused for a moment. That night in

the dungeon contained many eventful moments, but he couldn't think of anything that could have influenced a decision that would lead to this.

"I believe your question was, 'what Queen would sit back and watch another Queen be defeated in war by the last remaining King?' It was a thought that always lingered in my head that your words brought to the surface. And the opposite question came to my mind. If a Queen were to attack Burlus during a moment of weakness or poverty, which other Queen would lift a finger to support it?"

He's right, power-wise, thought Victor as he bit at his lip, pondering the circumstances. *There would be no reason to assist Burlus in any of its Kingdom's affairs. Honestly, if not for his father's contributions, they may have taken Burlus a generation ago.*

"I see you understand now. Truthfully when those two Kemlors approached me with the idea, they had to have known that I could have exposed their plot to all the Queens and be done with it. But the conviction to bare themselves before me also made me realize the fragility of my own circumstances."

"So, it's better to survive together than risk falling separately."

"The die must be cast eventually. Despite our circumstances, I've always respected that mind of yours. It was why I used you to pursue these past events. Which, by chance, was also the catalyst for them asking for my assistance?"

"How so?'

"That would be your visit to the city of Molask, where we first met," said Retallia. "I had to wonder why the great General Victor Krill would be visiting such a city and using a false name."

"So, you knew it was me all along."

"One does not plan what I was planning without knowing the great generals and attendants of every Kingdom. And as such, after your grand escape from the catacombs beneath the city. I began to have my followers ask questions. Then it wasn't long before I discovered that you had recently visited Burlus."

"And you thought to bring the King into your plan?"

"Every valuable piece on the board must be used."

"Fine. I admit defeat. I overplayed my hand, and you have won. What do you plan to do with me?"

"While I have a personal reason for wanting you dead. The King knows politics far better than I and has informed me that your value to the Queen is not insubstantial, and as such, you should be used as a bargaining tool in negotiations with her, should anything go awry."

Personal reason? What have I done that would affect him to this extent?

"Until then, you will be stored away. The King informed me of how you once visited his dungeon, and now I would ask that you visit ours. We have another guest there who is waiting for you, and you should see your handy work with your own eyes," said the Kemlor as he walked past Victor towards the door. "Guards, please help our friend along. We will speak later, your Highness."

Two guards grabbed and ushered Victor along behind the Kemlor. They made their way through the back of the building, passing by several rooms. Inside a few, Victor saw some clergy members testing the limits of their magic.

"You really believe you can start a war with the level of magic you have here? Most of your members seem to barely be able to lift a stone. The moment you announce your intentions, your city will be under siege by every Kingdom in the land," said Victor as they walked through the halls.

"Oh, did you believe that bit of theatrics? No, Victor, we never intended to kidnap the children. Why would we do such a thing when all is required is that we claim to test their blood from time to time? That simple change will give us an unlimited supply."

"Then why—"

"Why insight the rebellion of my people? Simple; I needed total commitment and telling them the whole truth would only have given me half-hearted dedication. But now, those that have survived will be even more dedicated to the cause, for they have survived where their brothers and sisters have perished. They are chosen. At this very moment, they are being informed of their true mission."

"I would tell you to be careful—that telling lies of such a scale would place you amongst the worst people the world has known."

"Depends on the lie. There is one particular school that we have interests in—one that has a certain person who I believe can be of great use to us. But that should not be so important to you now."

They made their way down a flight of stairs until they reached a door where two guards stood on either side. Grabbing a torch off the wall, the Kemlor opened the door and walked inside a large dark open area.

"Come in, Victor," said the Kemlor from inside the shadowed room. "Come and witness your handy work."

My handy work? A guard pushed Victor on the back, which sent him stumbling into the room. He could hear the sounds of moaning coming from ahead but could not see past the darkness.

"Forward, General," ordered the Kemlor.

Victor stepped in line with the Kemlor as the moans grew louder the farther in they went. Until finally, he reached the wall at the end, where Victor saw a man chained and shackled against the wall.

"When we found him, he had already killed several of us. And in subduing him, he killed several more."

Victor took a deep breath of the thick moist air as he stared into the man's eyes. It was the large man they fought in the catacombs. The man whose neck he had driven in one of those red crystals. He was indeed alive and caged. The chains jingled against each other as he shook against the wall. His mouth was wrapped with a cloth so that he couldn't speak.

"Whatever spell you cast on him, whatever you did, no one has been able to free his mind from the madness that you caused. He speaks in unknown words and attacks anyone in front of him, even me, who has been his closest friend for all these years. But rest assured, I will find a cure to the madness you have stricken him with."

I'm sure claiming that I did not cause his madness would be *as futile as your attempts to reason with him,* thought Victor as he glanced between the two men. "I wish you the best of luck attempting to cure him."

The Kemlor gave Victor a look of disgust, the hatred behind his eyes clear as he had ever seen. This was the first time he had seen the Kemlor drop his mask, and it wasn't for long. He closed his eyes, took a deep breath, and, just like that, the mask of calmness was back over his face.

"Ensure that our guest is comfortable. I plan for him to stay with us for an extended period of time," he said to the guards.

The guards grabbed Victor and pressed his back against the wall. The sound of chains and a door being locked would echo in his mind for the rest of the night. That and the moans of a man who he had once thought he had killed and saw resurrected in front of his eyes. It was going to be a long night.

CHAPTER 39

The scent of fresh trees, grass, and dirt lingered in the air as Isha and the rest of the class sat on the ground in the open area of the floating island behind the school of Sceana. In front of them stood Mr. Higgins and Miss Webblebottom.

"Okay, we brought you all here so that you can get used to outdoor training," said Mr. Higgins. "I'm sure you all know that you will be graded on how well you are able to mix combat with your standard magic. You will be put together in pairs and judged accordingly." Out the side of his eye, he glanced at Jacinta. "Although obviously, some of you won't be able to participate."

"Either way, this will be a great way for you all to show off what you can do," said Miss Webblebottom. "I know it must get so stuffy in those classrooms all the time. But out here in the fresh air surrounded by the trees, we can embrace nature and become more comfortable using our magic when not within an enclosed space."

"Over there," said Mr. Higgins pointing to a wagon filled with weapons. "You'll find whatever weapon you've been training with. Today we'll be partnering you up in groups and having you spar. Then tomorrow, it'll be singles, and then finally, you'll be doing real combat drills and be graded accordingly. So go on, stand up and pick out your weapons."

As the rest of the class stood, going over to grab their selected weapons, Isha came back with Chloe and sat next to Jacinta, unrolling her throwing knives.

"Oh, and what do we have here?" asked Mr. Higgins as he walked over, picking up a blade and inspecting it. "I heard from Soulden how you girls saved her and even killed a guard or two in the process. So, I guess I shouldn't be surprised you'd have something like this. Can you actually use them?"

"I've gotten okay at throwing them. I was hoping to use the trees here for practice. But when I use the magic strength, they don't aim right."

"That so, huh? Show me," he pointed towards a straw-filled mannequin that stood before the line of trees. "So, when you throw them normally, you don't miss?"

"I mean, not as much. I'm not as good as the one who taught me."

"That was... ahh... Dessi, right?" asked Chloe. "The one in the camp. She was the one who taught you?"

"Yes. That's her. She's really good at throwing blades."

"Okay, then," said Mr. Higgins. "I think this is a good learning experience. First, throw a normal one without using magic to make you stronger."

After walking over, Isha took out a blade, placing it between her thumb and index finger. She lifted her arm up, and brought it down as fast as she could. The blade left her finger and flew silently through the air before striking her target perfectly in the chest.

"Oh! You actually hit it," said Chloe. "That's much better

than the last time."

"Well, I'll say, it seems you do have some talent. Right in the heart." He walked over, plucking the blade from the dummy's chest before inspecting it. "A little shallow, but you'll get stronger as you grow up."

"Sister has gotten better at krump," said Jacinta.

"It's not... okay maybe it is like krump," said Isha, remembering her night in the tent after she first met her sisters.

"Okay, now show me a throw with magic behind it," said Mr. Higgins as he walked back, handing Isha the blade.

Isha nodded before focusing the magic into her body, feeling the tingle in the muscles of her shoulders, arm, and fingers. Then, with a deep breath, remembering her words, 'stupid Leo,' she swung her arm. The blade flew quickly, cutting through the air, creating a whistling sound before tipping the shoulder of the mannequin, spiraling out of control, and striking a tree behind it.

Yes, that's what happened last time," said Chloe. "

"Not so bad. At least you hit it, I guess," said Mr. Higgins, looking down at Isha curiously. "But you have a surprising amount of power for such a little thing. Tell me, how does your arm feel?"

"Fine, I guess. It doesn't hurt."

"Not sore or anything?"

"No, sir."

"Hmm." He walked over to the dummy, inspecting it again. He ran his finger over the cut before walking over to the tree and inspecting the impact on the tree, how it had broken the bark and exposed the base. Leaning down, he picked up and pocketed the blade. Then, with a smirk, he walked back to the mannequin, placing his hand on its shoulder where the cut was. "Okay, toss another blade at this dummy, and be sure to use magic again."

"But... I can't. I don't want to hit you."

"You won't. I'm the teacher here, remember? I'll be fine.

Just toss it as hard as you can."

Isha turned to Chloe, who looked as confused as she did, then back and forth between her sisters as they just shrugged their shoulders at her. Sighing, she closed her eyes before taking a deep breath and kneeling, taking out another blade from her pouch. Then rising, she raised her arm and took aim. *Please don't miss.* Dropping her arm again, she chanted 'stupid Leo.' She threw the blade, and it went flying through the air. There was a whistling sound for only a moment before Isha stood there in shock.

"That was pretty good," said Mr. Higgins as the blade floated in the air in front of the mannequin's arm. "The aim's a little off, but still, it would be a disabling hit."

The girls all made their way forward, staring at the blade as it hovered in the air. Around it rippled out small puffs of magic.

"How you do this?" asked Jacinta.

"Simple. I turned this dummy here into a shield by channeling my magic into it."

"But I thought magic shields only block magic?"

"No, it also blocks things infused with magic, which is your blade since you channeled magic into your fingers, which were on the blade. It was probably only a small amount, but that was enough for it to be stopped by my shield. It's the same principle as your training with those bucklers."

"Oh," said Isha as she remembered using her smaller shields. She always found it odd how they absorbed her magic.

"Can you channel your magic into anything?" asked Chloe as she reached her hand out, poking the end of the blade with her finger.

"Mostly anything, but there are exceptions. Such as you won't be able to channel your magic into anything that has a higher magical presence than you do." He dug into his pocket and pulled out the other blade, handing it back to Isha. "Keep practicing with your blades. I imagine you don't get much time when on the main grounds. You two, assist her and work on your own training. If I remember correctly, Soulden has you learning how to control ships. You have your orb with you?"

"I have it in my bag there," said Makeba pointing to a pouch on the ground.

"Good. Then get to practicing. You two are far ahead in combat training anyway." He then left the girls alone as he went over to instruct the rest of the class.

"Hmm. I want to use more magic on the jewel that Tannor man gave me," said Makeba as she fiddled with the jewel in her hand. As she channeled a bit of magic into, it began glowing purple over her fingers.

"Why... it glow like that?" asked Jacinta.

"I do not know, but it feels warm now."

Isha leaned forward, inspecting the jewel. "It has a crack now. Did you drop it?"

Surprised, Makeba turned the jewel over. "Oh, sister is right. It was not there yesterday. I guess this will break too, then. You think Tannor man will be upset if it breaks?"

"I don't know. Maybe we should go ask him after class if we can."

Makeba nodded before putting the jewel away in her clothing and pulling out her small wooden mock ship. Then she pulled out a small red orb, placing it in a slot inside the middle of the boat. Walking around with it, she tried to make it float over her hands while channeling her magic into it. She had gotten better, but occasionally the ship would fumble and dip before falling back into her palms.

Jacinta hobbled herself over, taking a seat under a tree as she watched both girls start their training. However, she didn't have long to sulk as Chloe made her way over to her, pulled out her practice swords, and began asking her questions. Although unable to move, Jacinta gave Chloe pointers on how to hold her weapon and how to stab. Their

510

exercises continued through the day as the sun passed over their heads and Jacinta gave out instructions.

Isha continued to throw more knives before walking over and picking them up, only to throw them again. The more she threw, the more she found that her aim was getting a little better, but it was still not perfect. She needed to adjust how she flicked her wrist at the end. The rotation between a magic throw and a non-magic throw changed so much depending on the distance from the target.

Dessi doesn't have magic, so she can't do magic throws. I want to get better so I can show her what I learned. Thought Isha as she turned back again to see Makeba, who was still struggling to keep the flying toy boat afloat. *I guess they want to show Gregga... Mother what they learned also.* She turned to see what Jacinta was up to. Apparently, at some time during the day, Freedo had snuck away from the rest of the group and was now pestering her and Chloe. Although now, Jacinta didn't seem to mind his company so much.

"Do you want to go over and talk to them?" asked a soft familiar voice in her ear.

"Huh, what?" asked Isha, jumping back, startled as she dropped a few of her blades from her hand. "Don't scare me like that."

"Hello again," said Pavel with a big smile. "What are you up to?"

"Nothing, just practicing." Ever since that moment in the bath between them, Isha couldn't help but stare at his face. His jawline was slimmer than other boys like Freedo, but he was taller than her—a little taller than when they first met.

"You're staring at me again."

"What? Oh, I'm sorry, I just-"

"It's fine. People do that when they find out about me. Leo did the same thing, but I guess now it's a different type of staring."

"Do... do many people know about you?"

"Only a handful back home. And you and Leo, here. That is unless you've told your sisters about me."

"No, I wouldn't do that."

"Then that's good. Although one wonders what they would call me then, Jacinta already refers to me as the girly boy."

"I'm sorry about that."

"Don't be. If I could say that's the worst thing I've ever been called, then I would count myself lucky. And you're staring again."

Isha looked away, hiding her face from him.

"It's fine," He laughed. "I enjoy that you've taken an interest in me."

"What about your magic? Are you getting better at the sword?" she asked, still not looking directly at him.

"I have. But it's a pain in the butt trying to extend my magic through the blade and use magical strength at the same time.

"You can do that?" she asked, turning back to face him.

"It's a little tricky, but I can manage it for a while. But I get tired quickly because I haven't mastered it yet. Mr. Higgins says I'll be stronger as I get older. We all will since we are smaller than the adults."

"You sound like an adult."

"Do I? Maybe I just had to grow up a little faster than most. Come on. Let's go and see what your sister is up to with her tiny magic ship. I think she's by far the most amazing one here for attempting to fly those things."

"She practices a lot. I tried once, but I wasn't able to get it to move."

"Yes, it was much the same way with my attempt. Hello, Makeba," said Pavel as they approached. "Still enjoying the airship training?"

"It is hard, ahh, or complicated. I think. But I wish to learn. I hope to take sisters through the sky one day. Soulden says I am fast at learning."

"Very nice," said Pavel, nodding to Makeba. "Be careful. Your sister may end up becoming the object of Leo's affection. He really has taken a liking to you girls."

"Leo stupid. But good... maybe." She shook her head. "No matter, Sister has said she will not decide until we are bigger. She wishes to focus on her magic. I think we should do the same."

No, Makeba, don't bring that up.

"Can't fault your three there. I am doing the same. Learning how to focus and control magic is hard. And it's impossible to learn it all."

That's not what she meant. But I'm not going to say anything, thought Isha before changing the conversation. "Come on. It's time to go. Everyone is going to leave us out here."

Gathering their wooden weapons and storing them inside the little house at the end, they left, making their way across the field and over to the small platform.

"Is everyone here?" asked Miss Webblebottom, taking a look over the students. "Good. It seems we're all accounted for. Take us away when you're ready."

Mr. Higgins placed his hands on the orb, and the platform lifted into the air and began traveling back to the school.

"Is making this thing move the same as when pilots move airships?" someone in the class asked Mr. Higgins.

"No," said Miss Webblebottom. "While the principle is the same, the amount of magic, effort, and concentration are leagues in difference. The platform is magically linked to that spot there at the back of the school. Injecting magic just allows it to travel back nod forth between the predestined landing areas."

"We're here," said Mr. Higgins as the platform landed behind the school, between the airships. "We still have a lot of training to do. So, we will continue bright and early tomorrow morning."

A few of the class members moaned as they stepped off the platform and made their way off into the brush maze that led back to the school.

"Makeba," said Chole can you help me with that strength magic when we get back? I'm still having trouble with it."

"I do not mind. But I am not so good it too."

"It's fine. Your better than me."

"Thank you. Oh, I need to go my old dorm later to pick up the last of my things. Would you all like to come?"

"Yes, I would like to see other houses. How they look? I do not think they have Sakari Tree like ours, though. Tree Sakari cannot speak to them like with us."

Sister, look!" said Jacinta, her crutches shaking under her arms as she pointed to a figure over by one of the ships.

"What is..." Isha's words stuck in her mouth as she froze for a moment before squinting her eyes to ensure she wasn't seeing anything. "Rima," Isha shouted, but she didn't hear her and soon vanished behind a ship. Isha turned to her sisters. "Come on."

And they all made their war over to the ships, looking between them as they passed.

"Where'd she go?" asked Chloe, when they looked past the last docking station for the airships.

"I don't know," said Isha. "I'm sure it was her. She must be here some... ahh, there she is." They spotted Rima around the end of the school by the fence, looking out at the land below. "Rima, hey, what are you doing back so soon? Is everything okay?"

"Oh... hello. Are you girls doing okay? Sorry, I left so quickly."

"We're fine. Are you back to stay now?"

"Yes, for now. I still have a few things back at home to take care of. But I will be here for a little while longer."

"That is good. Leo is bad cook, you should cook."

"Is he now? Well, I would be glad to cook for you girls. Would you mind walking me home? I would like to get started on dinner if that's alright with you."

"Okay, we just finished and were headed back ourselves," said Isha as they headed through the school and down the streets, and back to their home.

"Have you girls gotten any better at using your magic?"

"Yes, we have gotten much better. One day I will be able to fly ships that bring us up here."

"Now, that is a skill worth having. The kingdoms prize their pilots very much, considering how few there are. What about you, Isha? Have you learned to control your powers better?"

"Yes. But there is still so much I cannot do."

"Yes, sister Isha still burns down little trees."

"Hey, it's not easy. Plus, I don't even know if I can do that stuff yet. Leo just keeps making me try since he says my normal magic and that white magic stuff are different. Oh, Makeba, you should do the tree thing with me. It might work for you since you have that seed that Tannor gave you. Seeds are kind of like baby trees."

"I do not care about the tree thing. I just wish to fly the ships."

"But it will be fun, and I won't have to do it alone. Don't you think so too Ri..." Isha looked up, catching Rima staring off over the city. "Rima? Is something wrong?"

"Oh, sorry, I was a bit distracted. The trip here has me tired, I guess. I probably just need to lie down for a bit."

"Was your home far away?"

"Yes, because the school moves through the kingdom. It wasn't near my home anymore. I've been in the air most of the day getting here, and I was too nervous to sleep."

"Well, we are here now," said Isha as they passed by the statue of Elena, each of the girls running their hands across the base. "Let's go inside."

They opened the door to the smell of delicious cooking in the air and to see Leo on his knees, placing a small stone base around the small tree.

"Oh, you're here. Welcome back. How was... Rima? You're back already?"

"Hello, Leo. I'm glad to... oh my. What's that?" She asked, pointing towards the tree. "It's glowing."

"Oh, that's right. You left before their friend invaded our home. This is the one they call Lonta`Mar."

"This is Tree Sakari. She lives with us now."

"Lonta'Mar? You named the tree?"

"No, Lonta'Mar is Tree Sakari's name. She comes here instead of being in school."

"Oh, yes. Of course. Hello to you too, Lonta'Mar."

The tree slowly leaned forward before lifting back to its normal position.

"You will get used to her eventually," said Leo as he stood up and walked over to Rima, looking her in her eyes. He then placed a hand against her face and began rubbing the side of her cheek before kissing her on the forehead. "I must admit, I have missed you. Do you need to go back?"

"No," Rima placed her hand on his and smiled. "I'm back for a while now. Mother has things taken care of."

"Ah," said Isha, taken aback by the display of affection between the two. "We promised Chloe we would go to her home. Is that okay?"

"Oh," said Chloe. "Ah... we can do it tomorrow, if you would prefer to talk with Rima.

"No." said Leo. "You girls go on. That will give me and Rima time to catch up. You four go ahead."

"Okay. We'll be back later," said Isha as the girls headed back out the door toward Chloe's house.

"I didn't know Leo and Rima had gotten so close," said Chloe. "When did that happen?"

"I don't know. I was surprised too," replied Isha.

"Leo is funny man, like Uncle Funny Man," said Jacinta, nodding her head. "So, ladies like him. That is why momma liked Uncle Funny Man."

"I thought you said that Leo couldn't cook," said Chloe.
516

"It smelled pretty good when I was in there."

"Yes, it's weird, usually Leo bad cook."

Leo walked back into the kitchen.

"You came back fairly fast. Is everything okay?"

"Yes. Turns out that it wasn't my father after all. I was so worried, but when I got there, he was just fine."

"Go on, take a seat at the table. I'll fix you something since I was already getting food ready. And since the girls aren't here to eat it, it'd be a shame to have it go to waste."

"Alright," said Rima as she took her place at the table.

"I'm happy you're back. Jacinta still feels weird about having a man heal her ever since she hurt herself in class. Mr. Higgins can be a slave driver."

"I remember."

"Here you go. Eat up," said Leo as he slid a plate of hot food on the table before taking a seat beside her.

"Thank you," said Rima, placing her hands on the table and taking in the smell of the food. "Ah, where is the silverware?'

"Oh! Did I forget that? Let me get it for you," said Leo as he stood up, reaching forward and slamming Isha's throwing blade onto the table, piercing Rima's hand as the blade went straight through, so deep that it pierced the table.

Her eyes went wide as she took a deep breath to scream, but Leo's hands wrapped around her mouth.

"We are going to have a talk, whoever you are."

Rima struggled, her body shaking in Leo's grasp. Her moans of pain muffled between his fingers. Slowly, something began crawling up her legs, then over her waist. Her eyes went wide with horror as she saw roots sprouting out and up through the floorboards wrapping around her body, constricting her.

"You come into our home and expect me so foolish as

to not notice my own student. Well, I'm afraid they've made a mistake," said Leo as he began twisting the blade in her hand. More screams escaped from Rima's lips as tears began to flow out of her eyes, followed by short muffles. "Rima's father was killed, and her mother was marched naked through the street along with a bunch of other nobles. She's not coming back here."

"I... sorry," were the muffled words that barely escaped through the fingers covering Rima mouth. "Please... let go."

"Please? Well, it seems you have some manners," said Leo as he moved his hand from over her mouth, sliding it down to her neck when he kept a tight grip. "Now, tell me why you are here."

"I was... I was sent to watch... the... the girl with the power, the one with the Sakari."

"By whom?

"King... King Montavia?"

"And what were you going to do to her?"

"Nahhh.... Nothing. I... I was to make sure she... she was safe."

"I find that hard to believe." His grip began to tighten on her throat. "Have you ever felt what it feels like when someone forces the muscles inside the throat to grow and expand around the lungs?" asked Leo as his hand began to glow.

"It's true... it's... true," she managed to say before she started struggling to breathe. "I'm... sorry. I'm so..."

Leo released his grip as the fake Rima began coughing.

"Explain. And keep in mind, for those girls, I will kill you and throw your body over the edge of this city. Even if you are a healer, I doubt you'll survive that."

"He... he said all I had to do was report the girl was safe. I pro... promise I meant them no harm."

"But does *he* mean her any harm?"

"No, I mean... She's his daughter, right?"

Leo stared at Rima for a moment before reaching

forward and yanking the blade free from her hand. She didn't scream but bit down on her lip with eyes wide, and Leo watched as her healing magic began to work.

"So, you really are a healer. Remove your disguise."

The image of Rima began to fade away, turning into a colorful smoke that lifted from her body and exposed a young brown-haired woman underneath.

"What's your name?"

"Ray... Rayrah."

"Okay. Rayrah. And what if I were to report you to the healing circle? Don't you think—"

"No, please. Anything but that. I... I don't want to go back. I'm sorry. He... he said that she was kidnapped and that all I would have to do was look out for her and keep her safe until he could come to get her. And... and... oh, please don't tell the High Mother."

Suddenly, all the tension left Leo's body. He didn't know whether to laugh or scold her more. He knew that if he told the High Mother, her name would be on the lips of every healer in the five kingdoms as a traitor and an outcast. Healers are a needed commodity, but where she would find work wouldn't be in any place of comfort, that's for sure.

"You're a healer. What possessed you to get involved in this? You know that you don't have to listen to Kings or Queens. We are not under the control of that mess."

"Yes, but... he is a King, and it is his daughter. So, I thought I was doing something good. Aren't healers supposed to do good? And then I come here and find this is a healer's house, and I didn't know what to do. So I just played along and... and... oh please. You won't tell the High Mother, will you?"

Leo sat there and looked at her for a moment before shaking his head. "No. But you'll be going back as soon as I can get you on a ship. Until then, you're not allowed to leave this house. If you do, I'll have this tree wrap around your neck as soon as you reach the door, and I will kill you. Is that understood?"

"Yes... yes sir. I... I understand," said Rayrah as the root stretched upward, sliding over the back of her neck.

"Good, and you're going to wear the face of Rima until I find you a passage home. I don't want to have to explain to those girls why Rima came home and have them come back to find you here."

CHAPTER 40

The next morning, Isha and the rest of her class stood at the edge of the floating island behind the school, looking into the forest. They all wore their school outfits, but inside each of their sashes were two small balls and three holes where balls could fit in.

"Okay, you little babies," said Mr. Higgins. "Today, you're going to show us what you can do. You're going to be graded on how fast you make it to the other side of the forest."

"That's not fair. Isha is just going to team up with those two Sakari," whined someone from the class.

"Yes, well, war and life are not meant to be fair. You make the best of the situation you are in. Most of you are going to team up with your friends anyway. I don't care what you do. Your goal is just to make it to the end of the field with five orbs. Find help or not. That's up to you."

"So do we just take each other's orbs then?" asked

another student.

"There are a few orbs scattered throughout the forest," said Miss Webblebottom. "You can use those also."

"The orbs will automatically lock into a slot in your sash by injecting magic into it. And vice versa, if someone wants to remove an orb, it will release from the slot when you inject magic into it for about three seconds."

The students fiddled with their orbs for a moment, popping them in and out of place before they began conversing and finding their groups amongst each other, while a few stood along, choosing to go solo.

"Good. Now keep in mind you're allowed to use your magic and any other means to subdue and steal each other's orbs. Obviously, you shouldn't try to seriously injure your fellow students, but roughing them up a bit is encouraged. If you find yourself unable to finish. Just call out for help. There are a few of the teachers already inside the forest. They are there to ensure you all are safe at the end of this."

"It shame, Chloe not here," said Makeba. "I want to see her magic. Her arm getting better. Why Leo make her stay home with Rima?"

"I don't know. He said he needed help with something," said Isha, turning to Jacinta. "How is your leg?"

"Leg is fine."

"Mother make Isha, Care Sister, you do not lie to her," warned Makeba.

"I not lie. Leg feel better. Not normal, but better. I can walk. I can fight."

"Alright. If you've decided who is with who, shall we start? All of you break apart. Good."

After the students spread apart, Mr. Higgins lifted his hand and signaled for one set of students to enter the forest. Then after a few minutes, he raised his hands and allowed another set. He did this twice more until it was Isha's turn. She headed inside the forest with Makeba and Jacinta, leaving another five groups of students behind to come in after them.

This forest's side wasn't as dense as she knew the other side to be. It was easy maneuvering between the trees as they made their way forward. It wasn't long before they spotted a girl ahead who happened to vanish behind a set of trees after she spotted them.

"Should we follow her?" asked Isha.

"No. It trap. They maybe lure us ahead. Forest is big and must get orbs to finish. I think we wait and keep looking again."

"Okay, we need fifteen orbs for all of us to win."

"We will find them. We go to building. Will be people there, I think. Good chance to get the orb thingies. And they be closed with walls, so hard to run in fight."

They continued their way through the forest for a few minutes until they heard a rustling in the brush.

All the girls froze for a moment turning toward the noise. Isha felt a chill come over her spine as the rustling grew louder, only to feel foolish as a small rabbit came from around the tree and stared at them. A sigh of relief hit her, only to be followed up by Makeba pushing her ahead as a large stone flew past where her head had been.

Instantly, Jacinta jumped into the brush as Isha began picking herself up off the ground. Looking ahead, her heart beating fast, she could see the bunny still staring at her before it became transparent and vanished. Once on her feet, she and Makeba started looking for any sign of attack before Jacinta came back out of the brush.

"They run away. I only catch back of heads. They run fast. Sister, okay?"

"I'm fine. Thank you, Makeba."

"They try to make us weak by hurting one, then attacking. It good plan. I would do same."

"Well, that's good to hear," said the familiar voice of Freedo. "Everyone for themselves, I guess."

The girls each began looking around but did not see

Freedo anywhere.

"Where Freedo? You hide and attack sister?"

"Look up," said Freedo. "And no, they were not with me. I decided to go by myself. Marlene and Serpene are up ahead somewhere. I'll meet up with them later."

The girls looked up, spotting Freedo perched above them with his arm above him, grasping onto another limb for stability.

"Why you up there?" asked Makeba, giving her usual frown at him.

"I just happened to be moving by and saw you. I figured I would say hello."

"Look, he has orbs already," said Jacinta, pointing up to his sash that hung over his knee. All the slots were filled with orbs. "How you get those?"

"I found them up here in the trees. Pretty lucky, huh?" he said with a large grin.

Makeba stepped forward, then smiled before stretching her arms to him. "Freedo, come down. I will give you big hug."

Now it was Freedo's turn to narrow his eyes while looking down at the girls. "I'm not that stupid."

"Makeba thinks you are."

"Oh, poo-poo on all of you. Good luck getting to the end." And with a leap, Freedo jumped out of sight, back into the trees.

"Why he so good at jumping like that?"

"I don't know. You think we should have asked him to join us?"

"No. No need Freedo. We can get orbs too."

The girls made their way deeper into the forest. Sometimes along the way, they could hear the sound of wooden weapons clashing, the sound of magic being cast, and the grunts of pain from students on the receiving end of attacks. Eventually, they arrived at one of the houses scattered between the trees of the floating island.

It was a two-story wooden house that seemed to be made from lumber gathered from within the forest. Moss formed on the outer layer, hanging down from the roof. The door to the house was open, allowing them to see the darkness inside. The morning mist at their feet looked as if it was being sucked inside.

"Do you think someone is already inside?"

"Maybe, but we can look for orbs inside also. Maybe find some like Freedo. If people inside, then we take theirs," said Jacinta as she stepped forward, peeking her head in, before taking a step inside.

"Well, I'm happy you're confident that we can. I'm not so sure."

"Sister worry, but we are strong. We take—"

Jacinta's words cut off as Isha watched two boys appear from the side, tackling her to the ground in the doorway. Isha and Makeba both dashed forward only to have the door slammed in their face.

"Hold her dow- argh! She bit me," screamed one of the boys from the other side of the door.

Makeba and Isha banged and pushed on the door, managing to open just enough to see Jacinta with two boys on top of her with gritted teeth before the door slammed shut again.

Instantly Makeba started pushing her magic into the door, trying to force it open. It shook the whole side of the house, but the door remained closed.

"Dammit, why'd it have to be the damn Sakari, argh! Hold her legs, and get the orbs before they get in."

"I'm trying, but she keeps moving. Got one!"

Isha started following Makeba's example as they both placed their hands on the food and forced magic onto the door. The side of the house shook again as they heard the lumber crack underneath the pressure, yet the door held.

"Hurry up. I can't keep this them out much—"

"Got them, go! Go! Go!"

Makeba and Isha attempted to push one more time, but before they could, they both fell forward on the house floor as the pressure on the door lifted. Ahead of them, they could see three boys running hurriedly down the hall of the house into the darkness. Makeba and Isha both got up from the floor and ran over to Jacinta, who had just pulled herself up.

"Jacinta, are you okay?"

"I fine. They get orbs," she said through gritted teeth, the rage clear in her voice. "We catch them. Go now." She then took off into the darkness of the house, a hint of gold smoke dripping from her eyes.

Disappearing into the darkness, Isha tried to follow her but was unable to see in the shadows. She tried to perform the magic trick with her eyes like her sisters had tried to teach her but was unable to. Suddenly she found herself alone in the blackness, her hands on the wall for guidance.

Where'd she go? They know I can't see in the dark like them. Where did Makeba go? Suddenly there was a loud boom as the walls shook around her. Somewhere ahead, she could hear the sounds of a struggle, but all too soon came a quietness. *Should I call for them? But what if someone else comes? If they beat Jacinta, I won't be able to do mu-* "Argh!" She yelped in surprise as a hand ran over her shoulder, quickly covering her mouth before she could scream.

Her heart pounded in her chest until she heard the sound of Makeba's voice whisper in her ear.

"Sister be calm, not know who else in house."

Isha spun around, but it was so dark she couldn't see her sister's face. "You scared me. Where is Jacinta?"

"She up ahead. I show you, but here is very dark. Weird magic is in this house. Even with Eyes, it is hard to see."

Makeba held Isha's hand, leading her through the darkness. They turned, took a few steps forward, and stopped.

"I can't see anything. Is Jacinta here?"

"I am here," said Jacinta as she placed her hand on Isha's stomach. "Lean forward, sister, and see."

"See? See what?" she asked, confused, but she leaned forward and felt the sun's heat on her face. Blinking her eyes, she tried to adjust to the sudden change. Her blurred vision cleared to see the forest around them. Even more confused, she tilted her head and realized she couldn't see the rest of her own body; instead, it was as if her head was poking out of a wall of darkness that enveloped her. "What is this?"

"I know not. But boys make hole in wall and run away. I could not follow."

Isha stepped outside the house, jumping to the ground below, followed by Jacinta and Makeba.

"Should we keep looking or search the house for more orbs?"

"Sister cannot see in dark like us. Maybe best to look other places."

"That's fine with me," said Isha, turning to see a downtrodden look on Jacinta's face. "Jacinta, are you okay?"

"I fine. But I am sorry."

"Sorry? Why?"

"I lost orbs. I... I am War Sister. I should not have."

"No. It wasn't just you. We made mistakes. We will do better. Now come on. I don't want to lose."

"And I don't want to lose to Freedo," said Makeba as she reached out her hand. "Let us go, sister."

With their renewed determination, the three girls headed back into the forest. Making their way through the trees, they heard the sounds of fighting. Instead of avoiding it, Jacinta turned and made her way toward the sound.

They found Pavel alongside his two attendants, fighting another group of three students. They all had their wooden weapons and were smacking them against each other. It looked like children playing rather than a battle between fledgling mages.

The boy dashed forward at Pavel, swinging his sword widely, but Pavel blocked every strike with his wooden sword. The clanking of the wooden swords was loud over their grunts. Pavel's attendants squared off with their partners, using their selected weapons, a whip and two smaller wooden blades.

The fight wasn't that long, as Pavel's group seemed stronger, which was proven by the boy on his back and Pavel's wooden sword at his throat.

"Do you give up?"

"Fine. You… you win," said the boy, out of breath. "Take it." He then reached to his side, removing one of his orbs and tossing it to Pavel.

"Thank you." Pavel reached out a hand, lifting the other boy from the dirt. "The others are still going. Shall we watch?"

The fights with Pavel's attendants were not as gracious. The girl with the whip won against another girl by tripping her feet and jumping on her. But the boy with the twin wooden blades lost to the girl wielding a long pike. The result of which was the loser of each forfeiting an orb.

"Do you wish to try again?" asked Pavel, a smirk across his face.

"No. We'd only end up losing more orbs. We'll go now, maybe find someone we can actually beat."

"Hey, speak for yourself. I won," said the girl with the pike.

"Fine. Then you stay and fight all three of them again. I'd rather go find someone I can win against."

"This is why I told you that you needed to practice more. Both of you," said the girl with the pike.

"Oh. Not this again. I told you, I was busy," said the boy as their group wandered back into the trees, still bickering with one another.

"I guess we should go now, Pavel," said the girl with the whip. "We still need four more orbs."

"Maybe not," said Pavel as he turned towards the bushes. "I know you're there. It's you, right, Isha? I saw you poke your head out earlier."

Isha's eyes widened as she turned to catch disapproving looks from both Jacinta and Makeba.

"It's not like I tried to get caught."

A little ashamed, Isha stepped out of the brush, followed by Makeba and Jacinta.

"Ah, so it was you. Were you there waiting until we turned our backs, and then you would try to attack us?"

"No. We heard the fighting and came to see."

"I'm not sure that's the point of this exercise," said Pavel, shaking his head before knocking his sword against the ground. "Well, since you're here. You three want to have a go? Each of us puts up one orb and then picks out our dance partners."

"Pretty boy, good at fighting. Jacinta wishes to fight," she said, stepping forward.

"I am here to entertain after all."

"I'm not fighting those Sakari," said Pavel's attendant.

"Yeah. I remember what they did to that Evangale girl," said the other.

"Come on, it's just training," Pavel sighed before looking around. "Fine, I guess the rest can wait and keep a lookout. We don't want someone sneaking in and taking us by surprise. But, hey, where'd all your orbs go?"

"Oh, I will give you one of mine if she loses," said Isha.

"So, you both have orbs, and she doesn't?" asked Pavel looking at the sashes hanging from the girls' waists. "I bet there's a story there."

"Story later," said Jacinta, squaring off in front of Pavel. "After I take your orb."

"Well, despite not having orbs, you certainly don't lack for confidence. Should we use magic, or will we just fight with our sticks?"

"Magic makes it more fun."

"I agree."

"Take this seriously, Pavel. Jacinta is in a bad mood," advised Isha.

"I am tak-" said Pavel as he narrowly escaped a thrust of Jacinta's stick as she lunged forward at his face. He reacted quickly by grounding his feet as she passed and swung his wooden sword toward the back of Jacinta's neck. But she blocked it by bringing the stick behind her back. Twisting, she brought her pole upward toward striking him on his wrist.

Pavel released the blade as the poke struck his wrist but dropped low, catching it with his other arm as quickly as he could, bringing it back up to Jacinta's chest, dragging the dirt on the ground upward with his force.

Jacinta jumped back out of the way, but not before Pavel's blade caught a piece of her clothing, ripping a diagonal gash in the fabric across her chest, revealing a small amount of her under clothing beneath.

Jacinta landed on her feet, skipping back to balance herself. Pavel then took the time to stand back up, switching his wooden sword back to his dominant hand, staring at her through the dust in the air between them.

"You're good. Maybe all those rumors about Sakari Justice were true after all."

"Pretty girly boy, not weak. But will not be so pretty after either."

"I'll take that as a compliment. But you're not going to be looking so well after either."

As the final trickles of dust settled between them, Pavel leaped forward, his arms over his head as he brought the sword down. Jacinta parried the blow by holding the staff above her head, releasing one hand, and letting the force carry the blow down to the ground. She then planted the edge of the staff into the dirt, bringing back up a large clump of dirt that struck Pavel in the face, forcing him to stagger back, waving his hands.

Pressing her advantage, Jacinta took a step forward by digging her staff into the ground, bringing up clumps of dirt at Pavel, forcing him to keep his distance. Pavel tried to bring up his shield for protection but soon realized not all the dirt and rocks had been enhanced by magic and some slipped through the shield, pelting him in the face.

Bringing both arms up in front of his face, Pavel's magic began flowing out of his arms. Spreading his wrists apart as the magic flowed out in front of him, the wave of rocks halted in mid-air, floating in front of his face—an action that caused Jacinta to pause.

"You're not the only one with fancy tricks," said Pavel as he thrust his arms forward, sending the wave of rocks and dirt back at Jacinta. It was her turn to defend as she brought up her arms to cover her face as the rocks pelted off her, falling to the ground.

Pavel reached downward, channeling his magic into the soil, and brought up a larger rock. He drew back and prepared to launch it at Jacinta. But, realizing what he was doing, she pulled back her arm holding the staff and launched it at Pavel's large rock. It struck true with such force that it pierced the rock, exploding through it leaving a large hole in the center. The dust splattered Pavel in the face again as the staff flew over his head.

Blinking and shaking his head for a moment to clear his vision, he saw Jacinta rushing towards him. In a rush he attempted to throw rock, however, Jacinta was already close enough to stand before him and began channeling her magic into the large rock he had in front of him.

The rock shifted in the air between the two as they both continued to force their magic into the small boulder. Gritting their teeth and planting their feet, they both began to push harder, a sliver of each other's face visible through the small hole in the rock that Jacinta's staff had made.

"Sister Jacinta happy. She is enjoying this fight," Makeba commented.

"Happy?" asked Isha as she looked over at Jacinta, her teeth biting into her lip, her brows making those ripples above her nose, and her eyes wide. "I'm not sure that's hap—"

Suddenly a cracking sound was heard from ahead and Isha realized the sound was coming from the rock that floated between Pavel and Jacinta. The cracking grew louder as the rock rotated faster under the force of both their magics, the small hole inside closing upon itself as the whole rock began to shrink. Pieces of it started breaking off, spiraling around faster and getting louder.

"This is bad. It will go boom." Makeba cringed away from the scene.

"Boom? What do you mean it will go bo—"

Time answered the question on Isha's lips as the spinning rock between Pavel and Jacinta exploded, sending them flying back and rolling around the ground as a cloud of dust filled the area around them.

"Jacinta! Are you alright?" Isha screamed out.

"I... I fine," Jacinta said as she lifted herself from the ground.

Only their silhouettes could be seen through the magic dust cloud as Pavel raised to his feet as well. Then in the dust, they could see Pavel dashing ahead at Jacinta with his sword in hand. His sword swung, cutting through the dust cloud, granting momentary vision of the two as they fought. Jacinta was nimble on her feet as she dodged each strike, trying to escape.

And with another leap back out of the dust cloud into the open, Jacinta appeared with Pavel chasing after her. Sweat pouring down her face, she struggled with Pavel as his sword strikes grew in speed. With her stick, she seemed to be at a disadvantage with him so close.

Then Pavel thrust forward, but instead of dodging, Jacinta shifted her weight and leaned forward as the wooden sword pierced the side of her clothing, scraping against the skin of her ribs and through the back of her school attire. Jacinta winced for a moment but smiled as her face was only inches away from a stunned-faced Pavel.

Realizing where he was, Pavel tried to free his sword and move back, but Jacinta latched onto him, wrapping her arms around his elbow and then leaning back. She began lifting him, wrenching at the tendon of his elbow as she did so. He winced in pain as he raised on his toes, trying to pry the Sakari girl off. Jacinta lurched back even harder, till his feet were off the ground, raising him higher until he was almost over her. Then it all came crashing down as Jacinta fell back, and Pavel fell on top of her with a thud.

Jacinta gave out a yell of pain as Pavel quickly rolled off her, clutching his arm and looking bewildered. There, on the ground, Jacinta lay huddled over, clutching at her leg.

"What's wrong," asked Isha as they all ran over.

"Leg... leg hurts."

"Sister, you push too hard. Remember, Leo say not to use leg too much," Makeba said.

"I... I'm sorry. I didn't think about her just getting off her crutches," said Pavel as he raised his hand in the air. "We should call for help. Leo can't be that far away." Magic flowed through Pavel's arm, gathering above his palm before shooting into the air and exploding, creating a loud popping sound.

"Can sister stand?" asked Makeba, reaching out her hand.

"I... try."

Makeba pulled Jacinta up by the arm as one of Pavel's attendants came running over, handing Jacinta her staff for her to use as a crutch.

"What do we do now?" asked Pavel, looking around. "I guess we could... oh, here comes someone now."

A man and a woman came out of the trees walking over to their group.

"What's going on here? Is everything alright?"

"One of us has been hurt," said Pavel, pointing towards Jacinta, who was still trying to hobble on her staff.

"The Sakari?" the woman looked around. "There isn't anyone else here. I suppose we should take her to one of the healers."

The man walked over squatted down and lifted Jacinta up into his arms.

"Let's get you off that leg, little lady."

"Is Mr. Higgins not coming?" asked Isha.

"We have an area set up for injuries and such. If he doesn't come here, then he will probably be there."

"You should come along as well," said the woman to Makeba. "I think it would be best for you two to stay together."

"What about test? Will we not need to finish?" asked Makeba.

"No, this is just one of many. There will be other chances. First, we will need to ensure your sister is okay. Okay, let's head off to the medical area." The man turned around with Jacinta in his arms and Makeba following behind them.

"Sister, come," said Makeba as she turned, reaching out her hand to Isha.

The group headed back towards the trees, but as they got closer, Leo appeared out of the brush, wiping leaves from his hair.

"And what do we have here?" he said as he approached the group.

"Sister hurt her leg again. She needs help," said Makeba.

"We were going to take her to the house at the end area. We have a healer there," said the woman.

"Oh, is that so?" asked Leo, staring at Jacinta in the man's arms. "I do remember telling you not to put much pressure on that leg of yours."

"I was fighting. Did not want to lose," said Jacinta, looking into Leo's eyes with defiant pride. "Would have won."

"We should head over now," said the woman interrupting their conversation. "We should get her there before any other students fall victim to any more accidents."

Leo sighed, nodding his head before reaching out, placing his hand on Jacinta's head, and rubbing her hair. "You girls will be the death of me." In one quick motion, from his sleeve, into his hand appeared a small metal object which he turned upward and drove into the man's neck. It went so deep that his fingers also went into the man's throat, small amount of blood dropping down onto Jacinta.

The man gasped for only a moment before his breath was cut short, and he began to shake.

"I'll take that," said Leo, reaching out and taking a stunned-faced Jacinta into his arms as the man took one step forward before falling to his knees and planting face down in the dirt.

"What? What have you done?" screamed the woman.

"You made a mistake. I'm the only healer left at this school. Anyone else would have to be approved by me."

"You don't— that doesn't—"

"This school does have people I'm not acquainted with," said Leo as he knelt, sitting Jacinta down on the ground. "But, seeing as I'm the only healer here, you should have known me, which you didn't. I can only assume you sent that fake here to fool us. But don't worry, I took care of her."

The woman's face turned sour as she took a step back. "Who are you?"

"A simple healer, and you're going to tell me who else is with you here."

"You're going to regret this," said the woman as she raised her hand before slamming it down onto the ground creating a dust cloud and disappeared.

"Are you all okay?" Leo turned back to the girls.

"We're okay," said Isha. "Were they the ones who attacked the school before?"

"Probably. I wasn't too sure. But it seems my hunch paid

off. Either way, I knew they weren't from the school. That's for sure."

"Why did you let her go?" asked Pavel, stepping forward. "Will she not just tell her associates about what happened?"

"I'm not a warrior," said Leo, raising a finger. "And speaking of which. Excuse me for a moment." He then proceeded to walk over to a nearby tree, place his hand on the trunk for support, and throw up.

"Are... are you okay?" asked Isha as she walked over.

"I'm... I'm fine... Just... Just never killed anyone before," said Leo as he regained his composure, standing back up straight and taking a deep breath. "I guess I should finish it." He then walked over to the dead man's body, kicked it over, reached down, and pulled out the metal spike he had just recently plunged into the man's neck. It was covered with blood as he wiped it off on his clothing, then held it out for Isha. "I suppose I should return this."

Isha stared at it for a moment before realization came to her. "That's one of mine."

"Yes, sorry. Remember the one you blew a hole in our wall with? It took me quite some time to find it."

She reached her hand out to take it but stopped mid-way. "No. I... I want you to keep it."

"Are you sure?"

"Yes. I'm sure."

"Okay," said Leo, looking around again. "What do we do now?"

Suddenly two bodies came hurtling out of the woods flying through the air before sliding across the ground. They were in school uniforms, and their faces and arms were severely scarred.

They all turned toward the trees as another figure appeared out of the woods. Out of the shadows of the trees came Mr. Higgins bare-chested: his school uniform was in tatters as he stepped out into the sunlight.

"Stupid to try and attack me. And with only two. To take

me so lightly," he said before noticing Leo and the children. "Good, you're all safe." He looked at the body of the dead man at Leo's feet. "Good. I see that the training we've been doing has paid off. Do you know what's happening?"

"No. But my guess would be they are the same people who attacked us before," replied Leo.

"One way to be sure," said Mr. Higgins as he walked over to the body of the man Leo killed. Taking a small blade out, he cut down the center of the man's garbs, exposing his chest. "Hmm, no crystal embedded like the report said." He turned towards Leo and the group. "Strip the other two and see if they have jewels embedded in their skin."

"None here," said Leo after he searched for the bodies with Pavel.

"I suppose not all of them are using them then?" said Mr. Higgins rubbing his chin. "I don't like this. Too many things we can't control are happening. First, we need to make sure the children are safe. Then we can—" His words froze in his mouth as he stared up into the sky.

An airship appeared over the school's main area, then another, and another, multitudes, until over two dozen had appeared,

"How in the Goddess's name have they gotten so many ships?" Mr. Higgins asked.

"What do we do now?" asked Pavel.

"No doubt, Soulden is asking herself that very question. Our first goal doesn't change. We should secure the rest of the children. Leo and I will split up and bring back all those we find back here."

"Don't leave us out," said Pavel. "We're not as strong as you, but we can still fight."

"We're not leaving you out. From the look of things, that Sakari over there is hurt. So, she won't be of much help. That leaves you and your followers here to protect them until we get help. Unless you think they will be fine on their own?"

Pavel glanced back at Isha and then at the injured Jacinta. "We'll stay."

"Good lad. We shall return after we figure out the situation." Mr. Higgins said, then took off and headed towards the tree.

Leo knelt, giving Makeba and Isha a hug. "Take care of each other. I'll go make sure it's safe." He followed Mr. Higgins, disappearing into the brush.

CHAPTER 41

The girls moved from the opening in the trees to a more wooded area. Makeba and Isha stayed with Jacinta as she nursed her leg while Pavel and his companions were spread out, keeping guard not too far away. Not long after Mr. Higgins and Leo left, they began hearing magical explosions being cast.

"How long do you think we have to wait here?" asked Isha.

"Not know. Many kingdom people on this island. Not know who to trust or if other teachers are okay," Makeba replied.

"You think we should move again?"

"No. Moving sister is hard. Also, maybe someone spots us if we move together. It is good Pavel here with friends. It makes—" Makeba's words froze in her mouth as she looked around.

A nearby bush rustled violently before a man's head peaked out."

"Hello there," said the man, turning his head back around. "Professor, I found some of them."

"Oh good, I was afraid-- Hello there," said Mr. Caudbell. "Monet said that we would find you this way. Are you three, okay?"

"Yes. We're okay. Is everyone else okay?"

"I'm not too sure. I happened to run across a very angry Mr. Higgins. He asked that I help gather up the children. Apparently, those associated with the previous attack on the school have returned as evidenced by the ships in the sky."

"Is everything okay?" asked Leo as he jumped out from behind a tree. "Oh, it's Mr. Caudbell."

"Ah, Leo. Good, you're here. I was told you would be nearby. Come, I shall escort your group back to the platform and make our way towards the school."

"Is it safe at the school?"

"I am honestly unsure. But I imagine we would find a greater shelter there than out here in the open."

"Okay, then," said Isha as she swallowed nervously. "Let's go."

"What about Jacinta there? How is her leg?"

"I fine."

"You are not fine," Isha snapped back. "You are hurt."

"Well, I'm not known for my strength, but I think I can carry you for a while," said Mr. Caudbell as he knelt down, picking Jacinta up in his arms. "Right then. Let's be on our way."

And with that, the group began making their way back through the forest, trying to move quickly and quietly through the forest area. Unfortunately, the wooded area had more visitors than they had expected. All of whom were wearing the uniforms of teachers from the school.

"I don't recognize any of them," said Mr. Caudbell,

stopping as two supposed instructors made their way past them. "And I know all of the staff here, recent or otherwise."

They waited until they had passed before standing up to move again when they heard the cries of some children from nearby.

The group looked around at each other before they all then turned to Mr. Caudbell.

He sighed when all their eyes turned on him. "Yes. I would be the only adult here, wouldn't I? Fine. But quietly. I'm known for my mind, not my combat prowess."

Stealthily as a group their size could move, they made their way towards the screaming sound until they found what they were looking for. Up ahead, with their faces planted into the dirt, was Serpene along with two other girls Isha knew from class but had never spoken to.

"Get off us. Why are you doing this?" asked Serpene, her legs kicking out from under the woman atop her.

"Just shut up and stay still."

"What do we do?" asked the girl in Pavel's group.

"I don't know. I mean, we have to ensure their safety. That's paramount. So, we can't—" Mr. Caudbell's words stuck on his tongue as he looked forward, squinting. "What is that?"

They all turned their attention to where Mr. Caudbell was looking, only to see a large object falling out of the trees. It only took another moment to see the large object was a person holding a large wooden stick. And as the person came down from the trees, their stick broke on the back of the neck of the man that was holding the two other girls down. He gasped before collapsing on top of them.

Hitting the ground with a thud after striking the man. They caught a glimpse of the person now standing back up, holding out their sword.

"Let... let her go," said Freedo, his wooden sword shaking in his hands.

"You little brat. If you think—" were the only words, the

woman atop Serpene managed to get out before Makeba and Pavel descended upon her. Makeba jumped out of the woods as Pavel's wooden blade struck her, cracking on the back of the skull. Just the same as the man before, she fell down on top of the other girl.

"Oh, thank the goddess," said Freedo, dropping the wooden stick from his shaking hands and lowering his head. "I thought I was going to die. My shields aren't strong enough to fight off real mages."

After climbing off the man, Makeba walked over to Freedo, and punched him in the shoulder.

"Stupid Freedo. Could have died."

"Hey!" said Freedo pointing a finger back at Makeba. "You did the same thing. What's the difference?"

Makeba stared at him for a moment before turning back around. She grabbed the unconscious man by the hair, lifting his head, and from inside of her clothing, she pulled out a small-curved blade. Isha recognized the blade instantly. It was the one her sisters had sprung out of nowhere when the school was attacked the first time. And before she had time to object, Makeba slit the man's throat. Then, just as smoothly, she turned to the woman and did the same. Their blood gushed out over the blade and on the group below.

She did it so effortlessly and with no hesitation. So much so, that it left everyone stunned. Makeba then walked back over to Freedo, her hands and her blade covered in blood as she held them out to him.

"Will you kill who comes next?"

"Wha... how... did you really have to kill them," stuttered Freedo, a grimace of disgust across his face as if he were about to vomit.

"No, but to be sure, I did. Now they can no longer hurt us. So, will you take blade and kill who next we find?"

"No, I don't... I don't want to kill people."

"Then that is the difference between us. I kill people. Sister Jacinta kill people. And even Sister Isha kill people.
542

So, you will let us girls kill for you."

"That... that's not—"

"She's right, Freedo," Pavel interrupted. "We don't know what they want but do you remember what happened last time? Some of the teachers and students here are dead. We can't just assume they wouldn't do the same to us."

"I... can't promise that I can do that. It doesn't seem right."

"Well, either way," said Pavel. "We should move on. We don't know how many more there are."

"Where are you headed?"

"To the platform leading back towards the school."

"Oh. Have you seen Marlene?"

"No, we haven't come across her yet."

"Then I can't go with you. I have to find her."

"What?"

"Freedo being stupid. What you do alone?"

"I'm afraid I must agree with the others," said Pavel, stepping in. "You surprised that one before, but there is no guarantee that will happen again."

"I know. But I won't leave her. You all go ahead. I will head back over to the platform when I find them." And before another word could be said, Freedo took off into the brush. Makeba instinctively took a step to follow him. But stopped for a moment, looking back at Isha and Jacinta. Jacinta nodded at her, and instantly Makeba took off into the brush, following behind Freedo.

"Wait, don't—" said Mr. Caudbell in protest but Makeba was already gone. He sighed, rubbing his hair and smushing his glasses to his face. "This is why I was never a good teacher."

"What should we do now?" asked Pavel. "Follow them?"

"No. They know where we are headed. And if they do find the others, we should secure the transport platform so that it will be safe when they get there. I say that in hopes that Mr. Higgins or some other teachers will be nearby," said Mr. Caudbell.

In agreement, the group continued their way through the forest. They couldn't see the school anymore because of the thickness of the trees. But they could hear distant screams and explosions, along with the occasional sighting of an airship above their heads.

Their path led them to the same house of darkness where Jacinta was attacked. From where Isha was, she could still see the black shadows oozing out of the house. She was still curious about the tricks that other houses used, but the platform back to the school was up ahead. There were a few people on the way, but the group chose to avoid them. Eventually, they made their way toward the end of the forest, where they started the orb game.

"The platform's gone," said Pavel.

"It's just on the other side," replied Mr. Caudbell. "That means it's at the school. Some could have gone back before us, perhaps to get some help." Ahead they could see the airship that had surrounded the school. Dozens of them floated in the sky. "How did they manage to gather so many? The sheer act of training so many pilots—"

His question was answered immediately, as a bolt of magical lightning arched from the school ground, through the sky and pierced through several ships. However, instead of splintering these ships into thousands of pieces, the lighting only passed through them with no effect.

"Illusions," said Pavel. "But there are so many of them."

"Yes, but where are they coming from? Who's casting them?" asked Caudbell.

Ahead at the school, a cloud of thick gray smoke began to cover the grounds—so dense that they could no longer see the base of the school.

"Someone is coming," said Pavel, pointing up ahead.

Through the smoke came a group of five dressed in school uniforms, riding along the floating platform. Magic blasts of fire came after them from out of the smoke, but their shields managed to block the blasts as they approached the group.

Protected, the group landed on their side of the island, dismounting the platform and looking exhausted. Some of them had pieces of their clothing torn from a previous battle.

"Are they on our side?" asked Pavel.

"I'm not sure yet," said Mr. Caudbell, squinting his eyes as the group came forward. "I think... Yes, that is Tannor. You girls remember him? He's my assistant. And two of those with him, I know them as well." He stepped out of the brush, waving at his companions, who instinctively took up defensive positions at his appearance.

"Wait! Stop," said Tannor upon realizing who had come out of the brush. "That's Caudbell."

The two men embraced for a moment and conversed, but Isha and her group couldn't hear what they were saying. After a few moments, Mr. Caudbell turned around and lead the group back toward Isha and the others. They entered the brush, all meeting up in a small opening in the trees.

"Would you inform the children on what you told me about what's happening at the school?" asked Mr. Caudbell.

"Chaos is what I would call it," said Tannor. "We don't know who is who anymore. Teachers have started attacking other teachers, Miss Webblebottom blew a hole in the side of her own classroom. And we were attacked by Miss Fitz."

"What about Soulden?"

"She's the one who sent us over here. I don't know what she has planned. She just asked us to secure the students here." He looked over all the children. "Where are the rest? Are they safe?"

"We don't know. Leo and Mr. Higgins went to secure the rest. But I haven't had contact with him since I found this group. We were going to head back to the school, but that doesn't seem like much of an option anymore."

"I would advise against that. You see the sad state of

affairs that we're in. I think it'd be best to secure the area over here first, if possible. Do you know many we're up against?"

"No, but according to the children and from what I've seen. They've killed five of them."

"If it's Mr. Higgins they're fighting, then I'm not surprised. That man has always been a walking explosion," said Tannor, taking a quick glance at the children. "Well, if we wish to mount an offensive, I would say that we stand a better chance with you all here."

"Yes, but I think moving together would be unwise. It would be much easier to spot us," said Mr. Caudbell.

"I suppose so, and I would like to involve the children as little as possible."

"Agreed. I think they are watching the platform area for anyone that returns. So, our best course of action would be to first secure the island in hopes that Soulden will secure the school."

"Good, then we shall split up and meet after everything is clear."

"Yes. Be on the lookout for the other Sakari child, Makeba. She went along with another student, Freedo, in search of other children."

"Right, we shall certainly be on the lookout then."

In agreement, they all split up; Tannor with his group and Mr. Caudbell with the children, heading back into the forest. Although this time, they frequently took breaks for Jacinta and Mr. Caudbell, who was carrying her.

"Sorry," said Mr. Caudbell, who was out of breath. "I never did... take magical strengthening seriously. I suppose... I'm paying the price of that now."

"There are some people up ahead," said Pavel, peeking his head in from around a tree. "About five of them."

"Are they, our people?"

"I don't know. I think I've seen one of them before. But not the others."

They all moved closer to peak past the tree and see the group Pavel spoke of: four men and one woman. They wore school uniforms.

"No. One of them was recently hired by the school. For protection, I think. But the others... no, I don't think they mean any goodwill towards us. I would advise avoiding them."

"But shouldn't we do something? What if they find someone else?"

"We're not warriors, Pavel. We can only get lucky for so...Wait! There may be a way. Do you think you could lure them into that house over there?" Mr. Caudbell pointed to a house painted white. "The house is actually laced with an extract of sleep root. If one were to stay there for an extended period of time. Well, I imagine they wouldn't come out until someone roused them."

"But wouldn't that affect us as well?"

"Yes, but it will affect mages more slowly unless tailored to do so. And from what I've seen, many of them are not mages. So, you will need to be quick."

"I... I can do that," said Pavel.

In agreement, Pavel and his two followers stepped off into the brush, leaving the rest to watch. Only a minute passed before they saw Pavel appear on the other side of the house, opposite the group of imposters. They couldn't see his followers, only Pavel, as he stuck his head out, looking over the area.

Then, having made up his mind, Pavel through a stick at the group of guards, whacking one of them in the head. There were a few words exchanged that they couldn't hear, but the outcome was Pavel running into the house by himself. Three from the group chased him inside, leaving two outside. The man who was hit and a woman who was checking his wound.

"Let's hope they aren't mages," said Mr. Caudbell.

"What do we do now? Two of them are still out there,"

asked Jacinta.

"We have to do something. We can't just risk Pavel coming back out and running into those two," said Mr. Caudbell.

"Hey, over here. I found some of them," came a voice from behind the group.

They turned around to see three more men wearing the school's uniforms, none of which Isha remembered seeing before.

"What are you all—" said the man before looking ahead and seeing his comrade by the house cradling his face. "So, you're the ones that have been causing us trouble. Grab them. Get the Sakari."

And in a split second, Isha found herself in a flurry of arms and legs as she struggled to free herself from the grasp of one of the men.

"Leave the children be," shouted Mr. Caudbell as he channeled his magic into his hand and sent out a wave of force that sent one of the men flying off of his feet and crashing into the trees with such force that it rattled the limbs above.

"Another stupid mage," said one of the other men as he turned his attention to Mr. Caudbell before launching a torrent of fire at him for his palms.

Quickly Mr. Caudbell brought up his arm to shield himself as his magical barrier covered the area around him. The flames struck the side of the barrier, instantly dissipating or redirected, scorching the grass and dirt around him

"Such disdain for your own kind. Are you not a mage as well?" asked Mr. Caudbell.

Isha struggled and kicked under the man's weight, trying to scratch at his face, but her arms were too short. But above, she saw Jacinta jump onto the man's back, plugging a blade into his shoulder. Releasing Isha from his grasp, he screamed in pain, rearing back with Jacinta still latched onto him, her hands wrapped around his neck as she was flung in the air.

Jacinta screamed in rage as she ripped the blade free in an attempt to try and stab him again. But he jumped backward, heading toward the base of a tree. Seeing this, Jacinta attempted to loosen herself, and fall to the side. But this effort was slow. Instead, her damaged leg was caught between the man's lower back and the tree on impact. Jacinta let out a scream as she tumbled to the ground, only for the man to pick her up with his hands around her neck.

"I don't know why they want you, Sakari. But one should be good—" the man's words paused as he began to shake. With a loosened grip, Jacinta fell back to the ground gasping for air. With still shaking hands, the man looked down to see Jacinta's blade sticking out of his abdomen, the hilt gripped by Isha.

Go away. Just go away, thought Isha as she drove the blade deeper inside him. *Leave us alone.*

The man reached down, grabbing Isha by her hair, only to have Isha scream and plunge the blade in deeper. His crimson blood pooled out of him and over her hands as she twisted the blade in his flesh.

He convulsed, coughing up blood that landed over Isha's hair and face before dropping to his knees and falling back with Isha landing on top of him.

Isha's breath was heavy on her lips as the man's blood that he had coughed up on her seeped into her eyes, turning her world a light crimson. She ripped the blade free as she sat atop him, raising it above her head. The man's eyes were still alive but fading as his hands gripped at her side.

Her body began shaking as she looked down at him. Images of Molan began flashing through her mind. That night in the tent, with him climbing on top of her and, screaming, she plunged the blade down into the man's chest. She screamed again as she ripped the blade free before driving it down into his chest again over and over, causing blood to splatter all over her and the ground around them. She drove the blade in as many times as she could, only stopping when she could not stop the shaking of her hands.

Looking down, she saw the mess she had made. The man's chest was awash with blood, and so was she. His eyes had long since rolled back into his head, and she now saw atop a corpse. Her lips quivering, she looked around as if she was lost, not fully remembering where she was. She was only brought back to reality by the sight of her sister on the ground away from her. Jacinta's face was covered in dirt, and she was clutching her leg, but her eyes were focused on her sister.

Isha thought that her sister was saying something. But she couldn't hear her. The world had lost all sound. All she could hear was the beating of her own heart in her chest. But Jacinta was screaming now and reaching out her hand to her. Trying to focus and understand, to Isha, the world slowly began to move again, and sound began to return.

"Kru... sister. Kru ... Krump Sister. Sister Krump."

Krump? Why Krump? Isha asked herself, confused for a moment before realizing that Jacinta wasn't holding out her hand. She was pointing. Isha turned around to see Mr. Caudbell using his magic to hold one of the men from before down to the ground but sneaking up behind him was the woman from before who had been treating the injured man.

Now understanding Jacinta's message, without hesitation, Isha snatched the blade free from the dead man's chest once more and reared the blade back over her head. Then gritting her teeth and clenching the blade as hard as she could, she thought of the words to focus her magic. *Stupid Leo.* She didn't hear the wooden hilt crack beneath her grip or feel the splinters dig into her skin. She only felt her arm come forward and down as hard as she could as she released the blade from her hand.

There was a slight whistle, and the blade pierced the

side of Mr. Caudbell's clothing, grazing his rib cage underneath. Barely passing him, it struck the woman behind him and embedded itself perfectly into her chest with such force that the momentum lifted her off her feet, sending her backward, breaking through several low-hanging tree limbs before she came crashing back down on the ground.

Mr. Caudbell released his magic hold on the man beneath him and dropped to his knees, clutching his side. Isha could see the blood beginning to cover his hand as she ran over to him.

"I'm sorry. I didn't... Are you okay?"

"Fi... fine," said Mr. Caudbell as he looked back at the woman's body and the destroyed grass and dirt from the force of her sliding across the ground. "I can see how it could have been worse. But perhaps continue to work on your aim a bit."

"Is... is it bad?"

"Just a flesh wound. Cut the skin, but no major damage. Stings quite a bit, though. Thank goodness I did not have my shield up at the moment. I would have prevented you from saving me. What about the other one? Is everyone safe?"

"We're safe," said Pavel as he stepped out from behind a tree, the side of his head bleeding from a cut above his eye. "The house only worked on one of them. The other two we had to sneak attack." He held up the remnants of his wooden blade, which was now broken in half. "Not sure what else I can do now."

"I swear if we make it out of this, you all will graduate with high marks. I shall see to it personally."

Pavel laughed while trying to wipe the blood and dirt from his face before catching Jacinta looking at him. He smiled back. "I suppose I'm not such a pretty boy now?"

"No, but I no good now either."

"And I have no weapon. If we get out of this, we still must finish our fight," he said before walking out and reaching his hand out to her.

Jacinta accepted his hand, hopping up with Pavel's support and balancing herself on one leg. "When get better I will win."

"How is your leg?" asked Isha looking at her sister worriedly.

"It is fine, sister. But you, are you not okay after him?" said Jacinta, nodding back to the bloody mess of the man Isha had just killed.

Isha looked down at her hands and arms, covered in blood and dirt. She shivered for a moment until Pavel placed his hands on hers, his own just as bloody.

"Don't think about it now. It won't help. Later, if you need, we can cry about it together. But we can't fall apart here."

She turned to Pavel, truly looking at him again. She somehow managed to find solace in the fact that he was also covered in blood and dirt. So, she nodded, pushing the thoughts as far away from her mind as she could and only trying to focus on Jacinta and him as they stood in front of her.

"Okay. I... I'm okay."

"Good," said Pavel before turning to Mr. Caudbell, who was looking down at the man he had killed who was embedded into the ground. His eyes seemed sunken in, and his mouth was agape.

"Just your standard push magic, albeit amplified a little. It seems our assailants haven't the ability to cast any magical shielding," he said, as if he were still teaching them in class.

"What should we do now, then?" asked Pavel.

"That is the question, isn't it? I wish I..." Mr. Caudbell looked up from the man on the ground and walked to the children.

Suddenly, a loud rumbling sound came roaring through their area. Above their heads appeared a ship, so low that it rattled the trees around them before moving forward past them. The gold plate around the ship was instantly familiar to Isha and the others.

"That's Soulden's ship," yelled Mr. Caudbell.

"Does that mean the school is safe now?" asked Isha.

"I don't... I'm not sure. But we won't find out anything just waiting here. And I dare say our small group isn't in a position to refuse any assistance," said Mr. Caudbell.

Jacinta, on one leg, hopped over to the dead woman's body, retrieving her blade from her chest.

Now in more dire condition than before, the group made their way as best they could toward the area where Soulden's ship had been seen going.

Only a little while later, they arrived at the field where Soulden's ship had settled. Ladders had been lowered as Soulden and her group stood in front of her hovering ship.

"Oh, thank goodness you're safe," said Soulden as she waved to the group as they exited the forestry area into the open. "Are you all alright? What happened?"

"Attacked... by some dressed as faculty. More than a few. How... how is the school? Are... the children safe," said Mr. Caudbell, out of breath and tired as he applied pressure to his wound.

"Yes, everyone is fine for the most part. Although we have suffered. My current goal is to ensure that everyone here is safe. The rest of the teachers are still fighting at the school. But we had many students here without protection."

"Yes. I see. Well, do you have a plan? I'm afraid I haven't been of much use."

"The plan should be to get you healed up," said Soulden, placing her hand on Mr. Caudbell's shoulder and looking down at his wound. "Where are Leo and the other Sakari? I don't see her."

"She followed after one of her friends. We haven't seen her for a while."

"Ah, so she's still missing. Well, with that being the case, we can take the wounded aboard to safety."

"Do you not wish to wait for any others."

"No. While my ship is reinforced to absorb some damage, I doubt it would survive an assault from several mages. It's best to secure whom we can for the moment."

"I go," said Jacinta, turning back to Isha. "I not good fighter like this." She then gave her sister a smile before freeing herself from their support and hopping on one leg over toward Soulden.

"I shall have one of the men here carry you up. Don't worry. I'm sure we shall find your sister soon."

But before Jacinta could reach them, Mr. Caudbell's arms wrapped around her, pulling Jacinta tightly close to his chest.

"Wait... child. Let us not move so hastily," said Mr. Caudbell, narrowing his eyes at Soulden and her group.

"Is there a problem, Mr. Caudbell?"

"Sadly, there seems to be... and quite a few in fact. I'd like to assume I would have spotted them earlier, but my current circumstances are quite taxing at the moment." He took a breath. "Soulden, do you know the names of the Sakari?"

"Of course, they are my students. Makeba and Jacinta. I hardly think now is the time to be playing such games. Especially given you—"

"And yet you referred to her as 'the other Sakari,' and, given you've been training the girl personally these last few months, I fail to think that much impersonality would still reside in your relationship."

"I see," said Soulden, closing her eyes for a moment but then resuming her usual composure. "But I hardly think that is enough reaso—"

"There is also the fact that I saw you using the ladder to make your way down from the ship. Soulden's ship had a special adjustment added to it where the side of her ship can detach and lower itself down to the ground. But of course, if you've never ridden in her ship, you would not know such a thing. Shall I continue?"

554

Soulden stared at Caudbell for a moment before smiling back.

"And here I thought you were only perceptive to your little experiments," came Tannor's voice out of Soulden's mouth before the area began to flicker like glass shards in the sunlight and then fade away to reveal his visage. "A shame, really. I wished not to have to kill you since we've worked so closely together. But those Sakari are key to our plans."

"Key or not," said Mr. Caudbell as he released Jacinta from his embrace and stepped out in front of her. "I shall not be releasing these girls into your care."

"As if you had a choice," said Tannor as he fired a small blast of magic into the air. Then, as if on command, dozens of figures began to emerge from the line of trees around them. "You see, my arriving here on that ship wasn't just happenstance. It was also a signal. And with Soulden and the rest distracted, you will not be receiving any assistance. But if you release the girls to us, I will guarantee your safety. This doesn't need to become any bloodier than it already has."

"Students, I'm going to ask you all to run."

"You're making a poor decision. A shame, especially for someone as smart as you."

"Perhaps, but I shall not live with the knowledge that I was such a coward as to force children into whatever plans you have for them. RUN!" Caudbell lifted his hands and a crackle sounded through the air as lightning exploded from his fingers, arching against the ground, ripping it apart.

Isha and the rest ran as best they could toward the edge of the trees where they had come from but could quickly see a dozen or so men and women from the other side rushing to head them off. That was until several bolts of lightning flew over their heads, striking two of the chasers and ripping at the ground in front of the others, halting them in their tracks as they took cover.

The blasts cleared the way as they entered the brush. Isha's last image of Mr. Caudbell was him firing out another arch of lighting and watching it veer off Tannor's magical shielding.

This time as they entered the forest, they could hear the yells of the people behind them as they made their way through the branches. Although in more a panic than before, they were noticeably slower as Pavel and Isha struggled to keep Jacinta on her feet. Isha could see the toll this was taking on her. The beads of sweat dripped down her face. The tiredness over her eyes as her head bobbed with each step was sign of vulnerability that she had never seen in her before.

A man's hand, barely within reach found its way into Isha's hair. He attempted a grab, but in the strands of her hair, his fingers just barely slipped through before forming a solid grip. But in her frantic state it was enough to stumble Isha. And with her trying to support Jacinta's weight, she soon crashed down onto the ground with Jacinta falling on top of her.

"Grab them. Get the black-haired girl with the Sakari. She's that amplifier that they were—"

Isha gritted her teeth from the impact of Jacinta landing on top of her. She heard Pavel cream something as she couched from the impact. Opening her eyes, she saw a man and a woman flying overhead, their clothing in tatters around them. They quickly came crashing back to the ground with such force that Isha felt the impact as they landed near her. She looked ahead to see Pavel standing in front of her holding his half-broken wooden sword in his hand.

"They are after Jacinta and you. Run."

"But—"

"We will be fine," said Pavel, as his now loose hair began to lift around his head. Soon, a slight breeze began to flow between the trees, and he and his companions all took up defensive stances as more and more assailants appeared from the nearby trees. As they approached, the shine from some of their hands was now unmistakably the gleam of metal from small blades.

Isha began to frantically look around. *What should I do? If I run, they will chase us. Jacinta can't run like this. We need...* And there, ahead and through an opening of the trees, she saw an odd darkness that seemed to be pouring out of the hole in the house from earlier. *There, we can hide in there.*

Both girls slowly rose to their feet and rushed to the house with the weird darkness as best they could. Behind them, they heard the yells of "Follow them" or "Don't let them go," which were then followed by, "Watch out," and screams of pain from what she assumed came from Pavel's group.

Between the trees, the two girls made their way out into the opening where the house was. Opting not to head toward the front door, Isha hoisted Jacinta up first and then she lifted herself up into the hole in the side of the house. The wall of darkness consumed her as she entered. Nervously, Isha turned back to see two men rush out of the trees headed toward them. Quickly she turned back around, pulling herself upwards, leaned forward into the darkness, and began crawling forward.

Even with eyes wide in panic, she couldn't see her sister but could feel her, and she grabbed up against her as she pulled herself inside. Isha yelped when a hand wrapped itself around her ankle. She grabbed at the floor for grip, but to no avail. The man was too strong and slowly began dragging her across the floor.

As her body excited the house, Isha felt someone crawl on top of her, their knee pressing into her back.

"Let sister go," came Jacinta's pained voice.

Then came the sound of a scream as Isha felt herself be freed from the man's grasp, and her lower body fell down, slamming against the side of the house. Quickly, her sister climbed off from on top of her and grabbed hold of Isha through her pained moans, pulling her inside the house of darkness.

Shaking uncontrollably, Isha clung to her sister as she listened to the screams from outside.

"What? What happened?" she asked.

"Sister, we go… we go now," said Jacinta, her voice now low and dreary.

Now clinging to her sister, Isha could feel Jacinta's heartbeat. It was heavy, and her breathing seemed pained and wheezing.

"Just a little more, Jacinta," said Isha, dragging herself back to her feet and lifting Jacinta along with her. "Come on, we just need to get inside. Can you see? I still can't do the eye thing."

"Yes… We go."

And with that, the two moved forward, deeper into the pitch-black house. To Isha, it felt as if the shadows were crawling over her skin as she followed Jacinta's instructions, eventually finding their way to a set of stairs.

"Are the stairs here?" asked Isha?

"No. Hole under stairs. We hide there."

Feeling around in the darkness, she found the edge of the stairs and the spot that Jacinta had mentioned and the two of them bundled up together in the small, cramped space.

"Do you think…"

Before Isha could finish her words, she felt Jacinta's face slump over and rest on her shoulder as she passed out.

"What is this place?" came a man's voice through the darkness.

"It's one of their magic houses. They were supposed to play tricks on those brats during their tests," another man replied.

"Pretty stupid idea—a house of darkness."

"Perhaps," came the voice of Tannor. "I'm sure it was

another one of Soulden's last-minute changes. Do you hear me, girls? No one is coming to help you. Understand that Mr. Caudbell died trying to protect you."

He's dead? No, that's not…

"You can save the rest of your friends before the same happens to them. All you must do is surrender yourselves to us. Unless you wish the same fate for your friends, Pavel, Mr. Higgins, Soulden, and even that caretaker of yours, Leo. You wouldn't want anything to happen to him, would you? Reveal yourselves, and let us end this. You will not be harmed. We only wish to have the power that those Sakari girls have. It will ensure that we will not need to harm children. You would be saving so many others from pain."

There was a moment of silence as the dark house grew still.

"Fine. Have it your way. But understand that I offered to end this as peacefully as possible. Find them. Hurt them if you must. We are short on time. But do not kill them. They are valuable pieces to the future of our plans."

Isha heard the footsteps of multiple people entering the house and felt the tremors of their footsteps through the floorboards as they fumbled their way around in the darkness around her.

"There are stairs here," said a man before the sound of creaking steps came from above Isha's head.

I have to do something, but what? I… I don't have anything. I don't have weapons. I can fight like Jacinta or Makeba. And even if I could, I can't fight all of them. I still don't even…

"This blasted darkness. I can't see anything," complained one of the men.

"We're in a forest. Just grab some sticks and set them ablaze as torches for those of you without magic. The others use fire magic to see but be careful not to set the house on fire. We can't risk losing them to a mishap," ordered Tannor.

"We've tried that, but the shadows consume it too fast," said another man.

"What... What do you mean the shadow consumes it?" asked Tannor. And soon, throughout the darkness, Isha began to see a white orb of light through the cracks in the steps. Holding it was Tannor. "What nonsense are you..." Then, as if in response to the light, a small tendril of blackness began spiraling at the base of the light before consuming it and casting them all back into darkness.

"I made some torches from the branches outside," said a man who appeared with a lit torch in his hand. Though not as bright as the magical orb of light, Isha could see parts of the flame through the strands of shadow.

"Good, this house seems to absorb any type of magic. Probably something that Mr. Caudbell thought up. Bring in more torches," ordered Tannor.

"Leave this place," came an ominous voice from the shadows as a wave of blackness came over what little light came from the fire and smothered it.

"Who's that?" said a startled voice from the shadows. "I thought there were just the kids in here?"

"It's just one of the children trying to scare us. They're mages, remember. It's possible to change one's voice with magic," said Tannor. "I'm impressed by your attempt to dissuade us. But you can't imagine scaring us off so easily by changing your voice. Sooner or later, you will be found."

"Found? You presume I am hiding. No. It is you who shall be found," replied the voice.

As if in response to a call, the entire house began to creak. Its wooden beams rattled amongst themselves, echoing in the darkness. To Isha, from her hiding place with Jacinta, it seemed as if the shadows around them began moving. Small strands of blackness, some thicker than others, appeared to be moving in front of her, flowing towards the entrance where she knew Tannor was.

Suddenly a scream called out from upstairs, then a loud thud, another scream—although now more muddled and pained—then finally a crash. The sound of wood breaking, crackling, and the scream from outside was followed once again by a thick thud as something hit the ground outside the house.

"Many are here. All will be found. All will suffer," warned the voice.

"That don't sound like no little girl to me," said one of the men.

"No," said Tannor, the tone of his voice growing deeper with suspicion. "It doesn't. It seems I was mistaken. Perhaps there is someone else here."

As the black strands of shadow continued to retract from the house, making their way past Isha, she began to get a clearer picture of those in front of her. It wasn't just Tannor, but also three others.

And there was something else. While it was still fairly dark, she could see an even darker mass pooling near their knees. From that blackness, a figure rose up, a mass of some sort, and within it, appeared two red eyes.

As if sensing the presence behind him, Tannor turned around, thrusting his hand out and blasting a wave of force at the creature. It dodged with the reflexes of a startled feline, spiraling downward around Tannor, hitting the three guards near him with such force that they all went flying backward into the wall. One was impacted so hard that half his body went through the wall and hung partly over the hole he made. The shadowy creature quickly came around Tannor, a mound of blackness gripping him around the throat, lifting him into the air.

Isha could see the effects of Tannor's shield through the creature's black grip. It was probably the only thing preventing him from having his throat crushed as the creature lifted him high, pinning his head and neck against the ceiling as he clutched it with his hands frantically, trying to free himself.

"You are the one."

"Release... me."

"Death is the only release you shall be—"

Two men ran past Isha with their hands raised and cast fire spells. The flame from their hands set the air in front of them on fire, the blaze roaring at the back of the black creature. The effort that was joined in by Tannor. He sent a blaze of fire into the creature's face. An inhuman scream came from the creature as it was engulfed in fire, setting the wood below and around them ablaze.

The creature swung around, dragging Tannor along with it and launching him at the two men casting fire spells. He crashed into them and went sprawling over the floor past Isha's hiding spot into the back of the house where now, more light was shining. Isha, in shock, turned back to see the creature surrounded by flames. But instead of the fire keeping the shadows away, it was the opposite as the shadows intermingled with flames and slowly began consuming them, smothering the fire.

"Outside, all of you!" ordered Tannor, after regaining his footing and staring at the creature consuming the flames.

"But what about the Sakari?"

"The other Sakari is still out there. We shall leave them to that monster," he said before he and the other men escaped through the opening in the wall.

"Noooo," came a voice from the creature. Its voice piercing through the house from a mouth she could not see. Then the creature whirled around, extinguishing the last bit of flames before dropping down and coming down the hall, a trail of blackness following like yarn in the wind.

Unlike the men before, when this creature moved, there were no footsteps. The floorboards didn't creak under its weight as it came closer. Instinctively, Isha closed her eyes in fear, hoping it wouldn't notice her and Jacinta there. Even with eyes closed it was as if she could feel the weird darkness of the house consuming her. Sliding over her shoulders, wrapping around her waist, it felt like a thin, soft fabric creeping over her skin. And then there was stillness.

Trying to control here fear, she slowly exhaled and opened her eyes. But that did nothing to calm her because directly in front of her, inside the blackness were two red eyes staring back at her. A new wave of fear ran over her as her body twitched in fright. The creature's face was inches away from her own as it stared, its gaze piercing, its breath warm as blew down on her arms.

Isha held Jacinta close, trembling, not knowing what to do. The creature's eyes swayed back and forth in the black mass as if examining her, then turning its head, it moved on silently down the hall and out of the house.

With relief, Isha fell over on her side with Jacinta beside her and gasped for air. Her heart thumped in her chest as she pulled Jacinta out of the crawl space underneath the stairs, holding on to her with her back against the wall. As she looked around the house, she noticed that it wasn't consumed by darkness anymore. Instead, it now looked like an average house, wooden flooring, stairs, and candle mounts adorned the hallway she was in. Each room had a door of a different color, white, red, and green.

What do I do now? Thought Isha as she looked down at Jacinta. *Do we run? Where would we even go? We can't get back to school, not like this. I wish Leo were here or Makeba. She would--* Her eyes opened wide with the realization of Tannor's last words. *Makeba! She doesn't know Tannor is with them. She might... and Leo might not know, or Mr. Higgins. I have to tell them.*

Isha struggled to stand up, scrubbing her back against the wall as she looked around. Her body was now feeling the pains of exhaustion. Taking a deep breath, she grabbed Jacinta under her arms and began dragging her towards the house's front door. Once there, she poked her head outside to make sure no one was around, then turned about and tried shaking her sister.

"Jacinta, come on. Please wake up. I can't do this alone."

But despite her attempts, she wasn't able to rouse her

sister.

Okay, think. I can... I can do this. She sat Jacinta up, then squatted and turned her back to her. Placing her sisters over her soldiers, she lifted Jacinta up into the air on her back, grunting from the effort.

Take the magic inside you and make it circulate throughout your body. I can do this. Take the magic inside you....

She repeated the words in her head, trying to push her magic through the muscles of her body, one step at a time to feel the magic and control it with each step. It didn't feel normal, especially with Jacinta's weight on her back. She didn't know how much magic was enough or too little. Sometimes the muscles hurt, and sometimes they felt dull.

Am I doing this right? I need to. I have to.

And although it was painful, Isha continued to place one foot in front of the other, not running, not bracing, just accepting the pain that came along with each step as she made her way back and turned around the house. There, beneath the trees, were the remnants of the shadowy creature dwelling in the brush, leading deep into the forest. Isha closed her eyes, took a deep breath, and shifted Jacinta's weight on her back.

Right. I'm going to do this.

She then headed off back into the forest.

CHAPTER 42

It was the middle of the day and Isha could see the sunlight shining through the trees. Yet somehow the shadowy underbelly of the forest seemed darker than before. She knew it had to be because of the magical black trail left behind by the creature, but she wasn't sure how. As she stepped through another brush, she found herself standing in the remnants of the battle Pavel's group had with those fake school members.

Two were dead. But how she knew it was Pavel was not because of the broken piece of a sword sticking out of a man's chest. It was because of the dead girl in front of her. Pavel's attendant, who was always with him. Her mouth was agape, and her eyes were still open. The cause of death was obvious. Her throat had been burned so deeply that Isha could see the bone and burned flesh underneath. She still held her wooden whip in her hand, her fingers bloody from gripping the handle so hard it cracked.

I'm sorry. I don't know if this is our fault, but I'm sorry.

She wanted to kneel and close the girl's eyes, but she wasn't sure if she would be able to rise up again. So, with trembling lips and a heavy heart, Isha stepped forward once again and continued her way through the forest.

Not moving too fast, Isha was patient. Along the way, she spotted two different patrols of adults dressed in school uniforms, some of whom she recognized but she didn't dare call out to them. Instead, she hid behind trees, out of sight, only feeling as if she could reveal herself to a select few.

To her surprise, Isha felt a tingle on her back. Makeba was using her as their link, taking some of the power inside of her. She hadn't done it since they first discovered that it could be done, and it still felt as weird as before. But this feeling... She could feel where it was being drawn to and with that headed off in that direction.

This way, she thought as she turned around. *No, this way.* She shifted directions slightly as the pull changed. Immediately, she went off in search of Makeba. *Maybe she's found Leo or Pavel. Or maybe Soulden has come to get us.*

Thoughts of rescue filled Isha's mind as she pushed forward. The feeling of being safe lightened the load of Jacinta as she tried to hurry. Unfortunately, this recklessness contributed to her being spotted by a lone man ahead of her. Despite her best efforts to evade him, the man was faster and cut her off, no matter in what direction she tried to run away.

"Hand over the Sakari," he ordered her.

He was a big man, and with Jacinta on her back, Isha couldn't outrun him. He reached out to her, trying to grab the unconscious Jacinta by the hair. But Isha jumped back, landing on wobbly legs, trying to balance her weight along with her sister's.

A way out. I need to find a way out. Makeba is so close. I know it, thought Isha as she tried to keep her distance from the man. She could still feel Makeba ahead of her, not too far away. *Think... think... there has to be a way to...* She jumped away again, barely dodging the man's hand as it grazed the side of her face. *Ahh! Just stop. Why won't... you all just... leave me...* The anger and frustration inside Isha finally boiled over as she planted one foot and kicked at him with all her might. *Alone.*

The kick caught the man unprepared and landed perfectly in his groin with such force that it lifted him off the ground a few feet before falling back down. His hands clutched over his crotch as he kneeled over into the dirt.

Isha stood there, stunned for a moment, before recognizing her opportunity. She took off, running back toward where she felt Makeba was. As she got closer and closer, she could feel the power Makeba was taking was weird. First, she would start and then stop and then repeat the process. Isha didn't understand. And that unknowing made her push herself more. The branches of a nearby brush scraped against her skin, leaves caught in her hair, but she didn't care. She wanted to see Makeba and to make sure everything was okay.

But as she passed the last brush, she realized that things were far from okay. In front of her, lay the bodies of four people dressed in school uniforms. And in the center of them, lay Makeba on the ground, with Leo holding her in his arms.

The look on Leo's face when he saw Isha emerge from the brush was something of such relief that it made Isha's heartache as she ran over to them, her knees finally buckling under the weight of it all as she dropped down in front of them.

"Oh, thank the Goddess, you're both safe. I've... I've been so worried." said Leo, as Isha laid Jacinta down next to Makeba. "What's wrong with..."

"She hurt her leg again, and she passed out after fighting the people chasing us," said Isha. Leo's face and clothing were dirty, and his right eye seemed to be recovering or developing from a black eye as it was slightly closed. But she didn't care. She wanted to hug him, kiss him, feel some sort of relief.

But all those emotions would need to wait. Because while they were glad to see each other, the more pressing issue was the wound on Makeba's side and a large amount of blood covering Leo's hand.

"What happened? Is she going to be okay?"

"I'm not sure. I only arrived a minute or so before you did and found her like this. Freedo found me and said she was injured."

"Then where is Freedo?"

"He went chasing after Marlene."

"Marlene? Did he find them?"

"Apparently, she was the one who stabbed Makeba."

"What?"

"I don't know the exact details. I wasn't paying much attention after he said Makeba was hurt. But honestly, I don't know how she didn't bleed out before I got here."

"Will she... will she be okay?"

"I hope so. With enough time, I could be sure, but..." He looked around at their situation, somewhere in a forest, perhaps still surrounded by enemies searching for them, and sighed. "But I doubt we have much time, Isha. That power you have that enhances others; do you think you could use that on me?"

"I think so. But whenever I do, the person always passes out and well..." she looked down at the ground. "My clothes kind of burn away if I use too much."

"If the consequence of getting these girls back on their feet is passing for a few hours, then that's a small price to pay. And you can place your school clothing to the side until we are done. Do you have on the undergarments Soulden had made for you?"

"Yes."

"Good, supposedly that shouldn't burn."

Isha nodded and stood, reaching for the hem of her uniform, lifting it over her head, and letting it fall to the ground. The fabric Soulden gave wasn't much, but it wrapped around her chest and created a little skirt that stopped around the hips. Leo, whose clothing was already ripped, simply tugged at the shoulder of his garb, tearing it free, and exposed his chest and bare back to her.

"Whenever you're ready. Just... just try to start slow. I will do my best to manage the power."

"Okay. I will try," said Isha as she stepped around Leo, placing her hands on his shoulder blades. She took a deep breath and placed the tip of her forehead against the center of his back. *Please, Goddess, let us all come out of this okay.*

"Don't worry about burning me. I would guess that I'm fairly used to it now. Just focus on what you're doing. I'll manage the rest."

With a nod of her head against his back, Isha delved into her own mind in search of power again. Now accustomed to it, it wasn't hard to find the streams of magic there. Instead of trying to grab it whole-handedly, she reached out only a finger, feeling the magic respond to her call. It entered her, and Isha slowly allowed it to flow inside her and outward into Leo. Instantly, she smelled the scent of burning flesh. With her eyes closed, a few tears escaped, but she clenched her teeth and continued to supply the power.

Leo, for his part, had bit his lips so hard that blood was dripping down his chin. But his hands and arms were as still as ever as he patiently continued to heal.

Isha didn't know how long she had been supplying magic, but she knew she would go on as long as needed. She would continue to draw more and more energy, as much as she could, for as long as she could if it meant protecting her sisters.

"Oh, okay. Make... Makeba is safe."

Isha's heart lifted as she raised her head.

"No, don't stop, not yet. Let me try... Jacinta.... while... while I'm still conscious."

Hearing the determination in his voice, Isha redoubled her efforts, continuing her access to her power. She knew she could access more, but something told her that any more wouldn't help. It was as if she could feel the magic inside Leo. It was hot. It throbbed as if it was under stress. And any more would break it.

The smell of burning flesh was upsetting her even more. It was as if she could feel her palm sinking just slightly into Leo's back. But through all of this, she never felt him move away from her, not even for a moment. Just a shift of the shoulder blade from the movement of his arm. It was as if he was as calm as ever, as if she were sleeping against his back. The heaving of his backside as he breathed in and out, the steady rhythm as he went about his efforts.

"Okay... that's enough."

His voice sapped Isha out of her trance as she opened her eyes and instantly pulled her hands away from him. And, for the first time, she saw the damage she had done. She had seared the flesh, leaving her own hands sticky with the results. Even the nape of his neck where she planted her head had been burned. She quickly slammed them down into the dirt, trying to remove the remnants of scorched flesh from her fingers.

"I'm sorry, I'm sorry... I didn't mean.. I... I..."

Leo didn't speak. He simply turned partly around, reached out his hand to her, and began rubbing the hair on her head before giving her the usual smile he always had. His lip was split open on the side as the imprint of teeth marks appeared on his bottom lip along with the blood on his cheek. After looking at her, he slowly closed his eyes as he fell over on his side.

"Leo, Leo. Wake up," said Isha as she crawled over, placing her hand on his shoulder and shaking him. "Don't leave me alone, by my..." her words stopped in her mouth as she saw the flesh of his back begin moving. The burning flesh looked as if it was boiling. At the other edges, where the burned flesh met the intact flesh, it seemed as if new skin was growing from the inside out, pushing out the old flesh as it fell to the ground. The new flesh came in as if like strands of hair needing over each other.

Isha remembered the last times Leo was burned: when he and Elena were engulfed in flames, or when he allowed her to see the damage done to his arm—how he had to cut at it for it to heal properly. But this was nothing like that. This was far stronger and faster than before.

Is that because of my power? Until now, she had only heard accounts of what her power did or how it affected people after the fact. Even the Queen just absorbed the power; she didn't actually do anything with it. But here, in front of her eyes, Isha watched the results of the power inside of her and the vast difference it made. She leaned over, rechecking Leo's lip, and was surprised to see that it had completely healed. The only visage that it was ever there was the blood still on his chin.

Nervously, Isha sat there on the ground. The three people closest to her were all lying on the ground, unconscious in front of her.

What do I do now? I can't leave them like this. What if one of those people were to show up? Can I fight them? I don't have any weapons. She began to look around for anything she could use to defend herself. She noticed a few rocks and a few large broken branches she could use to hit people. *I know how to use the push and pull magic. I can use magical shields, but I don't have one now. I can do a little...*

Leo moaned a bit, snapping Isha out of her calculations as he rolled over. He blinked his eyes for a moment before looking over to Isha.

"Was I... was I out long?"

"No," she said, shaking her head with relief. "Only a few minutes."

He sat up, looking down at Jacinta and Makeba, "Good." He rubbed at his head. "That power of yours is causing quite the headache." He then turned to Isha. "You can put your clothes back on now. Unless you think you can move better like that."

"What? Oh, yes, you're right," said Isha as she reached over, grabbing her school garb and sliding it over her head. "What do we do now... Wait! Do you know about Tannor? Or what about Mr. Caudbell?"

"No. Has something happened to them?"

"It's Tannor. He is with them, the people who attacked us. He chased us, saying that he came here for Makeba and Jacinta. The he said he killed Mr. Caudbell and we were inside this house, and it was dark. And there was this monster that was all black, and when he left, the house wasn't dark anymore. It chased after Tannor and—"

"Wait. Slow down. You're not making sense. Caudbell is... dead?"

"I don't know. That's what Tannor said."

So, Tannor is with the bad people, and he's after Jacinta and Makeba?"

"Yes, that's what he said."

"Good."

"Good? Why is that good?"

"Because they are here. So, he doesn't have them. We just need to think of what to do next. And they should be waking up soon, I think."

"Did you... are they okay?"

"No, not especially. I stopped Makeba's bleeding, and Jacinta should be able to walk now for the most part. But healing can only do so much in such a short amount of time. Although, with your help, we could probably have them fully healed in a few days. But I don't think I could survive the headaches."

Jacinta began to rouse from her sleep.

"There, see. I'm sure her brain will keep trying to block

the pain. She'll still be hurt but nowhere near as much."

Soon both girls awoke from their sleep, and Leo and Isha filled them in on what was happening. But they soon realized that none of them had any real weapons, as Jacinta had lost hers by attacking the man that tried pulling Isha out of the house, and Makeba had given hers to Freedo.

"Makeba, is it true that Marlene stabbed you?"

"Yes. We found her. I and Freedo, we run away together. But then she stab me. Freedo take my blade, hide me and then go off to find Leo. He save me."

"Let's just hope Freedo's okay then."

"What we do now?" asked Jacinta.

As if responding to her call, a loud inhuman scream came through, shaking the trees around them. As they all turned, they could see an enormous cloud of darkness off in the distance, the way it wormed in the air before dropping back down below the trees.

"Yes, that it. The shadow thing. In the house, there was this creature. And it—"

"Yes," said Leo, looking forward, his eyes fixated on the area ahead. "That's my brother."

"You're brother?"

"It's a long story. But if he's out now, then he's probably the reason why they haven't found us here. Dealing with him is probably all they can handle at the moment. You girls stay here. I'll—"

"No!"

Leo turned around, his face surprised and confused.

"I'm tired of us being separated. It's not good. If you are going, then I'm going," Isha commanded.

"But—"

"Sister right," said Jacinta, stepping forward and grabbing Leo by the hand. "Leo take care of us, and we take care of Leo."

He looked back and forth between Isha and Jacinta before hearing another scream further ahead, except this time, it seemed that of a man. Leo shook his head before turning to Makeba. "I don't suppose you're going to talk some sense into them."

"Sisters have made up their mind. I will protect them."

"I'm going to hold you to that because I expect all of us to make it through this."

In the distance, three more ships appear in the sky, emerging beyond the trees where Leo's brother was last seen. But this time, one of the ships took a huge blast and went teetering before it crashed into the trees. Then, spurred on by the assault from the ground, the other two ships began to cast magic down on the floating island where the first blast had come from.

"That's Mr. Higgins. Enough power to take down a ship in one hit. I can't imagine anyone else besides him or Soulden doing that," Leo shook his head. "Okay, fine, let's go. But be safe."

With no more hesitation, they all ran deeper into the forest after the sound of the screams.

Along the way, they passed by several bodies of slain people. But now, some of them weren't wearing school uniforms. Instead, they seem to be just ordinary clothing. Nonetheless, they were just as dead, having cuts on their legs, arms, and necks. One of them was even missing a hand, which couldn't be found at a glance.

This pattern continued the closer they got to the noise. More shadows, more dead bodies, some of whom were the students of the school who they were supposed to be practicing with. It was especially hard for Leo when coming across those students, especially the lingering shadows over their bodies.

"We may heal the wounded, we may heal the sickly. But we cannot ever heal the dead," said Leo under his breath. He didn't say it to anyone specifically, but instead, under his breath, every time he passed a student who had been slain.

The ground shook a bit as they made it closer.

"What are they doing?" asked Leo. "Do they not understand we are in the air? This island was not meant to withstand this. If they don't—" Leo stopped, as he spotted a group of three people dressed in common clothing. They all had swords in their hands. He quickly shuffled the girls into a hiding spot behind the trees as the men all made their way forward, heading directly toward them.

"Okay," whispered Leo. "So far, most of them don't have magic. So, that should give us an edge, if we attack them from far off. We can't block their weapons since they are mundane. I'll lure—"

"Ahhhh!" screamed one of the men, cutting off Leo's speech.

In shock, they all turned around, peeking between the brush to see one of the men dropping his sword as he fell to the ground.

"What hap—"

As the man fell to the ground and the two other men jumped back, they revealed the image of Freedo. Isha was stunned at just how different he looked from the boy she had seen earlier in the day. His clothing was in tatters, and from each side of his eyes, blood ran down the side of his face. And there at his side, his hand bloody all the way to the elbow, and in his grasp, he held Makeba's blade.

"Magical poisoning," whispered Leo.

"You little monster. Get away from us," said one of the men, his arm raised as he brought down the sword at Freedo. But in that same instant, Freedo was gone, and his sword struck the ground. Freedo appeared to the man's left, and with his foot planted into the ground so hard that it cracked under his weight, Freedo jumped back at the man with a slash toward his leg. The cut was so fast and deep that it severed the leg entirely. The man screamed, but only for a moment, as Freedo jumped in the air, planting Makeba's blade into his chest and riding him down to the ground as he did.

In sheer panic and fear, the last man took off, running into the trees. Ripping the blade free in a splatter of blood and a force so strong that it partially lifted the man back off the ground, Freedo raised off the man and dashed off, following behind the other. The whole event happened so fast that neither Leo nor the girls knew how to respond. By the time they came out of the brush and tried calling to Freedo, he was gone. The only thing that could be heard in the distance was a man screaming, which they all assumed was probably the man Freedo was chasing.

"Was that Freedo?" asked Makeba. "He looked..."

"That's what magical poisoning looks like. When you push yourself so hard that the magic inside begins to poison your body."

"Will he... will he be okay?"

"I'm not sure. I've only ever dealt with poisoning once before. Most mages don't do it. And it's even worse for boys since our bodies aren't as naturally receptive to magic as you girls are. I'm a healer, so that offsets it a bit, but Freedo..." Leo knelt down, placing his finger into the crease that Freedo's foot left when he sliced the dead man's arm off. "Makeba, stomp your foot as hard as you can next to this."

Confused, Makeba did as asked and stomped a foot next to Freedo's imprint. Her efforts barely affected the soil, and yet here was Freedo's effort, which was past the tip of Leo's finger inside of the ground.

"I can't imagine the strain on his body at the moment," said Leo, standing up. "We need this to stop. If Freedo keeps going at this pace, his body won't hold out much longer. And even if he does, he probably won't be the same Freedo, you know. Either way, this has to end."

Again, they took off, their speed a bit faster than before, as the rumbling grew louder. Ahead, they could hear the yelling and screaming. But the forest edge came sooner than expected, as a horde of trees had been turned over in front of them. It was blocking their path. But that wasn't as important as the image that was laid out in front of them.

It looked almost surreal. A crashed ship was lodged between several trees. Magical fire, rocks, and bolts of lightning flew through the air, crashing against magical shields and stone alike. Ahead of them, the ground was covered with darkness as the sun shined above. And there, in all the chaos, was Soulden, Miss Huffles, and Miss Webblebottom. Bodies lay throughout the field, some bent over fallen trees or spawned out over the ground, others twitching out of the surrounding blackness.

But ahead and closing in on Soulden's group, were the men and women who were along with Tannor. Behind them, was one of their ships. They seemed to be protecting it from arrant magic spells that were being cast by Soulden's group.

But, for just the few of Soulden's people that were left, there were dozens that seemed to come out of the ships.

"I don't get it. Why go through all this? I understand your power is unique, Isha, but is all of this really worth the price," said Leo as he continued to look around. "I don't see Mr. Higgins or Pavel anywhere. Maybe they're still on the other side of the island."

"Look," said Isha, pointing to an area in the trees behind the ship being protected. Other mages were casting fire into the trees, setting them ablaze as the shadowy creature Leo said was his brother dodged between them. They kept him away from the ship and isolated him in the trees.

"We need a plan. Soulden can't keep this up forever," said Leo, turning back to the girls. "I know this is asking a lot, but Isha, do you think you can make it to Soulden and give her some of your magic?"

"I can try, but... the last time I did, we both passed out."

" Look at her. She already looks to be at her limit and passing out after some type of grand spell is a lot better than just dying here like this. You girls keep each other safe."

"What about you? You're not coming with us?"

"I will go try to do something with my brother. Hopefully, he's not so driven by madness not to recognize me."

After a moment, they all agreed on the plan and, with a last hug, made their way out onto the battlefield with Leo providing shielding against any errant casting of magic that would have struck them. Instantly the girls were spotted by Tannor's group when they ran across the field, the nearest of them began giving chase after them. Luckily, they weren't casting magic, either because they couldn't or were instructed not to.

But as the enemies got closer, Leo stood to block their way as they raised their sword. But, before they could come within striking distance, a rock wall lifted from the ground, blocking their way, separating them from Leo and the girls.

Stunned, the girls looked over to Soulden but saw that it was Miss Huffles who had erected the wall of rock and was now waving for them to hurry over.

"Okay, okay," said Leo. "We have a window. " He turned them around, giving them a push on the back. "Now go!"

And with that, the girls took off towards Miss Huffles. The rock wall followed them as they came, leaving Leo out in the open as he ran back into the forest with several pursuers.

"What are you girls doing out here?" asked Miss Huffles as they arrived. "You should have stayed hidden. We were so afraid you were on board one of their ships."

"No. We escape them," said Jacinta. "But they are after Makeba and me."

"What?" shouted Soulden, just before taking a blast to her magical shield and firing back a bolt of lightning. "Didn't they come for Isha? Are they not after the power you have?"

"No! Tannor, when he almost caught us, he said he was after Makeba."

"Well, either way. I'll be damned if he gets anything. I'll wring his neck and throw him over the edge. Where did Leo go? Any assistance would be useful at the moment."

"He went to help his brother. He said it's the shadow thing that they've been fighting."

"Shadow thing? I don't..." Soulden shook her head. "None of that matters now. All that matters is that we save as many of us as we can and that we'll kill as many of them as we can."

"Leo told me to give you my power again if you needed it."

"Well, that's thoughtful of him. I don't suppose you've mastered that whole I-will-pass-out-for-days-after-giving-you-power thing, have you?"

"No, ma'am. But I did it for Leo earlier, and he got back up."

"And how long was he down?"

"A few minutes, maybe."

"I don't know if you've noticed, but a few minutes here might as well be the same as a few days, given that either outcome would more than likely lead to our demise and the capture of you girls. And Leo is a healer. His acceptance of magic is probably different from a regular mage."

"Now, now," said Miss Huffles. "It's not as if the girls had really much of a choice. But there are three of us. You've told me about what happened to you. If I were to—"

"No. We still haven't properly tested if there are any side effects for—"

"Oh. Is that the issue now? Fighting against our impending doom, and you worried about side effects?"

Soulden was silent.

"See, and there we have it. Can you tell me how this is done, sweety?" Miss Huffles turned to Isha.

"Ahh, well. I'm not sure. I... I think I just give you magic, and you use it."

"Seems simple enough. What say you give me a moment to come up with a spell?"

"Whatever spell you cast, just know that it's going to be amplified," shouted Soulden. "But you're probably only going to get the one before you lose consciousness."

"Well, I suppose I should come up with something particularly nasty then, shouldn't I?"

"Allow me to go first, ladies," said Miss Webblebottom. "I have something particularly interesting I wish to try. Soulden, you said that shield of yours turned solid as crystal when Isha touched you, correct?"

"Yes, but I was barely able to control that much power for half a minute."

"Then, let us perform a test, shall we? Let's see what happens if I cast an illusion and shape my shielding around it."

"Can you do that?" asked Isha.

"I've toyed with the idea but found that I wasn't strong enough to hold on to both spells in conjunction. But I see no better time than now to try."

"If you're going to do something, do it fast. This is becoming taxing."

"Right. Let us get this started, shall we?" said Miss Webblebottom, as she raised her hands in front of her, palms facing upward. Then, as she closed her eyes, Isha watched as two sparks of light appeared above her fingers. After that, the light shifted and morphed until it finally took the shape of small animals. They looked like cats—they were black and had long tails. Each one was the size of a finger. "Okay, Isha, if you would be so kind."

Isha stepped in behind Miss Webblebottom, placing her hands up to reach her shoulder blades.

"Okay. I'm going to start now," said Isha as she went inside herself to find the power.

"Oh, and do remember to clench your teeth," said Soulden looking back with a smirk. "The pain really is otherworldly."

"What pa—" said Miss Webblebottom before her body locked in place, and she clenched her teeth. She inhaled as much as she could, furrowing her brows as the wrinkles appeared on her face. She shook, trying to focus on where to distribute the massive amounts of power flowing into her system.

The small cats leaped off her hands to the ground while growing in size. Then, bigger and bigger still until their heads were the size of Isha's body, they clawed at the ground. Their paws vanished into the dirt. Miss Webblebottom shook, twitching her neck as she redoubled her efforts. A slight glow began to flow over the large black cats, and once again, they tried pawing at the ground. But this time, their claws dug into the soil beneath them. And with a smile from Miss Webblebottom, there came a large roar from the cats.

"You always were one for the theatrical," said Soulden, a smirk across her lips as she focused on shielding them all while Miss Huffless ripped huge boulders from the ground in front of them and launched them into the air. The boulders crashed into the shields of their enemies, the dust piling down around them.

The two overgrown back cats took off into the battlefield. Isha couldn't hear them move, and they seemed to float more than run. Those they were heading toward seemed to think that they were just illusions and didn't bother trying to move out of the way. That mistake cost them dearly, as soon, men and women were tossed into the air, flung out high from the flailing of the imaginary beasts.

Their impact on those that were unprotected was vicious. A swipe of their claws ripping into the flesh of those that dared get in their way. The creatures caused such a disturbance that every nearby mage began firing blasts of energy at them. Large targets that they were, they weren't hard to miss. The blast tore into and sometimes through the shields surrounding the fictional creatures.

Isha watched how the creatures went after with other mages' shields. Essentially, it was just two shields clashing against each other, but since the animals were being boosted by Isha's power, their opponent's shield's shattered from around their bodies, like the breaking of glass that would eventually turn into sparkly dust before the bloodshed.

But not even a minute into the carnage, one of the cats tried for a swipe at an enemy, and his hand passed right through them, the image of its paw distorting from the contact.

Isha couldn't see Miss Webblebottoms face, but she could feel her control of the power waning. The spurts of energy she took matched the trembling of her body. And then it happened. The shield around one of the creatures burst after taking one last blast of magic. And then, as if in a ripple effect, so too did the shield around the other giant cat. Then, an instant later, the image of the feline shifted, vanishing into the air.

Miss Wobblebottom collapsed to her knees, falling into Miss Huffles' arms, who was waiting to catch her. The back of her robes burned away, revealing the disfigured flesh beneath.

"You weren't making light of that power of hers. It truly is a boon to those that would wish to abuse it," said Miss Huffles as she laid Miss Webblebottom down, then steeling her own resolve. "Okay. I suppose I'm next. I can't let Miss Webblebottom's effort outdo my own, now can—"

Suddenly a bolt of lightning appeared out of thin air, striking Miss Huffles on the side of her face, sending her sliding across the ground. Soulden, in shock, turned toward the blast only to have her hand freeze in the air.

"Oh no. No more of that" came the voice of Tannor. Then slowly, the area around Soulden began to whirl as an image appeared in front of her with a blade to her neck. There, with a bleeding wound on his neck and one eye shut, Tannor appeared. "I think we've had enough surprises for one day. Don't you agree?"

Isha stared up at the man who once visited their home as a friend alongside Mr. Caudbell. But now, behind her eyes was contempt and hatred.

"This was supposed to be so easy. We cause a distraction at the school and then swoop in and take those Sakari and maybe their friend there for good measure, and no one would have gotten hurt."

"You... you disgust me," said Soulden. "How dare you do this... to children... to this school. "

"I did nothing. This is all your doing. All you needed to do is sit back and hand over the girls. But, instead, you blow ships out of the sky and stand in the way of progression. Those girls hold the key to a new age, and you keep them locked away, learning basic magic meant for mages far below their means."

"What do you mean? Why you attack us?" asked Makeba, stepping forward.

"Oh no, she wouldn't tell you. Of course not. Why would she? But no matter, you are the key to it all. You won't be a failed experiment like the last one. But first, let's clear the board of any last obstacles," said Tannor before drawing back and plunging his blade into Soulden's stomach. Then, placing his to her face as she gasped, he let loose a lightning bolt into her face that sent her sliding across the ground.

"No!" screamed Isha as she tried catching Soulden as she fell.

"Take them," said Tannor as a dozen men appeared, grabbed the girls by the arms, and began dragging them back towards the ship. "Do not worry. The three of you will usher in a new... a new..." Tannor paused, extending out his hands for his men to stop. "No. Something's wrong. What happened to the flames that were keeping the creature at—"

As if called by his words, a dark shadow began to creep over the ship, consuming the side of it as the creaking of its lumber sounded throughout the field. The glass that housed the liquid surrounding the ship began to crack under the pressure before finally bursting. The red liquid inside spilled out as the tip of the ship teetered before smashing into the ground.

And then came the creature itself. Its red eyes loomed over that side of the ship, raising itself higher as it peered down at them. Then, out of the shadowy creature, a body dropped. It banged off the ship's side before falling and landing on the ground. The mangled body was crushed on one side as if it had been gnawed on by a beast.

With a scream of fear, the other mages began fire blasts of all kinds of magical attacks at the creature.

"No!" yelled Tannor as the creature began dodging the attacks. "Don't damage the ship." But it was too late. Fear and panic had taken over those around him. The creature dodged the attack, shifting low onto the ship's deck and then behind it. Blasts of energy exploded against the hull. Chunks of wood exploded into the air as the creature landed on the ground and began going after the mages, dodging the debris.

As it weaved inside the area of enemies, it picked them up and slung them into the air before slamming them back down. The black mist over the ground began growing thicker the closer the creature came toward them, spiraling around a group of enemies and, in their confusion of trying to hit it, they hit each other with spells.

"Stop! Don't you see what he is doing? He's trying to—"

As if attracted by Tannor's words, the creature froze, which was just enough time for it to take several bolts of energy from several mages that sent it rolling across the ground. Its shadowy claws gripped into the soil, slowing it down as it stared over at them. It felt as if it was focusing on Isha, the same way its eyes locked in on hers in the house beforehand. And then, its attention turned to Tannor. And with that, the creature took off again, twisting and turning through the battlefield, leaving a black mist wherever he went, zigzagging through enemies.

"Stay away from me!" screamed Tannor as he outstretched his finger, sending out a torrent of magical lighting that arched across the ground at the shadowy creature. His attack struck true into the black mist but did little to stop the advance of Leo's supposed brother as he reached Tannor and began spiraling around him, lifting him into the air.

From below, Isha could see the creature trying to attack him, but every attack was being repelled by a shield. The cloud of darkness grew thicker as, now, Isha could only catch glimpses of Tannor inside of it every time he would cast a magical bolt of light inside the black cloud. Then the other mages joined in from below, firing their own blazes of fire and lighting up into the blackness. Even the mages who held Jacinta and Makeba were now holding them with one hand and firing blasts with the other.

Now's your chance, you stupid girl. Feed it. Came the voice of Grettaline into Isha's mind. *Now while they are distracted. Feed the shadows.*

With the shadow spiral in front of her, Isha turned around, looking at her sisters, who both were struggling within the grasp of the men trying to free themselves. The world seemed to be moving in slow motion. The anguish and fear on their faces allowed her to come to the realization that anything would be better than allowing what was going on to continue. So, with a somber mind, she turned back to the spinning shadows in front of her and stepped inside.

The vortex spun around her, nipping at her hair. She then stretched her hand, trying to grab hold of something, but the darkness just flowed between her fingers. She wasn't able to find a point with which to latch onto.

Close your eyes, said Grettaline. *He's there. You need not touch this one to give out the power. Just release it into the void, and he will respond. He will know the feeling.*

Trusting her, Isha just followed the will of Grettaline. It was as if she was giving over control of herself and the power inside of her. The world became quiet. Instead of forcing the magic out through her hands into the hand, she completely gave in to the magic itself, feeling it envelop her whole body. Feeling it escape from the flesh of her body, from the top of her head to the tops of her toes, it released from her, a heat so complete that it burned away the clothing around her in an instant, leaving only the garb that Soulden had given her. And even that started to glow shades of different colors as it tried adjusting to the force of her magic.

Isha could feel it. Beyond the pounding of her chest, something felt right. Something felt complete. The magic inside of her poured out freely. No more trying to manage it. No more dripping strands of magic trying to direct them when she wanted. Just acceptance and, in return, being accepted. It felt freeing. She felt complete, but more than that, she felt safe, safer than she'd felt in a long time. A moment she embraced for as long as a moment would last her.

But a moment was all she received as with the freedom of releasing the power within her was followed by screams. The horrible screams seemed to drill into her ears, cutting through the small amount of serenity that she had found. But opening her eyes, there was nothing to be seen, only blackness.

The world itself seemed to be consumed by a void of spinning blackness that spiraled around her as if she were in a cage of it. She looked up but couldn't even see the sky. Where it was just blue before now, it was black. And then she saw it: a sparkle of blueness, like a veil that began to pierce the blackness. At first, it was small, a blue line that spiraled through the dark void, glowing ever so slightly. But then came the thunder, flashes of light in the dark sky— more of it than she had heard from the battle before.

And as the thundering sounded through the sky, so did the blue strands that began to take over the blackness. One of the blue strands fell, landing on her cheek. Reaching up, she plucked it from her skin. It was water, a crystalline blue droplet that sparkled over her finger. It was beautiful, and then that beauty came pouring down over her and the land around them. Thousands of crystalline raindrops in the wind, twisting down and soaking into the soil at her feet. The blue water washed away the blood and dirt from her face as it seeped into her clothing.

But those droplets that lingered on her skin for too long turned into a blue smoke that lingered around her body before being sucked into the force of everything around her.

"Isha?" Came the voice of Leo, calling out into the blackness, "Isha, are you there?"

"I'm here," screamed Isha. "I'm here." Over and over, she repeated as she reached out a hand. And then, out of the shadows appeared Leo, and with him, both Makeba and Jacinta.

"Oh, thank goodness you're safe," he said as he knelt to hug her. But she stepped back, "No, don't. I'll burn you again."

"Yes, yes, right. I'm just... I'm just happy you're all alright," he looked around, unable to see more than a few feet in front of him. "Where's Soulden? Your sister said she was stabbed."

"Ahead," said Jacinta, both her and Makeba's eyes glowing golden as they looked around at a world that neither Isha nor Leo could see. "This way, sister, follow. No, get lost."

Leo looked around in amazement. "Is this one of Miss Webblebottom's illusions, I can't imagine my brother could create so much."

"No, I'm giving him my power, I think. It's weird. It's like he just is able to take it without me touching him. Maybe I am touching him," said Isha, sticking out her hand and allowing the shadows to wash over her fingers. "I think all of this is him."

"Your power, your'e giving it to him now?"

"I think so. That's why... That's why I didn't want you to—" Isha's heart sunk into her chest as out of the shadows, they found Soulden gasping for breath on the ground, the side of her face covered with mud as her blood-stained hands clutched at her side.

They all rushed to her, with Leo dropping to his knees, instantly channeling his healing magic into the wound.

Soulden twitched in his arms, coughing up blood.

"Miss Huffles, is she... is she... okay?"

"I don't see her," said Leo. "But worry about yourself for now. You've lost a lot of blood." He turned towards Isha. "I'm going to need your help here. Burn me all you like, but she needs healing now."

Nodding, Isha knew he was right. She stepped in behind him, placing her hand on his back the same as she had done before. Almost instantly, his clothes burned away, exposing the flesh beneath. Closing her eyes, she found the power inside of her, the way it seemed to just be taken from her, but she could control it. She could redirect it as she had done before, and that was just what she did, guiding the power back into her hands, pushing as much as she needed back into Leo.

The effect of the environment around them was almost instant. The darkness around them began fading away, going from a thick blackness to a dull gray. It was changing and appeared as if a dull fog had settled around them. Even the crystalline blue rain now turned into a clear liquid, but it continued to pour, and the sound of thunder still pierced the sky.

"Will Soulden be alright?" asked Jacinta, looking worried.

"I think so, must stop... bleeding," said Leo, his voice trembling as Isha pushed more power into him.

"This ends now," came the voice of Tannor, and out of the grayish blue fog, he emerged, his body rippling through the mist as he appeared beside Isha. "I should have done this in the beginning. With you out of the way, none of this would have happened."

Isha's eyes went wide as she turned to see Tannor with his sword raised above her head. Plunging it downward, Isha watched as it passed her and went straight into the back of Leo's neck. The blade went clean through to the other side, with spurts of blood landing on Soulden's face.

Makeba and Jacinta both screamed as they rushed at the man. But he was so fast. He spun around, kicking Jacinta in the ribs so hard that it sent her tumbling over the ground deep into the gray fog. Isha screamed, but only for a moment, as she felt a fist plunge itself into her stomach so hard that she doubled over.

"Come here," said Tannor as he grabbed hold of Makeba's arm. "You are coming with me." She struggled in his grip, trying to punch and kick at him. Each of her blows landed against his shielding, showing that she was even using magic strength, but it was of no use. He was just so much stronger than she was. A fact that was proven as he struck her in the face. One, then twice, then again, to the point where the fighting quickly left her body as it went limp. "No more games, no more tricks."

Isha doubled over on the ground, struggling to move as she reached out for Makeba, and her sister reached out for her. But nothing could be done as Tannor and Makeba began to fade into the gray fog around them.

Then, once almost out of reach, a shadow appeared to the side of them, its small frame in the air and through the fog pierced a blade. Its curved design was unmistakable as Freedo burst out, slashing Tannor across the back.

He released Makeba as he yelled in pain, then shot a lightning bolt into the fog, but Freedo had vanished again.

"You insolent little brats. Just constantly getting— Arghhh!" he screamed as Freedo dashed in, slicing the back of his leg, making him drop to one knee. "Damn you." He threw out his arm as a torrent of fire lit up the area around him. But. extending his arm was a mistake as Freedo dived into the flame. His shield crumbled around him, the intense heat searing the flesh of his face. But the boy seemed to be driven mad, and none of it seemed to stop him. Instead, he swung Makeba's blade as hard as he could, and a second later, Tannor's right arm fell to the muddy ground by his knees.

Blood spurted out of his arm as Tannor gave a ghastly scream. But it all fell on deaf ears as Freedo appeared out of the fog again to stand again. The madness seemed to completely take him over as he raised up the blade.

And then the killing blow came, but not on Tannor. As Freedo's hand froze down into the air, he looked down to see a blade sticking out of his chest. Freedo's body convulsed, twitching as blood spurted out of his mouth before he dropped to his knees and fell face down into the mud. Behind him were two men holding blades, their faces were bloody, and their clothing was in tatters. They stepped forward, lifting Tannor to his feet.

"Sir, we have to leave while that shadow creature is gone," said the man turning around to lead Tannor back off into the fog.

"Sa...kari... can't leave... without her," said Tannor meekly as he was being dragged off.

One of the men holding up Tannor released him and turned back around, limping his way back toward Makeba, who was crawling her way towards Freedo. He grabbed her by the hair, lifting her up as she moaned. But he quickly released her as Freedo's body flailed on the ground, the blade in his hands swiping at the man's legs. The man stumbled back, fear in his eyes at the boy moaning and worming on the ground in front of him. He then shook his head and struggled to get back to his feet before disappearing back into the fog.

Makeba crawled over toward Freedo in a daze as he twitched uncontrollably. Her mouth agape, one swollen eye shut, and mud caked to the side of her face, she placed her head against his. Seeing her, looking at her face, seemed to bring him something of a peaceful presence as the twitching of his body started to calm down. Forcing herself to sit up, Makeba took Freedo's head into her lap. And finally, as his body grew still, he managed to give him something of a smile before finally closing his eyes.

Makeba's mouth opened as tears rolled down her cheeks, but no sound escaped from her lips. Only the face of loss, of a pain that tore into her so deeply that words couldn't be formed to express it. Leaning down, she once again placed her head against his, gripping at the torn clothing across his chest.

Then slowly, something between them began to glow a light shade of purple.

Isha couldn't help but stare at her sister as the purple light appeared around her. In the midst of the purple light came a white light against her back. It started out small and then grew brighter and brighter until Isha felt it. A tug that resonated inside of her, and it was growing stronger. A force that pulled at the magic inside of her.

But this time, Isha wasn't pulling on the magic. It was being drawn out of her. Much the same as it had been with the shadow creature Leo called his brother. Her sister was consuming so much of it. The effect of which seemed to spread out the purplish light over the ground and into the fog changing its color to match.

The ground began to quake. And not just a small shake, but something massive was happening. So much so that it felt as if the entire island was breaking apart. And right in front of her, Isha watched as a small root emerged from the ground. It glowed purple, and there it began to worm its way through the soil, growing larger and large by the second. And then another sprouted up and then another until the land around her began twisting and turning as it began to be reshaped by the roots.

The moving land began swallowing up the bodies around her. Even Isha herself was not immune as a root sprouted up under her lifting her into the air. The roots lifted her so high that she could see over the fog. It stretched out on the entire island. The trees that loomed over the mist had all started glowing purple as they began toppling over one another.

But something was happening to the trees on the outer edge.

Out of the fog appeared a single ship, Soulden's. It was severely damaged, as evident by the way it lurched in the sky, its front end drooping lower than the rest. Tannor was escaping with whatever crew was left to leave with him. His plans were completely ruined as both the Sakari's were still on the island. Makeba's glow was still present in the fog, and Jacinta, while unseen, was undoubtedly somewhere below, hopefully not lost in the ever-growing roots.

No, thought Isha, as a clearing in the fog appeared. The trees were tumbling over. It was the island itself. It really was falling apart. But just that, the trees of the island seemed to be unraveling. The bark peeling away as if being sliced as large pieces of wood began warming and being into the air.

The houses near the edge started falling as the ground gave way. The large chains that connected the island to the school had long since been released as Isha could now see the island, the schoolhouse floating farther and farther away.

The roots now had grown so big that they were destroying the island itself. The trees that had unwoven were floating into the air circling the area as large pieces of wood. As their spiral sped up and tightened the wood began latching on to itself as if forming a cocoon. And there at the center of it all was Makeba's purple glow as the roots rose around them, enveloping both her a Freedo.

Isha wanted to call out to her, but the most she could manage was a moan. She looked around for anyone else, but the fog was too thick. All she could hear were the roots that made their way above, the sound they made as they tore into the ground below.

But then the world moved around her once more, and the root that Isha was laid across shifted. She could feel herself slipping. With what little strength she had left tried to grip the root as it twisted, but to no avail. She slid off the surface, falling to the roots below. But she didn't hit any of the roots on the way down. Instead, she fell past them toward the ground. But there was no ground. She passed through the soil, getting glimpses as the giant roots around her twisted and turned, knocking free massive clumps of soil and sending them falling to the world below, and that was precisely where she was headed.

Faster, she was falling faster than she had ever fell. The wind against her body and her own exhaustion made it feel as if she was paralyzed. And the pressure against her chest was making it hard to breathe. As she continued her descent, the world started to grow blurry, and just before it faded away, her world went black.

CHAPTER 43

"Let's hurry," said Oscar as he passed over the hill on horseback, riding beside Dessi and Jacob with a dozen men behind them.

"There it is," said Jacob, pointing toward the sky at the floating school. "There seem to be quite a few ships around."

"Dammit, we're too late," said Oscar, whipping the reins of his horse. "Where's that damned ship? If they make off with those girls, who knows where they will end up."

"Rebby said he could procure a ship, but the nearest port city was a day away. Who knows if we would get—"

"Ah, you both might want to look at the sky again," said Dessi. "Something is happening up there."

They all watched the blue sky slowly begin to turn black as darkness from the island behind the school began pouring out. Then, it started stretching over the sky as lightning began to crackle.

"What in the Goddess is happening up there?" said Jacob.

"A magical storm," said Oscar.

"A what?" said Jacob.

"A magical storm. It's what happens when too much magical power is poured out in a small area."

"Then why have I never seen or heard of one before? I've been in a lot of battles with mages of the field," said Jacob.

"Your average skirmish isn't enough to cause it. But if you ever found one queen battling another, then you'd probably get something like this. The battlefields during the shadow king's reign were littered with them. Miles of land soaked in blood and darkness."

"Well, shadow king or not. It's starting to look pretty dark," said Dessi as she looked at the small island above them. A torrent of darkness began spinning over it. "And you think Isha is inside of that thing?"

"When has she ever not found herself in the heart of trouble?" asked Oscar, and they arrived under the island's shadow. "And unless there's two Queens fighting up there, then my guess is that she has something to do with this."

As the darkness continued to spawn upward, it reached across the sky. Then came the rain, shiny blue soft crystals that poured down from above that soaked into their clothing and over the ground.

"Is this also part of that magic storm you were talking about? Are they going to bring the sky down on us?" asked Jacob as he took his cloak, covering himself and Dessi.

"No," said Oscar as he reached forward, letting the blue rain fall and pool into his hand. "This... this would be something new." He then looked over to Gregga, who was just standing in the rain, quietly looking up into the sky. The blue rains streaked down her face, but she did not move or answer. She seemed to just be waiting.

It seemed as if the entire world was moving in slow

motion, but in truth, only a few minutes had passed as they all stared up into the sky. First, the rain stopped, and then the blackness that had once filled almost half the sky faded, leaving a gray mist over the skyward island. The gigantic chains that shackled the two land masses together broke. The island itself started to break apart. Chunks from the outer edges began breaking apart, and some type of brown tentacles appeared to be bursting forth from it, wrapping themselves around the gigantic red crystal at the bottom.

Pieces of land, large enough to rival a house, struck the ground ahead of them. The force of which was so strong that they could feel the force in their feet from half a mile away. Small hills of debris scattered across the land as more and more pieces hit the ground. Trees fell from the sky, houses fell. People fell, their bodies flailing in the air as they descended towards their impending doom. It was terrible to watch and even more horrifying when they saw the small people mixed in with the large ones: children falling to their deaths.

"Let's go," said Oscar as he once snapped the reins of his horse. "It will do us no good to sit here in fear of what could be. Best to confront it and pray to the goddess that they aren't ours while on the way."

It was a horrible feeling. Speeding toward the inevitable death of dozens, knowing that by the time you reached any of them, it would almost certainly be too late to do anything, whether they died from impact or were buried under a mountain of soil. But they pushed forward, their horse's hooves sinking into the ground. As they grew closer, most of the large land mast had fallen away, but out of what was left, something else was sprouting upwards toward the sky.

And this thing would have captured all their attention if not something equally odd descended out of what was left of the island in the sky. It looked like a black cloud, and it dove toward the surface. But on the way down, it enveloped one of the smaller human-looking figures before its black mass began to expand, bigger and bigger, until wings of black smoke burst out of its sides. It swirled around in the air before slowly descending to the ground, landing on top of a mound of soil amidst the rubble of uprooted trees, shattered houses, and broken bodies.

It stood there, the blackness pouring out of it, covering the land around it more and more with every second it remained.

By the time Oscar and his group arrived, a black mist had completely settled over the ground around them. The horses whinnied and reared up, refusing to go further.

"What is that?" Jacob asked as they all stared at the creature.

"It doesn't matter, look what it has," said Oscar, nodding to the image of Isha barely visible beneath the creature. She and the creature were looking at each other, neither one paying attention to the mercenary group ahead of them.

Oscar dismounted his horse, landing on the shadow-covered ground. "Stay here, I'll—" His words cut off as Gregga walked past him holding a blade in her hand. "Wait, Gregga."

"Why? It has my daughter."

"Has is a strong word," said Oscar stepping up beside her. "Look closer. She doesn't seem to be in danger."

Gregga stared up ahead at Isha on the smoke covered hill. "Still. I will see her. My other daughters. I will ask questions."

"Then let's go. But drop thew blade. I don't think it will be needed."

"But Father," said Jacob. "We don't even know what that is."

"All the more reason not to provoke it with numbers or weapons. Now stay here. We'll be fine," said Oscar before turning to Gregga. "Shall we?"

They both headed up the hill with Gregga slowing herself for Oscar as he took his time making his way up to Isha and the creature. The ground was soft and unstable as they made his way upward with Oscar placing his hand on his knee for leverage.

"You... you intend to make this old man come all the way up there, don't you?" He got no answer from Isha or the creature. "Of course, you do." After a few more steps, Oscar felt like it was getting harder to walk, as if the shadows around his feet were growing thicker. Soon he felt as if he were wading through mud. "You could at least—" said Oscar as he looked around and found a shadow of the creature speeding towards him. Isha raised her hand, and the tendril stopped right before Oscar's face, but the old man seemed more bothered by the thickness of the shadows at his feet than the one before his face.

"Go away," said Isha.

"No, daughter," said Gregga. "Not until I know you are safe. What is that shadow around you."

"This is my friend," said Isha. "Go away and you will not be hurt."

"Oh... I think not," said Oscar, starting to lose breath as he and Gregga walked past the shadowy tendril on his way up to where Isha and the creature stood. "I suppose it's time for me to be taking you home." After reaching the summit, he looked to the shadowy creature. "And you, I'll be asking you to take your leave now. You've done your job."

"Do you wish to die?" asked Isha. "What right do you—"

"I almost died climbing up this damnable mountain we're standing on. I'm old and tired and being afraid of shadows won't do me no good. If you wish to kill us, then be done with it. But I'd imagine that wouldn't do either of us any good. And my right is that that little girl's body that you're in belongs to me. She's under my protection."

Isha laughed, "Protection? Almost raped by some brute in some backwoods army to falling from the sky to her demise. I dare say that your protection is lacking at best."

"She is right," said Gregga. "Molan was your man."

"I'm very much aware of that," said Oscar,

"Tell me, daughter. This shadow thing. Do you control it. Is it a magic of yours," said Gregga, reaching out a hand towards the creature only to it flow through it, her fingers dragging along small traces of shadow as it passed.

"The girl needed training. I saw to it that she received it."

"You call our daughter 'the girl' as if she is not before us," said Gregga, watching the last traces of shadow drift from her fingers.

"That's because that is our daughter's body," looking down at Isha. "But she's not the one speaking now, is she."

"I am who I need to be," said Isha.

"Of course, you are," said Oscar, but for the safety of my daughter, I chose the safest place I could, considering the circumstances." Oscar turned, noticing a flying ship heading toward them. "Or do you believe going about the countryside with your shadow friend here and being hunted by every power-hungry mage in the five kingdoms is a better option?"

"You try to force me into thinking I don't have a choice," said Isha.

"From the moment you saw me, you didn't have a choice. If you did, then the moment you saw me, you'd have let your little shadow friend here do me in. So, seeing that you didn't, I'm guessing that the person who that body belongs to isn't letting you. So, even if you don't wanna come along, I dare say that soon, you won't even have a choice in the matter."

Isha's eyes narrowed. "You should be careful. Not everything will always go your way."

"Maybe not. But today it will."

"If this is not our daughter," said Gregga, twisting her head as if examining her daughter in a new light. "Then where are Makeba and Jacinta." She looked over the shadowy hill. "And you will not say they are in this mess."

Isha twitched, her mouth twisting as her eyes began to flutter. "Ahhh, yes. Those accursed leeches that you've saddled me with. They're alive... somehow." She tilted her head upward. "They're up there. Beaten but still breathing."

Gregga looked up the sky with narrowed eyes as a frown came over her face. She then turned to Oscar. "You will look after this one till I return." And without a response she turned around, and headed back down the shadowy hill, her movement hasten by what Oscar assumed was motherly concern.

"You companion seems to have abandoned you. Do you answer to her?"

Oscar turned back to his daughter with a smirk. "A mutual understanding. One that benefits us both. Now, I suspect that it's time for us to be on our way. There will be plans that will need to be put in place before all is settled here."

Isha stared at Oscar for a moment before turning to the shadowy creature. "He is right. You should go. Hide if you need, but it isn't safe for us."

Then it was the creature's turn to turn to Oscar, the black covering the ground retracting inward and pooling around the old man. The shadows rose up, almost constricting around him, but then in an instant, they leaped from Oscar back into the creature. The creature hovered over the ground for only a moment before it took off, gliding over the rubble, down into the countryside before disappearing into some nearby trees. Above it, was the same ship from earlier, lifting off and heading upward.

"Now, let's head back. We should leave here before others show up."

"Old man. You appear here with demands and do not deem it necessary even to ask my name."

"You're my daughter. As long as you inhabit that body, that fact won't change. If you wish to be your own person, then leave her. But I imagine if that were possible, you would not be here before me now."

"Fine," said Isha with a smirk as she stepped forward,

looking up at him and placing a finger against his stomach. "Then what now, *papa*," the word papa said with as much irony as humor in her tone. "It's only a matter of time before the other takes back control. What until then?"

"Same as always. You make a mess, and I clean it up," he said as he turned around and began walking back down the hill. Except this time, he couldn't help but notice the broken bodies around him. Dozens of corpses littered the surrounding area, with shadowy creatures' presence now removed, was exposed for all to see. Some were half-buried, others impaled by wood or simply torn in half.

None of which seemed to bother the little girl beside him as she grabbed ahold of his hand and joined him in his descent.

Below there, an anxious-looking Dessi left her horse and came running over to them.

"And what will you tell them?"

"Nothing. You will play the part until the other one returns. They already have more than enough to think about."

"And if I don't decide to... play along."

"Well, I imagine this will get very difficult for you. Tell me, have you ever eaten green stew before? I've heard it does terrible things to the stomach."

"Oh, sweet baby. Are you okay," said Dessi as she knelt, giving Isha a hug.

"Ahhh. Yes, I'm... I'm okay."

"The bodies," said Jacob as Oscar passed him. "What do you want to do with them? The adults look bad, but the..."

"Bury the adults. Any children you find, take their bodies or what's left of them and have them wrapped. No parent should have to wonder whether their child is alive or not. We'll take them to the city."

"Rebby came with a ship, but Gregga, she took it and—" Jacob's eyes went wide as he looked up into the sky, not knowing what to say.

"It's her right. Let her go to her babies. I'll deal with the fallout when it comes."

"No, father. Look up."

Oscar looked at his son in confusion before finally looking toward the sky, and even he found himself at a loss for words. Because where there had once been a floating island, there now sat a giant tree. It was the size of a mountain, its roots wrapping around the vast red crystal at the bottom and its branches reaching so high that they seemed to pierce the clouds.

CHAPTER 44

Victor lay chained to the wall in the Holy Chapel's dungeon. Nearby, he could hear the jingle of the chains of the other capture. The tall man who he had only met once briefly before, was in a sickly manner. Vivid in his mind was the feeling of jamming a crystal deep into his neck, thinking to ensure his death. Only to then watch as he rose again, feeding off the power of the red crystals.

But now, according to them, he was sickly in a different way. No longer able to speak common words, instead just mumbling through the cloth gag over his mouth.

How long have I been here now? Two—three days? Goddess, my arms hu-- He managed a slight chuckle. *I suppose this is the best and yet the worst time to call out to the goddess. Here I am in her most prestigious temple, locked up by her most reverent followers.*

I wonder if Frenka and Silk are okay? I miss them. Their bickering, that stubbornness. It's not as bad as I thought it would be. He chuckled again. *But I guess, given my current situation, anything would be 'not bad' by comparison.*

I wonder if I will be something of a political prisoner. I can't imagine they would just...

Through the silent shadows, from far away, Victor heard the sound of a door opening.

The water carrier is back. That's good... I was starting to become thirsty again.

Then came the sound of another door opening, and he could see the flicker of a flame through the shadows of a silhouetted doorway as three people emerged from it. From outside of the barred way, they unlocked the cell door, its keys jingling as they fiddled with the lock, one key after another. Then the cell swung open, squeaking on its metal hinges in the cold darkness as the three slowly made their way forward.

Three of them. No water bucket? Interrogation maybe? Or perhaps moving me or coming for him.

"That's him," said a familiar voice of a young man through the night.

Victor blinked, squinting his eyes from the stinging light of the torch as they approached.

"Seems a bit rough. How long did you say he was down here?" said the familiar voice.

"It's been three days since he entered," came another familiar voice. It was the voice of Muslin.

"I thought I ordered you to keep him safe."

"This place, too many moving parts. Figure it's best to wait. So I did. Good, I did. You come soon and find me. And now we are both here."

"Fine. Unshackle him," said the young man as he leaned out, cupping Victor's chin in his hand. "Hello there, again."

Victor blinked at the sight of Kenkel, the young man who had led him into the temple.

"Yo...... u."

"Yes, me. We've come to free you," Kenkel before pulling out two vials. He popped the cork on one. "This is for those arms of yours. They're going to be hurting soon. This will stop the pain" He placed the vial of liquid to Victor's lips turning it upward. "Drink."

Skeptical but thirsty, Victor drank from the vial. The liquid that flowed into his mouth tasted bitter as there were some harder chunks in the vial, which made it hard to swallow. He coughed afterward as he could feel the chucks slowly making their way down his throat.

"Good now, this," said Kenkel, placing the other uncorked vial to his lips. The smell of a sweet wine filled his nose as his body instantly reached, gulping it down. He felt his body soon grow hot as his wrists were freed and his arms went limp.

"Why so much trouble to save man? To have my shadow, and then come here?"

"Do I ask questions about your toys?" replied Kenkel as he knelt down with the third person that accompanied them. "I think he will be of use. All men have their uses."

"Of use to you? Or to us?"

"Why not both? There is no rule that says my fun can't serve us as well."

"Selfish. Grennok be angry."

"Maybe, but that's something to be dealt with later if need be. Focus on the saving part now, if you would be so kind."

"You the boss lady."

Tired and barely keeping up with their words, Victor allowed him to be hoisted up and supported on their shoulders.

"What about the other one? He growls with mouth bound."

"Up to you. Do you wish to have a new pet?"

"No. Has angry eyes. Not worth trouble."

"Then leave him. I have what I came for."

The world kept going in and out as Victor compelled himself forward, step by step. The sound of their muffled chatter gave him something to try and latch onto as he tried to remain lucid.

They made their way to the stairs and upwards to the door leading into the chapel. There, he saw a guard slouched in his chair, his sword tip on the floor, and hilt over his shoulder. Past him, through the corridor, they made their way into the main hall of the second building, where Victor, even through a sleepy consciousness, found himself blinking with disbelief.

Blood and bodies were scattered through the hall. Their white robes were stained with crimson as their lifeless faces lay against the cold marble of the flooring. Kenkel led them through the area, not even giving his former companions a second glance as he made his way over the bodies.

Up the steps, opening the door to the library, Victor was escorted inside only for him to see more dead clergy members, their bodies slumped over the tables and chairs. The only living people were up ahead, by a wall. Two women stood dressed in the same clergy white robes.

On his way toward the two, Victor happened to glance down at one of the dead bodies, and there he saw the face of Kenkel.

Wait... wait... no, not... But his mind was in a daze. He couldn't figure out why or how the person leading him out and the dead person on the floor had the same face. Sure, he had been tired, but he wasn't this far gone before. Then it hit him. *What... wha... drink...*

One of the two ahead pressed their arm against the wall, and Victor saw a hit of magic before the wall shifted, exposing a room. It was wooden—much different from the marble flooring before. There were bounds of hay stacked up against the walls. Ahead Victor could hear the sounds of the city.

Turning the corner, Victor found himself inside a stable. And there ahead, he saw a hay-filled wagon led by two horses, assisted by the two that held him up, he slid into the wagon.

"Where... where?" were the only words that he could manage as he was lifted and pulled forward onto the hay by the woman and Kenkel who had climbed up into the front of the wagon.

"Someplace safer than that," said the boy as he placed his hands over Victor's eyes. "We shall wake you when we are far away from here."

And just like that, the world went dark. From the darkness of a cave to the darkness of his own mind. His final thoughts were a jumbled mess of what events had just transpired.

CHAPTER 45

Victor awoke, staring up at a ceiling of wooden boards. Below him, was the soft feel of a bed and pillow under his head. He frowned, constricting his face as he closed his eyes, shielding them from the candlelight in the room. By the sounds of the stretching lumbar, he knew that he was on a ship. Whether it was in the air or on the sea, he couldn't tell. He moaned as he shifted his weight a bit in bed. His back was sore, his arms felt dull, and the skin around his wrists was still chaffed from the shackles.

Shackles… shackles. He thought as it all started coming back to him. The events in the holy city. His capture and then imprisonment. He opened his eyes, sitting up quickly in bed. Which was a mistake. His body rejected the action as he became lightheaded, and the world began to spin. Unable to find any balance, he leaned against the cabin wall and once again closed his eyes. And that was when he heard

608

a door open.

"Ah, you're awake," said the voice of a young man. "I was wondering how long you would be out for. Here, I brought you some water," he said as he extended a flagon of water toward him.

Victor opened his eyes, spotting the flagon as his eyes narrowed because of the light. After a few seconds to focus, he Kenkel's face staring looking back at him as if he were some kind of puzzle, and he was trying to figure him out. But then Victor remembered the sight of Kenkel's dead body on the floor as he was led out of that dungeon.

"Drink," said Kenkel. "Unless you think I'm trying to poison you."

"No," said Victor, reaching out and taking the flagon. "It's just hard to see is all." He then tilted it upward, allowing the water to pass his lips and into his throat. It was one of the most satisfying things he had ever tasted.

"Who are you? Why did you rescue me? You're not the face that you're wearing?"

"Oh! Yes, I forgot I was still in this form," said Kenkel. And slowly, the boy's skin began to change from a dull pink into an ashen white. His frame shrunk, and as silently as a cat in the night, the boy changed into a familiar face.

Victor felt all the tension leave his body as he laid back down and closed his eyes. "Oh, for the love of the goddess, Silk. You could have just told me who you were. Is Frenka okay?"

"Hmmm?" moaned Silk, placing a finger to her lips and pretending to think. "Yes. She is fine. I left her after we passed the border. She should be there now waiting for me to return."

"And you assumed I'd be such a fool as to find myself in trouble. Well, I admit it. You were right," said Victor, before turning his head to look at her and catching her staring at him curiously. "What... what's wrong?"

"Nothing, it's just... Victor, do you love me?"

"What?"

"Do you love me?"

"You ask me after saving my life. How am I supposed to respond?"

"Is honesty too much?"

Victor sighed, "Yes, I love you. I love Frenka. I very much love the air I am breathing that I am still breathing. Does that satisfy you?"

Silk couldn't help herself but laugh, "No, but it'll do."

"Well, I'm glad you are enjoying yourself," said Victor as the door opened to the cabin once again. This time, another woman walked in. She was tall and wearing the gown of the holy chapel.

"Ah. So, he's awake now. Good, dead weight is hard to carry. We take him back with us now?"

Victor didn't recognize the face, but in her voice, he recognized her instantly. It was Muslin. No longer a whisper in his ear, but now she was standing before him, holding white sheets and a blade in her hand.

"No," said Silk. "No. Make course for Mari, there are a few loose ends we need to handle there."

Muslin looked confused for a moment but then shrugged her shoulders while making a weird face and left the room, closing the door.

"Do you have any more assassin friends you wish to introduce me to?"

"Why? Do you wish to marry them as well?"

"A fair rebuttal," said Victor with a sigh. "I didn't know you were still keeping in touch. Won't this cause us trouble if they report it back to that Grennok fellow?"

"Let me deal with that when the time comes. But as for this moment," said Silk as she stood up and stepped over, placing a knee on the bed and straddling herself on top of Victor. "For now, I'd rather think of something else."

Victor blinked as he looked up as Silk climbed on top of him, her soft emerald and ruby eyes alluding to something he wasn't sure he could handle. "I'm flattered and grateful. But I've only just woken up from being locked away in a pit of darkness. I'm not sure I'd be satisfactory to you, given how I can barely keep any thought in my head straight."

"Do not worry, lover. Your thoughts are not the part of you that I'll be asking of you to keep straight."

CHAPTER 46

Days later, in the city of Orlana, Oscar stood looking out the window. In his hands were a few pieces of parchment. A knock came at the door.

"Come in."

"You've kept yourself locked in here for days," said Jacob. "You ever think of coming out?"

"I've been thinking."

"On what to do with Isha? She's finally calmed down. You really should go and see her."

"I will. But Dessi's with her. Let her play her role. There are some things women are just naturally better at than men. When she's ready, she'll come and see me. I just need to be here when she does."

"Fine," said Jacob as he closed the door behind him, plopping down in a seat. "Anything else been happening in the world? We haven't received a proper request in months, and you continue to turn down the few that do manage to come in. Is there a proper excuse for this lack of war, or have you decided to open up a brothel like Broderick?"

"When the board is changing, it's best to wait and see which side has the most favorable pieces."

"And what pieces are changing, if you don't mind me asking?"

Oscar turned around, handing the parchment to Jacob. "Read it and tell me what you think."

Taking the notes, Jacob began scanning them. It was a few moments before he finished reading through all the accounts, and then Oscar watched as his son's face twisted in confusion and hate.

"Is this valid?" asked Jacob.

"As far as I know, it is. I've got several different reports here. But they all pretty much say the same thing."

"An entire religion after magical children. So bolden to the point where they attack a flying school in the sky."

"And not a Queen or King worth the salt would be stupid enough to oppose them," said Oscar.

"Then what are we supposed to do? Surely you know that not just the children, but they were probably after Isha specifically."

"The thought had crossed my mind, especially after learning that last bit."

"You mean about King Montavia holding a ceremony tomorrow," said Jacob waving the paper at his father. "But it doesn't say about what."

"Doesn't matter. The timing of the two gives me enough reason to think he is involved with it in some way. Especially if you think that he has strong ties to the girl."

"So, what to do now?"

"Has Gregga returned yet?"

"No. Any rational person would think she's taken her children and run off somewhere. But she'd wouldn't leave Isha. If she were to leave, she probably come back to get her.

And goddess help anyone that tried to stop her. Speaking of which, do you know what's going on with her?"

"What do you mean?" asked Oscar.

"We find her amidst the rubble of a fallen city alongside a creature that I don't even wish to think about, and for the most part, she's fine. She was completely calm for a whole day. But after sleeping, she awoke in a panic, screaming and calling out for those Sakari girls. I don't blame her, given the accounts she gave us. I can't imagine it. But it all seems strange that she wasn't grief-stricken when we found her. And now she says she doesn't remember anything between falling and waking up here."

"The girl was in shock. You've seen it happen yourself more than a few times on the battlefield."

"No. I know that face. There's something you're not telling me."

"There are many things I'm not telling you," said Oscar with a chuckled.

"Yes, and that is something of a bad habit of yours that Dessi and I both wish you would fix."

"I'll tell you if it becomes important. For now, just worry about fixing the girl."

"About that; whenever I calm her using my magic, something feels different."

"How so?"

"It feels… I don't know, odd. As if when I tap into her mind, there are other thoughts jumbled up inside. I thought it was nothing, but it reminded me of that night when Molan attacked her, and she first used her powers."

"You think she's losing control of her powers?"

"No, it's not that. It's… it's hard to describe, like on the way before we found her, I got this feeling. Like a whisper or something."

"Your magic affects the mind," said Oscar tapping himself on the head. "Sure, you're not properly trained, but I imagine being around that girl and what she can do might have affected you somehow. It's not as if she knows what all she can—"

Another knock at the door, but before Oscar could beacon them in, it opened, and in walked Dessi holding Isha by the hand.

"She wants to see you," said Dessi, the tone of her voice sounding annoyed.

"I imagine so. Fine, come here, child. I imagine you feel as if you have something to say."

Isha stepped forward, looking up into Oscar's face. "I want to see my sisters."

"Yes. And I would like to see their mother. But it doesn't seem that either of us will be getting what we desire."

"Is... she not here?" said Isha, looking around the room. Instinctively she grabbed at her arms to try and stop herself from shaking.

"No, Isha," said Dessi as she knelt beside her, placing her hands on her shoulders, trying to comfort her. "But I'm sure she will return soon. They're okay. Remember, you told me that you can feel them if you closed your eyes."

"Yes... yes," said Isha, her voice soft and stuttering. She then closed her eyes, and they all watched as the markings on her back glowed for a few seconds. "They're there. I know they are. Can I go back to school now? I want to see them. And I need to make sure Leo is okay. He... he'll need my help to heal them if they're hurt."

"No, Isha, remember. Aukube is a healer too. If they're hurt, she can help."

"But... but it's not the same. And there... there were so many. When they came... when they... came," Isha tried, but she couldn't finish before the tears began streaming down her face.

Jacob stood up from his seat, his hand beginning to glow as he reached out for Isha. But Oscar waved for him to stop.

"No. Some tears need to be shed. This is one of those times," he said as he knelt in front of Isha. He didn't console her. He just waited. For one moment, then another.

Isha held herself together for just a few seconds more before she wrapped her arms around his neck, hugging him as hard as she could and started sobbing, her tears sinking into the collar of his shirt, and there she would stay as long as she needed.

CHAPTER 47

Victor stood outside of the landing docks of Mari, standing beside Silk. She had taken on the appearance of Muslin. The streets were littered with people going about their day as several passed them attempting to board their own ships.

"Are you headed back to where Frenka is?"

"Yes. I do not think you will need to be rescued for a while."

"You're not going to let me live down the fact of you having to save me, are you?"

"What? I think it's refreshing for you to be the damsel in distress. Did you call my name when you were locked away?"

"I'm just going to go. Be sure to come back safely with Frenka. At this point, I'm not sure I can imagine life without—" said Victor before his lips were covered by hers in a long passionate kiss that sucked the life out of him for a moment.

"Be on your way, lover. I'll go and do what needs to be done," said Silk before turning around and heading back up the flight of stairs leading to the loading dock of the airship.

I'm not sure I will get used to kissing her while she's wearing other people. Although, she is definitely more confident now, he thought to himself as he watched her make her way up the steps. He couldn't help but think the swivel of her hips was a bit more exaggerated than before as if she expected him to look.

With a shake of his head to try and clear his mind of more sensual thoughts, he turned and made his way toward the castle. The city seemed abuzz with chatter, more than during his last stay here. He didn't make it far before he ran into another friendly face.

"Well, the General is back?" said Carol. "I was wondering where you went off to. I stopped by house, and you were gone. Did you get tired of freeloading or did the Queen sending you off on another mission again?"

"You know she did," said Victor with a smile as he greeted his old friend. "Why are you still in the city? I thought you were gone already."

"I'm actually on my way to the ship now. Took a while for me to book passage on another one, and then there were a few issues that needed to be taken care of around the castle. But I think my wife will forgive me."

"I'm sure. But far be it from me to keep you from your wife. I think ships are about to leave."

"Argh, of course they are. I'm never early for anything," said Carol as he stepped to Victor patting him on the shoulder. "Take care old friend. Don't forget, when I get back, you still need to introduce me to those wives of yours." And with a cheerful wave, Carol disappeared into the crowd on his way to the loading docks.

"What?" said Victor, confused. *But you've met Frenka and Silk. If it wasn't you... then who? Why would someone come into... Why would they pretend to be him.* Victor face twisted as his mind began to think about all the possibilities. In his confusion he turned and saw the castle and remember why he had asked on come back. *No, not now. There's something more important to handle. I'll have to think about that later. Along with everything else, it seems.*

Blocking it from his mind, he eventually made his way through the city streets until he reached the castle doors. Recognized by the guards, he was let in. The halls were filled with people in fine clothing chatting about something, but Victor was paying them no mind as he pressed forward, only stopping to question a guard.

After asking, it wasn't long before he was told that the Queen was in her private chamber and thus made his way up the steps.

After a knock at the door, he heard her voice.

"Come in," said Clarissa, looking over some dressing worn by mannequins by the window as Victor stepped into the room. "Oh, well. A tad bit late to make a report, but I suppose it is such a rarity to have you come to my quarters that I'll allow it. Go on and take a seat there. I assume you have something to report."

Victor looked suspiciously at the Queen and decided to stay standing as he made his way into the room.

"Yes, it's about what happened at the holy city."

"Yes, word of that debacle has reached me."

"What do you mean?"

"Well, I assume you come to report that Prince Saffron has married that high chancellor woman from the holy city. That bastard, Montavia is trying to turn Burlus into a kingdom of the righteous."

"What?" said Victor, his voice louder than he expected.

"Oh! Is that not why you are here? Well, it's all anyone can talk about outside of the attack on the magical schools. But that mess will be cleared out soon enough. You can't kidnap the children of nobles and expect to live."

"That's what I'm here to report on. It is King Montavia and the High Chancellor themselves that are attacking the schools."

"Our reports say that the schools there were attacked as well. Why would he attack his own schools?"

"I don't know," said Victor honestly. "But I know for a fact that it was them. I watched them discuss the whole meeting in their chambers before... wait." Victor began rubbing his face and began thinking of possible outcomes. "I escaped so, perhaps, the wedding... maybe it was because of that."

"Oh! You're thinking again. Explain it to me. It seems pieces of information are missing. And do keep things in order. Your mind has a tendency to be a bit sporadic."

Finally, accepting her suggestion, Victor walked over to take a seat at the makeup counter of the Queen. He couldn't help but look at his reflection in the mirror. His eyes were a bit puffy, and his hair was out of place. The issue was that a beard had started settling in, but grooming would need to come later.

"The crystals," said Victor, turning back to face the Queen. "They are able to give people magic. Apparently, if implanted in the bodies of the mundane, they are then able to cast magic."

"Preposterous, you can't just—"

"I've seen it, Clarissa, with my own eyes. Crystal embedded in a man's chest, and he could set ablaze an item in his hand. I once told you about the man I fought under the city of Molask. Well, that same man also had crystals in his chest and was able to cast magic. The same exact one who seemed to come back from the dead after having that same crystal shoved into his throat."

Clarissa stared at Victor for a moment before closing her eyes and taking in a deep breath. Then she calmly walked over and sat at the edge of her bed, looking him in the eyes. "I see you are serious. And I trust you. So, can you tell me why the Goddess's faithful are kidnapping children?

Surely, they don't think they can replace all mages with those crystals, do they?"

"No, that was an issue of contention in their meeting, one that led to them murdering over half of the heads of the clergy."

"What?"

"There were those who opposed the idea of the crystals. And they were slain within moments of doing so. But that's not the worst of it."

"I fail to see how the abducting children, pseudo-magic, and a religious cleansing don't classify as 'the worst of it.'"

"The children, they are not kidnapping them for ransom. They are harvesting them. Apparently, only the blood of children who have yet to have their magical affinity solidify can be used to make the crystals."

Clarissa looked horrified upon hearing the news, putting her hands over her lips. Her eyes darted back and forth as she comprehended the horrors and the meaning of it all.

"That's unspeakable. That's horrible," she said as a smile began to creep over her face, signaling a new thought entering her mind. "But that's also perfect."

"What? What are you saying?"

"Queen Pershai, don't you get it? The starlight child. She's looking for her child. Now, no one in their right mind would dare oppose a religious order. Not without firm proof, but the disappearance of a child... Why the Queen of Ursjun would surely be out of her mind with worry?"

"The child who's kidnapping you orchestrated?"

"And they are perfect fools to take the blame for it all," said Clarissa as she stood up from the bed. "Oh, wipe that look off your face, Victor. You are the one who taught me to look at things from the other side. Or do you not remember our nights together during the war?"

"That was for survival."

"And so is this," said Clarissa as she walked towards the window, looking over the city of Mari. "And rest assured, we will survive."

CHAPTER 48

Oscar and Gregga sat at a table in a well furnished room with a fireplace and a thick rug over the wooden floor. Adjacent to them was Isha, who seated in a chair holding Makeba's blade in her hand. It was around midday as the sun outside hung overhead, but there was a serious tone to the atmosphere as Isha sat quietly with Oscar and Gregga staring at each other.

"I'm not going to ask you to stay," said Oscar, placing his hand on his chin.

"Good, because I would not."

"You sure you'll be safe up there?"

"No, but Jacinta will be safer than before, which is all a mother should care about," she turned to Isha, reaching out a hand, rubbing the side of her face gently. "This kingdom land has now taken a husband and daughter from me. I will not suffer to see it take any more from me than it has."

She then turned back to Oscar. "You will finish this one's training. I will see to the other."

"Are you sure Makeba's dead?"

"No, but she is beyond me, and that feels the same as death."

"Do you blame me for it?"

"Yes. But I also blame myself. I blame the world. I wish to see it burn. You will find the ones responsible, and you will bring them to me."

"I will."

"Then I will go. Jacinta waits for me in the sky city," said Gregga, as she stood from the table. "Come here, daughter."

Isha stood from her seat and walked over to her Gregga, still clutching Makeba's blade to her chest. "I'm not going back with you am I Mother?"

"No. Your time in that place is done," said Gregga as she wrapped an arm around her, holding Isha against her stomach. "You will be here. Tell me, can you still feel your sisters through your markings?"

"I can. When they use magic, I can. But Makeba, hers, feels different than before."

"Different is fine. We will look for a way to fix what has been broken. And as long as you can feel, then your sister is not lost to us."

"I'm sorry, I couldn't do anything. I tried. I tried so much, but... but everyone is... is..."

"No, daughter. You must understand it is not your fault. Many children have been taken. You are just one of many. You are special, but in this, you are not."

"Will you come back? I mean, will I see you and Jacinta again?"

"You will. Oscar will hide you, see after you until we can kill those we need. Until then, you will be looked after." Gregga's eyes glanced over to Oscar, who nodded his head. "Goodbye, daughter." She released Isha from her belly and leaned down, kissing her on her forehead. "Your mother will come back to you with both sisters. I promise this."

And with that, Gregga turned away and walked toward the door. Placing her hand on the frame, she turned, giving her daughter one last look before leaving and closing the door behind her.

Isha watched her mother leave before turning to Oscar, who was staring at her.

"Are you going to send me away now?" she said, dropping her head.

Oscar leaned back in his chair, taking in a deep breath. "That depends. There are still a few roads to pick from."

Isha looked up, confused. "But you told mother—"

"No, I told your mother that I would see after you. And I will do that. But like before, I will let you decide how it is done. I have the resources at my disposal to hide you away forever if need be. But now that you've got that power of yours under control, I figured that maybe I should send you back to that Green Village place."

"You're going to send me back?"

"That is what ya wanted, isn't it? To go back home, see if it's still there. See if that other father of yours is still looking for ya."

"But..." Isha's hands began to shake. "What about Jacinta, Makeba, and Mother? I need... I need to be here when they... when they.... What if they need me?"

"I'm sure they will understand. You've been through a lot. I'll get Dessi to find you a ship to—"

"No! I won't go back. You can't just... you can't."

"I can," said Oscar shaking his head. "War is coming, and all your little friends are dead. The Sakari can fight. But you can barely throw them little knives Dessi gave you. It's best to send you home and—"

"No!" screamed Isha looking up at Oscar, the hate beginning to flame behind her eyes. "Stop treating me like this. You said I can decide, and I don't want to go back. I want to stay here with you and Dessi and Jacob. Why are you trying to get rid of me?"

"Because you're a little girl who can't fight. The only reason you're still here is cause Jasper asked me for that favor. And look what that's gotten ya."

"Then make me like Dessi. You took her, right? Why can't I be like her?"

"If I tell Dessi to kill people, she does it. If I tell Dessi she needs to go out a fuck some noble, then that's what she does. Is that what you want? Can you do that?"

"I..." mumbled Isha, her lip quivering as her gaze fell to the floor. " I want to stay here," she murmured.

"That's not what I asked ya."

Isha lifted her face and just stared into Oscar's. He wasn't smiling. He wasn't mad. He just looked at her, waiting.

"If I... If I do what you say, will you let me stay here?"

"Only if you do what I say. With everything that has happened. I can't have you getting in the way. I need to know that when the time comes, I can depend on you the same way I can depend on Dessi or Jacob."

"Then... then I will."

"Then you will, what? Let me hear ya say it. I need to know that you understand what this means."

"Then... then I will do whatever you say."

"Good. Then the first thing we need to do is to finish that training. Because I'm going to have you hunt down and kill everyone involved in what happened at that school."

"What?"

"You said you'd kill for me. But first, I'm going to have you kill for yourself."

"Do you know who it was?"

"Not yet. But I will. Just go on and tell Dessi what I said. She will do the rest."

"But what about magic? I don't have—"

"I have someone in mind for your magical training. They have their own reasons for wanting to help. Now, go on. I have a few things to take care of."

Isha looked confused but did as instructed, heading toward the door, and opening it before turning back to Oscar. "Thank you... for not sending me back."

"Go on. We will talk about this later."

Isha closed the door behind her as she left the room. Oscar stood up from his seat and walked over to his desk, picking up a pitcher of wine. He grabbed two cups, set them down on the table, and poured wine into them.

"Alright, come out now."

"I don't know why you had me wait there like that," said a familiar but raspy voice as a section of the room near the wall began to morph.

"I wanted you to see it for ya'self."

"You mean how you manipulated that poor girl," said Soulden, revealing herself as the colors of the world washed away, with her appearing behind them. Her face was scarred with lines that ran across her lips to under her left eye, which was now white. "And what is with all that "you" and "ya" verbiage. Can your vocabulary not comprehend other mutiples?"

Oscar gave a chuckle. "My daughter, before all this she wished for her father to become a cultured man. Wished that I stopped using "ya." He took asip from his cup. "But it appears I may be to old to learn another trick."

"Humph. You're daughter? Hardly... Can you really not ever think of anyone else? Must you attach yourself to them as if you were a leech?"

"And where has that gotten ya'self?" asked Oscar, tipping his cup in her direction. "Seems to me this whole mess could have been handled better if you were a bit more selfish."

Soulden picked up the other cup, sat in the chair, and took a mouthful of the wine. "Well, no matter to any of it, I suppose. Seeing as I won't be going back. Not after such a grand failure as I have put on display."

"Life is filled with failure. You should have grown accustomed to it."

"For you, perhaps, down here in this filth. But I once aspired to be something greater," said Soluden, extending a hand flippant manor.

"Which makes your fall that much more dangerous."

"For once… we agree. But Oscar, tell me. After watching how you treat that poor girl, why do I feel this resounding urge to rip your throat out?"

"Perhaps she brings up old memories."

"Perhaps… But you do know that if you mistreat that girl by whoring her out, I won't hesitate to break you?"

"I take it you've taken a liking to my daughter, then? Good, it's nice to have another on my side."

"I am not on your side," said Soulden, the disgust evident in her voice as her lip snarled. "Our sides are just merely aligned for the moment."

"Either way, the situation serves my purposes just fine," said Oscar as he lifted a piece of parchment from the table to look over.

"The world is far too kind to men like you."

"And far too lenient on women such as ya'self."

"And yet here we are, at odds again," said Soulden, her eyes lowering as she looked at the parchment in Oscar's hand. "What? Is there another nobleman looking to have you protect a farm or whatever you do?"

"No," said Oscar, lying the parchment back on the table and eyeing Soulden. "Those graves… the ones we made for your children when they fell from the sky. Apparently, one of them was dug up. It says that a body was drug off. Probably some local tribe, but I don't know of any clan habits that involve digging up dead bodies."

Soulden was quiet for a moment. "I… I suppose I should thank you for that kindness. For the burial, I mean."

"I wasn't going to leave the bodies of children to rot out in the sun. I'm not so heartless as that if I can help it."

"So it would seem," closing her eyes and taking a deep breath. "But tell me, why did you have me wait there in the corner? Why not allow me to meet Isha now rather than later?"

"She's angry. She'll need to use that anger. And after I break her more than she is now, when her body is barely hanging on, then I'll give her to you. And then you will fix everything I've broken."

"Truly a devious man. It leaves one to wonder just how deep is that bag of tricks that you have."

"Deep enough. It's never a bad thing to have a plan or two in action in case of certain... circumstances," said Oscar, this time a smirk sliding over his own lips. "Although I must admit, seeing you down here in the dirt with us common folk, that certainly isn't a trick I thought I'd ever see repeated so soon."

Soulden stared at Oscar for another moment before reaching forward and grabbing the entire bottle of wine, taking it to her lips. She swallowed several mouthfuls before slamming it on the table and wiping the side of her mouth with the back of her palm.

"My wife is dead. My school is lost to me. And my only apprentice is locked away in a damnable giant tree in the sky. No, Oscar, I am down here in the dirt where a failure such as I belong. But I don't need your sympathy. Save that for the ones who put me here after I find them. Because whether the five kingdoms go to war or not, rest assured that I most certainly am... at war."